Praise for L.E. Modesitt, Jr.:

'An intriguing fantasy in a fascinating world'

Robert Jordan

'Fascinating! A big, exciting novel of the battle between good and evil, and the path between'

Gordon R. Dickson

'Extremely interesting . . . unique . . . a refreshing use of the traditional fantasy elements'

Andre Norton

L. E. Modesitt, Jr.

THE SOPRANO SORCERESS

ORBIT

An *Orbit* Book

First published in the United States by Tor Books in 1997
First published in Great Britain by Orbit in 1997

A CIP catalogue record for this book
is available from the British Library.

ISBN 1 85723 534 7

Typeset in Century Old Style by
Palimpsest Book Production Limited,
Polmont, Stirlingshire
Printed and bound in Great Britain by
Clays Ltd, St Ives plc.

Orbit
A Division of
Little, Brown and Company (UK)
Brettenham House
Lancaster Place
London WC2E 7EN

For and to my soprano sorceress,
who made this possible.
Any mistakes are mine,
the music hers.

I

LIEDTRAUM

1

WEST OF THE SAND PASS, DEFALK

A dozen musicians sit on stools under the oblong white silk awning held in place by four sturdy poles, each pole anchored by heavy cords to a pair of stakes. The silk flutters slightly in the almost still air that carries the scent of dust and horses.

The brown-and-red mountains that loom in the east above the pass entrance waver in the summer heat, and sweat drips down the faces of the musicians. All wear faded blue cotton tunics and trousers, with boots of a matching blue leather. Occasionally, one blots a forehead or cheek, but not one of the musicians speaks. Dark sweat stains mark the tunics of the heavier men. The three horn players exchange glances, not quite those of worry, then look toward the two men standing in the midday sun beyond the silk awning.

The bigger man, wearing leathers and a hand-and-a-half blade in a scabbard worn across his shoulders, puts a hand on the saddle of his warhorse. A good fifty paces to the east wait a squad of mounted troopers wearing the purple of Defalk. Their black sabres are sheathed in scabbards at their waists. Half carry black horn bows and quivers, and half bear long spear-lances with identical, leaf-shaped steel blades.

'You're sure these walls will stand against even the Dark Monks?' drawls the bulky, broad-faced man. His hooded eyes give his face a sleepy-looking cast.

'What I raise will be standing when you and I are long gone, Lord Barjim,' affirms the resonant baritone voice of the slender and balding man in blue silks.

'That'll be a long time, Brill,' laughs the Lord of Defalk. 'You look the same as when I was Jimbob's age.'

'They'll stand that long or longer.'

'Aye, and they should for all the silver I'm paying.'

'It's far less than a bringing in masons from Nordwei.'

'Not that much. Not in these times.' Barjim pauses, as if waiting for a response, then finally continues. 'Too bad you couldn't bring us rain. Need that worse than the fort, except we need both, with the dark ones on the move.' He looks down at the shorter lord. 'I still don't see why you can't bring rain. It's not as though you've avoided darksong. We both know that.'

'That's too dark, and I've explained why before,' Brill answers patiently.

'You have an answer for everything,' points out Barjim. 'That's why you're a sorcerer.'

'No,' responds Brill. 'That's why I've survived as a sorcerer.'

'Cold iron is more sure.'

'That is true, lord,' says Brill, his tone light, not quite mocking. 'Unless you consider the Dark Monks.'

'Someday.' Barjim shakes his head. 'I'll leave you to your task, master sorcerer. I'll be back to inspect your work later, and, of course, pay you.'

'Of course, lord.' Brill bows deeply.

Lord Barjim snorts and turns, swinging up onto his mount. As he rides toward his troopers, they straighten in their identical purpled leather saddles.

Once the troopers pass the outcropping of dark stone on the south side of the valley, they turn due west, back toward Mencha, away from the Sand Pass that leads to Ebra. When the sound of hoofs on the paved highway echoes back uphill, Lord Brill lets a smile cross his lips. He glances toward the representative piles of stone and brick, the dry powdered mortar, and the tubs of water, then steps under the silk sunshade and wipes his forehead. After he takes a long sip from the goblet on the portable table, his brown-flecked green eyes drop to the two-part drawing of the walled fortification fastened with leather thongs to the drafting board. The right-hand side of the drawing illustrates the foundation outline, the left-hand side a frontal view as if seen from a tall oak, though Brill stands in the middle of a depression between the hills, empty except for the sorcerer and his players, and the heaps of stone on the south side. Beside the drawing are the spells, with the proper accents marked. The softness in Brill's eyes vanishes as he faces the musicians.

'The ground-sorting tune,' he orders. 'Run through it once.' He lifts his right hand and began the count, marking the time deftly. 'One, two . . .' With his nod, the musicians begin the sonorous tones, the brass horns low and urgent, the woodwinds pantherlike, the strings whispering like shifting sands.

'No! Jaegal, you must emphasize the downbeats more, especially the first.' Brill's hands stop the players, and his eyes flash.

Not one of the musicians looks up, although one of the horn players scowls, his face averted from Brill. In the last part of the string section, a black-haired youth takes a clean gray cloth and blots his forehead quickly before replacing the cloth and repositioning his bow.

'Again!' Brill demands.

As the musicians play, the ground beyond the bricks and mortar and water appears to shiver.

The sorcerer nods. 'Good. Take a moment. Some water. Wipe your foreheads.' Without looking at the seven men and three women, he turns the drafting board so that he can direct the musicians, see the drawing and the spell, and the ground where the fort is to rise.

Brill waits. The silk awning above ripples in the hint of a breeze, and the only sounds are soft and muted as the musicians drink and blot foreheads, necks, and fingers.

'Places,' the sorcerer finally announces.

The ten players reseat themselves on their stools and take up their instruments. The last to lift an instrument is the black-haired young man in the back with the viola.

'Now . . . one . . . two . . .'

Brill's resonant baritone wraps around the notes the musicians play.

> '. . . cleave the ground, even, straight, and true,
> More cleanly than the diggers do.
> Scour the stones both smooth and flat . . .'

The sorcerer sings; the musicians play; and a silver haze settles onto the hilltop where the soil shifts, and the ground parts. The air stills completely, and the awning hangs limply in the heat, and even the scents of parched grass, dust, and horses seem to vanish.

At the end of the songspell, Brill's hand slashes for silence, and the songhaze vanishes. The silk awning flutters.

'You have a few moments,' the sorcerer says. He takes the spotless white cloth from his pocket and wipes, then blots, his steaming forehead, before lifting his iron-tipped staff and walking out into the full sun and toward the sets of trenches that had appeared on the hilltop after the songhaze lifted.

The sorcerer walks the trenches, and the staff taps the lines of exposed stone, stone remelted into the foundation pattern.

Under the awning, the players stretch and stand, except for the woodwind player whose braided white-and-red hair betray her age far more than her creamy skin. Her cold eyes follow the sorcerer until he begins his return, when she looks down and takes a quick sip from her water bottle, then moistens her lips and her reed.

'The foundation is solid.' Brill blots his forehead a last time before folding the cloth and slipping it back into his pocket. 'Places.'

With a soft shuffling the musicians square themselves on their stools and lift their instruments in response to the sorcerer's hands. Their notes follow his tempo, and his voice.

'. . . replicate the bricks and stones.
Place them in their proper zones . . .
'Set the blocks, and set them square
set them to their pattern there . . .'

The hilltop shimmers, as do the bricks and stones, and the heaps of mortar, and the tubs of water tremble. Dull crackings whisper through the haze from the south side of the valley.

When the silver haze lifts, Brill turns toward the structure that looms there – newly built. Stone-based brick walls rise the height of four tall men and stretch across the floor of the valley, almost joining the two hills. The dark stone outcropping to the southwest of the fort has almost vanished, two-thirds of its bulk sliced away.

'Behold Lord Barjim's new stronghold against the Dark Monks of Ebra.' Lord Brill frowns, then whirls toward the players. 'Someone was humming.' Brill's eyes scan the musicians. 'Someone was humming. And look! Look at that gate wall!' His hand jabs westward.

The left-hand side of the arched gate is crooked, out of true.

The sorcerer reaches for his goblet and drains it, setting it on the small table with a thud. 'Gero!'

A thin youth runs from the wagon and the tethered horses to the west. 'Yes, Lord Brill.'

'More water.' Brill grasps the staff and carries it as he walks across the trampled sun-parched grasses and onto the paved road that resumes a dozen yards from the magically-built fort's gate, beyond the bricked and dry moat. He keeps tapping the iron-tipped staff as he continues through the open brick archway, across the brick-paved courtyard to the low brick-walled building that stands roofless in the afternoon sun. The staff raps against walls, against stone and paving stone, against mortar and brick for a long time before he slowly walks back under the white silk awning that scarcely flutters in the still air.

'The gate, thank the powers of song, is the only flaw.' His

now dark-circled eyes sweep the musicians. 'I should starve you all.' His eyes lighten. 'Refresh yourselves, and then, then we will use the symmetry spell to repair the gate.'

Brill limps, ever so slightly, to the drafting board, where he studies the spell, and begins to murmur to himself. After a time, he takes a markstick from the wallet on his belt and begins to write out a revised similarity spell below the others.

Under the back section of the awning, the black-haired young man glances nervously toward the white-haired violino player in the front row, but the older man sips from his water bottle without acknowledging the scrutiny.

With a last slash across the yellow paper on the drafting board, the sorcerer turns and straightens. 'Places.' Brill takes a deep breath. 'Similarity one, please. No humming. Fast tempo.' His hands begin marking the time, and his sharp nod cues the musicians as the music rises.

> '. . . set true and straight
> both sides of the gate . . .'

This time, the spell is short, and the songhaze lingers only over the gate for what seems to be instants.

The sorcerer slashes the music to a halt, staggers, before taking another deep breath, then a gulp of water from the goblet on the small table. Only then does he turn and walk back toward the gate. A dozen paces are sufficient to confirm his handiwork. The gate is straight, with no sign of deformity.

With a quick nod to himself, he studies the gate for a time. His steps are stronger as he heads back through the hot, still afternoon to the shade of the awning.

The musicians wait, silently.

'Culain – you hummed again!'

'No, ser. No!' protests the white-haired man who clutches the violino. 'I did not.'

'I will not have lying, and I will not have carelessness

jeopardize me or those around you! Once is an accident. Twice is arrogant disregard.'

Brill's eyes turn hard as jade as his mouth opens in song, as Culain backs away, out from under the lightly fluttering silk awning and into pitiless afternoon sun.

> 'Once a man is not always a man,
> lower than dust, softer than ...'

As the songhaze rolls across Culain, shrouding him, tears well up in the eyes of the black-haired young man. The woodwind player's eyes remain cold, and dry.

2

Anna looked into the mirror, trying to ignore the fine lines running from her eyes. 'You look like a raccoon.'

She used the tissue to blot her eyes. If only ... if only ... With a deep breath, she tried to push the offending viola out of her mind. She had given the final examination for her last course, Introduction to Music, and the sheets were even graded. The Scantron helped a lot, even if she hated multiple-guess tests, but there was no way she was about to grade eighty essay tests for an intro course.

The viola ... Don't think about the viola, she told herself. But it was Irenia's viola – an instrument tied irrevocably to her daughter. She took a deep breath and blotted her eyes again.

Why had she accepted the dean's invitation to sing at the Founders' Dinner for major donors? Because it was extra money – only fifty dollars, but the ATM had said her balance was down to two hundred, and it was almost two weeks until the first.

Her eyes flicked to the viola. Funerals ... who would have

thought a simple funeral would have been so expensive? Outside of the small policy paid for years ago by her father, there hadn't been any insurance, and that just hadn't been enough. Avery – the self-styled perfect husband and tenor – had always paid for things like insurance, and while she'd taken out insurance on herself for the children, she hadn't thought about insurance on them, even if she'd been able to afford it.

A quick glance at the clock told her that she had less than a half hour to pull herself together. She blew her nose, then looked at the empty glass on the dresser. No . . . one drink was all she could take.

First . . . makeup to repair the ravages of grief – and age. The two seemed to go together. The crooked and cheap Queen Anne stool that Sandy had repaired with metal straps before they'd broken off the relationship cracked, as it always did, when she sat down. Everything Sandy did had been a little rough, but he'd been there when Avery hadn't . . . for a while. Was the cracking of the straps louder? Did that mean she was heavier?

Makeup – concentrate on one thing at a time. When she finished, Anna studied her face. She used a touch more mascara, then stood. What would she wear? As she rummaged in the closet, she began the vocalises. Once it had taken only a few minutes to warm up, but these days it took longer, a lot longer.

'Holly-lolly-polly-pop . . .'

Good, her throat was clear, her cords resilient.

The green formal gown was clean, and she hadn't worn it where the president had seen it. After hanging it from the top of the folding closet door, she rummaged through the plastic bags she'd never unpacked or put in the drawers until she found the new longline bra – she hated any kind of bra, but she couldn't wear the gown without it. Then came the slip – tight, almost too tight. She sucked in her stomach as she zipped it, then twisted it around, checking in the full-length mirror. Of course, it wasn't straight, and when she tried to straighten it, the bra twisted.

Finally, with both bra and formal slip in place, she took a deep breath.

'Holly-lolly-polly-pop . . .' She could breathe, and it wasn't as though she'd be doing Mimi or Butterfly. It was just five songs for the university's big donors – the Founders' Dinner.

She took down the gown and slipped it out of the plastic, before beginning the struggle. These days, everything was a struggle, especially zipping a formal gown without help.

Her eyes strayed toward the picture on the Queen Anne dresser – the four of them, one of the few with just the children and her. Most of the old family pictures had Avery in them. He'd been insisting that he was Antonio or Tony thirty years, but Anna had known him when he'd been Avery Marshall – long before he'd become Antonio Marsali. The great Antonio Marsali, king of the comprimarios, who'd never paid a cent toward any of the children's education – except for Irenia.

They all looked so young – Irenia, Mario, and Elizabetta, even Anna herself – standing in front of the lilacs at the lake house. Now, it was Avery's vacation home. How could she have been so stupid?

Shoes – the green ones were in the corner, she thought, and they were. Her eyes went back to the picture, to the blond-haired young man. Mario always joked that he was 'northern Italian' or a 'WASP Italian,' probably just to irritate his father. Marsali had been Avery's great-grandmother's maiden name, and she was the only Italian in the family, but Avery – the great Antonio – had insisted that an Italian name was a must for an opera singer, especially a high baritone.

After Mario had left to go back to Houston, the condo had seemed so empty, but he called, like a dutiful son, every few days. Anna blew her nose and looked away from the picture. Think about singing. Think about singing.

Jewelry? Something ornate enough not to get lost, but simple. The silver necklace didn't look right.

The gold-link necklace looked good, but where had she put the earrings? They were where she'd left them, next to the telephone.

She squared her shoulders. 'I can do this.' She lifted the lipstick and touched up her upper lip. 'I can do this.' Especially since the president was the only supporter she had left now that Dieshr had become chair of the music department.

She could sing for the major-donor dinner, and Dieshr would sit by the president and say sicky-sweet things – like 'Anna's so good with young voices.' Or 'She does very well without a doctorate.'

As if she'd had any choice—

She went to the window. Cloudy, but it wasn't raining, not yet. She picked up the green leather purse and hurried downstairs. Her raincoat, not exactly fashion-coordinated with the gown, was folded across the banister.

After slipping it on, she glanced at the clock – five-forty – checked for her keys, then locked the door and stepped out under the town house's pseudo-Georgian portico. The cramped townhouse condo was definitely not what she would have ideally chosen, but aging junior music faculty members lived where the bargains were, in this case, the Colonial Mansions.

A roll of thunder was followed by a spattering of rain on the sidewalk, and a gust of wind that whipped the long skirt of the green formal around her calves.

Her hand went to her hair. The umbrella was in the car.

The line of rain struck the far side of the parking lot and gusted across toward her.

'Damn!' She was going to be late – or wet . . . or both, and she was being paid to look good as well as sing. 'Damn! I'd just like to run away . . . anywhere. Anywhere,' she repeated grimly. 'Anywhere!'

As she reached for her key to let herself back into the condo, the world swirled around her.

3

MENCHA, DEFALK

The black-haired young man bounces in the saddle a last time as he reins up the horse in front of the thick-walled cottage. The dark-oiled wooden shutters are closed against the midday heat, and not even the chickens are out in the hot still air. Dust lies heavy on the planks of the small porch shaded by the overhanging eaves, and the oiled oak door is shut as tightly as the windows.

After wiping the muddy sweat created by road dust off his forehead, he struggles down from the horse and ties the mare at the heavy stone hitching post at the end of the porch under the single oak in the yard. Then he eases the viola case from the oversized saddlebag.

'Well, Daffyd, where'd ye be getting a horse?' asks the slender brunette from the half-open door. Her hair is pulled back and bound high enough on the back of her head to lift it clear of her neck. She wears a sleeveless homespun brown shirt that reaches mid-thigh over loose gray trousers that stop at mid-calf. Her feet are bare.

'It was Da's.' Daffyd looks to the half-open door.

'He give it to ye? A fine gift that'd be.'

'He be dead, Jenny. Lord Brill killed him.' Daffyd takes the two steps onto the porch, then stops several paces short of her, the canvas and wooden case in his right hand.

The brunette steps back toward the door. 'What be ye here for?'

'You owe me, Jenny,' Daffyd says. 'You be owing me more than you can ever pay. How many times have I played for you, just the way you wanted, to send or summon folks all the way to Nordwei or Elioch?'

'I've been more than nice to you, Daffyd.'

Daffyd flushes, then adds, 'Aye, and I've been nice to you, not charging you for the music.'

'If Lord Brill be after you . . .'

'He's not after me.' Daffyd waits.

'Then why are you here?'

The young man wipes his forehead. 'You could invite me in where it's cooler. You've no company.' His eyes traverse the dust on the porch planks, unmarked except by his boots.

Jenny tightens her lips and looks toward the empty lane, then jerks her head toward the door.

'Jenny, seeing as it's me, no one would be saying anything.'

'Come in, then, seeing as there's no stopping you.' She stands back from the door.

Daffyd crosses the porch and steps inside, closing the heavy door with his left hand. The main room is empty, but a faint scent of onions wafts from the kitchen area to the left rear of the cottage. While the cottage is cooler than the late-morning heat outside, Daffyd wipes his forehead with the back of his left hand, his right still clutching the old brown canvas viola case.

'Well, fine talking Daffyd, what do you want?' The brunette looks to the closed heavy door, and then at the mirror on the cottage wall. 'I can't bring your da back from the darkshadows. Lord Brill himself couldn't do that. I could send you to Farway. That's as far as I can do.'

'That won't bring back Da.'

'Nothing will bring back yer da. Not even Meringuay could do that. I'm a rote travel-sorceress – good enough to hold a house – but not more. You told me that yourself. 'Member that?'

Daffyd pulls his lips together, then speaks. 'He hummed – just a few notes. Just a little. That was all. And only once – not twice like Brill said.'

'That'd be strong, accusing Lord Brill of lying. He'd not like that.'

'Like it or not, he lied. Da hummed a little. He's hummed for years. Everyone knows that, but he doesn't hum tunes, and it's never upset patterning before.'

'Just a few notes in front of the land's strongest sorcerer.' Jenny shivers, pursing her narrow lips.

'He turned him into dust – just dust – and the wind blew him away . . .'

'All I can do is send you somewhere,' she repeats.

'Can you bring someone here?'

'Aye. If they want to come, but who wants to come to dry Defalk?'

Daffyd smiles. 'Bring me a sorceress. One out of the mists. Make her blonde and strong enough to turn Lord Brill into red dust himself.'

Jenny shivers again. 'Out of the mists? A sorceress? She'd have to want to come, and what one of them would want to leave the mists? Why would they help the likes of you?'

'Try it. Please . . .'

'I don't know.'

'You try it – or I'll keep you from sending anyone anywhere.' Daffyd's voice turns cold.

'You do, and Lord Brill will be a-chasing you.' Jenny backs away. 'And you don't be threatening me, Daffyd. You're not the only friend I've got.'

'You aren't the only one I've got, either.' Daffyd shrugs.

'Mayhap . . . but it's my cottage where you've come.' She crosses her arms and waits.

Daffyd sighs, and waits. Finally, he speaks. 'You're the best I know, and I need the best.'

'Ha! You tell all the girls that, and that's just when you want something.' She walked over the bare open space of the room to the stone hearth, then turns and recrosses her arms. 'What you want is trouble.'

'I need a strong sorceress.'

'What am I – failed bread?'

Daffyd's lips tighten, and his breath hisses out through his nose. After a moment, he asks, 'Do you want to take on Brill?'

'Am I looking as daft as a heatstruck fowl?'

The young man shrugs.

'Oh, Daffyd . . . you've always been trouble.'

Daffyd sets the viola case on the battered waist-high square table set against the wall that separates the kitchen from the main room. He opens the case carefully and extracts the polished viola, then the bow.

'I need a spell for the mists,' points out Jenny.

'I have one.' He gently sets the viola on the table beside the case, and fumbles in his wallet before extracting a scrap of paper covered with smeared markstick. He reads the words slowly.

> 'Bring us a singer, truly strong,
> from the mists beyond our song.
> Her voice like fire, hair like gold,
> her words filled with flame and bold . . .'

Jenny holds up her hand. 'This spell's pretty chancy, Daffyd. You could get a blonde-haired lizard that sings.'

'Let me read it all the way through.'

The brunette nods.

Daffyd glances down and keeps reading, his voice deliberate as he pronounces each word. When he finishes, he looks at Jenny and asks, 'Well . . . ?'

'It might work. Just you make sure you play it all the way through. Those first lines are chancy.' She takes a deep breath and looks at the mirror on the cottage wall. 'But you get her outta here quick-like. I'll be telling Lord Brill you tricked me. You understand that, don't you? I'd have to be telling him that.'

Daffyd nods.

'Recite it again. I need to get the words in my head. Then you'll be playing your tune. I'll be needing to listen a few

times.' She shakes her head. 'A sorceress out of the mists
... why ...'

4

Anna completed an uncertain step, swaying for an instant.
The outdoor light of Ames had been replaced with something
gloomier – and hotter. She stood in the middle of a room,
smaller than the cramped living room in the condo. The walls
were a dirty white plaster that was uneven and rough, and
there was no ceiling, just open rafters. The faint light that
seeped around ill-fitting shutters on the room's two windows
was the only source of illumination.

Where was she? How had she gotten there? Had she
fainted? Her hand twinged, and the door key was somehow
burning her hand. Anna slipped the key into the green
leather purse, then squeezed her fingers together, pressing
her thumbnail into her palm, stopping before the pressure
became pain.

White spots flickered in front of her eyes, and she forced
herself to take a deep breath, then another. What had
happened?

'You did it! You did it!' exclaimed a male voice, interrupting
her self-inquiries.

'A travel-sorceress I am. Give me a good spell and a decent
tune, and I will bring someone from anywhere,' answered a
woman. 'You'd better hope she's what you want.'

Wondering what the young man wanted, and fearing that
she did know, Anna slowly turned from the hearth. On her
left were the two shuttered windows, on her right a wall
containing only a single wood-framed mirror and near the
far end, a closed wooden door. In the middle of the room
stood two figures. The man, black-haired and somehow
both angular and round-faced, was barely out of youth.

He held what looked to be a viola and a heavily arched shed bow and wore faded blue trousers and an armless and collarless shirt fastened with oblong wooden buttons. The woman was several years older, square-faced, in short trousers and a baggy armless blouse.

Behind them was another wall, with an opening into another room.

'She is beautiful,' the man said as if Anna were not even present. Anna hated being referred to in the third person. It reminded her of all too many auditions, especially the year she'd been in New York.

'A sorceress has to appear beautiful, Daffyd. You do not know what she really looks like.'

Anna glanced down. She still wore the raincoat over her gown, and she was getting hot in the small and stuffy room. After a moment, she unfastened the buttons and the trench coat's belt and stuffed the ends of the belt into the coat's pockets. Then her eyes went back to the woman.

'I'm Anna. Who are you?' Her words sounded firm. Totally inane, but firm.

'I am Jenny, lady.' The brunette offered a slight bow.

Anna's eyes went to the man.

'Daffyd.' His voice was defensive, and he didn't bow.

Where was she? They spoke English, or she understood what they spoke, but it sounded like English.

'Could you tell me where I might be?' Another totally inane question – she was in a peasant cottage – or totally out of her mind. Had she been hit by a tornado, like Dorothy, and was she lying somewhere hallucinating? Or worse, had Sandy been right about parallel universes or worlds? She'd always believed that the world was the world. Another thought flicked through her mind, a thought that seemed to move so slowly – time travel?

'Why, you are in Jenny's cottage,' answered Daffyd sardonically.

'That much I surmised,' snapped Anna, reacting to the teenaged-student tone she'd heard all too many times in her life already, particularly from ungrateful students. 'But where is Jenny's cottage? And when?'

The two locals exchanged glances. Daffyd walked to the square table on the wall and slipped first the viola, then the bow, into a canvas case. He did not close the case.

Anna sighed, then stripped off the raincoat and folded it over her arm. The heat was making her feel faint, and the last thing she wanted was to collapse in front of total strangers in this unknown place. 'Could you please tell me where we are?'

'We are in Mencha, and it is on the eastern marches of Defalk,' said Daffyd, as if the entire world knew the obvious.

That helped a lot, reflected Anna, before answering. 'I'm sorry, but I've never heard of Mencha, or Defalk, and I don't know the name of your world.'

'It is the world, the earth,' answered the brunette. 'Some of the sorcerers call it Erde.'

'Erde,' mused Anna. Germanic, but the two didn't look especially Teutonic.

'Except for the worlds of the mist,' added Daffyd, 'it be the only world.'

The only world? Anna felt flushed. 'Might I have something to drink? It's been a long trip.'

Again, the two exchanged glances, as if Anna had said something profoundly stupid, and she wanted to scream. That would have made matters worse; it always did. Then Jenny bowed slightly, turned, and walked through the opening in the wall to what might have been a kitchen, although all Anna saw was what seemed to be a brick stove and a table with a bench on one side. Her legs felt stiff, and Anna looked for a place to sit. There were two short benches and a higher stool.

Daffyd kept looking at her as if she were not quite real, the way her new students did after she'd done a recital, as if they couldn't believe that she could sing, really sing.

Bother it! Anna stepped away from the unused hearth

toward the stool. She set her purse on the dusty plank floor and quickly folded the raincoat over the rough wooden stool, hoping that the trench coat would shield the gown from any splinters. As she sat, her nose twitched from the dust in the hot room, and she rubbed it gently, almost afraid to sneeze.

Jenny returned across the dusty plank floors, a brown earthenware mug in her hands. She extended the handleless mug to Anna. 'Here, lady.'

'Thank you.' Anna stared at the water in the mug. It looked clean.

'I spell my water clean,' offered Jenny. 'Most folks can't, you know, and they won't pay to get it done.'

Spelling water clean? What sort of place was this Erde – like a medieval pigsty? 'Thank you.' Anna sipped the lukewarm water, then drank the mug down to the bottom. She'd been thirstier than she'd realized.

The two continued to study her intently, as if looking for some sort of sign.

'Why did you bring me here?' Anna reached down and lifted the green leather purse into her lap, rummaging through it for a handkerchief. She used the rumpled cloth to blot her damp forehead gently. The room was hot, hotter than the Colonial, and she had the feeling that it was even hotter outside. She looked down at the purse. The leather around the metal clasps was browned, as if it had been scorched or burned. She didn't recall that, but she'd grabbed the purse in a hurry.

Daffyd looked down at the dusty planks.

'Daffyd needs a sorceress from out of the mists,' Jenny finally volunteered.

'A sorceress? You can't be serious.' A sorceress? They thought Anna was a sorceress? What sort of nuthouse was this?

'You have to be a sorceress. Jenny couldn't have brought you if you weren't,' stammered the youth with the short and ragged black hair.

'Why do you need a sorceress?' Anna had trouble believing she was behaving so rationally. Or was it irrational to talk sensibly in a lunatic situation?

Daffyd and Jenny exchanged glances.

'Well?'

'Lord Brill . . . he turned my da into red dust because he hummed during a wall-raising. He said Da ruined the spell, and that was why the gate was crooked, but Da never hummed in tunes. It was just an excuse.'

Anna moistened her lips. The more she heard, the worse it got. 'What sort of wall?' Another rational-sounding question that made no sense.

'It was a whole fort – stone and brick. They'll finish the roof later. You can't handle wooden roof beams with sorcery, not unless you go to strong darksong, and that's dangerous, even for a sorcerer like Brill.'

'They say he does a lot of darksong when no one's around,' Jenny added. 'Liende plays for him then.'

Daffyd looked at Jenny. 'That can't be.'

'I know what I know.'

Anna's eyes flicked from one to the other. Both felt they were telling the truth – that was her feeling, and that meant something was wrong, very wrong. 'Why is that a problem, Daffyd?' Her voice was as calm as if she were teaching her musical-theatre class, and that was wrong, too, because the more questions she asked, the fewer got answered.

'Liende wouldn't do that. She wouldn't.'

'I know what I know,' affirmed Jenny.

'Stop it!' snapped Anna. 'Daffyd, you still haven't told me why you wanted a sorceress. You haven't said why it's important enough to summon one from far away. You haven't told me exactly how far this world is from mine. You seem to be why I'm here. I'd like some answers.' She licked her dry lips. 'Try to make them clear.'

'Go ahead, Daffyd. It be your idea.'

The young man looked at the plank floor, then at Jenny, then back to the floor. His eyes did not rise to meet Anna's.

'I wanted you to turn Lord Brill into red dust, like he turned Da into dust.'

Keep to the point, Anna told herself, whatever the point is. 'How?'

'With sorcery, acourse.'

'You say I have to be a sorceress,' ventured Anna, pausing. The room was small and hot. 'Why?'

'The spell called for a sorceress, and you're here. Spells work, or they don't. It worked. That means you're a sorceress.'

Confused as she felt, even Anna could follow that logic, and she held in a shiver. Wonderful! She was either dead, dying, hallucinating, or truly in another world or time where they thought she was a sorceress. Anna pursed her lips. She didn't like any of the choices. And she'd thought Ames after Irenia's death had been bad. *I can handle this*, she told herself silently. *I can handle this*.

'Daffyd spelled for a strong sorceress,' Jenny added. 'You must be very strong.'

'Could I have another cup of water?' Anna asked, wondering what she was supposed to do next. A strong sorceress who didn't even know what sorcery was? She didn't know whether to cry or laugh, or just break down and sob.

I can handle this, she repeated, *whatever this is*.

5

MENCHA, DEFALK

A single chord ending in a discordant minor reverberates from the silver harp that stands on the pedestal in the middle of the marble basin.

'What now?' The resonant baritone voice is far more impressive than the slender and balding man who speaks.

Circles ring his brown-flecked green eyes as he walks to the harp. His eyes drop to the ripples that disrupt the image in the silvered surface – that of a blonde woman in a brown cloak.

'I did not do it, Lord Brill, sir. Not me.' The youth in the short blue tunic backs toward the narrow door through which he has just hurried.

'You could not have done this, Gero.' Brill's eyes study the vanishing image, taking in the green gown that shows from under the blonde woman's cloak, the rough-walled cottage – and the brown-haired songstress.

'Jenny . . . oh, Jenny . . .' His eyes flick to the fading black-haired figure in the corner. 'Daffyd . . . well, we'll just have to do something about this. Yes, we will.'

Gero backs up until he shivers silently in the arch of the doorway.

'The cloak,' Brill murmurs, then reaches for the harp and strums it gently.

> 'Hold this image in my sight.
> Keep it fresh; keep it bright . . .'

He replaces the harp and watches for a time as the image in the mirrored water sharpens and as the woman removes the strange cloak with arms to display the magnificent green gown she wears. She also carries a large leather wallet that looks to be of green leather that matches the gown.

Brill frowns once more as the blonde woman sits on the stool and apparently begins to question Daffyd and Jenny.

After a time, he speaks. 'Gero. Have my carriage made ready. I will need two guards.'

'Yes, ser.'

'You doubt that two will be enough?' Amusement etches the resonant tones.

'No, ser. But . . . is it not . . . not . . .'

'Dangerous to try to cross the mist barriers? Very – she could have been burned. She should have been burned. Those two innocent idiots have not the faintest image of what they have done. But she is here, and we will see.'

'Yes, ser.'

Brill's eyes drop back to the images in the mirror pond.

6

Anna tried not to sigh after she took another swallow from the earthenware mug. 'Let's get back to the point. Why couldn't you have found a sorceress here on ... Erde, is it?'

Daffyd looked down at the planks again, just like a student who hadn't learned his music. Instead of answering her, he glanced at Jenny. 'A mirror peek at Brill's hall?' His voice was almost plaintive.

Jenny glared at Daffyd, but he just looked back dumbly, his big dark eyes wide and imploring. After what seemed an interminable silence, Jenny cleared her throat. 'If you would not mind ... lady ...'

'Anna. No, I would not mind.' Maybe, just maybe, whatever Jenny did would shed some light on what these people called sorcery.

'Daffyd? The looking song?'

Daffyd turned slowly and lifted the viola out from its case. Then came the bow, and he lifted the instrument to his shoulder and tucked it under his chin. Then he stroked the bow across the strings.

Jenny turned toward the mirror and cleared her throat, then lifted her hand, and gave a rough tempo, then dropped the hand.

Daffyd began to play, and Jenny to sing.

'Mirror, mirror on my wall,
Show now me the Lord Brill's hall.

Show it bright, and show it fast,
and make that strong view well last.'

The mirror shimmered, then filled with colors.

Anna swallowed and looked at the scene in the wall mirror. A blue carriage rolled through a gate in a tall stone wall, pulled by four black horses. The gates looked to be of heavy timbers, and there were turrets or guard towers on each side of the wall above the gate.

Sorcery – was it just the combination of words, song, and accompaniment? Just? Anna almost laughed. Jenny's words, simple as they had sounded, had been perfectly pitched and matched to Daffyd's equally simple melody. She doubted that many undergraduate students could have done that well, and that didn't take into account the words.

'There be Lord Brill's carriage on its way here, no doubt,' Jenny said dryly.

'Here?' Anna asked.

'He has a magic pool that tells him everything,' Daffyd said glumly, closing the viola and bow up in the canvas case. 'We had best leave. You can go to my sister Dalila's in Synope. Lord Brill can't leave Mencha until Lord Barjim's fort is done,' Daffyd said hurriedly.

'Why would I want to go to Synope?' Anna glanced from Daffyd to Jenny. 'By the way, where is Synope?'

'You have to go.'

'I'd like to know why,' Anna persisted. Once again, it felt like all the people around her were making the decisions.

'You just have to.'

'Why?'

Daffyd looked to Jenny.

'You asked for a strong sorceress,' Jenny said.

'Young Daffyd, I'm not going anywhere just because someone says so,' Anna explained. 'Why should I flee? Will this Lord Brill try to turn me into dust with a song?'

Daffyd winced. 'That's what he did to Da.'

'It doesn't matter, Daffyd,' Jenny said. 'Lord Brill's carriage is already too close, and your mount couldn't outrun it carrying double.'

Daffyd sighed.

Anna wanted to sigh as well. Had her insistence on trying to figure out the situation just made it that much worse? Was her life always going to be like that – a choice between reacting blindly, not knowing the situation, or trying to figure out the unknown rules and finding she was hopelessly behind by the time she did figure them out?

'Let's go and meet him,' she suggested. Much as she hated confrontation, she'd learned long ago that running from it only made things worse.

Again, the other two exchanged the kind of glance that confirmed they thought she was truly out of her mind.

Anna stood, folded the unnecessary trench coat over her arm, and picked up her purse. She walked toward the door she hoped was the right one.

Daffyd stepped forward and opened the heavy wooden door, and Anna could sense the ovenlike heat outside. No wonder everyone wore such light clothes. She stepped out onto the porch. Despite the shade provided by the over-hanging eaves, the air seemed to scorch her, almost taking her breath away, and, under her gown, she could feel the near-instant perspiration building. The sun seemed high in the sky – it certainly wasn't late afternoon, as it had been in Ames. She glanced at her watch – the hands showed five-forty, and she didn't think they were moving. She looked again. The brass of the watch looked tarnished, somehow. It was an inexpensive watch, a cheap replacement for the one her father had given her when she'd gotten her master's. The graduation watch had broken beyond repair the same week Irenia had been killed.

Anna swallowed, trying to ignore the fact that her new watch had stopped, that her daughter was dead, that ... that ... all too many things – and the heat – by studying what she could see of Mencha.

Perhaps a hundred feet from where she stood was another

cottage – low and thick-walled with stucco or plaster peeling away from the cross-woven stick frame in places. A few browned stalks dropped in a square stone-ringed space that had once been a garden. To her right, across a rutted dirt lane, was another cottage, one whose plaster appeared intact, and whose small garden was green, rather than brown.

Daffyd joined her, carrying his viola case. As Anna looked at the young man, she realized that she was almost as tall as he was, and that she towered over Jenny. At five-four, she wasn't that tall, either. Was everyone on Erde short?

'How big is Mencha?' Anna asked after a moment.

'Maybe two deks across.' Daffyd turned toward the dirt lane.

'What is a dek?'

'Ten furls.'

Patiently, Anna asked the next question. 'How long is a furl?'

'For a sorceress, you don't know much.'

Anna asked again. 'How long?'

'Ten rods.'

'How big is—' Anna began.

'Ten yards in a rod.'

'And a yard is about this long?' Anna approximated thirty-six inches with her hands.

'Something like that,' Daffyd answered, looking from her back toward the lane.

'How many people live in Mencha?'

'A hundred households, perhaps,' answered Jenny, as she closed the door to the cottage behind her.

Anna wanted to scream. Trying to find out anything would take *forever*! And by the time she did, everyone would think she was a dizzy blonde. 'How far away is Lord Brill's palace?'

'He has a hall, not a palazzio,' snorted Daffyd. 'Only the Nesereans have palazzios.'

'I'd like to see how well you do in my world,' Anna

snapped. 'His hall can't be far, not if his carriage would catch us immediately.'

Daffyd gestured toward the cottage wall, as if pointing through the structure. 'It's on the hill, overlooking the Synope road. That's less than three deks.' He added, as if anticipating a question, 'That's not quite half a league.'

'A league?'

'Ten deks.'

Anna's thoughts swirled with the unfamiliar measurements, but she guessed that Brill's hall was south of Mencha, assuming that directions weren't as strange as everything else on Erde. What should she do? Daffyd hadn't wanted her to meet Brill, yet he seemed resigned.

'What should I watch for with Lord Brill?' she asked.

Daffyd's mouth opened, then closed.

'Go on,' she said. 'You don't trust him, but you seem to think that I'll do what he wants just because I wouldn't do what you wanted.'

'He talks fine, lady,' Jenny said. 'They say he's a fine wit, and offers a right good table, but many folk leave his hall changed.'

'Changed?'

'Or with the wind, like dust.' Daffyd bit off each word and spat it out.

'They think he's a right fine lord, when they didn't when they went to sup,' Jenny said.

'Sorcery?' Anna asked.

'What else?' answered Daffyd.

'Speaking of the Lord Brill, that dust'd be his carriage,' Jenny offered, pointing past the yellowing oak and beyond the lane.

Anna could see a smudge of brown beyond several huts or hovels. Compared to them, Jenny's cottage was palatial. Anna wanted to shake her head. Instead, she used her handkerchief to blot her forehead, gently. For what it was worth, she didn't need smeared makeup on top of everything else.

'Has to be,' said Daffyd. ''Sides Essoles, he's got the only carriage in Mencha, and Essoles sent his wife to Wei. She took the carriage.'

Anna looked at Daffyd, wishing he would explain.

The young man saw her look. 'You wouldn't know that. Some say the dark ones are going to send their gray legions through the Sand Pass before winter. That's why Lord Barjim's here. He paid Lord Brill solid silver to raise that fort. Last fall, in the dry months, not that they have not all been dry, he had Brill raise a dam just beyond the pass road. Elwiss told me that there's a moat there where they can open a water gate and wash away anyone below the wall.'

''Gainst the dark ones, it won't be enough,' offered Jenny.

The sound of hoofs on hard soil, and the faint rumble of iron tires, announced the arrival of the coach. Anna turned back toward the lane as the carriage rolled across the parched ground almost to the porch of the cottage, where the blue-clad driver reined in the four blacks. The carriage rolled to a halt. The blue-lacquered finish gleamed in the hazy afternoon sunshine, and the door flipped open. A slender and balding man attired entirely in blue velvet stepped out.

Without a word, the sorcerer or whatever he was stepped onto the porch. In her heels, Anna was slightly taller than he was, but he doffed his velvet cap, and bowed. 'You do us honor, noble lady. I am Lord Brill.'

Despite the kindly appearing smile and the faint twinkle in his eye, Anna didn't feel quite right about the sorcerer.

He didn't call her a sorceress, Anna noted. Did that mean he wasn't sure, or was he being polite? What should she do? With a curtsey, the affected kind all the Met sopranos used, she replied, 'You do *me* the honor, lord.'

'I would like to do you greater honor, lady, by offering my hall as your residence for so long as you find necessary.'

'You are indeed kind as well as honorable.' Anna didn't quite choke on the words. Just think of it like university politics, she told herself. Just more politics. 'Most kind.' How honorable Brill might be was another question.

'Might I inquire as to how you prefer to be called?'

'I am Anna.'

'Lady Anna,' mused the sorcerer. 'Neither the pools nor the books offer guidance for that name, and that may prove most . . . liberating. We all could use some freedom in dealing with the dark ones.' He smiled again. 'But I stray from your comfort.'

Anna offered a smile, the polite, political kind that wasn't quite automatic.

'Well, young Daffyd,' said Brill cheerfully, turning to the black-haired young man. 'Like always, you've done the right thing for the wrong reason. And both you and Lady Anna were lucky, most lucky. And so were you, Jenny. Great works from innocents. Still, the dark ones are on the move, and Lord Barjim would give his left leg for a true sorceress. I trust you'll be back in your quarters before supper.'

'Yes, ser.' Daffyd bowed.

'As for you, Jenny . . . we may be needing you as well.' Brill smiled and added pleasantly. 'I wouldn't be traveling too far.'

'Yes, Lord Brill.' Jenny inclined her head.

The sorcerer turned back to Anna, his eyes and mouth smiling. 'If you would . . . Do you need assistance?'

'I'm fine.' Anna took the two wooden steps off the porch and walked across the dirt that seemed to grab at her high heels. She paused at the iron step to the carriage, marveling at the details, from the scrolled ironwork to the velvet upholstered seats and the brass impressed panels above the seat backs.

'You will find it quite comfortable, I'm certain,' Brill said reasonably. 'I apologize for the long step up, but one doesn't find mounting blocks everywhere.'

'I'll manage.' Anna took a slightly deeper breath and, holding the right-hand railing, also lacquered in blue, pulled herself up and into the carriage. As she sat down, more heavily than she intended, she could almost feel the carriage flex.

Brill stepped up into the carriage and closed the lacquered metal door, sealing the heat in with them. He sat on the side seat opposite Anna, his back to the driver. Without explaining, he hummed for an instant, then sang:

> 'Cool this space and chill the air;
> keep us healthy, fresh, and fair . . .'

When the sorcerer finished, the heat receded, almost as though the carriage were air-conditioned. He wiped his forehead, and took a deep breath. 'That will not last long, but long enough for us to reach my hall. It is a far more suitable place for a lady such as you.' The brown-flecked eyes twinkled as the balding man boldly studied Anna.

Anna again caught the humorous overtones in the words. 'And why might that be, Lord Brill?'

Brill made a gesture toward the small carriage windows whose perfect glass revealed the sunbaked and cracked ground, the yellow-tinged oak tree at the end of the cottage and the two figures on the porch.

'Is it not obvious?'

Anna nodded slowly, but ever since leaving Avery – and before – she had come to distrust the obvious, especially when someone pointed it out.

'You offer a gesture of agreement, Lady Anna, but not one that is more than perfunctory.'

'I guess I'm inclined to reserve judgment on many things until I'm more familiar with your world.'

'Is that why you did not ride off with young Daffyd?' Brill laughed softly. 'I do not read thoughts, but he was angry. He wrote the spell that summoned you, and taught it to Jenny, obviously. She is a rotesorceress, adequate but without much inspiration. Still, it is enough to gain her a house as a woman alone, and that is much in these days. He is talented, but his voice is not good enough to hold spells.

His playing is far better than his father's, and he doesn't hum that distracting monotone the way Culain did. Young Daffyd still does not understand how often or how deeply his father has jeopardized me. Or how much he jeopardized you.'

'You turned him into dust for humming?' asked Anna, her voice as emotionless as she could make it.

'What else could I do? He kept getting worse, and, if I let him go, he'd have been picked up by the dark ones in days, and they'd have the fruits of my works to use against Defalk.'

Anna's eyes flicked from the earnest-sounding sorcerer to the windows at the change in the sound of the carriage team's hoofs. The carriage was headed down a stone-paved street, with a handful of buildings on either side, but both pavement and buildings passed quickly, and the carriage seemed headed away from the town.

'Here, unlike your world, Lady Anna, sorcery is a dangerous business. The slightest improper inflection, the wrong thought-image of a word, or any distraction can cause a spell to fail – or to have unintended consequences.'

Anna frowned. Hadn't Daffyd said that spells either worked or failed? Was Brill lying? The inside of the carriage was getting warmer, and she wanted to rub her forehead.

'You understand, I see. But young Daffyd does not.' Brill sighed. 'I can only hope he will come to understand before it is too late.'

Anna pursed her lips. None of it made sense. If Brill were so evil, and if he could turn someone into dust, why hadn't he just turned Daffyd into dust? Or was that because he needed Anna? Was Daffyd what he seemed? But she usually had a good sense of people, and the young man had impressed her as honest – confused, but honest. And what about Daffyd being lucky – or her being lucky? She already had too many questions.

The carriage started uphill, and the horses' hoofs clicked once more on stone.

Anna leaned forward to study the structure. The off-white stone walls were high enough not to be squat, but not high enough to soar either, and the three sides she could see seemed to form a hexagon, with the gate she had glimpsed in Jenny's mirror centered in the middle section. The walls were not crenelated, and besides the higher towers straddling the gate, there were additional towers – one at each apex of the hexagon. Impressive for something called a hall, she thought.

The iron-bound gates swung shut behind the carriage with a heavy clunk that sounded as she imagined a prison door would. Anna forced a smile.

'There,' said the sorcerer with visible relief. 'I hope the dark ones didn't scry you, but, if they did, they won't know too much.' Brill frowned. 'How long were you there in Jenny's cottage?'

'Not very long.' It was Anna's turn to frown. 'Why?'

'It would be better if they didn't know you were here.'

'Who? And why?'

Brill laughed the same amused and soft laugh. 'I beg your pardon, Lady Anna. I will explain more when you are refreshed. For now, let me just say that the dark ones would destroy all of Liedwahr, and kill all of its sorcerers, including you and me, in the name of what they call reason. Since you are here, you can help.'

'Why should I?' Anna's tone was curious.

'You could be one of the most powerful sorceresses in Liedwahr, not just Defalk, but you have much to learn,' Brill answered reasonably. 'Unless you want to take the risk of dying in fire, you'll need to learn about Liedwahr. I intend to help you.' The carriage rolled to a gentle stop.

All Anna could see through the small carriage windows were walls of identical stones, each like marble, each tinted light blue. 'I imagine so,' she said sweetly, trying to keep from grinding her teeth.

'Not for your body, lovely as it appears, but because I would prefer to remain whole and intact, and it will take the power of every sorcerer in Defalk, and all the armsmen Lord Barjim can raise, to stop the dark ones.'

'Who are the dark ones?'

'The Dark Monks of Ebra, though their sacred source is in the mountains around Vult.'

More names that meant nothing, Anna thought.

'I'll explain it at dinner,' Brill explained, opening the door, and stepping out. 'I imagine you are hungry.' He extended a hand.

Anna found she didn't need it, since the carriage had indeed pulled up to what she imagined was a mounting block – or a set of stone steps designed to unload carriages.

Brill gestured to a diminutive black-haired girl, not even to Anna's shoulder, who stood in the shadows at the top of the steps by the open oak door. 'Florenda, will you escort the lady Anna to the first guest suite?' Brill offered his pleasant smile once more. 'We will eat at the first bell.' He turned to Anna. 'That will be two glasses before true sunset.'

Anna guessed that meant something like two hours before sunset, and her eyes flicked toward what she felt was the west, assuming the hazy white sun was in the western sky.

'You will find some refreshments in your suite, Lady Anna,' Brill added, with another bow. 'Until dinner.'

Florenda bowed. 'If you would follow me, lady.'

Anna wanted to shake her head. The only time she'd ever gotten this kind of bowing and scraping was the time she'd sung the national anthem at the Peach Bowl, and that had been years ago, when Cindy what's-her-name had canceled less than a day before.

She grasped her handbag firmly and walked up the half dozen steps to the tall doorway that dwarfed her. Her heels clicked on the hard light-blue stone. Was the entire hall built of the same stone?

The heat of the day vanished as she stepped into the hall and Florenda closed the doorway. The entry foyer rose nearly three stories, with a glittering brass-and-crystal

defense works to support his forts on Defalk's side of the Sand Pass.'

'Much good they will do him.'

'And a portal to one of the mist worlds has been opened.'

'Where?' The Songmaster stops writing on the heavy linen-paper scroll.

'In Defalk.'

'Defalk? How? A mist portal takes the lyric voice, and none there have the power. Are you sure of this, Brother Burthen?'

'As sure as we can be. The opening plucked the strings of Erde, and the echoes still whisper on her strings.'

'Was the portal opened from the mist side?'

Brother Burthen shook his head. 'Discovering it took some time, Songmaster. All we could determine is that a strange blonde woman, in an exotic green gown, went from a cottage in the hamlet of Mencha to Lord Brill's hall.'

'A single sorceress will not stop us, even one that has escaped the fires of passage. But how she did . . .' A shrug follows. 'That matters not now.'

'If she is allied with Brill . . .'

'Brill always turns and runs when matters become difficult. Why should this time be any different?'

'The sorceress might change matters.'

The hint of a smile crosses the Songmaster's face, visible only on the unshadowed portion of his mouth. 'She would have to be powerful indeed.'

'His hall is warded,' pointed out Burthen, as if the Songmaster had not smiled at all.

'Watch it, as you can. We will proceed with the day's works. Contact the dark chapter in Falcor and see what more they can discover about the portal – and if the woman is a sorceress.'

'One sorceress cannot prove that great a problem,' suggested Burthen.

'I would prefer to have no problems.'

'Yes, Songmaster.'

The Songmaster continues to write, slowly, on the song scroll before him, long, long after Burthen has left the dimness of the tent.

8

Anna stepped into the room – a medieval or Erde-ish version of a presidential suite, more than thirty feet long, and nearly as wide from the door to the windows. On the outside wall, blue-tinted but clear floor-to-ceiling windows offered a panorama of both the walls to Brill's stronghold, and the cottages and lanes of Mencha downhill and to the north.

That had to mean that the hall's walls weren't that high. Anna frowned, recalling that the hall was on a hilltop. Probably the walls were a lot higher on the outside than the inside.

The windows were flanked with heavy blue hangings drawn back with thick blue cording. Before the window was an elegant stone table, flanked by a pair of blue-lacquered chairs. The large and high bed was covered with a pale blue spread trimmed in white lace. In the center of the spread was the letter *B*, in a royal blue.

On each side of the bed were delicate-appearing stone tables, on each a brass-and-crystal oil lamp.

'The wardrobing area is through that door,' offered Florenda.

Anna crossed the room and slipped through the smaller door into a room that contained a raised stone tub that would have fit four of her, a long stone vanity that included a sink, and two walls comprised of open closets half-filled with clothing. Beside the left end of the vanity was a full-length mirror. It showed a bewildered-looking and slightly disheveled singer in a green formal gown, carrying a rumpled raincoat.

Florenda pointed to a curtained alcove in the outer wall. 'The jakes is there.'

Jakes? The word wasn't familiar, but Anna understood the idea. There was some form of indoor plumbing, at least for the wealthy, although she certainly was no stranger to an outhouse, not after the summers at Uncle Garven's Appalachian farm up in the holler beyond Bear Paw.

'If you need anything,' Florenda repeated, 'just use the bellpull in the bedroom or the robing room.' She pointed to a long blue rope beside the stone vanity. Then she bowed. 'Unless you have any immediate needs . . .'

'No. No. You can go.' Anna just wanted a few minutes to think. Things kept getting more and more confusing. She walked to the door to the corridor, following Florenda. As soon as the maid stepped out, Anna closed the door and threw the iron bolt.

Wasn't there something about iron being proof against magic? Or was that a superstition?

She wandered toward the bed, noting that the frame was beautifully-wrought metal of some sort, again covered with the almost shimmering blue lacquer that seemed everywhere. After laying the coat on the coverlet, gently, she lifted the stiff fabric, noting the stitching wasn't that much better than her own, and certainly not as good as her mother's. The bed even felt lumpy, and she frowned again.

She turned and walked toward the window, still carrying her handbag, looking at the hangings, a sort of velvet, but with a weave that was almost shoddy in comparison to the rest of the room.

She pulled out one of the chairs. Delicate as it looked, it was heavy, as if it were solid iron, and the small cushion on the seat, embroidered with another *B*, appeared somewhat frayed.

The brass tray on the table contained a small loaf of bread, what appeared to be slices of dried apple, and a handful of narrow yellow cheese wedges.

Anna set the green purse on one side of the circular stone table, broke off a corner of the dark bread, and chewed the small morsel. Although slightly tough, the bread offered a good taste, like a cross between pumpernickel and rye. She had another mouthful, then looked at the crystal pitcher and the pair of matching crystal goblets.

She sniffed the pitcher, but the amber-colored liquid offered a bitter, familiar, but unfamiliar tang, even faintly musty. Gingerly, she poured a small amount into the goblet, and took the smallest of sips.

'Oooo . . .' While it might once have passed for wine, the liquid tasted more like vinegar. Anna licked her lips and picked up the clean goblet, carrying it into the robing room.

There were two levered faucets into the stone tub. Anna picked the left one and turned it. A thin trickle of steaming water flowed out. Hastily she closed the first lever and opened the second. A wider stream of cool water poured from the faucet, and she slipped the goblet under the lukewarm stream for a moment, then turned the lever off.

Water – but did she dare drink it? She looked at the water in the goblet, thinking about Jenny and the girl's claim about spelling water. The water looked clean. Still . . . she wondered.

She thought about that song Mario used to sing endlessly – he picked it up from an old Frankie Laine album, something about cold, clear, water . . .

> 'All day I faced the barren waste
> without a taste of cool, clear, water . . .'

That wouldn't do.

She rummaged through her purse, and finally came up with a stub of a pencil and the envelope that had contained her last paystub. She began to write, not that she was any writer. Avery or Sandy or even Irenia – she shook her head and tightened her lips.

Don't think about it, she ordered herself. Not now. Angrily, she scrawled out the words. She looked at the rough verse on the rumpled envelope. It was terrible, but not much worse than the couplets Brill had sung to cool the carriage.

She cleared her throat, and tried a vocalise.

'Holly, lolly, polly ... pop ...'

Finally, she looked down at the verse.

'Ready or not ...' She cleared her throat, then tried the words, with as much inflection as she could, emphasizing 'cold' and 'clean.'

> 'All day I faced this barren waste
> without a taste
> of cold, clean water.
> Give now my glass in lovely place
> a healthful taste
> of cold, clean water.'

Anna could feel *something*, and she looked at the goblet, where frost appeared around the rim. Then virtually instantly, the water froze, and the goblet shattered, and Anna looked down dumbly at shards of crystal and a lump of clear and solid ice.

She shook her head, as cold inside as the ice before her. As the saying went, she wasn't in Kansas anymore, nor in Iowa. She certainly wasn't.

Her eyes burned, even as a sense of subdued excitement held her. It was good news and bad news again. Like the good news had been that Avery had left; and that had been the bad news, since he'd left nothing for her or the children. Here, the good news was that she could cast spells; the bad news was that she was really in a different world where she could cast spells.

She looked down at the mess again. There didn't seem to be anything for waste disposal, so she used a crust of bread to sweep the crystal into a small pile, and then she carried the chunk of ice, free of glass, to the sink to let it melt.

After that, she took a sip of the vinegar wine, rather than repeat the water spell. Who knew what she'd get the next time? She also tried the cheese, but the slightest taste gave her the hint of mold, and she set the wedge down. The apple slices weren't bad, if slightly like rubber.

In the end, she ate most of the bread and half the apples, leaving the cheese. Feeling better, she realized the room remained cool, as if a breeze blew from the windows. She walked to the windows again. While they were hinged, they were closed. Underneath each was a louver, and cool air came through the louvers. She extended her hand toward the metal louvers, but stopped short as she felt the chill. Sorcery? The louvers opened to the outside air, but somehow changed the hot air to cold air.

She was supposed to have dinner with the sorcerer, and she felt like a mess, even if she hadn't done that much. But she'd changed worlds, and she'd sweated, and been shocked and surprised.

Anna glanced around the palatial bedchamber, then headed into the robing room, where she found a set of towels – small, clean, and tending toward the frayed. She looked at her watch. The hands still showed five-forty. Didn't Erde have time, or had the transition destroyed the watch or what? Or had the battery run out? More questions for which she had no answers.

She reclaimed her purse and brought it into the robing room where she found a bottle of what appeared to be liquid soap, strong smelling. She used the smallest dab with lots of lukewarm water from the tap to remove the grime she hadn't even realized had built up on her hands. Then, with the smallest towel as a washcloth, using mostly water, she dabbed and blotted her face clean before reapplying her makeup.

That done, she went back into the bedroom and looked from the two hard chairs to the bed. She didn't want to lie down and wrinkle the gown, but the chairs were small and hard.

She walked to the window and looked out, but the scene remained unchanged, although she did see a man in armor walking along the ramparts of the hold, with a bow and quiver slung across his back and some sort of sword in a scabbard.

What was Erde? A place where people could be transported by magic, but used horses and carriages? Where sorcerers turned people into dust, but the weapons were bows and blades? Where castles were elaborate and ornate and finely built, but where cloth was rough and where the hangings and embroidery were equally crude? The contradictions didn't make sense. Was that why she still had a feeling of unreality?

Finally, she sat down on the hard chair, letting her thoughts go where they would.

A gentle knocking roused her, and she realized she had been half dozing as she had been sitting before the table, half propped up with arms and elbows.

'Yes?'

The knocking persisted, and Anna remembered she had bolted the door. She stood, walked over to it, and answered again. 'Yes?'

'Lady Anna? It is about time for dinner.' Florenda's voice was muffled, but clear enough.

Anna undid the bolt and opened the door. 'I'll be there in just a moment.'

Florenda bowed. 'You look most beautiful.'

'Thank you,' Anna replied, taking the compliment more as a testimony to fear in her supposed powers than in her appearance. She gathered her handbag, not wanting to leave it behind, and followed Florenda back down the wide hallway and the grand staircase. They turned left at the bottom of the wide stone steps.

The grand dining room contained a wide stone table nearly thirty yards long, dark under unlit chandeliers. A single gong or chime echoed through the lofty space, adding to the sense of desertion. Anna had the feeling that the room was seldom used as she followed Florenda to the open double doors at the end of the dining room.

Warm light filled the salon, a space not much larger than her bedchamber.

'Lady Anna, punctual as well as beautiful.' Lord Brill, still in the blue velvet jacket and trousers, rose from a carved wooden chair, upholstered in a blue needlepoint. The armchair was the first wooden chair Anna had seen.

Florenda slipped back and closed the salon doors.

'Lord Brill, you are most complimentary and hospitable.' Anna inclined her head.

'These days we must be hospitable. Good company is most scarce. Please be seated. That should accommodate your gown.' Brill gestured to the wide blue velvet settee, also framed in dark-stained carved wood. 'You're from one of the mist worlds, and, despite your poise, it's clear that Erde is strange.' He walked toward the small wooden bookcase set between the tall blue-tinted windows – a bookcase with four tall shelves that contained perhaps a hundred volumes. 'Would you like some refreshments?'

'Not for a moment, thank you. I did appreciate those you had placed in my room. Thank you.' Anna slipped onto the settee, aware that the upholstery was uneven. Was it stuffed with horsehair, like all the antiques collected by Avery's Aunt Lorinda – beautiful, but uncomfortable?

'It was the least I could do.' Brill offered the ingratiating smile. 'Our dinner will be here shortly.' His left hand gestured toward the small table placed in an oversized bay window at the end of the salon. The setting was for two.

Anna nodded politely and waited.

'I've seen some of your worlds – with great metal birds that fly, metal warships of the kind where one would sink all the navies of Erde. Yet you are surprised by the form of sorcery here.'

'Yes,' Anna said, admitting nothing the sorcerer clearly didn't know already.

'Sorcery does work differently here, and far fewer people employ it,' Brill said in an offhand manner.

'Fewer?'

'Everyone seems to be able to employ magic carriages in your world,' Brill said, 'and other magical devices.' He looked quizzically at Anna, then smiled. 'I seemed to have misunderstood what I have seen. Do tell me about your world.'

The sorcerer's pleasant smile set off alarm bells all the way through her, and she forced an equally pleasant smile back, her mind spinning. What could she say? What on earth could she possibly say?

'You have seen my world,' she said slowly. 'There is not too much I could add. But I have seen little of yours.' She offered another smile. 'Perhaps, if you told me more about this world – is it called Erde? Then I could explain the differences better.' That was true enough, since she didn't have the faintest idea what such differences were.

'Information for information.' Brill nodded. 'I will tell you a bit, and then we will dine, and we will talk.' He cleared his throat. 'Where should I begin?'

'Explain about Erde. Daffyd mentioned something about dark ones and great dangers, but that was about all.' Anna smiled brightly. She felt as though she were pasting the smile in place.

'Erde . . . Erde is the world. She is governed by the laws of music, and by the influence of the moons – Darksong and Clearsong. She is also governed by iron, cold iron. That seems to be true to a degree in all worlds,' Brill added sardonically. 'The Dark Monks are a new force in the world, new in the sense that their brotherhood dates back only a few decades, but already they have taken over Ebra and threaten both Defalk and Ranuak, although the Matriarch of the Ranuans insists that the dark ones are no danger.'

'Why are they dangerous?' Anna asked.

'Because they use massed voices to create darksong. They can sometimes change the weather, and there are those that claim the hot and dry years that have recently plagued Defalk are their doing.'

'You're one of those who believes this,' Anna said flatly.

Brill shrugged and offered the quick, warm smile. 'I cannot prove that, but, yes, I do believe that they have meddled with the weather.' The smile vanished. 'They will do worse in the seasons ahead.'

'I'm not clear on the difference between darksong and clearsong . . .' Anna didn't even know what they were, except that they had something to do with the way sorcery was practiced on Erde, but there was no reason to confess to total ignorance.

A ghost of a frown flitted across the sorcerer's face before he spoke. 'You have seen that the world can be recorded to some degree by manipulating the music that binds its components together. The stronger the aspects of the spell, the more effective it is.'

Anna nodded. That made a strange sort of sense.

'But there are two sets of bindings on Erde – those that bind the living, or once living, and those that bind the nonliving. It is dangerous to attempt to manipulate the living – and difficult.'

'But those who do are the darksingers?' she asked.

'Ah . . . yes . . .' Brill looked vaguely disconcerted.

'Are the dark ones—'

'They use some clearsong, too, in dealing with the weather. That's because a single voice doesn't have enough power, even with a large number of supporting players.' The sorcerer paused, then added, 'Your gown would indicate that you are, in fact, one of the great . . . ones.'

Anna wondered at the pause, as though Brill were having trouble finding the appropriate word. 'I'm considered to have a moderately strong voice. In my world, it's hard to make it, especially if you have children.'

'You're a sorceress, and you have children?' Brill's voice was not quite unbelieving.

'Three.' Anna swallowed. 'They're grown.' They certainly were by the standards of this world, and she didn't want to try to explain. 'One was killed in a car accident – a magic-carriage accident,' she added.

'How old are they?' Brill asked, clearly confused.

'Twenty-four and eighteen. The oldest was twenty-eight.' Anna enjoyed the look of total confusion on the sorcerer's face.

'Years? Or seasons? Do they grow up more quickly?'

'Years. Probably we grow up more slowly, from what I've seen so far,' Anna said.

Brill sat down slowly in his padded chair. 'Daffyd . . . I wouldn't have . . .' The warm smile returned. 'You do indeed present a welcome surprise, perhaps a greater surprise than many would expect.' He stood and gestured toward the table, extending a hand to Anna. 'Let us dine.'

She took his hand, a normal, warm male hand, and rose. She could smell the faint odor of sweaty male – deodorants didn't go with magic, she gathered.

Brill dropped her hand, without squeezing, and gestured toward the place on the right. The place setting included a folded, faded blue linen napkin, a blue china plate with the *B*, fired in place in the center, edged in a gold trim, a silver spoon more like a soup spoon, and a small sharp knife. There was no fork.

The two chairs at the table were both finished in metallic blue lacquer with blue cushions. Brill pulled out her chair with both hands, and Anna almost nodded to herself. The chair was heavy.

The outer walls of the keep or hall shaded the blue-tinted windows from the glare of the sun, low in the sky, Anna suspected, from the angle and depth of the shadows in the courtyard. The area she could see from the window was empty – no retainers, no guards. She looked back to the sorcerer.

'I must apologize in advance, lady. Our fare here is limited.' The sorcerer lifted a crystal bell and rang it before seating himself.

As the tones echoed through the salon, a white-haired woman in the faded blue that all Brill's servitors and employees, if that was what they were, wore appeared with a small tray.

Silently, the server placed a half melon in front of each of them. The melon had a bright orange interior and a yellow-green rind, like a cousin of a cantaloupe.

'The melons are probably the best part of the meal,' Brill noted, reaching for a crystal carafe containing the same amber vinegar wine.

'No, thank you,' Anna said quickly.

'You do not like the wine?'

Anna scarcely would have called it wine.

'I'd prefer clean, cold water, if you don't mind.'

'Some sorcerers do, I've discovered. The blue pitcher has water in it.' He filled his own goblet with the amber wine.

'Do you have to spell all the water here?' Anna asked, pouring the water into the empty goblet.

'I do. All the water used in the hall is clean, even the bathing water.'

'I see why people call your hall a place of wonders.' Anna wasn't so sure she was happy about a world where it was considered excessively cautious to purify the bathing water.

'Jenny said that? Generous of her. It couldn't have been Daffyd. He wouldn't offer me a kind word.'

'You don't seem bothered by his dislike of you.' Anna used the small sharp knife to cut away a bite-sized slice of the melon, slipping it into her mouth. It was warmer than she liked melon, half honeydew, half cantaloupe, but sweet and refreshing. She cut another slice.

'I'd dislike me were I in his boots.' Brill took a sip of the wine. 'Not too bad.'

'Why would you dislike yourself if you were Daffyd?'

'I killed his father. It was necessary, because Culain's humming was getting worse, and he wouldn't listen.' Brill set down the fluted goblet. 'Lady Anna ... using spellsong is always dangerous. You said your daughter died in a magic-carriage accident. It is much the same way here on Erde. My father tried to use spellsong too long. There was less of him left than of Culain.' Brill laughed, a sound with bitter overtones. 'Of course, it didn't help that he tried to turn a thunderstorm on Lord Barjim's grandfather.'

Anna shook her head. 'Your father was—'

'Politics. They're always complicated. Barjim was raised by his uncle. Donjim was the older son, but none of his children lived. Barjim and I don't care much for each other personally, but he needs a sorcerer, and I, obviously, need silver.'

'Just as you need Daffyd?' Anna guessed.

'Precisely. I thought you might understand. Daffyd is a good player, and I would certainly not take askance if you remained friendly with him. Do keep in mind that, like all players, he has a tendency to . . . react . . . rather than consider the effects of his efforts.'

Anna cut another slice of melon and chewed slowly, trying to gather her thoughts together.

Brill cut himself a wedge of melon larger than Anna's and popped it into his mouth with relish.

'It's often hard to consider the future when you are struggling with the present,' Anna temporized.

'If you don't, you often have no future.'

'If you don't eat today,' countered Anna, 'you may not live long enough to worry about a future.' Even on Erde, it appeared, there were the elitists who preached about preparing for tomorrow while conveniently forgetting that too many people had trouble getting through today. Elitists like Avery, who used his money on vacation homes while insisting that she share in the children's college tuition costs, while preaching that she hadn't saved enough after she'd followed him everywhere and given up her chances at tenure to try to let him have his big chance.

'If I were to allow people to use seed grain for flour, we'd all have starved,' Brill said coolly.

Anna swallowed her retort, realizing that she couldn't afford to make the sorcerer angry, just like she couldn't afford to make her department chair angry, her thesis advisor angry, Avery angry . . . Instead, she took a last slice of melon and chewed it slowly, looking out the window into the still-empty courtyard.

'It can be a hard choice,' she finally said.

'Hard indeed, and I am often called cruel for it.' Brill refilled his goblet with the amber wine. 'All prudent lords are in this time of trouble.'

The white-haired server removed the melons, leaving the plates, then used a crude spatula to lever a brown-covered slab of meat onto Anna's plate. Next came a whitish green heap of something. Finally, she set a steaming loaf of the brown bread in the center of the table.

Brill nodded at the server, who departed as silently as she had slipped into the salon.

Anna looked at the brown sauce that covered the hefty slice of meat. The sauce reminded her of all the mystery meats she hadn't eaten when she'd been studying in England. She tried to sniff the meat without being too obvious.

'It's not the best beef,' the sorcerer admitted, 'but the sauce is good. Only the tougher animals have been able to weather the drought.'

'How long has the drought continued?' asked Anna, using the knife to slice a silver of beef.

'This is the fourth year.' Brill cut a large chunk of meat and eased the entire portion into his mouth.

Anna repressed a shudder, although she'd seen Mario do the same thing all too often. She chewed her small slice – tough despite a marinated sauce that was sweet and acidic simultaneously. If what the sorcerer was putting in front of her happened to be good food, she wasn't sure she wanted to find out what the common folk ate.

'Because of the dark ones?'

'It appears that way. Ebra is getting good rains, and the Ebrans are selling melons and grains to the Ranuans and the Norweians. Before they took over, the weather was spotty there.' The sorcerer cut another slice off his slab of meat and stuffed it into his mouth, wiping his fingers on the necessarily large napkin, then breaking off a chunk of bread. After that he took and ate another enormous chunk of meat.

'Why are they doing it?' asked Anna, not quite sure what she was asking. 'What do you think?' She followed Brill's example and took a corner of the bread. A mouthful convinced her that it was far better than the meat.

'Does what I think matter? I wish I knew. Oh, I can summon images that show what they do, and that's clear enough. They spell-move the Whispering Sands south and west, uncovering once fertile ground, and covering the groves and grasslands of Ranuak.' Brill sipped from the goblet. 'The Ranuans insist that the sands move naturally, but they must know better. The sand-moving gives better crops to the Ebrans, who thank the dark ones, and weakens the Ranuans. Beyond that, I can see that this prosperity allows them to equip and feed better and more troops. I can only guess at the planned use of those troops. The water mirrors do not read intent, as you know.'

'And you guess what?' Anna took a sip of water and another mouthful of bread.

'They will invade Defalk, sooner or later – before harvest this year, or no later than next.' He shrugged. 'That is but a guess.'

Anna lifted the deep spoon and tried the whitish green mess – which turned out to be something like tart and unsweetened fried apples. She had another bite.

'After seeing how you preferred water, I thought you might like the sour apples.'

'They are good,' Anna said, 'but I can't live on fruit alone. The dark bread is quite good, too.' She followed her second spoonful of apples with another thin slice of the tough beef. The brown sauce helped, but the apples and the bread helped more.

'What will you do to stop them – the dark ones?' Anna asked after several bites.

The sorcerer finished yet another large mouthful of beef before he spoke. 'I have helped Lord Barjim build walls on

Defalk's side of the Sand Pass, but they will only slow the armies of the dark ones.' He frowned. 'I had not meant to speak of it, but I had wondered whether you might have some special magic, such as the mighty weapons of your world.'

Anna thought. She didn't want to admit she was essentially clueless, but how could she answer him? Finally, she spoke. 'Our world is different, and the way our technology works requires many technicians. Each adds something. I am only one person.'

'What is a "technician"?'

'A technician is like a player, I'd say, except technicians work with special tools and magic boxes called computers.' Anna cleared her throat. 'Everything works differently here and there.'

'Yet Daffyd's spell brought you,' Brill pointed out.

'I *may* be able to help,' Anna said, 'but I need to learn more about Erde.'

'Can you even do spells here, lady?' asked Brill coolly.

'Yes,' Anna answered truthfully, glad that she had tried the water spell, 'but I made a large mess out of one of your goblets.'

'You broke one of them with a spell?' The frown was so momentary that Anna would have missed it had she not been concentrating on reading his reactions.

'That wasn't the intent.' Anna offered a gentle laugh. 'I was trying to get cold and clean water. I got it so cold it froze the crystal.'

'Again, you surprise me.' Brill inclined his head. 'I have never tried to freeze water. Working with water can be most dangerous. Metals and stone are generally easier.'

Anna glanced down at her plate, vaguely surprised that she had eaten everything on it, and then at Brill's. Despite the fact that he had easily eaten twice what she had, if not more, he was clearly trim and without a spare ounce anywhere. Sorcery had to be hard work here. A trace of a smile crossed her lips. Maybe she wouldn't have to worry about weight. Her half smile disappeared as she realized that she was being considered as a weapon in a war, and she knew little about either side.

The sky outside the window was turning a deep purple, and the salon had gotten dimmer and dimmer.

Brill hummed for a moment, then sang to the candle on the table between them:

> 'Candle light, candle bright,
> flame clear in my sight.'

The candle flame appeared from nowhere, then flicked and continued to burn.

'Can you do that?' Brill asked.

'I've never heard the tune, but I can try. Would you hum it once?' Anna asked.

The sorcerer obliged.

Anna glanced up at the chandelier in the middle of the ceiling, then thought. She hummed the tune once, and again. Finally, she took a deep breath, hoping that she could duplicate the feat, concentrated on the mental image of a blazing chandelier, and sang:

> 'Candle light, candles bright,
> flame clear in my sight.'

The entire chandelier blazed into light, then subsided to a warm glow.

Brill wiped his forehead. 'Ah . . . yes, I can see that . . .'

'I seem to have this tendency to overdo things,' Anna said politely. Inside, she was half excited, half fearful, wondering how she was so successful at something she'd never done. She also tried to remember the tune Brill had hummed.

'Even the dark ones might be somewhat surprised,' the sorcerer observed as he lifted the crystal bell and rang it.

The white-haired server appeared and removed the plates and bread, then returned with two small slices of pastry.

'Recerot,' the sorcerer explained.

Anna picked it up with her fingers and took a small bite of the layered pastry soaked in honey, almost like baklava – but without the nuts. The honey tasted slightly off, but she finished it anyway, and followed it with several healthy swallows of water.

'The honey is a trace strong,' Brill said. 'I think that's because there is so little moisture.'

'I appreciated it all,' Anna said truthfully, realizing that she had been hungry indeed, and that she could have eaten more.

Brill rose, almost abruptly. 'I would not presume to escort you to your chamber, Lady Anna, but I trust you will rest well.'

'I appreciate your hospitality, lord, and your willingness to assist a stranger.' She inclined her head.

'Tomorrow, perhaps, you would enjoy a ride around the hall's grounds?'

'If you have a gentle horse,' Anna answered. 'I'm out of practice.' Out of practice was definitely an understatement. Except for a few trail rides with Sandy and his daughters, she hadn't been on a horse for more than twenty years. 'I would enjoy learning more about Erde.'

'We will see what we can do.'

The ubiquitous Florenda was waiting at the salon door with a lamp, and Anna followed the slender woman back up to the guest chamber.

'Breakfast is served at the second morning bell, lady. I will knock on your chamber door at the first bell.' Florenda bowed deeply, even more deeply than before.

'Thank you, Florenda.' Anna offered the young woman a smile before closing and bolting the door.

The coverlet had been turned back, and both bedside lamps had been lit. The window hangings had been loosed and completely covered the perfect tinted blue glass panes. The small pile of crystal had been removed, and two clean and empty goblets and a pitcher of what appeared to be water stood on the window table.

Beside the lamp on the window side of the bed was a candle, like something out of an antique picture book, set in a metal holder that had a curved handle. Beside the candleholder was a metal device that looked like a combination between tongs and strange scissors.

Anna shook her head and felt the sheets – somewhat coarse linen, but at least they weren't wool. She hoped Lord Brill had spelled the bed for vermin, or whatever.

Of course, she couldn't sleep in her green gown – or wear it every day, either. With a sigh that was half yawn, she stepped toward the robing room, then realized that she couldn't see in the dark.

That was the reason for the candle. She stepped around the bed and picked up the scissor-tongs, and squeezed them. A spark leapt from them. Although she understood the striker, rather than fiddling with the device, Anna hummed the tune she and Brill had used to light the candles again. It seemed easier than fiddling with the striker. This time, she sang and concentrated on getting a normal flame – and she did.

With a smile, she carried the candleholder into the robing room, and after pawing through half the left-hand closet wall, she found what appeared to be a thin cotton gown. Then in the dim candlelight, she kicked off her shoes and struggled out of the green formal and the slips, and the longline bra, and the nylons. They were ruined with runs in at least three places. For the moment, with another yawn, she set them aside. As she pulled on the gown, she wondered if Brill were spying, then shook her head. She hoped he wasn't. She didn't like the idea of her privacy being invaded, but she didn't have any doubts that a sorcerer who had discovered her arrival could easily use his abilities to follow her motions – dressed or undressed. Still, the shapely Florenda indicated that Lord Brill probably had his pick of local young women. So, why would he bother with Anna?

Had he been telling the truth with his words about not wanting her body, but her abilities? Was anyone telling the truth?

She carried the candle back into the bedchamber and set it on the bedside table, cupping her hand and blowing it out, since she saw no snuffer. The cold of the stone floor on her bare feet was welcome. Sitting on the edge of the bed, she took off her jewelry last – all costume except for the ring Irenia had given her – and laid it on the bedside table with the non-functioning watch.

Then she climbed between the sheets. The mattress was lumpy, as she had suspected. She tried to arrange the equally lumpy pillows and pushed back the coverlet so that she was covered only by the sheets.

Finally, she blew out the lamps and lay back in the darkness – and the silence.

Everything seemed so real – and unreal. The smells and tastes were vivid enough, especially the vinegary taste of the wine. And the crystal fragments had seemed real enough. But a world where sorcery worked? And everywhere was the same strange contrast – delicate, cultured, refined items beside crude things. What was the pattern? She shook her head in the darkness, knowing she knew the answer, but unable to grasp it in her tiredness and confusion.

Finally, her eyes closed.

9

ESARIA, NESEREA

A sea breeze cools the columned, hilltop chamber. Between the fluted marble pillars the man in the spotless and feather-light white tunic can glimpse the whitecaps of the Bitter Sea. The music of strings, low strings, drifts from the adjoining Temple of Music, providing a soothing background.

The man wearing the cream-and-green Neserean uniform,

who stands below the marble Seat of Music, does not appear soothed.

'How did the dark ones first contact you, Jorbel?' The Prophet of Music, Lord of Neserea, and the Protector of the Faith of the Eternal Melody leans forward on the green cushion that comprises the only softness in the receiving pavilion.

'I don't understand, Lord Behlem.' The uniformed man bows, as he has several times previously.

'If you wish to keep using that head for understanding and other purposes, like surviving, you had best stop playing dumb, Jorbel.'

The perspiration on Jorbel's forehead turns into rivulets. 'Ser?'

Behlem nods, and two armored and armed figures step forward. Jorbel's hands grab for the knife at his belt, for his scabbard is empty, then claw at the empty air before him. The corpse sinks forward to reveal the blade in its back.

'Donkey-copulators!' snarls Behlem. 'How do they do it?' His fingers stroke the neatly trimmed reddish blond beard. 'Three of them in the army command in the last year.'

An older man, white-haired and white-bearded, steps forward. His eyes are bloodshot, with deep black circles beneath them. 'He might have said more, ser.'

'They never do. The dark ones do something to them. They don't even respond to the persuasion of the strings or spells of loosening the tongue. They just start making trouble, always insisting that they have received commands I never gave.' Behlem snorts. 'Why would I order Jorbel to take the blades from the armory reserves and have them forged into plowshares? Why?'

'Perhaps the dark ones are sending a message?' suggested Menares.

'That we should peacefully accept the rule of darksong and its dubious benefits?' Behlem glances toward the storm gathering beyond the breakwaters of Esaria. 'Still . . .' He pauses. 'Are you sure this is wise, Menares? We are far from Ebra, and building up the army has not been inexpensive.'

'Consider this, ser. All of the traitors have opposed it. Also consider the situation that faces us. Nordwei is too strong for the dark ones—'

'At present,' interjects Behlem.

'The Norweians continue to expand their navy, and they refuse to trade except for solid silver. Ranuak is protected by the Whispering Sands and the Sand Hills. Esaria is our only trade port, and the Bitter Sea is often ice-packed or frozen near half the year. The overland route to Encora can be easily severed if the dark ones take Defalk's eastern marches. In your uncle's time, we had access to Wei through the River Nord, to Synek and the Syne River to Elahwa.'

'Please, Menares, don't give me a lecture on trade or economics. I trust you for that. Perhaps I shouldn't, but we both know how good I am at that sort of thing.'

A wry smile passes the older man's lips. 'Very well, ser. It's very simple. If you don't take Defalk, at least the access to the Falche and the South Pass, before the dark ones do, Neserea will be a province of either Ebra or Nordwei in a decade, and you're a young man.'

Behlem nodded, despite the frown on his face.

'Of course, if you would like to rely upon Cyndyth's heritage . . .'

Behlem's eyes glitter. 'You are my advisor, but some matters are best left to me, Menares.'

'I shouldn't have suggested.'

'No. You shouldn't have.' Behlem's eyes focus somewhere far distant. 'I'd send her home, as you well know, except that I need the annual stipend from Mansuur, and Konsstin would love an excuse to cut it off.' He smiles brightly, tightly, and his eyes refocus on his advisor. 'You're sure this latest thing won't stop the dark ones?'

'The blonde sorceress that Lord Barjim has conjured from the mists?' Menares shrugs. 'I have my doubts that

any sorceress could stop the dark ones, but if she does
... we have nothing to lose. Barjim has not the silver or
the troops to hold his eastern marches against Ebra and
the west against us. Nordwei would not risk an army in
Defalk, and certainly not in Ebra.'

Behlem strokes his beard again, as the soothing sounds
of the strings drift across the hilltop from the Temple
of Music.

As the Prophet of Music looks away, Menares wipes his
forehead.

10

Anna woke abruptly in darkness. Where was she? She
reached for the lamp, and her hand fumbled on the smooth
stone of the bedside table, sending the link necklace skidding
off the edge and clanking onto the stone floor.

Her face itched from the scratchy pillowcases, and she
could feel a lump of mattress padding – lint or horsehair
or feathers or something – digging into her side. She shifted
her weight and struggled upright in the dimness, sensing
light beyond the heavy window hangings.

Rather than try a lighting spell or the striker – groggy
as she was, she could definitely understand the value of
the striker – she eased her feet off the high bed and onto
the cold floor. She padded across the smooth stones toward
the windows, where she pulled back the hangings to a gray
morning, gray because the sun had not risen.

The stone walls looked blue-gray in the predawn light,
and forbiddingly empty. Weren't people supposed to get
up early in less technological cultures? Anna yawned and
looked toward the robing room.

Today, she was supposed to go riding – riding and
learning more about Erde. If she were hallucinating, she

certainly must have taken some fall. Anna shook her head. Erde didn't feel like a hallucination.

'It sure doesn't feel like Kansas, Toto – or Iowa.'

And it didn't. The mattress had been lumpy, the sheets scratchy, and the room stuffy. Her joints ached; her eyes were gummy, and she wanted a toothbrush.

She walked slowly into the robing room and turned on the tap – the wrong one, and quickly added lukewarm water to the steaming stream. There was a flat, rubberlike plug that fit over the drain. In struggling to get the plug to fit in place, she ended up soaking half her gown.

'Damn . . .' she muttered, looking toward the mirror as she waited for the tub to fill. The gown clung to her in all the wrong places, especially if she were being watched, magically or otherwise.

She shook her head, definitely not at ease with the idea of real magic. 'Are you sure you're not hallucinating?'

The faint steam from the tap, the cold stone underfoot, the aches in her back, the damp gown against her skin, and her itchy nose were good indications that wherever she happened to be was real – too real.

She finally turned off the water, stripped off the gown, and eased into the tub. The warm water felt good, although she'd probably need another bath after riding, as much to relieve soreness as to remove dust. She had to sprawl half out of the tub to grab the small towel she'd used as a washcloth the day before. Then she used the oil soap sparingly, very sparingly, as she washed her face. She wished she had more than the small bottle of hand cream and the little jar of lip moisturizer. Even lotion would have been good, but she hadn't seen anything like that on Erde – and doubted that she would.

The too-small towels were scratchy, and her skin prickled in the cool of the robing room. Still, it was better than the heat she imagined continued outside the sorcerer's hall. She laughed ruefully. Hadn't that been the story of her life – difficult as things seemed, they were always better than the alternatives could have been?

She also needed to find some clothes that would fit for riding. The green formal gown was definitely not designed for that. With a deep breath, Anna turned toward the open closets, where she found what looked to be a dressing gown. That helped with the chill.

In among everything else – and Anna had to wonder just how many ladies Brill had prepared for – she found some soft green cotton trousers and a matching armless tunic, as well as a loose-fitting natural cotton blouse she could wear under the tunic. She frowned. Would both a blouse and tunic be too hot? She fingered the fabric of the blouse . . . or shirt – the buttons were on the right-hand side.

The cotton underdrawers she found were either too tight or too baggy. Clearly, Erde hadn't discovered elastic, either. She opted for comfort. Too tight might look wonderful in a fashion magazine, but she wasn't in a fashion magazine. She was in some strange world where everyone else seemed to know what was going on. Finally, she shrugged off the dressing gown and pulled on the baggy underdrawers – softer, at least, than any other fabric she'd felt, and then the rest of the outfit.

Shoes? She certainly couldn't wear heels.

On a shelf at the far end of the open were four pairs of boots, all in shades of blue, but nowhere could she find socks. Only one pair was large enough, and even those were a squeeze around her calves.

When Anna had dressed and applied a little makeup and lip gloss, she studied herself in the mirror. She had to admit she didn't look too bad. The faded green flattered her complexion, even with the minimal makeup she'd had and used, and – wonder of wonders – the trousers didn't even accentuate her hips.

She snorted. 'A strange world, and you're worrying about how your hips look.'

Anna looked at the green handbag on the table in the bedchamber. She didn't want to carry it, nor to leave it, especially some of the contents, like the lotion, the lip moisturizer. She doubted that any of the coins were worth anything, not since the U.S. had given up honest silver and copper. That brought another rueful look to her face. Who would have thought she'd be thinking about coins?

While she had carried more than a few things in her purse, the handbag she'd carried had been stripped down to essentials – as she always did for functions. She offered a wry grin to the mirror. Too bad she hadn't been headed for a theatrical performance with three bags full of stuff. For a moment, she wished she were one of those women who carried *everything* all the time.

The trousers had no pockets, nor did the blouse, and the two patch pockets on the tunic didn't feel like they'd hold much. So how did people carry things?

She went back to the closets that seemed to hold everything and began to rummage, eventually coming up with something that looked like a cross between an overgrown wallet, a purse, and a leather pouch. The leather loops were clearly designed for a belt to fit through them.

As she untied the leather belt – no buckles on Erde – and slipped the wallet-purse in place, she smiled ruefully. The meaning of the term *cut-purse* was a lot clearer. By carefully nestling items together, she could even fit everything that had been in her green handbag in the oversized wallet, except the brush. She set that on the table with the handbag. Then she looked at it again, finally picking it up and easing it into the left tunic pocket, bristles down. The handle stuck out, but the way things had been going, who knew where she'd be by evening?

Her eyes went to the bedside table, and the jewelry and her watch. She walked over and picked up the watch that still showed the time as five-forty. That was another question. Why didn't it work? Why had it and the key gotten so hot when she had been spelled into Erde – but not the necklace or her rings? Did the gold plate have anything to do with it? Finally, she strapped the watch on her wrist and the rings on her fingers, but the costume gold links went into the green handbag. If they vanished, so be it.

Anna jumped at the knock on the outer door, then took a deep breath and walked to the door. 'Yes?'

'Lady . . . your breakfast is being served in the salon, and Lord Brill would greatly appreciate your company.'

Anna fumbled with the bolt and opened the door. 'Florenda, I will be there momentarily.'

'Might I wait and accompany you, lady?' asked the dark-haired girl, her black eyes pensive.

'That would be fine.' Anna could sense Florenda's unease. Would the girl be punished if Anna failed to appear? Or was she politely trying to get Anna to hurry, but fearful of offending someone she thought might be a powerful sorceress?

Anna left the door ajar as she studied the bedchamber, then turned. 'I guess I'm ready.'

Florenda bowed and turned. Anna followed her down the corridor and through the dimly lit rooms to the salon, where light poured through the bay window behind the table.

Lord Brill rose from the small table and bowed. 'Good morning, Lady Anna. I trust you rested well.'

Anna returned the bow. 'I appreciate your courtesy and hospitality, Lord Brill.' She looked down at herself. 'I hope you do not mind my use of the clothing, but I did not arrive exactly dressed for . . .'

'You may have anything you need, lady.' His mouth crinkled and his eyes smiled. 'You will doubtless repay it manyfold through your talents.' He gestured to the table. 'Please . . .'

'Thank you.' Anna slipped into the chair across the table from him, trying not to think about repayment.

The sorcerer wore blue, as he always did, Anna suspected, but the cloth was more functional, harder than the velvet of the day before. Shirt, tunic and trousers were all of a faded cotton like that of Anna's green trousers. The circles under Brill's eyes were even more pronounced than the evening before, and the brown-flecked green eyes were themselves bloodshot.

'You must have stayed up awhile last night,' Anna observed.

'Something like that.' He sat again and took a sip of the hot beverage in his mug.

Anna followed his example, pouring the steaming yellow-green liquid into her mug and taking a small sip. While the warmth was welcome, whatever it was, it wasn't tea, and it wasn't coffee, and it was bitter, with a taste like boiled pine needles.

She poured a goblet of water.

Before her was another half melon, and in the middle between them, a loaf of bread, some sliced dried apples, some cheese wedges that looked like those she'd rejected the day before, and a jar of reddish preserves.

She broke off some of the bread, dabbed some of the preserves on it, and took a bite.

'You never did say much about your world,' Brill began slowly.

'No,' Anna admitted after swallowing a mouthful of the tasty and chewy dark bread. 'What would you like to know?'

'Can you create any of the magics like the iron birds?'

'No. Even on my world,' Anna said slowly, 'to create one of them takes a long time and hundreds of special workers.'

Brill nodded. 'I thought as much. What about the magic staffs that throw fire?'

Anna frowned. Magic staffs that threw fire?

'People put them to their shoulders, and smoke and fire comes from the end,' Brill added. 'Sometimes they kill people from a distance.'

'There are two parts to that,' Anna said. 'You need to make the gun, and then it needs ammunition, bullets, and that takes a special powder . . . gunpowder.' Avery probably knew the formula for gun-powder, but she didn't. Anyway, would gunpowder even work on Erde? Slowly, she dabbed more of the berry preserves on another hunk of bread. She was hungry.

'You look very doubtful, lady.' Brill set his cup on the table.

'I don't know enough about Erde to know what might work here, and what won't.' Anna tried to keep from pursing her lips. 'It took thousands of people hundreds of years to develop the things you're talking about.' She took another mouthful of bread and preserves, then cut a slice of melon.

Brill frowned openly. 'You make it sound as though magic is very difficult on your world. Yet my few glimpses in the mirror waters show many magic devices.'

'Few?' asked Anna, stalling and trying to think of an appropriate answer before she was pushed into admitting something unwise, although everything she might say appeared unwise in some way.

'It is dangerous to look more than infrequently,' answered Brill. 'What about these magic devices? Why can you not spell some?'

How could Anna explain? She sipped some water. Finally, she took a deep breath. 'It's hard to explain, but I'll try. What you call magic in my world is called technology. People don't make the magic devices through spells. They use machines to make them. First, hundreds of years ago, we had simple machines. We used them to make more complicated machines. Then people improved those machines.' Anna stopped, before adding, 'It took lots of people a long time.'

Brill nodded pensively. 'The reflections show many people in the mist worlds, and your face shows you are telling the truth.' He sighed. 'But it is disappointing. We have few people compared to your world, and little time. Is there not something from your world that we could use?'

'I don't think our worlds are quite the same, Lord Brill,' Anna offered. She pointed to her watch. 'On my world, this tells time. Here it doesn't even work.'

'Perhaps the shock of crossing the mist barriers . . .' suggested Brill.

'It doesn't *feel* like it will ever work here,' Anna added. She pursed her lips before continuing. 'Also, I can tell you that my songs have never been as powerful on earth as on Erde. That takes some getting used to.' What she said was true, if misleading, but she felt it wasn't a good idea to admit she wasn't a sorceress at all on earth. Not now, anyway.

As Brill pondered her words, she cut and ate several more slices of melon and even had another sip of the pine-needle tea. Then she had more bread and preserves.

'Hmmmm,' he said after sipping his own tea with far more relish than Anna could see reason for, 'this bears more thought. You are a powerful sorceress here, and your mist world has many things that would seem impossible here. Both are true.' Brill laughed. 'So we shall see.'

Her mouth full, Anna offered a nod. She was still hungry, more hungry than usual in the morning. Was it nerves? Or something about Erde?

'Well? Are you ready for your ride?' asked the sorcerer with a smile after she had finished the last of the bread. 'Perhaps I can show you something of Erde, enough to stimulate your thoughts on how you might help us.'

Anna nodded, wondering why she should help Brill. The sorcerer hadn't really given any good reason for her to help, and he had admitted killing Daffyd's father over what seemed a trifling thing, and yet he was acting as if she would.

As Brill stood and turned, his hand brushed the crystal water goblet.

Anna lurched toward it, but was too late. The shimmering goblet seemed to fall in almost slow motion toward the polished stone floor – where it rang as it bounced . . . and bounced . . . and rang . . . and did not break.

'It's all right,' Brill said calmly. 'Serna will wipe it up.'

Anna tried to look away from the delicate-seeming crystal that still rolled back and forth on the light-blue stone floor.

After a moment, she forced a smile. 'Your crystal is rather durable.'

'I had thought so,' Brill answered with a smile. 'I had thought so.'

What did he mean? Then she remembered. She had shattered one of the goblets with her botched spell. She wanted to blot her suddenly damp forehead. 'Would you excuse me for a moment?'

'Certainly, lady. I'll meet you in the front entry.' Brill bowed, not quite sardonically, as if well aware of the confusion he had created, and picked up a cap from the side table.

Anna wanted to scream that she wasn't slow, that she wasn't stupid, that she'd like to see how he would do plopped into her world. He'd probably get run over in a parking lot in thirty seconds – especially in Ames. Instead, she pasted on a smile, and inclined her head momentarily. 'I won't be long.'

Ignoring Florenda, who had appeared as she left the salon and fluttered alongside her, Anna walked slowly back to her chamber.

In the robing room, Anna washed her hands mechanically, once, twice. How could this be happening? Every time she turned around there was another reminder that people thought she was something special, another hint that she had to do *something*.

How? She was just Anna Thompson Marsali, born Anna Mayme Thompson in Cumberland, Kentucky, a soprano not quite good enough, or lucky enough, to have made it to the Met, but good enough to place second or third in every competition she had been able to afford – before she'd given in to Avery and gotten pregnant.

She walked back into the bedchamber and stood before the window. The scene remained unchanged – the stone walls, the dirt roads, and the distant view of Mencha to the north . . . and the sun, already beating down on the dry countryside.

Anna went back to the closets, searching again, until she

found a floppy brown hat with a brim wide enough to shade her face. At least she hoped it would.

Florenda waited in the corridor and followed her back down to the entry where, as he had promised, Brill waited, knee-length riding boots polished and glimmering.

Anna stepped out into the morning behind the sorcerer, and felt herself begin to sweat almost instantly in the summer heat – worse even than Ames in August.

'This way,' Brill suggested.

They walked along the shaded north side of the main hall building, across more of the flat stones that paved the entire courtyard, and back into the sun, toward a low, blue-tile-roofed structure.

The stable was like the rest of the hall – well designed and of finely finished stone. Like all stables, there was the odor of straw and manure, and of leather and oil.

'Morning, lord.' A short, white-haired man stepped from the dimness of an open and empty stall into the sunlit doorway, offering a perfunctory nod to the sorcerer.

'Good morning,' Brill answered, gesturing from Anna to the wizened man. 'Quies, this is the lady Anna. We'll be riding out to the south dome, but she'll need a horse.' He added. 'Quies is the stablemaster, and a fine one.'

'I'm pleased to meet you, Quies.' Anna nodded at the wizened stablemaster, who scarcely reached her chin, although his shoulders were broad and his arms heavily muscled.

'How good a rider are you, lady?' asked Quies.

'Not very,' Anna admitted. 'And I'm out of practice.'

Quies pulled at his stubbled chin as if to ask how anyone could get out of practice when riding was the only sensible way to travel. 'Well ... you're a tall woman ... and a sorceress ...'

Anna held in a frown. Tall? She'd never thought of herself as tall, but on Erde, she seemed to be above average, especially for a woman.

'Maybe the palomino gelding ...' Quies nodded as though he expected Anna to follow him.

She did, stepping into the stable that was cooler than the courtyard, and followed the stablemaster toward the rear of the long building. Her nose itched from the straw dust, and she rubbed it, hoping she wouldn't sneeze too much.

'Here . . .' Quies opened the stall door and slipped inside. 'I'll saddle him.'

Anna looked toward Brill, but he had stepped to an adjoining stall. He nodded before turning back to Anna. They waited.

Finally, Anna asked, 'Is there any magic to make riding easier?'

'Not that I know of, lady.' Brill offered the crinkled smile.

When Quies led the palomino out, Anna looked at the horse doubtfully, and even more dubiously at the saddle, something higher than an English saddle, but not as solid as a western one, and there was no saddle horn. The palomino swished his tail, but didn't edge away as Anna stepped up toward him. She frowned at the fine tracery of lines across his shoulders, half concealed by his coat.

'What's his name?' she asked.

'Name?' Quies shrugged. 'He belonged to one of the raiders out of the high grasslands. Barjim sold him at auction, and he was cheap because he was cut up.' The stablemaster looked to Brill.

The sorcerer shrugged. 'It wasn't that hard to heal him – minor darksong. He was strong.'

'Now he's worth a good five golds – be thirty if the raiders hadn't gelded him,' observed Quies.

Anna had the feeling that she and the palomino would be spending a lot of time together. Why she couldn't say, but she'd learned to trust her feelings. So the horse had to have a name. What did one call a horse?

She laughed. 'Farinelli!'

'What?' said Brill.

'That's his name. Farinelli.' She really didn't know if the

original Farinelli had been blond, but it didn't matter. The name felt right. —

Brill and Quies exchanged a look that said, '*If you say so*.'

She studied the palomino once more – a lot taller than a mule or even most of the broken-down horses she'd climbed on for her handful of trail rides when Elizabetta had gone through the horse-loving phase. She swallowed. Her redheaded baby – except Elizabetta was scarcely a baby, not after a year at Emory. But what had she thought when she had come home from her job at Fransted's and found her mother missing?

'Lady Anna? Is this horse . . . ?' Brill asked solicitously.

'It's not the horse,' Anna said. 'My thoughts wandered.' She looked back up at the gelding, who *whuff*ed. Riding Farinelli couldn't be too much worse than riding old Barney had been, and she'd managed Barney bareback. Then, she'd been a lot younger, and her grandfather had been more than a little upset.

After she took the reins from Quies, she patted Farinelli on the shoulder again. The gelding *whuff*ed again. Then she led him toward the front of the stable.

Brill paused by the other stall, opening the door. Shortly, he followed, leading a black mare, already saddled.

Outside the stable, back in the dry, dusty heat of the morning, Anna looked up at Farinelli, trying not to swallow. Finally, she grasped the saddle and levered herself up.

'Doesn't need a mounting block . . .' Quies observed.

Anna turned to see a frown cross the sorcerer's forehead, then vanish. Quies seemed to ignore the expression as Brill swung up into the mare's saddle.

'Just be firm with him, lady,' Quies added, 'and if he tries to nip, clout him on the nose. Once is enough.'

Anna let Farinelli follow Brill's mare along the side of the hall toward the front gate. Brill reined up at the main hall entrance, slid out of the saddle, and used the braided, blue-corded bellpull. Anna remained in her saddle, waiting.

After a moment, the door opened and a brown-haired youth appeared.

'Yes, ser?'

Brill turned to Anna. 'Gero, this is the lady Anna. She is a sorceress, and to be respected and obeyed.'

Gero bowed. 'My lady.'

'Gero is my assistant. He's perfectly tone-deaf, which saves us both a great deal of misunderstanding.'

'I'm pleased to meet you, Gero.' Anna said politely.

Gero bowed again.

'We'll be riding for a time, Gero. I'd like you to tell Kaseth to gather the players, at the ninth glass.'

'At the dome, ser?'

'That would be best.' Brill nodded and climbed back into the mare's saddle.

'Yes, ser.' Gero bowed again. 'At the ninth glass, ser.'

The sorcerer remounted without looking back, although Gero remained standing stiffly by the door, and turned the mare toward the hall gates.

The twenty-foot-high gates stood open as they rode into the morning sun. Despite the floppy-brimmed hat, Anna had to squint against the glare as the horses' hoofs clipped against the stone pavement that stretched for a few hundred feet beyond the gates.

'Where are we going?' she asked.

'First, I'll show you the dome building. There.' Brill pointed to the small and heavy-walled building on the hilltop. 'That's where I work on new spells. While I certainly wouldn't wish to impose, Lady Anna, I thought you might find one of the workrooms . . . useful, at least for a time.' Again, the sorcerer offered the friendly crinkled smile, although Anna didn't feel the undercurrent of alarm she had before.

So . . . he's being honest? Why? Because he doesn't want you trying to figure out things and damaging his beautiful hall?

Brill turned the mare onto a narrower dusty lane that wound down the hilltop where the hall sat, and then up toward the dome building.

Dust rose with every step Farinelli took, some of it seeping into Anna's nose. After a time, she sneezed.

'It is dusty,' Brill said. 'It's been that way for the past few years.' His arm stretched eastward, encompassing the low brown hills, some with scattered trees, others with a handful of dead and leafless trees. 'I can remember when all that was green, and the taller hills were filled with trees.' He shrugged. 'Then we began to hear more of the dark ones, and the summers, and the winters, got drier and drier.'

Anna cleared her throat. 'Hasn't anyone tried to do something about them?'

'The Ebrans were warlike before the dark ones. No one has ever conquered Ebra – unlike Defalk,' he added sardonically, 'which has been conquered and reconquered. The Norweians lost several thousand troops under their last Council, and the Ranuans have always relied on the protections of the Sand Hills and the Whispering Sands.'

'Isn't there anyone else?'

'The only three countries that border Ebra are Nordwei, Ranuak, and Defalk.'

Anna lurched forward as Farinelli reached the bottom of the trail and started back up the winding way toward the dome house. She grabbed the front rim of the saddle and steadied herself. 'That doesn't sound good,' she temporized, reading Brill's face as much as his words.

'It is not good. Lord Barjim cannot even defend Defalk, much less consider attacking Ebra. So the dark ones will move on us first.'

'Why are you still here?' Anna blurted.

'I intend to show you why, Lady Anna. That may take some time.' The sorcerer reined up halfway up the hillside and pointed eastward. 'Those are the Sand Mountains, and a bit to the south is the Sand Pass to Ebra.'

'How far is the pass?'

'Somewhat less than ten leagues.'

Anna tried to remember what Daffyd – had it been Daffyd? – had said about measurements. Ten deks were a league, and a dek was almost a kilometer, and that was something like six-tenths of a mile, and that meant . . . less than sixty miles from the border with Ebra?

'You look disturbed.'

'I hadn't realized Ebra was so close.'

'It's a good two days' ride to the Sand Pass, and another half day beyond that to the true border.' Brill frowned.

Anna shook her head. She'd forgotten that sixty miles or ten leagues or whatever was a long way on horseback. She needed some perspective. 'How far is the border with the country to the west?'

'Neserea? I suppose it is around sixty leagues.'

So Defalk wasn't a postage stamp-sized country, either. 'What's to the north? And how far?' Anna pressed.

'Nordwei – it runs across most of the north of Liedwahr – more than three hundred leagues from Cape Eastwei to the mountains north of Esaria.' Brill pursed his lips. 'The border is about thirty leagues north of Falcor, and a little farther from here.'

'Is Falcor the capital of Defalk?' Anna asked.

'Capital? You mean the coins amassed by a usurer? There are few coins indeed in Falcor. Falcor is the liedstadt of Defalk, because that is where Lord Barjim's liedburg is.'

Every time she tried to get an answer, somehow the answer led into something else. If the Germanic word roots meant the same things, then Falcor was the capital of Defalk, but *liedstadt* translated roughly as 'song-city,' while Lord Barjim's castle or hall was a 'song-castle.' Anna grabbed the saddle as Farinelli lurched forward, her thoughts spinning as she tried to construct a mental map – Ebra to the east, and Neserea to the west, and Nordwei to the north.

'What's south?' she blurted.

'Ranuak,' Brill answered tersely. 'I have a map in my workroom.'

His tone bothered Anna. Was she just supposed to sit on Farinelli and follow the sorcerer around and meekly take what information he offered? She'd stopped doing that with

Avery which had been one of the many things that had led to the divorce – and she wasn't about to start again.

The sorcerer reined up by a stone hitching post outside the squat building, and dismounted. The dusty path to the oaken door bore boot tracks, almost all the same boot tracks, probably Brill's, Anna reflected as she climbed off Farinelli and tied him beside the mare.

Anna followed the sorcerer, almost as in a daze, as he led her through the small entryway and into a room filled almost entirely with a pool contained in a raised stone pedestal, where, on one side, rested a harp, half reflected in the silvered water. Anna squinted as she glanced at the silvered surface, where images seemed to flicker and then vanish. The cool of the building was a relief after the searing heat outside.

'Reading the pool takes some effort, and it's hard to separate what *is* from what you hope. There is the map.'

On the wall was a crude map. Anna refrained from smiling as her study of the map confirmed – generally – her mental picture. Defalk was indeed surrounded on all sides, both by mountains and other countries.

Brill touched her arm, interrupting her study of the map. 'The practice room is through this door.'

She bit back a comment about being hurried and followed the sorcerer.

The next space was a large room empty except for an array of stools and a large wooden stand that could have held music, except that Anna had seen nothing resembling music.

Brill explained, 'This is where the players practice new spellsongs. Confinement helps reduce untoward effects.'

Anna cleared her throat. 'I thought there weren't any effects if people weren't singing.'

'Unaccompanied music cannot cast a spell, but it can disarray the emotions,' Brill answered smoothly, with an air of superiority that momentarily reminded Anna of Avery again – or Antonio, as he now called himself, the king of the comprimarios.

She repressed a snort, and managed a nod, as they entered another room, with two wide windows to the east, a flat desklike table, two chairs, and a small book case.

'This is the eastern workroom, and it might be most suitable for your use,' suggested the sorcerer.

'That is thoughtful of you,' she said slowly.

'You are still not convinced that Erde is real,' he said.

'At some moments I am, and at others I'm not. It's getting more real the longer I'm here,' she added after a pause.

'It is very real, lady, and you could be here for a very long time.' He laughed harshly. 'Or a very short time, if you do not believe it is real.'

Anna understood that threat and found herself flushing, half in anger. 'You would have some of the same problems in my world.'

The sorcerer nodded. 'I well might, but you are here.' Next he guided her back to the center atrium and pointed to the doors for a washroom and attached jakes, and to a storeroom which contained supplies for her work.

'Such as?'

'A key-harp, a set of bells, some paper ...'

Anna had seen nothing resembling a piano, a harpsichord, or an organ, but went with her gut feelings – not to comment on that deficiency.

Brill's own workroom contained two desks and several spoked wooden chairs, a northern exposure with a view of both the hall and Mencha, a small instrument that looked like a zither with a short board, presumably one of the so-called key-harps, and a book case. A rack of hand-bells was mounted on a side wall, and sconces held three wall lamps.

The third workroom was similar to the first – stark, but spacious, except that it seemed much warmer, perhaps because of the southern exposure that showed browning fields and groves of gnarled trees climbing halfway up the hill to the dome building.

'Apple trees?' Anna asked.

'Apple and some apricots. The apricots take the heat better, if they get water.'

Anna studied the southern view, the scattered houses and the brown line that seemed to be a highway heading south.

'Do you prefer this or the east room?'

'The east,' she answered.

'I thought as much.' Brill turned back toward the small entry hall without another word.

Were all sorcerers like that? Did they flick from solicitous to indifferent from moment to moment?

She followed the balding sorcerer from the dome building, and the late-morning heat struck Anna like a furnace, but the dryness made it bearable – just. She united the gelding and mounted.

Brill gestured toward the other trail, the one leading down to the groves. 'I had thought to show you what we face from the dark ones.'

Anna eased Farinelli up beside Brill's mare. 'The effects of the weather?' she asked.

'Not five years ago, all these fields, all the way to the south, as far as the eye could see, were green.' As the horses carried them farther down the trail toward the groves, he continued. 'The leaves of the apple trees were so thick you could not see the ground under them from here.'

Anna glanced out to the south, her eyes reaffirming the brown dryness, broken only with intermittent stretches of green.

'The roads were filled with wagons and carriages.'

'*Kkkkchew!*' Anna rubbed her nose. The dust was getting to her. 'Sorry. It is dusty.' She was glad for the floppy hat, but she wished she'd brought sunglasses as she squinted against the constant glare. 'It looks pretty barren.'

'That's the work of the dark ones.' Brill laughed harshly. 'The Ranuans refuse to see the danger, and the Norweians play off everyone else, and each year Defalk dies a little more.'

On the right side of the trail, perhaps fifty feet from

where the apple orchard began, was an empty pond, one with slightly darker dirt that indicated recent water, formed on three sides with the elaborate and precise brickwork that Anna was associating with sorcery.

'You made the pond?'

'What else could I do? You see . . .' explained the sorcerer, his hand pointing to the nearest of the gnarled trees, and the damp and narrow ditch that ran from a sluice gate at the bottom of the brick dam down to the orchard.

Anna studied the irrigation system as Farinelli carried her down into the orchard itself.

'Where do you get the water?'

Brill smiled wryly.

'Is that what you were doing last night?' Anna guessed.

'I claim I have a spring that flows at night.'

Anna nodded. With water so scarce, Brill would not wish to broadcast his sources, especially if he were drawing from the same aquifer as other's wells.

'Even so, see how small and few the apples are?' The sorcerer lifted his shoulders and let them fall. 'And I cannot bring water more than a few times a week, and the waters barely feed the orchard.'

'How far do your lands extend?' Anna asked.

'Not even a dek beyond the base of the hills. My grandfather obtained the hills, and my father added the groves and fields beyond the base. Not that the fields have offered much in the past few years.' He turned the mare back uphill without another word.

Her knees were shaking by the time she dismounted at the hall stables. Her head was spinning, and sparkles flashed in front of her eyes. She staggered as her feet touched the courtyard stones outside the stable.

'Are you all right, Lady Anna?' Brill took her arm.

'I need some water,' Anna rasped. She wasn't that good with heat, and the dryness had kept her from realizing just how dehydrated she had gotten. She'd been used to the wet heat of Iowa, where she would have been drenched in sweat.

'The mist worlds are cooler. I should have known,' Brill took her arm and helped her back to the hall and to the salon where Anna slumped into a chair at the table.

The sorcerer watched as Anna sipped her way through nearly a pitcher of water.

'I'm not used to this much heat,' she finally said as the worst of the dizziness and disorientation passed.

'Will you be ready to hear the players this afternoon?'

'How long?' she asked.

'That won't be until the ninth glass.'

'I'm not used to your timekeeping. How many glasses in a day?'

'At the beginning of spring or fall, the day is ten glasses long, and, of course, so is the night.'

Anna thought for a moment. So a glass was somewhat longer than an hour, say, maybe ten minutes or so, and it was near noontime. 'It's what, about the fifth glass of the day now?'

'Actually, midday in summer is the sixth glass.'

'I should be fine by the ninth glass, especially after I eat.' She paused. 'If we ride in this heat anymore, I'll need a water bottle of some sort. That should do it.'

'You are different, Lady Anna.' Brill shook his head slightly. 'Very practical.'

Anna wondered. Avery and even Mario had thought her often very impractical. Or was a problem-solving attitude just considered unfeminine on Erde? Or was Brill flattering her?

He rang the bellpull, and the white-haired server appeared.

'Serna ... we will eat ... and the lady Anna will need a pair of water bottles for our afternoon ride – around the eighth glass.'

'Yes, ser.' The dark eyes looked from Brill to Anna and then at the floor.

Anna supposed she looked bedraggled, but, for the moment, she didn't care. She probably would later, but her stomach was empty, and she still felt dehydrated. She refilled the goblet and took another sip of the cool water. The last of the light-headedness was beginning to disappear.

In less than two sips, Serna returned, with two platters and an array of food – more of the dark bread, two more half melons, some cold slices of meat, yellow cheese wedges, and dried apple slices.

Anna tried a small nibble of the yellow cheese – hard, but without the moldiness that the softer and whiter cheese possessed.

The melons were the same as always, but welcome nonetheless, as was the tasty bread. Again, Anna found that she ate more, far more, than she should have.

'I'd like to rest for a while,' she said, after glancing again at the empty platter before her.

'Of course.' Brill's smile was understanding, but not cryptic, and she made her way up to the bedchamber, accompanied by Florenda.

11

NORTH OF THE WHISPERING SANDS, EBRA

Ten rows of dark-hooded figures stand silently as the drums begin to roll. Then come the horns, the low falk horns and muted brazen trumpets.

The Songmaster raises his left hand, then drops it into a slow rhythm, while the drums and horns meld into a sound like the incoming tide rushing across the Shoals of Elahwa. The black baton in the Songmaster's right hand falls, and the massed voices take up the spell.

> 'Blessed be the land that receives the damp,
> Strike the watered clouds with heaven's lamp.

> Blessed be the land that receives the damp,
> Strike the watered clouds with heaven's lamp.'

Shortly, a bolt of lightning flashes through the black clouds that roll southward and pile up in the skies over the newly uncovered soil just north of the Sand Hills.

> 'Blessed be the land that receives the damp,
> Strike the watered clouds with heaven's lamp.
> Blessed be the land that receives the damp,
> Strike the watered clouds with heaven's lamp.'

More lightning bolts cleave the clouds that have turned nearly nightblack.

The Songmaster's left hand gestures once more, and the timbre of the accompaniment deepens. The baton flicks, and the chant shifts.

> 'Blessed be the land that receives the rain.
> Open the clouds onto the thirsty plain.
> Blessed be the land that receives the rain.
> Open the clouds onto the thirsty plain.'

Droplets begin to fall on the newly uncovered soil, on the fragments of dried wood that had once been shaped, and upon the sand-polished, white fragments that had, centuries earlier, belonged to some living creature.

12

The ninth glass found Anna in the dome building, standing beside Brill as she watched the players tune their instruments. Gero sat on a stool in the corner, his eyes on Brill.

While she hadn't been able to sleep, with all too many questions swirling inside her head, the combination of the midday meal, lots of water, washing up, and several hours' rest had left her feeling surprisingly good, surprising for someone thrown from one world to another. She just hoped Elizabetta would be all right. Mario was on his own, anyway, except that she still worried.

'After they practice,' Brill suggested, 'you might have a word with young Daffyd.'

'About what?' Anna asked innocently.

'Whatever you choose,' the sorcerer answered. 'He's like a skittish colt, and if he bolts, he's going to get in trouble.'

Anna held in a frown. In trouble with whom? – Brill? Lord Barjim? the dark ones?

'The dark ones would see him as your summoner, and . . .' Brill shrugged.

Lovely, reflected the singer. *If I don't keep the young man here, and anything happens to him, it's my fault!* It was so convenient for Brill to forget about what he did to Daffyd's father, but not unexpected. That sort of rationalization was typical for tenors, conductors, and directors – and, apparently, for sorcerers. Her eyes went back to the group assembling around the stools in the dome building's practice room.

There were twelve players, and eight were strings – four violinists, with instruments like the early Italian violinos, two violas, and two cellos. Then there were the horns – two instruments resembling clarinets, one wooden flute, except it was played from the end like an American Indian flute, a last woodwind that resembled a cross between a bass clarinet and an English horn, and one brass horn halfway between a French horn and a tuba, except the brass tubing seemed thicker and shorter.

Daffyd, carrying his viola, looked sideways at Brill, then at Anna. Anna offered a smile to the young man, but he looked away quickly, and took his seat on a stool.

'Are they ready, Kaseth?'

'We are almost ready, lord.'

'We will begin with the building song,' Brill announced. After a minimal number of tunings, the sorcerer raised his hands, and with tight but fluid gestures, directed the group through the very short song.

Anna listened. Although she was no musicologist and she couldn't have provided an explanation of Schenkerian analysis, let alone provided such an analysis – the music seemed similar to early Western music, mostly polyphonic and modal in nature. Then, did they have either the mathematics or the instrumentation to develop equal-tempered tuning? There was so much she didn't know, didn't even know how to ask without creating more problems.

Each instrument seemed to carry its own melody, although the predominant melody seemed to rest mostly on the high strings, the violinos. Occasionally the predominant theme was carried by both the woodwinds and the strings. The cello seemed totally used for a simplified bass version of the melody, rather than for true harmony, as was the deep sound of the bass clarinet/English horn. The brass horn – Brill had called it a falk horn – followed the violas, or so it seemed to Anna.

'. . . the section where the falk horn and the bass wind join – you're not together there . . .'

The two hornists exchanged glances, and the woman clarinet player with the white-streaked red hair followed the interchange. Daffyd looked stolidly at Brill.

'Again,' the sorcerer ordered.

'Now the paving song . . .'

'. . . the forging song . . .'

Through the rehearsal, if that were what it was, Anna wasn't impressed, but she kept her face impassive, or she hoped she did.

'That will be all for this afternoon, Kaseth.' The sorcerer nodded to the man with the wispy white hair, the concertmaster, of sorts, then at Anna.

Anna slipped from the side of the practice room to the

stool where Daffyd was easing his viola into the brown
case. Brill followed Kaseth out into the small entry hall.
Gero followed the sorcerer.

'I'm sorry about your father,' Anna said.

'You are with Lord Brill, most high sorceress,' Daffyd
said stiffly, closing the instrument case.

'Yes, I am staying in his hall. That's all. I'm a stranger
here. I have no clothes, no money, and very little knowledge
of Erde. What would you suggest?'

'You are a sorceress. Lord Brill says so.'

'That may be.' Anna took a deep breath. 'But I don't know
who to trust, and how much. I don't know the politics or even
much about the geography. Don't you understand, Daffyd?
Even if my language is much like yours, I'm a total stranger
here. I'm not a composer. I'm not even an arranger. I'm a
singer, and the songs I know won't do much here.'

Daffyd looked over his shoulder. Only the woodwind
player with the white-streaked red hair remained in the
practice room, and she looked directly at them. Anna caught
her eyes, and the woman turned quickly and hurried out into
the entry foyer.

Daffyd still did not reply.

'What is it? Is "singer" a dirty word here?' The look on the
youth's face gave her the answer. 'Some people act as though
it's a dirty word where I come from, too. Especially when
it's time to pay you. They want it for free, or cut-rate.'

'They don't pay sorceresses?'

'If you mean singers . . . no, not very much.'

Daffyd looked bewildered, and his eyes flicked toward
the empty doorway. 'But you are a sorceress,' he protested.

'Right now, I'm a sorceress with a few spells, just enough
to keep Lord Brill off balance.'

Daffyd paled slightly. 'They must be powerful.'

'Enough,' Anna temporized. 'But not enough to go wandering all through Defalk, not without getting into even
more trouble.' She could tell that Brill remained outside

the practice room, and that bothered her. What was he expecting from her?

'But you were powerful in your world . . .'

'Song magic isn't as strong as technology magic on my world.' Anna thought of her stopped watch. 'Here, it seems like some forms of technology don't work at all, and song magic is stronger, much stronger. It takes some getting used to.'

'Why are you talking to me,' Daffyd asked, 'if Lord Brill has all the answers?'

'Because no one has all the answers, and because I trust you,' she answered bluntly, but quietly enough that her words would not carry. 'I couldn't explain why, but I do.'

Daffyd opened his mouth, then shut it. Finally, he asked in a whisper. 'And what about Lord Brill? Do you trust him?'

'About some things.'

Daffyd gave a small nod. 'I have to think.'

'Do that.' Anna watched the young string player as he left the practice room.

Brill returned shortly, even before Anna reached the door. 'He seems more settled. What did you tell him?'

'I told him that I had to learn more about your world, and that I trusted him.'

'That was dangerous.'

'His heart is good,' Anna said.

'But not his judgment.'

'He's young,' Anna said, reflecting to herself that some judgment could be learned, but not trustworthiness. 'We've all had to learn.'

'You're more charitable than I,' Brill continued as he closed the doors to the building.

'That may be because you are more experienced in the ways of your world,' Anna answered, hating herself momentarily for trying to placate the sorcerer.

Despite the sun's low position over the western plains, the air was still and penetrating as though Anna stood in a massive oven. She patted Farinelli and took several deep swallows from the water bottle before mounting.

As they rode back to the sorcerer's hall, Brill edged his mare closer to Farinelli. 'What do you think of our music?'

'It's more ... functional, I think. Ours is designed more for ...' Anna paused. How could she say it? What was earth's music designed for, anyway? After a time, not long before they slipped into the shadows of the hall's gates, she finally answered. 'I need to think more.'

As they rode past the main entry to the hall toward the stable, from somewhere in the back of the hall grounds came the single crow of a rooster, following by clucking and *brawwk*ing.

'You are very thoughtful, lady,' Brill said as he dismounted outside the stable. 'Best you get the thinking done while you can. Events may not always allow for lengthy contemplation.'

'I appreciate the advice.' Anna dismounted and led Farinelli toward his stall, where she was met by Quies.

'How was he, lady?' asked the stablemaster.

'He was fine, thank you. I enjoyed riding him.'

'Good.' Quies led the gelding into the stall, and Anna started toward the front of the stable.

'You seem rather distant,' Brill offered, joining her. The two walked back across the stones toward the main part of the hall.

'It is rather unsettling to accept a whole new world.' *Especially when you're still not sure it's real.* Anna took off her hat, holding it in her hand. Where the hat had touched her hair was sweaty, and probably dirty from the sweat and dust. 'It's even hard to know where to start.'

'I have done my best to make you welcome.'

'I would have done the same for you, Lord Brill, and you would have had as much readjustment in my world as I do here – perhaps more.' Anna realized she shouldn't have spoken so sharply, but her feet hurt, and she was tired of

being expected to be grateful or scintillating or brilliant –
or whatever Brill expected.

'Dinner will be ready in a glass or so.' Brill said stiffly in
the entry hall, his eyes taking in Anna's dusty clothes and
floppy hat.

'That will allow me some time to get cleaned up,' Anna
said sweetly. She was amazed at how dusty she'd gotten just
from the short ride to and from the sorcerer's outbuilding.
She nodded politely and headed up the wide stone stairs.
Before she had gotten three steps up, she was joined by
Florenda.

While the tub filled, she rummaged through the long
closets, not wanting to wear the green performing gown
– especially not the longline bra – to dinner. The tub
was almost full before she found a dark blue gown that
was almost a wrap-around style – but it seemed to fit –
the only one that really did. Most of the clothing was for
women far shorter than she was. She'd still have to wear
either the heels, a pair of sandals her toes hung over the
front in, or boots.

She opted for the sandals, since green heels clashed with
the dark blue.

Then she stripped off the dusty riding clothes and eased
into the tub. For a time, she just lay in the warm water
of the tub, letting it carry away the soreness in her feet
and legs.

A knock on the door roused her, and she had to hurry,
finally pinning her hair up into a bun that would probably
come undone halfway through dinner.

Again, Florenda escorted her to the salon.

'You scarcely look like the horsewoman I saw this afternoon.' Brill bowed deeply. He had also bathed and wore the
dressier blue velvet trousers and tunic, and short boots.

'You're kind.' Anna nodded.

'Truthful. I'm still amazed that you have grown children. You have no secret spells to make you younger,
you're sure?'

'Not that I know of.' *Not except hair coloring, and I'm not about to mention that.*

'After a day here, what have you discovered about us?' asked the sorcerer, pulling out the chair and waiting for Anna to seat herself.

'That I have a great deal to learn.' Anna kept her voice light as she slipped into the heavy chair.

'What else?'

'Defalk seems to face some serious problems.'

Brill rang the bell, and Serna appeared immediately. Dinner was a repetition of the night before, except that the sauce on the unnamed meat was white instead of brown, and the bread was more toward rye than pumpernickel.

'Have you had any more thoughts about the difference between our music and yours?' Brill probed idly.

'Ours is more concerned with affecting how people feel,' Anna said carefully, knowing that was certainly true enough.

'That's more like darksong. Is that because your tech-knowledgeable magic is more powerful than clearsong?'

Anna blinked. 'Oh, it's *technological* magic – the machines. Now, we can do much more with technology, but it hasn't always been that way.' She still felt as though she were walking on eggs, trying to avoid admitting that song had no direct physical power in her world without being blatantly untruthful. 'Does your clearsong – it is clearsong, isn't it? – work better on things than people?'

'Clearsong usually does not work on people. Darksong does, but only if the sorcerer is both powerful and careful. Healing is the most dangerous type of spellcasting.'

'Don't you have doctors?' She paused. 'Healers?'

'Some healers know herbs and poultices, and there are some surgeons, but except for setting bones or sewing up wounds, most people heal better without them.'

Anna shook her head, and took another mouthful of bread. She ate slowly, her eyes heavy. The long day, and the heat, were catching up to her.

'Tomorrow, I need to work on a new spell,' Brill mused.

'For what?' Anna asked.

'That's something sorcerers generally do not share, at least not until the work is done.' Brill took a sip of the vinegar wine that Anna continued to avoid. 'You could use the other workroom.' The sorcerer's words weren't quite a suggestion.

'You'd prefer that I not ride anywhere alone, and that I not experiment with spells in the hall?' Anna tried to keep a smile from her face.

'I have great respect for your abilities,' Brill returned. 'So might the dark ones, and they know you are here. Outside the walls, until you are more . . . accustomed to Liedwahr . . .'

'Do you think people would come after me?'

Brill smiled sadly. 'I know they will. What I do not know is how soon they will begin.'

'It sounds like you think I should work on sorcery to protect myself.'

'That is always a good idea, particularly now.'

Anna yawned. 'I'm sorry. It's not as though I've done that much today. Just ride and listen and look around. Maybe I'm still recovering from . . .' She spread her hands.

'That could be. I have never dared to try to transport someone from the mist worlds.'

Anna waited.

'It can be dangerous, and some sorcerers have been pulled there, rather than pulling objects or people here. Most times the objects or people carried are burned as if by fire.' Brill laughed, but his laugh died away. 'For those reasons, hard as matters may be here, I prefer my own world.'

'So would I, but I wasn't given much choice.' Anna finished the last of the water in the goblet and sat back. 'How do I get back?'

'I do not know. I would worry about trying. It could kill you.' Brill spread his hands. 'You are here, and a few others have come from the mist worlds. Likewise, there are records of older sorcerers traveling there, and records of those who arrived as charred corpses. I know of no one who has traveled more than one direction.' The sorcerer paused. 'That does not mean it is not possible.'

Anna understood. Brill was not about to spend time on something that was impossible. He wouldn't hinder her, but he had paying work to do, work that she had interrupted, and he was suggesting that she work on getting her own spellcasting in order – before too long. Like ... starting tomorrow.

'If you don't mind, Lord Brill, it's time for me to turn in.' She stifled another yawn. 'Time to get some sleep,' she added as she pushed back the chair and stood up.

Brill rose and bowed. 'I will see you at breakfast.'

'I'm sure you will.' Anna inclined her head.

Florenda appeared and followed her up to the bedchamber.

After changing into the thin gown, Anna sat on the edge of the bed and looked at the covered windows, wondering how Elizabetta was doing, hoping that her daughter would be all right. Then, again, Avery would certainly step in. Yes, he would. Her fingers clenched.

Finally, she pulled back the covers and slipped between the sheets.

Neither her worries nor the lumpy mattress and pillows could keep her awake.

13

FALCOR, DEFALK

Barjim looks into the pewter goblet, then across the table. 'I shouldn't have any more.'

'No one will tell you not to, lord,' offers the blocky gray-haired man.

'No one but my conscience, or the ghost of my father, or worse yet, that of my uncle. Or the headache I'll have tomorrow.' Barjim's hands curl around the goblet as if he would squeeze it into scrap before he forces his fingers to relax. 'Everyone is watching every move I make. If I move troops from Denguic to Mencha or farther east, the Prophet of Neserea will have an army marching from Elioch. Oh, I forgot. He already marched it to his border station at the West Pass to ensure . . . What did he call it? The music of tranquility?' Barjim's heavy, hooded eyes widen fractionally, and he sets the goblet down on the ancient table. 'The dark ones are massing to overwhelm me through the Sand Pass, and I can't raise enough levies and can't buy enough troops to reinforce the eastern marches, and Brill's got about as much backbone as a sand adder.'

'He does a good job on fortifications,' points out the older man.

'Only if he's paid, Gelen. Only if he's paid, and you know how little silver we have left. With the drought, the fall harvest won't bring much, and even those bitchy usurers in Encora won't lend me anything else.'

'So . . . abdicate. Turn Defalk over to Behlem and his prophecies of music. Or petition the Traders' Council of Nordwei to make Defalk a protectorate of Nordwei.' Gelen's voice is ironic.

'I can't do that.' Barjim picks up the goblet once more, turning it in his fingers. 'Behlem would have my hide – and have Jimbob turned into a castrato and sold to the Sea-Priests. The Norweians would just put me in command of the forces against Behlem – or the dark ones.'

'Have you asked Alasia?' asks the gray-haired man.

'I don't have to ask her, Gelen. I certainly don't. She tells me, and how can I not listen? Her father has no other direct heirs, but the holding would go to Ensil like that' – Barjim snaps his fingers – 'if he thought I'd as much as indirectly criticized her.'

'She is not stupid,' Gelen says levelly.

'No. She's brighter than I am, and all of Defalk knows it. Oh . . . what does she say? She says about what I just said, because I listen, because I'm smart enough to know that she makes sense.' The Lord of Defalk looks at the pitcher beyond the goblet and shakes his head. 'Everyone needs an excuse – even me.'

Then he stands. 'Except I've got to live with myself.'

14

'Everything here is yours to use, or you may ride back to the hall. Make sure either Wiltur or Frideric accompanies you. All I ask is that you do not disturb me when the door to my workroom is closed.' With that, Brill had bowed and left her.

The workroom was clean enough, and spacious, nearly the size of her bedchamber in Brill's hall, with a window that viewed the distant hills – or mountains – to the east.

On the stone table were a goblet, a pitcher of cool water and more of the dried apple slices and bread. Both a crude pencil and a quill pen and inkstand rested on the table beside a stack of light brown paper. The key-harp on the corner of the table was something like a miniature piano, except the volume was so low that it was clearly useless except as a composing or learning aid.

Anna pulled out the chair and sat at the table. Was she just supposed to practice? What? Spells she didn't know? Or was she supposed to create spells?

As she'd told Daffyd, she wasn't a composer. She was a singer.

She filled the goblet half-full and took a deep swallow, then another. Her fingers strayed toward the bread, and she pulled them away.

She touched one of the hand-harp's black keys, and winced. Either the instrument hadn't been used in years or Erde used a strange scale, and that didn't seem possible. The music played the day before had been a simple polyphony, functional, but not out of tune. She looked at the tuning pegs, almost like levers.

Her hand crept toward the bread again, and she pursed her lips. Eating because she was worried and stressed – one of her worst habits, and one reason why she was a size twelve instead of the eight she'd been four years ago. She shook her head and picked up the pencil, absently creating a series of fat-lined, interlinked loops on the top sheet of the brown paper.

Anna tried to recall the general rules Brill had given – grudgingly – at breakfast. Sorcery didn't work on the singer – except indirectly; if you caused something to explode you could get killed by the fragments. Spells worked best on ordered or semi-ordered nonliving materials. Spells had to have rhyme and what amounted to meter. Songspells worked best with solid accompaniment, and the more complex and involved spells didn't work at all without that kind of support.

Great! She put down the pencil, pushed back the chair, stood, and walked toward the door. Then she stopped. What would she do? Ride back to the hall and stew? Complain to the two guards? Or to the ever-attending Florenda? And about what? Being fed, clothed, treated like a lady? She wouldn't even get sympathy.

With a deep breath, she turned to the bookcase. Maybe the books would help. The handful of books in the case were leatherbound – handbound, she was certain. She scanned the titles – *Boke of Liedwahr, The Naturale Philosophie, Proverbes of Neserea, Donnermusik*. She pulled out *Donnermusik*, and opened it to the first page. Her eyes blinked.

While what she spoke seemed close to what Brill and the others spoke, the words on the page before her seemed like a cross between seventeenth-century English and German – or maybe the way English would have been without the Norman invasion.

Musik is the mathematik of sound ... and sound the manifestation in Erde itself of the structure of musik that doth support all that be and all that be within Erde ...

She struggled on for a page or so before she realized that the book wasn't just about music, but a treatise on the musical theory behind storms. From what she could piece together, the writer was discussing how the harmonics of a storm were music-driven. She flipped through more pages, stopping occasionally and reading paragraphs.

As lightning beginneth with a long note value, so must the music which calleth it forth ...

Harmonic variants be most important as a musical consideration, for they must in truthe effect a change of musical resemblement though the constant repetition, with most suitable variants, of the bass pattern ... through trommel ...

The relationship between the thunder, and that needs must be represented by the falk horn, supplemented by a continuous bass provided by a trommel, and the lightning ... must be joined by a melodic line of the violincello ...

Anna frowned. The last phrase sounded like a sorcerer needed an entire symphony to deal with storms and weather, but Brill had been uneasy in talking about the weather, and he had certainly implied that the dark ones were the only sorcerers who did – and that they used massed voices because a single voice didn't have enough power.

She looked at the book again. The writer certainly seemed to think that instruments could support weather spells. But the writer was hinting at something that amounted to harmony, and nothing Brill had shown her had demonstrated anything that was effectively complete harmony. She shook her head, and began to leaf through the pages again, but so far as she could see, the slim volume held no words for spells, and nothing resembling music, not even the flaglike medieval tablature she vaguely remembered from her graduate days.

She closed the book and walked back to the window. The roads were empty, and the sun was higher, and hotter, no doubt. After a time, she turned and reseated herself at the desk-table.

Part of the problem was the songs. She'd never realized how many dealt with love, and feelings. She needed a song that dealt with solid objects, or weapons, or something.

Her mind was blank. With all the songs she'd learned over the years . . . Her mind was blank . . . not blank of songs. There was the jewel song, and all the arias from *Bohème*, and *Barber, Don Giovanni*, and even *Lakmé*. Delibes had some violence in *Lakmé* . . . Were there some sections that could be used? She murmured the words, not singing them until she reached the section she sought.

> '*Que le ciel me protège*
> *Me guide par la main*
> *Chasse le sacrilège*
> *Au loin de mon chemin!*'

'*Sacrilège*' wasn't it. Could she use '*les ennemis*'?—that was a near rhyme even in French. But . . . the words wouldn't do much except in a battle, and she didn't expect to see one. At least, she certainly hoped she wouldn't. Still, she wrote down the words, with the change, and the rough notes of the melody line. Would they be enough? She couldn't write the whole score, and even if she could, could anyone read it? She hadn't seen any written music. Was there any?

She rubbed her forehead and took a swallow from the goblet, turning it in her hand. Why did she have so many questions? In novels, heroines or heroes just did things, but what was she supposed to do?

She looked back at the key-harp. She might as well tune it, even if it were only good for composing or learning. A piano would have been better. Why an underpowered harp?

Then she nodded, almost ashamed at her slowness. If the strength of spells were determined by the combination of music and voice, and if most spells took twelve players or more, a sorcerer or sorceress had to be limited by what he or she could develop and teach. That meant that there couldn't be that many sorcerers, not when it took talent, trained skill, the ability to read both language and music, and write both in a semi-literate culture.

With a piano ... or something like it ... She shook her head. A good pianist and singer – or even a good guitarist and singer – would be the equivalent of ... what? A guided missile, atomic weapons? She didn't know ... and she didn't have a piano, or a clavier or a harpsichord.

She strummed the strings, then counted – twenty-four – three octaves. It sounded almost like equal-tempered tuning, but not quite. Perhaps an early form, without the minute adjustments that made the system work smoothly? She hoped so as she reached for the tuning levers.

After getting the key-harp in what she hoped was a rough tune, a very rough tuning, Anna looked at the short stack of paper and rubbed her forehead. Surely, surely ... Surely she could come up with something.

What about repeating her cool-water experiment, if only to prove she still had the talent? She had left the envelope with the last words in the green handbag. Shaking her head, she began to write with the greasy pencil, since she hadn't even brought her one working spell with her. Some sorceress.

The words were as awful as ever, but she scratched out 'cold' and replaced it with 'cool.' Then she ran through the vocalises quickly. Should she use the key-harp?

She turned the chair and picked the harp up, resting it on her leg, and trying to duplicate the melody. She stopped after a dozen notes. Even using a one-note-at-a-time melody was laborious with the unfamiliar instrument. She set the harp back on the table. Maybe later.

After clearing her throat again, she sang the words again, emphasizing 'cool' and thinking about ice water.

Surprisingly, the goblet didn't split, but frost rimmed both goblet and pitcher, and the water was cool indeed, and a pair of ice cubes bobbed in the pitcher.

Anna grinned, but the grin faded quickly. So she could chill water. That wasn't going to do much of anything, let alone get her back to Ames and Elizabetta. With a deep breath she looked at the paper again.

Love songs . . . Why did almost every song she knew deal with love or something like it?

Her eyes drifted to the road below the hill, and the single rider who headed up toward the hall, a rider wearing a sleeveless purple surcoat.

There had to be some songs she could change . . . didn't there? To what . . . for what? She shook her head angrily. No one was telling her anything, and she didn't know enough to know what to ask.

Could she do something with the candle-lighting spell? She wrote down the words and looked at the paper. After glancing around the room, finally wadding up a sheet of paper and setting it on the floor. She hummed through the tune and tried her improvisation.

'Paper white, paper bright,
flame clear in my sight.'

The single sheet of paper went up in an instantaneous blaze.

Anna wiped her forehead. Would it work with other items? She wrote out a set of lines to the same rhyme scheme, but pondered . . . If every word were critical, what about armsmen? Would such a spell work on them? She took a deep breath, and penciled in another thought.

She snorted. Great! She could turn paper into fire, and

maybe an armsman or two, if she had time to sing, if she had some accompaniment.

Her eyes went to the window once more, toward the clear hot day outside. Finally, she took another swallow from the goblet and reached for the *Boke of Liedwahr*. Maybe that would help with ideas ... or something.

15

With the rap on the workroom door, Anna glanced up. 'Would you care to accompany me back to the hall for the midday meal?' asked Brill.

Anna looked at the half loaf of bread and the empty platter that had held apple slices. She was still hungry. How could she be? 'Yes. Unfortunately. I seem to be hungry all the time.'

'Magic is hard work,' Brill offered. 'There are few weighty sorcerers.'

That might be so, but Anna hadn't been doing that much sorcery. She was still trying to figure out the basis for a few verses or adapt a few songs that might possibly be converted to the magic of Liedwahr – she hoped. She'd figured out a way to cool water – safely – and burn paper. Neither was particularly inspiring. 'I haven't been working that hard.'

Brill glanced at the dark spot on the stone floor.

Anna flushed. 'I burned some paper. The spell worked.'

'Why paper? Paper is hard to come by, lady.'

'I'm sorry. I didn't realize that.'

'There are a number of objects and materials in the closet,' Brill inclined his head toward the closet door Anna could not see.

Anna donned the floppy hat, following the sorcerer out to the horses – and the two guards – who waited outside in the shade offered under what amounted to a portico. Gero stood behind the guards, eyes downcast.

'Is all well?' asked the sorcerer.

'We'd not be seeing anything strange,' offered Wiltur, the older guard, one hand still on the blade at his waist. ''Cepting a messenger.'

'Messengers do not bode well,' Brill said lightly, 'but we all know that.' He laughed gently.

Anna smiled briefly at the two men, then untied Farinelli, and climbed into the saddle, trying to ignore the blazing sun and dust as she rode beside Brill and toward the hall. Gero and the guards followed.

'To the northeast there,' said the sorcerer with a gesture to the hills that hugged the eastern horizon, 'lies Lake Aulta. Vult is the home of the dark ones, and it lies some thirty leagues north of the lake through the mountains.'

Anna concealed a frown. Why were the dark ones attacking some thirty leagues to the south? Or were the distant mountains so impassible that they made direct travel difficult? She smiled to herself ruefully, thinking about horses and foot soldiers crossing the Rockies – or the Appalachians. Cumberland Gap had been the gateway to Tennessee, and that had been less than two hundred years earlier. But it was still hard to believe she was stranded in a place where such considerations were necessary. 'I take it the mountains are impassable for an army?'

'For a large force,' Brill conceded. 'And clearsong sorcery does not work that well there, except where there are no trees.'

Anna rubbed her nose, to try to keep from sneezing, then shifted her weight in the saddle.

Farinelli *whuff*ed, and she patted his shoulder. 'Easy there ... good boy.'

That got her a snort.

Even the chickens were silent in the midday heat as she reined up before the stables, and by the time Anna had walked from the hall stables, she felt like a morning glory subjected to the South Dakota badlands in August. She shivered, recalling the time Avery had dragged them all camping and Elizabetta had come down with roseola in the middle of nowhere.

The cool of the hall was welcome, and she stopped for a moment in relief, pulling off the floppy hat.

Brill bowed and said, 'I will meet you in the salon, Lady Anna, shortly.'

Anna started up the stairs, followed by the ever-present Florenda. Anna pursed her lips. She hated being followed. That was one thing that Mario had done as a preschooler that had driven her crazy. She'd cross the family room, and he'd followed. Then Avery had used the same tactic, as things were falling apart, following her from room to room, except he'd kept saying, 'We just have to look at this logically. You're feeling, Anna, and you need to think about it.'

At the top of the steps, Anna turned to the serving girl. 'Florenda?'

'Yes, lady.'

'Are you to do my bidding?'

'Yes, my lady.'

'Good. Follow me.' Anna marched to her bedchamber and into the robing room.

Florenda tagged along. 'You wish some help in robing?'

'No. I need some more clothes. In this whole place there are two pairs of trousers that fit, and two shirts, and not much more in the way of gowns and drawers.'

'Drawers?'

'Underclothes, smallclothes, the stuff you wear under your trousers or dresses.'

'Yes, lady?'

Anna turned and glared. 'I don't need help. I don't need you following me around. What I do need is more clothes. I'd appreciate you taking care of that, rather than following me around.'

The girl swallowed. 'But Serna ... and Lord Brill ...'

'Tell Serna I've told you what I need. If she has a problem with that . . . then she can talk to me.' Anna smiled. 'And you can also tell Serna that I will be very displeased if I find out that she is even thinking about punishing you for carrying out my wishes.'

Florenda swallowed.

'And I will punish her if you are replaced.'

That got a tentative smile, tinged with hidden amusement. Anna wanted to sigh, hoping she'd covered all the possibilities. 'Now . . . get on with finding me some clothes. You can still wake me in the morning or announce meals, and you can check with me when I come back to the hall – but otherwise, get me some clothes that fit.'

'Yes, Lady Anna.' Florenda remained standing in the middle of the robing room.

Anna pointed to the dusty outfit she had worn before. 'Take that and go. Now.'

Florenda backed out. When the door closed, Anna took a deep breath. 'I hope it works.'

After washing up, Anna returned to the salon where, for once, she arrived before the sorcerer. She seated herself, pouring more water into her goblet, and sipping it while she waited.

Brill's face was solemn, almost impassive, when he finally entered the salon. 'You need not have waited.'

From the formality of his statement, Anna decided it was better that she had. 'You have always waited for me.'

The sorcerer pulled out the heavy iron chair, which grated slightly on the stone floor, then sat and immediately filled his goblet with the dark wine that Anna had not tried.

'Bad news?' she asked, adding, 'I saw a rider in purple, earlier . . .'

Brill lowered his goblet. 'Lord Barjim sent a messenger.'

'You don't sound pleased.'

The sorcerer shook his head. 'The dark ones are beginning to mass their forces on the far side of the Sand Pass. Lord Barjim estimates they will begin to march in two weeks, perhaps three.' He took a long sip from the goblet.

Serna slipped through the doorway, her sandaled feet almost silent as she carried two platters to the table – one with narrow wedges of both yellow and white cheese, surrounded with dried apple slices, the other with a long loaf of dark bread.

Brill waited until the server set down the platters, then broke off a chunk of bread from the one and nodded to Anna. She took a chunk herself, and added several wedges of the yellow cheese, and some apples, to her plate.

'Did you expect them so soon?' Anna asked, hoping the sorcerer would provide more information. She still knew so little.

Brill chewed through some cheese and bread before answering. 'That they would attack before harvest was to be expected. This soon . . . Barjim had hoped for more time, and so had I.'

Anna chewed through another mouthful of bread, nodding for him to continue.

'With the bad harvest of last year, and the dry winter, supplies are scarce. We have a half a season to harvest – and Lord Barjim probably owes half his share of the harvests to the usurers in Encora.'

'Encora . . . you haven't mentioned that.'

'That's the liedstadt of Ranuak, and the richest city in Liedwahr.'

'That's the one women run?' Anna asked. 'If it's so rich, why aren't the dark ones attacking there?'

'They are,' snorted Brill. 'They're moving the Whispering Sands south.' The sorcerer refilled his goblet. 'Defalk is an easier target. With all the coins the usurers have, the Ranuans can afford a large standing army, not just levies. Of course, the bitches also need the army and the ships to prove they can collect on their loans.' Brill took another deep swallow from the goblet, then broke off another chunk of bread.

Anna ate silently for a time, trying to put together what

she had learned. Finally, she spoke. 'Do you think that what the Ebrans plan is to take over Defalk, then bring back the rain and prosperity, and use that—'

'Exactly,' snapped Brill. 'It's so obvious, that an outsider like you can figure it out in less than a week, and no one in Liedwahr has been able – or willing – to say so.' The goblet went down on the table with a thump. 'Then, they might have to join forces against the dark ones. Instead, they each hope that the lizard snake eats the others first.'

'You're upset,' Anna prompted.

'I am requested, in return for silver, to join Lord Barjim's forces at his summons.'

'"Requested"?' Anna gave the word an ironic twist.

'I don't exactly have a choice, dear lady. If Defalk falls to the Ebrans, they will have no use for sorcerers of my type – or yours. If, by some miracle, Lord Barjim holds them off without my assistance. . .' Brill frowned.

'You're not exactly in the best of graces?'

'Exactly – if you consider being dead or exiled as being in poor graces.' The sorcerer's eyes flicked to the window.

Anna followed, but the sky outside remained clear, the walls empty.

In the silence that followed, Anna asked, 'What do you expect of me?'

'Lady Anna, I expect nothing. You will do as you see fit. You owe Lord Barjim nothing, and so he can ask nothing.'

'I owe you hospitality and information,' she replied, biting back the thought that the information remained hard-fought and scanty.

'In a struggle such as this, one cannot ask,' Brill said gently.

Right! She would be forced to volunteer by Brill's expensive hospitality. 'What will you do, then?' she asked.

'All that I can,' answered the sorcerer, with a rueful laugh. 'There is little point in doing less.' He lifted his goblet, then held it momentarily, while asking, 'How was the workroom? Is there anything . . . I might help with?'

The sorcerer's condescending tone irked Anna, just as Avery's had, but she wasn't married to Brill, and she smiled and asked, 'Why couldn't you use just a drum to replicate thunder, rather than requiring both a falk horn and a violincello?' Anna watched Brill intently.

Brill swallowed hard, then squinted at Anna. For a moment, he said nothing. Then he took another swallow of the vinegarlike wine. 'No one has tried to create storm magic in a century – except for the dark ones – and they use the chorus – the power of massed voices.'

'Why couldn't you use a drum?' Anna broke off a corner of the dark bread, still the best part of the meals Serna offered.

'It is like matching voices with different melodies and the same words.'

'We call that "harmony",' supplied Anna.

'If the match be not perfect,' Brill continued as if she had not spoken, 'then both singers could be destroyed.'

'But you said that the darksingers used massed voices.'

'They sing the same notes and words in chorus. That is different.'

She wondered how different – or were sorcerers so paranoid, or untrusting, like rival tenors, that harmony was effectively avoided? She ate more of the bread, wondering why she was not becoming a balloon.

'You continually surprise me, Lady Anna. Burning paper, and actually reading.'

'Don't most sorceresses read?'

Brill laughed, not unkindly. 'Very few sorcerers or sorceresses could have read what you obviously did. The talent to cast spells does not necessarily require reading. Young Daffyd's friend Jenny cannot print or read her name, but she is good at summonings and sendings – if someone else supplies the spell and music. That earns her a fair living.'

Anna shook her head at the reminders that Liedwahr was still mainly an oral culture, even in spell magic, and one where a prosperous woman was one who owned a small house. She noted that, once again, Brill hadn't answered the question. 'Why wouldn't a drum be enough?'

The briefest of frowns vanished from the sorcerer's face. 'It has to do with the nature of magic. There is no link between one drumbeat and another. All are the same tone, and by the construction of the drum, all must be of the same tone.' He pulled at his chin. 'The first Evult was said to have wrought spells with drums of different pitches, but no one has tried that since, not that I know of, although who would know what they do on the Eastern Isles or in far Sturinn?' Brill turned to Anna, and with that cheerfully false smile, added, 'You still puzzle me, lady. You understand some aspects of music, yet not others. Your voice is firm, precise, yet spells seem foreign to you. Once given a hint, you can perform a spell as powerfully as the best, yet you seem to know no spells.'

'I didn't say I had no spells,' Anna said slowly. 'I think I could come up with several dozen love spells, but love spells aren't really what I need.'

'Several dozen?' Brill's voice sharpened.

'Maybe more,' Anna admitted. 'You might say that those songs are the ones most in demand in my world.' There! She'd told the truth, but not in a way that revealed anything new. 'I was working on a different spell this morning, and I think I have it right, but I need to make sure I have the support correct.' She hoped Delibes' ghost weren't whirling too much in his grave.

'I thought you burned the paper?' Brill looked confused.

'Oh, I did that, all right. That was just an adaptation of the candle spell. And I figured out how to really chill water without smashing your crystal. This was something else.' She smiled brightly, and took another mouthful of the bread.

'And you said you hadn't been working that hard?'

'At a recital, I'd have to perform for at least an hour. A glass, roughly,' she explained. 'Perhaps two.'

The sorcerer shook his head. 'Glasses' worth of love spells, performed one upon the other. Yet you have few other spells? What a strange world must yours be.'

'It is,' Anna agreed. Put that way, earth did sound strange. 'It is.'

16

SOUTH OF SYNEK, EBRA

'Eladdrin?' the voice song-whispers from the harp that stands on the pedestal in the small pond, above the image of the hooded figure in a brown robe so dark it is almost black.

'Yes, Evult?' The Songmaster bows slightly, his golden hair a pale blur in the darkness of the closed tent.

'I can still sense the ripples in the music of Liedwahr. Those ripples have already reached Sturinn. What have you done about the mist-world sorceress?'

'I have taken steps, Evult. The ripples will be removed.'

'It may not be easy, Eladdrin.'

'I have made ready a second effort, Evult.' The Songmaster bows again to the image in the luminescent pool. 'If necessary, there will be a third.'

'Good. It would be better were she removed before the faithful combat against the infidels of Defalk.'

'It would be better, Evult, but one who ripples the weave of the music is strong, and we must march soon.'

'I understand, Songmaster, but bear my words in mind.'

'I hear the melody of your music, Evult.' Eladdrin offers a last bow, but the image in the pool has vanished, and the harp is silent above the water.

After wiping his forehead, then easing the soft cloth into the left waist-pocket of his robe, Eladdrin steps into the cool outside the tent, breathing deeply of the damp air that has followed the rains to the east, taking in the scents of the orchards and the fertile fields.

As he steps toward the campfire, the two armed monks slip from the shadows and follow.

17

Anna sat at the desk in the eastern workroom, her eyes blank. Why was every song she could recall a love song? Or a lullaby? Or useless? She refilled the goblet, and took a sip. With each day, she felt more and more useless. Yes, she could burn wood objects, and paper, and freeze water or chill it. She could light and snuff candles, and she had two or three spells that *might*, just might, do something in a battle. She'd pried some more information out of Brill, but each syllable that meant anything was an effort.

She'd terrorized a poor servant girl into not following her every step – just every other step – and she had another riding outfit, and a casual gown, and a pair of soft leather shoes for wearing around the hall. But the sheets were still scratchy, the mattress lumpy, and each day, she owed more of that intangible debt to Brill – one he clearly didn't want paid with her body, but with the skills he pressed her to keep developing.

The indirectness was driving her crazy.

She jerked upright at the rap on the workroom door.

'Are you ready—?'

'Not yet.' Anna forced a smile. 'Would you sit down?' She gestured toward the chair across the desk.

Brill sat gingerly, his eyes flicking to the window, and then back to Anna.

'Customs are somewhat different in the mist worlds, or mine, anyway,' Anna began. 'And I've tried to discuss certain matters with you, but you are so charming that they never get discussed. So I have a few questions, and I'd be even more deeply in your debt if you could bear with me and answer them.'

'I have tried to be most forthcoming.'

'As I know you have,' Anna said flatly. 'First, in simple terms, if Daffyd and Jenny, who have far less skill than you, could summon me, why can't you send me back to my world?'

Brill looked at Anna. 'Song magic isn't just a sorcerer singing and players playing. The words have to be righ:, and the sorcerer has to be able to see what he wants. I have to be able to *see* the fort Lord Barjim wants, almost to feel it. I use the drawings and plans to help create the image in my mind.' He shrugged. 'Daffyd could bring you here, because he was asking for any sorceress to be placed in a setting he could see. The problem with sending you back into the mist worlds is that you're the only one who can see where you need to go, and you can't send yourself.'

Anna half understood the visualization aspect, but it still bothered her. It had been almost a week, and Elizabetta had to be upset – a totally vanished mother, with no trace whatsoever. 'That's almost saying that no one can send me back unless I can show them an image that they can hold to.'

'You must trust them, totally,' the sorcerer pointed out. He frowned, then added. 'Perhaps you can see why sometimes the smallest of distractions can upset a sorcerer. They should not, but they do. And there is the problem of the burning. Too many attempts, and the fires turn on the sorcerer. That is why my glimpses of the mist worlds have been infrequent and seasons apart, fascinating as I find such glimpses.'

Anna nodded, trying not to swallow at the double impact, as she understood also what Brill was saying about Daffyd's father. And the business of burning – was that why her key had been so hot?

But she had to get more answers while Brill was sitting still. 'Second, what can song magic do to stop the dark ones, and what is it that you want me to do to help you?' Anna held up a hand to cut off Brill. 'No more nice fancy statements. Plain and simple.'

'If all women of the mist worlds are like you, I see why the old books caution against summonings.' Brill added a slight laugh.

Anna presented a hard professional smile.

Brill's laugh died away.

'I will have to use clearsong if they are near the hills, or darksong, if they are not, to bring destruction on the Ebran soldiers.' The sorcerer spread his hands. 'Some of my players . . . darksong would destroy, and that weakens what I can do.'

'What would you like from me?'

'Any spell or magic that will stop the Ebrans or the dark ones.' Brill smiled ruefully.

Anna understood the smile. He found her attractive, but her possible power even more so. She stood. 'Last question. Why do I need guards?'

'For the same reason as I do. These days people want to kill sorcerers . . . or sorceresses. And you don't know how to use a blade, either.' Brill eased to his feet.

'There must be something I can carry,' Anna suggested. 'You carry a sword.'

'Not willingly, and not well. It takes seasons, if not years, to really master a blade.'

Anna frowned. She'd used a sword once, when she'd played Clorinda. She'd been younger then, twenty years younger, and her arms had ached for weeks, and that had been a choreographed fight. 'What about a knife?'

'That's worse.'

'So . . . what do you suggest, lord and master of the hall Brill?' Anna's eyes flashed.

The sorcerer looked away.

Anna waited.

'A truncheon or a short staff. You should have some personal-protection spells worked out before long, and you won't ever master the blade enough to hold off trained armsmen.' Brill added hastily. 'I can't, either. So what you need is something to keep people off you enough to allow you to use your voice.'

Anna had to admit that the sorcerer made a sort of sense, even if he were suggesting that she get some personal-protection spells in a hurry. 'How about one of each?'

'It couldn't hurt, just so long as you remember that you really don't know how to use a knife.'

Anna tried to repress the glare she felt at Brill's conde-scending tone.

The sorcerer stepped back. 'If you hold a knife and a truncheon, that might give you time to use a spell.'

Again, what he said made sense, but she still hated that air of condescension. 'How do I get them?'

'Quies' son Albero is the armorer, as close to one as we have. I believe we have some knives and truncheons. Those would be better.'

'I know. It's been twenty years since I held a sword, and I didn't do well with it then.' Anna forced a rueful smile.

'I had not realized blades were used in the mist worlds.'

'They're not, not normally. I was in grad school, and I played a part that required using a sword. That was a long time ago.' Anna's stomach growled. 'I'm hungry. We can go.'

'You have no more questions?'

'I have a lot more questions, more than you'll want to answer, but I'm hungry.' Anna gestured toward the workroom door.

Outside the dome building, the midday sun beat through the clear air, as it had every day without fail. Even in the shade of the portico, the air seemed hotter than the day before – as if the atmospheric oven had been eased up a few more degrees. Anna looked down at the empty water buckets for the horses.

'We refilled 'em twice, lady,' said Frideric apologetically. 'Gero's gone to get some more.'

Brill glanced to Wiltur. 'Any visitors?'

'No, ser. The roads are clear, mostly, except for a messenger of Lord Barjim's. He was riding toward the Sand Pass.'

'We'll be seeing more of that.' Brill untied the mare and mounted.

'A-feared so, ser.'

As Anna bounced toward the hall, she realized, not for the first time, that she needed more practice riding. Then, again, she needed more practice at everything.

18

ENCORA, RANUAK

'What was that awful disharmony in the chords, Veria?' The round-faced and gray-haired woman offers a cheerful smile as she lifts with both hands the steaming cup that has no handles. 'Did you ever manage to find out?'

'Which discord, Matriarch?' The black-haired woman at the other long end of the oval ebony table pours her own mulled cider. 'Between the Evult, his Songmaster, Lord Brill, and the constant scrying of the Norweians, there have been more than a few incidences of discord.'

'You could say that,' adds the silver-haired man on the short side of the table. 'I'd even call it dissonance.' He adds another pinch of cinnamon to his cup, then twists the end of his silvered handlebar mustache. 'Then, there has been more discord since the effects of ill harmony were discovered. Too bad that we could not have the Prophet and the Evult sing together.'

'Father . . .' protests Veria.

'Do not be vulgar, Ulgar,' suggests the Matriarch.

'Accuracy, my dear, accuracy. Not a silver for vulgarity,

but golds for accuracy. Isn't that what the counting houses say?' He lifts the cup and slurps his cider. 'Too hot. Like Defalk.'

'You make no sense, Father. It is warmer here,' says Veria.

'The warm damp is good for the bones. The dry heat of Defalk turns you into a mummy.'

Mother and daughter exchange glances.

'Counting houses, dissonance, Lord Barjim – it all be linked with the silver chains of harmony,' continues Ulgar.

'You do not have to be obscure, dear.' The Matriarch adjusts one of the wooden clips that keeps her iron-gray hair neatly in its bun. 'We all know the links.'

'I don't,' protests Veria.

Ulgar lifts one silvered eyebrow and looks to his consort.

'We lent Lord Barjim the golds he requested so that he could buy enough supplies from us to move his forces from Denguic and Falcor to the Sand Pass. He will use his sole sorcerer—'

'That was it, Mother – Matriarch,' Veria corrects herself and continues. 'He has two sorcerers. Or rather, Lord Brill has a sorceress. That was the disharmony. Someone opened a weltsperre—'

'Call it a "worldgate," daughter. Pretension does not become you,' suggests Ulgar, putting yet another pinch of spice into his cup.

'Yes, Father.' The slightest edge tinges her words. 'Someone opened a worldgate and brought her through. She is blonde, a soprano sorceress, I think.'

'You think?'

'Ulgar . . . let her finish.'

Veria drops her head, then continues. 'The dark ones have set their assassins on her, but they have not reached Mencha.'

'I said it was all linked,' points out Ulgar.

The Matriarch smiles, still cherubic. 'She must be a strong sorceress to have created such discord.'

'The scriers do not know her strength, but Eladdrin, the spymistress of the north, and Lord Behlem all use their mirrored waters to watch her.'

'The better to keep them occupied.'

'Matriarch?' asks Veria. 'What will you tell the others about the shifting of the sands?'

'What I have said before. Matters balance, and they will again. The Evult has strained the chords of Liedwahr, and they will redress the harmonies, and before too long.'

'Then why did you agree to lend Barjim two thousand golds? He cannot repay them.'

Ulgar slurps his tea, and both women wince.

'Sometimes, one must buy time while the harmonies regroup.' The Matriarch smiles and stands.

19

Anna's fingers struggled with the key-harp as she tried to keep the words of the aria in mind.

> *'Donde lieta usci al tuo grido d'amore,*
> *torna solo Mimi al solitario nido*
> *Ritorna un'altra volta a intesser finiti fior!'*

Paper flowers! Love! All the arias she'd learned were useless! And she didn't know Italian well enough to make most of them meaningful in the crazy world that was Erde. Or enough German. French she knew better, but she wondered if the French melodies would work that well in a Teutonic-musicked world.

Anna wanted to scream and crumple the heavy paper up into a ball. Instead, she refilled the goblet with water, and slowly drank it all. Then she stood and walked from the workroom.

Once in the entry hall, she glanced toward Brill's work-room, but the door was closed, and Gero was nowhere in sight. She slipped out through the front door, her boots heavy on the stone, and into the midafternoon heat.

'I'm going to ride down to the orchards,' she announced, checking the water bottle fastened to Farinelli's saddle. She had to keep reminding herself to drink in the dry heat.

'More than a few folks on the road, lady,' offered Wiltur. 'Some even stopped under the trees down there.'

'Don't see them anymore,' added Frideric.

Anna patted Farinelli on the shoulder, then mounted. It seemed easier, but she'd had some practice over the days. She eased the gelding out of the shade and into the sun, adjusting the floppy-brimmed hat as she did.

Wiltur glanced at Frideric, then mounted with a fluid grace that Anna envied.

'Do I really need guards?' Anna asked.

'You more than most, Lady Anna,' answered Wiltur. 'You're beautiful and a sorceress, and that's enough to have a lot of folks after you.' The guard with the silvered hair and graying stubbly beard smiled, not that the smile improved his appearance much, not with the long scar across his left cheek.

'You're kind,' laughed Anna, 'but my son's as old as Frideric.'

From his position by the dome building's door, Frideric looked quickly toward her, and then away.

'You must have been young,' replied Wiltur. 'Very young.'

'Young enough,' Anna said, her fingers going to the truncheon at the left side of her belt, and then to the knife, before she flicked the reins, and Farinelli started down the winding trail toward the orchard below.

Wiltur edged his mount up beside Anna's. 'Hottest day of the year so far.'

'It feels that way.'

'Is it this hot where you come from?'

'In some places, Wiltur. It's not as dry.'

'When I was a young fellow, it wasn't this way. My folks had a small holding out on the Synope road, ran sheep.' The guard coughed. 'My brother Uthor got the place. Thought he was the lucky one. All the grass went, and Falinya died when the heat fever came three years ago. His boy died too. She was a pretty one, Falinya was, and Eber looked like her.'

'What happened to your brother?'

'Sold the place for a handful of coppers – no water – and he left to go to Falcor. Been more than a year, and haven't had any word.'

'I'm sorry.'

'Thought he was the lucky one. Me and Biel, least we got a solid cot below the hall, and enough food for us and the girls. Brill's not a bad lord, leastwise, long as you keep your mouth shut. Doesn't take the girls the way they say his sire did, and the ones that like him, well, they say he treats 'em well. Strange, though, seeing as he's never taken a consort, and none of the girls have children.' Wiltur coughed again, looking back toward the hall.

'You're trying to tell me that Lord Brill's a good sort, especially compared to a lot of lords?' Anna asked.

'I've not seen many lords, but, after a while you get to hear. Know other lords' guards like to come with their lords when they visit.' The grizzled guard cleared his throat.

Anna looked to the hills in the east, distorted by the heat lines that wavered across the plains all the way to the horizon. She eased Farinelli to the edge of the trail to avoid a dust-filled hole. Her nose itched, and she rubbed it gently. 'I take it some of the other lords are best avoided?'

'Avoided, aye, if you can. They say that Lord Genrica beds every maid on his lands 'fore she can have another. That's not as bad as old Jylot, though. Lord Barjim had to have his hall pulled down around him.' Wiltur shook his head. 'He had dungeons, and they smelled like a renderer's, and it weren't from sheep nor cows.'

Anna winced, then unfastened the water bottle and forced

herself to take a drink. As Farinelli carried her down and around the curve in the road, she could see the empty irrigation pond. This time, even the bottom of the pond was dry and cracked from the heat.

'Are there others as good as Brill?'

'Some . . . so they say. Lord Jecks – his hall's on the big hill above Elhi. Peddlers say he's fair, and he even gives each maid raised on his holding a dower.' Wiltur laughed. 'Without tryin' 'em, so to speak. His levies, they say he's good, and that means he doesn't mess with their women, and takes only his fair share of the harvests.'

Even from beside the empty pond, Anna could see the fine dust on the small leaves of the apple trees, and on the cracked branches of the dead trees. Almost a third of the orchard seemed to be dead or dying, despite Brill's sorcery to bring water to the trees.

Downhill, at the end of the row of trees that Brill's road paralleled on its course down to the main road, Anna thought she saw another pond, then realized the image was some sort of mirage.

'Quiet, here,' said Wiltur.

As Farinelli stepped past the beginning of the trees, Anna could feel the hair on the nape of her neck prickling, and she turned in the saddle, looking west past the dusty apple trees, squinting against the afternoon sun. She could see nothing, and she scanned the apparently empty orchard.

Farinelli *whuff*ed and side-stepped, his hoofs raising dust. Anna's nose itched, but she fought the urge.

'Lady—' began Wiltur.

Although she couldn't say why, Anna threw up her free arm – and fire slashed across it. Another line of pain slammed into her shoulder. Dumbly, she looked down at the shaft in her upper arm.

'Guards!' Wiltur yelled, as he spurred his horse away from her and toward two figures that began to run between the gnarled trees. 'Frideric!'

Somehow, Anna clung to the gelding's mane with her

uninjured hand as Farinelli side-stepped, and she turned
him uphill. She had to get help.

Somewhere in the distance, she could hear a horn, and the
damned thing kept blowing and blowing, horribly off key.
She wanted to laugh at herself for thinking about it when
her shoulder hurt so much.

Wave after wave of pain slammed through her, but she
kept riding, kept hanging on as Farinelli plodded up the trail
back toward the hall. Behind her, the horn sounded again,
and somewhere there were horses, lots of horses, but she
was afraid to look, afraid that she would lose her balance
on Farinelli as the gelding carried her back to the hall.

The last thing she recalled was looking at the front entry
of the hall, wondering how she could dismount with an arrow
through her shoulder, and watching the door open.

20

Anna stood on the stage, looking down at the dusty riding
clothes she wore. What had happened to her gown? She
couldn't sing in front of the Founders' Dinner in riding
clothes, not dusty and sweaty. Why, that alone would kill
her chances for tenure. As Music Chair, Dieshr would see
to that. How had this happened? Had her injury thrown her
back to earth?

She tried to open her mouth, but found she couldn't, and
only a croaking groan issued forth. Then, she turned to walk
off the platform, but her feet would not move.

When Anna finally shook herself awake, her back hurt
as well as her shoulder. And her hand hurt. She could feel
the sweat and dust matted into her hair. As her eyes opened
fully, Florenda stood by the bed, a goblet in her hand. She
was still on Erde, and her eyes burned.

'You must drink, lady.'

Anna drank. Whatever it was tasted like vinegar laced with used crankcase oil and spiced with extra-soapy cilantro.

'More,' insisted Florenda.

Anna forced herself to take another deep swallow, then closed her eyes for what seemed a moment.

When she woke again, Florenda sat on a chair, sewing.

'I'm thirsty,' Anna announced.

But she got more of the oily wine, first, before Florenda let her have water.

'I must get Liende and Lord Brill.' With that the serving girl scuttled from the bedchamber.

Anna wanted to shake her head, but she had the feeling that her head might not remain on her neck if she did. How could one arrow do so much? And hurt so badly? Bullets . . . she understood the damage that high-powered guns could cause, but arrows?

As she reflected, the door reopened, and the woodwind player with the red hair streaked with white entered, followed by Brill and Florenda.

'You are awake,' said the older woman. 'Good.'

'I'm afraid . . . don't know your name,' Anna said slowly.

'I am Liende. Lord Brill asked me to . . . assist. I had some little training as a healer years ago.' The clarinetist offered a warm but crooked smile.

'How do you feel, lady?' asked Brill. The circles under his eyes were deeper yet.

'I'll live.' Anna looked at the dressing across her upper arm and shoulder and the rough stitches in her palm.

'I'd trust so,' he said ironically.

'You helped heal some of this?' she asked.

'Some. As I could. Liende's skill helped also.'

Anna frowned. 'There was just one arrow. How could it . . . ?'

Liende laughed gently. 'It was a war arrow, and no one thought you would live.'

'I'm glad . . . to prove them wrong.'

A silence fell across the chamber.

'I don't understand,' Anna finally said. 'What did I do? I haven't lifted a hand against anyone.'

'You are here,' answered Liende. 'You came from the mist worlds, and that'd be the one place that the dark ones fear.'

'But why?' Anna shook her head. She felt so stupid. All she'd been doing was trying to improve her riding and learn something about Erde, and people were trying to kill her. On earth, they wanted to destroy your career or take your job, but most people she knew weren't killers. 'I haven't cast a single spell against them . . . against anyone.'

'I did not think the dark ones would try to strike so soon,' Brill answered. 'They fear you, and they want you dead before you realize your powers. Wiltur and Frideric killed all three of them, but they wore the dark robes. They cast a glamour and hid there, waiting for you. For the dark ones to send three so far from Ebra – that is a tribute to your powers.'

Powers? Anna wanted to laugh, but that would have hurt. All she'd done was to shatter a goblet, light a few candles, turn a few pieces of wood to ashes. Yet some people were telling her she was powerful, and others were trying to kill her.

Her lips tightened, even as she sank back against the lumpy pillows.

Erde was no dream. It was different, though, a place where sixty miles was considered far way, and where arrows could kill.

She was going to have to learn to be a sorceress, a real one. If she didn't, sooner or later Brill would turn against her or just abandon her; or the dark ones, for whatever reason, would kill her – or both.

She tightened her lips. She had a lot of memory-searching to do – a lot. Her breath hissed between her lips.

Except she had to get better, first. Except that she was so tired. Her eyes closed.

21

WEI, NORDWEI

The woman with the close-cropped golden hair steps into the well-lit room whose single wide window overlooks the harbor piers that mark the well-dredged juncture of the River Nord with the Vereisen Bay.

The dark-haired woman behind the table, her back to the window, speaks, though her lips barely move. 'Sit down, Gretslen.'

The golden-haired Gretslen slips into the armless wooden chair. 'You sent for me, Ashtaar?'

'I did. How are matters going in Esaria?' Ashtaar raises a hand to the short dark hair, then pauses, her fingers going to the polished black wooden oval on the desk.

'Well enough. Young Behlem is poised to march, once Barjim reinforces his troops to stop the dark ones.'

'How soon?'

'The dark ones are marshaling in the Sand Pass now, and Barjim has called for his levies. He must wait for Lord Jecks' forces, and it will take more than two weeks for them to be gathered and march the distance from Ehli, say three weeks or more before Barjim gathers east of Mencha.'

'The dark ones could move into Defalk long before that.'

'Eladdrin won't. Then he'd have to chase the lords' forces all over Defalk.' Gretslen offers a brief smile. 'He'll let Barjim mass his forces – and then destroy them.'

'What about the rumors of this sorceress? The one who supposedly was summoned from the mist worlds?' Ashtaar laughs. 'Mist worlds, indeed.'

'She is reputed to be powerful enough to frighten the dark ones. They sacrificed some of their agents in Defalk to attack her.' Gretslen moistens her lips ever so slightly. 'No one has seen her before . . . anywhere.'

'You really don't believe that song sorcery can cross worlds, do you?'

'I only know that she appeared from nowhere.'

'Are you sure?' presses Ashtaar.

'We're sure.'

'Kendr said she will die.'

'Kendr is a good seer, but the sorceress is not dead, and she is safe within Brill's hall.' The golden-haired woman adds sardonically, 'The attack was enough to drive Brill back to darksong to save her.'

'Because it shows her value?'

'Exactly. Brill was already extremely deferential to her, extremely deferential. That alone indicates that she is more than beautiful, and this attack would confirm it.' Gretslen shakes her head.

'The dark ones are sometimes so stupid.'

'They are powerful, though,' answers the blonde one.

'So is a cyclone, or a tidal wave, and one should fear both, but not because they are smart.' Ashtaar's eyes focus on Gretslen. 'What if Brill should want another such sorceress?'

'We have taken steps to stop that.'

'Good.' Ashtaar leans back in her chair. 'Who else knows of this strange sorceress, or whatever she may be?'

Gretslen laughs. 'Everyone knows, except Barjim. But no one knows anything except that she is an exotic beauty who some claim came through a portal from one of the mist worlds.'

'Even Behlem?'

'He probably knew before I did,' Gretslen admits. 'He has sources all over Defalk.'

'That means Konsstin may. And some others.'

'I doubt it. Behlem wouldn't tell him, and Cyndyth wouldn't, not after being effectively sold to Behlem. And if those two don't want him to know, who would risk their necks to tell him? He'll find out within weeks, but he'll be among the last. I don't know about the Matriarch, although I'd guess so. Money has eyes everywhere.'

'So it does.' Ashtaar laughs and raises a hand to dismiss the blonde woman.

Gretslen rises with a polite smile.

22

As the tinted glass of the bedchamber window filtered the worst of the late-afternoon sun, Anna sat at the table with the keyharp, a stack of the tan paper, a pencil, and the inevitable pitcher of water and accompanying goblet.

Her left shoulder ached, as did her left hand, but her insistence on distilling alcohol from the vinegary wine, and bathing the wounds in it – combined with Brill's initial magic, seemed to have warded off infection. The soreness around the deep slash surprised her, as did the shades of purple and green, and the burning sensation that accompanied cleaning the wounds and the area around them didn't leave her in the best of moods.

Nor did looking in the mirror and seeing all too many gray and auburn roots at the base of her hair.

She glanced toward the robing room, where Florenda had delivered a third riding outfit, this one in an even lighter green. She asked the girl for a gown, even sketched a rough outline, but she'd have to come up with something else for Florenda to do before long. Requesting too many clothes was wasteful, and probably put her even more in Brill's debt.

No matter where she was, she was in debt in some way or another.

Her eyes dropped to the paper before her, but her mind kept veering off. How had she gotten to Erde? What had she been thinking? The words rolled back to her – '*I'd just like to run away . . . anywhere. Anywhere!*'

The tears welled up in her eyes, and she blotted them angrily with the cloth in her good right hand. What was it – be careful about what you wish for or you may get it? Erde was certainly anywhere other than Ames, but she was still dancing to everyone else's tune.

She blotted her eyes again and then picked up the paper. She needed something strong. What about a hymn? Or something? She needed a hymn for battles. Then she smiled. That one she knew, and there must be some set of words that would do what she wanted. She had time, and she *would* get the words right!

Brill wanted a sorceress, and the dark ones wanted to kill her. Her lips tightened. She'd repay both – somehow!

23

Anna carried the sketches down to the salon for the noon meal, arriving, as was becoming the case more frequently, before Brill.

Even though her left shoulder and hand had healed enough to use the key-harp for short periods of time, the instrument seemed almost worse than useless. Not only was the key-harp frustrating her, but it had no power of projection.

She sat on her side of the table and poured more water. Serna peered in.

'He's not here yet,' Anna said pleasantly. 'You know, I like your bread.' She smiled. 'I hope it's yours.'

Serna nodded, then vanished.

With the faint whispering of boots, the sorcerer appeared, wearing the hard, faded-blue clothing that was his working apparel, but his boots were still those of gleaming blue leather.

'You have that certain look upon your face, Lady Anna.' Brill bowed before pulling out the heavy blue-lacquered chair. 'Before you begin, how is your shoulder?'

'It doesn't hurt at all with small movements, or gentle ones, and it's still itching. So it's healing.' She offered a rueful smile. 'How's Farinelli? He probably helped as much as anyone.'

'Quies says that he misses you.' Brill shook his head. 'You do have a way, Lady Anna. Wiltur was impressed, also. He said you threw up your hand to deflect the arrow from your throat or heart, and that you didn't cry out. You just rode back to the hall with a wound that would have felled many armsmen.'

'It felled me all right.'

'But not until you could be helped.' Brill shrugged. 'You might have died if you'd fallen from the gelding down at the orchards.'

Serna scuttled in with the lunch. This time, there were melons again, as well as yellow cheese, hot apples, and bread. Anna smiled at the server, and got a fleeting smile in return.

Brill filled his goblet from the wine pitcher. 'So what are you planning, lady sorceress?'

'Who makes instruments? Stringed instruments.'

'Kaseth does. I imagine even your young friend Daffyd does. Why?'

'I have an idea,' Anna said.

'I thought you might.'

She spread the papers on the table. Once she'd been a fair artist, but that had been years before, and she was guessing at some of the dimensions and features from what she recalled.

'You have a fine hand. You could have been a scribe or an artist.'

'I did some drawing, years ago, but I wasn't talented enough, and I liked music better.'

'Hmmmm ...' Brill sipped the red vinegary wine and

looked at her drawings. After a time, and several more sips, he cleared his throat. 'It looks something that partakes of the lute and the violoncello, and something else I have never seen.'

'An acoustic guitar.'

The sorcerer looked blank.

'It's like a lute, except it's more powerful and would project more sound.' Anna took another sip of water. 'If you want me to be useful, this would be most helpful.'

'You are not even healed yet,' Brill protested.

'I'm doing better, and I don't know that the dark ones will wait for me to recover.'

'I have tried to let it be known that you are still at the brink of death,' the sorcerer said blandly. 'I had hoped that would encourage the Dark Monks to take their time.'

Anna frowned. 'Why? I'd think they'd hurry.'

'Anyone with armsmen can take land. Unless the Ebrans destroy those who can take it back, what good does marching into Defalk do them? It is better to fight one decisive battle than many that bleed one dry.'

Anna thought for a moment, realizing that she had thought that battles and taking territory were synonymous, and maybe they were, on earth – but then, she recalled Prof Martin and his lectures about Lee and the Civil War, how Lee had prolonged the war by preserving his army. 'Then shouldn't Lord Barjim refuse to fight?'

'If he retreats, the Ebrans will take the best fields and the orchards, and their harvest. He owes half a harvest's worth of coins to the moneylenders in Encora.'

Anna got the impression that Lord Barjim was damned one way or another. She gathered the drawings up. 'What should something like this cost?' Then she shook her head. 'Why am I asking? I don't have any way to pay for it.'

'I would guess that it would cost a gold.' Brill set down his goblet. 'I will supply the woods from the players' stocks, and pay for it.' He laughed. 'If it helps defeat the dark ones, it is a small price to pay, and if it does not, then

I won't miss it, either. Tell Daffyd, and he would be better than Kaseth for a strange instrument, that he may use the seasoned woods.' Brill's hands dipped out of sight and returned with several heavy silver coins. 'Best you offer him a silver as a token. I will send a messenger in your name after we eat.' The sorcerer reached for the bread.

Anna ladled out the hot and tart apples, then took both bread and cheese. She seemed always hungry, but she wasn't gaining weight. If anything, she had lost a bit – not nearly what she would have liked – but the trousers seemed slightly looser. That had to be from the time when she was unconscious and hadn't been able to eat.

When the finally looked down at her platter and around the table, Anna flushed, realizing she had eaten almost as much as Brill. Eating that way, she'd gain everything back!

'I will send for Daffyd,' Brill said as he finished the last of his wine and rose from the table.

'I think I'll be ready to ride in a few days, and then I can go back to work in the workroom.'

'So soon?'

'So long as there's no infection, there's no reason to sit around.'

'As you wish, Lady Anna.'

Anna drank another goblet of water and watched the empty walls, and sun-drenched Mencha, for a time. Serna removed all the dishes except for the water pitcher and Anna's glass. She'd meant to talk to Brill about harmony, to ask whether a harmonic spell would work. The *Donnermusik* book had implied it was workable. But somehow, she hadn't felt right about asking – or maybe she wasn't up to a fight, not that she ever was, when she was still recovering.

'The player Daffyd,' Florenda announced finally.

'Have him come in.'

Anna stood and waited.

'You sent for me, lady?' Daffyd bowed, deeply enough almost for it to be sardonic.

'Yes. I did. I didn't know how else to find you, and it's not exactly wise for me to go riding all over Mencha in my condition.' Her eyes dropped to the wrapped shoulder. 'Not yet, anyway. Not since I'm still weak in the sorcery department.'

Daffyd frowned at the word 'department.'

'I have a favor to ask. I need an instrument made. It's special.' Anna bent over the table and spread out the papers again, ignoring the twinge in her shoulder and the faint throbbing in her left hand.

Daffyd looked at the drawings. 'How big is this instrument?'

'A little more than a yard.' Anna started to spread her hands to indicate how large, then thought better of it as her shoulder twinged.

Daffyd's eyes rolled. 'Six strings? What kind of strings?'

'The four from the cello and the two deepest ones from your viola, except longer. I'll tune them differently. When can you start?'

'I must find woods, and—'

'Lord Brill said that Kaseth would give you the material from the players' stocks, and he said you could use the most seasoned woods. I don't have much I can give you, not yet, but . . .' Anna extracted one of the silver coins from her purse.

'Why do you need this . . . what would you call it?'

'It's not a guitar, not with gut strings, but it should be a lot stronger than a lute. Call it a lutar.' Anna almost laughed, thinking that 'lutar' sounded much better than 'guilute.' 'I need it for sorcery.'

'You haven't asked for a bow.'

'It's to be strummed or plucked.'

Daffyd frowned. 'I've heard of sorcerers using lutes, lady, but they don't help much because your fingers will touch the strings.'

Anna pursed her lips. She didn't like picks, but they might solve part of the problem. 'There might be a way around that. How soon can you do this?'

'It should take a season.'

Anna shook her head. 'I need something a lot sooner. A lot sooner.'

'I can try,' Daffyd said. 'The seasoned woods will help, but it will not be as good as I would like if I hurry.'

'Daffyd ... most times I would agree with you, but this is one time where a poor instrument is better than none.'

The young instrumentalist's eyebrows lifted.

'Go ...' Anna laughed. 'Listen to your elders.'

When the young man had left the salon, Anna stood, gathered the papers, and walked slowly up to her chamber, accompanied by Florenda. What other tasks could she devise for the girl?—not too onerous, but ones that would keep her out of Anna's hair all the time.

She tried not to sigh, wishing that she felt stronger. Still, she intended to be riding again within another few days. If she had to stay in the hall much longer, she'd scream – except she wouldn't. She always tried to be reasonable.

24

FALCOR, DEFALK

'Why does it take your sire, the powerful and wise Lord Jecks, so dissonantly long to gather his levies? Three weeks more before he can move them down the Mencha road?' Barjim looks at the half-eaten loaf of bread on the table between them, then scoops up a handful of the heavily salted almonds.

The broad-shouldered brunette, whose short hair shows streaks of gray, brushes the crumbs off the worn leathers that match Barjim's. 'Because it's the only way he can buy you time. You can't be expected to move against the dark ones without the largest company of your lords' levies.' She takes a deep swig from her pewter goblet and sets it on the table. 'The dark ones wish to crush us at one blow, and they will wait – for a time, but not until harvest, or even close to it.'

'Alasia, I songpraise the day we were joined – when I'm not cursing it.' He refills his goblet.

'I know. Do you want me to be less than I am? Would that help?' Her voice is calm, free of edge or bitterness, gentle, but not soft.

'No. You know that. So does half of Liedwahr, unfortunately.' After a sip from the goblet, he asks, 'What can I gain from such time?'

'Send a message to your sorcerer, for one. Suggest that he had best use the time to good advantage.'

'I did that already. Twice, as you may recall. He responds that he stands ready for my summons.' Barjim takes another swallow of the harsh wine.

'Can you replace some of the liedburg guards in Denguic with levies in similar garb, levies from Sudwei, perhaps?'

'That might help. That cripple Geansor won't complain.'

'Not with his heir and daughter in the south tower,' says Alasia dryly.

'You've never approved of that, but what choice do I have? In any case ...' Barjim pauses and rubs his left temple. 'In any case, we could move them in with the supply wagons over the next week. Behlem wouldn't notice the difference through a scrying pond, no matter what he claims about being the Prophet of Music. It's easy to claim that sort of thing with the Liedfuhr of Mansuur behind you.'

'And his coins,' murmurs Alasia.

'Those too.' Barjim takes another handful of nuts.

25

'The first battle song – again,' ordered Brill.

Daffyd shifted his weight on his stool, his eyes flicking to Anna and then away, before he lifted his bow.

From the chair at the side of the practice room, Anna listened as the eight players followed Brill's gestures. Kaseth, one of the other violinists, one clarinetist, and the bass-horn player were missing.

Gero sat on a stool in the corner, his eyes on Brill.

Liende and the falk hornist carried the main melody of the short battle song, and the strings supported them, rather than the other way around, as it had been in the previous practices Anna had attended. Even so, the structure still seemed mostly polyphonic, and she couldn't help but wonder if homophonic music would provide stronger spell support – or even vocal harmony.

Anna suppressed a bitter laugh. Theory wasn't her bag, and she was speculating again on what kind of music would cast spells better in a world she scarcely understood. Avery would have done that, but was she any better?

Mentally, she tried to construct some verse that would follow the music, but found she could not – not anything that made sense. She could adapt something she knew ... but creating it from scratch, that she hadn't been able to do – not yet anyway. Had Brill actually written the battle song – or inherited it from his father?

After the practice, Anna made her way across the room to Daffyd. 'How are you coming on the lutar?'

'I have the frame done. Do you want the fingerboard rounded like a violin?'

'Flat, if you can, and ...' Anna shook her head. There

wasn't any point in fretting the board, not when she didn't know and couldn't begin to calculate the intervals. That would make fingering hard, and even harder on her fingers, but violinists managed it.

'I have also found some of the best spruce for the bass peg and the sounding peg.'

'Good.' Anna recalled spruce was supposed to be good for that. 'Hardwood for the front and back?'

'Maple and rosewood.'

'How soon?'

'I cannot say.' Daffyd closed the case for his viola. 'Sooner than I had thought.' He glanced toward the entry hall where Brill and Liende stood. 'Lord Brill said that I should only work on your lutar and my playing.'

Anna nodded. So Brill thought her lutar was that important. He hadn't told her.

Daffyd, Liende, and several of the players followed them back to the hall, riding discreetly behind Anna and the sorcerer.

Brill pointed to the east, and the dark clouds over the distant mountains. 'The clouds – the dark ones are working the weather again. The eastern rains never reach us.'

'. . . black bastards . . .'

Anna caught the words but not the speaker, although she thought it might have been Frideric.

Once they were back inside the hall's wall, Anna led Farinelli into the cool of the stable and to his stall, almost wishing she could unsaddle him, but she hesitated to try with her injured arm. She'd never had that much upper-body strength anyway.

'Let me do that, lady,' offered Quies.

'Thank you. I really should be doing it myself by now, but this shoulder . . .'

'Quite a wound you took,' Quies said. 'Even left some blood on Farinelli, more than a little. Good thing you're a strong woman.' With quick motions he undid both front and rear cinches and lifted the saddle off the gelding.

Anna patted the palomino's shoulder. 'Good steady fellow you are.'

Farinelli *whuff*ed.

'You want to be fed, I'll bet.'

'You've that right, lady. He's a glutton, or would be if I'd let him.' Quies shook his head. 'He likes you. Doesn't like many. Albero wouldn't ride him. Neither would Husto.' The stablemaster grinned. 'Figured you two would get along, and I was right.'

'I like him,' Anna admitted.

'He likes you,' Quies repeated. 'I like to see that.'

With a last pat, Anna headed out of the stable and back to the hall, far enough behind the others that the courtyard was empty. She could feel the sweat beading up under the hat, and she swept it off when she stepped inside the entry hall, where Florenda waited.

Anna repressed a sigh as she climbed the steps to the second floor, absently peering down the hallway as she stopped at her door. Brill's rooms lay at the end of the corridor. That Anna knew, though she had never been there. In fact, the issue had never come up, and in some ways that bothered her almost as much as if it had.

Was she getting that old? Brill was as old as she was, or close to it.

'Florenda?'

'Yes, lady?'

'I'm going to need some clean clothes.'

'They're all clean, or drying, except for what you have on, lady.'

'All right.' Anna couldn't help but smile. 'Go find something to do. Get me an apple, if you can.'

Florenda grinned briefly, then bowed. 'I will ask Serna.'

'Fine.'

As Florenda hurried away, a figure stepped into a doorway at the end of the hall. Anna thought the woman was Liende, but she wasn't sure.

If so, Brill wasn't going after the young ones like Florenda.

She could have been wrong, but he didn't strike her as the type to chase a number of different women at the same time. 'Interesting,' she murmured.

Her chamber remained cool, and she set the hat on the flat surface in the robing room, then began to wash up, getting rid of as much dust as she could. After she blotted her face dry, she returned to the bed-chamber and stood in front of the window, gazing out the tinted window at the same clear sky, the same sunbaked view of Mencha, the same dusty and empty roads.

After a time, she turned to the table and lifted the water pitcher.

Thrap . . . thrap.

'Who's there?'

Someone answered, but she didn't catch the name. So she walked to the door.

'Yes?'

'It's Liende, Lady Anna. Might I enter?'

Anna opened the door, then gestured for Liende to come in and to take a seat at the table. The player took the one facing away from the window, crossing her trousered legs and showing a pair of pale tan leather boots.

Anna closed the door and took the chair across the table from the other woman.

'I needed to talk to you,' Liende said.

Anna felt tongue-tied. Why did the clarinetist feel this way – because she was Brill's lover? Or was she? Was Liende worried? 'I should have thanked you earlier,' Anna started. 'Without your help, I understand I could have died.'

'You are stronger than that, Lady Anna. I was pleased to have been able to help.' The red-haired woman cleared her throat gently. 'It is about Lord Brill . . . You saw me . . . and . . .'

'There's nothing to explain,' Anna said. 'Lord Brill has offered great hospitality, and I value his friendship, especially because I'm a stranger here. But I'm not interested in him, not in a romantic way.' She added, 'I also get the impression that he is far more interested in my sorcery than in anything else I might offer.'

Liende gave a gentle smile. 'I am not certain about the last, but with women he is a true noble. He has been with me.'

'I can only offer you water. Would you like some?' asked Anna.

'Thank you.'

'You know, Lord Brill loves Loiseau.'

'Loiseau?' Anna set her own goblet on the table before her.

'That is the name of the hall and holding. That is why he will turn to darksong against the dark ones. That is why he hopes you can help. Loiseau is all he really has. He cannot have children. At least, he never has, and it appears unlikely.'

Anna understood that. In a world without modern birth control, if Brill had no children at his age, he probably never would have them.

'You say Lord Brill is kind,' Anna temporized. 'Yet Daffyd says that he killed his father. He says he killed him for humming.'

'Some things are true, and that is true,' Liende admitted. 'But it was not quite that way.'

'I don't understand,' said Anna. 'Humming?'

'Daffyd did not lie. Lord Brill did kill his father, and Culain hummed for years. He could not really even hum. There was no music there.' Liende shook her head. 'The only melody was in his violino.' She lowered her voice. 'The humming was the last note. Brill had stood it long enough. He couldn't stand it any longer.'

'Stand what?' Anna took a long sip from the goblet, wondering what else she would find out.

'Brill took a fancy to Nyreth – that was Daffyd's mother. She was never happy with Culain, but she used Brill to buy her way out of Defalk. She was beautiful even then, and Brill was lonely. All sorcerers are. You are already, and you will become more powerful and even more lonely.'

Powerful and lonely? Anna wondered if that would be all bad. At Ames, it had seemed like she was powerless and lonely.

'You should know how hard sorcery is,' Liende continued. 'The slightest mistake in his thoughts, and Brill could destroy his own spell, or what he strove for . . . or even himself. That is why sorcerers are so touchy. And Culain was a hard man. A fair man, but hard. Hard,' Liende repeated. 'He beat Nyreth more than once.' Liende shrugged. 'Brill was gentle. He is kind in his own way. But Culain kept nagging him silently. Culain kept humming to annoy him and distract him. He told Daffyd how terrible Lord Brill was.' Liende shrugged.

If what Liende said were so, that put a different light on things. Still, Brill had killed Culain. Anna wasn't quite sure what to think. 'What happened to Nyreth?'

'Folks say she's a lady in Elioch, but no one really knows. With a sorcerer, anything's possible, but when she left, a week later, my cousin Zania saw her on the long-carriage to the west, and she gave Zania a silver to keep her mouth shut for a week. That must have been five years now.'

'Why did you agree to be Brill's . . . lover?' asked Anna.

'Gaelin died four years ago. Brill is gentle, and,' Liende touched her hair, 'sorcerers can make you young again, and it stays. Nyreth looked like first youth – that's why no one recognized her.'

'But Brill isn't young.'

Liende cleared her throat, then looked toward the closed door. 'Those are the rules. Sorcerers can't do anything for themselves.'

Anna pursed her lips. Brill wanted her to make him young – or worse. Every time she learned something, life got more complicated. That hadn't changed from earth to Erde. It didn't look like it would, either.

26

Anna struggled to unfasten the cinches and got them both loosened before Quies entered the stall.

'Would you mind, lady,' he asked ironically, 'if I did my duties and racked the saddle?'

Anna had to smile. 'No. That would still be hard.' She added after a brief pause. 'I'm not trying to do your job, but I guess I feel that if I ride Farinelli, I should know how to take care of him.'

Quies racked the saddle with the effortless motion that came of long practice, and healthy shoulders. 'That feeling might not sit so well with other lords and ladies, excepting Lord Brill, and maybe one like Lord Jecks.'

'They don't have to live with me,' Anna said. 'I do.'

Quies smiled briefly. 'Then let me show you how to take off the bridle. Anyone can fumble a saddle into place.'

Anna thought of Farinelli's teeth, but nodded. Good intentions and an open mouth always led to trouble.

'Horses are just like people. They're not much for others fiddling with their mouths,' said Quies. 'Now, watch.'

Anna watched.

'You try it now.'

She felt like her hands were all thumbs, and reaching up to get the top over the gelding's ears strained her shoulder. She winced involuntarily, but managed. Farinelli *whuff*ed, as if to ask that she get it over with, but, surprisingly, did not toss his head or attempt to nip.

She patted his shoulder. 'Good boy.'

'He likes you. That helps.'

'I like him, and I owe him a lot. He got me back here.'

'You did that, Lady Anna. Your mount helped, but you did it. Took a lot to do that.'

Anna flushed. Although she felt she was a survivor type, she'd never thought of herself as courageous or one of those people who rode into battle. Then, again, she hadn't. She'd just survived ... again, and there wasn't much sense in taking herself too seriously for that. 'Thank you, but I did what any sensible person would do. I rode to where I could get help. I didn't fight off people or protect anyone.'

'Sense is the last thing most people have with a war arrow through their chest.'

Realizing that Quies would always think her actions were special, Anna shifted the subject. 'Lord Brill said that your son could help me with learning something about the knife.' Anna's fingers touched the hilt. 'He sent them to me, or someone did, but I don't know where to find him.'

Quies laughed briefly. 'The armory, such as it is, is on the other side of the stable. He's there now.'

'Good. I have some time before the midday meal.'

'Nearly a glass,' confirmed Quies. 'Albero will help. He likes sensible women.'

'Thank you.' Anna didn't shake her head. Were sorceresses not supposed to be day-to-day sensible?

She tried two doors before she found the armory. The first was a storeroom filled with barrels, and the second she left sneezing from the hay or grain she stirred up just in opening the door. The third door opened into a dim and narrow room.

A redhead with his back to the door sat on a stool pumping a grindstone with his foot as he sharpened a long blade. He looked up as Anna entered, then stood and set aside the blade. 'Lady.'

'I had hoped that you could help me with the knife,' Anna said.

The red-haired young man smiled. 'If you had not already been wounded, Lady Anna, I would say that you needed no blade.' The smile vanished. 'Times are changing, my sire says, and not for the better.'

'So it seems. Where do we start?'

'I cannot teach you the knife in days, or even in seasons. I can help you enough so that you can stop a desperate or stupid man, or hold off someone long enough to use one of your spells.' Albero eased the yardlong blade he had been sharpening onto a set of brackets on the side wall, then stepped out into the open space to the right of the grindstone. 'Take the knife out of the sheath.'

Anna struggled for a moment, then wrestled the blade out. She looked down at the short length of polished iron – or was it steel?

Albero laughed. 'That is the first problem. You have to draw your blade quickly enough to use it.'

Anna flushed.

'I do not mean to jest. The simple matters are important. You must keep the blade oiled and sharpened. Do not use too much oil, just enough that there is a thin layer, one you can almost not see. Do not touch the edge. Your fingers will dull it. A clean blade draws quickly.'

That made sense to Anna.

'Also you must have a sheath that lets you draw the blade quickly. That one is pretty, but it catches the blade.' Albero turned toward the shelves on the wall to Anna's right. After a moment, he returned with a battered but stiff black leather sheath. 'Let's try this one.'

Anna fumbled the softer, tooled leather sheath off her belt and replaced it with the more functional looking one. The knife slid in and out smoothly.

'Can you feel the difference?'

She nodded.

'Now ... there's holding a blade. How would you hold a blade to strike me?' asked the armsmaster.

Anna shifted her grip and raised the knife.

'No! A good knife fighter always strikes directly – or under-handed. Look.' Albero drew his own dagger, shimmering, wide-bladed. 'If I raise the knife ... see ... my whole chest is open. If you keep the knife low and between you and the other, you can always strike.' He laughed. 'Besides, a

low blade says you know something, and that will make
him cautious. And if you use your stick' – he pointed to
the short truncheon that hung from Anna's belt – 'if you
use it on his blade, then he cannot hurt you.'

'Like this?' Anna asked, shifting her grip on the knife.

'Put your thumb on the flat side there.' Albero demonstrated. 'Like this.'

She held in a deep breath. Why was she learning about
knives? Because, like everything else in her life, from taking
the crummy position at Ames to going deeper and deeper
in debt to get Elizabetta and Mario through college, she had
no choice if she wanted to survive. With that thought, she
emulated Albero's grip.

'Good. Now . . . Your feet are important. You have to keep
them far enough apart so that you are not unbalanced, but
you have to be able to move . . .'

Anna shifted her weight.

'Better if one foot be forward of the other . . .'

The singer tried to follow Albero's instructions, on position, on moving, on keeping the blade before her.

A faint clang of the bell penetrated the thick stone walls.

'That's enough for now, lady. If you just practice those
few things – the drawing, the holding the knife, and those
one or two moves – leastwise no one will just rush you.'
Albero grinned. 'Best you practice casting spells while you
use the knife, too.'

Anna had to return the grin. He was right.

She hurried back to the main hall, washed quickly, and
scurried down to the salon, where Brill waited.

'I'm sorry.' There, she was sorry again. She was always
sorry. Why? 'I was learning more about using a knife.'
She slipped into the chair across the table from the sorcerer.

'That is wise, as long as you don't spend too much
time at it.'

'Albero said the same thing,' Anna admitted.

'Lord Barjim and the last of his forces will arrive here the day after tomorrow.' Brill filled his goblet with the vinegary wine, the amber version, as Serna quietly slipped the serving platters on the table.

More cheese, hot apples, and bread – Brill had warned her about the lack of variety in fare, and he'd been right.

Anna waited.

'That means putting up tenscore armsmen and Lord Barjim and Lady Alasia,' the sorcerer continued.

'Where?' ventured Anna.

'Oh ... the corner rooms opposite yours at the far end – those have been for the Lord of Defalk since my father's time. It's easier that way. As for the armsmen, there's more than enough space in the barracks. When my grandsire built Loiseau, Lord Donjim's grandsire was always guesting – it was a way to extend the treasury of Defalk. Barjim's a fairer man than old Firash or his uncle, but some of that's because of Alasia. She's Lord Jecks' oldest daughter, and she handles a blade better than most armsmen. She rides with him, and he listens to her.' Brill shook his head ruefully. 'Good thing, too. Barjim's honest, and fair, but some mules have more between the ears.'

Anna offered the bread to the sorcerer.

'You might be wise to appear in the green gown,' Brill mused. 'There's nothing like that here.'

'Alasia is suspicious?' Anna asked, refilling her goblet with water. Lord, she'd drunk a lot of water lately.

'She has to be. Old Gelen can't or won't ride. He'll stay in Falcor and keep tutoring young Jimbob.'

'Gelen?' About the time she thought she understood something about Defalk, something else popped up.

'Gelen's been one of Barjim's advisors since he was a boy. Between them, Gelen and Alasia keep him riding the right direction.'

Anna frowned. Women behind the man in power always bothered her. They were often worse than overtly power-hungry bitches.

'How long will they stay?'

'Just overnight. Then we'll all ride east to the Sand Pass to smite down the dark ones.' Brill refilled his goblet.

'You still haven't been very forthcoming about what you expect from me,' Anna pointed out.

'I expect nothing,' Brill said gently. 'I hope you can find some way to use your powers to kill either the darksingers or their armsmen – or both. If we do not destroy most of them, like dark locusts they will crawl across Defalk, consuming everything in their path.' His single swallow from the goblet half drained it.

Anna sipped her water, and then helped herself to the apples. Brill was drinking more of the wine each day, and withdrawing more and more.

'I have some spells,' she finally admitted. 'I can't really test them, though.'

'How true!' Brill's laugh was overloud. 'Unlike the dark ones, we must wait till battle to see if what we devise will work.'

Anna wished she could stomach the wine. Instead, she refilled her goblet with water again. 'About harmony – vocal harmony ... According to your books, two voices with the same words, but—'

'Harmonies are too dangerous.' Brill shook his head. 'If we had worked together for years, perhaps, but there is no time to ensure that they would be perfect, and perfect they would have to be.'

'Perfect?'

'They would have to be perfect.' Brill's voice turned flat, stubborn.

Anna wanted to scream, but she only smiled. 'I understand ... but would you think about it?'

'With all else I must consider?' He shook his head.

Anna decided not to push, since he didn't seem likely to listen. 'When you do have more time.'

'If that time comes, Lady Anna, then ... perhaps.'

Was he afraid of losing control, like all men? She managed to keep from shaking her head, just barely.

27

Anna looked at the words on the paper, mentally fitting them to the familiar melody she strummed on the mandolin.

'In the terror of the tempest, death is brought between the hills,
with a slashing through the bosom that flattens monks it kills.
As we lived to keep men free, let dark ones fall in rills ...'

Anna winced at the word 'rills,' but she felt the word was Germanic in origin, and should help – she hoped – in a world where song seemed to have its roots in a similar tongue.

Finally, she set the mandolin on the desk beside the unused key-harp. Absently, she wondered why the sorcerers of Liedwahr never developed something like the autoharp, with chording bars. Then, without a pianolike instrument, the whole idea of chords seemed almost foreign to the mostly polyphonic spell music of Erde.

She touched her shoulder. Under her shirt and tunic, the healing wound, and scars from the ugly stitches, were covered only by a light layer of cotton. The area around the wound was tender, and much of it remained a faded purple with a yellowish cast – but she could move her arm without more than discomfort, and she could play the mandolin. The small instrument helped in working things out, far more than the key-harp.

She wished that Daffyd would complete the lutar, but she had the feeling that it would not be ready by tomorrow, when they would have to leave with Lord Barjim.

Why had she agreed to go?

She shrugged, ignoring the twinge in her shoulder. What real choice had she had? She had no funds, no supporters except Brill, and from what she could tell, most of Erde didn't seem terribly fond of sorcerers or sorceresses. She was in a medieval-style culture, and she had no real skill with weapons – or with such crafts as sewing, stitchery, or weaving. With song relegated to sorcery, she couldn't even sing for her supper, so to speak, and she certainly didn't feel like being a harlot.

As usual, nothing had changed, even though she had changed worlds. Her nonself-destructive choices remained virtually nonexistent, and when she had ideas, like using harmony to amplify magic, the men didn't want to listen, and she was even more isolated from her children.

Her eyes turned to the window.

In the late afternoon, to the east and north, along the road toward Ebra, scattered clouds of dust rose, for all that the air was still.

'Soldiers . . . armsmen . . . whatever they're called,' Anna murmured as she lifted the mandolin again. What other spells could she devise?

28

Anna glanced out the bedchamber window, but nothing seemed different, except there were several guards stationed on the walls, there to present an appearance of watchfulness to Lord Barjim, no doubt, reflected Anna.

She walked slowly back to the mirror in the robing room.

After a quick *thrap* on the door, which Anna ignored, Florenda opened it slightly. 'Lady Anna, Lord Brill says that Lord Barjim is almost to the gates.'

Anna took a last quick look in the mirror. Brill had suggested that she wear the green gown, and she understood that. Just like all men beholden to a higher authority, he wanted to play up his strengths, and Anna was clearly one of his strengths. When would she be able to be one of her own strengths? Ever?

She shook her head and bent closer to the mirror. Although the gray and natural auburn was showing at the roots of her hair, it wasn't that obvious, not yet, not the way she had arranged her hair, although she wouldn't be able to conceal the graying and darkening that much longer.

There was something about Erde, though. There had to be. She'd had to cinch the longline bra into the next-to-tightest hooks, and she didn't even feel constrained, and she'd been eating heartily enough, more than heartily enough.

Only the slightest edge of the cotton covering the scab and scar showed. Thank goodness the green gown wasn't that low-necked.

'My lady!' Florenda called.

'I'm coming.' After a last glance in the mirror, Anna turned, left the chamber, and followed Florenda down the stone stairs, holding the balustrade loosely because of the high heels. Gero and Brill stood in the entry hall, waiting.

Brill bowed. 'You look both lovely and formidable, Lady Anna.'

'Thank you . . . I think.'

A smile creased Brill's face, one that vanished with the sound of the bellchime. He nodded to Gero, and the youth darted to the doorway.

'Welcome to Loiseau, Lord Barjim, Lady Alasia,' piped the sorcerer's assistant, as he held the door wide for the pair to enter.

'My lord,' Brill offered a bow to the big dark-haired man in a purple shirt. 'Lady Alasia.' Beside the broad-faced bulky man stood a broad-shouldered woman with short, gray-streaked hair, also in purple and bearing a short black sabre, as well as a belt dagger.

'Lord Brill. I see you are as prepared for war as a sorcerer is.' Barjim's eyes flicked to Anna, his eyes taking in the green gown.

She met the sleepy-looking hooded eyes, angry at the insinuation, and glad that the heels and her own height, and the shortness of people in Erde, allowed her to look the Lord of Defalk straight in the eye. After the briefest of moments, Barjim returned his scrutiny to Brill.

'This is the Lady Anna,' Brill explained. 'She is a sorceress from the mist worlds.'

Both Barjim and Alasia looked at Anna.

'I am pleased and honored to meet you both,' Anna said evenly. 'I hope to be of some help.'

'She already has been,' Brill said. 'The dark ones sent three spell-casters after her, and they are dead.' He paused. 'We can discuss this as we eat. Would you like to refresh yourselves?'

'That would be most kind,' said Alasia before Barjim could speak.

'Then, might I escort you to your quarters?' Brill bowed and gestured toward the staircase. 'Lady Anna, would you be so kind as to inform Serna that it will be a slight while?'

'Not that long,' said Barjim. 'Eating's a lot better than washing.'

'Captain Dekas and Captain Sepko will be joining us, also,' said Alasia.

'I had expected them.' Brill smiled at Anna and added in a lower voice, if one loud enough for the others to hear. 'And would you take care of the candles? It would take Serna forever with the lighter, and I did not get to spell them.'

'My pleasure.' Anna inclined her head, both to Brill and to Barjim and Alasia. Alasia returned the nod and smiled faintly. Despite Brill's description of Alasia as a power behind the throne, Anna found herself wondering. Alasia seemed almost too plain, common-sensical.

As the three ascended the stone steps, Anna turned and walked slowly to the grand dining room, where she noted that the table was set for six, with actual silver cutlery, and bleached cloth napkins set in carved rings. The goblets were the same crystal, but looked more formal in the grand dining room than in the salon.

Anna glanced up at the massive crystal chandelier, on which there were at least three dozen gleaming white candles. For a moment, she studied the chandelier, trying to form the mental image of all the candles blazing, before she hummed, trying to get the pitch right, and wishing she'd brought a pitch pipe. Then, she sang the spell.

'. . . flame clear in my sight!'

Light gushed through the once dim room.

'Oh . . . oh . . . oh . . .'

Anna turned. Florenda looked whiter than the candles in the chandelier.

'Are you all right, Florenda?'

'Oh, lady . . . I did not realize . . .' Florenda turned toward the door to the kitchen area, where Serna appeared.

'Lord Barjim and Lady Alasia are refreshing themselves,' Anna said. 'Oh . . .' The eight wall sconces remained unlit. 'Do those get lit also?' she asked the white-haired server.

'Usually, Lady Anna.' Serna paused.

'Thank you. I'll do them in a moment. I don't think the delay for dinner will be great. Lord Barjim seemed rather more eager to eat than to wash up.'

'Aye . . . that's always the case,' affirmed Serna, glancing down at Florenda, who slipped over beside the older woman. In turn, Florenda looked toward Anna, then dropped her eyes.

'Easy, daughter, powerful sorceress or not, I'd venture she's the same woman she's always been.' Serna patted Florenda's shoulder.

'Your daughter? I didn't know.'

'No reason you should, lady.'

'She's a good young woman.'

'She's that, too, for all that I'm her mother.' Serna paused at the sound of a chime. 'Best you light the sconces, Lady Anna. The captains have arrived. Florenda, you get the big flagons of the good wine. The good wine. Go, girl!'

As Florenda scuttled off, Serna nodded toward her daughter's departing figure. 'I saw you spell the candles before. She hadn't. Young ones don't believe their parents, for all the years we have.'

Anna laughed. 'I know. I have children, too. They're grown.'

'You don't look more than a girl, lady.'

'The gray's there, if you look closely,' Anna said ruefully.

'Let Lord Barjim find that out for himself.' At the sound of voices in the entry hall, Serna raised a hand. 'Best I'm back to readying dinner.'

As the server vanished, Anna took in the wall sconces, did her best to visualize them, and repeated the spell.

'*Donnermusik . . .*' muttered a voice from the arched entry to the dining hall.

Anna turned and beheld Gero with two men who looked to be in their late twenties or early thirties. She stepped forward. 'I'm Lady Anna.' She hated titling herself, but that was the way this opera played, fantasy soap opera or not.

'She is a sorceress,' Gero announced. 'From the mist worlds.' As the youth stepped back, he winked at Anna, who kept her lips tight for a moment to avoid an amused smile.

'Dekas, captain for Lord Barjim.' The black-haired man in the tan shirt and purple vest bowed.

'Sepko.' The blond bowed quickly. He wore a creamcolored shirt with his vest.

While Dekas was nearly six feet tall, Anna judged, she was taller than the squat and muscular Sepko.

For a moment, there was silence. Then Anna decided to seize the opportunity. 'Everyone talks in general terms. Can you describe the dark ones, the Dark Monks?'

Dekas cleared his throat. 'Why, Lady Anna?'

'It would help my spellcasting if I knew more.' *It would help a lot of things if I knew more*, she thought to herself. 'How are they likely to attack?'

'Well ...' began the tall captain. 'They all wear brown, brown so dark it is almost black.' He shook his head. 'How they manage in the sun, I don't know. First, their singers bring in clouds and a storm, and they try to lash you with lightning. Then they bring up crossbows while you're still watching for lightning. After that ... well, it could be horse or pikes – it depends on the lay of the land. That Eladdrin, he's said to be a good commander, for all that he's a spellmaster, too.'

'Sometimes, it gets so dark, you think the sun would set,' added Sepko.

Both men turned at the sound of voices and boots echoing off the stone steps.

'I believe your lord and lady and Lord Brill are arriving,' Anna said easily.

From the shadows of the doorway, Gero offered another wink, and eased farther from sight.

Anna inclined her head slightly as the three passed under the archway and into the room. Brill's eyes took in the still-blazing candles, and he nodded ever so slightly before gesturing to the end of the table closest to the salon. 'My lord.'

Barjim waited until Alasia stood by the chair to his left. Following Brill's faint nod and her feelings, Anna took the chair to the right. Brill sat beside Alasia, while both captains seated themselves below Anna.

She noted that only Brill offered anyone a chair, and that to Barjim's consort. Somehow, that didn't exactly surprise her.

The small party took less than a third of the table, and Anna wondered how often the entire white stone table was ever used.

Almost before the chairs were pulled into place, Florenda

set three flagons on the table – one between the captains, one by Barjim, and one by Brill.

'Is this the good stuff, Brill?' asked Barjim. 'Not that vinegar you usually drink?'

'This is the good wine,' the sorcerer affirmed.

The Lord of Defalk filled his consort's goblet first, then his own. Brill filled his goblet, and Ann found hers being filled by Dekas.

'Thank you,' she murmured.

The tall captain nodded.

Barjim raised his goblet. 'For your hospitality, and a good refuge from a dissonant dusty road.'

'Here . . .' murmured Alasia.

To Anna's surprise, the red wine was actually drinkable.

Serna and Florenda carried in more delicate plates than Anna had seen, almost porcelainlike white, with only a fringe of the blue Brill affected. On each plate was a half melon.

'Your melons are always good,' said Alasia.

'I like the dark bread,' replied Barjim.

'How has your travel been so far?' asked the sorcerer.

'How's travel anytime?' grumbled the big lord. 'Saddle's hard. Dust is everywhere. Someone's mount's always lame. Supply wagons break wheels. And you know it's going to get worse. Rather not talk about it.'

At least he was honest, reflected Anna.

'How do you find Defalk, Lady Anna?' Alasia's voice was self-assured, firm, yet somehow gentle.

'From what little I have seen, Lady Alasia—'

'Alasia, if you please. We could "lord" and "lady" each other to death here.'

The two captains exchanged glances.

'From what I have seen, people are friendly. They worry and struggle, just like people anywhere. Lord Brill has been very hospitable and helpful. Learning your way around an entire new world isn't always easy.'

'Nor safe,' Brill interjected. 'As I mentioned, the dark ones sent three of their spelled-killers after her. They put a war arrow through her shoulder.'

Anna's eyes involuntarily dropped to her shoulder, and Alasia's followed.

'How long ago?' asked Barjim.

'Two weeks ago, roughly,' answered the sorcerer.

'And her hand as well?' asked Alasia.

Anna realized the woman didn't miss much. 'Yes. I was stupid enough to try to stop it barehanded.'

'Actually rather amazing,' Brill said. 'They were under a glamour, and she felt the arrow and deflected it. She couldn't see it. It still tore up most of the shoulder.'

'And you're walking around?' asked Barjim.

Anna flushed. 'I have been for a while. Lord Brill's healers are good. I've been riding for several days, but Farinelli's gentle.'

Brill snorted. 'That's what she calls that palomino I bought from your auction.'

'You ride that beast?'

'We get along,' Anna said, realizing that Brill was building her up for all he was worth, and hoping that she could live up to his image-creation.

Again the two captains exchanged glances.

'As a matter of fact,' Brill added, 'she rode from the orchards all the way here with a yard-plus arrow through her shoulder. She lost more blood than some have.'

'I believe you've made your point, Brill,' said Alasia dryly. 'I can see the outline of the wounds, and they're not small, even after your magic healing.' She turned to Anna. 'How did you come here?'

'I was summoned,' Anna said. 'I never even knew there was a place like Erde. I have to admit it was a shock, leaving everything behind, especially my children. It's a good thing they're all grown. Do you have children?' she asked in turn. 'I hope I'm not being forward.'

'One, and he's enough,' offered Alasia.

'How old is he?'

'Ten, the middle of Neun.'

Anna nodded.

'You said you had grown children?' asked Barjim. 'I was always given to understand that sorceresses did not have children or they lost their powers.'

Anna shrugged. 'I don't know. I have children, but I can do spells here.'

Dekas nodded involuntarily.

'You nod, Dekas?'

'She did not see me, lord. But I was standing in the shadows, and she sang a few words, with no players, and suddenly every candle here was lit.'

Barjim nodded. 'I begin to see why the dark ones sought your death, lady. Perhaps fortune will actually smile on us again.'

'I hope to be of some assistance,' Anna answered.

'We will need all of that and more,' added Alasia.

'If you will pardon me,' Anna said, 'could you tell me how many men the Ebrans will have?'

'Two hundred fifty-score, more or less,' offered Alasia. 'That's men under arms. They'll have tenscore dark singers, and those are usually in two groups, one after the van and one behind the main body.'

'If Lord Jecks' levies make it, we'll be lucky to have tenscore,' added Barjim.

'But we have fortifications,' pointed out Brill, 'and the floodgates.'

'Let us hope that they, and your sorceries, are enough. Enough of gloom,' finished Barjim. 'We can do that on the two days' rides ahead. Let's talk of more pleasant matters. Are you going to send me a keg of this wine afterwards? This is the best yet.' He refilled a goblet Anna had not seen him empty, then sliced off a chunk of melon and popped it in his mouth.

'I'll send two,' Brill answered with a laugh, 'since you like it so much.'

'One in the fall, and one at midwinter,' suggested Alasia. 'He'll appreciate it more.'

Anna took some of the melon – the best she'd had so far.

'I appreciate it anytime.'

'You appreciate it too much anytime,' quipped Alasia. 'But it is good. That I will grant.'

Anna agreed by taking another sip. Despite the cool of the room, she could see the faint sheen of perspiration on Brill's forehead. Why? Was he uncomfortable entertaining? Was he worried about her performance? Or was she missing something?

'You are quiet, sorceress,' said Alasia.

'I don't know a great deal about Erde or Defalk,' Anna answered.

'Tell us about the mist worlds, then.'

'I only know of my own. Lord Brill would have to tell you about the others.' Anna paused for a sip of the wine, careful to make it small. 'As I have told him, our magic is different, and it is created these days through small machines. We have carriages that run without horses, and metal birds called airplanes that carry dozens of people across our globe ...'

Anna talked for a time, trying to word what she said carefully, never to say earth had no magic, but pointing out that some of the magic devices she had brought did not work on Erde.

'That is strange,' mused Alasia. 'Magic changes from world to world?'

'It seems to,' said Anna.

'From what you have said,' Alasia continued, 'and from what the sorcerer has said, it would seem that you are more powerful here. Is that true?'

'That's true,' Anna said. The woman was perceptive.

'They say there is a price for power,' continued Alasia. 'What might be yours?'

Anna swallowed. 'I hadn't thought of it quite that way because I've been trying to learn about Erde – and then I was recovering from the arrow. I don't know everything,

but I can't see my parents again, or talk to my children.'
She swallowed again, trying to maintain her composure.

'You are paying a great price, then. I am truly sorry.'

Anna covered her surge of emotion by lifting the goblet,
and sipping slowly. The other woman seemed truly sorry for
her, and not at all manipulative, the way Brill had hinted, and
that sympathy or empathy smashed through all the barriers
she had erected.

'. . . terrible exile . . .' came from Sepko, whispered to
Dekas.

'. . . maybe lucky for us, though . . .'

Anna held the goblet, trying to keep her hands from
trembling. She'd tried to keep from thinking about her
parents, or Elizabetta or Mario. She'd tried, and one glass
of good wine and a sympathetic question and she was about
to come undone.

'How did you manage to ride the palomino?' asked Alasia
softly.

Anna swallowed. 'I don't know. I liked him, and, somehow,
he liked me. We just fit.'

'She talks to him, and he listens,' offered Brill.

'Of course,' said Barjim. 'You talk to your mount. That way
he knows he's special. Treat a horse right, and he'll carry you
through the mistuned drums of the worst storms.'

'How big is he?' asked Sepko quietly.

'Big as Rowin, if I recall,' said Barjim.

'You're a tall lady, sorceress,' said Dekas, 'but that's a
big horse. You are fortunate.'

In some ways, thought Anna, in some ways. She gripped
the goblet more tightly and plastered a smile on her face as
the small talk continued, as Serna and Florenda removed the
melon plates and brought in brown-sauced meat with flaky
white rolls, and the hot apples.

Some of the tightness in her stomach eased, and the
cheerfulness in her voice was forced to her own ears, but
she managed to keep smiling as the dinner went on, to

answer appropriately, and even to make a witty comment now and again.

She noted that the sheen on Brill's forehead continued as well.

29

MENCHA, DEFALK

'Cold in here,' grumbles Barjim, looking toward the closed window hangings and then the bed. 'Cold as an untrustworthy sorcerer.'

'You think that of the sorcerer?' Alasia strips off the purple shirt, and then the armless chemise.

'Brill? He's got a good heart, but he'll turn under pressure. She will, too, I'd wager.'

'The sorceress, the lady Anna? I do not think so.'

'She seems pleasant, but . . .' Barjim shrugs and looks pointedly toward the bed.

'Barjim! I know you've had too much good wine, but listen.'

'Yes, dear.' He slumps into the chair, bare-chested.

'This woman has been dropped into a strange world. She's been shot at and wounded. She's lost everything, except her sorcery, and that's stronger. Yet, she's repaying Brill's hospitality by supporting you. How many lords do you have that have so much a sense of duty?'

'Dissonantly few, frigging dissonantly few.'

'I think we need to let my father know about her . . . just in case. And it might be wise to offer a few silvers for expenses, just a token.'

'Silvers here, silvers there. Don't have many left.'

Alasia walks over behind Barjim and begins to massage his shoulders. 'I know. I know. I have a few.'

'You like her? You don't like many women,' says Barjim slowly.

'Under that fancy gown, she's like me. Any woman who can ride that palomino and take an arrow – I saw that gash; it's more than a span wide – she's no backroom sorceress. She's more of a man than fussy old Brill is.' Alasia keeps massaging his shoulders. 'Brill does what he can. He's good at heart, as you say, and he'd be better in a peaceful land.'

'Fat chance of that,' mumbles Barjim.

Alasia massages his shoulders more gently. 'We need to rest.'

'Know what I need, woman.'

She bends down and kisses his neck, letting her skin touch his. 'I know.'

30

Under the floppy-brimmed hat, Anna could feel the sweat collecting, and they hadn't even reached the main road where the main body of Barjim's forces had drawn up.

Anna shifted her weight in the saddle, wondering how well she'd last on a long ride. Her fingers slipped over the harness holding the pair of water bottles before the saddle. There was another set behind her, fastened over the bedroll and the saddlebags that contained food, clothing, and the mandolin. She hoped she had enough water, and she wished Daffyd had completed the lutar. He had brought the pieces, or so he had said. That bothered her, but she couldn't quite say why.

She rode beside Brill, with the eight players on smaller mounts behind them, led by Daffyd and Liende. Gero had remained at the hall, because, according to Brill, he was too young to wield a weapon, and unable to do sorcery.

Anna smiled to herself, thinking about the contradictions that Brill embodied – cruel and kind, devious and honest, and who knew what else?

She glanced down the trail to the cloud of dust ahead. Barjim and Alasia and their host had left the hall less than half a glass earlier.

'See,' observed Brill as the road from Loiseau flattened to join the main highway, if a rutted dirt road less than five yards wide could be called a highway. 'They're less than a dek ahead.'

Anna rubbed her nose, trying to avoid sneezing from all the fine dry dust raised by the horses before them. 'I think I would have liked to have left with them. Then we wouldn't be breathing their dust.'

'I guested them.' Brill answered, as if that explained everything.

'*Kkkchewww!*' Despite her best efforts, she sneezed, hard enough that her shoulder twinged. Even her hand ached momentarily. '*Kkcheww!*' Her eyes began to water, and before long, she'd have reddish mud streaking her cheeks and probably her riding clothes.

What on earth – or Erde – was she doing, riding to a battle on a strange planet, while still recovering from being punctured by an arrow? Put that way, it made little sense. Then, nothing for the past several years had made much sense. So why would that change?

She rubbed her nose again as their small group drew abreast of the slower-moving rear guard.

'We'll be out of the dust before long,' Brill promised, clearing his throat.

'I hope so.' Anna patted Farinelli on the shoulder, and got a low whuffling in return.

'Who's the woman with the sorcerer?'

'. . . say she's a sorceress . . .'

'. . . tall for a sorceress . . .'

'. . . water-sorceress . . . look at how much she carries.'

'. . . and that's a beast she rides, big as the lord's mount.'

'Quiet,' snapped another voice. 'She's ridden with wounds that would leave you stretched on the clay. She's riding a raider horse, too. I watched her create a bonfire with about five words. You want to mess with thunderflame, be my guest, fellow armsman.'

Anna turned in the saddle and saw Captain Sepko, already wearing a slight coat of road dust. 'Greetings, captain.'

'Greetings, Lady Anna. I hope this ride will not be hard on you.'

'Farinelli will take care of me.' *I hope.*

'He is an imposing beast.'

'We get along.' She patted Farinelli again, then nodded to Sepko, before easing the gelding more to the shoulder of the road to ride around a wagon filled with barrels – water barrels.

'You seem to have impressed the captains,' Brill whispered, leaning toward her with an ease she envied.

'You took care of that,' she countered, 'with all your tales.'

The sorcerer shrugged, pleased with himself, and they continued to ride, somewhat faster than the armsmen, drawing toward the front of the column.

Anna sneezed again, trying not to wince at the jolt it gave her shoulder.

Dekas led the main body, and he nodded to Anna as, using the edge of the road, she and Brill eased forward toward the purple banner that marked the immediate host of the Lord of Defalk, just forward of the main body.

Anna peered eastward, squinting into the low morning sun, and barely making out another group of horsemen more than a dek ahead on the flat and dusty road.

'Scouts?'

'That's the vanguard. The scouts are another two deks ahead. They are most times,' said Brill.

Anna reined Farinelli in slightly, to let Brill lead the way toward Barjim.

'Let the sorcerers through!' called the Lord of Defalk, and the guards swung their mounts aside slightly.

Anna edged Farinelli up beside Brill's mare, and followed the sorcerer.

'You look rather . . . different today,' observed Barjim, his eyes falling on Anna. 'More . . . more . . .'

'More commonplace?' asked Anna wryly.

The Lord of Defalk flushed enough that his color change was visible despite the bright morning light and the dust that powdered his face.

'Good for you, lady,' said Alasia warmly. 'You see, my lord, she is a real person and not just a pretty image.'

'You wear a hat, but it is not warm yet,' said Barjim.

'It's warm already, compared to my world.' Anna blotted her forehead, just under the brim of the hat. The dry heat evaporated her sweat elsewhere.

'She comes from a mist world,' added Alasia.

'It will be much hotter before the day is done,' Barjim announced.

Anna was afraid of that.

'I see you carry a number of water bottles.' Alasia pointed with her left hand.

'Not all water, I'd wager,' said Barjim.

'You do, and you'll lose, my lord,' said Brill.

'I lose every time I speak,' answered Barjim with a deep laugh.

Anna could sense why Brill liked Barjim. The man was genuine, and didn't take himself that seriously.

'You're with friends,' Alasia said.

'Best I enjoy it. That will not last.' The Lord of Defalk frowned. 'Do you think we will see your sire by the day after tomorrow?'

'I would guess so, my lord, but you know what I do.'

Anna looked at the road ahead, again, stretching to the low line of brown hills in the distance, a road that seemed endless already.

After another sneeze, she opened the first water bottle

and eased it to her lips, taking a deep swallow. Then she glanced back, back toward Loiseau, but the hall was only a smudge on a low hill.

31

With a groan Anna rolled onto her side. Her whole body ached. The thin bedroll hadn't even softened the ground. Her eyes were gummy, and her head pounded. Her shoulder didn't seem to ache as much, but that might have been because everything else ached more.

After prying open one eye, seemingly glued shut with gunk and dust, she tried the other. In the grayness before dawn, most of the camp still slept, except for the guards. On the bedroll beside her, Liende snored softly. Beyond, Brill and Daffyd slumbered. Anna shook her head. How could anyone sleep? How had she slept at all?

She looked at the saddlebags beside her, and the water bottles. She'd refilled them the night before, carefully order-spelling the water, since she didn't trust the look of the barrels. Her mouth was dry, almost cracked, and she half lurched, half crawled into a sitting position, then reached for the nearest water bottle.

She sipped slowly. Even more slowly, the throbbing in her head eased. Defalk was so dry she got dehydrated sleeping, and that was saying something.

As she shifted the thin blanket that she didn't need, fine reddish dust rose, and her nose twitched. By gently squeezing it, she managed to keep from sneezing.

Here and there, across the camp, figures were rising, and Anna thought she saw movement inside the thin silken tent that housed Barjim and Alasia. Anna could have cared less about the tent, but she did envy the two for the cots that went with the tent. Bedrolls and hard ground just didn't cut it.

'Good morning,' offered Liende, her voice low as she sat up.

'It is morning,' Anna agreed. She missed coffee, especially on mornings like this where everything ached, and her stomach turned.

'Do all sorcerers and sorceresses dislike mornings?' asked the red-haired woman.

'Yes,' grumbled Brill without even lifting his head. 'They also hate travel.'

Anna looked at the boots. After days of wearing them, they seemed to fit better, especially around the calves, which didn't bind anymore. She seemed to be losing weight still, that or her trousers were stretching, and she couldn't imagine plain cotton stretching.

Anna took another long slow swallow from the water bottle. She felt sweaty and dirty all over, and they had another long day on the road, according to both Brill and Barjim. Already, she missed the luxury of the tub and hot water at Loiseau, and this adventure had barely started.

Given how she felt, she didn't even want to think about how she looked.

32

Anna shifted her weight in the saddle again, trying to relieve the soreness that ran from her knees through her lower back. Although the sun had just set, the air remained still, hot – and dusty.

The ride from Mencha had given Anna a new appreciation of the term 'eat dust.' Even near the head of the column the dust was everywhere. She felt like she had been eating, breathing, and even drinking dust.

'The fort isn't that far.' Brill's voice was uneven and raspy.

'How far?' Anna hoped she didn't have to sing or cast spells. The way her own voice sounded, who knew what the results might be, not that she had that many spells to cast.

'Another five deks, less than a league. It's right at the base of the hills that guard the access to the pass. You can see the low spot up ahead there.'

Anna nodded, looking to the gentle rolling plains to the north of the road, half covered with browned grass, a few tumbleweeds, and sharp-leaved clumpy plants that reminded her of cactus. There was no sagebrush, although the scene could have come from western Kansas, if not for the mountains ahead.

'No ... we're not in Kansas, Toto,' she murmured to herself. Not even in western Iowa – or anywhere close.

'Lady Anna?'

Anna turned and guided Farinelli back toward Alasia. 'Yes?'

'How is your shoulder?'

'It's feeling better than my legs right now,' Anna admitted.

'My legs get sore still, after all these years of riding,' said the brown-haired woman.

'Don't let her deceive you, lady,' grumbled Barjim. 'She was born on a horse. She'll ride us all into the ground.'

'My legs still hurt,' said Alasia. 'Yours do, too. You won't admit it.'

Anna reached for her water bottle again, drinking the last from the one fastened in front of the saddle, but carefully recorking and replacing it.

For a time, in the reddish purple of twilight, the mountains seemed no closer, and they were mountains, Anna realized, mountains as high as and drier than the Rocky Mountains, mountains of hard red rock and gray cliffs.

As the twilight deepened, and the column came to a hill crest that dropped gently away, suddenly, a red-brick structure loomed ahead, filling the entire expanse between the two hills that seemed to merge on each side of the fort with the ridges that guarded the approach to the higher mountains. Watchfires lit the regularly spaced towers.

'The Sand Pass fort,' Brill said.

'You built it?'

'He built it,' confirmed Alasia her mount to the right of Farinelli. 'In times other than these, it would be more than enough.'

As they rode closer, Anna studied the walls, as precise as those of Loiseau, if of brick rather than stone, and rising perhaps fifty feet above the base of the valley.

Cannon? She realized she had never seen any kind of firearms – yet the precision with which Brill formed things with magic, and the crafting of blades and other items would argue that they could be made – or was there something about gunpowder that didn't work?

Erde was like that. She was so preoccupied trying to understand the place and to figure out what she could do with her talents that things she didn't happen to be familiar with slipped by. Except they didn't stay slipped.

She realized that her head was beginning to ache again, and she reached for the water bottle.

The pale purple banners bearing the crossed spears of Defalk hung limply in the growing gloom, lit intermittently by the watchfires. The road arrowed straight toward the middle of the wall. In the gloomy heat of twilight, Anna could barely tell where the red brick of the ramparts separated from the sunbaked dirt and the hard and dusty road.

Despite the broad-brimmed hat, her face was red and nearly raw. Defalk was no place for a fair-skinned singer.

A trumpet sounded, seemingly right behind Anna, and she twitched in surprise. Farinelli whuffled, and Anna patted his neck automatically, moistening her lips.

By the time the column reached the walls, the gates were swung open, and two squads of mounted troops, one on each side of the road, had formed up. The high brick walls loomed reddish purple in the last glimmers of twilight.

A trumpet fanfare echoed across the twilight, then repeated.

'I suppose they want to announce to all the dark ones that our lord and master has arrived . . .'

Anna held back an ironic smile at Daffyd's hissed comment to Palian, the only other woman player besides Liende, then guided Farinelli to her right, easing him behind Barjim's guards as the column narrowed to enter the gates.

The inside courtyard – or open space – of the fort was no more than twice that of Brill's hall. At first, Anna thought that the structure was only a set of walls. Then she squinted through the darkness, broken in patches by the intermittent light cast from the watchfires and the torches mounted on brackets at regular intervals along the walls.

The quarters, stables, armories, whatever buildings there were, were extensions from the outer walls toward the center courtyard.

'Our quarters here are not large,' apologized Brill. 'We have two rooms in the quarters section, but they are on the upper level. That should be quieter and afford more privacy. You and Liende and Palian will share the smaller one, and the other players and I will share the large one.'

Anna nodded, wondering how much privacy there was with so many people together. She also hoped her legs would bear her weight when she dismounted – and that there was something to sleep upon besides the floor – or hard ground. Her stomach growled, and her head ached.

Brill eased his mare around Barjim's guards, and toward the low structure on the southwest side of the fort. 'The stables are there.'

Anna followed numbly, her face burning, and her neck, shoulder, back, and legs all aching.

'Oh, ser sorcerer . . .' said a round-faced young man as they neared the low building.

Anna could tell from the odors they had reached the stable, and she reined up.

'This is the lady Anna,' Brill explained as he dismounted. 'She's a sorceress from the mist worlds, come to help us.'

Anna didn't feel like a sorceress, but like ground beef or the Erdean equivalent, and her legs shook after she dismounted. Slowly, she led Farinelli into the stable, where, surprisingly, the light was provided by candles with glass mantles.

Somehow, she did get the gelding unsaddled and rubbed down, before staggering up two flights of brick stairs after the sorcerer, carrying her gear – gear that felt like lead weights.

Liende and Palian followed her.

The end room was narrow and held six pallets, raised off the floor on brick pedestals no more than a foot high – or was that two spans? Anna wondered. However it was measured, the pallets were low, and narrow – and they looked wonderful. There were two small high windows, both unglazed and unshuttered, on the north wall.

'It's not much,' Brill said, 'but better than the barracks.'

'Is there anywhere to wash up?' she asked tiredly as she dumped the saddlebags and bedroll on the pallet under the back window. Then she stripped off the floppy hat, trying to ignore the dust that came with it.

'There's a washhouse in the western corner,' Brill explained, leading her back to the doorway and pointing toward a pair of torches. 'There.'

Anna took a deep breath and started back down the steps while Liende and Palian arranged their gear.

'So . . . what captain do you belong to?' leered the armsman by the door to the washhouse.

Anna looked at the youth. She needed spells to shut up idiots like the armsman. 'I came with Lord Brill and Lord Barjim.' That was the best she could do, but it seemed to be enough as she stepped by him and into the room. For a washroom it wasn't much, just two awkward-looking pumps, with spouts and tubs beneath. Each small tub had a lever device that was probably a drain.

Anna stepped to the far tub and began to pump. A reddish stream of water poured out. 'Damn . . .' she muttered.

At least, she had the water spell. As she pumped she sang, and the cold clear water flowed.

There was a gulp from the door that she ignored as she splashed away the dust and grime from her face and arms as well as she could. She had to repeat the spell once before she felt halfway refreshed, and she felt like she'd drunk as much as she'd washed with.

'Lady Anna?'

She looked up to see Brill standing there. Behind him stood Liende, Palian, and Daffyd. She thought she could see the shadows of the others out in the courtyard.

'Yes?'

'The water's not that . . .'

'I took care of it.' She lowered the handle again and a stream of clear icy water gushed out.

Brill moistened his lips, then added, 'We're to join Lord Barjim for dinner. As soon as we can.'

She looked down at herself. 'Like this?'

'You look better than most of us.'

She waited while Brill splashed the worst of the road grime off himself, and then they walked toward the center section of the eastern wall.

Two guards stood by the closed wooden door.

'Lord Brill and Lady Anna,' said Brill.

The older guard nodded and opened the door.

As they stepped through the door, Anna's mouth watered at the smell of bread, and some form of cooked food, a stew, she thought, and she swallowed.

The low-ceilinged room held a trestle table and benches. The only light came from four individual candles spaced down the table. Barjim sat at the only chair at the head of the table. Alasia, dusty and as hard-looking as any soldier, sat on his left. Seven men sat at the benches. Anna recognized Sepko and Dekas. There were two empty places across from Alasia.

'Sit down, sorcerer, lady sorceress.' The Lord of Defalk gestured but did not rise.

'Thank you,' Brill said.

Anna forced a smile, and she tried not to slump onto the bench.

'. . . sorcerers . . . useless . . . better cold iron . . .'

Anna turned to the man with the salt-and-pepper beard at the end of the table, catching his eyes. She held them, saying nothing, until the man looked down. She hadn't realized just how angry she was until that moment.

'One moment, Lady Anna,' said Alasia, turning her head toward the foot of the table. 'Captain Firis, apologize to Lady Anna. I won't bother to explain. I would suggest you talk to Captain Sepko after you leave tonight, and I suggest you offer thanks to the harmonies for my intervention.'

Firis opened his mouth, then looked at Barjim's hooded eyes, then back at Anna.

Anna saw the contempt there, and began to think about spells. She could substitute the word 'captain' for 'armsman' in the variation on the candle spell. She hummed slightly, trying to get the pitch right.

Dekas looked at Firis and shook his head sadly. Sepko opened his mouth.

At the sound of the humming, Firis paled. 'I apologize, Lady Anna. I apologize.'

'Very wise, Firis.' Barjim turned to Anna and Brill. 'The stew's rather good.'

Firis looked down, but Anna could sense his anger. At the moment she didn't care, not after having spent two days riding in dust out of obligation to Brill . . . and then to have some . . . medieval . . . idiot . . . insult her almost before she'd seated herself.

'You might try the wine,' Alasia suggested. 'It's not quite vinegar.' Barjim's consort smiled.

Brill took the flagon and poured some for Anna and then

himself, while Anna broke off a chunk of bread and ladled the stew across it.

She looked back at Firis. He was still seething, and he glared at her, his dark eyes burning. She thought she caught the word 'Bitch . . .'

Anna looked at his goblet which was wooden, like hers and the others, and concentrated on holding image, words, and melody.

> 'Goblet there, goblet fair,
> flame bright in this air.'

The goblet blazed into a pillar of fire, illuminating the entire room.

Firis fell backwards over the bench, carrying Dekas and Sepko with him.

'Lady Anna . . . was that not a bit . . . much?' asked Barjim, standing.

'No.' Anna almost didn't care. 'This isn't my world. I've ridden across a damned desert for two days because—' She broke off. No sense in admitting her obligations. 'I've been shot because I support you, and I don't have to take insults from half-educated idiots who don't even know me.' She glared at Firis. 'You have no right to be angry at me, and you have no right to insult me or Lord Brill.'

'If you were a man, I'd challenge you,' hissed Firis, scrambling off the floor as the light from the burning goblet died down into a low flame, his hand on the hilt of his blade.

'Well . . . Lady Anna?' asked Barjim.

Anna rose. 'Perhaps I should go. By your leave?'

Alasia looked at Barjim, mouthing no.

'I think not.' Barjim turned to Firis. 'I'm not the brightest lord who ever lived. You know that.' He laughed. 'You all know that.' His face turned somber. 'Whose side are you on, Firis? It's strange. I finally get a sorceress with power, and she's not in the fort a glass, and you want to kill her.'

'You know, she could have turned you into flame as quickly as that cup,' Alasia added.

Anna bowed to the captain. 'I apologize, Captain Firis. I am tired. I am not used to riding so far, and the past weeks have been hard. Very hard.'

Firis's eyes flicked from Barjim to Anna to Alasia and back to Anna. 'You obviously need not apologize, Lady Anna.'

'Lord Barjim needs all his captains,' Anna said. 'And I am truly sorry to have upset . . . this group.'

'I would like to point out one matter,' Alasia added, turning to Firis. 'When you were wounded at Cheor a spring ago, how would you have felt if Captain Dekas there had suggested you were useless?'

Firis frowned.

'It is not obvious, but Lady Anna took a full war arrow through both shoulder and hand less than three weeks ago, from the dark ones. She has made quite an effort to be here.' Alasia spread her hands.

'The dark ones?' asked Firis.

'They are dead,' Brill said. 'Lady Anna also deflected that arrow barehanded, or she would be dead.'

That was an exaggeration, but it would serve, and Anna did not think a correction was in order.

Firis bowed his head. 'I apologize.'

'I am sorry,' Anna said. 'I really am.'

'Sit down, both of you, and eat,' ordered Barjim. 'I need you both, and half the problem is you're both starving.'

'Might I ask for another cup?' asked Firis sheepishly, with a grin.

Anna avoided a deep sigh of relief as she sat, her legs trembling. She'd botched that, and without Alasia and Barjim, she'd have been in real trouble.

'Eat,' commanded Brill quietly, 'or you'll fall over. You're pale as snow.'

Her head was pounding, and her vision was almost double, but she managed to take one mouthful, then another. Before she was quite sure how it had happened, her wooden platter was empty, and she found herself reaching for the bread.

Brill passed the stew kettle back to her.

While she couldn't quite believe she was still hungry, Anna took seconds, trying to listen as she did.

'We're still not at full strength,' offered the thin, almost dapper man across from Sepko. His iron-gray hair glinted in the candlelight.

'We had a messenger from Lord Jecks this afternoon, Rohar,' replied Barjim. 'He will be here with his levies in less than two days.'

'Will the dark ones wait that long, ser?' asked Dekas, after taking a deep swallow of the amber wine.

'Oh, they will wait. They will.' The Lord of Defalk refilled his goblet.

'How many does Jecks have?'

'Twentyscore, or more, and some good archers.'

'Solid man, Jecks is.'

Anna began to have trouble listening after that, just trying to keep from yawning and falling asleep at the table. She shouldn't have had the goblet of wine, not as tired as she was.

By the time she and Brill returned to the upper level, both Palian and Liende were asleep and snoring.

'Good night, Lady Anna. You made quite an impression.'

'Not a good one, I'm afraid.' Anna yawned in spite of herself.

'Quite good, I think. It will help morale.'

'What?' She yawned again. 'That I insulted a captain, flamed a goblet, and made an ass out of myself?'

'You showed spirit, and they need that more than anything.'

'Good night,' Anna said, closing the door. She managed to get her trousers and boots off, but that was all, before she sank onto the pallet.

33

Anna stepped around a clump of manure as she followed Brill through and around the groups of armsmen and toward the steps leading up to the northeast corner watchtower. Despite the dust and dry climate, the fort was beginning to smell – the result of too many animals, too many people, and inadequate sanitation.

The smells didn't help her throbbing head, probably the result of bad wine, sorcery the night before on an empty stomach, and exhaustion. Sleeping on the raised pallet had been better than on the ground, but not much. A breakfast of bread, hard cheese, and dried apples had helped, but not enough. So had nearly a bottle of cold water, but the spell to clean and chill it had renewed her headache.

'You need to see how this battle will develop,' Brill said over his shoulder as he trudged up the narrow steps. Carrying the mandolin, she followed. Somewhere, she needed to find a corner to practice, even to run through some vocalises. Could she sing separate lines of a spell without triggering the effect? . . . How far apart?

There was still so much she didn't know . . . so much.

As she reached the top of the steps, she stopped by the weathered, iron-bound door in the side of the tower and asked, 'Can you practice a spell in phrases – without creating something?'

'Serento used to do that. I never have. I'll speak the words, or sing the pitches with nonsense syllables.'

Anna pursed her lips. 'Could we try that with harmony?'

'Not now.' He shook his head. 'If you had come sooner . . .'

Anna doubted that somehow.

'The players will be here.' The sorcerer gestured to a space no more than five yards square on the western side of the watchtower, protected by the tower itself on the east, and the crenelated wall on the north. There were no protecting walls or rails on the inside, and the drop-off was more than twenty feet. 'And I'll stand here.'

Anna nodded. Where should she stand? She still didn't exactly know what she was going to do, even though Brill acted as though she did, and she needed to practice, especially given his clear aversion to considering anything resembling harmony or joint spellsinging.

After easing toward the outside parapet and stepping into the shade of the tower, Anna took off her hat, blotting away the sweat that had collected where the leather inside band had pressed against her hair and skin.

'See anything?' The low voice came from above, and Anna looked up, but could see nothing except the crenelations of the watchtower.

'Nothing, except some dust on the road to Mencha.' A laugh followed. 'I'm in no hurry to see anything coming down from Ebra.'

'You said it.'

Anna's lips quirked. Like the sentries above her, she wasn't in any hurry for the Ebrans, or whoever, to show up.

'Where would be best for you?' asked the sorcerer.

'I don't know. I need to practice.'

He nodded, and half turned to the west, almost as though he had not heard her, slowly walking along the parapet, then stopping, and leaning forward on the bricks of the wall, his eyes turned to the west.

Anna put on her hat and followed him out of the tower's shadow, slowly, halting beside him.

'Less than ten leagues, and Loiseau might be a world away.'

She looked westward, the morning sun at her back. The road climbed up the low hill they had come down the night before and then seemed to vanish.

'Sometimes it seems that way with lots of things,' she answered.

'Sometimes.'

They stood silently for a time, and Anna could feel the sweat beginning to collect under the brim of her hat again, and her hand went to the water bottle at her belt as her eyes studied the barren terrain. Only a few stunted and twisted pines, scattered cactus, some sagebrushlike bushes in the hills, and a few patches of browned grass. Everything else was rock, sand, or bare dirt.

The fort seemed to be almost in the middle of nowhere. The last hut or hovel Anna had seen had to have been a league back toward Mencha. The thinnest of dry streambeds ran along one side of the road that twisted into the mountains.

The eastern gates of the fort were closed, and the wooden span removed, so that the road ended on the eastern side of the dry moat that encircled the entire fort. The western gates were closed, but the bridge spans were in place. The moat was wider on the north and south sides of the fort, nearly a hundred yards, and much deeper on the eastern side, with precisely fitted brick or stone walls.

Anna studied the approach to the pass again. 'Why didn't you build the fort farther uphill? It looks like this ridge wouldn't be that hard to ride up and circle away from the fort.'

'The slopes are sandy, and they slow down mounts.' Brill said. 'The ramparts are here because the ground seems solid, and because there aren't any higher cliffs that the dark ones could shake down on the walls. Or use to fire arrows into the fort.'

Anna supposed everything was a compromise, even warfare, and she nodded slowly as she looked farther to the northwest, catching sight of a patch of blue, a small lake that seemed so incongruous in the red-soiled and dry hills, nestled almost at the northern base of the long ridgelike hill that ran to within a hundred yards of the fort's walls.

A lake? Why in the middle of nowhere?

Then she recalled the comments about water gates, and

studied the regularity of the moat on the east side. She studied the moat more closely, finally discovering a circular stone opening, more than ten feet high, on the south side of the northwest corner. She pointed. 'How well will it work?'

'Well enough, while the water lasts.' Brill shrugged. 'Even underground, there's not much here anymore.' He straightened. 'I need to gather the players together. We'll be practicing in the bigger room.'

'I think I'll stay up here. It's cooler.' She gestured toward the shaded side of the watchtower behind her.

'For now.' Brill turned.

After the sorcerer left, Anna sat in the shady corner and began to try to work out some form of chording for her battle hymn. She knew the melody well enough, but trying to develop chords from scratch was another thing. She'd always had music to refer to, and so far, she hadn't seen any on Erde. If it existed, it was well hidden . . . for good reason.

She eased the two folded papers from the belt wallet, unfolded them, and laid them on the bricks beside her.

The mandolin was out of tune, and the tuning pegs wouldn't hold unless she jammed them sideways.

She ran through several vocalises, but her voice was tired, and she felt clumsy, even as she kept at it trying to get clear, get warmed up.

Then, when she picked up the mandolin again, her fingers fumbled on the strings, and her mind skittered over the words.

'I have loosed the fateful lightning so the darkling ones
  will die, My songs will strike them dead . . .'

She paused and shook her head. It was all so insane.

What was she doing? Sitting in a brick fort in the middle of a desert, trying to compose or arrange a song that would kill people she didn't know, except that those people had already tried to kill her.

How long she spent, she didn't know, only that her voice was tired, and her fingers ached, and that the sun had almost reached noon and taken the last vestige of shade when she folded up her would-be spells and started down the steps, trying to ignore the low voices from the watchtower.

'There she goes ... sorceress ...'

'... almost turned one of the captains into charcoal ... insulted her ...'

'... say she killed dozens of dark ones with an arrow through her shoulder, then rode all the way here ...'

Anna winced. Stories always seemed to grow. Then you were in trouble if you didn't live up to them, and you were in trouble if you refuted them.

She eased her way along the upper ramp toward the small room with her gear.

34

Anna hugged the shade on the eastern side of the northwest watchtower, still struggling with the chords on the mandolin, trying to forget how hard the bricks she sat on were, or how much her nose itched from the dust raised in the courtyard below.

'That doesn't sound like much of a melody.' Daffyd stood there, viola in hand, grinning.

'It would be easier if you'd been able to finish the lutar.'

'A melody's a melody.'

Abruptly, Anna realized what he was talking about. Players in Liedwahr played melody lines that stood alone, while she was working on supporting chords – the difference between the polyphony of Brill's players and the mostly homophonic approach of, say, a Beethoven symphony – or a Britten song cycle. Idly, she wondered how Sophie Weiss or Nancy Evans might have done in Liedwahr, then pushed the thought away. She was here, and they weren't.

'Lady Anna?' prompted Daffyd.

'I'm sorry. Sometimes, I think about other things. How is the lutar—'

'I can't do much here except work on the tuning pegs and smooth things.'

'Daffyd! We need to work on the battle song,' called Brill.

The viola player nodded and hurried back to the group.

Anna set down the mandolin and uncorked her ever-present water bottle, drinking slowly as Brill conducted the eight players. Palian was taking Kaseth's place, and Daffyd seemed to hold the lead viola position. Liende carried the bass melody.

After corking the water bottle, Anna went back to the chords, trying to work out the chorus lines of her much-adapted 'Battle Hymn of the Republic,' shutting out as well as she could the off-notes of the players, and Brill's corrections.

'What's that dust?' asked one of the lookouts in the tower above Anna. 'It wouldn't be the Ebrans.'

'Not coming from the west, idiot. The scouts say that the dark ones are moving their lancers up the pass, and there are troops of archers on the trails headed down to us.'

'That has to be Lord Jecks, then, doesn't it?'

'Look for a blue banner with a golden bear.'

A series of trumpet calls echoed from the west, reverberating off the angled sandstone cliffs east of the hills straddled by Brill's fort.

'There's a blue banner, but it's all wrapped up.'

Anna stopped chording and eased to her feet. Between the sentries, the trumpets, Brill's players, and the heat, she couldn't concentrate anymore.

'That's it,' Brill announced. 'Put away your instruments. We'll meet here in the morning, one way or another.'

'That's Lord Jecks,' offered Daffyd, from behind Anna's shoulder. 'He's always the last to bring in his levies.'

'He does bring them, in person,' said Brill as he walked up to them. 'Unlike most of the lords, who only send captains.'

Anna looked at the sorcerer quizzically.

'There is an obligation to send levies, but a lord of holdings does not have to come at every call.' Brill shrugged. 'Barjim could request their presence, but most of their captains are better commanders than they are – except for Jecks and Kysar.' The balding man paused, then added, 'I wanted to tell you that we are to eat with Lord Barjim tonight, again.'

'The food's better, but . . .' Anna spread her hands.

'I doubt anyone will insult us.' Brill laughed. 'You made your point.'

'She always does, ser,' Daffyd said quietly.

'Yes, Daffyd, and I hope she can with the dark ones.' The sorcerer looked into the low western sun, squinting to make out the oncoming riders, then turned and headed down the steps.

'He's not happy,' said Daffyd.

'Would you be?' Anna wondered if she should have brought up the possibility of harmony again, before Brill had slipped away, but she had the feeling the sorcerer would always refuse that possibility.

'I'm not. We'll be lucky to get out of here with our heads attached to our bodies.'

'So why are you here, then?' Anna asked.

'My head wouldn't be attached to its body, lady, if I had not come. What about you?'

'Did I have any choice?'

The young man shook his head.

'I have to get ready for this latest . . . command performance.' Anna shifted her grip on the mandolin and started down the narrow steps, keeping to the inside and away from the unrailed outer side that overlooked the courtyard.

By the time she reached her quarters, there were three buckets of water in the middle of the floor.

'I had some buckets brought up to the room,' Palian said. 'I went down to the washroom.' She shook her head. 'They asked me who I belonged to. One of them pawed me.'

'They tried that on me, at first.'

'No one would touch you, now, Lady Anna,' said the slender violinist. 'There are so many stories . . .'

'I know.' Anna's tone was wry. 'I killed dozens of dark-singers with a war arrow twice my size through me after losing all my blood, and then I hopped on the biggest and nastiest beast in Defalk and rode here without resting.'

Palian laughed.

'It's half true,' said Liende from the doorway, where she eased the wooden door shut behind her. 'You lost half your blood, and it was a full-sized war arrow with a barbed head, and they're more than a yard long.'

'Wait a moment.' Anna looked at the buckets, then hummed, and sang the water spell gently.

The water in all three buckets foamed, then subsided.

'It'll be cool,' she added as she pulled off the floppy-brimmed hat and the armless tunic. 'I'm still glad you had the water brought up.'

Liende looked at the buckets, then bent and dipped a finger into the water and licked it. 'It's almost a shame to waste such clean water.'

'I'll spell more later, if you want,' Anna offered, 'but I want to clean up.'

'So do I,' said Palian.

'It certainly couldn't hurt.' Liende stripped off her faded tunic. 'But I don't know how long we'll stay clean.' She coughed at the dust from the garment.

Anna had barely finished getting dressed and into a cleaner tunic when Brill rapped on the door.

'Lady Anna?'

'I'm coming.' Her hair was pinned into a bun, although it wasn't quite long enough for that, and despite her best efforts she was slowly losing pins, and she was afraid it would come undone halfway through dinner.

'You look most presentable,' the sorcerer said when she stepped out onto the third-level walkway.

'Thank you.' Anna wasn't sure whether that was a compliment, or a statement of appreciation that she had tried to look good but hadn't quite pulled it off.

The dining area was the same low-ceilinged room, except the shuttered windows were open, and the faintest of breezes fluttered through them. This time, more than a dozen men, and Alasia, stood around the table when Brill and Anna stepped inside.

'Lady Anna, who can set hearts afire – along with the rest of you.' Captain Firis bowed, then grinned at her.

Anna couldn't help but grin back at the impulsive young captain, so willing to kill one moment, and forgive the next. She could appreciate him without trusting him. 'Captain Firis.' She turned to the two others she knew. 'Dekas . . . Sepko.'

Then she bowed ever so slightly in the direction of Barjim. 'Lord Barjim, Lady Alasia.'

Barjim nodded to the sorcerer and sorceress, but continued to listen to the redheaded captain who had not turned.

Beside Alasia was a stocky, white-haired man, his leathers still dusty. Alasia motioned to Anna, and the sorceress stepped toward her.

'Lady Anna, this is my sire, Lord Jecks.' Alasia turned from Anna to the white-haired warrior. 'Lady Anna is the sorceress from the mist worlds, the one who almost turned Firis into a cinder.'

'He still hasn't learned that much caution, it appears.' Jecks bowed. 'My daughter has told me about you, and I am pleased to meet you.'

'I'm pleased to meet you.' Anna bowed.

'Let us sit down and get on with the business of eating!' said Barjim, his voice carrying across the conversations.

Anna followed the command and found herself second

down on the right-hand side, with Lord Jecks on her left, Brill on her right, and another older man across from her.

'Get the wine moving,' Barjim suggested.

Alasia smiled at Anna, then turned to the man on her left, the one across the table from Anna. 'Lady Anna, this is Lord Kysar. He holds the strongholds and the lands around Pamr. Lord Kysar, this is the lady Anna. She is the sorceress from the mist worlds I had mentioned.'

Anna inclined her head. 'I am pleased to meet you, Lord Kysar.'

'Just don't tell her she's useless, lord ...' A sotto voce whisper crept up the table.

Anna tried not to flush.

'I believe I missed something there.' Kysar's voice held the false heartiness that many big men cultivated, in Anna's opinion.

'Rumors fly all over Defalk about you, lady,' added Lord Jecks, kindly. 'Is this another one?'

'It is not a rumor, unhappily, Lord Jecks,' Anna admitted. 'When I arrived here, I was tired and not thinking too clearly. One of the captains made a remark, one I think now that was in jest, but it made me mad.' She forced a shrug. 'I overreacted.'

Jecks and Kysar looked to Barjim, who, with his mouth full of bread and lamb curry, nodded at Alasia.

'The lady Anna turned his wooden goblet into a bonfire, and was starting on a spell to do the same to him,' Alasia said. 'But she was gracious, and so was the captain, after a few words.'

'And you, daughter, are diplomatically keeping everyone happy.' Jecks laughed.

'My lady Alasia is good at preserving my resources,' boomed Barjim. 'Get the wine down to my captains.'

'Lord Brill, I believe we last met in Falcor in the spring,' offered Jecks.

'I believe so.' Brill poured some wine, first for Anna, and then for himself. 'Did you have any luck with the dam?'

'In fact, I did. It was a good idea, and there was water where you suggested, but it's taking longer to fill the pond.' Jecks broke off a large chunk of bread, and took but a small sip of wine.

'Without more rain, that will happen.'

'More disharmony from the dark ones.' Jecks looked at Barjim, then lowered his voice slightly. 'Now that the last of the levies are here, will they attack at dawn?'

Brill frowned. 'Not at dawn, but by late morning, I would guess. They are already moving the clouds westward. I could see the darkness over the Ostfels.'

'Be a long day tomorrow,' Kysar interjected.

Anna felt like every day had been long since she arrived in Liedwahr, but she nodded and took the smallest sip of wine.

35

ENCORA, RANUAK

The Matriarch settles her considerable bulk into the polished ebony chair under the awning. Her eyes focus beyond the balcony at the harbor below the hilltop residence. In the blue-green waters are anchored a handful of ships, while another handful load at the grain docks.

'What else have you and Veria discovered?' asks the gray-haired woman after she settles in the oversized chair. 'About the disharmonies?'

'They continue, Matriarch,' answers the slender brunette. 'They center on the Sand Pass and the new sorceress.'

'She is not new, properly,' says Ulgar from where he stands in the sun at the stone railing. 'Merely a recent arrival to Liedwahr. And Lord Barjim will doubtless use her talents in his desperate efforts to fend off the dark ones.'

'Lord Barjim is an honest man,' says the Matriarch cheerfully. 'An honest man, a caring man, and entirely the wrong leader for Defalk in these days. His consort knows this, and she supports him.'

'As consorts often do,' interjects Ulgar.

'Alya, about the disharmonies?'

'They continue, and all the scriers follow the soprano sorceress.'

'How do you know she is a soprano?' asks Ulgar. 'Has anyone heard her sing?'

'Hush, dear,' responds the Matriarch. 'She is a soprano. The harmonies demand that she be a soprano, and so she is. Just as the harmonies demand that Lord Brill and all male sorcerers reject true harmony. Just as the harmonies demand that poor brave Barjim perish and Lord Behlem succeed him.'

'And what else do the harmonies demand?' Ulgar smiles indulgently as he turns to let the hot sun bathe his tanned face and short silvered hair.

'That we let them work out the destiny of Liedwahr.' The Matriarch leans back in the big chair with a smile.

'Why did you lend Lord Barjim the golds?' ventures Alya. 'The Evult will scarcely repay them. Nor will Behlem, if he can hold Falcor.'

'Two thousand golds are a cheap price to send Barjim and his levies against the dark ones. If he even inflicts enough damage to slow them for a year, the coins are well worth it.'

'We will be lucky if his poor armsmen can slow Eladdrin for a season,' points out Alya.

'There is a balance to things, daughter. Matters do balance, and sometimes it is but a question of knowing when to wait.'

'If there is such a balance—'

'Why did we need to send the golds? Because the harmonies work slowly, and the golds allow them the time to work their will.' The Matriarch leans back in her chair and closes her eyes.

36

Anna stood by the northeastern watchtower. Her eyes flicked from Brill and the players on the open space behind her and then back to the empty road that led up to the Sand Pass. The distant pass was already overshadowed by the red-and-gray bulk of the Ostfels, and by the growing darkness of clouds that rose out of the eastern horizon to challenge the mid-morning sun.

From the parapet, Anna squinted out from under the floppy-brimmed hat at the road, and the hills and ridges that flanked it, but could see nothing moving – no armsmen, no horses. That motionlessness made the shadows that darkened the mountains to the east and marched down toward the fort all the more ominous.

Even the sentries on the watchtowers were silent, as were the archers stationed at every crenelation along the eastern wall. Anna glanced to the blank-faced bowman less than a yard from where she stood, but the archer's eyes remained on the canyon, as did the eyes of all the archers who ranged the walls.

'You're making ready?' asked Liende, stepping up almost beside Anna. 'Can you help stop them?'

'I don't know. I'll do what I can,' Anna said. 'But I'm not sure that waiting to see if a spell will work is "making ready".' There was so much she really wasn't sure about – like why she was so calm when a battle was about to break out around her.

'You will turn their storms against them?' pursued Liende, as she fitted the horn's mouthpiece into place. Like Anna, the clarinetist wore the faded cottons from Brill's hall, and like Anna's, hers were green, unlike most of the other players, who wore blue.

'No. I don't know about storms.' Anna shivered, thinking about the truly terrible words she had crafted, wondering why she was doing what she was doing? Was there ever a good reason for destruction? She tightened her lips. The dark ones had tried to kill her, just because she was alive and in Defalk. She had the right to try to stay alive, didn't she? But did that give her the right to use her new talents to kill? Or would they even work? Was she just a fraud?

Liende stepped back as Brill approached.

'The dark ones have begun their attack.' The sorcerer's eyes rested on the clouds. 'Soon we'll see firebolts, stronger than normal lightning.'

'How long before we see anyone?' Anna glanced back to the empty road, and the seemingly empty ridges to the east.

'The storm comes first, with lightnings, then archers, and more lightnings . . .' He spread his hands. 'That is what I understand, in any case.'

'You don't know?'

The faintest breeze picked up, carrying more sandy dust out of the pass. Anna's nose itched, and she rubbed it gently. Her eyes itched, too.

'That is what the dark ones did when they took over Ebra. That was more than ten years ago.' Brill did not look at her.

'You mean that for ten years they haven't done anything?' asked Anna.

'They have trained a mass of darksingers, and they have spent the last year pushing the Whispering Sands and the Sand Hills south into Ranuak, enough to give them a clear road to the Sand Pass.'

Anna shook her head. 'I don't think I understand.'

Brill glanced back at his players, standing with their instruments, waiting, and then at the clouds. The sunlight began to dim as the first edges of gray-and-black clouds touched the edge of the sun. 'Ebra was isolated. That was why no one could help Ketansa when the Evult and his darksingers came out of the depths of the Ostfels. The mountains are too rugged in the north and west, and the ocean and the rocky cliffs bar entrance to most of Ebra, except for Elahwa, and the channel is narrow there. So the dark ones could raise storms against the ships. The sands in the south had drifted northward over the years, blocking the Sand Pass and most passage south to Ranuak, except for the hardiest of travelers. Besides, the Ranuans look unfavorably on strangers, especially Ebrans, and they discouraged maintaining the roads when Ketansa repudiated the cult of the Matriarch.'

As the gloom fell across the fort, Brill paused.

'Go on.'

The sorcerer studied the road and the hills, then continued. 'In the old times, Ebra and Ranuak were one. That was before the winds changed and the Whispering Sands grew and joined the Sand Hills and blocked the Sand Pass to Defalk. They say that deep under the high dunes in the midst of the Whispering Sands, there is a temple. That was where Wahren cast the mighty spell to dry the highland swamps of Ebranu. They say he trained his players for a season, and that it took him more than a year to build the spell.'

Brill shrugged. 'Others say that Wahren was only a myth, that the sands have been there forever. I don't know. What we all know is that a little more than a year ago, the sands began to move, and mighty storms were raised, and that the dark ones reopened trade with Sturinn, and most of that trade was for weapons.'

A distant rumble of thunder rolled out of the east.

'We need to make ready, Lady Anna.' The sorcerer turned, his eyebrows lifted as if questioning.

'The dark ones will have to get closer for anything I do to work.' Of that Anna was convinced. Neither the mandolin nor her voice would carry that far.

'As you wish.' The balding sorcerer turned and walked several steps back to where the players waited. His eyes focused on them, one by one. 'Sit down. The wall will shelter you.'

Anna glanced to the northwest, her eyes seeking Brill's lake, wondering when or how he would employ it – if he could.

'Form up! Wall details!'

'Third Mounted – to the gates.'

Below Anna, the courtyard swirled with activity. Armsmen scrambled up along the walls. The western gates opened, and nearly threescore men rode out, most bearing bows and quivers. Once they were across the bridge, the timbers were slid back inside the fort and the gates closed, while the riders split into two groups – one circling north, the other south.

'Woman!'

Anna turned, and the armsman swallowed.

'I beg your pardon, sorceress.'

Anna eased herself back beside the base of the tower. 'This is all the space I need now.' The walled corner doubtless offered more safety against arrows, but who knew about sorcery?

The young armsman swallowed, then stationed himself to the left and back of the archer who had strung his bow and set his quiver on a projecting brick shelf. The armsman's fingers gripped the hilt of the long blade, but he did not draw it.

The clouds were darker now, and the day darkened as they slid across the face of the sun, a sun that seemed somehow to Anna rather more red than the sun she knew – but that could have been from the dust that never settled.

From where the road seemed to vanish over a crest leading up to the pass itself came a trickle of darkness. Then Anna realized that the darkness was composed of dark-clad armsmen, with the occasional flash of indirect light on metal – swords or burnished shields.

Recalling the comments about archers, her eyes turned to the hill ridge to the north of the fort, and she watched. Was that an Ebran archer? Then more figures darted from rocks to rocks to the few gnarled trees, moving south, toward the point nearest the fort. Anna inhaled, then exhaled, as she realized she was holding her breath. That wouldn't help singing, not at all, but she'd never been called upon to do a concert – even a single song – in the middle of a battle where people were getting killed.

The Ebran forces seemed to pour down the road toward the fort, darkening the road as the clouds continued to darken the sky.

A single sword of lightning crashed into the hill ridge to the south of the fort.

'Storm song! Now!' demanded Brill, his voice almost shrill.

The cracking roll of thunder underscored his command.

The players began, and Anna wanted to wince. The stress definitely had an impact on their tunefulness, either that or their playing from a sitting position. She checked the tuning of the mandolin, crouching into the brick-walled corner to shut off the outside noises as much as she could.

Then she tried a vocalise, gently, hoping the dust hadn't dried her cords too much, that she could clear her voice without too much effort. Her voice cracked, and she stopped and took a long swallow from the water bottle at her belt before resuming her warm-up.

The clouds dropped lower, thickening, darkening, until Anna thought she could almost stretch and touch them.

Crack! Another blast of lightning smashed down, and the entire fort shook.

'Aeeiii . . .'

'Stand firm! Stand firm!'

'Lightnings . . .'

Anna turned. The top of the southwest watchtower was gone, leaving nothing but a mass of brick and dust.

To her right, Brill sang, trying to project his voice over other voices and the rumblings of the storm that swept down out of the Ostfels.

'. . . mighty fortress is our song . . .
. . . stands against all nature's powers strong . . .'

Spang! An arrow smashed against the edge of the parapet, then dropped onto the bricks less than a yard from Anna's feet. The arrowhead itself was a triangular, serrated, ugly chuck of metal, tough enough that it was barely deformed by its impact against the hard bricks of the fort.

Flattening herself against the watchtower where the archers from the north could not see or hit her, she shivered momentarily, thinking that one of those had gone through her shoulder.

Crack! Another flash of lightning slammed down, this time not far from where the eastern road ended at the dry moat, and the fort shook.

'Again!' demanded Brill. 'It's working!'

Arrows began dropping over the north wall and sleeting into the courtyard.

'Shields up!'

'Under the overhangs!'

The violinist beside Palian, whose name Anna didn't know, crumpled with an arrow through his chest.

'Keep playing!' ordered Brill, as yet another lightning bolt seemed to bend away from the fort. He began to repeat his spell.

Anna lifted her head and studied the eastern road, but the Ebran soldiers appeared to be still more than a dek away, and the rumbling of the storm would probably limit how far she could project.

'Why aren't you doing anything?' hissed the young armsman.

'They have to get closer!' Anna hissed back. Belatedly, trying to hold on to her concentration, she started a second vocalise.

The rain of arrows seemed to slow, then stop, and Anna shifted her position enough to look northward where she saw a handful of mounted archers, wearing the purple of Defalk, on the ridge.

As she watched, several Defalkan archers went down, and more of the dark-clad archers began moving down the ridge from higher ground toward the position taken by the mounted Defalkans.

A few drops of rain darkened the dusty bricks of the fort, then, suddenly, the few drops became a heavy rain, and then almost a wall of water, under which the melodies of Brill's players half dwindled, half squeaked to a stop.

Crack! Another lightning bolt slammed down into the wall right above the closed eastern gates, and bricks cascaded everywhere.

Whatever the lightnings were, they weren't just electrical energy, and Anna wished she'd read the *Donnermusik* book, but vain wishing wouldn't change the past.

Another wall of water, like a line squall, washed over the fort.

Within moments of the rain's passage, the hail of arrows resumed – and the bass hornist went down.

Anna looked up the eastern road. Under the cover of the storm, the Ebran forces had almost reached the dry moat.

'Under the wall there!' Brill ordered the players. 'Now!' The sorcerer scurried up beside Anna and peered toward the dry moat. Below and to the east, under the hanging dark clouds, the Ebrans were fitting together siege ladders.

Yet another lightning bolt smashed into the fort, right at the eastern gates – and then another. Anna grabbed the wall to steady herself as the entire fort shook.

'Archers! Fire!'

The Defalkan bowmen began to release arrows into the massed Ebran troops, who immediately lifted heavy round shields.

Some arrows deflected into the air; some imbedded in shields, some in Ebran soldiers, and within a handful of moments dozens of dark-clad bodies lay on the far side of the dry moat.

Crack!

'Down!' Brill almost flung Anna around the side of the watchtower, following her and jamming them into the shielded corner formed by the north wall and the watchtower wall.

Crack! Crack! Lines of lightning flashed across the entire eastern wall, slamming the fort with jolts hard enough to jerk Anna back and forth across the bricks, raising dust everywhere, despite the fort's earlier drenching. Then another line squall, another instant wall of water, crashed across the Defalkan fort.

Anna scrambled back into a sitting position and glanced down the wall, catching sight of Palian, Daffyd, and Liende crouching next to the wall. Dozens of still figures lay in the courtyard below, and the eastern wall was riddled with fissures.

In the light rain, Brill scrambled back to the edge of the eastern wall, and Anna followed more slowly.

Her stomach turned as she saw the blackened body that had to have been the young armsman who had asked why she hadn't done anything.

One of the gates had fallen forward into the dry moat, and hundreds of the Ebrans, if not thousands, swarmed forward into the brick-lined depression.

Farther up the road, well out of bowshot, a dark-clad group appeared, and Anna could hear a low chanting of some sort. The darksingers?

Brill stood behind the parapet that was now only knee-high, and began to sing.

Anna looked back to his players, but they held on to instruments and crouched under the protection of the northern wall as more arrows sleeted into the fort, mainly from the north.

'. . . sweep forth in power and might!' concluded Brill.

A dull rumbling began, accompanied with a whistling sound.

Anna glanced around, but while the clouds threatened, for

the moment nothing fell from them but light rain. Should she use her spell? The wind gusted around her, and blew the brim of her hat down across her eyes. She ripped it off and stuffed it into her belt.

The Ebrans in the dry moat started to run, and Anna looked down to see a brown-colored wave rumble out of the north side of the moat toward the invaders. Within seconds, the moat was filled with threshing figures.

Anna swallowed. Most wore armor, and few could swim. A handful struggled out on the east or south sides, but before long the brown water was mostly still, where a few items floated, and one or two bodies were buoyed by air trapped in their garments.

The ground shook again.

Brill straightened and scurried back to the north wall.

Anna's mouth opened. Another wall of soldiers marched around the dark-clad monks toward the fort.

The ground shook again, and more bricks fell from the walls.

'Power song . . . the power song,' gasped Brill.

Somehow, some way, a melody began, and Daffyd's viola dominated the intertwined melodies.

Anna shook herself. The world was coming apart around her, and she'd done nothing. Nothing!

She gripped the mandolin. If she didn't use her spellsong now, there wouldn't be anything left to use it for.

The tower and the fort lurched again, and she steadied herself against the tower one-handed, as massive cracks appeared in the ground beyond the fort.

With a gulping, guzzling sound, the moat began to drain – and the thousands of new Ebran soldiers began to march forward.

Anna hummed, wishing she'd done more vocalises, but there wasn't time, and she'd been too disoriented. She faced the darksingers and the oncoming troops and began.

'I have sung the glory of the thunder of the sky,
I am bringing forth the voltage so the bolts of death can
    fly
I have loosed the fateful lightning so the darkling ones
    will die,
My songs will strike them dead ...'

Even by the end of the first verse, the dark clouds were
twisting back, and the lightnings turned, and white bolts
flashed toward the dark singers.

Anna forced herself to keep singing.

Behind her, Brill sang something else, and beneath them
the ground buckled and heaved as Brill's spell and that of
the darksingers meshed in dissonance.

When Anna finished her second verse, she looked up.

Only smoldering flames remained of the darksingers, but
the Ebran soldiers were untouched, although they had halted,
if momentarily, still more than a dek from the shattered
Defalkan fort.

Anna turned. The western gates were being opened, and
armsmen began to pour out, scrambling through the moat
that was dry again, except in places, scurrying around limp
bodies. Two bridge extensions dropped into place, and the
horsemen followed, heading back west, as if retreating.

Why?

Anna looked back at the eastern side of the fort, a mass
of fallen masonry, gaping holes filled with bodies and loose
bricks. Someone led another set of horses from the stables
on the north side, relatively unscathed compared to the
devastation below and to the south of Anna. She shook
her head, and was rewarded with a sharp throbbing.

A handful of arrows whistled past, and she flattened
herself against the watchtower, the sole intact section of
the fort's upper walls.

'Lady Anna!'

At Daffyd's voice she turned, seeing Brill standing with
a heavy arrow through his chest.

Her legs like lead, she half walked, half ran, crouching, to where the sorcerer sagged onto the bricks. His eyes were almost blank as she knelt by him.

'Liende . . . promised . . .'

Anna looked around. Liende was still lying on the corner of the rampart, where Palian struggled to bind or splint the clarinetist's leg, broken by one of the lightning-thrown stones. Daffyd crouched between the two groups, keeping his head down as arrows flew over the northern wall intermittently.

'Liende . . .'

'She's right over there,' Anna said, taking the sorcerer's hand.

'. . . promised . . . all I can do . . .'

Anna bent to catch the words, but could hear only fragments.

> '. . . always golden, always young,
> spells always cleanly sung,
> from my death, bring her life,
> . . . through all strife . . .'

'No—' she protested, even as Brill slumped back on the damp bricks of the fortress that he had built and that was falling with him.

Yet, with his words, her body tingled – that was the only term for it. What had he done? Why? But had it been for her? He'd called for Liende.

His hand went limp in hers, and his eyes stared sightlessly skyward.

More arrows whispered overhead, and a trumpet call sounded from the east.

Anna scuttled back to the holed and sundered eastern rampart and looked out. Although no darksingers remained, the dark-clad Ebran soldiers were hurrying forward, ignoring the sodden bodies in the moat, where only scattered puddles remained, and stepping around the cracks in the brickwork and ground.

Overhead, the dark clouds had already begun to thin, and

patches of blue showed to the south, but the Ebrans kept moving westward.

Didn't anything stop the devils?

She looked across the broken Defalkan ramparts, but nothing moved.

When she glanced back to where Brill had lain, she saw nothing but clothes and an arrow. From where he was helping splint Liende's leg, Daffyd's mouth opened. So did Palian's.

Anna wanted to shake her head, but she did not, trying to ignore the tingling that had raced through her body and had begun to subside.

The courtyard below was deserted, except for two armsmen, one struggling to help the other through the open western gate. Anna could see, farther to the west, scattered puffs of dust from fleeing soldiers, and one organized group, under a blue banner, slowly marching to the northwest.

Daffyd and Palian eased Liende toward the steps, but the other players had vanished, except for the dead violinist and bass hornist. Anna shook her head. Everything seemed to be moving in slow motion ... so slowly.

The Ebrans would be inside the fort long before Daffyd and Palian could get Liende down the steps – and Liende should have gotten Brill's bequest, not Anna.

The sorceress moistened her lips and picked up the mandolin from beside the watchtower wall, humming slightly. Then she stood beside the wall, shielded from the arrows from the north. As the first Ebrans began to dash through the gaps in Brill's once clean and well-formed brick walls, Anna began to sing.

> 'Armsman one, armsmen all,
> from flame to ashes shall you fall ...
> from the strings, from the sky,
> fire flay you till you die!'

A crackling bolt flared like a snapping harp string from

the still-dark clouds, whipping across the Ebran soldiers. A second followed the first, and then a third, and fourth ... until the sky seemed hatched with lines of fire.

Anna winced at the screams that seemed to go on and on, covering her ears and crouching down by the base of the watchtower, trying not to watch what she had unleashed.

Her head ached, and her stomach turned, but she could see that Daffyd and Palian had gotten Liende almost down to the main level. A ray of light flickered through the clouds, and the air was silent, except for the moaning of wounded. Anna slowly fumbled open the water bottle and drank, and drank.

A dull thudding sound echoed through the broken stones, and Anna lifted her head and looked toward the Ostfels where distant dark clouds still swirled across the eastern sky. The ground rumbled, and more bricks toppled into the courtyard.

She peered over the crenelated section beside the watchtower, the only tower intact, from what she could see. Like ants, more columns of dark-clad armsmen wound their way down the road, past the burned bodies that lay everywhere, toward the dry and cracked moat, and toward the fort – and Anna.

Her battle hymn had worked on the monks, but not the regular soldiers. Her burning song had almost floored her, and left hundreds dead, or more, and that didn't count the thousands swept away in Brill's onetime torrent. Yet here there were thousands of the Ebrans left, all marching out of the Sand Pass and down toward the shattered remnants of the fort.

What could she do? She wasn't quick, and she couldn't think. Her head was already splitting.

Maybe, if she stood close to the edge of the tower, and projected – used everything with the same spell she burned the armsmen – maybe ...

She shut away the sounds of the screams that still echoed in her ears, and eased herself toward the open space that had been the front rampart. There weren't any Ebran archers close by, not that she could see, but some of the dark-clad soldiers were almost at the base of the walls, winding around the scattered puddles and getting ready to swarm up into the stronghold. Their blades gleamed in the intermittent sunlight.

A dull thunder sounded, and Anna looked north toward the empty reservoir. Under the black banners were horsemen – far too many to count, and they were on the safe side of the disasters Brill had wrought.

'Lady Anna!' called Daffyd, scrambling up the steps and across the brick-strewn rampart. 'We've got to leave. The levies have all deserted, except for those under Lord Jecks, and they are forming up to fight outside the fort.'

Anna turned to the youth, pointing to the north. 'Look. We won't get a mile.' She took a deep breath. 'Get the others ready, and get Farinelli saddled. I'll be there. One more spell.' *Just one more – that's all I've got time or energy for – just one.*

Daffyd opened his mouth, then backed away as Anna threw everything she had left into the spell.

> 'Armsman one, armsmen all,
> from flame to ashes shall you fall . . .'

· As she sang, sending her voice across the openness, trying to stay free while projecting everything she could, trying to visualize lines of fire striking mounted Ebrans and Ebrans on foot, it seemed as though behind the blue-green sky, behind the nearer hazy clouds that were disintegrating, giant strings thrummed and cascaded.

·Fire – lines of fire – slashed again from the sky, and screams, screams that went through her like a knife, flayed Ebrans – and her soul.

Without really looking, just visualizing lines of fire, she began to repeat the awful words and melody, but her knees began to buckle, and the crescendo that descended carried blackness ... and silence, a silence behind which echoed screams ... endless screams.

37

SAND PASS, EBRA

Eladdrin staggers to his feet, putting a hand to his forehead. It comes away not only bloody, but with flakes of skin, as though his face had been scorched by the sun.

Slowly, he steps through the black tatters of the tent, and gazes from the ridge toward the west, toward swirls of dust, and smoke, and seemingly endless death.

A subcaptain lurches uphill toward him.

The songmaster clears his throat, then waits.

'We have the devils' fort, songmaster. That's about all.'

'What happened?' asks Eladdrin.

'You ... ser ... you must ...'

'Tell me what you saw.'

'The sorceress, the blonde soprano – her voice was like a giant harp in the sky and she called the lightnings on the forward darksingers and twisted them back onto them.' The subcaptain swallows.

'And then?'

'Then ... twice she called forth something like whips of fire, and the whips touched everyone in the first army, and they all burned, and then when the second army attacked ... she did it again.'

'Where is she?'

'We do not know, ser.' The subcaptain hung his head. 'We didn't find her body.'

'What is left of the Defalkan forces?'

'From the bodies we found, maybe half survived, but most scattered and ran. One group retreated to the north

– a blue banner with a gold bear. Not many, say a dozen score. Scattered riders here and there.'

'Our forces?' Eladdrin forces himself to ask.

'It's hard to tell, ser, what with all the rocks and the fallen walls.'

'Guess, then.'

'A third left, maybe less. None of them worth a dissonance.' The subcaptain spits on the rocks to his left. 'Everywhere you look, burned bodies, bodies flayed with whips of fire. I'd flay that bitch sorceress, and then some.'

'Why?' asks Eladdrin tiredly. 'We would have killed her. We already tried once and failed. She has no reason to be kind.' He blotted the blood away from his eyes, looking at the spirals of dust and smoke that swirl over the end of the Sand Pass. 'Still, part of me hopes she is in dissonance's deepest discords.'

'You lost all those darksingers, and . . . ?'

'I'm excusing no one. We did what we had to do, and she did what she had to do. There's no room for hatred in war, Gealas. It destroys your ability. But, if I could hate anyone, I'd hate her.' He pauses. 'Marshal up the forces, and find a campsite north of the battle. We'll need to regroup – and we'll need a lot of reinforcements.' As the subcaptain leaves, Eladdrin adds under his breath, 'A lot . . . and the luck not to run into more sorcerers like those two.'

II

WAHRWELTTRAUM

38

Anna's eyes were gummy, and her head pounded, and someone was talking to her. She opened her eyes slowly, but could see nothing for a moment. Was she blind? What had happened? Then points of light wavered in the darkness – it was night.

Daffyd was talking.

'Are you all right? Lady Anna, are you all right?'

'I don't know,' Anna finally said. 'I think I can see. It's dark out, isn't it?' She was lying on something, a bedroll, that didn't soften the ground underneath very much.

'It's well after sunset, could be close to midnight.'

'Midnight?' It had been around midday, or early afternoon, she thought, at the end of the battle, except it hadn't been a battle – more like alternating slaughter. Her lips twisted. Had she really done it? Really summoned whips of fire? She shuddered.

'Are you all right?' Daffyd repeated.

'What happened? Tell me what happened.'

'But are you all right?'

Anna slowly rolled on her side and struggled into a sitting position. Her head ached. In fact, her entire body ached. She felt like she even had bruises on her stomach. 'No. Do we have any water? Where are we? What happened?'

Daffyd fumbled and then extended a water bottle – her water bottle. It was only half full, and Anna drank nearly half of that. The throbbing in her skull subsided to a dull aching.

'Where are we?' she asked again.

'A little off the foothill road from the Sand Pass to Synope,' Daffyd answered. 'A long time ago, before the pass sanded up, this was the main road between Synek and Sudwei. Now it's not much more than a trail.'

'Fine . . . What happened?'

'The weather changed. Lord Geansor got crippled—'

'No. At the Sand Pass.'

'You turned a whole lot of the Ebrans into cinders, and then you just fell down. I barely caught you before you almost rolled off into the courtyard.'

'Great . . .' muttered Anna. Fainting just because she sang a spell?

'Everyone was so surprised that I carried you down and . . . anyway, we got out of the fort. Palian and Liende headed back to Mencha. They said no one would bother plain old players. I didn't know about that, but I didn't think that was a good idea for you, not after . . . what happened.'

Anna's ribs were sore, too. 'How did you get me here?'

'I couldn't carry you,' Daffyd said defensively.

'You didn't drag me, did you?'

'No. I sort of tied you in your saddle. It wasn't easy, and I had to go really slow. We're not very far from the fort, really.'

'Everything hurts,' Anna murmured, more to herself than to Daffyd, then asked, 'Why aren't we headed back to Mencha?'

'I'd thought we'd be riding to Synope. We can't be going back to Mencha.'

'Why not?' snapped Anna.

'All the darksingers saw you on the walls. Enough of them lived that they'd be killing you on sight, and, well, without Lord Brill or Lord Barjim . . .'

'What happened to Barjim?'

'He was heading out with his guards when one of those thunderbolts brought the south tower down on 'em all.'

Anna recalled the tower falling, but hadn't realized Barjim had been beneath it – but she should have guessed. There had been too much chaos, and Barjim – or Alasia – had been too organized to allow that to happen. 'Lady Alasia, too?'

'I fear so. Lord Jecks managed to break through the dark horse, but you gave them some help.' The player's face

THE SOPRANO SORCERESS · · · 201

twisted into a smile. 'That was something. I wish I could do sorcery like that.'

'No, you don't,' said Anna bleakly, thinking about all the screams that had echoed in her ears and soul. 'You don't.'

'That's what Lord Brill said. You sorcerers just don't want anyone else to learn what you do.'

Anna sighed, but that hurt, too. After uncorking the water she drank a little more. Brill certainly hadn't wanted to share. Would some sort of harmonic spell have been better? But how could she have persuaded Brill with so little time when it had been all too clear how little she had really known?

'Are you all right?' he asked again.

'I'll live.' She took another swallow. 'Synope? That's where your sister lives? Delia?'

'Dalila,' corrected Daffyd.

'What would happen if we went back to Brill's hall?'

'Even if the darksingers didn't get there first, could you hold it?' asked Daffyd.

'Hold it?'

'It's a lot of sorcery. He calls forth the water, and keeps it cool in summer, and warm in winter—'

'He did that all with sorcery?'

Daffyd nodded, a gesture Anna had to strain to see in the dark.

'What will happen if we don't go back?'

'Nothing for a while. Nobody would want it, except another sorcerer, or sorceress. I guess it belongs to the Lord of Defalk – except we don't have one right now, unless it's Lord Jecks.'

Anna rubbed her forehead, and tried not to breathe deeply. Her diaphragm was sore, and she wasn't certain that Daffyd hadn't just slung her across the saddle.

Whhuuuffff.

She smiled as she recognized Farinelli's whuff in the darkness, but the smile faded quickly. 'Why won't people in Synope recognize me? Or ask questions about a stranger?'

'You could be my other sister,' suggested Daffyd. 'No one's seen Reneil in years.'

'I'm years older than your sister.'

'Not anymore, Lady Anna, not anymore.'

Anna shivered again, and her eyes burned. She was glad that Daffyd couldn't see that closely. She was young again – because a dying sorcerer thought she was someone else. She was young again, in a strange place, where she might never see her children again. She was young again, in a world she barely understood.

The tears flowed, silently, in the darkness.

39

WEST OF THE SAND PASS, DEFALK

The harp strums in the darkness of the tent, then whispers.

'Songmaster?'

'Yes, Evult?' Eladdrin rises and faces the instrument centered in the small pool.

'The sorceress must be destroyed.'

'I know. Do you have any suggestions as to how?' asks Eladdrin.

'Songmaster . . .'

Eladdrin's eyes are fierce as he faces the pool. 'Never have I felt such power – that was more than a league away – and that power was supported only by a tiny stringed instrument. With a dozen voices like that, we could hold the world. She destroyed five hundred massed voices – and you order me to destroy her. I would do so gladly, if I knew but how.'

'We may have to use others for that. And do not think of trying to enlist her. She will break you like an arrow snapped across my knees.' The distant voice recedes momentarily. 'I will send another cohort of darksingers and more armsmen.'

'I had planned to take the harvests to resupply.'

'This time, until we discover where the sorceress is, you can move slowly.' The words that whisper from the harp stop, then resume. 'There is a sorceress, a travel-sorceress, in Mencha who called the blonde one from the mist worlds. Ensure that she can call no others. That you can do, Songmaster.'

With a discordant clinging, the harp falls silent.

Eladdrin walks out into the twilight and stares at the distant stars as they begin to appear. 'As if I could move other than slowly ...'

40

The next morning was worse. Anna could barely roll over because her stomach muscles were so sore. Her head felt like it had been used as the chimes in the *1812 Overture*, and her eyes were so gummy that they felt glued shut. Unseen needles jabbed into her brain every time she moved her head.

The sun had barely cleared the horizon, but she could feel the heat building, and she smelled like she'd run a marathon.

And Daffyd was humming to himself, almost tunelessly, as she fumbled with the water bottle. The two swallows left in the bottle that had been at her belt weren't really enough. She levered herself onto her knees and looked around.

The rest of her gear, including the other water bottles, was sitting almost within reach, beyond the head of the bedroll. From the weight, she could tell the first two she tried were empty. The third was full, but why was it always the last place you looked that you found what you needed?

'Are you awake, Lady Anna?'

'No. I'm still sleeping,' she answered after taking a long swallow.

Wisely, Daffyd did not reply.

For a time, she just sat and sipped the water, looking around. Daffyd had set up camp under a rocky overhang that was several hundred yards uphill from the winding trail he had said once had been a main road. It didn't look like it had ever been anything but a trail, but she wasn't exactly the expert on Erdean roadworks.

The air remained clear, and the sun pounded down. She was glad their crude campsite remained in the shade.

To the south Farinelli and the mare grazed on the scattered clumps of mostly brown grass. To the north, Anna thought, there was a thin twisting plume of smoke – the fires of the Ebrans? Or the burning ruins of the fort?

She looked at her boots, sitting by the bedroll. Finally, she corked the water bottle and pulled on one, then the other. She tried standing up, and every muscle in her body suggested that she was well over a century old. The faded green trousers sagged, and she had to retie the belt even tighter.

'You should eat something,' Daffyd ventured. 'There is travel bread and cheese in the cloth there. I left it out for you.'

'Thank you.' Anna limped toward it, bending slowly to retrieve the food off the rock ledge.

The cheese was hard, and the bread stale, but Anna had no trouble eating everything. Daffyd was packing his gear on the gray mare before Anna finished off her breakfast with more water.

After beating the dust out of the floppy-brimmed hat that seemed to have followed her, she went through her saddle-bags, but everything was there. 'Did you pack these?'

'No. Palian threw everything in there while I was carrying you down the steps. I put the mandolin in, though.'

'Thank you.'

'You're welcome, Lady Anna.'

Anna carried everything over to Farinelli. The gelding ignored her and kept trying to nibble on anything remotely green.

'I can't get you water unless we get you saddled.'

Farinelli kept grazing.

After looking at Farinelli, and wondering if she really wanted to ride however many leagues it was to Synope, Anna fumbled the blanket in place, and then the saddle.

As she lifted the saddle, she frowned, realizing that her shoulder didn't even twinge, that there wasn't even a trace of soreness there. Once she fastened both cinches, she looked at her left hand – there was only the faintest thread of a white line there – if that. Hadn't there always been a line there? She crooked her head and pulled her shirt and tunic forward. There wasn't even a scab where the arrow wound had been, and she could tell her stomach was flatter than it had been in years.

She shivered, but Farinelli brought her back to reality with a long whuffling sound and a toss of his head.

'I know. You're hungry and thirsty.'

'What?' said Daffyd.

'We need to find water for the horses.' Anna fastened the saddlebags in place. *And for me, before I get so dehydrated I can't function.*

'We will.'

The sorceress wished she were that certain. Perhaps she could use a variant of the cool-water spell to bring some to the surface – but she'd have to be close to where there was water underground, and she was a singer, not a geologist. She took a deep breath. The needles still stabbed into her brain, and she knew she was only a singer, when she needed to be so much more.

41

Anna pulled off her hat, wiped away the thin film of muddy dust that collected on her forehead, then readjusted the hat, and reached for the water bottle. Farinelli walked stolidly down the gentle downgrade into another dry valley, filled with sandy red dirt, a handful of twisted juniper-like trees, more than a few barren and dead tree trunks, and scattered clumps of browned grass.

'Is it like this all the way?' she asked.

'I suppose so.' Daffyd's voice was hoarse, and he glanced back over his shoulder. 'It didn't used to be this way. There were more trees and grass.'

'Drought,' Anna said, half standing in the stirrups to relieve the hardness of the saddle, except that her legs protested the extra effort. If the second day on the back road to Synope had been hard, the third had been even worse, and it was only early afternoon. They had no travel food, just the water Anna had been able to call from dry creek-beds – enough for the horses, and to fill the water bottles.

The sun continued to beat down, and Anna's face felt raw and burned, despite the hat, and the needle-stabbing headache seemed constant. Her muscles remained sore, especially around her stomach and in her legs, since she still wasn't that used to riding, although she had the feeling, if she stayed in Erde, that would change.

If? she thought. Brill might have been able to figure out a way to get her back . . . and he was dead. Daffyd was bright enough, but, as for visualizing earth . . . ? And the business of some people being burned when they tried it – that was another question. She shook her head, and her eyes stung, wondering what Mario and Elizabetta thought, wondering why she was being so punished for thinking that she just wanted to get away – anywhere.

She forced a deep breath. Anywhere was where she was. She'd laughed about the old saying *'Be careful what you wish for because you might get it.'* It didn't seem quite so funny at the moment.

Daffyd glanced back over his shoulder again.

Anna turned in her saddle to follow his eyes. Was there dust in the air, not from their slow progress, but from some other traveler? Not many travelers took the trail they were on. Anna hadn't been able to make out either a hoofprint or a wagon track, but she was no tracker. 'Does anyone use this road anymore?'

'It's not overgrown,' Daffyd said.

'Nothing grows here,' Anna pointed out.

'Oh . . .'

Anna looked back again.

The group that appeared at the hill-crest of the trail behind them, little farther than a dek back, was more than just a few riders. Anna squinted. The others were moving at a trot, clearly aimed at catching up with them.

'There are eight of them,' Daffyd said. 'They don't look like soldiers.'

'What are they?'

Daffyd urged the gray mare to move at a quick walk.

'I take it that means they aren't friendly?'

'They don't have pack animals, and they're trying to catch us. I think they must be bandits, but I've never seen or heard of any here.'

'You told me this was a main road, too,' Anna said, urging Farinelli to move more quickly. 'Times have changed, it looks like.'

'I didn't know.'

Anna snorted. How many times had she heard that from students? *Then, are you any better? You didn't know that wishing to be anywhere else would lead to this. Why couldn't you have just been happy to stay in Ames? . . . Singing for the Founders or whatever, even dealing with Dieshr and her snide comments from her high position as chair, is better than fighting battles, starving, and being chased by bandits with no good in mind.*

She looked back again. The dust given off by the bandits was rising higher, as if they had spurred their mounts into a quick trot now that they were on the flat.

'Can't you do something?' asked Daffyd.

'What do you suggest?'

'Anything. They'll kill us for sure.'

Anna's stomach congealed in a cold lump. After an instant of frozen silence, she asked, 'Are you sure?'

'Bandits are killed, even if they spare their victims.'

Anna twisted toward the saddlebags, fumbling open the right one, then closing it and opening the left one in her search for the mandolin. Where was it? Finally, she lifted the mandolin out and slipped the strap over her neck, trying to ignore the tightening in her shoulder.

If only Daffyd had been able to finish the lutar – although it really wasn't either a lute or a guitar – she would have felt happier. The mandolin was tinny, and it didn't project far enough.

What could she sing? Their pursuers weren't armsmen, and she'd learned that the words targeting a spell-subject had to be fairly precise. Bandits, evildoers, villains . . . what were they?

The pursuing horsemen were closer, perhaps half a dek, and she could see several bare blades, and at least one bow.

'Aren't you going to do something?' asked Daffyd.

'I'm thinking,' she snapped. Only nursery rhymes seemed to go through her head, like '*Sing a song of sixpence . . .*'

An arrow skidded across the ground, leaving a line of dust in the road thirty yards behind them.

'"Sing a song of" . . . what?' she murmured. 'Villains?' *Then what?* It was hard to think and ride.

Then she had the words. They weren't great, but they just might work.

She began to strum the strings, hoping the mandolin was close enough to being in tune, but her fingers fumbled and the chords were off, and she was about to fall off Farinelli because she wasn't good enough to ride and sing and play all at once.

She reined up and turned Farinelli so she faced the oncoming riders.

'What are you doing?' Daffyd looked back, but didn't slow his mare.

A handful of arrows flew toward her, the closest going by her left shoulder. Holding back a shiver, trying to keep her voice relaxed – how was she supposed to do that with people shooting at her? – Anna cleared her throat and began the simple chords to an even simpler song.

'Sing a song of villains, stop them as I can;
four and twenty arrows shoot into each man.
If that is not enough, then wrap their necks in stringing;
now isn't that a better way to stop their evil singing?'

Anna winced at the lousy rhyme, but tried to visualize what she had in mind. Again, she got the sensation of a giant harp vibrating behind the bright blue sky, and a shuddering wrench of the ground.

Farinelli half whinnied, half whuffled, and Anna patted his shoulder, then squinted through the sudden dust. She swallowed, trying to keep her stomach in place. Eight trussed bodies lay on the road, eight bodies that looked like pincushions.

That was the way her head felt, even more so after the spell.

Behind her, she could hear the ugly sound of Daffyd retching. Do something, he'd said. They'll kill us. She had, and now he was retching.

Anna turned Farinelli toward the bandits' horses. Queasy or not, she and Daffyd could use food, coins, whatever the raiders might have. She swallowed again, but she left the mandolin out, strapped around her neck.

One by one, she went through the wallets. At least with the big belt wallets, she didn't have to dig through the bandits' pockets.

She noticed something strange. The bandit's quiver was empty, and he had neither bow nor bow string – yet she had seen both.

After the second bandit, a good-looking blond young man of that sort vaguely similar to Mario, she did lose it, retching into the dusty dirt beyond the shoulder of the road. She looked over. Daffyd still leaned against his gray mare.

She tightened her lips and went back to looting, thinking as she did. *No one asked me if I wanted to be here. No one's providing for me, either, and Daffyd wanted me to use sorcery. And this bandit wasn't Mario. Mario wouldn't rob and kill people.*

In the end, she had a half dozen gold coins and over a dozen silvers, not to mention a large handful of coppers. She stuffed most into her wallet, looking up as Daffyd rode the mare toward her slowly. His face was pale. 'Do you need any help?'

'Yes. Gather all the food and water bottles they had and pack it on two of their mounts – the two best ones.'

'What about the others?'

'Take off their bridles and saddles and let them run.'

'They're valuable,' Daffyd protested.

'What would happen if we rode into Synope with ten horses?' Anna asked, proud of herself for thinking about it. She recalled her grandfather's words, and expletives, about horse thieves. 'We can explain two extra mounts as left from casualties from the battle, but ten?'

Daffyd nodded stolidly.

'Do you need some coins?' Anna asked.

Daffyd shook his head.

Anna walked over to the young player. 'Take these, at least, as payment for finishing that lutar.'

'I haven't . . .'

'You will.'

'Yes, Lady Anna.' After accepting the two silvers and some coppers and putting them in his wallet, he slowly rode toward the most distant bandit mount, and Anna turned to the one nearest her. *What does he expect? He's like a kid whose watched violence on TV, and then he sees it close and learns what it's like.* She shook her head. She had no doubts about what the bandits would have done to them, to her.

All the bandits' quivers had been empty, she realized.

Then she nodded to herself. Brill had said spells basically rearranged things from nearby material – probably
most of the arrows had been the bandits' own, and the
particolored string they were wound in had probably been
their blankets.

Her knees began to shake, and she ate the first food she
could find in the bandits' saddlebags – travel bread so dried
that the stale stuff she'd finished the morning before seemed
fresh by comparison.

What had she become? Killing people with spells, eating
barely edible food, and justifying it?

Her eyes burned ... but she continued to eat, if more
slowly, more deliberately. Shortly, Daffyd joined her, but
he did not look directly at her.

42

WEI, NORDWEI

Gretslen slips into the armless wooden chair, her face
expressionless under the short blonde hair, the green eyes
intent upon Ashtaar.

'While your reports are quite clear about what the Ebrans
are doing,' begins the spymistress, 'I find that I need more
explanations for the Council on what they are *not* doing.
We had anticipated that Behlem's forces would already be in
Falcor and that Eladdrin would be at least to Pamr by now.
Instead, the Ebrans, after having crushed the Defalkans and
killed Lord Barjim and his too-capable consort, squat a few
leagues inside the border. Is that not so, Gretslen?' Ashtaar
steeples her fingers, and her dark eyes flash.

'They have taken Lord Brill's hall and outbuildings in
Mencha, and the surrounding farms and dwellings. The
sorcerer's hall is easily suited for a base of operations,

still within ten leagues of the Sand Pass. They are also rebuilding the Defalkan fort there.' Gretslen's tone is level.

'Both are late Lord Brill's masterpieces, no doubt?' Ashtaar frowns. 'What do they do there that is so vital?'

'They have established a continuous resupply from Synek, and they are rebuilding their forces. Their losses were substantial, as I noted.'

'From the purported mist-world sorceress? Any sorceress that powerful would be transformed to cinders crossing the worldgates. Are you certain it was not Brill?'

'Lord Brill was dead when more than half the Ebran armsmen were flayed with fire.' Gretslen's eyes flicker to the window, through which she sees an afternoon storm above the harbor.

Ashtaar's fingers close around the dark oval of polished stone before her. 'The waters could be wrong.'

'They could be.'

'You do not think so, do you?'

'No, honored Ashtaar.'

The spymistress sets down the dark oval no larger than her clenched fist. 'This is troubling. A sorceress that powerful cannot cross from the mist worlds. There was no sorceress that powerful known in Liedwahr, and there has not been one that strong since the time of Vereist. You do not know where she is? How can that be? The waters can surely trace that kind of power.'

'The waters show her image. She is riding, with a single companion, somewhere in Defalk.' Gretslen shrugs. 'After the drought, one part of Defalk looks much like another.'

Ashtaar nods. 'Then keep watching, and let me know. What of the travel-sorceress?'

'A team was dispatched the afternoon you requested it, but they have had to avoid the fleeing soldiers.'

'This is vexing, Gretslen. Is the sorceress also the reason for Behlem's caution?'

'I could not tell you that with certainty, but his seers have used their waters to scry the battle.'

'So this unknown sorceress gives Behlem pause, and nearly destroys the Ebrans. We don't know who she is, or where exactly she is. We don't know where her loyalties lie. In the meantime, Eladdrin is wary enough not to move until he has far more armsmen than he needs, and Behlem has learned caution.' Ashtaar pauses. 'Very vexing. Defalk should have fallen easily.'

'Most of the armsmen fled as we planned,' points out Gretslen.

'Except those of Lord Jecks.'

'We could not subvert them, as we noted.'

'What is Jecks doing?'

'His forces are quick-marching to Falcor.'

'Gretslen . . .'

'I only scried that a few moments ago,' answers the blonde hurriedly.

'What a dissonant mess . . .' mutters Ashtaar before looking up. 'Is there anything else? Anything else that the Council could spring on me?'

'Well . . . this sorceress works only with a mandolin, not with players.'

'Donner save us . . . You're certain?'

'Yes, Ashtaar.'

'I suggest you consider a method for removing the sorceress. No . . . don't send anyone . . . not yet . . . but consider it. Consider it carefully.' Ashtaar offers a hard smile.

43

From the hillside to the northeast, where Farinelli carried Anna steadily down the dusty road that they had reached earlier in the day, Synope looked like a larger and even hotter and drier version of Mencha. She checked the rope that ran from her rear saddle ring to the brown mare. The mare plodded after the gelding, bearing two sets of saddlebags, filled partly with stale travel bread, some daggers, a few hand tools and an awl – and two swords. Daffyd led another mare, a piebald one, similarly loaded.

'Are you sure this wasn't the road you had in mind?' Anna asked for the second time, or maybe it was the third, glancing at the late-afternoon sun that hung over the dusty fields.

'Lady Anna . . . I said I was sorry.'

'So am I.' Anna wasn't quite sure why she found it hard to forgive Daffyd. Was it because she hadn't wanted to kill the bandits? Or because she'd been glad to be able to stop them before they hurt her or anyone else? *They deserved it*, a part of her mind said. *But you were pleased*, another part said. She took a deep breath. 'Daffyd, I don't mean to be sharp with you, but . . . I've already done things here that I'm not proud of.' *Except you are, in a perverse way.*

'Those bandits, lady? You stopped them from killing many people. How can you say it was something you aren't proud of?'

Anna thought. 'If I kill a snake or a mad dog, it has to be done, but it's nothing to be proud of.' *There!*

Daffyd looked down at the mane of the gray mare. '. . . sorcerers . . . sorceresses . . .'

There was so much Anna didn't know. She had weapons and tools she didn't know how to use. She had coins, but what were they worth?

'Daffyd?'

'Yes?'

'What are the gold coins called?'

'They're golds, that's all.'

'What can you get for a gold or a silver?'

'Things, of course.' Daffyd sounded exasperated.

'I meant, what are they worth? How much can you buy with them?'

'Oh . . . like boots or blades or food?'

Anna nodded.

'A good meal at an inn will cost three or four coppers.'

Daffyd frowned. 'My last boots cost Brill three silvers. A good horse runs from three golds up.'

'Are there ten coppers in a silver?'

'Of course. Ten silvers in a gold. Always have been, far as I know.'

The sorceress's lips tightened.

'You could sell some of those blades, Lady Anna. Not here, but in places like Falcor or Cheor or maybe Sudwei. They'd bring over a gold each, maybe more.'

'I don't know what we should do.' And she didn't. She was carrying, apparently, a fair amount of coins for a local, plus goods that might be worth even more. But business wasn't her strongest point, especially in a strange place like Liedwahr.

The road curved around an orchard. The trees had leathery gray-green leaves. An olive orchard? Anna didn't know, but Russian olives had those kinds of leaves, and olives grew in hot climates.

As she rode around the gentle curve, she could see scattered trees lining what might be a river off to the right, but the road curved back and continued south and parallel to the river toward the scattered dwellings that marked the outskirts of greater Synope.

'Is that a river?' Anna pointed.

'The Synor River. It never was very big, and it's smaller now. Even with the dam, there's barely enough water for the mills.' Daffyd fell silent.

'What will your sister say about your showing up with a complete stranger?'

'Every time I come, she says I should come more often. She doesn't mind if I bring friends.' Daffyd smiled. 'After all, I am her little brother.'

That didn't exactly reassure Anna. 'Where does she live?'

'On the east side, but not so far east as the hills where the mills are.'

Anna glanced to the east and the low hills beyond Synope. The Ostfels were no longer visible on the eastern horizon and

had not been since well before midday, which meant that
Synope was farther from the mountains than Mencha was.

'Does she have children ... a husband, consort?'

'She and Madell have a daughter. Ruetha is three, I
think.'

'What do they do? She's not a player, is she?'

'No. Madell's father is a miller, but there hasn't been that
much milling lately.'

They passed a small cot on the left side of the road. The
door hung open, and one of the shutters lay on the ground
beneath the window. The next cot had neither windows
nor doors.

Farinelli tossed his head and took a side-step.

'I know. You're a hungry and thirsty boy.' She patted the
gelding's shoulder, looking ahead to where a wagon stood
outside a building. A youth carried a bench from the building
to the wagon.

'That used to be the woodworker's place, but I never met
him,' explained Daffyd.

'How long has it been since you were here?'

'Two years, I'd guess,' Daffyd admitted.

The woodworker's apprentice looked up at the two riders
and their de facto packhorses. His eyes crossed Anna's, and
he took a long look before flushing and looking away. Then
he scurried back into the shop.

Anna pursed her lips, then moistened them. What had that
all been about? Certainly, the young man had seen women
before, even women on horseback. From what she'd seen in
Erde so far, all women who rode wore trousers – none of
the sidesaddle idiocy spawned by the English.

Synope had a central square – of sorts – with a mélange of
shops clustered around a dusty red stone platform standing
in the middle of an intersection of an east-west road and
the north-south road that had carried Anna and Daffyd into
the town.

Yuril's proclaimed a faded green sign bearing two crossed
candles. Under the sign was a shop with narrow and grimy

windows. Beside Yuril's was a larger building, from which projected a white-painted sign bearing only line-drawing outlines of a mug and a bowl.

'The Cup and Bowl,' offered Daffyd. 'Could be the worst food in Defalk, maybe in all Liedwahr.'

A heavyset woman in frayed brown trousers and an overlarge tunic that had grayed from too many washings dragged her daughter away from the horses. Her eyes went to Anna, and then away, and she pulled the girl under the narrow porch beneath the sign for Yuril's.

Anna tried not to frown. She knew she was dirty, dusty, and probably had circles under her eyes that reached to her jaw, but when people looked at her and then ran, it wasn't exactly encouraging.

'That way.' Daffyd pointed to the left.

Anna urged Farinelli around the red stone platform and its chipped sandstone balustrade that looked like a town bandstand without a roof. She couldn't imagine a bandstand in Defalk, though.

Two armsmen in soiled light-green tunics, trimmed with purple, stood in front of another shop – this one with a barrel displayed over the door. Neither looked away. Both stared at Anna. She ignored the pair, but could feel their eyes on her back until she and Daffyd were at least another hundred yards from the center of Synope.

The few shops gave way to houses, almost all of one story, and most were finished on the outside with a plaster or stucco. Some were gray, others painted, but the paint on all had faded.

'There it is,' said Daffyd, turning the mare down a short lane off the main thoroughfare – if a dirt strip ten yards wide constituted a main thoroughfare.

The house to which the young player pointed was similar in shape to that of Jenny, the travel-sorceress in Mencha, if somewhat longer. The red dust had stained the outside white stucco or plaster walls a faint pink, and two weathered wooden benches stood on the warped planks that formed a porch under the overhanging eaves. The front door was closed against the late-afternoon heat, as were the four shutters, two on each side of the door.

The wood had once been painted a bright blue, but the paint had faded and peeled, giving the house a faintly disreputable look. Behind the house was a long shed, with an overhanging roof and one side without doors, showing six stalls. Five were empty.

'Are you sure your sister won't mind?' Anna asked again.

'She's always saying that I should come more often.'

'But I'm an outsider.'

'You've saved my life. That counts for something.'

'When did I do that?'

'When you talked to Lord Brill, and when you killed all those dark-singers and Ebrans. Otherwise none of us would have lived. And you stopped the bandits.' The violist grinned briefly. 'Three times ought to merit some hospitality.'

Anna shook her head.

Daffyd tied the mare and his packhorse to one of the two stone hitching posts, and Anna used the other.

'Young Daffyd.' An angular and wiry man stepped out onto the narrow porch. 'Your sister will be pleased to see you.' He looked at Anna.

'Madell, this is the Lady Anna.'

Madell bowed deeply, without looking Anna in the eye. 'Lady . . .' He was barely taller than the sorceress. Despite the superficial respect, Anna distrusted Dalila's consort, mate, whatever he was. He reeked of trouble.

'Daffyd!' Dalila was pert, if stocky, and short, barely above Anna's shoulder, and very pregnant. And she bounced off the porch and hugged her brother.

A dark-eyed, dark-haired girl peered from the doorway.

Daffyd hugged his sister carefully, then disengaged himself. 'Dalila, this is the Lady Anna. She's a sorceress. Fortunately, for you, and especially for me, she's managed to save my life several times.'

'Then we do indeed owe her. You've always needed a

saving.' Dalila turned to Anna, and her eyes twinkled, as she gave a head bow. 'You are most welcome to what we have, lady. It isn't much, and certainly not fit for—'

'This is a palace,' Anna said. 'We've slept in the rocks, and before that in a tiny room with lots of people in a fort.'

'But shouldn't you be paying your respects to Lord Hryding?' The small brunette held out a hand, and the girl scurried across the porch and grasped it. 'This is Ruetha.'

'I don't even know who Lord Hryding is,' Anna admitted. She smiled at the girl. 'Hello, Ruetha.'

The three-year-old buried her face in her mother's trousers.

'Lady Anna is from the mist worlds,' Daffyd explained, 'and she hasn't been here very long.'

'The mist worlds, fancy that,' murmured Madell, openly disbelieving.

'I summoned her,' Daffyd retorted. 'Me and Jenny, anyway.'

'Then she should surely see Lord Hryding,' said Dalila, stroking Ruetha's dark brown hair.

'She cannot do that now,' said Madell. 'I know it for a fact that Lord Hryding is on his way back from Sudwei and will not be in his hall for at least two more days.'

'And how might you know that?' asked Daffyd.

'His saalmeister came to tell us that he would be bringing back Ranuan grain in his wagons for us to mill.'

Anna frowned. Wasn't flour easier to transport than grain?

'You see,' Madell expounded, 'if we mix the hard winter grain of Synope with the soft grain of Ranuak, then the flour doesn't spoil as quickly.'

'And it doesn't taste so bitter,' added Dalila.

'Right now, I'd rather not deal with another lord,' Anna admitted.

Dalila studied Anna for a moment, then smiled again, warmly. 'I can be seeing that. Well ... you're welcome. You're certainly welcome. It must have been a hard trip.'

Anna nodded. So did Daffyd, but not, she thought, for exactly the same reasons.

'There are bandits along the back roads, especially now, and you were carrying some fair-looking goods and horses. Did you see any?' asked Madell speculatively.

'One group,' Anna said. 'We managed to leave them behind.'

Daffyd swallowed slightly and started to open his mouth. Anna looked at him, and he closed it. The less Madell knew about her abilities, the better.

'There are matters you're not talking about, but those are yours.' Dalila smiled.

'There's a lot we're not talking about,' Anna admitted. *Including the coins and the weapons in our packs.* 'We were in the middle of a battle with the dark ones . . .'

'Aye, and the words come to Synope even.' Dalila turned to her brother. 'The Prophet of Neserea has sent his forces to Falcor, and he is now traveling after them. Sasia was saying so at Yuril's this morning.'

'That's all Defalk needs,' snapped Madell. 'Another ruler to bleed us all dry.'

'Do you think Lord Barjim was that type?' asked Anna.

'He was better than most,' grudged Madell, 'and look what happened to him.'

'There is that,' Anna agreed.

'Well . . . we're talking, and your legs are most likely to be falling off, and you'd need to rub down your mounts and wash up, and then we'd be pleased to eat.' Dalila offered another warm smile.

'Thank you,' Anna said. 'I do appreciate it.'

'You can have the one spare room. Reneil, she had it, but it's been two years now, and I'd be guessing she'll not be back. Afore long, it'll be Ruetha's, not that it's large.'

'Are you sure?' asked Anna.

'After saving Daffy's miserable neck, you deserve that and more.' The pert brunette gestured. 'You be doing what you need, and I be getting back to the cooking.'

Madell followed them out to the shed-stable. 'Best four are the stalls in the middle. Good mounts you got there.'

'Lord Brill's finest,' Daffyd said ironically as he began to unsaddle the mare. 'It was . . .' He broke off. 'I'll tell you all at dinner.'

Anna swallowed. Of course. There were no telephones. No one knew that Daffyd's and Dalila's father had died. She went to work on Farinelli, more slowly.

'Fine beast there,' observed Madell from the stall wall.

'He was a raider horse, I was told. He likes women, but not men.'

Farinelli punctuated her words with a whuffling snort.

After she had him settled, she started on the pack mare, thinner and less well fed than the gelding.

'Most people wouldn't travel just in a pair these days,' said Madell, eyeing her from the back of the mare's stall.

'We didn't have much choice or much time to pick up traveling companions with all the Ebran soldiers pouring through the Sand Pass.' She was sweating in the close confines of the stall, and had to wipe the salty dampness out of the corners of her eyes.

Somehow, despite her tiredness, the saddle was easier to handle. Even the heavy saddlebags seemed lighter. Was she getting back into some semblance of shape? When she was finished with the horses, she lifted the saddlebags, putting a pair over each shoulder and struggling along with the last set in her arms, following Daffyd back to the house.

'Strong woman, you are,' said Madell.

'I do what I have to.' Anna liked the man less and less, but, again, she wasn't exactly in a position to be choosy. She had the feeling that if she went to the local inn, as a single woman alone, things would be even worse. Damn! Why were there so many like Madell?

'Here.' Madell gestured to the door to the small room.

'Thank you.' Anna stepped inside and lowered the saddlebags to the floor beside the narrow pallet bed. The single window was shuttered.

'I'll be leaving you to wash up.' The wiry man smiled.
Anna nodded.

As the door closed, she laid the hat on the peg nearest the
door and walked to the narrow dresser where the washing
bowl and the pitcher stood. On the wall over the dresser
was a mirror. Anna wasn't sure whether she should even
look, given the way she still felt, and the way so many of
the people in Synope had looked at her.

Finally, she stepped up to the mirror.

A stranger looked back at her – a stranger with blonde
hair, not dyed with streaks of white and auburn showing,
but silvery blonde all the way to the roots; a stranger with
firm cheeks and a chin without any signs of aging; a stranger
with no wrinkles, either in the forehead or around her eyes.
A stranger with a thinner face than she remembered ever
having.

The stranger looked sunburned, exhausted, and filthy, but
the stranger was young, probably in her mid-to-late twenties.
Anna shook her head, and the stranger shook hers.

'No . . . no . . .' *Yes . . . You've paid for it . . .* But had she,
really? Really?

She put her head in her hands.

44

Anna tried to half lift, half shrug the damp shirt away from
her sweaty body without being too obvious, then slipped
into the end seat on the bench beside Daffyd. Madell sat
at the single chair, at the head of the table and to Anna's
right. Dalila sat across from Anna, with Ruetha by her side
and across from Daffyd.

The sorceress smiled at the dark-haired little girl, but
Ruetha leaned over and hid her head behind her mother's
arm.

A tantalizing aroma of spices and hot meat circled up and out from the large earthenware crock in the middle of the trestle table, but everyone sat quietly.

Anna waited. Something was going to happen.

'In the name of harmony, let this food pass our lips.' Madell nodded as he finished, and Dalila offered the basket that held a warm loaf of dark bread to Anna.

'Thank you.' Anna broke off the end chunk and then offered the bread to Daffyd. She still felt hot, even without wearing the overtunic.

Madell frowned ever so slightly, but smiled when Anna turned and presented him with the basket.

'There's the cider in the pitcher, Lady Anna,' said Madell, a slight emphasis on the word 'lady.'

Anna half filled her earthenware mug, then sipped the slightly fizzy amber liquid. It was cider, relatively hard cider. 'Good.'

Dalila smiled, then added, 'And the stew in the big crock is my special.'

'It is good,' Daffyd added.

Madell ladled out some for Anna, Dalila, and Daffyd, before filling his own crockery platter.

'There was something you were to tell us,' prompted Dalila. 'I do not think it was good, but I would hear it.'

'It's about Da,' Daffyd began slowly. 'The gray mare was his, a gift from Lord Brill.'

'He's dead.' Dalila nodded to herself. 'He's dead.'

Anna glanced from Dalila to Daffyd. They might have been talking about two different men, from their reactions.

'Yes, he's dead,' choked the young player. 'Is that all ye have to say? He's dead. Is that all?'

'Daffyd . . . I know you loved Da . . .' Dalila spread her hands, then put her arm around her daughter. 'Be gentle. Ruetha would not understand.'

Daffyd shook his head. 'I thought you would be sad.'

Dalila handed a small piece of bread to Ruetha, who began to eat.

Madell wore a cynical smile, and helped himself to another chunk of bread, then some of the stew.

Anna took a small mouthful of the steaming stew, using the carved wooden spoon by her plate. The stew was more peppery than she would have liked, and there was a trace, but only a trace, of something like cilantro, not enough to spoil it for her. She took another mouthful, then stopped.

'I am sad. I am sad for you, Daffyd. Da was good to you.' Dalila took a swallow of cider.

'I never understood,' Daffyd said. 'You said it was better when Mother . . . and you left as soon as you could . . . but . . . you never said.'

'No. Mother asked me not to before she . . . left.'

'Some family stories are best left untold, are they not, lady?' said Madell in a quiet voice, leaning his sandy haired head toward Anna.

'Sometimes. Sometimes not.' Anna edged ever so slightly along the bench toward Daffyd.

'Da was good to me,' Daffyd said.

'He was, and it's best left that way. None of us be changing the past, now,' Dalila said firmly. Then she offered a soft smile and, with her free hand, reached across the table and touched Daffyd's wrist. 'You be remembering him as he was to you. No one can take that.'

The emotional undercurrents tugged at Anna, and she finally looked back at Ruetha. This time, the girl didn't hide, but looked solemnly back at the sorceress.

'Ah . . . you were saying about the Prophet,' Madell finally interjected into the silence.

'Sasia said that his armsmen had reached Falcor, and that he was claiming Defalk in order to stop the dark ones.'

'What about young Jimbob? He didn't die in the battle,' pointed out Madell. 'He's the heir.'

'Sasia was sayin' that the young lord was too untried to rule, and besides, his grandsire made off with him, and that meant the lords had abandoned the liedstadt.'

Madell snorted and took a gulp of cider, large enough that Anna winced, then swallowed and turned to her. 'Did you see how Lord Barjim died?'

'The dark ones destroyed a tower around him with their thunderbolts,' replied Daffyd. 'They sent thousands of armsmen, and archers—'

'Could we be talking of something more pleasant, for now?' asked Dalila, pointedly glancing down at the wide-eyed Ruetha. 'How do you find Defalk, Lady Anna?'

'Those people I have met – not the dark ones – have been nice. It is hot,' Anna offered, 'much, much hotter than where I'm from. And the air is much drier.'

'It has been hot for the past years, because of the black ones. They've stolen our rain, and the winter snows, and every year the grain harvests have been less, the kernels smaller,' added Madell.

'And Lord Brill? How was he? He is said to be a great sorcerer. Daffyd has said much, but I would know what you thought,' asked Dalila.

'Yes, what did you think?' asked Madell, with a smile not quite a smirk.

'Lord Brill was most hospitable to a stranger, and very helpful, to the end. He was a learned man, and I don't think he was ever comfortable in using his sorcery for warfare. In his own way, he seemed honorable about most things, but I couldn't say for sure, because I didn't know him that well or for very long.'

'I daresay you knew him better than most,' offered Madell. 'Being as you're a sorceress,' he added quickly.

'I don't know,' Anna said, stifling a yawn. She was tired, but still hungry, and she took another mouthful of stew, followed with more bread. The bread was good, though not so good as Serna's, but the stew was far better than any meat dishes she had had at Brill's hall. And she was hungry all the time, anyway.

'He was a good sorcerer,' Daffyd said. 'But . . . he didn't . . .' The player shook his head.

'You're tired, Daffyd,' suggested Dalila. 'How long a ride was it?'

'Almost four days,' answered the young man. 'We had to take the old road because the Ebran armsmen were marching on Mencha.'

'A long four days,' added Anna, mechanically taking another bite. Her head ached slightly, still, and her muscles all were tight. She yawned, covering her mouth.

'Tired you are, lady?' asked Dalila as she rocked Ruetha in her arms. Her daughter's eyes were closed, and a faint smile crossed the child's lips.

Anna nodded. How long had it been since she had held hers like that? How long since Elizabetta ... ? She shook her head. 'I'm sorry. I'm not thinking very well.'

'Have you had enough to eat?' asked Daffyd's sister.

'Yes. It was good.'

'Then shoo ... You need some rest. Four days in the saddle. Course you'd be tired.' With her free left hand, Dalila gestured toward the guest room. 'You just climb into that bed and sleep till you wake. We'll leave bread and cheese for you. So don't worry. Get some rest.'

'Thank you. I will.' Anna eased out from the bench, almost stumbling because her feet felt so heavy, vaguely amused at the pert and motherly tone from the young woman.

'Now ... you be sleeping well, lady,' Madell said heartily as he stepped closer to her, almost grinning.

'I'm very much looking forward to getting a good night's *sleep*,' Anna said. She turned away from Madell and looked at Dalila. 'Thank you again for dinner. It was the best food I've had in a long time.'

Dalila flushed. 'You'd just be saying that, Lady Anna.'

'I meant it. Thank you.' She turned to Daffyd. 'Good night, Daffyd.' And then to Madell. 'Good night.'

She stopped in the doorway of the guest room, but someone – Madell, she guessed – had lit the single candle on the dresser. So she stepped into the room and closed the door, letting the latch click.

Anna hadn't liked the looks from Madell, or the tone of his words, and she stopped and checked the door. There was only a simple catch, not a bolt, nor a lock. She grinned as she saw the simple chamberpot behind the door, but the smile faded.

What if Madell came after her? Would he, in the same house as his wife or consort or whatever the term was? Anna snorted. Madell's type well might. Were men the same everywhere? She shook her head. Brill had been a gentleman; he'd even tried to give youth to Liende with his death. Anna's eyes burned for a moment. Nothing ever turned out the way anyone planned.

Her eyes drifted back to the door. She yawned, not wanting to deal with Madell. But she didn't want to deal with a surprise visitor in the middle of the night, either.

Her fingers strayed to the truncheon and the knife at her belt, then she shook her head. Unless she wanted to hurt or kill the man, they wouldn't do much good, and he was probably physically stronger than she was.

Sorcery? Her lips tightened. Same problem. Assuming she could sing, she could kill him ... but that wouldn't make things any better, especially for Daffyd's sister. She took a deep breath and rubbed her forehead. Why did things keep getting more complicated? Why?

The room was close, still hot, although some air circulated through the louvers of the shutters. The single candle fluttered on the narrow dresser.

All she wanted was to be left alone, to get some rest, but she had a gut feeling that it wouldn't work out that way.

First, she stacked the saddlebags with the tools in them against the back of the door. Then, with one eye on the door, she rummaged through the other set of saddlebags. She had the one gown, not in the best of shape, that Palian had – bless her heart – stuffed into the saddlebags. But she couldn't keep sleeping in her clothes. Finally, still watching the door, she slipped out of the filthy riding clothes and into the somewhat cleaner gown.

She still didn't have an answer.

All she wanted was for him to leave her alone. Just – go away. Then, she smiled, and began to call up the words. They were appropriate, and she didn't even have to change them. She spoke them all the way through twice, then hummed the melody.

After turning back the covers, she slipped the truncheon and knife under the corner of the thin pillow, then blew out the candle and stretched out on the pallet – lumpy like every mattress or bed she'd found in Erde. But it didn't matter. Her eyes closed almost immediately.

Scccttcchhh . . .

Anna woke to the scratchy sliding sound of the door being opened and pushing the saddlebags. She sat up and pulled the knife from the sheath, her sleepy hands fumbling as she did. Grasping the truncheon was easier. She slid to the end of the bed, trying to get her eyes to focus, and to clear her head.

She was so groggy – and tired. The words? The song? Something about going away? Why? Why?

Scccttcchhh . . . Now the door was being closed.

She could make out the vague outline of a figure padding toward the bed.

'Oh . . . you're awake and waiting, lass . . .' Madell's soft words oozed toward her.

Her head ached, and she kept trying to remember what she was going to sing. Why did it take her so long to think when she woke? She wanted to cry in frustration, even as she edged away from Madell.

'Now . . . with your fine protector gone, who will look after you, lass?' Madell whispered, his hands grasping her wrist. 'You're no sorceress, just a pretty trollop pretending to be one. You need a real man . . .'

Anna tried to think. What were the damned words? Damn! What were they? Why couldn't she think? Because she was so damned tired?

'The door?' she asked.

His hand relaxed slightly as his head turned toward the door. Anna jerked away from him, standing and holding the knife low as Albero had taught her.

'Go away ...' she murmured to herself. Finally! She had them.

In the gloom, Madell looked at the shimmering blade, and at the way she held the knife, and paused.

Anna began to sing as she stood there, trying to keep her weight balanced, hoping the words would be enough, mentally insisting that they suffice.

> 'Go away from my window,
> go away from my door.
> Oh, please go away from this heart of mine,
> and trouble me no more.'

Madell stopped short of her, as if he had run into an invisible wall. He reached toward her a second time, then recoiled.

Anna slashed with the knife, drawing a bloody line across his wrist, but Madell's lunge stopped short of her again.

'What ha' ye done to me?'

'Not nearly so much as I will,' snapped Anna, 'if you don't get out of here and leave me alone.'

Slowly, Madell backed toward the door as Anna advanced, still keeping the knife low. She wanted to kill the bastard.

Madell backed up more quickly, fumbled with the latch, opened the door, and slipped into the main room, leaving the door ajar behind him. Anna closed it slowly and pushed the saddlebags back into place.

For a long time, Anna sat on the pallet, trying not to shiver. Did she shiver because Madell might have assaulted her or because she knew, after the spell, clumsy as she was, that she could have killed the man?

What was she becoming? Did she have any choice? Why didn't anyone leave her any choice? Why?

She wanted to scream. Instead, she slipped the knife and truncheon under the pillow and lay back. Sleep eluded her for a long time, a long time filled with images of broken walls, and men flayed with fire, and Madell lusting and panting about 'a real man.'

45

Anna looked around the empty main room of the house. It didn't seem that late, but she had slept at last, surprisingly, and longer than she would have thought possible after the night before. At least Madell didn't seem to be around, for which she was thankful.

She walked across the wide plank floor toward the table. As Dalila had promised, a half loaf of bread lay there, along with something folded in cloth. Anna unwrapped the cloth – yellow cheese. Using her belt knife, she sliced off several chunks and ate them with an end of the bread. Then she sliced some more, and ate them. A third set followed. Why was she so hungry?

She hadn't been that hungry when she was young the first time. Or was it the magic? She orderspelled the water in the pitcher and poured some into a clay mug. In the end, she ate more than half of both bread and cheese, and drank nearly three mugfuls of water – she'd pay for that later, with a trip to the little house in back.

After hearing humming from the doorway at the end of the house, Anna edged toward it. The door opened into a room – or addition to the house – the size of the guest room, and two steps down to a lower level, the ground actually, as shown by the packed-clay floor. Two big wooden barrels set above the packed clay floor on square stones filled the space. Ruetha sat beside the barrel closest to the outside door, and scratched lines – or a design or picture

– in the clay. Then the little girl threw down the stick and stood.

Dalila walked through the door and poured a bucketful of water into the barrel farthest from the door, then turned and walked out, not even looking toward the doorway.

On a crude long shelf on the wall were piled heaps of clothes. Outside, Anna could hear someone – Daffyd? – chopping or splitting wood. She stepped down and looked into the tubs. The one closest to the door was empty, the one farthest about half full.

'Laundry?' Anna asked as Dalila reentered with yet another bucket.

'Washing, aye. I hate it, and there'll be more of it once there's another.' Dalila looked down at her protruding abdomen.

'I never liked laundry that much,' Anna said quietly, stepping up to the end of the table and smiling down at Ruetha, whose face was already grimy.

The little girl smiled back, shyly, then buried her head in her hands for a moment.

Anna hadn't thought about what washing would require in Liedwahr – one step above the riverbank – hot water to be heated on the stove, tubs to be filled, clothes to be hung on lines. Did Dalila heat an old-fashioned cast-iron iron on the stove, or were the clothes worn wrinkled?

'I didn't know as ladies worried about laundry.'

'The "lady" business is recent,' Anna said. 'Sin – sorceresses are far more common in the mist worlds, and I did my own laundry, but we had magic machines – everyone did – that gave us hot water ... and a few other things.'

'That would be nice.' Dalila sighed, and reached across the table to extract a work shirt from Ruetha's grasp. 'Could you sing magic like that here?'

'I don't know.' So far, she'd never really used her magic for anything useful – except for the business of lighting candles and lamps or cooling and purifying water. 'Let me think about it for a moment.'

Could she bring water to the two barrel-tubs? With a variant of her water spell?

Anna walked back to the guest room and retrieved the mandolin, still puzzling out alternative words for the water spell.

Finally, she stood in the wash room doorway, and sang.

> 'All day she'll face the laundry's tasks,
> and she'll need her casks
> of water, clear, pure water . . .'

Despite the hokey words and the inadequate rhyme scheme, water splashed in both tubs.

Dalila stopped at the nearer barrel with her bucket in hand, a puzzled and worried look on her face. 'Lady . . . I'd not ask . . . but . . . most times I have to heat the water for the one barrel.'

Anna should have known, but why not try again?

'Do you mind experimenting?' she asked.

'Experimenting? Is that a form of sorcery?' The pert brunette put down the bucket and picked up her daughter.

'Perhaps. Do you put soap in the tub with the hot water?'

'Aye.' Dalila nodded.

'And then you put in the clothes, and use the paddle there to stir and wash them?'

'Know ye another way?' Dalila's tone was both interested and faintly sardonic.

'Let's try. Put in the soap, and then the clothes.'

As Dalila glanced at Anna, a smile crossed her face. 'Perhaps you should put your clothes in?'

Anna looked down at the stained and dusty shirt and trousers, smiling in turn. 'I should. Do you have a robe – or something?'

It was the younger woman's turn to smile.

Before long, the white clothes – or those that had once been white or light-colored – were in the front tub, and

Anna stood barefooted in the doorway wrapped in a light linen robe. She hoped Madell didn't show up too soon, but in the dry heat of Defalk, she suspected that her clothes would dry soon – assuming her sorcery worked.

For some reason, Blake's *The Tyger* had kept slipping into her thoughts, and she found a way to use it.

> 'Water, water steaming hot,
> in the confines of the pot.
> Boil and bubble up to clean
> the clothes as bright as ever seen.'

A wave of heat flared back from the barrel, followed by a wave of steam.

'Mummmy!' Ruetha shrieked.

Dalila swallowed and eased back from the barrel.

Anna wiped her forehead. Had she overdone it – again? She felt tired for a moment, and she sat on the step from the kitchen into the washroom. She also realized she was hungry – again.

'Are you all right, lady?'

'I'm fine,' Anna said automatically.

'I think not.' Dalila stepped around the sorceress into the main part of the house and brought back more of the bread and cheese.

As Anna ate, wondering why such a short spell of singing should take so much energy, Dalila went back to the front tub. There, with the wooden paddle, she lifted out one sodden shirt, holding it as water vapor steamed away from it. She squinted, then moistened her lips as she carried it over to the rinsing barrel, where she dunked it before lifting it out and hand-wringing it. Then she carried the shirt out to the rope-line hung between two posts behind the kitchen door where she smoothed it before stretching it and fastening it in place with a wooden clothespin.

Dalila studied the shirt for a long moment, then walked back into the washroom.

'There were stains, lady, but they aren't there now, and I never could get them out.'

Anna looked up. 'I'm sorry.' As she said it, she wondered why she was apologizing. She'd done the best she could, but her head hurt. Was she still tired from the Sand Pass battle? Or had she done something wrong?

Dalila scooped up Ruetha and sat on the floor near Anna's feet. 'Madell was angry this morning ... He tore off some bread and he left. He was saying he was worried about the grain, but he was angry.' Dalila tightened her lips. 'I'm not fancy the way you are, and I'm not a player like Daffyd, but I've eyes to see ...' The young mother looked imploringly at Anna.

Anna took a deep breath. 'Your Madell thought I was something I'm not.'

'Aye. I saw the looks ... but you ... it was plain you were not.'

'Some men—' Anna broke off.

'Why was he so angry?'

'Because I told him to leave me alone ... and he wouldn't ... so I cast a spell to keep him from touching me.' Anna looked down at the table. 'I'm sorry. Perhaps I should go.'

'You're still tired, aren't you?'

'Yes,' Anna admitted.

'But you used your magic to help me?' Dalila gestured to the tubs.

'I wish I could do more. The song magic here in Liedwahr is new to me.' Anna glanced down at the three-year-old, who looked back with steady eyes for a time.

Dalila offered a wan smile. 'Best I finish these clothes, and put the others in.'

Daffyd looked in from the doorway between the washroom and the kitchen end of the main room. He held the ax loosely. 'I thought you needed wood to heat the water.'

'The lady Anna heated it,' Dalila said, bending down to disengage Ruetha's hand from the washing paddle that Dalila had momentarily leaned against the barrel as she wrung out a shirt. The three-year-old grabbed a dangling lock of hair and pulled, but her mother disengaged her daughter's grip with a gentle movement and a smile.

'You mean that I chopped this all for nothing?'

'No. It'll be used, little brother. After you and your sorceress friend leave, there will be many weeks where I need wood.' Dalila forced a smile. 'Please, would you split some more?' Dalila added, 'Please?'

'As you wish.' Daffyd looked from one woman's face to the other. 'As you wish.' He picked up the ax and retreated, shaking his head.

Anna slowly finished the remainder of the bread.

'Are you interested in Daffyd?'

Anna's mouth dropped open. 'You . . .' Then the sorceress realized that Dalila did not see Anna as Anna saw herself. 'I had better explain, Dalila. I am older than I look. I have a son older than you are, and a daughter who is Daffyd's age. I did have a daughter who was even older, but she died several months ago.'

'Months?'

'Seven or eight weeks ago.' Had it been that long? 'Daffyd can tell you. I looked older when I came to Liedwahr, but some magic in the battle changed me. It was a surprise to me.'

'A not unwelcome one, I wager,' Dalila said.

'I don't know. Had I looked the way I did, Madell would not have been so interested. I wonder if any man will take me seriously.' *Especially in this culture.*

'I had not thought that way.' Dalila frowned. 'Having Ruetha was not easy, for all that Hersa said it was a good birth. To raise children, and then to have one die . . . and have the chance to start again . . .' She shook her head, then offered a brief smile as she reached for another shirt – Anna's.

'I can wring that out.' Anna stood.

'Ye be sure of that?'

'I'm sure.'

Ruetha began to whimper, and Dalila looked at the barrel still filled with warm water and clothes.

'You feed her,' Anna said, taking her shirt. 'I can manage this.' She added, 'Enjoy your daughter.'

That got a smile of sorts as Dalila retreated to the kitchen.

The mechanical work of lifting out each article from the hot tub and rinsing it, then wringing it and carrying it out to hang, was almost a relief to Anna.

As she finished the last of the whitish items and dropped the darker clothes into the hot tub, Daffyd appeared at her shoulder, looking toward the kitchen area where Ruetha sat at one side of the table chewing on more of the dark bread, then back at Anna. He smiled as he looked at the ground.

Anna had to smile, too, thinking about walking around in a gown with boots, but she had neither sandals nor slippers.

'What did ye do to Madell?' asked Daffyd, again glancing toward the kitchen.

'He tried to overpower me last night,' Anna said quietly. 'I managed a spellsong, one that demanded that he trouble me no more.'

'He hates you, and he'll be telling tales to Dalila, if he hasn't already.'

'We've talked about it, in a quiet way,' Anna said. 'Madell won't be any trouble to me.' She wondered, though, how much trouble the miller would cause for Dalila. Anna liked the pert brunette. The problem was that using spellsong led to using more song. Wasn't there any end to it? Anna tried not to sigh. 'I should go back to Mencha.'

'That's where the dark ones will be, as I stand here.'

'Stand back,' Anna said before repeating the laundry spell. Then she retrieved a pair of trousers and rinsed them, then wrung them.

'I can do that,' said Daffyd.

'So can I. But I can't finish that lutar, and I suspect you're better at chopping and splitting wood than I am.'

'You should go to Falcor,' suggested Daffyd, 'or, better yet, Elhi. Lord Jecks would help you.'

'I don't know,' Anna said. 'That doesn't feel right.' She didn't even know why it didn't feel right, but things felt unfinished in Synope, although she knew she shouldn't stay.

46

In the morning light, Anna sat at the table, her hair damp. Sooner or later, the way it was growing, she was going to have to cut it, or wear it permanently in a bun of some sort.

She broke off another piece of bread and offered it to Ruetha. The little girl grinned shyly.

'You can have some, Ruetha,' said Dalila.

'She looks funny,' said the daughter.

Anna supposed she did, with damp thick hair that had more curl than she remembered, but Dalila had said she could use one of the tubs in the washroom for a bath, and the water spell had gotten her hot water. She felt cleaner than she had in weeks, even if water were dripping down her neck onto the collar of the clean shirt. She'd left off the tunic; it was too hot to wear inside.

She'd blotted herself as dry as she could – Defalk wasn't big on large towels – but then she suspected that, given the difficulty in getting water, Defalk wasn't big on washing. In dressing, she'd noticed that she could almost make out her ribs. Had she ever been able to do that?

'So do you,' Dalila pointed out to her daughter, standing at the worktable kneading dough. Dalila also looked damp, since the brunette had followed Anna into the tub and given her daughter a good scrubbing.

After the solemn-eyed Ruetha took the bread, Anna – still hungry – broke off another piece, and slowly chewed through it, occasionally eating from a small wedge of very hard yellow cheese.

'You will spoil us, Lady Anna. Warm water without fires, and laundry that does not take all day.' Dalila glanced toward the corner of the room where Daffyd had laid out the pieces of the unfinished lutar. 'Daffyd, you should have bathed.'

'There wasn't any point to it. I'll get hot and dirty, and besides I have to finish this.' The young player slowly eased the backpiece of the lutar into place. The odor of glue permeated the room, already hot, even though it was not even mid-morning. 'I'll bathe later, if I can persuade the sorceress to provide the same luxury for me.'

'Such industry deserves some luxury,' Anna said lightly.

'Well, you said you needed this.'

'I do. Or I will. Unfortunately.'

'It is unfortunate to be a sorceress?' asked Dalila as she rolled the dough into a ball.

'I hope not.' Anna half forced a laugh. 'But it is unfortunate to be a sorceress who seems to be more regarded for the damage she can create than the good she can do. Laundry and bathwater are more constructive than trying to hurt soldiers.'

'Mayhap,' said Daffyd from the corner, where he was setting some glue clamps. 'Sometimes the soldiers kill people, though, and it's useful to keep them from killing.' He grinned ruefully. 'Especially when it's me you kept them from slaughtering.'

'Aye, force has to be stopped with force, and those who can't . . .' Dalila's lips tightened.

Anna thought of the slamming door. She had been awake since not much after dawn when the slamming door had reverberated through the house. Madell had not been at dinner the night before, and he had left early.

'Is Madell busy with that Ranuan grain?' the sorceress asked blandly.

'He left early, lady.'

Anna backed off. 'Thank you for the bread. It's good. Everything you cook is good.'

'I doubt it's like that in a great hall.'

'No,' Anna said. 'It's better. I mean it.'

That got a brief smile before Dalila turned to Ruetha. 'Best you come here, girl, and give your mother a hug.'

Anna swallowed.

'There!' interjected Daffyd, stretching. 'That's about all I can do for now. A few more days, and we'll see what this beast sounds like.' He turned to his sister. 'I'm making a strange instrument for her.'

'Oh?'

'She paid me, in coin,' Daffyd said.

'And what is it?' Dalila's voice was somewhat warmer, and Anna was reminded that food was not cheap, from what she recalled, in less mechanized cultures.

'It is like a lute, with six strings, but the backplate is flat and the strings tuned lower.'

Dalila nodded and began to mix up something else, dismissing both of them in her concentration.

'Daffyd? Can you remember that mirror song? The one Jenny used.'

'I can play the melody, but the words have to change for what you want to look at.'

'That's fine. Does your sister have – oh, we can use the one on the wall in the guest room.' Anna paused.

The two walked into the small room, and Daffyd played the tune twice and spoke the words for Anna. After several tries she thought she had some words that would work.

'Are you ready?'

'Ready as you are, lady.'

Anna nodded; Daffyd played; and Anna sang.

> 'Mirror, mirror that I see,
> Show now me now who looks for me.
> Show them bright, and show them fast,
> and make that strong picture last.'

As Anna completed the song, and Daffyd lowered the viola, the surface of the mirror swirled into four quarters.

In the upper right corner was a figure clad in a dark hooded robe, apparently within a darkened room. In the upper left was a man with reddish blond hair and a matching beard. He sat in a thronelike chair before pillars and wore a cream-colored tunic. In the lower right was a short blonde-haired woman with penetrating green eyes, who seemed to look straight out of the mirror at Anna. And in the lower left was a white-haired woman with a thin face in a deep-blue and high-collared shirt.

For a time, Anna studied the figures, and only the green-eyed woman seemed aware of the scrutiny. Just before the images faded, she offered a sardonic smile.

Anna blotted her forehead, damp not just from the unending heat of Synope and Defalk. 'Who were they? I suppose the one in the dark robes was one of the Dark Monks from Ebra, but what of the others?'

Daffyd wiped the sweat off his forehead before answering. 'The older woman in blue – that's the color of the motherhood, and they run Ranuak. The blond-bearded man – if I had to guess, that would be Behlem, the Prophet of Music. He be the one who sent his troops to Falcor. The woman in green . . .' He shrugged.

'I'd guess she's from whatever country that surrounds Defalk that the others aren't.'

'Nordwei? Why would the Norweians be seeking you?'

'Why would any of them – except for the Ebrans – be looking for me?' Anna replied.

'Aye . . . you are the sorceress.'

'Where's Madell?' Anna asked, knowing the answer, but wanting Daffyd's reaction.

'He left early. Mayhap he never came home. He'd never wish to see your face again.'

Daffyd's words were cool, and that bothered Anna. She pursed her lips. She didn't like what she felt. Because she'd repulsed Madell, was he taking his aggressions out on Dalila – one way or another? But what could she do?

Everything she did led to something else.

The thought nagged at her. She just couldn't go off and leave Daffyd's sister unprotected. She'd have to think of something. Something that wouldn't backfire, or lead to something else.

She also needed to do a few other things.

'Daffyd?'

'Yes, lady?'

'We need to go shopping.'

'Shopping?'

'I can't let your sister keep feeding us.'

'But that's guesting.'

'She can cook. I'm spoiled enough that I enjoy good cooking, but can't we buy some food?'

The young player smiled. 'Aye. I don't think she'd mind.'

'Besides, I can't afford to get out of shape for riding.'

Daffyd shook his head.

47

You can't keep doing this . . .'

The low words seemed to hiss through the gray of the early morning, and Anna bolted upright in the narrow and lumpy pallet bed, not that she had slept that well, with nightmares of various shadowy figures chasing her through improbable settings, none of which she could remember clearly.

Her head ached, and her eyes were gummy.

'I'll do as I please, woman . . . and you and that witch won't stop me . . .'

Anger seared through Anna, and she pulled on her clothes and slipped out of the guest room and into the main room barefoot, saying under her breath the words she had composed the night before, repeating them as she moved, mandolin in hand.

'. . . your brother, never up to any good . . . bringing *her* here . . .'

As Anna tiptoed through the predawn gloom, Dalila stood on one side of the table, and Madell on the other, his back to Anna. Daffyd was presumably still sleeping the sleep of the dissolute young in the small loft after staying up late talking with Dalila.

Dalila's eyes widened.

Madell turned, his eyes met Anna's only briefly before darting away. 'I was just leaving, Lady Anna.'

Anna's finger's caressed the strings.

> 'Madell wrong, Madell strong,
> treat her right from this song.
> Madell warm, Madell cold,
> gentle be till dead and old.'

Dalila's mouth opened, then shut.

Madell swallowed, started toward Anna, then slowly sank onto the bench. 'Why . . .' he whispered. 'Why me? Why did you have to enter my life?'

Anna looked at him, feeling some pity in spite of herself. 'I could ask the same question, Madell. Why did you try to force yourself on me? Why was I picked up and taken from my own world? Why me?' She swallowed. 'I don't have an answer, except I felt guilty because you were hurting Dalila because I rejected you.'

Madell looked down, and Anna could feel the hatred.

'You should be thankful that I like Dalila. Very thankful,' Anna said slowly. 'I could have killed you.'

'Better you had. Better you had.'

'Let me get this straight. All I have done is insisted that you not bother me, and that you treat Dalila kindly. You would rather die than behave decently? Does the ability to abuse women mean that much to you?' Anna caught a flicker of movement in the doorway to the kitchen area, but Daffyd ducked back into the washroom before anyone but Anna saw him.

'I have no choice . . .' Madell said slowly, looking down.

Anna snorted. 'I didn't have much choice about coming to your world. I didn't have much choice about leaving my children behind. Half the powers in this world are looking for me, and I didn't have much choice about that.' She paused. 'You have plenty of choices. You can whimper about being forced to be decent, or you can learn to live with it.' After a moment, Anna added, 'I didn't compel you to be good to anyone else . . . but if I find that you're hurting other people, sooner or later I will find out, and then you'll find out just how nasty I can really be. Do you understand?'

The miller just sat on the bench, looking at the empty tabletop.

Anna turned to Dalila. 'I'm sorry. Every time I try to protect myself or someone else, then some other person gets hurt.'

For a moment, Dalila looked puzzled. Then she nodded slowly. 'You do not like to hurt people, do you?'

'No. In a way, that is why I should have left. But I had nowhere to go . . . or I thought I didn't.' Anna's eyes went back to Madell. 'Within a day or two, I'll be gone, and I hope you can put things back together.'

'But . . .' protested Dalila, 'where will you go?'

'Where I must. Where I must.'

48

ITZEL, NESEREA

After fingering his beard, Behlem touches the silver goblet. The terrace of the Temple of Music where he sits overlooks the triangle in the river. Nearly a dek downhill, the Saria and the Essis Rivers join to form the Sariss. 'What do you think of it?'

'Itzel's a pretty-enough place,' Menares agrees guardedly. 'I prefer Esaria.'

'You just don't like to travel. You'd better get used to it, though. You'll be headed to Falcor as fast as you can, and then wherever necessary.'

'Wherever necessary?' The older man covers a swallow with a bright smile.

'We need to find the sorceress that Brill brought to Liedwahr, and get her to support us.' Behlem nods. 'That's your job, old friend.' He lifts the goblet and takes a small sip.

'Is that wise, ser? To bring someone like that into your . . . circle?' asks Menares. 'Why would she even consider it?' His goblet remains untouched.

'First, it's very wise. Second, since everyone else wants to kill her, sooner or later our hospitality will make her either grateful or at least willing to throw in with us. She's staying in a hovel somewhere at the moment, and that indicates how few appreciate her talents.'

'Those talents could turn on you, ser. You have no idea what this . . . woman . . . is really like.'

'I could care less if she's an old hag or a bitch that would make Cyndyth look like a meek maiden. She destroyed almost half of the darksingers of Ebra in one battle. Can you find me a sorcerer like that anywhere else?'

'I don't know. Do you want one that powerful?'

'Do you have any better ideas for defeating Eladdrin?'

Menares spreads his hands. 'Besides, how would one find her?'

'It shouldn't be that hard. Sorceresses aren't that loved. I'll leave the details to you, Menares.' Behlem smiles. 'She is to be treated as if she were the highest lady in the land. If she's found dead, or maimed, or injured, you have the choice of death or exile to Ebra or Mansuur.'

'Ser?'

'You know coins, trade, that sort of thing, Menares, and scheming. There's more to you than meets the eye, old friend and tutor. But there are some things I know. If I can defeat the Ebrans and unite Defalk and Neserea, and if this sorceress can break the darksingers, then the rains will return, and Neserea will be more powerful than Mansuur or Ranuak.'

'There are a great many *if*'s there, ser.'

'So there are . . . but you are the one who pointed out my limits. Why are you so doubtful about my attempts to change them?'

'I remain your servant, my lord.'

'Menares, you are no man's servant, not mine, nor even that of the spymistress of Nordwei. So let us have no false modesty.' Behlem raises his goblet dramatically, but little of the wine actually passes his lips.

'Ser . . .'

'You are leaving with a detachment of lancers in the morning. I won't be far behind you.' Behlem pauses. 'And Cyndyth won't be that far behind either of us. Nor Rabyn. Nor the couriers from Mansuur.'

'Yes, ser.' Menares looks at the goblet before him on the white linen cloth, but does not lift it.

49

We need to go riding,' Anna insisted.

'We?' asked Daffyd.

'I need to go riding, and you need to guide me and keep me out of trouble,' Anna said with a laugh, before lowering her voice and adding, 'And Dalila needs us out of her hair.'

'Oh . . .'

'Is there anything else you need to do with the lutar right now?'

'The glue has to set.'

'How soon before it's ready to use?' she asked.

'It needs at least a coat of varnish. Might be as I could get some from Pelnmor. Say . . . a few days to dry after that.'

'We can't stay much longer.' Anna frowned. 'Or I can't. Perhaps I can pay my respects to Lord Hryding in the next day or two.' She broke off as Dalila carted Ruetha into the main room.

'Young woman . . . I cannot set you down for a moment, and you are in the dirt pouring dust in your hair.' Dalila set her daughter on the tabletop with a thump.

Anna wanted to laugh. Mario had been the same way – into everything all the time. It was funny, and it wasn't. Instead, she asked, 'We're going out for a while. Is there anything else we could get you?'

'Lady Anna . . . you are the guest. You brought so many things yesterday . . .'

'You have been kind and hospitable to a stranger in a strange land . . .' Anna tried to conceal a wince. That phrase – hadn't it been the title of one of those damned science-fiction books Avery had buried his nose in when she'd tried to talk to him? Avery – Antonio Marsali, the great culture king, who read more science fiction than opera librettos, and she was the one living it. The irony was almost too much.

Dalila shook her head. 'If only more ladies were as you—' She lurched for her daughter, who was inching toward the end of the table. 'No, Ruetha. You will be the death of me.'

'She is lively,' Anna commented.

'Like the sun is bright.' Daffyd laughed.

Dalila gave a rueful grin as she picked up her daughter again. 'We need to make bread. You can make a little loaf all by yourself.'

Anna's mouth watered at the idea of bread. Why was she always thinking about food and eating?

'Can I?' came the childish question.

'Yes,' answered Dalila.

'Are you certain we cannot get you anything?' Anna asked.

'Not today. I must cook what we have.' Dalila smiled over her shoulder. 'And let Ruetha bake her bread.'

Anna pulled on the now clean floppy-brimmed hat, and the player and the sorceress walked out to the rear stables.

Again, the late-morning sun had turned Synope into a dry, hot oven.

Farinelli whinnied as Anna approached.

'Thirsty? Hungry?' she asked, although there was some grain in his manger. The bucket had some water, but Anna walked to the well for more, which she orderspelled before pouring into the horse bucket.

'Why must you offer so much to Dalila? Madell has not been kind to you.' Daffyd led the gray mare out into the sunlight that seemed unending.

'I haven't been kind to him, either, I suppose.' Anna tightened the second cinch, straightened up, and untied the leads.

'You cursed him with kindness, did you not?'

'I forced him to be kind to Dalila.'

'He has not always been kind. So that is good.'

'I don't know.' Farinelli whuffled as Anna climbed into the saddle. She patted his shoulder. 'Don't be so eager. Before long, you'll get plenty of exercise.' Then she turned to Daffyd as they rode out of the yard. 'People don't change, and one thing leads to another. I protect myself from Madell, and he gets angry at Dalila and wants to hurt her. I stop that, but that doesn't make him less angry. Will he beat his horse? Someone else?'

Neither spoke as they rode to the end of the lane, and Anna turned the gelding back toward the center of Synope.

The fine dust rose with each step the gelding took, rising in the still hot air and hanging for an instant, then clinging to Farinelli's legs, while some rose enough to irritate Anna's nose.

'Does it ever rain here?'

'Not unless it comes from the north, or sometimes the south. The rains used to come mostly from the east, and the dark ones—'

'—stopped that,' Anna finished.

'What do you know about Lord Hryding?' asked Anna.

'He's supposed to be fair, but he's never gotten along well, so they say, with either Lord Barjim or his uncle who used to be Lord of Defalk.'

'That's a barrel-maker's?' asked Anna as they rode past the shop with the half barrel mounted above the partly open door.

'That's old Fesrik's. He's some sort of cousin of Madell's. Dalila said he's been the only cooper in town since the drought began.'

As they rode westward, Anna studied the center of Synope, more carefully now that she was more rested. 'What's the stone platform for?'

'Used to be where they made announcements on market day, or where traveling dramaturges performed. Most towns have platzes, but market days haven't been much lately, and no one can spare coppers for a dramaturge or a troupe.'

'And Yuril's? What does he sell?' Anna guessed that the green sign signified something for sale, although she didn't know what the crossed candles meant.

'Some of just about everything. Most chandleries do. Leather goods, travel food, bedrolls, candles, of course . . .'

'What's to the south?' Anna gestured to her left.

'That leads to the bridge, the one over the Synor River, and the road to Sudwei. Sudwei is at the north entrance to the South Pass. That's the only real trade road left to Ranuak.'

Anna struggled, trying to fit Sudwei into her mental map of Defalk. 'You mentioned some lord there once?'

'Geansor. He was crippled in putting down a peasant uprising. They say the leaders were paid by those women in Ranuak.' Daffyd shrugged. 'I would not know, but I guess he had to be most careful in balancing between Barjim and the matriarchs, especially since he cannot ride or lead his levies.'

Anna wanted to shake her head. Did it always come down to military ability?

50

Just after mid-morning Anna and Daffyd rode west past the center of Synope toward the Synor River – and Lord Hryding's holding. Although it was far earlier in the day than when she and Daffyd had first entered the town, or on their previous rides, the town center still looked nearly deserted.

A single horse stood outside Yuril's, and two women crossed the square from the Cup and Bowl, wearing hats with brims wider than Anna's as protection against the endless sun. Each step they took raised a puff of the fine red dust.

Anna patted Farinelli and could feel the long tail swish behind her, seeking one of the infrequent flies that bit hard enough to draw blood. Anna involuntarily raised her hand to brush the unseen insect from the vicinity of the back of her neck.

She shifted her weight in the saddle. With each hour – or glass – the past days had felt more and more confining, as if an unseen noose, or something, were being tightened around her. The mirror images of the four seeking her hadn't helped that feeling.

His nose itched, and she rubbed it gently.

A yellow dog lay in the shade of an empty water barrel beside a vacant dwelling, its shutters askew. The dog barely looked up as the two rode past.

'Will the lutar be ready tomorrow?' Anna asked.

'You ask every day, but . . . yes, it will be ready.' Daffyd paused. 'What it will sound like – that I do not know.'

'I don't, either, but let's hope it's halfway melodic . . . and loud.'

'Why are you going to see Lord Hryding? I asked before, and you did not say.'

'Call it politics,' Anna explained.

'Is that another one of your strange magics?'

'I wouldn't call it magic, but it is an art, one at which I haven't been as good as I should have been.' She looked westward. 'Is that it?'

From a distance, the building on the low hill overlooking the river resembled an Italian or Mediterranean villa, with blank white walls that appeared to surround a central courtyard.

'Yes, and the banner says that he is home.'

As they rode nearer, Anna could make out a low wall, slightly less than three yards tall, which circled the hall.

Less than a dek farther along, a side road led to a gate in the wall – less than a few hundred yards from the main road. The unguarded iron-bound wooden gates were hinged open, and did not look as though they had been closed in years.

Halfway up the hill on the right side, they passed an orchard similar in layout to that of Brill's except the trees were those Anna had seen on the way into Synope.

'Olive trees?'

'That is what Dalila told me.'

On the southern side of the road was a long wooden shed, and in the shade several chickens pecked at the ground. Farinelli *whuff*ed and tossed his head slightly.

'They're only chickens.' Anna patted the gelding.

About fifty yards short of the white-walled villa, a hitching rail had been provided under a slanted tiled roof, with a stone water trough beneath as well. A curved stone path ran from the roofed area toward the hall or villa.

Anna reined up, dismounted, and tied up Farinelli near the middle, where it would remain shady as the day progressed.

She patted his shoulder. 'You stay here. You get water, anyway.' After extracting the mandolin from the left saddlebag, Anna started up the walkway, and Daffyd hurried to catch up to her.

A young and stocky armsman watched from beside the covered archway that was presumably the entrance to the villa. There were no windows on the ground level, and but a few on the second level, all with heavy shutters. The third level had a number of windows, and several were even open.

The other concessions to defense or the violent nature of Liedwahr were the thick walls and the crenelated parapets above the walls, although the highest point on the villa walls could not have been more than ten yards above the ground in front of the arched entrance.

The two heavy and iron-banded doors to the archway were open, and the single armsman in a pale green tunic stood in the shade of the curved roof that projected out from the archway that held the doors.

Anna let Daffyd take the lead.

'This is the lady Anna. She is a sorceress here to pay her respects to Lord Hryding,' Daffyd announced.

'You don't exactly look like a lady,' observed the guard. 'These days everyone wants to see Lord Hryding.'

Daffyd frowned. 'Give him a spell.'

The armsman did not quite smirk.

'Are you thirsty?' Anna asked. 'Would you like some cold clear water?'

'Sure, and how will you deliver it? With that little sound box?'

Anna strummed the mandolin.

'Since now he's faced this duty's waste
without of a taste of cool, clear water,
shower him now with water cold and clear ...'

The equivalent of several gallons of freezing water cascaded over the armsman.

Anna stepped back, and began to sing the repulsion spell even before the guard stepped forward.

He bounced almost against the stones.

'Now . . .' Anna said sweetly, 'I could have turned you into a flame, but I didn't. Do you think I'm a sorceress or not?'

'Calmut!'

Anna looked up. A silver-headed man, dressed in pale green, with a broad smile on his face, leaned out of the parapet above.

'Yes, ser?' The guard looked up.

'I would be most happy to receive the lady. I also think you need to help Sestor muck the stables later. I appreciate your checking on the lady's abilities, but I have to question your brains in trying to attack after she proves them.' The green-clad lord added, 'And I appreciate your forbearance, lady. Loyalty is hard to find these days.'

Calmut stepped aside, then opened the door, his lips tight. 'Take the stairs there, all the way to the top.'

As Anna and Daffyd started up the wide stone stairs, the guard slowly retreated to the front door, shaking his head, and the water from his hair.

The silver-haired lord waited at the top of the steps, a smile upon his tanned face. 'I am Lord Hryding.'

Anna bowed. 'I am Anna, and this is Daffyd.' She felt that Hryding was honest, though she couldn't have said why.

'Let us go out to the roof garden, and you can tell me why you have chosen to honor an old man.' Hryding gestured down a short arched hallway that showed greenery and sky at the end.

Anna stepped out of the arched corridor into relative coolness and shade. An awning stretched from above the arched doorway out to the roof garden, and a round-faced woman with frizzy, henna-colored hair sat at the round wooden table under the awning. She was younger than Hryding, in her early thirties, or younger, Anna judged, since life was obviously harder in Liedwahr than on earth.

The garden behind the table where the woman sat was

small, four yards wide and a dozen long, bordered by brick-edged flower boxes filled with red and pink blooms, and containing several small palmlike trees.

Anna looked around. The third level of the hall consisted of rooms opening onto a tiled terrace that encircled and overlooked the central courtyard. Each room had both shuttered windows and a louvered door – probably for ventilation. Beyond the edge of the garden was a waist-high wall that also followed the terrace all the way around the hall's upper level, providing a barrier between the terrace and the two-story drop-off to the courtyard below. Some trees growing up from the courtyard's lowest level protruded above the wall, and a hint of moisture suggested to Anna that the lower courtyard might have a fountain.

'This is my consort Anientta. Dear, this is the lady Anna, and her player Daffyd.'

'You are young,' said Anientta, nodding her head politely. 'What brings you to Flossbend?'

Hryding picked up a small bell and rang it gently. 'Please be seated.' He gestured to the chair beside Anientta, then looked at Daffyd and nodded toward the empty seat on his consort's right.

Anna slipped into the curved wooden armchair, surprisingly comfortable despite its lack of upholstery. 'Thank you.' She turned to Anientta. 'I am new to Liedwahr, and I wanted to pay my respects.'

'New to Liedwahr . . .' mused Hryding. 'Your words do have an odd flavor to them.' He took the chair across the table from the three, looking up as a slim youth in a sleeveless pale green tunic and matching trousers appeared. 'Nerio . . . some of the cold berry juice, if you please, for all of us.'

The youth bowed and turned, then headed back through the archway.

'From where have you come? Far Sturinn? Or the Western Isles? Or cold Pelara? You look Pelaran with that blonde hair.' Anientta smiled indulgently.

Anna forced herself to return the smile, even though

she disliked the other woman's condescending tone. 'Much
farther . . .'

'She is a sorceress,' suggested Hryding. 'I had to laugh
when she doused poor Calmut with ice water. He was so
angry he tried to jump her, but Lady Anna was merciful.
She just bounced him back a few paces.'

Anientta's frown was brief. 'A sorceress? Are you perhaps
looking for a patron?'

Anna shook her head. She hadn't even answered the last
question. 'No. I am very new here. Do most sorcerers or
sorceresses have patrons?'

'Some sorcerers do,' Hryding said. 'Most sorceresses do. I
think the Lady Peuletar was the last independent sorceress,
but she died when I wasn't much more than a boy. Lord
Brill, the harmonies rest his soul, was independent . . .' His
words stopped, and his eyes sharpened. 'I am unintelligent.
Are you the sorceress who was at the Sand Pass battle?'

Anna nodded.

'Is it true that you were summoned from the mist worlds?'

'Yes,' Anna admitted. 'You can see why I am not familiar
with the customs of your world.'

'It was said that you perished with Lord Brill.'

'I had some difficulty,' Anna said, hating to admit the
weakness, 'and Daffyd carried me out.' She paused as the
young server Nerio appeared with a tray, a pitcher, and four
goblets.

As Nerio filled the pewterlike goblets, Hryding cleared his
throat and lifted a goblet. 'Would you honor us with your
presence here at Flossbend, Lady Anna, for a few days?'

'I appreciate the offer, Lord Hryding, but it might be best
if I did not impose upon your hospitality – not for long,
anyway.'

Hryding's face clouded, and he half lowered the goblet.

'I do not wish to offend you,' Anna said. 'But so far almost
every lord who has offered me hospitality for any lengthy
period is dead.' That was true. Although Anna doubted
she was exactly the reason, she felt staying at Flossbend

would not be a good idea with Anientta's unspoken hostility, although the lord's offer was certainly tempting, especially given the strain created by Madell.

'Surely, one day would not cause great problems?'

'For a day or so I would be most pleased and honored,' Anna said, 'but more than that would trouble my conscience.'

'We should begin with a midday meal, then.'

Anna grinned. 'That would be no problem, and I deeply appreciate your warmth and hospitality.'

Again, Anna caught the tinge of irritation or anger from Anientta.

Hryding lifted the bell, and before the echo had died away, Nerio had reappeared.

'The midday repast for all of us, and the children, and Gestatr and our guests. Tell Gestatr that I would greatly appreciate his presence. We will use the west awning.'

Nerio nodded and slipped away.

Anna wondered what other people were hidden away – guards and the like.

'How do you find our land?' asked Anientta pleasantly.

'Hot ... very dry,' Anna said. 'I am told that the dark ones have caused the dryness.'

'So say the sorcerers, and, I must admit, I do not recall any years since my boyhood that were as dry as the last four or five,' Hryding said slowly. 'It is hard to believe that they have such power.'

'They do,' replied Anna, thinking of the massive storm clouds and the lightnings that had smashed the fort.

'How is it—' began Hryding.

'And the people, what of them?' asked Anientta. 'Are we so different?'

'I have not met that many people besides sorcerers, players, and armsmen, but those I have met seem like people anywhere.' Anna turned to Hryding. 'You were asking, lord?'

'Oh ... it will wait.' The older man smiled pleasantly.

'Are you really from the mist worlds?' asked Anientta.

'Not all of them, if there are more than one. My planet is called earth.'

'You were a sorceress there, also?' pursued Anientta.

'Sorcery is not quite the same there, but, yes, I used singing to make my way.'

'"Make your way" ... that is an odd way of saying it. Are not sorcerers respected there?' Anientta raised an eyebrow.

'Sorcerers and sorceresses are not as powerful as the technology wizards, not in my land,' Anna said carefully. 'Our worlds are very different in that way. The technology wizards build steel birds ... that carry hundreds of men thousands of leagues in the air, or they can destroy whole cities in the blink of an eye.'

'Could not you have brought such magics here? Rather than uncertain sorcery?' asked Anientta.

'Such technology magic does not work here. I brought a few things, but they are useless.' Anna forced a smile, repeating, 'Our worlds are different.'

Anientta opened her mouth, then closed it as a square-faced man with short-cut black hair walked up and stopped short of the table. His leathers were worn, but clean, and he wore a pale green sash. A blade hung from the left side of his worn and broad belt, matched by a knife on the right. 'You sent for me, lord?'

Hryding rose. 'I did. Might I present you to the lady Anna? This is my captain Gestatr.'

Anna stood also. She had seen the man before, although she did not know where, but it had to have been at the Sand Pass fort, since it could have been nowhere else.

'Lady.' Gestatr inclined his head.

'Captain. Did I see you at the Sand Pass?'

'Yes, lady.' Gestatr looked at Anna. 'Lady ... you are the same ... and different, but I cannot say how.'

'Battles have a way of changing things,' Daffyd suggested.

'That they do, master player. That they do.' The captain

slipped into the chair that Nerio had brought. 'But the lady appears ... more rested ... younger.'

Anna and Hryding sat down.

'You were in charge of Lord Hryding's forces ...' ventured Daffyd.

Gestatr glanced toward the lord, then nodded. 'There were not many of us there. Synope has one of the lower calls.' He laughed, almost bitterly. 'That was what saved us. We were marshaled above the stables, to provide assistance to larger groups. Afterwards, Captain Firis – he was some lord's captain – just told us to head home, that our lord would need us in the days to come.' Gestatr laughed. 'So we did. No one seemed to want us, and there wasn't much point in throwing away less than twoscore lives.'

'Your call was only twoscore?' asked Anna. Lord Jecks had been required to bring ten times that.

'Unhappily ... no. We had fourscore. Twoscore is what I brought back, and reckoned us lucky for that after the thunderbolts and the Ebran archers.'

Nerio reappeared. 'The table is ready, ser.'

'Good.' Hryding stood.

So did everyone else.

Anna and Daffyd followed the lord and his lady out from under the high awning and into the sunlight, along the terrace wall. Gestatr walked on Anna's left.

In the courtyard below was a central plaza surrounded by a miniature park, with grass, trees, flowers, and the fountain Anna had predicted. The group walked halfway around the upper level of the hall until they stood under a second awning almost directly across the courtyard from where they had been sitting. The long table, covered with a pale green cloth, was set for seven, a place at the head, and three on each side.

Hryding stopped behind the head chair and gestured to the place at his left. 'Lady Anna.' Then to the place beside Anna. 'Ser player.'

'The children?' asked the lord, still standing.

'I hear them,' answered Anientta.

The ubiquitous Nerio arrived, following a boy and a smaller girl, almost as though the servitor were a rear guard.

'This is Kurik.' Anientta smiled at the sandy-haired boy. 'He's ten. His older brother Jeron is out riding with my sire today.'

Kurik was a square and stocky boy with a too-round face and a spoiled look about him that Anna didn't like. His smile was perfunctory, and his bow more so.

Standing at the corner of the table was a petite red-haired girl with bright green eyes. Like her brother, she wore a pale green armless tunic, trimmed in silver, and trousers. She was barefoot, while Kurik wore boots. That bothered Anna. So did the fact that Kurik plopped himself into his chair beside his mother's place without even a glance at either his father or mother.

'This is Secca. She is my youngest.' Anientta's smile was marginally tighter.

The redheaded girl nodded, and bowed to her father.

'You may sit,' Hryding said. 'Everyone . . . please.'

Anna was glad of that. She'd not drunk much of the berry juice, and her head hurt. Hunger did that to her, and she'd been a lot hungrier of late, a lot hungrier. She slipped into the high-backed wooden chair, following Hryding's example.

Secca reminded Anna of Elizabetta, and the sorceress's eyes filled. Anna swallowed, and looked down. 'She's precious . . .' the sorceress said huskily, and looked down.

'You are upset by a child?' asked Anientta, drawing her chair up to the table.

'No – not upset, not that way. I was summoned here . . . and my children . . . they . . .' Anna tightened her lips and shook her head. Battles she could handle, and lecherous men, and riding, and wounds – but not children.

'You are so young . . . so very young.'

Anna ignored the condescending tone and blotted her eyes, hating herself for revealing the pain. 'My oldest daughter would have been almost as old as you, Lady Anientta. My son is twenty-four, and my youngest daughter, who looked like . . . Secca here . . . she is eighteen.'

Hryding was the one to swallow. 'Even for a sorceress . . . that is hard to believe . . . Your seeming youth . . .'

'The price was high. Very high, and it wasn't even my choice.' Anna looked down at the neatly arranged apple slices on the plate at her place, then toward Secca.

Hryding and Anientta glanced toward Daffyd.

'She did not seek it. Somehow it happened when Lord Brill died and the darksingers were trying to bring down the fort. Lady Anna destroyed the darksingers close to the fort and almost half the Ebran armsmen before she could do no more.' Daffyd offered a shrug.

'I thought sorceresses could do anything they wanted,' Secca announced.

'Oh, how I wish . . .' Anna smiled at the girl. 'You do look like Elizabetta.'

'Elizabetta – that's a pretty name. Is she pretty?'

'She is, just like you are.'

Secca blushed.

'Ahh . . .' Gestatr cleared his throat. 'I did see part of that, Lady Anientta. The sorceress stood on the open battlements and threw her own whips of fire at the Ebrans. She destroyed more than half their forces. That's why we got away after they crushed the walls. They had to bring up reinforcements from deks back.' He nodded toward Anna. 'I saw her fall. That's why I thought they'd felled her.'

'I did fall,' Anna said.

'But why, if you are so great?' asked Anientta.

Anna wanted to flame the bitchy lady, who seemed determined to put Anna down with every word.

'It's like a horse, or a runner, that gallops at full speed. That's sorcery,' Daffyd explained. 'You run too long, and you fall. Sometimes, sorcerers die from trying to do too much. Lady Anna was trying to hold back the Ebrans by herself after Lord Brill died. She killed so many that the

moat was filled with bodies, but the dark ones kept coming.'
The player shivered.

'You must be the most powerful sorceress ever,' said
Secca.

'I don't think so, young lady.' Anna smiled again at
the girl.

Nerio had moved silently from one diner to the next as
they talked, filling the goblets, pewter like the ones that had
held the berry juice, with a dark red wine. The two children
got splashes of wine, and a second set of goblets filled with
the berry juice.

'To our guests,' offered Hryding once the goblets were
filled.

Anna took the smallest sip of the wine, then a slightly
larger one after she realized that it was decent, not vinegary
like Brill's.

Hryding broke off a chunk of bread, lighter, ryelike, and
passed the basket to Anna. She took some and passed it
across to Anientta.

'Surely, you could do good works here, Lady Anna?
Would not a patron make your life more secure?' asked
Hryding.

*It probably would, but not with your consort's attitude
toward me*, Anna thought, saying instead, 'Right now, Lord
Hryding, most of what I know is how to destroy, and a
number of powerful people are seeking me. Some have
already tried to kill me.'

'She took a war arrow through the shoulder several weeks
before the battle for the Sand Pass,' Daffyd announced.

'You are more durable than you appear,' Hryding said.
'Or enchantment covers your wounds.'

'They've healed – with some help.'

Hryding raised his eyebrows.

'I know some ways to make healing ... antiseptics ...
and Lord Brill ... provided some help.'

'Darksong is dangerous, it's said,' mused Gestatr.

'He seldom used it,' Daffyd said. 'But he felt the Lady

Anna would be of great help – otherwise, why would the dark ones have tried so hard to kill her?'

'I saw why,' added Gestatr. 'I doubt that the dark ones have ever taken such losses.'

'So . . . why are you here?' asked Anientta.

'Where else would I go?' countered Anna politely. 'Mencha was about to fall to the dark ones, and I know no one else in all of Liedwahr, except for people who died in the battle. Daffyd's sister has been kind enough to guest me.'

'You intend to stay here . . . ?' Anientta raised her eyebrow again.

'No. I had thought to head back to Falcor.' Anna realized how lame her words might sound, and tried to strengthen them. 'I would like to stop the dark ones. They need to be stopped.'

'Why do you not wish to return home . . . to your children?' asked Anientta, a skeptical tone in her voice. 'You are, still, a mother.'

'I would like that – except that I cannot send myself home, and no one I have yet encountered knows how. Some claim it cannot be done at all.' Anna shrugged. 'And if the dark ones win, I have been led to believe that there will be no way to return.'

'You cannot send—'

'Anientta,' said Hryding firmly, 'even *I* know that the most basic rule of sorcery is that a sorcerer – or a sorceress – can do nothing to affect herself directly. Now that Lord Brill is dead, there are no other powerful sorcerers in Defalk or anywhere close. Lady Anna's choices are, perforce, rather limited.'

'What would you hope to find in Falcor?' Gestatr's voice was openly curious.

That is a damned good question, Anna thought. *What do I think I'll find there?* 'I do not know.' She offered a rueful smile. 'Except that I feel I must.'

Hryding nodded slowly. 'Sometimes, what we feel is

indeed what we must do.' Then he smiled. 'Enough of this serious stuff. Pass the meat!'

'Might have I more berry juice?' asked Secca, squirming ever so slightly in her chair across the table from Anna and Daffyd.

'That could be arranged,' laughed Hryding, nodding at Nerio, who eased toward the little redhead.

Anna studied the girl's open face, thinking about how long it had been since Elizabetta or Mario – or Irenia – had been that young. Irenia . . . why Irenia? Why any child or young person?

And why was she getting more and more deeply involved in a war in a place she'd never even heard of – or dreamed about? Why her?

Anna the sorceress took a sip of the wine, only a sip, and mellow as it was, the vintage tasted bitter.

51

The faintest breeze ruffled the roof awning, and Anna looked up toward the end of the garden where Anientta worked on something that seemed to be cross-stitch. The lady of Flossbend never looked at Anna, but the sorceress felt a constant scrutiny.

Anna laughed silently. Let Anientta scrutinize. Anna hadn't the faintest interest in Hryding, except that he seemed a decent sort in a place where decency was a luxury. Then her eyes went to the little redhead across the table from her.

Secca stared intently at the game board, then picked up two of the black stones and placed them in adjacent slots in the lattice to Anna's far right. 'There!'

Vorkoffe was similar to the box game Anna had played in college, where whoever got the most boxes completed won, but in Liedwahr the object was to distribute stones by twos. Five stones completed a lattice.

So far Anna was holding her own. She'd lost the first several games, but had won the last, not that winning or losing was any great gain or loss, but she hated to seem incompetent.

Anna spread her two stones, placing them in the lattices at the opposite corners of the board.

'I don't like it when you do that, Lady Anna.' Secca said, with a hint of a pout.

'No pouting.' Anna laughed. 'Do you know that when I was your age, every time I started to pout, or stick my lip out . . . do you know what my mother said?'

'What?' Secca grinned. 'That must have been a long time ago,' she added.

'She said that she could ride my lip all the way to town.'

Secca laughed. 'Was your mother blonde? Only people from Pelara are blonde.'

'She wasn't blonde. She had reddish brown hair, and she was from a place called Cumberland, in the mountains.'

'Oh . . . here's father.'

Anna turned her head.

Hryding stood in the archway, his eyes flickering from Anna to Anientta, and then back again. Finally, he walked over, a scroll rolled tightly and held in his left hand. 'Secca . . . I need to talk to the lady Anna for a moment. It will only be a moment.'

'Promise?'

'I promise, little one.' Hryding laughed, and Secca scampered toward Anientta.

'I beat her, Mommy. I beat the lady Anna!'

Anientta set down her needlepoint.

'Have you ever played Vorkoffe before?' Hryding asked.

'No, but I'm learning.'

'I have just received a message – or a proclamation,' said

Hryding wryly, 'from the self-styled Prophet of Music, Lord Behlem.'

'Oh?' Anna's stomach tightened. If Daffyd had been correct, Behlem was one of those seeking her.

The awning fluttered lightly in a breeze that died almost immediately.

'Some of it applies to me . . .' The Lord of Synope's words faded as he unrolled the parchment and began to read.

'"All lords, regardless of past acts or loyalties, are requested to accept the sovereignty of Neserea as necessary to protect their lands and lives from the depredations of Ebra. Lords are requested to offer their levies and trained armsmen to the Prophet of Music, as they would have to the former Lord of Defalk . . ."' Hryding paused, then commented, 'A very polite way of saying that we can keep what we have if we support his claim to Defalk. The next part is the one of interest to you.'

Anna waited.

'"Further, it is also requested that the sorceress known as the lady Anna also offer her loyalty, and with that loyalty from henceforth her standing as a lady of Defalk and Neserea is recognized and affirmed, and none shall impede her in her travels to Falcor or in the performance of her duties in support of the lands. Furthermore, any who impede, or otherwise attempt discourtesy or harm, shall be considered as enemies of the realms . . ."' Hryding cleared his throat and paused. 'There's not much more, except flowery words suggesting that Behlem will return Defalk to its former glory and that we all should be grateful that he and his armsmen have arrived to save us from the Ebrans.'

'Can he?' asked Anna.

'Who knows? His consort is the daughter of the Liedfuhr of Mansuur, and Behlem has more armsmen than anyone east of Mansuur, except for the Norweians and, of course, the Ebrans. With his levies and those remaining in Defalk – and you . . .' He shrugged.

The sorceress pursed her lips.

'Have you ever met the Prophet?' asked Hryding.

'I don't know who he is, except by title, and a brief glimpse in a mirror,' Anna admitted. 'He and his sorcerers have been looking for me.'

'I would judge that your value is high, higher than that of his captains and advisors.' The lord rolled up the scroll. 'It appears that your feeling about going to Falcor was correct.'

'I didn't know,' murmured Anna. 'I just felt it.'

'I'd not go against your feelings.' Hryding laughed gently. 'Or you, lady.'

'I don't know that I should just ride into Falcor, but I also wonder if I have much choice.'

'You're wise to be cautious.' Hryding scratched the back of his silver thatch. 'I think we might both profit.'

'Oh?'

'Please allow me to send at least a few armsmen with you.'

'Your losses have been great,' Anna said. 'How could you spare them?'

'I am not being totally charitable, lady. If you arrive with my guards, under my banner, then Behlem's armsmen will give your presence greater credence. Behlem will also look more favorably upon us, I hope. That is very important, since Synope is poor, and I could not oppose the Neserean forces.' He smiled. 'You see. By helping you, I hope to help myself.'

'Put that way, Lord Hryding, I would be pleased to accept some few armsmen – but only a few.'

'I had thought three. Two might be enough for you, but they will need to return, and most ruffians will not attack three armed men.'

'You are most generous.'

'With this' – he raised the scroll – 'I can see that your concerns about remaining in Synope were well founded. Would tomorrow morning be too early?'

'I think not,' Anna said. *Not with your consort following my every move.* 'I will need to send a message to Daffyd.'

'That can certainly be managed.' He turned and raised his voice. 'Secca. You can finish your game.'

'Are you done with your business?' asked Anientta.

Anna winced at the sicky-sweet tone, but answered. 'We were discussing my departure tomorrow.'

'The lady's presence has been requested in Falcor – by Lord Behlem,' explained Hryding as he walked toward Anientta.

'How immensely flattering. His consort must still be in Esaria.' Anientta's teeth flashed.

'I wouldn't know,' Anna said. 'I've never met him. I've never met anyone from . . . his land.' She couldn't remember the name of the country Behlem ruled. Then she looked down as Secca dashed up.

'You aren't leaving so soon?' asked the little redhead.

Anna wondered if children ever just walked. 'I'm afraid I must. Not until tomorrow.'

After reaching the end of the awning, Hryding slipped into the empty chair beside his consort. '. . . might be some good out of all of this . . .'

'. . . do hope so, dear . . .'

Anna tried not to bristle at the condescending tone.

'Then we can play some more?' asked the redhead.

'We can play some more.' Anna agreed, conscious of how much she missed Elizabetta.

52

After washing her hands and face, Anna glanced around the room – taking in the wide wood-postered bed, the washtable with the delicately curved legs, the small writing desk, and the two wide windows with inside louvered shutters and outside solid shutters.

Like the cushion on the stool and the braided rug on the

brown tile floor, the coverlet on the bed, a coverlet she'd never needed, was pale green.

She looked in the mirror above the washtable. The strange young face, too thin somehow, framed with blonde hair that was getting too long, looked back at her. Somehow, she was young – but she didn't look the way she had when she'd first been young – and it wasn't just the hair. Her features had retained a certain sharpness – fineness – character – something. The faded green cottons looked good, if looser than when she'd first worn them. Anna shook her head. *Looking at yourself isn't going to help anything.*

She still needed more spells – common, everyday things. She tried to figure out one for 'Mary Had a Little Lamb,' saying the words until she had them worked out.

> 'Anna had a dark green gown, dark green gown
> whose cloth was strong and light
> and everywhere that Anna went
> the gown stayed pure and bright.'

Did she want to try it? She shook her head. If it worked, then she'd have to bring it with her. Besides, she'd have to be near some cloth or wool or something, because, according to Brill, sorcery didn't create out of whole cloth, but reshaped things.

Instead, she took out the stub of greasy pencil and crabbed the words on the last sheet of paper left from those she'd taken from Brill's hall.

It was so easy to think that sorcery could solve her problems, but when she actually got down to trying to create spells, it got harder. Was that because sorcery effectively created absolutes, and life was seldom filled with absolutes?

Thrap. The knock on the door was almost tentative.

'Yes?'

'Might I enter, lady?' asked Hryding.

'Of course.'

The silver-haired lord stepped into the room and paused, leaving the door wide open behind him. 'I wanted to tell you that the armsmen are ready.'

'I was just getting ready to come find you.' Anna nodded toward the bags on the floor.

'Your player has also arrived. He's waiting in the stable with my men.' Hryding glanced toward the door. 'I did not realize you had packhorses.'

'We picked them up after the battle,' Anna said. That was true enough, if misleading, but she did not want Hryding to think she was too powerful. Sorceress or not, she was learning that using the local equivalent of tactical nuclear weapons created as many problems as it solved, and Hryding's armsmen would be far more effective and less disruptive in getting her in to see Lord Behlem.

'You are resourceful.'

'Lucky, I think,' Anna said. 'I appreciate and thank you for guesting me.' She added with a rueful smile, 'Right now, there is little I can do in return. I am afraid I am still an incomplete sorceress, good at destruction and a few other things.'

'If you go to Falcor with my armsmen as escort, Lady Anna, that will be more than repayment.' With a sardonic smile, Hryding stepped forward and extended a small leather bag. 'You clearly have not had time to gather what you might need for expenses.'

'You are too generous,' Anna said, not taking the bag.

'There is little enough there for your trip, and you will be required to pay any lodging costs for the armsmen. It would not be well for them to pay for you.'

'Thank you. I had not thought of that.' Anna nodded, and accepted the heavy bag. It seemed far too weighty, but just as Hryding would not be stingy, out of self-interest, neither would he be overly generous, not with Anientta looking over his shoulder. She slipped it into the belt wallet.

'Also, here is a scroll. I would be indebted if you would present it to Lord Behlem. It says that I will be most cooperative.' Hryding snorted. 'As though I had any choice at all.'

Anna slipped the scroll into one of the saddlebags.

'Let me escort you,' said Hryding as Anna lifted the saddlebags.

Through the years with Avery, she'd felt like a gypsy, and as they stepped out of the guest room, it seemed that even in a strange world, she was still a gypsy, never getting settled anywhere before some other circumstance, out of her control, sent her reeling in another direction.

The early-morning sky was bright and clear – as usual – with the sun's heat already raising mirages on the fields she could see over the upper-level walls to the west.

As Anna reached the stairs, Secca scurried up, still bare-foot.

'I wanted to say good-bye, Lady Anna.'

The sorceress looked down at the little redhead. 'I'm glad you did, Secca. I'm glad you did.' She grinned. 'Next time I might be better at Vorkoffe.' *If I ever get a chance to play it again.*

'You are good enough. You won the last game.'

Secca threw her arms around Anna's legs. 'Come back and see us, Lady Anna.'

'I'll try.'

'Promise?'

'Secca, I will do the best I can, but we can't always do as we wish in this world.' *Or in any other world, either.* Anna bent over and awkwardly hugged the girl.

'If you try really hard, you can,' Secca observed.

'I'll try.'

'Promise?'

'Promise,' Anna conceded.

'Secca! Where are you?' Anientta's voice echoed across the upper terrace.

'I have to go.' Secca gave a last shy smile, and dashed off as quickly as she had come.

'She admires you,' said Hryding softly as they continued down the stairs.

'I think she's special. I hope she stays that way.'

'Lady?' Hryding paused at the foot of the steps, in the small entry hall just inside the main-floor archway.

'Yes.'

'If . . . if things go well for you . . . would you consider fostering Secca?'

'Me?' Anna was flabbergasted.

'I know it is presumptuous. Many foster their sons with other families, but few consider daughters . . . Still . . .'

'Lord Hryding, if I ever can foster any child or young person, Secca would certainly be one.'

'Thank you.'

Anna wondered exactly what she'd gotten herself into. Did she want to raise another daughter? She tightened her lips at the recollection of Kurik's smugness and insolence, and his shiny boots. Jeron, the one time she'd seen him, had been even more insufferable.

Calmut looked steadily into the distance as the two walked from the hall.

Anna paused. 'Calmut . . . I don't bite. I just won't be bitten.'

'Yes, lady.' The armsman's voice was exceedingly polite.

The sorceress wanted to kick him in the shins – or worse. Instead, she added, 'Calmut, there is always someone stronger, someone faster, someone with more weapons. As long as you put your fate in strength, you will fail.'

'Yes, lady.'

Anna gritted her teeth and said nothing.

As Hryding led the way to the stables on the south side of the white-walled hall, the lord asked, 'Why did you say that to Calmut?'

Anna held in a sigh, moistened her lips, and thought for a moment. Finally, she said, 'Lord Hryding, my world was once much as yours, and, if I am truthful, some parts of it still are. Often, men rule women by the virtue of brute strength . . .'

'You are taller and stronger than many men,' Hryding protested.

'On my world, the men are larger and stronger. Many are over two yards tall.' Anna paused, then sighed. 'I suppose what I think doesn't matter, but I have a problem with brute force determining life. I know it usually does, but what I don't understand is why people accept it so easily. Only one person can be the strongest, and yet it seems that everyone thinks he can be that person.'

Hryding said nothing for several paces, and Anna wondered if she had offended him deeply.

'When you say something like that, lady, I almost feel as though all Erde shivers.' The lord glanced up at the open stable doors. 'Either the muses of Harmony or the harpies of Discord sent you. I trust in Harmony, but either way, after you, I fear, nothing will be quite the same.'

'I'm one woman.' Anna forced a gentle laugh.

'With the powers of Harmony behind you, I suspect.' The silver-haired lord returned her laugh.

Standing beside his gray mare and in front of the two mares serving as packhorses, Daffyd nodded as they approached. 'Good morning, Lord Hryding, Lady Anna.'

'Good morning, Daffyd,' Anna responded. 'You seem to have everything in order.'

The player nodded.

'Here are your escorts,' Hryding said as they reached the packed dirt outside the stables. Three men in pale green tunics waited by the stable door. Each bore a blade and a bow. Anna thought she detected mail under the tunics.

'This is Fridric.' Hryding nodded to a young black-haired man barely as tall as Anna.

'Stepan.'

The sandy-haired man bowed slightly to Anna.

'And Markan.' Markan was in his late twenties, clearly older than the others.

'Markan is the senior armsman,' the lord continued, 'and is familiar with the route to Pamr and then to Falcor.'

'I am pleased to meet you, Lady Anna.' The slender, brown-haired armsman bowed. His gray eyes twinkled. 'I am led to believe that we will have an interesting trip.'

'I hope not,' Anna said involuntarily.

Hryding made a sweeping gesture. 'Lady Anna, I must leave, but I believe all is ready, and I wish you well.'

'Thank you, Lord Hryding, for both hospitality and advice.'

As the lord retreated toward the hall, Anna stepped into the stables, where Farinelli whuffled in his stall, unsaddled. Anna grinned to herself. Somehow it didn't surprise her that no one had wanted to groom and saddle the big gelding.

The sorceress fumbled around until she found a brush. She slipped inside the stall and patted Farinelli's shoulder. 'Are you terrorizing the stable help again?'

Whuff!

By the time she had the gelding ready to ride and the saddlebags fastened in place, Daffyd and the three armsmen were ready and waiting.

'I'm sorry.' She led the palomino out of the stable into the sun. 'It takes me longer.'

Anna glanced at the two laden packhorses, glad that Daffyd had been willing to take care of those goods. She looked again. Each horse carried a large bundle tied over the saddle.

'Lord Hryding insisted on supplying travel provisions,' Daffyd confirmed.

'Where's the lutar? Did you finish it?'

'It's finished – in the brown canvas case there.' Daffyd pointed to the piebald mare.

Anna pulled her floppy-brimmed hat from her belt and adjusted it, then mounted. As she started down the road to the hall gates, Markan rode on her left, and Daffyd eased his mare up beside her on the right. The two other armsmen fell in behind the pack mares.

The road toward Synope was empty, but bore recent hoofprints and wagon traces.

'How fast do you wish to ride, lady?' asked Markan.

'I don't have that much experience with riding, but we made it from the Sand Pass to Synope in a little over three days. Would that be fast or slow?' Anna asked.

'That is a good pace,' Markan reflected.

'I can handle that.' Anna paused, then added, 'Before we leave Synope, I need to make a stop to pay a debt. It's just east of the center of town.'

'Lady . . .' began Daffyd.

'I have to,' Anna said. 'I wouldn't feel right about it.' Even with what she planned, she still didn't feel right, but didn't know what else she could do.

Even before they reached the center of the town, Anna wore a fine coat of dust, and her nose itched. She was squinting as they headed into the sun.

Several dozen individuals filled the central square of Synope as the five rode past Yuril's.

'I haven't seen that many people here since we arrived.'

'Market day,' answered Daffyd.

At least a dozen faces turned toward the riders as they passed the brick stand and headed toward the cooper's shop.

'That's her . . . the sorceress . . .'

'Warrens and spades . . . warrens and spades!'

'Looks almost like a girl.'

'Say she's hundreds of years old . . . buried her grandchildren . . .'

'Get your spices here! Fresh spices from Mansuur!'

'Bet Lord Hryding's pleased to see her leave.'

'Wager that Lady Anientta's even more pleased.'

Anna had no doubts about the last.

'People hereabouts don't get that much chance to see a real sorceress, lady,' said Markan.

'They don't see much of anything.' Fridric's voice drifted up from where he rode beside the pack mares.

The white-haired cooper looked up and then away from the group.

Anna tried to rub her nose gently to stop the itching and keep from sneezing, then guided Farinelli down the narrower lane toward Dalila's house.

'That's the young miller's house,' said Fridric.

'My sister is his consort,' explained Daffyd.

Anna reined up outside the long and narrow miller's house, then dismounted. She handed Farinelli's reins to Daffyd. 'I won't be long.'

'You don't—' he began.

'I do.'

Dalila already had the door open before Anna reached it, and the pregnant woman stood in the doorway with Ruetha on her hip.

Anna inclined her head. 'I never had a chance to thank you properly, Dalila, and I didn't want to leave Synope without seeing you.'

'I only did for you as any friend of Daffyd's . . .'

'You were gracious and gave me a place to rest and sleep when I knew no one,' Anna said. 'That kind of hospitality – it's rare on any world. What I'm doing probably isn't proper, but it's all I can do right now.' She pressed the silver coins into Dalila's free hand. 'These are for you.'

'But I couldn't.'

'Then keep them safe for the children. They might need them someday.' Anna paused. 'And do not give them to Madell. They are for you and the children.'

'But why?'

'Because you offered hospitality to a stranger, because you trusted your brother.' Anna squeezed Dalila's hands, then released them. 'Because you are a good person when you did not have to be good.'

'The harmonies be with ye, lady,' Dalila said softly. 'Always.'

Anna's throat felt thick, but she smiled and offered a head bow. 'And with you.'

'Bye . . . ' said Ruetha.

'Good-bye, Ruetha. Take care of your mother.'

Anna swung back up onto Farinelli. Markan led her entourage back toward the center of Synope to take the road north and west to Pamr.

'You did not have to do that,' Daffyd said as they passed the cooper's once more.

'I feel better about it.' Anna flicked the reins, and Farinelli *whuff*ed. Sorcery was taking getting used to, and she was realizing that it wasn't exactly what she had thought it would be. The circles under Brill's eyes made even more sense now. As did her own thinning frame. She was beginning to think she needed to eat more, but stuffing herself made her feel like a hog and a glutton.

'How long to Pamr?' the player asked Markan.

'Three, four days, if the roads are clear,' answered the older armsman. 'If the discordant Ebrans are still in Mencha.'

Anna wanted to groan – not another four days in the saddle.

53

Anna took the lutar out of the crude canvas case, then sat crosslegged on the bedroll on the low knoll where they had camped. They had stopped at sunset, far enough west that the Ostfels had disappeared. In any direction that Anna had looked all afternoon, she had seen only gently rolling hills, some few covered with tress, but mostly just fields and meadows. Many of the fields were clearly untended dry soil partly covered by sparse flowers and weeds.

In the gloom barely lifted by Clearsong – that point of light in the west that was far brighter than earth's evening star and far dimmer than earth's moon – she could see Farinelli outlined against the stars. Glancing overhead and then to the south, she made out the small reddish disk of the second moon – Darksong.

The moons were a discordant reminder that Erde was real. Never would Anna have dreamed a dream with two moons – they were something Avery or Sandy would have thought up.

She tightened the tuning pegs and then strummed the lutar's strings. The tone was ... different, not as tinny as the mandolin, but not as resonant as she would have expected from a guitar.

'That's strange,' Daffyd said. 'Harsh, it is.'

She wondered how he would have heard a true guitar, without the softness that the gut strings provided.

'I thought sorcerers had to be separate from the music and the players.' Stepan adjusted his thin blanket on the dry grass that seemed to crackle with each movement.

'I'm told that it works better that way.' Anna frowned as she wrestled with the stiff tuning peg. 'Some spells it doesn't matter.'

'Stepan,' called Markan out of the gloom, 'we need some help with the tieline for the mounts.'

'Coming.' The sandy-haired young man bounced up and away from Anna and Daffyd.

'Lord Brill said that it didn't matter with darksong,' Daffyd whispered.

'You didn't tell me that before.'

'I didn't know you could do darksong.'

'I can?'

'Anything that affects living things has darksong in it. The spell with Madell ...' Daffyd's shrug was pronounced enough to be visible in the dim moonlight and starlight.

Wonderful – she'd have a reputation as dark sorceress before she ever got to Falcor. 'So now everyone will call me a darksinger?'

'Most sorceresses are considered darksingers, whether they are or not, lady.' Markan folded a blanket and sat down on it.

'Any woman with power is evil,' Anna said wryly.

'Except in Ranuak, where men with power are evil. Or Nordwei, where both men and women with power are evil. Or Ebra, where anyone in a dark robe has power and is evil.' Markan's boyish grin was wide enough to be visible in the dim light.

A faint breeze swirled through the campsite, and for the first time since dawn, Anna began to feel comfortable.

Fridric sat down next to Markan.

'Stepan?' asked Daffyd.

'He gets first watch, since we did most of the work on the tieline.'

In the silence that followed, since Anna didn't feel like talking, mentally she reviewed some of the spells she had developed – the repulsion spell, the various burning spells, the looking-glass spell, the untried spell to create a gown. Would a gown spell be considered darksong? All the fabrics she knew came from something living – except polyester, and somehow that didn't seem likely on Erde.

Anna tried the chording for the burning-spell song.

'That's not quite a melody, is it?' observed Markan.

'No. It's homophonic.' Anna felt difficult.

Daffyd and Markan exchanged glances, but Anna kept working on the chords and the tuning until she had the progression and the fingering the way she wanted them.

Then she shifted to 'Go Away from My Door' – her repulsion spell, but had to stop after a handful of chords as the lutar slipped out of tune. That was to be expected with new strings, but it was irksome to keep retuning.

After a time, Markan and Fridric lay down, and so did Daffyd.

Finally, she stopped struggling with the lutar and looked up at the cold and unfamiliar stars. Was her sun, her earth, somewhere in those heavens? Was her daughter looking at the same stars from somewhere else?

The stars blurred as her eyes burned with not-quite-shed tears. She put the instrument back in its case and stretched out herself, the blanket only across her waist as sleep slowly crept over her.

54

Anna stood in the stirrups, trying to stretch her legs and relieve the tightness in the muscles above her knees. Either she wasn't riding the way she should be, or everyone's upper legs were ready to fall off.

The road was a strip of dust rising from packed red clay five yards wide and stretching from one low hill to the next. To her left was what had once been an orchard, with over half the trees dead or dying. The stead's house, visible a hundred yards back from the road, had a sagging roof and empty, shutterless windows.

'Is it like this all the way to Falcor?' asked Anna.

'For the next day or so,' said Markan, 'until we get to the Chean River valley. Lord Kysar built ditches from the river three years ago.'

'Didn't the river dry up, too?' Anna brushed away a persistent fly, and Farinelli's tail swished at the pesky insect.

'My legs are sore,' mumbled Daffyd, from the gray mare to Anna's right. 'When do we stop for something to eat?'

'We stopped just a while ago.' The senior armsman looked at Anna.

'We can keep going for a while.' Anna took off the floppy hat and fanned her face with it, then replaced it. Despite the long sleeves of the shirt, and the hat, her skin was still getting burned by the endless sun, especially the back of her neck.

'Good idea,' said Markan.

Fridric and Daffyd both groaned. Anna glanced back. Stepan grinned and shook his head at the sounds coming from the two youngest riders.

'About the river?' she prompted Markan. 'Why hasn't it dried up?'

'It rises in the Ostfels, and the dark ones couldn't cut off the rain there without hurting Ebra. Both the Chean and the Fal run lower now, and there's been a spate of fights over the water. Lord Jecks had to raze Lord Jurlt's hall two years ago.' The armsman shook his head. 'Wager there's thousands fewer folk in Defalk now than five years ago, and more leaving and dying each year. More dust storms with the great west winds.'

Anna tightened her lips. Dust bowls because of natural occurrences were one thing, but using magic to starve a land to death was another. *Isn't it?*

'Can't we stop soon?' asked Daffyd.

Anna shook her head. If she could deal with it, the player could.

Her eyes strayed to the east, across barren, weed-filled fields and another set of collapsing hovels. For some reason, the view reminded her of the back roads of eastern Colorado, when she'd let Sandy navigate.

'Arms!' snapped Markan.

'What?' asked Daffyd.

Stepan and Fridric pulled bows from their leather cases and strung them, following Markan's example.

Anna twisted in the saddle and fumbled with the lutar case, extracting the instrument more slowly than the armsmen had readied their weapons.

From the southwest a narrow trail joined the main road just past a long row of waist-high bushes. Anna glanced back down the southern trail. Three figures on horseback had reined up. The three appeared ragged and bearded, and only one bore a bow. The burly rider in the center carried a huge blade in a shoulder harness.

For a time the three studied the larger group, then turned their mounts back south.

'I suppose this means we can't stop for a while,' muttered Daffyd.

'Not unless you want to chance getting robbed or worse,' said Markan ironically.

Daffyd slowly took one leg from the stirrup and awkwardly massaged his thigh as the gray mare plodded along, carrying him up yet another gentle hillside.

'They'll bear watching,' said Markan. 'Might follow and try to take us by surprise tonight.'

'Not another night on the ground?' asked Daffyd, replacing his foot in the stirrup.

'If we're lucky, we'll reach the waystop below Stendir.' Markan snorted, still turned in the saddle to watch the retreating bandits – if that were what they were. 'Halas is just ahead, and after that, there's Yrean, and then Poskit. Even in the good years, they didn't have inns, and few live anywhere near any longer.'

'There haven't been many people on the road,' Anna said. 'Is that because they all left?'

'Some. This isn't the main road to Sudwei, either. So we won't run across traders. People are too poor to buy now.'

Anna looked back, but the would-be bandits were cut off from sight as Farinelli started down the far side of the slope. Ahead, the reddish dirt strip stretched past another set of orchards, these apparently tended, and toward another rolling hill.

'Might be we could rest at the crest of that next hill,' suggested Markan.

'Good,' mumbled Daffyd. 'If I can stay on this beast that long.'

Were they traveling that much faster than they had coming from the Sand Pass? Anna wondered. Was she stronger because she was younger? Or was Daffyd just bored by the endless and monotonous nature of the journey?

She wiped the sweat out of the corners of her eyes, then repeated the acrobatics to replace the lutar in its case before she finally reached for her water bottle.

55

Anna looked to the north, across rows of corn taller than Farinelli's shoulders. The river valley was a lot more like Ames, flat and humid, though much of the humidity had to come from the irrigated fields extending away from both sides of the road that stretched ahead to the flat western horizon. With the humidity and the greenery, it was hard to believe that the drought-struck desolation of Mencha and Synope lay but a few days ride behind her.

She brushed away another of the flies that had plagued them from almost the moment they had descended from the river bluffs on the east side of the Chean River the afternoon before, even before they had forded the wide brownish waters outside the little hamlet of Sorprat.

Farinelli swished his tail almost constantly as the five rode almost due west under the noonday sun, and the flies continued to buzz and circle.

Anna readjusted her battered hat, then turned in the saddle. 'How much farther to Pamr?'

'Unless I miss my guess, that's it.' Markan pointed to a brown-and-green smudge on the horizon, where trees lifted above the greenery of the endless crops.

'It is,' Daffyd confirmed. 'I was there a couple of years ago.' He shifted his weight in the gray mare's saddle, wincing.

'Are your legs still stiff?' Anna asked.

'They're stiff, and they've been aching since the first day. I don't know how you manage.'

Anna's legs hurt, too. It was almost torture to walk for the first few steps whenever she dismounted, but she didn't see much point in talking about it. What could anyone else do?

'Ouch . . .' The player swatted vainly at one of the flies. 'They bite.'

'Hard,' Anna agreed. She had a few welts on her neck, and one on the back of her left hand. 'I wonder if we could find out what the dark ones are doing? Or if the Prophet is going to attack them soon?'

'Or if the Norweians have bought both countries,' suggested Daffyd.

'Might be a good idea,' Markan said. 'Can you use your sorcery?'

Anna frowned. 'I could call up images, but I don't know how to get what they say.' She paused. 'I also don't know *who* would give us that kind of information. Sorcery doesn't do that. Not what I can do, anyway,' she added.

A gray blot on the road ahead slowly grew into the shape of a wagon as they continued to ride west.

'Could we ask the drivers of that wagon?' Anna asked. 'They might know something.'

'We can ask,' Markan said. 'They might just be local farmers.'

By the time, they neared the wagon – also headed west – the man beside the driver had turned in the seat and had a bow ready.

'Off with ye!' snapped the driver. 'We don't want trouble.'

'Arms!' snapped Markan, and the guard lowered his bow in the face of the three armsmen.

'We don't want your goods or anything else,' Anna said, 'except information. And civility,' she added sweetly. 'Do you know how far the Ebrans have marched?'

'Couldn't say. We only went as far as Sorprat. Some say they stopped at Mencha.' The driver spat onto the road, flicking the reins. 'Not get us out there again. Levies running everywhere, except for Kysar's. Some captain had them in tow. Half decent, they were, but they marched back, and the others, every time you looked around, some fool was trying to grab something, even raw carrots.'

'Some of them just drooled and plodded along,' added the driver's guard.

'Have you heard about Lord Behlem?' asked Markan.

'Some say he's bringing in a regular army. Some say he's goin' to make Defalk part of Neserea. Who cares? Just leave us and our horses alone. One lord, another lord ... don't make much difference.'

As they rode around the wagon team and toward Pamr, Anna kept looking back. So did Markan, until they were well beyond bow range.

'They weren't very friendly.' Anna said.

'No wonder, if there are that many levies and armsmen wandering loose,' said Stepan from where he rode behind the pack mares.

'It's bad. Probably get worse,' Markan mused. 'Be better to take the long south road and then the river trail back.'

'Why didn't we go that way?' the sorceress asked.

'It takes twice as long, and we didn't know which might be worse.'

That made sense, especially in a world where rapid communications were nonexistent. Anna kept from shaking her head, and instead looked at the fields beside the road, now filled with what looked to be some form of beans.

As she watched, a fat bird, like a golden pheasant, flapped out of the grass between two fields, and across the road before them.

'Oh ... for a net,' said Daffyd. 'The goldens are delicious.'

'Best not say that too loudly, player. Most places they're reserved for the lords.' Markan laughed. 'In the light of day, leastwise.'

'Lord Brill said they belonged to those who caught them, but he punished any who took the females or the chicks.'

'Wise man,' said Markan.

The more Anna traveled Defalk, the wiser Brill sounded – yet he had killed Daffyd's father in cold blood. She shook her head. Would she seem like that to others – if she survived?

A well-tended home, with a lane to a barn, stood on the north side of the road. Two men struggled with shovels on an irrigation ditch beyond the single-story house.

'*KKhhhcheww!*' Anna's whole body ached with the force of the sneeze. She wiped her nose gently and blotted the involuntary dampness from her eyes. She hated to sneeze like that.

Slowly, as they rode west, Pamr rose out of the fields, a wide clump of tended trees, overshadowing houses and shops. Anna could see a second line of trees running from the southeast to the northwest, marking the turn of the river back toward the west just beyond the town.

The road remained dusty, and Anna tried to avoid rubbing her itching nose, but she still sneezed intermittently, as did Daffyd and the armsmen.

On the right they neared a fenced field, and Anna smelled the cattle even before she saw them.

A reddish stone stood on the left side of the road, proclaiming, *Pamr – 1 D.*

'See?' exclaimed Daffyd.

Anna nodded, and kept riding, riding past the small huts and larger homes, all white-plastered as in Synope, although the walls were more reddish tan than white. Irrigation didn't do much for road dust, or any other dust outside the fields.

While none of the houses in Pamr appeared deserted, many had a worn sense to them. Was that just the nature of homes in a more primitive culture – or was that because of the hard years? Anna didn't know.

Unlike the chandlery in Synope, the one in Pamr was freshly painted – blue with white trim – and the sign read *Forse*. Beside the chandlery on the left was a cooper's, and on the right was a narrow brick building without any sign. Across the street was an inn – whitewashed with green trim, and a sign bearing the picture of a green and well-endowed bull.

Anna reined up outside the chandlery and dismounted, glancing across the empty street toward the Green Bull, where two bearded men watched. A wagon creaked down the dusty street and swung into the inn's courtyard.

'Would you like us to come in?' asked Markan.

Anna shook her head. 'I'm only going to ask directions.'

She stepped inside the building, which reeked of leather and wax and sweat, and looked at the long counter to the left, on which were haphazardly piled items, including a mildewed bedroll, several sets of water bottles, a saddle, and three open boxes of candles of varying lengths.

'What would you like?' asked the stocky and unshaven man standing in the dimness by the counter.

'Directions. Which way to Lord Kysar's hall?' Anna forced a pleasant smile, not an alluring one, but one she hoped was businesslike.

The stocky man stepped forward. 'Aren't you a beauty. Sure you aren't looking for the River's Rest?' He leered.

'I'm looking for Lord Kysar's hall.' Anna's voice was cold.

'Why you be looking for that? Old Kysar's dead, and some captain I never heard of is holding it for his consort. Arrogant pup. Bet he'd like to see the likes of you. Don't know as you'd like it, not the way those captains are. Now ... I could be real friendly.' Another leer followed.

Anna tightened her lips, fighting back the temptation to use some spell on the chandler, before asking, 'It wouldn't be Captain Dekas, would it?'

'One's the same as the other.' The leer faded, and the chandler's eyes took in her riding clothes and the knife and truncheon. 'You know that captain?'

'I know some of the ones that were at the Sand Pass.'

'Oh ... a favorite, were you?' The leer returned.

'No. I was there.' She couldn't say she was there to fight, for all that she had killed.

'You confuse me, woman. You say you were there, and you don't wear a blade, but you're not one of their women.' The chandler scratched his head.

'I'd still like to know—' Anna broke off and stepped back toward the entrance as another man, taller and wiry, stood from a chair behind the counter and moved toward her, cutting her off from the door.

'Get her . . . too good—'

Forcing herself to be calm, Anna slipped out the knife as she backed up and began to sing,

> 'Go away from my soul;
> Go away from my door;
> Go away from my body;
> and trouble me no more . . .'

Both men stopped, almost in their tracks.

Anna glanced toward the door, but the tall man had his dagger out. 'Shit, Forse . . . you picked a friggin' sorceress,' he muttered, steadying himself on the wall, but still blocking the exit from the shop.

The chandler laughed and reached for the bow that sat in the bracket by his shoulder.

Seething, Anna swallowed, trying to clear her throat, and sang the second song, as strongly as she could.

> 'Chandler wrong, chandler strong,
> turn to flame with this song!'

As Forse flared into a pillar of fire, the tall man bolted out the door he had blocked.

'No . . . aaeeiiiii . . .' The chandler groped for the bow, but the flames cascaded over it as well.

Anna pushed back the door as it swung toward her, and staggered out into the heat of the day.

'What happened?' asked Daffyd. 'What did you do to him?'

'Are you all right, lady?' asked Markan.

'Let's go,' Anna choked, tears streaming down her face, as she sheathed the knife and climbed onto Farinelli, trying to ignore the shaking in her legs. Why did so many men think that force was the only answer? Why was she always having to use a violent form of sorcery just to stay alive? Or enter a store with armed men at her back? She hated Erde! 'I'm fine. I'm fine. This ... damned ... world is the problem.' She turned Farinelli back toward the central cross-roads two blocks south.

The two bearded men who had stood on the inn porch ran across the street, skirting the armsmen and not looking at the group.

'Let's go!' Anna snapped. She wasn't about to stay around, not with locals who might be offended that a woman had the nerve to defend herself. If only she'd had more time ... but she hadn't, not with Forse lifting the bow. The fire spell was all that had come to mind.

The others followed silently. All ignored the screams from the chandlery that had died quickly.

'You are crying, yet you're angry.' Daffyd cleared his throat as he drew the gray mare up beside Anna and Farinelli.

'I am angry. I'm furious. I tried to be calm. I wasn't even trying to be a sex object, and it was like they couldn't see it. One of them – when I used sorcery to push him away – he wanted to kill me with a bow. So I had to kill him, because I didn't have any other way to stop him.'

'You could have run out the door.'

'The other one had a knife, and he was in the way.' Anna straightened in the saddle. 'Besides, I've run too many times, and I'm not running now. But I'm angry. Are those my choices? Kill someone or run? Submit to some dirty beast or kill him? Or scream for armed men so that they can use force?'

'All men are not like that,' Markan said.

Anna sighed. 'No. You're right. They aren't, but there are a lot who are. Too damned many.'

'There are too many women who lie and scheme, I'd wager,' Markan said softly.

'No more than—' Anna stopped. What was the point of

arguing about it? Some men were violent. Some women schemed. Both lied, and it seemed as though they all responded only to force, and she felt trapped between them. She shook her head. 'We need to find Lord Kysar's hall.'

She turned Farinelli onto the road that led toward the river, and before long they were on the outskirts of Pamr, headed toward a stone-pillared bridge. Anna saw no sign of a hall or extensive tended grounds, only an older woman carrying two heavy bundles who trudged along the road. The woman looked up warily as Anna slowed Farinelli.

'Where would I find Lord Kysar's hall?'

'You're headed in the wrong direction, girl. He's out the north road. Best be careful. There's a bunch of armsmen and some levies gathered there.' She looked at the armsmen. 'You going to join them?'

'Not that we know of,' Anna answered.

'That be good. Wish the old lord had returned. None of this nonsense. Well, girl . . . don't just look at an old woman. You got places to go. So do I.'

'Thank you.' Anna laughed, much preferring the older woman's approach to that of the late Forse. She turned Farinelli, and they headed back through Pamr, avoiding the chandlery. There was no smoke rising, and that meant at least she hadn't destroyed the building with its chandler.

Lord Kysar's hall was more like Hryding's than Brill's, white-walled and austere from without, with a lower wall around the immediate grounds. Even from the road, it was clear that the hall was larger, with more than a dozen outbuildings. The biggest differences were the dozens of tents and the camped levies arrayed on each side of the road from the wall gate to the hall proper.

A sole sentry stood by the gate, a bow leaning against the dusty stucco-plaster wall.

Anna rode up to the guard. 'I'm the lady Anna. Could you tell me who the captain is here?'

The soldier looked from Anna, then to Daffyd, and then

to the three armsmen and the pale green banner that Fridric bore. 'What business is it of yours? Whose banner is that?'

'The banner is Lord Hryding's,' Anna said firmly.

The soldier looked doubtful.

'Your captain should be the one to deal with the lady Anna,' suggested Markan.

'That's right, boy,' said a deeper voice. A grizzled armsman stepped out of the shade of the gate arch and nodded to Anna, and then to Markan and Daffyd. 'This here sorceress killed a dozen score or more of them dissonant Ebrans. I was in the fort tower, and I saw it all.' The older man bowed to Anna. 'Not as I know your name, lady, but I owe you my life. So's a lot of us. Captain Firis, he'll be glad to see you.'

Anna wondered, but she only said, 'Thank you. I don't know your name, either. You may recall Daffyd. He was one of the players who helped destroy some of the dark ones. Markan here is a senior armsman from Lord Hryding in Synope.'

The young guard still looked doubtful, his eyes traveling between the older armsman and Anna.

'Look at the banner, lad.' The older man turned back to Anna. 'I'm Meris, lady. You would be wanting to see the captain, would ye not?'

'I had thought it would be useful.'

'Aye, and it might, with what we don't know, and all the tales that are flying about. Follow me. His tent's up yonder. You keep the gate, lad.'

The young sentry opened his mouth, and Anna glared at him. If one poor sorceress and four men could disrupt a small army, then the army wasn't worth much anyway. She guided Farinelli through the archway and after Meris who strode briskly along the narrow rutted road.

A small awninglike tent stood beside the road leading up to an ancient white-walled hall on a hill so slight it was barely a knoll.

'You wait here. I'll be announcing you,' Meris stated.

As he marched toward the pair of guards outside the tent, Fridric murmured to Stepan. 'People know her.'

'Would you forget her?' Stepan whispered back.

Anna tried not to flush.

The young captain with the salt-and-pepper beard practically rushed from the tent. Then he stood and looked at her. 'Lady Anna . . . more beautiful than ever.' Firis bowed. 'And more deadly, I wager.'

'Angrier, anyway,' Anna said, feeling somehow ashamed as she did.

'I had heard so many stories – that you had escaped, that you had fallen on the wall holding back the Ebrans, that you had turned half their forces into charred corpses . . .'

'Actually,' the sorceress said, 'in a way, all of those are true. I've been recovering in Synope as the guest of Daffyd's family' – she gestured toward the young violist – 'and of Lord Hryding. Captain Firis, this is Markan, representing Lord Hryding.'

'You must be tired. At least, you could join me for some refreshments. We do not have much, but you are more than welcome to what we have.'

'Thank you.' Anna swung off Farinelli and held on to the saddle for a moment while her legs readjusted.

'You still have that beast?'

'He lets me keep him around.' Anna smiled, then led the gelding a dozen paces to the rough hitching rail, glancing up at the afternoon sun.

'I'll have water brought for your mounts.' Firis turned to Meris. 'Could you see that the water detail brings some buckets here?'

'Yes, captain.'

'And thank you for escorting the lady Anna. Your name is . . . ?'

'Meris, ser.'

'I'll remember that.' Firis laughed. 'And not the way most captains do, armsman.'

Meris smiled faintly.

'So will I, Meris,' Anna added. 'You've been helpful when many would not be.'

'Thank you, lady.'

The armsman turned and left, not before a broad smile crossed his lips.

'You two fellows can refresh yourselves here.' Firis gestured to Stepan and Fridric, then led Anna, Markan, and Daffyd through the lower front of the tent to a portico at the rear, open to a faint breeze on three sides, where a portable table and a half dozen stools stood.

'I would offer you water, lady, but . . .'

'Bring some,' Anna suggested, 'and I'll cool it and purify it. Tired or not, that I can do.' She stood behind one of the stools, not ready to sit again quite yet.

Firis motioned to a youth. 'Some water and two clean pitchers. Also, a jug of the better wine and some bread.' He turned back to the three. 'It will be a moment.'

After a moment of silence, Daffyd spoke. 'Why would you say Lady Anna is more deadly?'

'I saw what she did to the Ebrans.' Firis tightened his lips and turned back to Anna. 'I am glad you were kind to me. You know, you are being sought by the Prophet.'

'I know. I don't like it. Lord Hryding showed me the proclamation.'

'Yet you appear to be headed to Falcor.' Firis stopped as the young orderly reappeared with a grimy-looking bucket and two pitchers.

Anna winced. 'Fill the pitchers first.'

After the youthful armsman did, she sang the water spell, and immediately moisture beaded on the outside of both the battered metal pitchers. Anna's head pounded with the effort, but she said nothing.

'You amaze me,' offered the captain, handing the first goblet to Anna, who drank it all, then perched on the stool.

She waited for the others to drink before she refilled her battered goblet and took several more sips. With the water

alone she felt refreshed, but her mouth still watered when
the orderly reappeared with two long loaves of bread.

None of the travelers said much until everyone had at
least one good-sized chunk of the bread.

'Would you be willing to tell me why you are here?' Firis
finally asked.

'I felt that I needed to go to Falcor. I understood that the
Ebrans are in Mencha—'

'They are. They now hold the walled camp that Lord Brill
created for Lord Barjim.' The captain shook his head. 'What
a waste.'

'Then Lord Hryding received that scroll.' Anna shrugged.
'If I remain long with anyone, they risk angering Lord
Behlem. So . . . I thought it best to go meet him. He says
he'll oppose the Ebrans.'

'I am certain he will.' Firis snorted. 'And how will we
be any better off under him than under the Evult of the
dark ones?'

'From what very little I have seen,' Anna said, 'almost
any ruler would be preferable to the dark ones.'

'Unhappily, you are on the mark.' Firis sighed. 'But choosing one's slavemaster is not the best of situations.'

Anna didn't have an answer for that. 'What are you
doing here?'

'I have been asked to support Lady Gatrune and Lord
Kysar's son and heir, young Lord Kyrun, and Lord Barjim
was no longer available . . .' Firis shrugged. 'We all do what
we must.' He smiled. 'I can offer you supper, and I am
sure that we can find a better place for you to rest here
than in Pamr. I suspect Lady Gatrune would be pleased to
guest you, and I can offer food and shelter to the rest of
your party.'

'That would be welcome,' Anna said slowly. 'Very welcome.' She didn't like separating from Daffyd and Markan,
but if she didn't use and develop any possible political
advantages, her career and life in Liedwahr might be very
short – short indeed.

56

As the sun hung above the western horizon, the distant trees that bordered the Chean River were black outlines above the fields of a green so dark that they also appeared black from the low hill. Anna carried her saddlebags and walked beside Firis.

'You know, Lady Anna, I owe you something, but bright as I am, I cannot tell you what it is. I can only tell you how it came to be.'

'I'm a little too tired for puzzles or riddles, captain, although I hope I may have been helpful in some way.' Anna's legs and feet hurt, and despite the bread and water, and some cheese, her head still ached. Her shoulders were as tight as an overtightened timpani, and her neck felt worse.

'Bear with me, lady. You could have destroyed me, and no one would have gainsayed your right to do so.' Firis laughed softly. 'I saw what you did to my goblet, and the Ebrans, and you could have done that to me. You did not. You apologized, and you said that Barjim needed all his captains. I was angry. Though I jested, I was angry. Then I saw you give all that you had to save people you scarcely knew, and I was one of them, and I had wanted to slay you.' The captain paused short of the tiles of the small covered archway before the door where another sentry stood. 'As the walls were falling, the black ones advancing, you remained, and I thought. Rather than flee as so many had, as I had every right to do, because you stood fast, I gathered all those I could, and I held them together, and brought them here because most of those I gathered were levies from Pamr. They – and the lady Gatrune – made me their captain. I accepted, since with Lord Barjim dead, and my company destroyed, I had nowhere else to be welcomed.' Firis shrugged. 'That is why I owe you.'

'Captain, I am flattered, and I admit I'm pleased that whatever I did inspired you, but you had the courage and the abilities to undertake those duties. No one can take that from you, and they shouldn't.' Anna smiled. 'I am glad you are here.'

Firis bowed. 'If ever I can offer aid, you know where I am.'

'You already have. Thank you.' She lowered her voice. 'Thank you very much.'

The captain stepped up to the sentry. 'I am escorting the lady Anna to see the lady Gatrune.'

'She is expecting you, ser.' The blond sentry opened the wide louvered door that stood behind the open, iron-banded main door.

A young, white-capped woman stood in the small entry hall. 'If you would follow me, captain and lady . . .'

The serving maid led them down the narrow corridor to a wide set of brick steps and then up two flights and along another hallway to a room resembling a salon – except that the northern side was open to the courtyard below, the only barrier being a waist-high, wrought-iron railing.

A big-boned woman with white-and-blonde hair stood from the padded leather chair and stepped forward, the first woman the sorceress had seen in Liedwahr who was both substantially taller and bigger than Anna was.

'This is the lady Anna,' Firis said. 'Lady Gatrune.'

'Thank you, captain.' Gatrune's eyes studied Anna for a moment. 'We are indebted to you, and I am pleased to meet you.'

'If you do not need me . . .' Firis said quietly.

'You may go. Thank you.'

As Firis slipped away, Gatrune gestured to the leather chair that faced and matched hers. 'You look tired. Please be seated. I would like to talk with you for a bit. Then you can wash up and change – do not worry. There are plenty of gowns in your room. And then we will have something to eat. You look as though you have been starving.'

Anna did not stand on ceremony, but dropped into the chair, easing the saddlebags to the floor by her feet. Starving? Did she look that bad?

'Would you like some mulled cider?' asked the aging blonde.

'Yes, if you wouldn't mind.'

Gatrune poured the amber liquid from the pitcher into an empty goblet sitting on the low table between the two chairs. Then she refilled the other goblet and took a deep swallow.

Anna sipped hers, enjoying the faint bite, but fearing that too much too soon would leave her on the floor.

'I had heard that there was a sorceress at the battle, but until Captain Firis introduced you, I never would have guessed. You look so young . . .' Gatrune extended the enameled wooden tray that held sliced apples.

'I'm not.' Anna took several of the apple slices, eating them between words as she summarized and sanitized her long tale, beginning with her arrival and ending with a shrug. 'It's proved very disconcerting, and provided more than a little trouble.' Should she tell Gatrune of her encounter with the chandler? She frowned.

'Your frown says there is more to your tale, and it is not pleasant. I would not impose.'

Anna smiled ruefully. 'One lord's consort was convinced I was going after him, and your local chandler attempted to rape me. I was successful in defusing the issue with the consort.'

'"Defusing" . . . a strange word . . .'

'We reached a rough understanding,' Anna amplified. 'The chandler was not so . . . reasonable. When I stopped him gently – the spell was to keep him from touching me – he tried to kill me with a bow, since he couldn't touch me.'

'That would have been Forse, no doubt. I won't let any of

the serving girls go near the chandlery.' Gatrune frowned.
'So what did you do?'

Anna sighed. 'I turned him into a bonfire. It was the only
way I had left to protect myself after he and his friend barred
the door.'

'Kysar had always told me that Forse was to be watched,
but I had thought of that in terms of the serving girls or
Herene – she is my younger sister, and ward, now that our
father has passed on.'

'I'm sorry,' Anna said automatically, even as she wondered
exactly why she was sorry.

'You are dangerous.' The widow laughed. 'So Forse
received his due, even after a warning.' She took a sip
from her crystal glass. 'Many of the men in Pamr will be
distressed, I'm sure. I cannot think of a single woman who
would be.'

'But it's sad,' Anna said. 'Why is it that some people only
respect force?' *And why do I have to be the one to apply
that force?*

'Most of them are men,' Gatrune said.

'Is that because they're men, or because they're powerful
and don't want to give up any power? If women were as
powerful, would they be any different?' *Am I any different? If sorcery makes me more powerful, will I turn out
like them?*

'I think I might like to find out. Even now, strong as I
am, I must rely on a strong captain, and the fact that I
have a brother who is a lord. That's Nelmor – he holds the
estates at Dubaria – they're a good two days' ride north
of Denguic, and the ground is rocky enough that our next
ruler, that so-called Prophet of Music, hasn't bothered even
to seek fealty. The ground won't support much except goats
and sheep, but those in Denguic and Elioch and even Falcor
will pay for good goat cheese.' Gatrune laughed. 'I prefer cow
cheese, personally. That comes from all the years of making
the goat cheese.'

'I'm not much for goat cheese.' Anna shifted position in

the leather chair. Comfortable as the chair was, every part of her body seemed sore.

'Anyway, with my next dispatch, thanking him for the cheese, and it is useful, especially for feeding the staff, I will tell him of you, and that you are to be trusted.' Gatrune lifted her goblet. 'I can tell who is and who isn't. Kysar was always surprised, but I've never been wrong yet, and it's been years.' She shrugged. 'What good our support will do, one never knows, dear, these days, but . . .'

Anna felt dazed by the outpouring, but she nodded. 'You trust your feelings.'

'Exactly. Too many people rely on proofs or words. Words are spoken on the wind; feelings are rooted in the soil and the harmonies.' Gatrune refilled the goblet. 'Then there's Firis. He is convinced that he owes you.' Gatrune smiled. 'Because he does, and because he returned with enough levies to protect the hall and holding, Kyrun and I owe you.'

'Kyrun is your son?'

Gatrune nodded. 'You will meet him later, but don't expect much. He's but five.' The lady of the hall took a long pull from her goblet, then looked at Anna. 'Will you serve Lord Behlem?'

'You must have read his proclamation.' Anna was taken slightly aback by Gatrune's directness.

'I did. I also agreed to his terms, as you will, if I'm not mistaken.'

'I am new to this world,' Anna said slowly, taking another sip of the strong spiced cider. 'But it would appear that Lord Behlem might be preferred over the dark ones.'

'He doubtless is, but—' Gatrune shrugged. 'It won't be easy, especially for you. No matter how old you really are, and it is hard to believe you have children as old as my younger sister, you look young, and you are beautiful, and that will have Cyndyth ready to have you killed, if she can manage it. If you don't help Behlem, they'll both want you out of the way. I don't envy you.'

'Cyndyth? I beg your pardon . . . but I am new . . .'

Gatrune laughed ruefully. 'I apologize. Even in this time of
sadness, it is refreshing to talk to a woman who doesn't look
over her shoulder for her lord, and I forget that you do not
know everyone. Cyndyth is Lord Behlem's consort, and she
is also the daughter of the Liedfuhr of Mansuur.' With a look
at Anna's face, she continued. 'Mansuur is the westernmost
country in Liedwahr, well beyond the Great Western Forest,
and about the size of Ebra, Nordwei, Defalk, Ranuak, and
Neserea all together.'

'Oh . . .'

'It's not exactly a great holding, but almost a confederation.
I think that by joining Cyndyth to Behlem he was hoping to
induce young Behlem to join Mansuur. Either that, or have
him assassinated, and then move to annex Neserea in the
guise of protecting Rabyn – that's his grandson, Cyndyth's
only child. Something like that. The Norweians oppose
Mansuur, and they've offered some support to Neserea.
Even the Matriarch of Ranuak has been warmer to Neserea
– with some caution.'

Anna tried to concentrate on Gatrune's words, but she was
tired, and some seemed to slip through her brain without
totally registering.

'You're still hungry and tired, and I'm prattling on. It's
lonely here, and Kysar was really the only one I ever
could talk to. For all his bluffness, he was a good sort,
and I never thought I'd find a consort.' For a moment,
wetness clouded Gatrune's bright eyes – but only for a
moment. The older woman stood. 'You need to wash up,
and then we'll eat, and you can tell me about the mist
worlds.'

Anna had to struggle to her feet as she followed the taller
lady from the salon. She hoped she would last until dinner.
Starving? How could she force herself to eat more? It seemed
as though all she did was eat . . . eat and ride . . . and watch
her back. She almost tripped as her boot caught the edge
of a floor tile, but she caught herself and continued after
Gatrune.

57

As she stood by the arched doorway, her stomach full from the warm bread and hot spiced apples, Anna wanted to yawn. She did not want to climb on Farinelli and ride for another two or three days. She just wanted to go back to bed . . . almost any bed. How long had it been since she had really been able to sleep? Even in Ames, if it hadn't been teaching, or rehearsals, or the job at the Lutheran Church, or . . .

Gatrune, in garb similar to Anna's brushed and washed riding clothes, was bright-eyed and smiling, as though she had been awake for hours – glasses, Anna corrected herself – and the lady of Pamr probably had. Everyone in Liedwahr rose at ungodly hours – or should she try to think of them as dissonant glasses? Either way . . .

'Here are two scrolls – one's for Nelmor, just in case you run into him before my messages reach him, and the other is for Lady Essan. You remember, you were sleepy last night, but she is Lord Donjim's widow, and she still has friends and influence in Falcor. Don't seek her out at first, though, because that would set Behlem to worrying, and there's nothing worse than the suspicions of a young and insecure Prophet.' Gatrune extended the scrolls to Anna, who balanced the saddlebags across her thigh and slipped them inside.

'I appreciate your kindness, and I will do what I can when I get to Falcor.' Anna glanced toward the shadowed entry hall behind the lady of Pamr, 'I did enjoy sleeping in a real bed, and eating hot food. Inns are not exactly plentiful on the roads.'

'The inn in Zechis is good. Kysar and I stayed there. It is the Black Pony, and Visula runs it. You might try it,' suggested Gatrune, 'although it is a long day's ride.'

'A very long day's ride,' added Herene. The younger blonde woman offered a wry smile.

'Thank you. There's a lot I have to learn about Defalk.'

'That is true of all of us,' replied Gatrune, ruffling Kyrun's hair. The boy, already tall for his age, stood beside his mother, wearing a sleeveless tunic and shorts. He was barefoot, and a cowlick gave his short blond hair a tousled appearance. He shifted his weight from one foot to the other, as though he wished he were someplace else.

Anna grinned down at him. 'I'll be gone in a bit, and then you can go play or do whatever you do.'

'Lessons, first,' Gatrune said, 'then play.'

'Do I have to?'

'Yes.' Gatrune and Herene spoke simultaneously.

'Yes, Mother.' Kyrun's tone was polite, but resigned, without being pouty.

'What you learn in your lessons can be useful later in life.' Anna paused, then added. 'Especially when you have to act before you have the time to learn what you should have learned as a child.'

'Remember that,' suggested Herene. 'Great sorceresses do not come along often.'

A great sorceress? Anna had more than a few doubts about that.

'You are. You will see,' predicted Gatrune. 'But you need to begin your journey, and my talking will only make it longer.' She nodded toward the door, and the stable across the expanse of packed earth.

'Thank you . . . again,' Anna said.

'No thanks for what best be done. Don't forget Lady Essan.'

'I won't.' Anna hefted her saddlebags and headed toward the stable.

Daffyd was leading the gray mare out of the cracked-walled stable that seemed far older than the hall itself as Anna crossed the packed earth from the hall. Markan looked up from securing the saddlebags behind his saddle.

'How did you sleep?' she asked.

'Well enough,' answered Markan.

'Better than on the road,' Daffyd agreed. 'Hot food was good, too.'

'Better than travel bread or cheese,' added Stepan, bringing out one of the pack mares.

As usual, Farinelli was unsaddled, and *whuff*ed as Anna neared.

'I can't believe you ride that beast, lady,' offered the stablehand as Anna slipped the saddle blanket in place. 'He like as chased Greize right out of the stall last night.'

'We get along,' Anna said, trying to stifle a yawn. 'We're both temperamental.' She eased the saddle in place, half realizing that it no longer felt particularly heavy, then went to work positioning it and tightening the cinches. Farinelli edged sideways a fraction, then planted himself as though in resignation. 'It's not that bad, old fellow.'

As usual, by the time she was ready and had led the gelding out into the too-early morning sun, everyone else was outside and mounted. Two brown-and-gold dogs sat by the corner of the stable, both already panting, with long pink tongues lolling from the corners of their muzzles.

Whhhhunnnnnn ... Anna glanced toward the whinny from the stable, but could see no one and guessed that some mount wanted to say something to another, or something. With the sun falling on her uncovered forehead, she found her hand feeling for the floppy hat tucked into her belt.

'Lady Anna.' Firis had arrived as well and bowed.

'Captain Firis.' Anna returned the bow. 'We appreciate your hospitality, and I wish you well here in Pamr.'

'I wish myself well, also,' responded Firis, his hand smoothing the salt-and-pepper beard that made him look older than his years. 'It was good to see you, lady, and may your journey to Falcor be speedy and free of difficulty.'

'Thank you.' Anna looked around. Only she was unmounted. She climbed into the saddle, with a great deal more ease and skill than just a few weeks previously.

'Ready, lady?' asked Markan.

'Yes.'

Firis offered a half salute as they rode across the packed yard toward the road leading downhill to the gates.

Anna glanced around. She did not see Meris, but realized Gatrune still stood by the hall entrance. Anna waved and got a wave in response.

No one spoke for a time as they rode south into Pamr and turned westward into the center of the town. As the five passed down the main street, the handful of men standing outside the chandlery, where a grimy white bow had been placed in the front window, turned toward the horses.

'That's her!' someone shouted.

Three of the men stiffened and glanced toward Anna, as if to step into the packed dirt of the street, then paused as they saw the armsmen.

'Hail the sorceress!' cried an unseen feminine voice.

The face of the tall, bearded man in the center of the three clouded, and he raised a clenched fist, looking around quickly for the woman who had shouted.

Anna turned Farinelli toward him, then reined up. Farinelli snorted loudly, as if to warn the townsman.

'Don't curse me,' Anna said. 'And don't raise your hand against me, or any woman. Your lord is now Lady Gatrune, and her captains will support her to your death. She was ill pleased with Forse. So was I. Why would you seek your own death to avenge someone so cruel?' The sorceress waited.

'No woman should raise her hand to a man,' sputtered the bearded man.

'Then . . . no man should raise his hand against a woman. After all, a woman bore him, and another will bear his children.' Anna waited, then added, 'Times are changing, and you should change with them.' She flicked the reins, and Farinelli carried her westward past the chandlery.

'. . . arrogant bitch!'

Anna ignored the words, much as she would have liked to do more, but some men would never change, and she couldn't do more for the local women – not yet. Still, it continued to irk her that what would have been sternness in a man was considered bitchiness in her.

'. . . you believe that stuff about her flaying the dark ones with fire whips now?' whispered Fridric to Stepan.

'. . . don't understand sorceresses . . . burned that chandler to a crisp, and she was crying. Here she's telling them to shape up, or mayhap die.'

Put in Stepan's terms, Anna thought, some of her actions were strange, but how could she explain what she felt without appearing a total emotion-driven idiot? When she didn't have time to think things out, she had to go by what she felt. When she didn't, she got into even more trouble.

'Lady!'

Anna looked up to see a small girl scurrying from a small house toward her. The barefoot brunette carried a basket and lifted it up to Anna, even as the girl's eyes flicked back toward the center of town.

Almost instinctively, Anna bent to take the basket.

'Thank you . . . My mother thanks you, too,' whispered the child before she raced back away from the riders.

Anna's mouth opened, but the girl was gone behind a dusty hedge, and Anna found herself looking at a dirty gray cat that also immediately vanished into the roots of the hedge.

'I don't think the chandler was well liked by the women of Pamr,' said Daffyd.

'It would not seem so,' agreed Markan.

As she rode, Anna lifted the cloth covering the rush basket. Within were two round cakes, a coarse weave bag that appeared filled with nuts, and a waxed wedge of cheese.

What could she do with the basket?

'There's room in the provisions bag,' suggested Daffyd. 'What's in it?'

'Cakes, cheese, nuts.'

Markan helped bring the piebald mare up beside Farinelli, and held open the provisions sack while Anna eased the basket in place. She slipped the flowers under the leather strap of her own saddlebags, wishing that she had a better place to put them.

Between the flowers and the dust, her nose itched again, and they hadn't even left Pamr.

A quick glance back reassured her that no one was following, but Stepan shook his head. 'No one be following you, lady, not from here.'

Was she that fearsome?

Her eyes went to the road ahead as they neared the bridge over the Chean. Despite the length of the stone span – more than two hundred yards, the river itself was a narrow strip of brownish water between dry mud flats, weeds, and sun-dried water plants. A nondescript brown duck paddled toward the reeds of a small marshy span north of the bridge.

Farinelli's hoofs clacked loudly on the stones of the bridge, and Anna felt as though she were leaving more than a town where she had spent but a single night, as though the unknown she had already faced were the familiar compared to what lay ahead.

58

The sun was still above the western horizon when the five riders passed the roadstone that declared Zechis a mere two deks ahead.

Daffyd's lips were clamped tightly together, and he swayed in the saddle of the gray mare. Fridric's and Stepan's conversation had died away. Anna's legs were sore, and the thigh muscles above her knees threatened to cramp. Her hair felt like it had crawled through a swamp, then been powdered with dust, and her eyes burned from the road grit.

'A good day's ride, indeed,' Markan declared. 'We'll like as to be at the inn before sunset, well before sunset.'

Anna pulled her sweat-dampened hat farther down on her forehead to shield her eyes against the sun as they neared the town. Unlike Pamr, the only large trees visible in Zechis were those to the north of the town proper that outlined the banks of the Chean.

Anna glanced at the house nearest the road, shutters askew, walls brown-splotched and dusty. Nothing moved, except a chicken pecking at the ground on the west side.

The five rode quietly, the only sounds those of hoofs, harnesses, and horses occasionally snorting.

Another hundred yards farther into the town, Farinelli danced sideways as a gray dog growled, straining at a rusted chain that held him close to the door of a small hut with cracked and dust-smeared plastered walls that once might have been white.

'Easy, Farinelli . . . easy.' Anna patted the gelding's shoulder.

The dog growled once more, then sank back onto his haunches as the travelers passed, their dust subsiding in the hot stillness of late afternoon.

The inn dominated the central square of Zechis. Perched above a roofed front porch, the sign alone was distinctive, with a painted border of intertwined black and gold triangles, and an enormous black pony. The outside walls had been recently whitewashed, and a youth in rags swept the front steps.

Markan reined up at the railing beside the front steps, and Anna followed his example, conscious that a quiet had fallen across the handful of men standing in the shade of the east-facing porch. A heavy man in a gray leather vest and a shirt that once could have been white openly leered, while a younger, trimmer man in a sleeveless tunic merely looked.

Anna bowed to the inevitable, and snapped firmly, but not sharply, 'Markan . . . you and Daffyd come with me.'

The player appeared puzzled, but Markan answered crisply, 'Yes, Lady Anna.'

The heavy man in gray looked away. Markan's eyes

twinkled, but his face remained stern as the three dismounted and tied their mounts.

Anna let Markan and Daffyd flank her on the way into the inn. Inside, the main floor was warmer than the porch, and Anna removed the soggy hat. Behind a narrow counter at the end of the entryway stood a narrow-faced woman in a brown shirt.

'Looking for lodging?'

'What have you for a party of five?' Anna asked.

The woman glanced from Anna, then to the armsman and the player. 'And who else?'

'Two more armsmen,' Markan said. 'My lady travels light.'

'You can have the corner place, lady. That's a gold, for the private bed and the common room. You get a basin and a towel, and common fare for all.'

The no-nonsense manner indicated that was to be expected, but Anna paused.

'Our mounts?' asked Markan. 'The usual copper each?'

'For five? That's for hay. If you want grain, say an extra two coppers. Visula might ask four, but it's late.' The innkeeper paused. 'That's a gold and seven coppers . . . if you want the grain.'

Anna managed not to fumble with the wallet, and laid a gold and a silver on the counter, waiting.

The three coppers came back slowly, as if the innkeeper were expecting some largess.

The sorceress smiled. 'Extra service is paid for after it is rendered . . . if it's merited.'

Markan's lips stiffened momentarily.

'You won't find better on the whole highway to Falcor, lady. No you won't!'

'Then I'm sure we'll both be satisfied,' Anna answered with a smile.

'You want I should show you the room?'

'Daffyd . . . you come with me. Will you take care of the mounts and baggage, Markan?' Anna asked.

'We'll stable them and bring things up.' Markan turned to the woman keeper. 'The front corner or the back?'

'Back, a'course. Quieter for a lady.'

Anna followed the older woman up stairs barely wide enough for the innkeeper's broad hips, and down a narrow hall where every plank creaked.

'Here you be.'

The room directly off the hall held six pallets of a dubious nature, an oil lamp on a wall sconce, and a single narrow window.

Through the door from the outer room, Anna stepped into the corner room. Small, not much more than three yards square, it had a window with the two-shutter arrangement – louvers on the inside and heavy open shutters on the outside. A single worn towel lay folded across the base on the lumpy narrow double bed that had no pillows. A nightstand containing a basin and pitcher on one side and a single squat lamp with a sooty mantle stood between the bed and the window. Two wooden chairs and a cracked and battered chamberpot completed the furnishings.

'Be bringing up the water soon as I leave.'

'I'd appreciate that,' Anna said.

The woman sniffed and headed back down the dim hall, the floorboards creaking under her weight.

'It's not much better than the tents in Pamr,' Daffyd observed sourly, massaging his thighs.

Anna refrained from shaking her head. Compared to the Black Pony, the El Reno Motel she'd stayed in for Irenia's senior recital had been a palace – if only she'd known! If the Black Pony happened to be better than most, Anna wasn't sure she wouldn't prefer a bedroll in the open air to the rest of the inns. Of course, inns probably had greater appeal before the dark ones had cut off all the rain and snow.

Markan clumped down the hall and into the room, handing Anna her saddlebags and lutar case. 'Lady ... the way you handled Quisa ... even Lady Anientta couldn't have done that.' The armsman shook his head and surveyed the room with a laugh. 'Hasn't changed much. It's still better than most.'

Anna carried the saddlebags back into her room and set them in the wooden chair closest to the window.

'Here's a good solid bucket of water!' announced Quisa. Markan intercepted it. 'Thank you, Quisa.'

'You're with that lord down south, aren't you, fellow?'

'Lord Hryding,' Markan agreed. 'We're headed to Falcor.'

'Takes all kinds, it does.' Quisa shook her head and waddled back out the door.

Fridric, provisions bags in hand, had to flatten himself against the wall to allow Quisa to pass.

Stepan was laughing as he brought in the last of the saddlebags. 'I waited until she came down, but, no, you just had to get up the stairs.'

'You were right,' Fridric conceded.

'What's in these?' Stepan lifted the two irregular bags. 'They clank, like blades and stuff.'

'Blades and stuff,' Anna admitted. 'I thought they might be worth something.'

'More than in your purse,' Markan said. 'Could I ask . . .'

'You can ask.' Anna forced a smile.

'Never mind, lady. Better I not know.'

'I'm hungry,' Fridric said, almost plaintively.

'Best we eat early. Food just gets tougher,' Markan suggested.

'I'd like to wash up a little,' Anna said.

'Not enough water for all of us,' Markan observed, glancing toward Anna's room.

'I think I can handle that.'

Anna washed first, then managed to clean the water in the basin and bucket twice with the water spell. She sat in the empty chair and looked out the window while the others washed.

Two armsmen in purple rode past the inn, but neither stopped. A setterlike dog dashed across the street after something she couldn't see, and loud voices echoed from the porch.

Her head kept aching, even after she held it in both hands and massaged her forehead. She finished the water in the bottle. Markan had brought with her saddlebags, and that helped.

'We're ready, lady,' Daffyd offered softly.

Anna stood, her legs suddenly unsteady. After two steps, they uncramped somewhat.

'Can you ward our stuff?' asked Stepan.

'Ward?' she answered.

'Keep it safe.'

'Let me think a moment.' It took more than a minute, but Anna did come up with what she hoped would serve.

> 'Sing, sing a song;
> keep them safe to last our whole night long.
> Don't worry 'cause it's sure strong enough
> for those who don't belong.
> Just sing, sing a song.'

She rubbed her forehead, which had begun to throb, probably from all the spells and no food for several glasses. Sorcery on an empty stomach hurt, she had discovered.

'Strange ward,' murmured Fridric.

'Strange or not, it will work,' opined Markan.

Anna hoped so.

The entire inn seemed to creak as they walked in single file down the hall and to the lower level. The public room was half empty, with a large table in the near corner.

'Take the corner chair, lady,' Markan suggested, though Anna had already decided on that.

The five had scarcely wedged themselves around the circular battered and grease-stained wooden table before the squat serving woman arrived, her trousers and tunic brown from a variety of sources beyond the color of the fabric. 'Standard fare?'

'What else is there tonight?' asked Anna.

The serving woman glanced toward the squared arch through which smoke oozed and lowered her voice. 'Nothing anyone should try.'

Anna felt the comment was honest. 'Standard fare all around.'

Markan nodded minutely.

'Drinks? Beer, red stuff about all we got.'

'Red stuff?' asked Daffyd.

'Call it wine, but it's half vinegar, so I call it red stuff. Visula's always on me for it, but . . . customers like to know.' A toothy grin followed, showing too many blackened teeth.

'Beer,' suggested Markan.

Anna agreed, and, after that, so did the others.

'Five more for the drinks,' said the server.

'When they come,' answered Markan.

Anna wanted to massage her forehead, which throbbed more fiercely. She needed to eat. Instead, she withdrew, trying to ignore the greasy air, the odor of sweat and burned meat, and the too-loud conversations.

'Visula thinks he's got the only inn on the road.'

'He does, the dissonant devil.'

'Who's the lady, there?'

'. . . three, four armsmen, but she rode in, no carriage . . .'

'Who cares? . . . prefer a good blade any day . . .'

Five tin mugs clunked onto the table.

'Where's your five?' asked the serving woman.

Anna laid five coppers on the wood, which vanished in a different kind of magic, and pulled one of the mugs in front of her. She studied the soapy-looking liquid even as Markan took a deep draught.

'Good . . .'

She didn't quite believe him, and tried a sip. Lukewarm or not, it wasn't bad. She had another sip.

Stepan swallowed half a mug.

'Lad . . . easy,' cautioned Markan. 'The lady Anna isn't about to pay to get you sick.'

Before Anna took a third sip, the serving woman was back with five large steaming bowls filled with a thick dark liquid leavened with lumps. 'Road stew,' she announced, staring at Anna.

Anna got the message, and looked to Markan. The armsman mouthed 'two.' Anna fumbled out a pair of coppers.

With a smile the serving woman swept them away. 'Enjoy. The bread's a-coming. Hot, too.'

Within moments, it had – two long black loaves.

Anna glanced around – no cutlery . . . nothing. Markan had out his own dagger. *Do as the Romans, or whoever, do*. Anna ended up spearing the chunks of meat with her own dagger, nibbling on them, and sopping up the gravy with her bread.

Her headache began to subside. What *was* it? She'd had trouble with blood sugar before, but it seemed even worse on Erde. Was doing sorcery worsening the effect?

As she ate, around them, the half spoken, half shouted conversations swirled.

'. . . a dissonant fool ol' Berfir was . . .'

'. . . Prophet'll save us, but that's to keep the Liedfuhr off his ass, not 'cause he gives a single note about us.'

Anna looked down at the empty bread basket and the empty bowl. Had she really eaten it all? Her eyes felt heavy. Maybe the bed wouldn't be too lumpy. Maybe.

59

With the sun beating into her eyes, low enough that the battered hat's brim was useless, Anna squinted toward the west and the road that merged with a red stone bridge.

Moving past her on the left was a wagon drawn by two horses that plodded stolidly forward and raised road dust that seemed to hang just high enough for her to breathe. The driver stared at the road without ever looking at Anna, Daffyd, and the three armsmen.

Anna rubbed her nose gently.

Daffyd sneezed once, twice.

'The dust never ends,' Markan said.

The player sneezed again, and so did Stepan. Anna squeezed her nose and tried not to sneeze as well – and failed. Her eyes watered with the explosive force of the sneeze.

'. . . wish we would get enough rain to lay the dust,' gasped Stepan.

Anna agreed, but blotted her eyes on her sleeve, then straightened in the saddle.

A rider wearing a sash of cream and green pounded past the armsman and toward the east. The sorceress's eyes followed the rider for a moment.

'Prophet's messenger, for all the good it will do him.' Markan paused, then added. 'No one will listen, and no one will tell him anything.'

Anna smiled ruefully – that sounded familiar, just like academic politics at Ames or anywhere else.

A small square tower stood at the eastern end of the bridge, door bolted shut, upper windows shuttered. Dust coated the stones, softening the harsh red. As Anna's eyes passed over the structure, she wondered why the small tower had ever been built, since it would have been useless against any army. A tollhouse that could no longer even pay for itself?

'Up there, three deks or so, is where the Fal and the Chean come together,' Markan said idly as his mount's hoofs clacked on the broad stones that paved the approach to the bridge.

Wide enough for two wagons abreast, the stone bridge across the Falche River consisted of three sections. The first ran about a hundred yards from the east bluff of the river to a wide stone pier built up from a small island covered with brush and willows. The second section extended somewhat less than a hundred yards to another stone pier that rose out of the placid-looking muddy water. The last section stretched from the pier to the western bluff of the river – and the eastern part of Falcor.

The ruts in the stone pavement testified to the bridge's age, as did the loose mortar in the railing. A single cargo raft, steered with a tiller and containing pallets of something, floated south of the span, a dark brown splotch on the light brown water that shimmered almost silver in the late-afternoon sun.

As Farinelli carried her off the bridge and onto the rough cobblestones of the road, Anna studied the small square that consisted of one statue on a pedestal in a paved area from which five streets branched. Like every other town she had seen in Defalk, Falcor lacked walls. Was that because sorcerers could break them down or because the countries were so far inland that walls were seldom needed? Or for some other reason?

'Which way?' she asked Markan, slowing Farinelli.

'The river road, the one to the left. The liedburg is south of the city proper.' As he spoke to Anna, Markan turned in the saddle and pointed toward Fridric. 'Unfurl the banner.'

The streets of Falcor were paved, if dust-and dirt-covered, and the sounds of the city echoed along the narrow streets.

'Knives sharpened . . .' *Cling, cling!* 'Knives sharpened . . .'

''Ware the wagon! 'Ware the wagon!'

Anna looked up and saw the chamberpot, reining up Farinelli just before the sloppy mess splashed into the open sewer that ran along the right side of the street.

Flies swirled around them, smaller and swifter than the large horseflies on the highway. The street narrowed more, and an odor compounded of horse manure, sewage, spoiled food, and kitchen fires drifted around Anna. No wonder medieval minstrels extolled the countryside.

'Beautiful Falcor . . .' murmured Anna. Brill's hall seemed impossibly distant, impossibly clean. As with so many things in her life, Anna was reminded that the better aspects were often transitory – like Irenia . . . like earth itself. She drew herself erect on the gelding, steeled herself for the ordeal that would come.

The equivalent of a dozen blocks farther south, they reached another square, containing women, children, and carts drawn up randomly on the pavement. From several carts the smoke of fowl being cooked on braziers rose, and Anna was reminded of how Mario had smelled every night the year he had worked for KFC.

'Roasted fowl! Roasted fowl, two a quarter, two a quarter . . .'

'. . . hot fowl rolls . . . hot rolls . . .'

'Stenjabs! Get your stenjabs here!'

What were stenjabs? Anna had no desire to find out, and neither Markan nor Daffyd made any comment.

'Lady? A fowl for your men?'

The sorceress shook her head.

'Probably diseased,' Markan said under his breath as they rode from the open area back onto a street wider than that which had taken them from the bridge.

The dwellings were larger south of the square, with lower level walls built of large square red building stones, like brownstones, and only shuttered entrances on the street level. Up a level were balconies and windows, and higher, tile roofs.

The street sewers were covered – mostly – with slabs of stone.

As the street sloped downhill, Markan gestured to the castle – the first real castle Anna had seen – on the opposite hill, overlooking Falcor, with the Falche River to the left. 'The liedburg.'

A banner comprised of two cream-and-green triangles, over which was superimposed a golden trumpet, flew from the staff above the gates.

Anna nodded and took off the floppy hat, using her hands to try to push her hair into some semblance of order.

'Good idea,' said Daffyd.

Don't condescend to me! she thought, but only smiled.

The street widened into an avenue as it flattened in the space under the liedburg. An expanse of grass a full hundred yards wide surrounded the castle on three sides, with the eastern side of the bluff overlooking the river.

Markan slowed his mount at the stone-paved road to the gates.

The walls around the liedburg were not perfunctory, but a full twenty yards high, made of massive red stone blocks, designed to withstand sieges. In the flat below the walls on the side closest the river, were set up rows of tents, and armsmen lounged in the shade created by the canvas. Several peered toward Anna and her entourage as they headed across the open area to the gates.

A full squad of guards in leathers and sea-green sashes was drawn up, half on each side of the gate. While the gates were open, a network of bars that resembled a portcullis with a small doorway in the middle blocked the gate opening.

'We might as well ride on.' Anna flicked the reins, and Farinelli stepped forward, his hoofs loud on the hard stone.

'Who are you?' asked the weathered subofficer who stepped forward when Anna reined up short of the guards. Then he added less peremptorily, 'Lady?'

'I am the lady Anna. I am here responding to the Prophet's proclamation. The armsmen escorting me represent the fealty of Lord Hryding, and his demonstration of goodwill.'

'The lady who?'

'The lady Anna,' she repeated, forcing herself not to explain. No lady would explain in public.

'Who is she? Some lord's daughter ...'

'... another doxie for Behlem?'

'... got none, not with his consort ...'

'... she that sorceress?'

Anna smiled, ignoring the whispered speculations, waiting for the subofficer's response.

'I cannot say that I ...' The subofficer broke off his words with an embarrassed smile.

'It might be best if you conveyed my message to Lord Behlem,' Anna said. 'Just tell him that the lady Anna has arrived, as he requested.' There was no way she was entering the castle or its grounds until Behlem knew she was there. 'I will be happy to wait here.'

'It's hot out here, lady. I was only thinking of your comfort.' His smile turned slightly sick looking.

'I've ridden from the Sand Pass to Synope and then here. A little more sun won't hurt.' She smiled and patted Farinelli.

After a long moment, the subofficer bowed slightly, turned, and made his way into the shadowed archway and through the door in the portcullis.

'She's got guts . . .' whispered Fridric, before Stepan jabbed him in the ribs.

The guards remained drawn up, holding positions loosely at ease, all except for a graying armsman who stepped forward to take the subofficer's position. He did not look toward the five riders who waited.

Sitting on Farinelli in the late-afternoon sun, Anna could feel the heat on the side of her face and her neck, and the sweat in her hair. Her legs threatened to cramp again, but she held her seat, as if it were a performance before unfriendly critics – and it well might be.

In time, two green-coated officers, with silver-braid swirls on the shoulders of their tunics, appeared, flanking a white-haired older man in cream and green. The subofficer trudged behind.

The whispers rose as the four neared the far side of the portcullis.

'Counselor to the Prophet . . .'
'. . . more than pretty she must be . . .'
'. . . think old sharp-tongue's in for it now . . .'
'. . . she can get the captains here, she's someone . . .'

The armsman who had taken the subofficer's place stepped back as his superior stepped in front of the guards.

'Honor . . . arms!'

Twelve blades flashed in salute.

The white-haired man stepped toward Anna. 'I am Menares, counselor to the Prophet.' He bowed, then straightened. 'I recognize you from the waters, lady, and bid you welcome to our temporary abode.'

'I am pleased to be here.' Anna swung out of the saddle, hoping her legs would hold. They did. 'I have arrived as quickly as possible.'

'Your haste is appreciated in these times,' Menares said, before lowering his voice. 'If you would all follow me . . .'

Anna turned and nodded to Markan, and the four dismounted, Daffyd slightly behind the others.

'Let them enter!' Menares ordered.

'Raise the gate!' said the stockier of the two officers who had accompanied the counselor.

After a moment, with a creaking series of squeaks, the gate lurched upward and into the stone grooves behind the heavy wooden gates.

'Return . . . arms!'

Anna led her entourage forward through the narrow stone archway, hoping that she were doing the right thing. Farinelli only side-stepped once.

Once they were in the courtyard, Menares turned to Anna again. 'The Prophet will meet with you – only briefly at the moment – but he will receive you more formally at dinner tomorrow when you have had a chance to rest and refresh yourself.'

And when he's had time to gather everyone to examine me, Anna thought. *Or decide what he really wants to do with me*.

Menares motioned to the slender officer. 'Namir will ensure your armsmen—'

'—and my player,' the sorceress interjected.

'—have their mounts stabled and are refreshed, while I escort you to Lord Behlem.'

'Now?'

'What better time, Lady Anna?'

The sorceress shrugged, finally handing the reins to the Neserean subofficer. Farinelli neighed and side-stepped.

'Easy,' Anna commanded, and the gelding subsided.

With a last look back, and a quick smile at Daffyd, she followed the white-haired counselor across the courtyard and through a wide double door. Their steps echoed through the high ceilings of the hall, or liedburg, echoed off worn and polished stone floors that had no mats or carpets. The walls were bare red stone, except for sconces holding unlit lamps set at irregular intervals. The lamp mantles were uniformly sooty.

A sour odor permeated the hall, one that would have been more unpleasant, Anna suspected, had the climate not been so dry.

At the end of the main hall, Menares started up the grand staircase. Anna tried not to wince as she lifted her sore legs and feet.

'I must admit that I was . . . taken by surprise . . . at your speedy arrival,' said the older man.

'I didn't see much point in waiting,' Anna said. *Not since I really had few choices.*

'Sorceresses do not have so much freedom as many surmise,' Menares continued. 'Nor do lords.'

Anna nodded. Counselors to rulers weren't stupid, not even in backward realms, not if they survived, and she had better remember that.

They halted outside a set of double doors, where two armed sentries stood. The one on the right eyed Anna silently.

'This is the lady Anna, the sorceress the Prophet summoned. She has ridden for the past week to answer his summons.' Menares waited.

'As you wish, counselor.' The sentry turned and opened the right-hand paneled door.

Menares gestured, and Anna entered, hoping it was not an elaborate trap, mentally readying the burning spell, hoping it would not be needed.

The room was long and not much more than five yards wide, with high shelves on both sides, and a single, man-high window at the far end.

'What do you want, Menares?' The voice came from the end of the long battered table, where maps were strewn almost haphazardly. A pitcher and a single goblet stood in the midst of the various sheets of parchment and paper. In person, Behlem looked even less impressive. Hardly into his late twenties, the light beard concealed a weak chin and highlighted shifting watery eyes.

'This is the lady Anna,' Menares said, stepping forward into the space at the foot of the table. 'She just arrived with an escort from Lord Hryding. He's the lord in Synope.'

Behlem looked toward Anna, and the watery eyes focused.

Anna could feel her skin crawl, but she smiled. 'Greetings, Lord Behlem. I am here because of your proclamation.'

'You are . . . younger than the waters showed.'

'I am who I am,' she responded.

'Will you help us against the dark ones?' The Prophet's words were blunt, almost harsh.

'Yes,' Anna answered, equally bluntly. 'I wouldn't be here otherwise.'

Behlem blinked. then he nodded, and said more matter-of-factly, 'We are crowded here, Lady Anna, but I believe there will be room for you in the north tower with some of the other distinguished ladies and envoys.'

'And my player?' Anna asked.

'That is easier. There are smaller rooms with my players. All players seem to enjoy each other's company. Unlike armsmen and counselors.' The prophet smiled. 'Menares will ensure you are both comfortable.' He glanced at Menares. 'She had an entourage?'

'Some armsmen from the south. I had thought to feed and quarter them for a day or two and then allow them to return to their lord with words from you.'

Behlem's hand wandered to his beard again, even as his eyes strayed across Anna. Then he straightened in the chair.

'I am sorry if I appear preoccupied.' He offered a broad smile. 'If you would ensure that the lady's needs are all completely satisfied, Menares, I would be most grateful.' Behlem turned back to Anna. 'Have you supped yet?'

'No. We came to the . . . liedburg . . . as soon as we reached Falcor.' Anna's head ached, and her legs still threatened to cramp.

'Then perhaps you could use the small hall to feed them before seeing to their quarters and needs?' Behlem smiled at the older man.

'Yes, my lord.'

'I look forward to seeing you tomorrow at dinner, Lady Anna. Surprise us.'

Anna suppressed the swallow and returned a smile. 'I will try to, Lord Behlem.'

A faint frown crossed Behlem's face and vanished. 'Do so. I will see you after you have settled Lady Anna and her party, Menares.'

'Yes, my lord.'

The Prophet looked back at his maps, and Anna followed Menares from the dim study.

As they walked down the stone steps, Menares asked, 'What are your impressions of the Prophet, lady sorceress?'

'He is preoccupied . . . perhaps worried about having the resources to do what he must.' That was certainly safe enough.

'What else?'

'He's younger than I had thought.'

'So are you. And more beautiful. Perhaps too much so,' the counselor added dryly.

'I am not so young as I might appear, counselor, but I am here to do what I can to stop the dark ones.'

'Why? You come from afar.'

'Someone must,' Anna said. 'And without making this land safe, how can I ensure my own safety?' She hoped that also struck the right chord, true as it was. No one was going to feel happy with a sorceress they didn't feel grateful to – or something like that.

'You see to the heart of matters.'

Anna wanted to shake her head, but she followed the counselor back toward the courtyard.

60

In the courtyard below, another set of messengers had arrived, their horses' hoofs clacking on the ancient stones. The unwavering sun cast the shadows of the walls across most of the eastern side of the courtyard.

Anna wiped her forehead and turned from the narrow window back into the hot confines of the modest tower room. Falcor was more humid than Synope or Mencha – not so bad as Ames in the summer, but hot and damp enough to make her uncomfortable. Could she come up with some spell to cool the place?

Less than four yards square, the stone walls contained a bed somewhere in width between a double and a twin, perhaps a three-quarter bed like the one in her grandparents' guest room on the Cumberland holler farm. Every bed in Defalk seemed to be a different size, but she supposed each was built individually for the room it was to occupy.

She had a flat dressing table with a mirror that distorted her image slightly, a stool, a straight-backed armless chair, a large chest, a wash-table, and the ubiquitous chamberpot. There was also a jakes on the level below her, but the smell outside it was overpowering. A single braided purple-and-beige rug lay on the floor, its braid frayed and close to unraveling. The purple coverlet on the bed was also frayed and worn with remnants of stains that no washing could remove.

A large pitcher of water with a single goblet stood on the

chest. She'd definitely orderspelled the water, especially after the ride through Falcor. She'd cobbled together yet another spell to rid the room of vermin the night before, and the immediate headache she'd received had convinced her that there had been vermin, and that she would be better using the mandolin or lutar whenever she could.

Still, she had slept better than since she had left Brill's hall, despite some nightmares where faceless figures in dark robes had chased her through the night. Were the dark ones still looking for her?

Anna snorted to herself. Had they stopped seeking her?

Breakfast had arrived on a tray, as had a midday lunch, and she had enjoyed both the attention and the time to relax and practice the chords on the lutar, far trickier than she had imagined. But she didn't doubt she was a prisoner of sorts – although the only bolt on the door was on the inside.

That didn't matter for the moment. What was important was getting ready for the dinner reception, just like for a performance, and that's what it would be.

Thunnnnkk! The heavy knocker on the tower door clunked. 'Lady Anna . . .'

The two pages who had apparently been assigned to her, as some sort of disciplinary duty, she suspected, stood there. Their arms were filled with ill-assorted fabric, with shades ranging from mottled brown to mottled green.

'Just bring me some cloth, linen and cotton,' Anna had said. 'Any kind.' Well . . . they had brought all kinds.

'Put it on the bed.'

'Would you like anything else, lady?' asked the thin redhead.

Anna ignored the slight overemphasis on 'lady,' and answered. 'Is there a bathing room in the tower?'

'Ah . . . no, Lady Anna.'

'Then bring me two large basins of clean water. And some good soap.'

Both pairs of shoulders slumped.

'I know. It's a long walk.' She smiled. 'But I would appreciate it, since I must appear in court tonight.'

'Court?'

'Before the Prophet,' the sorceress explained. Every so often she used some common phrase, and everyone looked blank. It was so like the year she had studied in London.

The two exchanged glances.

'We could bring a big bucket for your basin,' said the redhead.

'If you could get one more basin with the bucket . . .'

'We'll try, lady,' promised the more voluble redhead.

After they left, Anna sorted through the dozen yards or so of assorted fabric. Some appeared to be cotton, and a small swatch of blue was something like velvet. All was poor quality.

After picking up the lutar again, she had to spend more time tuning it, and she probably would every time until the strings finally broke. Three spells later, two goblets of water, and more retunings than that, she had a passably decent recital – or court – gown, a dressing robe, and a nightgown. And still several yards of cloth left.

She'd have to think about what else she needed. In the interim, she folded the spare fabric and tucked it under the bed.

Shoes? What could she do about shoes? She snorted.

Green suede shoes, instead of blue? Why not?

That worked easily, even if she never had seen green suede heels. The spell, or her visualization, had even matched the suede with the green of the gown. She tried not to worry about the source of the leather. At least her boots remained intact.

Then, reminded of the heat by the sweat on her forehead, and the need for another goblet of water, she tried a cooling spell, using an offshoot of the basic water melody.

Mist rolled off the walls, and a hammer slammed through her skull. She slumped into the chair and massaged her forehead. Maybe enduring the heat was easier.

She just sat for a time, until another thunk on the door announced the return of the two youths with the water.

After standing and setting the lutar in the corner by the window, Anna opened the door.

The redhead gaped at the bed, where the green gown lay, with the shoes beneath. 'Where . . . lady? Did you bring a seamstress?'

'Sorceresses make their own gowns, didn't you know?'

'It's cool in here.' The dark-haired page set the heavy bucket on the floor. 'Cooler than down in the water room.' His arms trembled.

'Don't spill the water, lad,' Anna cautioned. She paused. 'I can't keep calling you two "lad" or what have you. What are your names?'

Both swallowed.

'Uhhh . . .'

Anna shook her head. 'Names mean nothing. If I wanted to, I could cast a spell on you without your names.'

'But . . .'

Anna waited.

'I'm Birke,' said the redhead. 'My father is Lord of Abenfel.'

'Skent. My father was guard-captain of the liedburg.' The brightness of Skent's eyes warned Anna.

'Bear with me,' she said. 'I have much to learn. I am a stranger here.'

'Is it true you're from the mist worlds?' asked Birke. 'That's what the armsmen who brought you said.'

'Yes.'

'What are the mist worlds like?' Birke persisted.

'I only know my own world. Where I live is cooler than here, especially in the winter . . .' Anna paused and looked at Skent, who was holding himself still and trying to keep his lip stiff.

She touched his shoulder. 'I'm sorry.'

'Don't touch me.' His words were cold and trembling.

'I am sorry,' she said. 'I don't want to upset you, but I can tell it hurts.'

'How would you know?' burst forth from the dark-haired boy.

'My children are in my world,' Anna said. 'My oldest daughter died not very long ago, and it still hurts.'

Birke stiffened, but Skent continued to tremble.

'I wanted to hold her ...' Anna swallowed, then said quietly, 'I never can.' She pulled back into herself. 'I'm sorry, Skent. I didn't mean to upset you.'

'That's ... all right. You are a lady.'

'Can we do anything else?' Birke asked quickly.

'No.' Anna glanced to the window. 'How long before dinner?'

'They eat when the sun sets,' Skent said coldly, the chill radiating from his words.

'Thank you.' She paused. 'I need to wash up and get ready, then.'

The two slipped out, and Anna did not close the door all the way, listening to whispers over the steps that slapped down the stone stairs.

'Maybe she is a sorceress ...'

'... better act like she is, Skent ... she's something, and I wouldn't want to get in her way ...'

'She seems nice ... a lot nicer than the others, anyway ...'

Anna hoped the story would get around. She needed all the help she could get, and that might not be enough. Her eyes flicked to the lutar and then to the heavy bucket of water. She had a lot to do.

Even washing up wasn't that simple. She had to use another spell to clean the water again in order to wash her hair, but she wasn't going to her first dinner with the Prophet of Music without looking her best.

The bell in the liedburg differed from that used by Brill, but Anna was ready, looking out the window toward the sun that touched the tops of the houses on the west side of Falcor.

Thuuunk. 'Dinner will be served, lady,' called Birke, his high voice carrying through the heavy wood.

'I'll be right there.' Anna glanced at the mirror and patted her head a last time, trying to nudge the blonde strands into a better semblance of order.

Birke gulped audibly as the sorceress stepped into the narrow hallway. She smothered the smile, knowing that she was treading a fine line, but the gown was conservative, with slightly puffed short sleeves and a square-cut neck that did not show any cleavage, even if the cut of the fabric hinted not quite blatantly that she was feminine.

Skent smiled shyly.

'Are you feeling a little better?' she asked.

'A little, lady.'

'Can you two tell me who will be at this dinner?'

Both shook their heads.

'They don't tell us. We have to stay in the tower during the day, except when we fetch things,' Birke explained. 'That's why we don't mind going for water or cloth or things. Not too much, anyway.'

'Where is this dinner?' Anna asked, putting out a hand to the rough stone wall. The last thing she needed was to tumble down the narrow stone steps.

'In the middle hall,' said Birke.

'No one uses the great hall,' Skent added.

Anna wanted to sneeze as each step seemed to raise more dust. Her eyes were watering by the time they left the tower and walked along a paneled side hall – windowless, with only intermittent lamps. After less than twenty yards, Birke turned left into a larger corridor, where the sconces contained larger brass lamps. The lamps on the left side had been lit, and a page with a striker stood on a stool at the far sconce on the right side. Anna's heels clicked on the tile floors that had been recently swept.

Halfway down the corridor, an older page or a young armsman stood before the pair of guards outside a set of arched double doors.

'That be the middle hall,' whispered Skent.

Anna stopped. Now what?

'Giellum, this is the lady Anna. She's the sorceress from the mist world,' explained Birke.

'Lady Anna.' Giellum bowed, and turned toward the doors. The guards opened the doors, and he stepped through. 'The lady Anna!'

Anna smiled at Birke and Skent, then straightened and walked into the formal dining hall. The room was dim, with only three triple candelabra upon the table lit, a table under the pair of unlit chandeliers that contained close to twenty men – not a single woman. Within herself, Anna stiffened, but she kept the smile in place.

'How do you know she's a sorceress?' The single remark from somewhere near the head of the table hung in the sudden silence.

Before anyone else could speak, Anna sang the candle spell almost loud enough to shiver the crystal chandeliers – and the room flooded with light. A quick look up told her that her spell had burned down the top third of every candle.

About half the jaws around the long table hung down.

'For the moment, will that do?' Anna asked, inclining her head slightly to the sandy-haired Lord of Neserea.

'Yes. That will do, Lady Anna.' Behlem smiled broadly. 'Does anyone else wish to question the lady's capabilities?'

The silence answered the question.

The Prophet gestured to the empty place at his right.

As Anna passed up the table toward the head, she caught a few whispers.

'. . . Prophet has the luck of the dissonant . . .'

'. . . take luck over skill any day . . .'

'. . . never seen a sorceress that lovely . . .'

She kept the professional smile all the way up the table, where at another nod from Lord Behlem, she took the empty seat to his right, noting that not one of the men around the table even made a gesture toward her chair.

'Lady Anna, you have met Menares,' the Prophet said after she sat.

Anna nodded across the table to the white-haired counselor, who returned the nod and gave a half smile.

'This is Hanfor, overcaptain of the Prophet's Lancers.' Behlem inclined his head toward a square-faced officer in the cream and blue that marked the Nesereans. Hanfor was seated to the right of Menares.

Hanfor's black hair was short and streaked with gray, and his weathered face offered a professional smile. 'I hope you can assist us.'

'I will do my best, overcaptain.'

'This is Delor, overcaptain of the Mittfels Foot.'

'Sorceress.' Sitting to Anna's right, Delor was whipcord thin, with black eyes that glittered beneath balding brown hair.

'Overcaptain,' Anna offered her professional smile.

'And this is Zealor, captain of the Prophet's Guard.'

Zealor had a sad round face, blue eyes, and short and limp blond hair. He nodded from the other side of Delor.

Anna returned the nod.

'I am Nitron, overcaptain for the levies.' The brown-haired man beside Hanfor had a sweeping mustache and pale green eyes. His smile was the type that said, 'How can you resist me?'

Delor quietly filled Anna's crystal goblet with dark red wine.

Three servers entered the hall with platters, and a fourth with two baskets full of bread. Two of the platters went down between Behlem and Anna, one with slices of beef covered in a brown sauce. The second platter contained mixture of apples and green beans sprinkled with nuts.

'Eat while the food is warm. It won't be hot because the kitchen is a long walk.' Behlem laughed briefly, then speared a slice of the meat and dropped it on Anna's plate, then took two for himself. She returned the favor by ladling some of the apple-bean casserole onto his plate and then hers.

Several of the younger officers at the foot of the table continued to stare at Anna, but she forced herself to ignore the scrutiny. She cut and ate a bite of the meat, glad that at the Prophet's table there was cutlery, since she had not brought her dagger with her. The hot mint sauce was spicy enough that Anna's eyes watered after one mouthful, and she quickly broke off a chunk of bread and ate that, followed by a sip of the fruity and too-sweet wine.

Then she tried the apples and beans – an odd, but not unpleasant combination.

'Not bad for Defalk,' murmured Menares, after finishing a complete slice of meat in less than three mouthfuls. 'A little on the mild side.'

Anna took smaller bites of meat from then on and reminded herself to be cautious when eating in Neserea.

'Perhaps the lady Anna would be so kind as to tell us in a few words where she is from and how she came to grace our presence.' Behlem lifted his goblet and punctuated his words with a long swallow.

'As some of you know,' the sorceress began after gently clearing her throat and wondering when her sinuses would stop burning from the spices, 'I was summoned here from earth. It's one of the mist worlds . . .' She went on to summarize her tale, careful not to identify Daffyd and Jenny as the summoners, emphasizing the cold, dark nature of the Ebrans, and concluding with her trip from Synope.

'Sorcerers tell of wondrously mighty weapons seen in the images of the mist worlds,' said Menares. 'Powerful as you are, why have you not employed such weapons?'

'Because it takes thousands of people to make those weapons on my world and because that kind of technology magic does not work on Erde.' Anna offered a shrug.

'Does song magic work on your world?' asked Menares.

'Not nearly so well as it does here,' Anna answered.

'I am curious,' ventured Delor. 'Why are you willing to help us?'

Anna paused, thinking, *Careful . . . this is where it gets tricky.* 'I am frankly not so interested in helping you as I am in stopping the Ebrans. In my world, years ago, there was a country like Ebra, whose soldiers wore black and who decided to try to take over the world. No one tried to stop them when they were smaller and not so powerful. In the end the world was devastated and over fifty million people died.'

'Million?' asked Zealor.

Anna frowned momentarily, then realized the number was probably meaningless in a culture where the largest cities were in the tens of thousands and battles were decided by a few thousand people. 'One hundred thousand – a million is ten times as large.'

'You must be . . . deceived. There are not that many people anywhere.'

'The country where I lived had over two hundred million people. Two others had more than five times as many people.'

'They would be crowded together like rats,' protested Zealor.

'In some places, they are,' Anna admitted.

'The sorceress answered the question, I believe,' interjected Menares smoothly. 'It is not that she loves us so greatly, but that she has already seen in her own world what damage those like the dark ones can create.' He rubbed his chin. 'Still . . . why do you choose to fight? Most women do not.'

'I think I have already shown that,' Anna answered. *And I'm not about to admit that I don't have many choices.*

'Surely . . . some would offer protection . . .' That came from the lower end of the table.

'When one accepts such protection, the price is high, and the choices few,' Anna answered.

Behlem laughed. 'What our sorceress is saying is that, like you, captains, she prefers to make her own choices and pay for them with her abilities. We need her abilities, and I would rather pay her than lose armsmen. Wouldn't you?'

'With almost no support,' Menares added, 'she destroyed more than half the Ebran forces in the battle for the Sand

Pass, and all of the darksingers in the pass itself. Eladdrin is yet seeking replacements.'

Anna covered her confusion with a sip of the wine. Menares and Behlem were using the others' questions to sell Anna. Why? She especially needed to watch the older man, she felt. Menares didn't feel untrustworthy, but he didn't feel trustworthy, either. He also knew too much. Behlem was totally untrustworthy, and he'd do away with her as soon as he didn't need her. So she needed to remain indispensible. What a miserable situation – the worst of university politics combined with magic and medieval court intrigue.

'I suppose she'll use her sorcery from a safe redoubt while we take the arrows?' asked Nitron.

'At the Sand Pass, she was as exposed as any armsman,' Behlem said mildly. 'Sorcery doesn't work unless the sorcerer's voice can be heard. Except in the mist worlds,' he added with a disarming laugh.

'That works out both ways there,' Anna added. 'Our weapons can destroy whole cities, so nowhere is safe in war.'

'Barbaric . . .' said Hanfor under his breath.

All war seemed barbaric to Anna, and arguing about which way of killing was more or less civilized was an academic exercise. She took another sip of wine.

'How soon will the Ebrans advance?' asked Delor.

'Not until they are at full strength, and that will be several weeks yet,' said Menares.

'We should attack sooner.'

'Good advice,' said Behlem wryly, 'except that we're not up to strength yet, and their forces are closer than ours. We also need to get more support from the local lords.'

'Ha! You've got a fat goose's chance of escaping that fire.'

'The lady Anna brought us the support of the Lord of Synope, and we have the support of Pamr and Dubaria—'

'. . . never heard of them . . .'

'—and we expect that support to grow with the arrival

of additional forces from Elioch and Itzel.' Behlem raised his goblet. 'To the defeat of the dark ones.'

Anna managed to drink less than two goblets of wine in the endless toasts, and the questions that, as the evening proceeded, repeated the questions already asked, and the answers already given. She also forced herself to eat far more than she wanted. A good look in the mirror while dressing had convinced her of that necessity, even while she fought the impulses that screamed, '*You're overeating. You'll get fat.*' Even though the words in her mind had sounded like Avery's, she had to fight to eat what she had.

In the end, though, her steps were steady when, after asking the Prophet's leave, she stood and walked toward the arched doors.

'Think she'll warm his bed?'

'Not if he's got any brains. Would you want to get caught between her and Cyndyth?'

Even keeping her face calm as she walked toward the door, Anna seethed. In some matters, even in Falcor, she had choices. And she would have more.

61

FALCOR, DEFALK

I had not expected her to be so ...' Behlem fingers his beard, as he leans back in the leather chair.

'So beautiful?' asks Menares.

'How can it be real? Is it a glamour?'

'Her reflection in the wall mirrors is the same as her appearance. Even with spelled water, her reflection is the same. I took her hand, and it feels like the hand of a young woman.'

'But ... how? She looked older in the mirrors.'

'She was. She is. She has indicated that she has children older than Cyndyth.'

Behlem looks sharply at Menares. 'How did you find that out?'

'From my efforts when you sent me here. Does it matter?' Menares shrugs. 'You wanted the sorceress, and she will assist you.'

Behlem fingers his beard and shakes his head.

'Don't even think about it,' cautions Menares. 'She may be powerful, but if Cyndyth and Konsstin—'

'I know ... But she's beautiful, and she doesn't simper or cringe.'

'She is almost old enough to be your mother, no matter how she looks,' says Menares dryly. 'And you need her abilities a great deal more than you need her body.'

'There is that.'

'Keep thinking that way, Behlem. Otherwise, Eladdrin will pull Defalk down around your ears – our ears, I might say.'

The Prophet swallows the last of the wine in his goblet. '... never have what I want ... always some problem ... What about this Lord Hryding?'

'He lost half his levies and most of his trained armsmen in that battle for the Sand Pass. He couldn't stop four-score of your armsmen. So he escorts the sorceress to you and hopes for your favor. Send back a few golds and a scroll. He'll support you, and it will cost you almost nothing.'

Behlem nods. 'What does it gain me?'

'You can announce tomorrow what you did last night to the captains, that yet another old lord of Defalk has seen the wisdom of supporting you. If you can announce one every few days, before long, no one will dare oppose you, not openly.'

The Prophet refills his goblet. 'She is beautiful, and it is not just her appearance.'

'You had best hope that Cyndyth does not discover that is how you feel.'

'So had you, dear friend. So had you.'

62

You summoned me, Lady Anna?' Daffyd asked, looking at the dusty stones of the landing where he stood outside Anna's door.

'I just asked if I could talk to you.' Anna shrugged. 'Before I knew it, the pages were running off, and I guess they dragged you up here.' She gestured to the chair by the table. 'Why don't you sit down? Would you like some water?'

'Ah . . . yes.'

Anna could see the dampness around his forehead. She handed him the extra goblet. 'It's clean.'

'Your room is cool.' Daffyd finished the entire goblet in two long swallows. 'That was good. Thank you.'

'I've had time to work up a few more spells. I don't know that I could take it if it were as hot as it was when I got here.' She refilled the goblet. 'I figured that if Brill could cool rooms I ought to be able to find a way, and I did. It's so hot here.'

'It's hotter here than in Mencha. It always is this time of year, and it gets hotter until harvest time.'

'How are your quarters?'

'I have a small room to myself, and it's got a window. That's something. I managed to get some spare strings, too. One broke when I was practicing yesterday.'

'How are the players?'

'They're players,' Daffyd shrugged. 'Most aren't as good as I am, or Liende or Kaseth, or even Jaegel. Lord Brill had the best. This bunch only knows a few dozen spell tunes.'

'Who do they play for?'

'Lord Behlem.'

'He knows sorcery?' Anna asked, puzzled. If Behlem knew sorcery, why did he need Anna?

'Most rulers know a few spells. Even Barjim learned a few, but they're simple. Anyone can learn a spell, I guess, but what good is one spell, or even a few? And people who aren't sorcerers can't always sing the spells right, even the ones they know.'

And they probably can't match their singing well with the players unless it's very simple, Anna thought, then asked. 'Do you need anything?'

'No. We're fed well, and we can practice, and walk around the courtyard. It's boring, though.' He looked at Anna. 'Was this a good idea, Lady Anna? There's no locks here, but . . .'

'We'll have to see,' she answered. 'I couldn't do much in Synope.'

The player finished his second goblet of water.

'See who you think would make a good players' group.' Anna held up her hand. 'I don't have anything in mind, yet.' She poured herself another drink. Even with the coolness of the room, it was dry, and she needed a lot of water.

'You know, Dalila really liked you,' Daffyd said slowly.

'I like her. I don't care much for Madell.'

'I never did, either. But she had to get away, and he was interested. Ma worried about Lord Brill.'

Anna shook her head. From what Liende had said, Daffyd's mother probably worried that Brill would be interested in Dalila instead of him and she wanted out more than her daughter had.

'I don't know,' the violist finally said. 'You think you know things and then you don't.'

'We all find that out,' Anna said with a half-bitter laugh. 'We all do.'

63

WEI, NORDWEI

The bright flames of the lamps on the wall scarcely flicker, and no smudge of soot mars the crystal mantles of the brass luminaries. Through the window, points of orange and yellow mark the larger lamps lighting the the harbor piers, and the lines of darkness undotted by lamps denote the River Nord and the outlines of Vereisen Bay.

The heavyset seer waits in the chair until the dark-haired woman with her back to the window looks up. The blonde woman in the adjoining chair moistens her lips.

'What have you seen, Kendr?' asks the dark-haired Ashtaar at last.

'The sorceress from the mist worlds ... She is strong ... and she has been welcomed by the Prophet Behlem,' answers Kendr.

'We knew she was strong. All the strings of Liedwahr echoed when she called the fires of dissonance down upon the Ebrans.'

Gretslen looks down.

'You are displeased, Gretslen?'

'I am concerned. I did not feel dissonance when the sorceress called the fires.'

'What about you, Kendr?' questions Ashtaar.

'I sensed no dissonance, ser.'

Ashtaar frowns, then asks, 'What else have you discovered about the sorceress?'

'She is in a tower in Falcor, in the liedburg, and she has a strange instrument, like a lute, but larger. She practices with it. People visit her.' Kendr smiles apologetically.

'Is that all?'

'Yes, Your Mightiness.'

'I'm not a mightiness, Kendr, but you may go. I would like a few more words with you, Gretslen.'

The two wait until the seer departs and the door closes.

'Why did Behlem offer her sanctuary?' asks Ashtaar.

'It was his idea alone. We tried to discourage it, and we've planted more seeds, especially since the sorceress has been renewed and made young again.'

'Those seeds will take time to grow into trees and bear fruit.'

'I know,' Gretslen admits.

'That's fine, I think. The battle for the Sand Pass showed that the Ebrans are stronger than the Council thought. So let the sorceress be, for now, Gretslen, whether she be of harmony or dissonance,' says the dark-haired woman. 'If she defeats the Ebrans, and Behlem is victorious, then she must be eliminated. Behlem with a sorceress of that power – he would be insufferable.'

'Even with our influence?' asks Gretslen.

'Behlem disregarded our "influence" on this already,' answers Ashtaar ironically.

'We should remedy that, too,' suggests Gretslen.

'Later . . . if necessary,' Ashtaar agrees.

64

Anna studied the clean riding clothes she wore, then yanked the bellpull. Daffyd had intimated that she was a prisoner in a gilded cage. Well . . . there was no way she was going to spend another day sitting in a tower room practicing lutar and trying to adapt more songs into spells. She'd go mad.

She walked back to the window, standing slightly back from the open shutters and the cooling barrier she had managed. The portcullis had been lifted to admit another troop of horse, and there were more tents in the flat outside the walls. To the north, clouds formed on the horizon – had her efforts reduced the Ebran control over the weather?

Thunk! 'Yes, Lady Anna?' came the voice through the heavy door.

'Come in.'

The redheaded page stepped inside and bowed.

'Birke,' Anna announced, 'I'm going riding. Farinelli needs the exercise. I'd appreciate it if you would make the arrangements so that we can leave the liedburg as soon as possible.' She smiled. 'I'll saddle Farinelli myself. It might be dangerous for anyone else.'

'But . . .'

'If anyone gives you trouble, they can come to me – or to the Prophet's counselor Menares. It's not as though I'm going to ride out and attack the Ebrans. All the other captains come and go. So will I.'

Birke gulped. 'Yes, lady.'

A smile played across Skent's face as he stood behind Birke.

Anna stood waiting until the page bowed, and both of the youths left. Then she shut the door and walked back to the window. The portcullis had been lowered again, and the arriving armsmen had vanished somewhere into the castle.

She could have marched down to the stable herself, but that would have created a direct confrontation with the stablemaster, or whoever was in charge, or would put the man in an impossible situation, and she didn't want to put any of the staff in such a position. She would need every ally she could find. The pages were supposed to carry out her wishes, and she'd provided them with a safe response – she hoped.

She did not have to wait long before the knocker thunked again.

Menares stood at the door, breathing heavily. 'I understand—'

'I am going riding. Nothing more. I will not spend all my

days in a small tower room. If I am to ride to battle, I need practice.'

'Not all of Falcor is safe . . .'

'Fine. Tell me where I shouldn't go.'

'You need an escort . . .'

'All right. A small one. Have them meet me in the stables in a few moments.'

'Your actions might be considered . . .'

'Menares, you're a smart man. You know, and I know, that the Prophet needs me, and I need the Prophet. But I'm not a bird in a gilded cage. Besides, it wouldn't hurt the Prophet's image to have me riding around. It will give the impression that people are joining him by choice, not force. Oh, and I'd like one of the pages to accompany me, probably Skent this time. He needs to get out.'

'Lady Anna . . .'

'Menares, it's much safer for you and Behlem to have me perceived as willful and independent.'

'Still . . .'

'Do you want me to have to resort to sorcery? Do you think I won't?'

'I will have an escort as soon as possible.' The heavy shoulders dropped. 'I would appreciate your not trying to leave the castle without them. We might need the portcullis at some point. Or the walls.'

'Thank you. I'm not about to do anything foolish.' *Not too foolish, anyway, besides riding in a strange town in an impossible world under the indirect and questionable protection of an unloved conqueror. Except I can't allow myself to be seen as his creature or his captive, and I can't allow them to intimidate me.*

Anna permitted herself a tight smile as the counselor's heavy footsteps and labored breathing echoed back up the tower staircase.

Before she had taken a step back into her small room, two sets of footsteps raced up the stairs. She opened the door before Birke could lift the knocker.

'Lady . . .' panted the redhead, 'the counselor said we were to get you ready, that he would send word to the stablemaster—'

'I know. He just left.' Anna glanced at Skent. 'Did he tell you that one of you will be accompanying me on my rides?'

'No, lady.'

'Today, it's Skent's turn. Tomorrow, it will be yours.'

'But . . . Virkan said we weren't supposed to leave the liedburg,' said Birke.

'It won't be for that long. You can tell Virkan that both Menares and I feel one of you should go.' Anna smiled. 'If Virkan gives you any difficulty, or tries to make your life harder with things like extra duties or less food, let me know. I'll find out anyway, but telling me immediately will stop such nonsense immediately.'

The two pages exchanged glances again.

She had the feeling Virkan would be a problem from the shiver that went through Skent.

'Just a moment. Wait right there.' Anna went to the dresser and rummaged through her scraps of paper until she found the notes on the 'kindness' spell she had used on Madell. The two names even had the same number of syllables.

Then she uncased the lutar, retuning it quickly, not that it needed much since she'd practiced earlier. Vocalises were just about the only thing she dared sing full volume on Erde.

Both pages swallowed as she stepped onto the landing outside the door.

'Let's find Virkan.'

The two exchanged glances.

'Don't worry. I won't turn him into ashes. We're just going to put a stop to this nonsense. Let's go.'

Birke led the way, down to the lowest level of the tower, and then through a musty narrow tunnel that ran south, Anna thought, under the main section of the hall. Finally, they halted outside a room that looked to be under the foundations for the hall's main grand staircase – or something that required an equally imposing footing.

'The lady Anna wished to see you, Virkan.' Birke's voice trembled.

'Oh . . . up to no good again, Birke. Trying to use your exalted position to get out of work. Or is it worse this time?'

Anna stepped through the doorway, ignoring the sour smell that filled the room. Sitting in an old wooden armchair before a battered table, almost a caricature of the English butler, Virkan looked like Anna had supposed, pudgy, but not fat, with deep-set weasellike eyes that shifted from one side of the small lower room to the other.

'No. I am taking Skent and Birke with me on my rides – one at a time, of course, so that one will be left in the tower, but I was led to believe that you would be displeased.' Anna smiled, lifting the lutar into position.

'Displeased, my lady? We are only here to serve.' Despite the smile, the words were empty sounding, false. Anna could tell that Virkan was the type that would always present a cheerful and pleasant front while abusing people who couldn't resist. And all the men in the liedburg would ignore the problem because they thought anything less than whipwelts was acceptable.

'So am I,' Anna said, letting her fingers caress the chords. 'So I thought I'd help the Prophet a little.' Then she sang:

> 'Virkan wrong, Virkan strong,
> treat all right from this song.
> Virkan warm, Virkan cold,
> gentle be till dead and old.'

The lutar's chords and Anna's voice slammed through the small, stone-walled room, and, halfway through the song, the pagemaster staggered up as if to reach for Anna, then slumped into the chair.

'You have cursed me . . .' His voice was instantly hoarse.

'No more than you deserve,' Anna said quietly. She could see the desperation behind his eyes as she watched every scheme, every cruelty being weighed and denied by the spell. 'You will be kind to everyone. It's really no different from a command from the Prophet or Lord Barjim, except you can't weasel your way around it.' She nodded. 'Good day, Virkan.' Then she turned. 'Skent, you and I will head for the stable. Birke, I forgot the case for the lutar. Would you fetch it, and meet us at the stable?'

'Yes, Lady Anna.' Birke bowed and scurried off.

Anna followed Skent back up the steps to the main floor.

'You look discouraged, Skent,' Anna offered as the silence persisted.

'You upset Birke, Lady Anna, maybe as much as Virkan.' He paused. 'Sorcery is scary.'

'I didn't mean to scare you, but I could tell that Virkan would punish you and that neither one of you would admit it.'

'That frightened me, too.'

'That's not sorcery. I saw that because I have children. My son is twenty-four, and he got that look every so often.' Anna laughed, thinking about how transparent Mario had been.

Skent swallowed as he held the outside door to the courtyard. 'Is that true? Really true? You look as young as Lady Cataryzna.'

'I take it you like her?'

'She's beautiful. Not as beautiful as you,' Skent added.

'I'm sure she is beautiful, and you don't have to worry about flattering my ego, young man.' She almost winced as she stepped into the heat of the courtyard. Why was Birke so upset? Should she ask, or just listen over the next few days? She decided on listening.

The stables were within the southwest corner of the outer walls, and Anna could smell straw, horses, and manure, although the odors were mild, and the packed-clay floors swept clean.

The page led her to a small room just inside the doors, where he held the door and bowed. 'Tirsik, this is the Lady Anna.'

The stablemaster was probably younger than Anna, but looked older, with short graying hair above a wrinkled forehead. The blue eyes twinkled, and his right arm was shorter than the left and seemed permanently crooked. He bowed as Anna stepped inside, still carrying the lutar. 'Lady Anna.'

'Stablemaster,' Anna returned.

'Of sorts.' He grinned. 'You're the one riding the beast.'

'Farinelli? The big palomino?'

'The beast,' Tirsik affirmed. 'We feed him and water him, but the stall's a mess. Won't let no one in. Hisse got slammed leading him in and unsaddling him, had to scramble up the wall.'

'I'm sorry. I'm taking him out today, and from now on, I'll make sure I'm here to groom him and ride him every day. It's taken a little time to work things out. I'm new to Falcor.'

'You from Neserea?'

'No. I'm from a distant place, but most recently I've been living in Mencha and Synope.'

'She's *the* sorceress,' Skent volunteered.

'Oh . . . my pardon, lady.' Tirsik bowed again. 'I did not know. You are the one from the mist worlds?'

'Yes. But I'm still a real person.' She forced a laugh. 'And I need help, just like everyone else who rides a horse.'

'If you ride the beast,' Tirsik returned with his own laugh, 'I don't know what help I can give.'

'You feed and water him.' She inclined her head to Skent. 'Skent here, and on alternate days, Birke, will be riding with me. They'll need mounts, if that's possible.'

'We can do that.' The words were slow, not quite questioning.

'I've already met with Virkan and Menares.'

'She has,' Skent confirmed.

'You have great powers of persuasion, then.'

'I appealed to their better nature.'

Tirsik raised his eyebrows.

'Virkan, I am confident, will have a much better nature from now on.' *Of course, he'll hate me to the end of his days, but if the spell holds, he won't be able to do much, and who knows, he might actually find being kind works.*

'If that be so, lady, many will be grateful.' Tirsik looked at Skent. 'Get your boots, imp.'

'Yes, Tirsik.' Skent grinned and was gone.

'Happiest I've seen him in weeks.' Tirsik stepped toward the door. 'Let's see to your beast.'

Even before Anna reached the stall, Farinelli started snorting and whuffling. She set the lutar carefully on a bale of hay. 'Yes, I'm coming,' Anna told the gelding as she opened the stall door.

'You must have ridden a lot,' Tirsik said, staying outside.

'Not for years until recently. We just get along.' She patted the gelding's flank and scratched his forehead as Farinelli turned to her. The gelding *whuff*ed violently and edged her toward the stall wall. Her boot hit something sharp, sharp enough that she could feel it through the heavy leather.

After bending down, she extracted what looked to be a four-pointed metal star, bigger than her fist, with cruelly sharp points. Anna glanced at Farinelli, then called, 'Tirsik.'

'Yes, lady?'

'Why is this in Farinelli's stall?' She gingerly handed the object to the stablemaster.

'Dissonant bastards,' muttered the stablemaster. 'Can you check his hoofs?'

'Why?'

'That's a caltrops.'

'What?'

'Foot soldiers use them, scatter them around to stop horse troops.'

Anna swallowed, then moistened her lips. Why would

someone try to lame Farinelli? To get at her? Anna shook her head, then began to ease her way around the stall – carefully with the slippery footing underneath.

Surprisingly, to her, Farinelli let her lift each foot. Each appeared uninjured. 'His hoofs are fine.'

'Good. None of my people would do that. Not to any animal, and certainly not to one this fine.' Tirsik's voice was edged. 'We'll check all the stalls.'

Anna began to brush the gelding.

'Looks like some armsmen coming,' commented Tirsik.

'Oh . . . I'm supposed to have an escort. Menares doesn't want someone to attack his prize sorceress. I told him a *small* escort.'

'Subofficer walks like he's got a burr under his saddle.'

'He probably does. Proud warriors don't like protection details.' Anna snorted, looking for the saddle blanket. She patted Farinelli, hoping he wouldn't throw off the blanket, and eased out of the stall.

'Subofficer Spirda, Lady Anna.' The words seemed forced out of the stiff young officer's mouth. His tanned face registered disapproval, even to the blond hair and brush mustache.

'I am pleased to meet you, Spirda.' Anna inclined her head gravely. 'I'll be a few moments, since I'll need to finish saddling Farinelli.' She could see the thoughts in his mind – *She* names *horses; what am I doing here?*

'Naming horses is one of my many peculiarities,' the sorceress added. 'Along with carrying my own weight.' She stepped back into the stall, where she slipped the saddle off the rack and onto Farinelli, who whuffled. 'Easy . . . you'll get some exercise, plenty of exercise before we're done.'

'That one's not what she seems, officer,' said Tirsik wryly. 'Not a one of my men that beast will let near.'

'A disguised unicorn? I doubt that,' said Spirda.

'You want the bay mare, boy?' asked Tirsik, looking at Skent who had hurried up.

'If you please, ser.'

'The page is coming?' asked Spirda.

'Yes, ser,' Skent said. 'The sorceress said I had to.'

'Sorceress . . .'

'Ser,' offered Skent politely, 'she filled the middle hall with light in instants, and she turned useless cloth into the finest gown, and her room is cooler than the deepest cellars of the hall.'

'You saw all this, boy?'

'Yes, ser.'

'Hmmmm . . .'

Behind the stall wall, as she tightened the saddle cinches, Anna frowned. Spirda sounded like another man who needed both cultivating and watching.

As she led the big palomino out of the stall, Birke appeared, breathless. 'Here's your case, Lady Anna.'

Tirsik offered, and Anna handed the reins to the stable-master. 'Easy, Farinelli.'

The gelding *whuff*ed, but remained planted as Anna quickly retrieved the lutar and put it in the case, then strapped the case to the empty saddlebags. She took the water bottle, and handed it to Birke. 'I'm not as organized as I should be. Can you fill this quickly?'

'Yes, lady.' The redhead dashed off.

Anna frowned. Fear from the youth, she didn't want. She turned to Spirda and smiled. 'I'm pleased to meet you, Officer Spirda. I apologize for imposing on your time, and that of your men, but the Prophet's counselor felt . . .' She shrugged.

'The instrument? I understood this was to be a ride.'

'It is.' She glanced down to his belt and the rapier he wore. 'You are an armsman, and you wear your weapon on your belt. I'm a sorceress. I'd prefer not to use mine. That is why you are here, and why the lutar is in its case. I will use it if I have to.'

Spirda frowned, and Anna wanted to sigh. Had she gotten the biggest dunce in Behlem's forces? Probably, and that meant explaining.

'What the sorceress means,' Tirsik interjected with a smile, 'is that sorcery's often not too . . . particular-like, I'd guess you'd say, officer. I heard that this lady killed at least a couple thousand Ebrans. I don't suppose that the Prophet would want her having to kill a few thousand folks just to fend off a few brigands.'

Anna could see the light dawning, dimly. 'Officer Spirda,' she said gently, 'we are just going on a ride. I need the exercise. The Prophet is convinced I need a certain amount of protection. For me to do what I can, I need to see more of Defalk. Right now, that means Falcor.' She smiled again, feeling that she was smiling too often, as she had at Ames, and before, until her face felt like it would fall off. Why couldn't she just spell out the situation? Because she was dealing with people, and people didn't like truth. Once she'd thought it was only men – before she met Dieshr – but women were just as bad, and often more vicious.

'All right, lady. We will accompany you. Let us get our mounts.'

You don't have any choice, but if that's the way you want to save face, for now, we'll leave it like that, Anna thought, saying, 'Thank you. Skent and I will wait for you in the courtyard.'

Tirsik smiled sadly and briefly as the Neserean officer turned and marched off. 'Need to get you on that bay quick, Skent.'

'Yes, ser.'

Anna led Farinelli out of the stables and into the still-shadowed corner of the courtyard. Two armsmen working a grindstone in the shade of the wall glanced up, speculatively, then went back to their labors. She tried to look at the inside of the liedburg in a more analytical fashion.

From what she could tell, the general plan was simple – the hall sat in the middle of the walls, with towers attached to each corner of the four walls. The working aspects of the castle, such as the stables, were built inward from the outer walls, and the irregular space between the hall and the expanded walls formed the de facto courtyard. Guards walked the upper section of the outer walls, but without much conviction.

Anna, again, got the impression that Falcor, and Defalk, were just too tired from drought, whatever, to put up much resistance. Behlem had apparently just marched in and taken over.

Skent arrived first, leading out the bay mare. 'Tirsik let me take the bay. Birke says she's steady. I didn't get to ride much this last year, not like he did.'

'Why was that?'

'He's the son of a lord. They get to ride more often.'

There was more, but Anna didn't press, especially as Birke hurried back with the water bottle. 'Thank you, Birke. I appreciate it.' She took the bottle and slipped it into the leather holder hanging from the front of the saddle.

Birke nodded.

Spirda and two armsmen rode up almost immediately. So Anna climbed into the saddle with a grace she wouldn't have believed weeks earlier, and eased Farinelli alongside Spirda's chestnut.

'Whenever you're ready, Officer Spirda.'

Spirda nodded stiffly and eased the chestnut into the sun and toward the portcullis gate.

'Spirda, Prophet's Guard, escorting sorceress, the lady Anna.'

The portcullis lifted, and Anna nodded to the gate officer. 'Thank you.'

The officer did not smile, just studied her. Anna stared back until his eyes fell.

Another set of guards were drawn up outside the portcullis, but only one or two even looked up as the six rode out. Was that because no one was interested in anyone free enough to ride *out*?

As Farinelli's hoofs clicked on the stone – and the gelding almost pranced – Skent rode on her immediate left, and

Spirda on her right. The other two armsmen, bored looks on their faces, rode behind.

She turned to Skent. 'If we go south, where will the road take us?'

'Through the merchants' quarter, Lady Anna, and then back to the fork in the highways. One crosses the south bridge and goes on to Sudwei, the right fork follows the river to Cheor, and then down to Abenfel. I haven't gone that far, but that's what Birke says, and he's from Abenfel.'

Anna turned Farinelli left at the end of the causeway, with the castle to her left and a row of structures to the right. Her eyes focused on the shops across from the liedburg, a strange mixture – a perfumery beside a tailor, and then a cooper, and a bootmaker, and then the inevitable chandlery.

'Officer Spirda, where are you from?'

'Zeltos.'

'Where is Zeltos? You have to remember that I'm new to Liedwahr.'

'It's a trading town south of Itzel.'

Anna waited.

'Itzel is where the Essis and the Saria Rivers join. Once it was the capital of Neserea.' Spirda closed his mouth.

'First woman I've seen riding out of there,' came a comment from under a purple awning at the right edge of the street.

'Got a page, too.'

'Discord! The whitecoats might actually be human.'

'Pretty woman, though.'

'Do you come from a military family? – I mean a family where use of arms is the practice?' Anna eased Farinelli around a pushcart bearing baskets.

'All Neserean men are skilled in arms,' Spirda said stiffly, his mount following Anna's. Skent went around the other side of the cart.

'I'm sure. That wasn't quite what I meant. You're a leader, and often families have a tradition of producing arms leaders.' Anna patted Farinelli because she could sense he was getting edgy with the combined street traffic of pedestrians and carts.

'Oh ...' Spirda paused, and Anna could almost feel a thawing at the recognition/compliment. 'No. My uncle was a subofficer with the old prophet, but my sire is a merchant. I was never meant to peddle carpets. So I joined the Guard.'

'I got the impression the other night that the Guard is special, but no one said much. Probably they thought I knew.'

'The Prophet's Guard is the oldest company-at-arms in Neserea, and it takes much skill to be accepted.'

'I'm complimented that the counselor felt I needed such talented escorts. I didn't know.' Anna tried not to retch, but subtlety clearly wasn't within Spirda's reach.

'The Guard gets the special assignments.'

'Do you guard the Prophet in battle?'

'Not all of us, but some Guards are always around him, except when he does sorcery.'

Sorcery? Behlem did sorcery? He didn't feel like he did sorcery, but Daffyd had indicated that anyone could do a few spells, if they practiced, and were ready to take the risks.

At the end of the liedburg grounds to the left, they continued down the street, with structures now on both sides, with a higher noise level.

'... best spices in Falcor ...'

'Fresh fowl! Get your fresh fowl ...'

'... *told* Alastor that flour would go to five silvers! Think he'd ...'

Anna wanted to put her hands to her ears as they eased down the street.

Despite the noise, when she saw the cloth merchant, and the deep green velvets, she wanted to stop, but decided that the Erdean equivalent of shopping wasn't a good idea – not on the first ride with the stiffnecked Spirda.

'It's better a block down,' Skent said loudly. 'In three, the way's clear to the bridge and square.'

Anna hoped so, and offered another smile to Spirda. More

politics! Would she ever be free of politics? It didn't seem to matter where she was; the need for politics continued!

65

'... the gown stayed pure and bright!'

Anna set down the lutar and looked at the deep-blue gown on the bed – neck cut low enough to sing, high enough to get the message across that she wasn't looking for anyone, with quarter-length sleeves loose enough to let her move, yet like nothing she'd seen on Erde.

In some ways, she hated creating gowns ... but it was like performing for the University president – sorceress or singer, she had to keep up appearances.

She glanced in the mirror, struck by the contrast between her riding clothes and the gown – and by the thinness of her face. She felt like she were stuffing herself, making sure she ate seconds, and everything on the trays the pages brought. But her clothes were looser. In the beginning, the idea of youth and eating anything hadn't seemed so bad ... but now, it was almost as though she couldn't eat enough. She was more muscular, but she still looked too thin, bordering on anorexic. Could she order extra food?

Nothing she did seemed to be enough. She took a deep breath.

Still, she'd been riding for the past three days, and even Spirda had become almost friendly. The two pages seemed to enjoy it, and she had a better idea of what Falcor was like – and what it had once been.

Although it was hard to tell, she sensed that perhaps a quarter of the structures in the small city were empty, and that some had been vacant for what seemed years.

She shook her head.

The knocker thunked.

'Yes?'

Not recognizing the voice, Anna opened the door.

Menares stood there. 'Might I have a word with you, Lady Anna?'

'Of course. Please come in.'

As Anna closed the door, the heavy, white-haired counselor took one of the wooden chairs, sat, and wiped his forehead. 'Your rooms are cool.'

'One of the benefits of sorcery. I can cool a small room; I'm not sure about a larger one. Would you like some water? It's cold and pure.'

'Another benefit of sorcery?'

'A necessary one. Defalk is dry, and I need to drink a lot of water.' She filled the spare goblet for Menares, and refilled her own before sitting down across from him.

'You are attending the dinner this evening?'

Anna's eyes flicked to the gown.

'I see you are. More sorcery?'

'Of course. I don't sew that well.'

'You should be aware that the last of the Ebran reinforcements have started out from Synek.' Menares took a sip of the water, then a long swallow. 'I never thought water would taste so good.'

'Thank you.' She paused. 'How long before they reach Mencha?'

'About two weeks.' The counselor paused. 'There are nearly ten thousand in the last contingent.'

'We're outnumbered?'

'Greatly. I was wondering just how effective your sorcery is.'

'It's not *that* effective.' Anna tightened her lips. 'Do you have any maps of the land between Mencha and Falcor?'

'A number,' admitted the counselor. 'But you are not a field commander.'

Anna shook her head. 'That is not why I need them. I have some ideas of how I might apply magic in some areas.' *Actually, I have no ideas at all, just feelings, but I'll have to trust them.* She paused. 'That might mean fighting somewhere of our choice, though.'

'After what the mirrors showed in the Sand Pass, Lady Anna, most commanders would listen if you could assure them that fighting on this or that hilltop would grant them a victory they could not otherwise assure.'

'I may have to ride out to Zechis or Pamr,' Anna cautioned.

'You will have to take a larger escort,' countered Menares.

'For something like that, I'd need one,' Anna admitted. She stood and refilled his goblet.

'Were I younger . . .' the counselor began.

'Remember, counselor,' she cautioned, 'I'm not that much younger than you are. I was just a beneficiary of a sorcerous accident.'

'Would that such an accident befell me.'

Anna frowned. 'Would you really want to be young in a place where you could never see family, friends, or do what you loved fully and freely?'

The white-haired man tugged at the uppermost of his double chins. 'Hmmmm . . . that is a point.' He sipped more of the water. 'Yet . . . it is almost a pleasure just to be here. Cool . . . with a beautiful woman.'

Anna laughed, softly. 'What else do you want, you devious schemer?'

'Me? The truthful counselor of the Prophet? Devious?'

'You.' The sorceress sipped her own water and waited.

'You see . . . I worry about the Prophet. Everyone around him has only seen how easily Defalk fell . . .'

'Without Lord Barjim and his consort, I suspect, Defalk was already defeated, or at least Falcor was.'

Menares's eyes widened. 'How . . .'

'You can feel a lot when you walk or ride through a city.' Anna looked toward the window, and the afternoon shadows on the walls. 'Falcor is dying, or something.' She looked back to the white-haired man. 'You were saying?'

'Be careful, Lady Anna. The Prophet needs you. I know he needs you, but few others understand that need.' Menares eased his bulk out of the chair. 'Alas, I must go.' He bowed. 'Might I visit again?'

'Of course.' Anna inclined her head. 'Of course.'

'Until dinner.' Anna waited until he was down the stairs before summoning Skent to get some water so she could wash up. She missed having a tub – even a real shower would be heaven – but neither was going to happen soon.

She also hoped the dinner would not be long, that she would not be the subject of more sexual speculation, and that she would not have to demonstrate sorcery. She also feared all three would come to pass.

66

Her suspicions had all come to fruition, and despite absolutely gorging herself the night before, a decent night's sleep, breakfast, and a good ride, Anna still had a nagging headache, and the desire to turn Delor into the Erdean equivalent of a toad.

As if nursing sour white wine all evening, and fending off the innuendos of the not-so-good overcaptain Delor had not been enough, someone had searched her room while she had been at dinner. There was no way to lock the tower door from outside, and they certainly knew by now that she had a packful of assorted arms, and spells of sorts scrawled everywhere, although she doubted many could use them, given modern English spelling and cryptic musical notation.

The whole idea made her seethe, though she certainly should have expected it – even sooner. It was almost as bad as university politics. Worse, in some ways, because the locals had this idea that everything was all right unless they were caught red-handed. She shook her head. That wasn't just an Erdean problem, but one she'd seen everywhere, and more often in men than women.

Thunk!

'Coming!' She wrapped the light robe around her and walked to the door, where she unslid the bolt, opened the door slightly, and peered through the slit.

A slender youth – a page Anna hadn't met, she guessed – stood outside on the landing. 'Lady Anna?'

'Yes?'

'The lady Essan will receive you following the midday meal.' His message delivered, the boy straightened, waiting for some response.

'I would be pleased,' Anna said. 'I'm new here, and I do not know where her chambers are.'

'Oh ... that is easy, lady. She has the quarters on the highest level of this tower. She removed herself there when the lord Behlem occupied the liedburg.'

'I'll be there.'

The page still stood on the landing.

'Convey to Lady Essan that I will be at her quarters following the midday meal.'

'Thank you, Lady Anna.' The page scurried up the stone steps.

Anna closed the door.

Why did Lady Essan want to see her? What should she wear? how riding clothes didn't seem appropriate, nor did the gowns she had created for Behlem's dinners.

In the end, she went back to spells and sorcery to come up with a looser set of trousers she could wear with her boots and a light overtunic – both in green. That effort left her perspiring, made her headache worse, and exhausted her stock of unused cloth.

She left her riding clothes on and made her way down to the courtyard. As she passed the lower door, both Birke and Skent leaped to their feet.

'Lady Anna!'

'I promised I'd meet Daffyd, my player, where they have the midday meal.'

'That's over by the stables.' Birke wrinkled his nose.

'You'd do that?' asked Skent.

'Why not? He helped me when there was no one else.'

The two pages looked at each other.

'My turn,' said Birke.

'All right.'

Anna let Birke take the lead, but looked back and gave Skent a smile just before she stepped out the door into the hot courtyard.

'It's really not far,' Birke said with a grin, 'but we can't leave the tower unless we're on an errand or escorting you or Lady Essan, or Lady Cirsa.'

'How's Virkan?'

'He's *much* better, lady. He's not really the same person, but we're not complaining.' Birke stopped, as did Anna, while a squad of Neserean armsmen rode in front of them through the courtyard and toward the liedburg's gate.

Had she been right to lay a geas on Virkan? She *knew* he needed controlling, and that nothing short of sorcery or death would stop the man from terrorizing people who couldn't protest – but that sort of defense wouldn't have stood up in court. But she wasn't in court; she was stuck in a place where power ruled. *And you're becoming just like them*. Was she?

Birke guided Anna around the horse droppings and toward the stable. 'It's good to be able to ride again, and the Prophet even let me send a scroll to my sire. I told him about you, and about riding. You don't mind, do you?'

'Heavens, no.' Anna laughed.

'It's not quite like it was when Lord Barjim was here, but it's getting there. We still don't have lessons like we used to, but Galen's gone.'

'Galen?'

'He was Jimbob's tutor, as well as counselor to Lord Barjim, but he managed to take Jimbob out of the liedburg before the Prophet arrived. Some armsmen clattered out of here in the middle of the night, and the Prophet's forces were here in the morning.' Birke stopped as the dark-haired Daffyd stepped from the shadowed doorway ahead.

'I'm glad you could come, Lady Anna.' Daffyd bowed.

'She keeps her word,' Birke said. 'By your leave, Lady Anna?'

The sorceress and the player watched as the redhead hurried back toward the north tower.

'I'm hungry,' Daffyd confessed.

'Then lead on, master player,' Anna said lightly.

'We're there,' he said, turning and opening the weathered door. The room had two trestle tables in it, and four long benches. The roughplanked ceiling was low enough that Anna could have reached up and touched it. Three men and a woman sat at the tables, the three men in one group, and the woman alone. All looked up as Anna and Daffyd entered.

'You don't mind bread and cheese, with beer?' asked the violist.

'That's fine. I can't stay too long, though. I have another command performance.'

'Lord Behlem?'

'Lady Essan. She's important, but I don't remember quite why.'

'She's the widow of Lord Donjim. He was Lord Barjim's uncle and the Lord of Defalk before Barjim.' Daffyd pulled at his chin. 'Do you know why she wants to see you?'

'Not a clue. I hoped you might know. You know more about Defalk than I do. But you're hungry.'

'Let me introduce you to Fiena. Just sit down and I'll get you a platter.'

'Make it a lot, please,' Anna said. 'Twice as much as you'd eat.'

Daffyd's eyes widened.

'Sorcery. If I don't eat like a stuffed horse, I lose weight.'

'If you say so.' Daffyd gestured toward the woman sitting

at the table nearest the stone wall – clearly part of the exterior wall of the liedburg. 'Fiena, this is the lady Anna. Fiena is the lead string player for the Prophet.'

'I am most honored.' Fiena, a strawberry-blonde with wide blue eyes and a pinched face, sat with her back to the wall. Her eyes went to the platter before her, filled with wedges of yellow brick cheese and a large chunk of dark bread, then back to Anna as the sorceress eased herself onto the bench across from the string player. 'You do look so young, lady. Everyone said that, but it's hard to believe until you see.'

'Appearances can be deceiving,' Anna said blandly, deciding she didn't really trust the blonde. 'Where are you from?'

'I'm from Esaria. Most of us are. There's a players' school there. It's the only one in Liedwahr, they say.'

'There was one in Elahwa once,' Daffyd interjected as he set a platter before Anna and another to her right. Both were filled with bread and cheese, Anna's overflowing in all directions. 'The dark ones destroyed it.'

'Where did you hear that?' asked Fiena.

'Lord Brill.' Daffyd slipped back to the serving table.

'Oh, he was the one who failed.' Fiena gestured vaguely.

'He was very successful in many things,' Anna said gently, taking a good-sized mouthful of bread, then breaking off a generous churk of cheese.

'I suppose so,' answered Fiena. 'I don't know much about Defalk.'

Daffyd set a tumbler before Anna and another before his own plate.

'How many players are there with the Prophet?' Anna asked.

'Just eight of us. That's more than enough. He can only do small spells. They say his sire was a great Prophet.'

'That was Mikell,' Daffyd explained. 'Even Lord Brill admitted he was a great sorcerer. That's why the Norweians assassinated him.'

'He died in his sleep,' said Fiena.

Daffyd shrugged. 'Lord Brill said he was killed, that no

one but a Norweian assassin could bring down that great
a sorcerer.'

Anna felt like she was following a tennis match, with
her head traveling back forth. She tried to concentrate on
forcing more food into the system. 'I don't know much
about Nordwei.' Fiena dismissed Nordwei with a gesture
that reminded Anna of too many over-the-hill divas, or
Mozart's prototypical Madame Goldentrill. 'I do know that
it is impossible for assassins to have killed Lord Mikell.'

'How did you get to be a player?' Anna decided to change
the subject. 'Was anyone in your family a player?'

'My father was the lead string player for Lord Mikell.'
Fiena shrugged. 'I was the youngest daughter. I would
far rather be a player than the consort of a flax merchant.'

Did that mean that her father had had too many daughters?
'How many sisters did you have?' Anna asked.

'Four. Grendee is the consort of Dene—'

'Dene was the son of Lord Mikell's brother,' Daffyd added.

'Sort of a duke,' mused Anna.

'Duke?'

'Never mind.' Anna took a healthy swallow of the beer.
'It means something like the brother of a lord.'

Fiena shook her head minutely, stopped her intermittent eating and looked at Anna silently for a moment,
before saying, 'I don't know much about foreign words.'
The string player dismissed foreign words with the same
gesture that she had dismissed Daffyd's speculations about
Mikell's death.

'I take it that most players do not have consorts,' Anna
offered.

'Not women. It disturbs the harmonies.' Fiena looked at
Anna's platter. 'You eat like a sorcerer. All of you eat so
much and are so thin.'

Anna broke off another piece of bread and chewed it
slowly, along with some of the hard cheese. What Fiena
said about women players didn't make sense. Liende had

been Brill's lover, as had Daffyd's mother. She looked toward Daffyd.

His mouth full, the young violist shrugged.

Anna took a long sip of beer, then asked, 'What is Esaria like?'

'Esaria is beautiful, with white stone buildings on the hills, and wide bridges over the Saris. It's the oldest city in Liedwahr, and scholars come from across all of Erde, even from far Sturinn, to study at the Temple of the Prophet.' Fiena smiled faintly. 'Each season has its beauty, and no other city is beautiful in all seasons. That is why the Prophet chose it, and why it has endured.'

'What makes Esaria so beautiful?' Anna pressed.

'Just everything.'

'Is there anything in Falcor that resembles Esaria?'

'I haven't seen much of Falcor. I didn't bother.' Fiena dismissed Falcor.

Anna took a last mouthful of bread. Had she eaten the entire platter of cheese and bread? She felt still hungry, and yet as though she could not swallow another morsel. She finally nodded to Daffyd before rising and turning to Fiena. 'It was nice to meet you, Fiena.'

'It was pleasant to meet you, Lady Anna, but I hope I didn't offend you. I don't know much about sorceresses.' Fiena smiled her faint smile.

Anna returned the smile.

Daffyd gulped the last of his meal and scrambled after Anna.

'Are they all like that?' she asked Daffyd after they left the room and stood in the courtyard.

'Like what?'

'Never mind,' Anna said.

'Fiena's nice, once you get to know her.'

'I'm sure she is.' *Nice and empty-headed*. The sorceress stepped back as two messengers guided their mounts toward the stable. The faint *brawwk*ing of chickens echoed through courtyard and the heat of the day.

'Sometimes, Lady Anna, I do not understand you.'

'I'm sorry, Daffyd. It's hard to explain. Just because, by some fluke, we speak a language that is similar, we don't see things in the same way. It's not your fault.' She paused. 'I need to go meet with Lady . . . Essan.'

'You should be careful. She is very clever.'

Anna nodded, instead of snapping out at the condescension in his tone, then added, 'I'll talk to you later.'

Her boots echoed on the stones as she walked back to the north tower.

Back in her room, she washed quickly, then slipped into the new tunic and trousers, combed her hair again, swearing as she broke one of the comb's teeth. She hadn't seen any combs in Defalk. Then, she hadn't seen a lot of things, but she couldn't go around trying to create everything through sorcery. After more than a few spells, especially spells without the lutar, the headaches started, the ones that carried needles that stabbed.

The sound of hoofs caught her ear, and she walked to the window. Another troop of horse was gathered outside the portcullis gate, reminding her that she remained in the middle of a war on a strange world.

You'd better find out where those maps Menares promised you are, and get to work. The Ebrans aren't going to wait forever.

After a last look in the mirror, she left her room, still troubled that she had no way to lock it, not that it mattered, she supposed, since Behlem's people would certainly be able to force their way into any place. Anna took the steps up to the upper level slowly. She didn't want to arrive panting.

The white-haired woman who opened the heavy tower door was neither stocky nor frail, and stood nearly as tall as Anna, though her face was heavily lined.

'Lady Essan, I am Anna.' The sorceress inclined her head.

'You are tall,' said Essan. 'Too tall for a blonde woman from Mencha. Please come in.' She stepped aside and gestured toward the pair of chairs covered in embroidered upholstery. Between the chairs was a polished table of dark wood, on which rested a pewter pitcher, two goblets, and a platter containing nuts.

Anna stepped into the tower room, the same size as hers, and bowed. 'I am pleased to meet you.'

'Yet you did not seek me.' The words were not quite acerbic as Lady Essan closed the door and walked stiffly toward the chairs with the pillow on one side of the seat.

Anna followed and waited for the older woman to sit before extending the scroll. 'The lady Gatrune suggested that I not be too forward.'

'How do you know Gatrune, if you are such a stranger?' Essan unwrapped the scroll and slowly read it.

'I had met her consort, Lord Kysar, at the battle for the Sand Pass. When I passed through Pamr later, I stopped to pay my respects. I didn't know that he had died. That was when I met Gatrune.'

'That's what she says. Foolish woman. She believes what people tell her.' Essan gestured to the pitcher. 'Help yourself, as you want. Don't if you're not thirsty. Makes no difference to me.'

'Thank you.' Anna eased into the chair across from the older woman.

'Olive butter wouldn't melt in your mouth. Here you are, young and beautiful, and half the tower's running scared of you. Some nonsense about your coming from the mist worlds. They look in those fancy waters and mirrors, and anything they don't understand belongs to the mist worlds.' Essan snorted. 'You look normal enough, too normal to come from a mist world, and you talk like we do, except for that odd accent. So where are you really from?'

'A world called "Earth." They say it's a mist world, but I couldn't tell you. In some ways, our worlds are similar. In others they are very different.'

Lady Essan stared straight at Anna as the sorceress spoke, then leaned forward and took a sip from her goblet. 'You believe what you say. Why should I?'

'Because it's true. I wish it weren't.' Anna smiled wryly. 'At least, in some ways.'

'According to the legends, no one can be transported without wanting it. Why did you want to come here?'

Essan's blunt frankness was disarming in some ways, and Anna found herself answering in the same spirit. 'My daughter was killed recently, and I thought things couldn't get much worse. Just when I thought that, apparently, a sorceress in Mencha was asked to summon a sorceress from the mist worlds, and I found myself in a totally strange world.'

'Your daughter . . .' mused Essan. 'Some have insisted you are near as old as I am, and enchanted to look younger. How old was she?'

'Irenia was twenty-eight.' Anna poured some of the amber liquid from the pitcher, trying to guess whether it was cider, wine, or something worse.

Essan nodded to herself. 'You have other children?'

'Two. I miss them.' *And I need to do something, somehow . . .*

'Sorcery does not work, or it works weakly in your world – is that not true?'

'That's true,' Anna admitted. 'How did you know?'

'You are said to be powerful, and too many people have seen your sorcery for that not to be true. Yet you are not arrogant, and you are most careful. You work miracles with sorcery, and often forget, or do not think to use the simplest spells. Why do you not use your mirror to view your children?'

Anna barely kept her jaw in place. She hadn't even thought of that. She should have, but it just hadn't occurred to her.

'If you are powerful here, yet are not familiar with simple spells, and have little pride in sorcery . . .' Lady Essan shrugged. 'Then sorcery is not strong on your world.' She laughed once, twice, harshly. 'The hopes of Defalk lie in the Prophet of Neserea and an unknown sorceress. I am almost glad Donjim did not live to see this.'

Anna took the smallest of sips from the goblet – and was

glad she had. The liquid was something like a strong apple brandy that seared her tongue. With the amount that Lady Essan had sipped already, Anna wondered how the woman could talk, let alone be so lucid.

'So . . . how might I help you?' asked the older woman. 'Gatrune thinks I should.'

'I did not come seeking help,' Anna said.

'Why did you offer your services to the Prophet?'

'I didn't see many other choices. I also disliked the Ebrans.'

'Not many as do like them, but that's no reason for a stranger to stay.'

'I don't like running.' *I've had to run too often because I've never had any power.*

'I like you, girl. Except you're not a girl. How old are you?'

'Forty-seven,' Anna admitted.

'Young enough. You don't know enough, Anna.' Essan cackled. 'No, you don't. No one told you about youth spells, I'll wager.'

'No one had a chance. This was a death spell.'

'That harmonizes. Brill'd be noble to the end, the dissonant noble fool.' Essan paused to munch several of the nuts. 'Youth spells mean you stay young until you die. You live a little longer because you're healthy, maybe even twenty years longer, but one day, young as you look, you die. Very sudden-like. Me, I prefer the natural state. It'd be too long that I have been around anyway, and being young and pretty isn't always what it could be. Men,' Essan snorted, 'if you're pretty, they think you have no brains. And if you let it be known that you do, then you're uglier than a wall-eyed goose, and more dangerous than a pointed blade. So . . . woman-girl from the mists, ask me questions.'

'What I don't understand is how Lord Behlem took over Falcor so easily.' Anna tried the nuts, found that they were salted and spiced almonds, and that she remained hungry.

'That is not difficult to explain.' Essan adjusted an embroidered pillow behind her back. 'Defalk has not been blessed with a solid lineage of lords for generations, and it is a difficult land. I had three children. Niedra died in childbirth. Senjim was killed in the first peasant uprising in the south, not the one ten years back – the first must be thirty years now. Carlon – poor boy. He never was quite right, for all that the sorcerers tried, even Lord Brill. So Barjim was the best of the lot, even if his father was a scoundrel. Barjim was honest, and people liked him. We got him to take Jecks' bright daughter, old maid or not, as his consort. All that work . . . and for what?' Essan refilled her goblet.

'Doesn't he have a son?'

'Jimbob? Aye, and Jecks has him safe, for now, but Jimbob has no guardsmen beyond those of his grandsire. I remain near a prisoner, and the old lords of Defalk needs must acknowledge Behlem . . . as you must, powerful as you may be.' Essan added more of the applelike brandy to her goblet.

'And if Jimbob could become lord?'

'He's yet far too young, and at the mercy of his counselors he'd be, for Jecks would not live to see him safe.'

'What will happen if the Prophet can stop the Ebrans?'

Essan sipped more of the brandy and shrugged. 'Who might say? Behlem is a trickster, but some say Menares understands what Behlem does not, and Menares is beholden to the north.' The older lady laughed. 'Behlem knows that well, yet can find no better counselor. It be that way ever. Donjim's best counselor was Werum, and he was beholden to Konsstin.'

Anna wanted to shake her head. It seemed like everyone was tied to someone else, and everyone pretended it wasn't so – just like university politics – or opera companies.

'That would be why all fear you, Lady Anna. No ties have you, and power that will grow. Yet ties you will need. Choose those ties carefully.' Essan set down the goblet and stood. 'I be a meandering old lady, and you are gracious, for all your strangeness.' She yawned. 'Time for my rest.'

Anna got the hint and stood. 'You were most gracious

to receive me, and I appreciate your kindness and your insights.' *Exactly what they mean is going to take a little time to sort out.*

'Nonsense. I enjoy the company. Do come and see me again.' Essan eased toward the door.

Anna walked across the purple-and-gold braided rug to open the door for herself. 'I will, and thank you.'

As Anna stepped out onto the landing, Lady Essan smiled faintly, then added. 'Someday, I hope you can meet Jimbob. He has the cleverness of his mother and the honesty of his sire.'

'I hope so,' the sorceress answered, before turning and heading down the stone steps to her own quarters. The coolness felt welcome, and she stood back from the window for a time, enjoying it and watching the gate, and thinking about all that Lady Essan had told her while pretending to offer nothing.

She could see Elizabetta – maybe. She could try, in any case. But she needed to think about the Ebrans, too, and what she should do, and a dozen other things. She rubbed her forehead. She shouldn't rush into anything, but looking at maps wouldn't hurt.

Her eyes went back to the portcullis. No one had departed or arrived, and after a bit, still thinking about Elizabetta, she stepped back and reached for the bellpull.

Skent arrived alone.

'Lady Anna?'

'Did you know Lord Barjim's son Jimbob?'

'Yes, Lady Anna.'

Anna studied the page, hoping to read more from the dark and serious eyes. 'Would he have made a good page?'

'Lord Barjim made him work with us. He even got punished,' Skent said. 'I got to ride some then, too.'

Anna felt like nodding to herself. At the very least, young Jimbob had gotten some discipline, and Skent did not seem to dislike the heir apparent.

'Skent? Does Menares have a page?'

'He has three. There's Cens and Barat and Hoede.'

'Good. Wait just a moment.' The sorceress went to the table and found a blank sheet of paper, one of the few remaining from those she had brought from Mencha. She wrote out her request, then rolled the paper up and handed it to Skent. 'This is for Menares. I need some maps he promised. Can you make sure he gets this?'

'Yes, Lady Anna.' The dark-haired page nodded somberly. 'Barat owes me.'

After Skent left, Anna pulled out the lutar and began to practice. She still wasn't as familiar with the instrument as she knew she would have to be, not by a long ways.

She managed to ignore the voices from the courtyard, the hoofs on stone, and the occasional horn call. She still hadn't figured out the purpose of most of the horn signals.

She managed to struggle through her revised battle hymn twice, and had gone back to work on adaptations of burning spells, when the door knocker thumped.

Thunk!

She set the lutar aside and went to the door where Skent and a second page stood on the landing. Each carried an armful of scrolls.

'Your maps, Lady Anna. The counselor only asks that they remain in your rooms.'

Anna laughed. 'I can promise that.' She held the door wide. 'Put them on the bed.'

'It's cool here,' said the other page.

'I'm Lady Anna. And you are?'

'This is Barat, lady.'

Barat bowed deeply.

'I appreciate your helping Skent, Barat, and convey my thanks to Counselor Menares.'

'Yes, lady.' The round-cheeked Barat looked up at Anna. 'Did you use a spell to get it so cool here?'

Anna nodded. 'It's much cooler where I'm from.'

'Me, too. My sire's lands are in the south Mittfels, and the

snow doesn't melt until the trees are green in the lowlands.'
Barat paused. 'It's nice here.'

'Thank you.'

With a slow long breath, Barat bowed again, as did Skent,
before the two left the room.

Anna stood with the door ajar as the two headed down
the steps.

'. . . she's pretty! . . . so lucky, you two are . . .'

A faint smile crossed Anna's lips as she closed the door.
She replaced the lutar in the case and unrolled the first
scroll. She had a lot of studying to do.

67

Anna looked into the mirror, wishing she had a clear pool
of water, much like the one Brill had used. But she had no
way to have either a clear pool or a harp, and the wall
mirror would have to do. She hoped it would work.

The sorceress ran through the two sets of vocalises with
the lutar, then brought out the scrap of paper with the words
and notation for the spell.

She cleared her throat, once, twice, took a sip of water,
and then began the spell, trying to mesh the lutar with
the words.

'Mirror, mirror . . .'

The mirror surface shivered into a silvered darkness,
reflecting nothing of the tower room. In the midst of the
shimmering darkness, an image appeared, first as a small
point of light, then expanding to fill the dark wooden frame
that held the silvered glass.

The image was clear – too clear.

Elizabetta sat on the deck of the New Hampshire house,

across the white table from Avery – Antonio. Even through the shimmer of the mirror, Anna could see that Elizabetta had been crying, and Avery was talking. He was always talking, trying to rationally turn everyone to his way of thinking.

Anna watched, but the two just talked, and Paulina didn't appear. The light dimmed, and the shadows around her daughter and former husband deepened as the two figures talked, as Avery smiled and offered yet another statement, and as Elizabetta frowned and tried to hide her disagreements.

From what Anna could see, Elizabetta was protesting, saying something like, 'She wouldn't do that ... it's not like her ... something's happened ...'

The sorceress bit her lips. That bastard! Avery was trying to convince her daughter that Anna had run off. What could she do? Could she?

She couldn't send herself, and Daffyd couldn't send her back, and she couldn't reach Jenny – not with Mencha in the Ebrans' hands.

No one she'd talked to even knew another living sorcerer, and Brill hadn't been exactly encouraging about her being able to return to earth. He'd once muttered something about transport between Erde and the mist worlds creating fires, but when she'd pressed, he'd just shaken his head, and then they'd had to fight the Ebrans, and Brill had been dead before she'd been able to get a straight answer.

The mirror seemed hot, heat radiating off the silvered surface, the heat growing ...

She looked around, then tried to improvise, as the heat beat from the mirror surface at her.

'End this view with a song,
for the heat's too strong.'

A *crack!* followed, slashing across the glass, leaving it blank.

For a moment, she just stood there.

Why was everything so fucking difficult?

Her eyes welled up with tears, and when she could see, the mirror still bore the crack, splitting the reflection of a stone-walled tower room.

She wanted to scream. Instead, she walked past the bed, and the heaps of map scrolls, out the door onto the narrow landing and up the stairs to the top of the tower.

Elizabetta . . . Elizabetta . . . so near, and so far. An image in a mirror, yet a world away, and Avery, the snake, telling her that Anna had willfully abandoned her! All Anna had wanted to do was get away from the nastiness, the pettiness of the university politics – and she'd made the mistake of saying that at the worst possible time. But that seemed to be her lot in life – saying or doing something at the worst possible time. She hadn't wanted to leave Elizabetta, but the spell hadn't heard that.

She was breathing hard when she reached the open roof of the tower, blotting her eyes, and trying to stop the tears.

The sun was a red ball touching the horizon that cast long shadows across Falcor. Anna crossed the ancient tower stones to the north side and peered out over the parapet at Falcor, still blotting her eyes. Only a handful of chimneys smoked, fewer each night, Anna thought. While the dwindling fires might reflect the late-summer heat, Anna suspected that they also reflected a slow diminution of the population as more and more people slipped out of Falcor, fearful either of Behlem or the Ebrans – or both.

With each daily ride, the sorceress saw fewer souls on the streets, more shuttered windows, and yet no one else remarked on the changes. Did they fail to see them, or fear to report them to the Prophet?

'Probably the latter,' she murmured to herself. No one liked to report bad news to the ruler – just like the department chair, she reflected as she used the tear-soaked cloth to bolt her forehead.

The hot air of twilight reminded her of Brill. She'd been able to duplicate some of his spells – cooling her room, seeing Elizabetta in the mirror, lighting candles – but so many she had not. Anna laughed, a sound both soft and harsh. How many spells had he created about which no one knew? Were they still there at Loiseau, somewhere in his notes? Would one be able to return her to Ames? Or anywhere on earth?

Anna shook her head.

She couldn't hope that, not now, not with the Ebrans gathering their forces. What could she do to stop them? Eladdrin, according to Menares, was almost ready to move westward, and more of the darksingers, younger ones, were arriving daily from the training stronghold in Vult to replace those Anna had destroyed.

Water? Could she do something with water? Brill had said that water was hard to handle, and perhaps they wouldn't expect that. There was a place where the main road crossed the small river – the Chean – near Pamr. The whole curved section of the river valley there was low. The irrigation ditches proved that.

The sorceress pulled at her chin. What could she adapt? And how? She gazed out at the small city – or town – then stopped and turned.

A girl stood on the last step leading out onto the tower, almost frozen as Anna moved toward her.

'You can come up,' Anna said, stepping toward the thin-faced young woman who clutched something to her chest.

'I didn't know anyone was here. I'd ... better go.' The dark-haired girl started to turn.

'Please don't go. I'm Anna.'

'I ... know ... Lady Anna. I am Garreth. Birke warned me, but he didn't think you'd be up here.'

'Warned, Garreth? I'm not a monster.' Anna didn't have to force a smile. 'Please come up.' She paused, looking at the drawing board that the girl held tightly. 'Do you draw?'

Garreth glanced around. 'I'm not supposed to, not now. The lady Essan says that drawing girls and singing boys will come to no good end.'

'I don't know,' Anna mused. 'I used to draw, but I sang better than I drew, and there wasn't time for both. Do you like to draw?' She stepped back, afraid that she was crowding Garreth, and motioned for her to step onto the stones of the tower.

'Oh ... sometimes.' The brunette stepped out of the stairwell, but at an angle to avoid nearing the sorceress.

Anna shook her head and laughed, gently. 'You'll have to do better than that to hide it. That's what I would tell my teachers, and the whole time I was saying inside that I liked singing more than anything.'

'You're truly, truly a sorceress.' Garreth tilted her head as if trying to see Anna in a different light.

'That's not sorcery,' the sorceress explained. 'I was young once, and I remember.'

'Birke said that you were old. You do not look old.' Garreth's deepset green eyes narrowed slightly in the red light of sunset.

'I am older than I look,' Anna admitted. 'It wasn't my idea. It happened in the battle for the Sand Pass.' Her eyes fell to the drawing board. 'I won't press you, but could I see what you're working on?' She shook her head. 'Around here, it seems no one has time for beauty.'

'It's not beautiful. It's awful.'

'I doubt that. Could I? I won't say anything.'

'Birke did say you keep your word. He said you would die before you would break it. That be important to him.'

'I know.'

Garreth slowly lowered the board. A single sheet of paper lay there, held in place by leather triangles glued to each of the four corners of the wood. On the paper was a half-completed view of Falcor, as seen from the north side of the tower. Anna took a quick breath. 'It is lovely. You are an artist.'

'It be not my best.'

Anna smiled, even more warmly. 'Your best must be very good.'

Garreth blushed, ever so slightly.

'What do you do here?' Anna asked. 'Are you a page?'

'Dissonance, no, lady. My mother was the maid to Lord Donjim, and I help Lady Essan. I am too young to be a proper maid, and the lady needs but one. Yet she tells Lord Behlem that she needs us both. Synondra is her real maid. She be quiet.'

Anna studied the girl, noting the deep-set and hooded eyes. Had Barjim's uncle had those eyes?

'Everyone says I have his eyes, those of Lord Donjim. Lady Essan has been good to me. Elsewise ... I would have nowhere to go.'

Anna nodded, a glimmer of an idea in her mind. She would have to see, and it might take time.

The evening bell rang, reminding her that she was expected for dinner with the Prophet and his senior captains and overcaptains. Why on some nights and not others? Or was it that the Prophet didn't offer full dinners to everyone every night? She didn't know, only that Birke had brought her the invitation – or summons.

Her eyes flicked eastward, catching the dim red spot that was the moon Darksong – hanging just above the horizon. Darksong ... she hoped it wasn't too much of an omen. 'Garreth ... I must go. I enjoyed talking with you, and I hope I'll see you again.'

'You eat with the Prophet?'

'Sometimes. Tonight is one of those times.'

After hurrying back down to her room, Anna briefly enjoyed the cool while she washed and donned the dressier tunic and trousers she had created for meeting with Lady Essan. Somehow, she felt the time for gowns was past, at least for now.

Then she used the bellpull to summon a page – Birke this time.

'You are ready, lady?' gasped the youth as she stood waiting for him on the landing.

'Sometimes I can be early, Birke.' She nodded to the steps, and added, 'I've decided that I should dine in more ... functional clothes.'

'Yes, lady.' The redhead started back down the tower steps.

'I noticed that more armsmen in Neserean colors have been arriving,' she said, ignoring his unvoiced disapproval of her garb.

'They have had to quarter some of them outside the liedburg. That's how many have arrived. Are we going riding tomorrow?'

'Tomorrow? Probably.' *After that, who knows? I really need to go back to Pamr and study the river, and I'll have to argue with Menares about it, tomorrow, since it's not something to be done publicly.*

'I'm glad I can ride again. Did I tell you that they even let me send a scroll to my sire?'

'You told me the other day. I'm glad.' She paused. 'Are you the oldest, Birke?'

'The oldest son? Of course. I need be here so my sire would not declare fealty to Ranuak or Neserea. But Wasle is only two years younger.'

'I see.'

None of the lamps in the wall sconces were lit in the corridor leading to the middle hall, and they walked through the gloom almost silently.

'We're here,' announced Birke, to both Anna and to the guard at the door.

'The lady Anna,' announced Giellum after opening the door to the middle hall.

Anna smiled back at Birke, then stepped into the gloom of the middle hall. She'd refrained from lighting the chandeliers since the first dinner, especially given the late-summer heat. This time, she had arrived before Behlem, and the senior armsmen stood in groups around the table. Nitron, the dashing captain of the Prophet's Guard with the sweeping mustaches, stood in a corner with some of the captains Anna had not met.

The sorceress nodded politely to Hanfor and to Zealor, who stood together near the middle of the single long table. Both shifted their weight from side to side, uneasily. That bothered Anna, since neither had seemed that nervous at previous dinners. Hanfor inclined his head slightly more than a perfunctory nod, while the sad-faced Zealor offered a bow. Anna smiled briefly.

'Lady Anna?'

Near the head of the table, and Behlem's vacant high-backed chair that was not quite a throne, a wiry man with graying hair stood beside Menares. The counselor beckoned to Anna, and the sorceress walked toward the pair.

'Lord Vyarl, this is the lady Anna,' offered Menares. 'She is the sorceress from the mist worlds that Lord Behlem had mentioned.'

'From the mist worlds? Are they all as young and beautiful?' asked Vyarl.

Anna was slightly taller than Vyarl, and she smiled her professional smile before answering. 'While I appreciate the compliment, I am rather older than I look. My people are like yours – good-looking and not-so-good-looking.' After the briefest pause, she added, 'I am a stranger here, and I'm not familiar with you, or your lands.'

'Lord Vyarl is the Rider of Heinene,' explained Menares. 'He holds the grasslands to the east of the Mittfels and north of Denguic – the counterpart, in a way, of the High Grasslands of Neserea.'

'Except we do not suffer raiders to use ours as refuge.' Vyarl's voice bore a hint of anger and humor.

'The lady Anna rides one of the raider beasts,' Menares said smoothly.

'Oh?'

'Farinelli's a palomino gelding. They say he was a raider mount, but I wouldn't know.'

'Can anyone else ride him?' asked Vyarl, almost intently.

'He won't let anyone else in his stall,' Anna admitted.

'And he is tall?'

'The tallest mount in the stables, I think,' Anna answered, wondering why Vyarl was so interested in Farinelli.

Vyarl pursed his lips, but only momentarily, then inclined his head. 'You are most fortunate, lady. He sounds superb.'

'He is. I hadn't ridden for years, but riding him has gotten to be a pleasure.'

Another frown crossed Vyarl's face and vanished.

'You have not worn a gown this evening, I see, Lady Anna,' offered Delor, gliding up, almost snakelike. 'I had taken you briefly for a Ranuan ... envoy.'

Anna could feel the words contained double connotations, but had no ready answer. 'The time for finery has passed,' she finally said.

'Ah, you are announcing that you are a warrior ... with real weapons.' Delor's eyes glittered.

'I'm not one for announcements, overcaptain.'

'But I am,' declared Behlem, striding in to stand by the head of the table. 'It is past time to dine!' The Prophet gestured to the place at his right. 'Lady Anna.' Then he gestured to the seat to his right. 'Lord Vyarl.'

Even as they sat, servers were appearing around the Prophet, with platters containing slabs of meat smothered in a cream sauce and baskets of bread.

Vyarl looked from Behlem to Anna, then pulled on his chin. He said nothing, but broke off a chunk of bread and served himself two large slices of meat. Anna followed his example, except she didn't bother with politeness, and took three, then watched as Hanfor, to her right, filled her pewter goblet.

'Thank you, overcaptain.'

'My pleasure, Lady Anna.' The faintest twinkle appeared in the green eyes, although Hanfor's weathered face bore no smile.

'Lord Vyarl,' the sorceress began, 'as I am sure you

know, I am new to Liedwahr. What can you tell me about your lands?'

Vyarl's lips curled into a smile; then he laughed. 'You know not what you ask when you offer a rider that much of a chance to boast. Still . . . you did ask.' He moistened his lips with the dark red wine in his goblet. 'The grasses in Heinene are the deepest in all of Liedwahr – or they were until the dark ones began to meddle with the weather, but they remain tall, and they stretch from just north of Dubaria to the Nordbergs. A sea of grass, designed for long-legged mounts and their riders. The gazelles slip through the grass so silently and so swiftly that only the sharpest of ear and the fleetest of horses can seek them.'

'What about the grass snakes?' asked Menares.

'They are large, also, but they avoid riders, unless one is stupid enough to ride over one.'

'How large?' asked Anna.

'I have one skin that is five yards long, but Fiesar swears that he has seen a snake twice as large.' Vyarl offered a wry grin. 'If he had, we would have few gazelles, and less of all game.'

'Has fire become a problem?' mused Anna.

'In the south, near Dubaria, but the taller grass does not burn easily. The weeds do. So fire is our friend. So far.'

Anna understood. Even the toughest grasses needed some rain.

'How is your research faring, lady?' asked Menares.

'I'd like to see you tomorrow after my ride.'

'Good,' said Behlem. 'The last of the Ebran reinforcements are gathering in Synek.'

'Now that the Ebrans are moving . . . you had said the time had passed for finery, Lady Anna,' interjected Delor, his fingers toying with the base of the pewter goblet. 'Yet women have so many weapons . . . and even finery can be a weapon.'

Anna eased the smallest of sips of the wine past her lips. 'I rather doubt that the cut of your uniform, Captain Delor, or whether I might wear a gown, would impress the dark ones – or slow their advance an instant.'

A guffaw came from the foot of the table, and Delor's face darkened for an instant before he answered. 'Finery has doubtless created many delays.'

'It probably has,' Anna admitted, 'but not for the winning side.'

The guffaw was louder, followed by a hissed, 'Best you cease while you can, Delor.'

Anna took another sip of the dark red wine, ensuring that it was small, much as she felt like gulping it. The idea of riding to Pamr didn't sound that bad at all, not at all.

68

MENCHA, DEFALK

The harp strums from the middle of the pool, and Eladdrin nods to himself.

'Songmaster? I see you have made the sorcerer's work yours.' The pool shows a hooded and shadowed figure in a dark room, seated behind a small table beside a pool larger than the one Eladdrin has turned to his own use.

'Not exactly.'

'What of the sorceress?'

'She is in Falcor, under Behlem's protection in the liedburg,' admits the Songmaster. 'She intended to return here, for she left her gown.'

'A gown? Why does that concern us?'

'It is unlike anything I have seen. Even the material is otherworldly.'

'You have no doubts she is from the mist worlds?'

'None. That concerns me.'

'You are in control. Do what you must.' There is a pause. 'What of the travel-sorceress?'

'She is dead, but . . .'

'What?' The words are chill, yet sing.

'She was killed before we reached her – it had to be the Norweians.' Eladdrin looks down at the dusty tile floor of the domed building.

'Who killed her matters not, not this time. The other sorcerers and sorceresses in Defalk would not try such a spell, if they knew it, and the strange sorceress will not try to bring another.'

'You think not, honored Evult?'

'If she has ethics, she cannot bring another until she knows more. If she has no ethics, she will not bring another to share her power, not until she is secure in it.' The harp offers a discordant whisper of tones, a parody of a stringed laugh.

'She meets with the Prophet, and she has the freedom of Falcor.'

'She has freedom until she defeats us or falls to us. You will ensure the latter. While you finish your preparations for the attack on Falcor, send a detachment of archers and horse to shadow her, to kill her if they can. Perhaps they will succeed. If not, they will worry her – and that arrogant Prophet.'

'What of the Norweians?'

'I will send a flood down their River Ost as a warning. That will occupy them for a time. Do not worry about that. Worry about destroying the Prophet and adding Defalk to our domains.'

'Yes, Evult.'

After the strings have ceased their whispers and the images have left the waters of the pool, Eladdrin walks from the dusty workroom out into the twilight. For a time, he studies the lifeless hall that had once belonged to a sorcerer, a hall Eladdrin has yet to fully fathom or to return to functioning as it once had.

69

Whhhnnnn!

Anna paused, short of Farinelli's stall, then jumped back as she saw a shadowy figure, and a hand slammed across her mouth.

She staggered back, dropping the lutar case as her own right hand grabbed for the dagger, her left pushing the arm and hand back away from her. She swallowed, trying to sing the repulsion spell, but she couldn't. As the knife finally cleared the sheath, she kept backing up, swallowing and trying to get enough saliva to sing.

The bigger figure lunged again.

Anna choked out the words of the spell, and the armsman staggered, but kept moving toward her, thrusting a hand toward her mouth again.

Whhhnnnnn!

As she vaguely remembered, she brought the dagger up and toward the biggest target she knew – the diaphragm, right under the ribs – and thrust as hard as she could.

'*Oooffff* . . .' Even with the deep thrust and the knife in his guts, the armsman's right hand pinned her left, and his hot acrid breath cascaded across her face.

She twisted and yanked the knife more, and managed to bring up one knee into the man's groin. With a stunned look, the attacker staggered back.

Instinctively, Anna held tight to the knife, watching as the unfamiliar blond and bearded armsman clutched at his guts, before crumpling, his hand grasping toward the stall wall as his feet slid out from under him. After a moment, he lay face-up, his mouth moving with a low series of moans, his feet twitching.

'Get her!'

Anna cleared her throat, and turned, keeping her back to
Farinelli, and this time, she sang the burning song, on tune.
Both soldiers went up in flame. She slashed the forearm of the
one in front, the dark-haired one, to keep him from clutching
her even as he burned. Then she danced back, her stomach
turning.

The straw on the floor began to smolder under the
burning bodies, and she tried the water song, visualizing
water spilling across the corpses and straw.

The words were enough to stop the flames and convert
the straw into a sodden mess – and the odor of manure,
charred meat, and burned straw was enough to turn Anna's
legs nearly to jelly. For several moments she just stood, one
hand holding the stall wall.

'What . . . ?' Tirsik came trotting from the far end of the
stable. He looked at Anna, then at the three bodies – two
charcoaled bundles, and one lying face-up, still moaning.
Tirsik's eyes went to Anna and the bloody knife. His mouth
opened and closed.

Whhhnnnnn! offered the gelding, from behind her. Anna
thought that horses didn't whinny except to other horses,
but it sounded like one. She wondered why she was thinking
that, even as she half turned, looking down at the bloody
knife almost as though she had not seen it before.

'Mmmmm!' A muffled sound stopped both the stablemaster and the sorceress.

Anna turned back toward Farinelli, but Tirsik found Birke,
bound and gagged, just inside the empty stall adjoining
Farinelli's.

The stablemaster lifted the youth to his feet, ripped off
the gag, and slashed the cording. 'Now . . . what happened,
young fellow?'

Birke's eyes widened as they took in the destruction and
death, fixing on the bloody dagger Anna still held.

She glanced down at the blade.

Tirsik handed her a rag, and the sorceress wiped the
blade clean, slowly, looking back at the wide-eyed dying

armsman, whose moans grew louder. How had she managed it?

Tirsik let go of Birke and knelt by the bearded man. 'Who sent you?'

'Hurts . . . so much . . .' gasped the young armsman. 'Didn't tell me . . .'

'Who sent you?'

'—'Elmat . . . said . . . he did . . .' The eyes widened, and the body slumped.

Tirsik stood, shaking his head, before turning to Birke. 'What happened?'

'I came down to saddle the bay. They were by the stall, and the big one grabbed me.'

Tirsik nodded. 'Subofficer came in to ask me about reshoeing a horse. Asked me to look. So's I wouldn't be around, I'd guess.'

'I came in to saddle Farinelli.' Anna took a deep breath and pointed to the dead man. She supposed she should do something, but she didn't know what, and she didn't feel all that charitable. 'He was waiting behind the empty stall door there. Farinelli warned me enough, but I couldn't get a spell off quickly enough for him. Those two were slower.' She looked at Birke.

Birke put his hand to his head, then winced.

'Got a stiff lump there.' Tirsik peered at the boy's skull. 'Don't like these things happening in my stable.'

'Neither do I.' Anna looked up as Spirda and his men approached. The young subofficer's mouth opened soundlessly.

'You aren't going to ride now, are you?' asked the stablemaster.

'I need fresh air,' Anna said. *I'm not going to be intimidated. I won't be.* 'Especially now.'

'What . . . ?' began Spirda, turning toward the dead figure in Neserean colors.

'Looks as though someone doesn't want the sorceress to be successful,' Tirsik said dryly.

Birke massaged his neck gingerly.

Anna sheathed her dagger and went to reclaim the lutar case, and to saddle Farinelli. Was she being a fool to ride? Probably. But she'd be a bigger fool to show fear – or the terror that she'd pushed to the back of her mind. Even the nastiest of university politicians hadn't tried to murder her, except occupationally.

'Them's think she's a normal weak woman . . . they'll be sorry . . .' muttered Tirsik.

Anna hoped so. She picked up the lutar case, trying to ignore the mixed stenches of blood, death, charred meat, and sodden straw. She swallowed the bile in her throat and straightened, her fingertips brushing the dagger hilt. Her head ached, and she wanted to rub it, but didn't.

70

After unsaddling and grooming Farinelli, Anna marched across the courtyard to the tower, the sound of her boots echoing from the stones with each determined step. Her tunic and hair were plastered to her, and she smelled worse than the stable.

After the attack in the stable and before her ride, she'd been startled, afraid, and angry. Now, she was just angry. As she had ridden down the Falche River with her escort, she'd been thinking. The whole attempted murder in the stable had had nothing to do with the Ebrans. It reeked of someone like Delor, of jealous male egos, or jealous females – but so far she didn't know of any females, except Hryding's bitchy consort, who'd be that jealous.

Back in her room, she stripped off her sodden riding clothes, and splashed herself as clean as she could, before drying and donning the other clean riding clothes. Then she yanked the bellpull and waited for a page by the door.

When she heard steps, she opened the door. A dark-haired youth trotted up the stone steps.

'Take me to Menares,' Anna told Skent before he had even reached the landing.

The dark-haired page gulped.

'Now. He knows I'm coming.' *He just doesn't know why.* Anna closed the tower door behind her.

'Did you really kill that armsman with a dagger?' Skent asked as they went up the broad red stone staircase.

'I didn't have much choice.' *And I was lucky, because he wanted some fun, I think, first.* She repressed a shiver. Lucky, because her attacker had thought of her as a sex object? Or wanted to terrify her? Would the next time be a straight murder attempt? Could she afford a next time?

The hot outside air had seeped into the hall itself, despite the thick stone walls, and outside of Anna's room, the rooms and corridors were scarcely cooler than the oven outside. She wondered why she'd even tried to clean up, as perspiration oozed from every pore. She'd never been one for medieval romances or fantasies, and the heat and lack of modern bathroom facilities reinforced her predisposition – except she was stuck in the real-life equivalent, with no apparent way out.

A squat blond youth in Defalk purple sat on a stool by the closed two-panel wooden door, blotting his forehead with a ragged square of cloth. He jumped up as he saw Anna and Skent.

'Cens,' began Skent. 'The lady Anna ... She ... is here ... ah ... to see ...'

Cens's eyes darted from Skent to Anna. He swallowed before finally saying, 'I'll have to ask – it might be a moment – he is meeting with Overcaptain Hanfor ...'

'What I have to discuss should not take long.'

'I will have to ask, lady.'

Anna nodded. 'I'll wait.'

Cens slipped behind the door, and Anna thought she heard voices, although they were cut off as soon as the page closed the door behind himself.

In moments, Cens reappeared, sweat beaded up all across his forehead. 'He will be but a moment, Lady Anna.' The blond page's eyes darted to Anna's belt dagger, then to the floor.

Scarcely had the page finished speaking than the door opened behind him, and he eased to the side.

Hanfor's weathered face and graying dark hair appeared in the doorway. The overcaptain bowed. 'Lady Anna. I am pleased to see you.' His mouth crinkled, and his eyes sparkled. 'Although it was certainly distressing, I have taken the liberty of informing my captains and officers about this morning's incident. I have also suggested that I would not be so swift and kind as you – were there to be any further such incidents.'

'Thank you, Overcaptain Hanfor. I will do my best to ensure such incidents also do not recur. The Prophet will need all his armsmen.'

'My thoughts as well, Lady Anna.' He nodded, then turned and strode down the dim corridor.

'My lady . . .' Cens gestured to the still-open door.

Anna stepped through, letting the page close it behind her. The room was long and narrow, with closed doors at each end. Five narrow and high windows dotted the long outside wall, their shutters open, but the air in the room remained still, with the faint odor of perspiration.

Menares stood behind a small circular table on which rested a pitcher and three goblets. There were three straight-backed chairs drawn up around the table.

The sorceress wondered who the third man had been, and why he had not exited with Hanfor.

'Please . . . If you would . . .' The graying counselor gestured to the chairs across from him.

'I won't be long.' Anna sat.

'Lady Anna . . . I heard about the incident in the stable . . . The Prophet was most distressed . . .' Menares eased himself back into his chair.

Menares was playing both sides against the middle, Anna

felt, but she had no real proof, only her feelings. How far should she push it?

'I am certain he was distressed,' Anna said sweetly. 'And others were probably distressed by its failure.'

The counselor's face froze. 'Lady Anna . . .'

'Menares,' Anna cautioned. 'I am well aware that there are some within the Prophet's circle that would feel no grief at my death or disappearance. Such as Delor.'

The faint widening of Menares' eyes, and his look away told her all she needed to know.

'But,' she emphasized, 'that is not why I am here. I have been studying the maps and thinking, and I need to go back to Pamr to study the area.'

'The maps are not enough?'

'Sorcery doesn't work on maps. It works on people or land or the sky, but not on the maps. As Lord Behlem pointed out last night, it won't be long before the dark ones march on Falcor. If we fight here, we'll lose.' Anna had no logical reason for her conclusion, but it felt right, and she had to go with her feelings.

'Lose?'

'Lose. That's why I need to go back to Pamr. That's where all the roads from the east meet.' Anna waited.

'You would need an escort . . .' mused the counselor. 'I do not know.'

'I am here to help the Prophet defeat the dark ones. I cannot defeat them without knowing the land where we may fight – or finding the best place for a battle. You pointed that out already.'

'I am the Prophet's counselor, but I command no armsmen.'

'You are too modest,' Anna said. 'You command more than armsmen.'

'I can only promise that I will bring the matter to the attention of the Prophet.'

'Menares, honored counselor, I plan to leave the day after tomorrow. I do hope you will discuss it with Lord Behlem before you have to explain my departure.' Anna smiled.

Menares blotted his forehead. 'I will bring it to his attention this very afternoon.'

'I knew I could depend on you, Menares.' Anna stood and smiled.

'Ah ... thank you, Lady Anna.'

Skent had left already when the sorceress stepped back into the corridor. Cens stood stiffly by the door.

'Good day, Cens.'

'Good day, Lady Anna.' The youth's words were stiff, formal, as if he were afraid to say anything to her.

He probably was, reflected Anna as she marched back toward the tower.

Back in the cool of her tower room, Anna washed her face in the basin of fresh water that Birke or Skent had brought, then blotted herself dry. She still felt sticky all over.

Thunk.

'Just a moment.' After pushing her hair back out of her face – and it needed cutting – Anna answered the door.

Wearing a pale purple sleeveless tunic over a white shirt, and trousers that matched the tunic, Lady Essan stood on the landing. 'I had hoped for a moment with you.'

'Please come in.' Anna waited, then closed the door behind Essan.

'This looks more like a sorceress's room – or a warrior's,' said Essan, settling herself into one of the wooden chairs. 'Then again, despite your looks, Lady Anna, it is becoming apparent that you are a warrior.'

She paused. 'Birke told me you were attacked in the stable, and that you killed one Neserean with your dagger and two with your spells. Is his tale true?'

Anna nodded.

'It is cool here, cooler than anywhere in the hall.' Essan smiled, then leaned forward. 'I am old, and I can say what I wish. Can you leave the liedburg?'

'I'm leaving for a time tomorrow,' Anna said. 'I need to see what I can do to stop the Ebrans, and that means traveling east again.'

'I would suggest that you take your time. The field is far less dangerous than Falcor. All liedstadts are perilous. It seems to come with their glamour.'

'I think I'd like to change that,' Anna snorted.

'If you can change that, Lady Anna, you will indeed be the greatest sorceress or lady in the history of Liedwahr.' Essan straightened, as if she were about to leave.

'I met Garreth the other night. She seems very talented, in her drawing at least. She was quite complimentary about you, and your efforts to help her.'

'I pay my debts.' The lady Essan's face could have been carved in stone, for what Anna could read at that moment.

'I'm sorry,' Anna said.

'You, thank the harmonies, had nothing to do with it. Men can be such fools.' Essan frowned. 'Just remember that, although I doubt I'll have to tell you.'

'I take it that you have no problems if I spend some time with Garreth?'

'That would be your choice. She is a sweet girl, and talented. I have no difficulties with what she is.' Essan eased herself erect. 'Much as I would like to stay, you have much to do – as do all young people.' The older woman shook her head as she walked – her posture erect, proud – toward the door. 'It is easy enough to see your experience, yet it is hard not to think of you as young.'

After she closed the door and started down the tower steps, Anna frowned. Had she always seemed young, or was it Brill's spell? And Garreth – what a difficult situation for Lady Essan.

71

FALCOR, DEFALK

Menares bows as he steps onto the balcony overlooking the courtyard.

'Now what?' asks Behlem cheerfully. The Prophet does not rise from the chair and the stack of scrolls on the table before him. His face is damp, and he scratches his beard. 'Is this about the lady Anna?'

'Yes, your honor. She came to see me.'

'I suppose she wanted vengeance of some sort. Women usually do.'

'No.' Menares stops opposite the table. 'She only mentioned the incident in passing, to say that was not why she came to see me.'

'Sit down. Do you know who did it?'

'The one she killed was from Delor's company,' Menares says. 'Shall I have Delor executed?'

'No.' Behlem shakes his head. 'Tell her that the armsman was from Delor's company, and tell her that we do not know whether Delor was behind it, or whether someone suborned his man. Then ... we will watch.' He takes a long swallow from the goblet and pushes aside a scroll. 'What did she want?'

'She is insisting that she ride back to Pamr,' Menares says smoothly. 'She says that she needs to study the land there to defeat Eladdrin.'

'And you want her here where you can watch her? Did you refuse her request?'

'I told her that such travel might be unwise, but that I would consult with you.'

'Oh, Menares, old friend ...' Behlem laughs. 'So cautious

you are. If you were only that cautious for the right reasons. This woman needs us. She could bring the whole liedburg down around us. Don't you know that?'

'If she can,' replies Menares, his voice carrying the faint hint of sourness, 'why hasn't she, with all the restrictions she clearly chafes under?'

'Because she is as old as she says she is, not as she appears. She knows a sorceress, especially a sorceress, cannot hold off an entire land, no matter how powerful she is.' Behlem refills his goblet, his eyes on the portcullis, which has been lifted to allow a troop of riders to enter.

'But . . . if she is that powerful . . . and you win . . . then what will you do? Can you afford to have her near?'

'No. But I will not ford rivers before I reach them. One way or another, she will not remain near.' Behlem smiles and fingers his beard.

'Talk to her this afternoon. Send Spirda and a full squad with her, and remember to tell her that her attacker belonged to Delor. Also . . .' Behlem frowns. 'I believe I will sup alone tonight, rather than in the hall.'

'Oh . . . you suspect Delor will make trouble?'

'He could. He could.' Behlem shrugs, his eyes on the portcullis as it drops back into place. 'Is there anything else new?'

'No, ser.'

'Good. Will you tell the page to bring me more of the wine on your way out?'

'Yes, ser.'

72

Anna set the lutar aside and glanced out the window into the hot mid-afternoon. On the one hand, she hated feeling cooped up. On the other, she hated walking out into the oven that the liedburg became every afternoon. Even the ramparts were empty, as sentries hugged the few shadows. The banner of Neserea hung limply from the flagstaff that rose above the wall that surrounded the portcullis gate.

She glanced back at the lutar on the bed, surrounded by scraps of paper on which were jotted words and musical notations that represented potential spells. She rubbed her neck and shook her hand to loosen her fingers, fingers that had developed calluses from the lutar practice over the past weeks.

The heavy knocker on the tower door thunked twice.

After taking a deep breath, the sorceress crossed the floor and opened the door.

Menares stood on the landing.

'Come in, counselor.' Anna held the door, then closed it behind the heavyset advisor.

'It is so pleasant here.'

'I'm glad you find it so.'

After settling himself into the wooden armchair, the counselor cleared his throat. 'The Prophet and I have discussed . . . your scouting mission . . .'

'He's agreed,' Anna said, tired of the circumlocutions. 'What sort of escort will I have?'

'Ah . . . Officer Spirda and a full squad. I trust that will be sufficient?'

'I would hope so. We'll leave right after breakfast.'

Menares nodded.

'Also, you should know that I won't take the pages, but I will take my player. He has experience with what players can handle, and I'll need that.'

'You did not mention . . .'

'Menares . . . I would like it if you would stop thinking about why I shouldn't do something and help me do it.' She paused.

The white-haired Menares coughed and cleared his throat again, then shifted his bulk on the chair, which creaked. His fingers touched the short white beard.

'And I'll need some golds,' Anna said. 'I'll be looked to for food and lodging, and since I'm not from Liedwahr, I don't have resources.'

'Then perhaps you should not—'

'I'm offering assistance you couldn't buy with all the golds in Liedwahr, and not only are you trying to hinder my efforts to help Behlem, but you're quibbling about lodging costs.'

'The treasury is not . . . boundless, Lady Anna.'

The sorceress stood and walked to the bed, lifting the lutar off the coverlet. Then she eased to the window, before turning back and facing Menares. Her fingers strummed across the strings. 'How much are two thousand armsmen worth? A handful of captains?'

The counselor's eyes flicked from Anna's face to her fingers and back again. 'I think we could spare a few golds, Lady Anna.'

'A dozen would be about right. You can have them ready in the morning when we leave.' She nodded absently, chording the background for the water spell. 'Who was behind the attempt to kill me?'

'That we do not know.' Menares shrugged. 'The armsman belonged to the Mittfels Foot.'

'That's Delor.'

'Someone could have suborned his men.'

Anna considered, then shook her head. 'I don't think so. Do you, really?'

'I could not say. I really could not.' Menares wasn't about to admit what he knew, but his reactions and body posture had already told Anna what she needed to know.

'There is no dinner tonight, since the Prophet will not be eating with his captains,' Menares volunteered as he slowly eased his bulk out of the chair.

Anna tried not to swallow. The statement meant more than the words conveyed . . . but what?

'I would like to remain, Lady Anna. I have not been more comfortable in days, but . . .' The white-haired counselor shrugged.

THE SOPRANO SORCERESS · · ·   393

'I understand.' Anna walked to the door and held it open, standing back as Menares half walked, half waddled onto the hot landing.

Once the echoes of Menares' footsteps had faded, Anna closed the door, yanked the bellpull and waited. This time, Birke appeared.

'Birke, I need you to find my player, Daffyd. Would you ask him if he would come here for a bit?'

Birke glanced down the stone steps, then cleared his throat. 'Yes, lady.'

'Good.'

After the page left, she closed the door, wondering once more why she had to act like a bitch to get anything done. And why Menares had been told to let her know that Behlem would not be at dinner. Finally, she nodded. The problem was hers to resolve. Hers alone. Delor could try to kill her again and again, and Behlem would do nothing – unless she either went to his bed or begged for his mercy . . . or both.

She took a deep breath, and began to look for a scrap of paper. *Do you want to do this? Do you have any real choice?*

Anna actually had the spell complete before Daffyd thunked. After setting the paper aside, she crossed the stone floor and opened the door, motioning him in.

'It's cold here.' The dark-haired player shivered as he sank into one of the chairs.

'It's comfortable.' Anna turned the chair to face Daffyd. 'Tomorrow, we're riding back to Pamr. I'm sorry I didn't give you much warning, but I just persuaded Menares and Behlem that it was necessary.'

'You want me to go?' asked Daffyd, a hint of a boyish sulk in his voice.

'Yes. I trust you, and you know more about Defalk than any of the Neserean officers who'll be with us. I need to see how I can turn things to help us.'

'You haven't talked to me that much lately.'

Anna held in a sigh. Why was it that men required so

much emotional hand-holding? Either that, or lots of power to reassure themselves? 'Daffyd, I have been very busy trying to keep from getting murdered. If you didn't hear, this morning three armsmen tried to kill me in the stable.'

'This morning? What happened? You look all right.'

'I almost wasn't. I managed to stab one with my dagger, and I got free long enough to use a spell on the other two.' Anna frowned. 'This happened in a castle where I'm supposed to be safe. Then, earlier, someone tried to cripple Farinelli by dropping those iron pointed things into his stall.'

'Caltrops?' The player shook his head. 'I don't understand. The Prophet needs you.'

'That may be, but someone doesn't agree. Or they don't care.'

The young player glanced toward the door. 'Do you think Behlem ... ?' He shook his head.

'No. Not yet, anyway. He needs me now, and he's an opportunist. But I trust him about as far as I could throw Farinelli.'

'Why would you do that?'

'You're not ...' Anna shook her head ruefully.

Daffyd grinned.

'Why do I stay here? Work with them? Because the alternative is worse.' *A lot worse, if what I feel is right.* And she had to trust her feelings. They were about all she could trust, from what she'd experienced of Liedwahr. She stood and stretched. 'I need to prepare some things. I'll see you in the morning, right after breakfast.'

'That's all?'

Anna really wanted to sigh. She didn't. 'Daffyd, I'm sorry if I haven't had more time to talk, but it's hard trying to learn all these things you grew up with and I didn't. It's also hard being a sorceress in a place that's ... very different. We'll have more time on the way to Pamr.'

'Do you want me to bring my viola?'

'I think that would be a good idea, don't you?'

The player nodded.

After Daffyd left, Anna didn't know whether to shake her head or scream. She was old enough to be his mother, and looked young enough to be his girlfriend, and the poor boy was confused. No matter what she did, he'd be confused.

She picked the lutar back up, running through the chords again, then the words, but never both together, and never singing the words.

When the sun had almost touched the horizon, Anna took another deep breath, then lifted the lutar, and slipped out of her room into the heat of the tower steps.

Although she passed two armsmen and a page she did not know, none said a word to her, all three looking away as she strode determinedly toward the middle hall.

'Lady Anna . . . ah . . . there is no . . . accompanied dinner . . . this evening . . .' stammered the young armsman standing outside the doorway.

'I know. I didn't come for that.' Anna smiled, but the smile felt cold, colder than university professionalism. 'I take it the captains and overcaptains are eating now?'

Giellum swallowed. 'You can't enter.'

'Do you announce me, or do I turn you into charcoal?' Anna's fingers flicked across the strings of the lutar.

The young armsman's eyes widened, then he croaked. 'Ah . . . a moment, lady.' He swung the door open.

'The lady Anna.'

She almost wanted to smile as his voice cracked, but she wasted no time stepping inside, halting, and surveying the table to make sure Delor was there.

He was. The overcaptain bolted upright at the table, his blade clearing the sheath, his face twisted in anger.

Anna sang.

> 'Delor, killer, now you learn . . .
> from flame to ashes shall you turn . . .
> from the strings, from the sky,
> fire flay you till you die!'

Delor leaped from the far side of the table, flicked out his blade, grasping a dagger in the other hand, and charged across the tile floor toward the sorceress even before she finished the spell.

Cracckk!!!

Anna flicked the last chord from the lutar strings and dodged.

Delor stopped in his tracks as one line of fire slammed his body, then a second. Although he went down after the second, he didn't begin to scream until the fifth or sixth fire-lash cut away fabric and flesh.

Except for Delor's screams, the miniature lightnings and the crackling of flame, the hall was silent. With his death, only heavy breathing remained.

Anna swallowed, and stepped up toward the horrified faces around the table. She noted that Behlem was not present. Nor was Menares. She turned to Hanfor.

'Unlike some, I don't hire innocents to do my killing. And I don't hide behind a smile and witty words. I didn't kill Delor just because he tried to kill me. I also killed him because he was stupid. How do you feel about a captain who would try to kill the best weapon his lord may have? How many of you will die if I am not there?' *You're setting yourself up ... but what choice do you have? You have to stop this assassination shit before it gets anywhere.* 'Do you want to play stupid masculine games or do you want to survive?'

Hanfor stood. He was silent for a long moment before he spoke. 'I appreciate your directness, Lady Anna. If they stop to think, many others may do so as well.'

'Thank you.' The sorceress bowed and turned, giving Delor's corpse a wide berth as she left the hall.

'... stupid ... He was so stupid ...'

'... you still dream of bedding her, Diuse?'

'... colder than the top of the Ostfels ...'

'... more of a man than Delor ...'

'That is most frightening ...'

Anna kept her lips tightly together as she walked back to

the tower, and up the stone steps to her cold empty room. She didn't even dare to try the mirror to see her daughter, not until she'd thought that out more.

She'd been given youth, and beauty back, and power – and it was getting more and more evident that the price was high – higher than she could have dreamed. She had the sickening feeling, unfortunately, that she had only begun to pay.

Why . . . why was it so fucking difficult? She was already being called a bitch and worse. Yet, if Behlem had been Delor's target, the overcaptain would have been tortured to death in the most grisly way without anyone thinking an ill thought of the Prophet. So why was she the bitch?

The cold stones that surrounded her gave no answer.

73

The day was gray when Anna woke, her eyes gummy, her nose stuffed. For a time, she lay on the lumpy bed, but her thoughts kept drifting back to the dream, a dream where she searched through an unfamiliar house, a house hotter than an oven. She was looking for Irenia, Mario, and Elizabetta. She hadn't been able to find them, but she'd just had to keep looking, going back through closets overflowing with clothes into which she could no longer fit, toys the children hadn't used for years, and stacks and stacks of music written in a notation she'd never seen. After a time, she forced her eyes open.

Finally, she sat up and swung her feet over the side of the bed. The gray outside was that of morning before sunrise. All that searching in her dream – it meant she had to see them – Mario and Elizabetta, anyway. She swallowed, and her eyes burned, at the thought of Irenia. No magic would let her see Irenia again.

She stood and padded to the window. The sun had not

lifted itself above the horizon, but the eastern sky was pink. Time to dress ... and then time to try another spell.

Once she had her riding clothes on, she turned to the mirror and began to sing, first focusing the spell on Mario.

'Mirror, mirror ...'

Nothing happened, except a brief swirl of white across her own reflection in the cracked and shimmering glass. Had she lost her ability? Or did a cracked glass spoil the effect? She swallowed, then walked around until she located the greasy pencil and began to scrawl. After that came the lutar.

'Mirror, mirror with cracks in glass,
remove the fissure with this pass,
Make it shine smooth and fine ...'

The glass misted, and reappeared – blemish-free. But the frame was still heat-warped and dark. She ate some stale bread and repeated the effort to see Mario. Again, there was the swirl of white – and nothing.

The sorceress walked back to the table and swallowed half a goblet of water, and chewed some of the bread left from the night before.

Then she tried again, with the same result.

She paced to the window, then back to the mirror. What about Elizabetta? Her heart pounding, Anna studied the mirror for a time before she sang the second spell.

'Mirror, mirror ...'

This time this swirling white mists in the mirror cleared to reveal Elizabetta sitting in her bedroom in the Colonial. Her red hair was unkempt, and around her were piled heaps of clothes. Elizabetta's eyes were red, and she was looking at the open cardboard boxes on the floor.

Anna felt her own eyes fill with tears, but she just watched as her daughter sat on the rumpled tulip quilt that Anna's mother had given Elizabetta for her tenth birthday.

The sorceress squinted as Elizabetta said something. Was she asking 'Why?' or swearing?

After a moment longer, the redhead jerked herself upright and began to fold clothes, almost savagely, before stuffing each item into one of the boxes.

Again the heat poured from the glass, far sooner than before, and Anna sang the release spell quickly. Watching that distant image just twisted her stomach tight up inside herself.

She shook her head, tiredly, and massaged her neck and then her temples. Spells weren't infallible, nor was she, as she had discovered in the stable.

The door knocker thunked.

'Who's there?'

'Menares,' came the answer.

Anna slid the bolt quietly and eased the door ajar, one hand on the hilt of the knife, but the counselor was alone. 'Come in.'

The older man stepped inside, fingering his white beard as he glanced at the empty saddlebags and the water bottles. 'You are still intending to scout out the area around Pamr?'

'I don't know any other way.'

'Last night . . .' Menares looked into Anna's eyes.

Anna looked back, and the counselor's eyes fell.

Finally, she said. 'You and Behlem set that up cleverly.'

'My lady . . . how could you suggest . . . Delor was a fine commander. He will be sorely missed.'

'By whom? The Ebrans?' She shook her head. 'If I hadn't done something, every egocentric officer in the Prophet's army would have thought he could try to kill me, in order to do Delor one better. Now that I have acted, you and Behlem are figures of great temperance and moderation, forced to put up with a mad sorceress for the sake of Defalk and Neserea.'

Menares did not meet her eyes. 'Perhaps it is best that you leave Falcor for a few days.'

Anna had her doubts. In her absence, the two would probably concoct enough rumors to ensure no officer felt safe within a mile – a dek, she corrected herself – of her.

'Menares, you are a wise man. I hope you can assure both the Prophet and his captains that I am a reasonable woman.' She forced a smile. 'I am sure you can find some way to get across the idea that . . .' She paused. 'Let me put it another way. If it had been the Prophet that Delor's man had assaulted, how long would Delor have lived?'

'Not long,' admitted Menares.

'I even gave Delor some time to make amends. Did he?'

'Captains are not usually given to making amends, Lady Anna.'

'Not to women, you mean? Perhaps they should reconsider their ways. That wasn't the point, though. I was hoping you could find a way to explain to the captains and overcaptains that I am a most reasonable woman.' She smiled again. 'Especially when people are reasonable in return.'

Another silence filled the tower room.

'How long will you be gone?' the counselor finally asked.

'As long as it takes, and not a moment longer.' Anna looked at the leather bag in Menares' hand. 'I presume those are our travel expenses?'

The counselor nodded and extended it. 'There are fifteen golds.'

Anna tucked the bag into her overflowing wallet. 'I'll return any that aren't needed.' She looked at the saddlebags. 'I do need to pack these and be on my way.'

'I'm certain you do, lady.' Menares smiled tightly as he turned toward the door.

After seeing him out, she slid the bolt into place and resumed her hasty packing – not that she was taking that much besides the lutar, spare riding clothes, a towel, and soap. There wasn't that much in Falcor she could take.

When she was through, Anna glanced at the saddle-bags and the water bottles by the door, then yanked the bellpull.

Before long, both Skent and Birke stood on the landing.

'I'd like some help with these.'

'You're leaving today?' asked Skent.

'I'll be back.' *Unfortunately*. 'Before too long.'

The two glanced at each other.

Anna could read the unspoken thoughts. 'If you're wondering whether I'm really leaving because of the mess last night, the answer is no. I'd arranged this before last night. Of course, it probably won't hurt that I'm out of view for a few days.'

'I'm glad Delor's gone,' Skent volunteered.

Birke smirked, and Skent added quickly, glaring at the redheaded page, 'He was mean. Once he kicked Cens.'

Birke looked away from Skent, and then down at the stones of the landing.

What was that about? What was she missing? Anna wondered.

'Let's go.' Anna lifted the lutar case. The two followed her down the stairs and across the morning-shadowed courtyard to the stables.

In the gloom inside the stables, Tirsik stood. Beyond him, Daffyd struggled with the saddle to his mare.

'Good morning, Lady Anna.' Tirsik smiled. 'He's been fed, seeing as I heard you'd be riding out early.'

'Thank you.' Anna turned to the pages. 'Just leave the bags by the stall. I'll load them once I get Farinelli saddled.' She smiled. 'Keep things in order while I'm gone.'

Skent smiled and nodded. Birke nodded soberly. Then they walked toward the stall. Anna looked back to the stablemaster.

'The one worships you. The other fears you,' said Tirsik.

'I hope I treat them the same.'

'Oh, you do, lady. I've watched. But Skent comes from an armsman's stock, and he's seen the worst. Young Birke, his sire's a lord, and the lords of Defalk haven't held much for strong women. Armsmen need strong women, but lords fear them.' The wiry stablemaster laughed. 'I talk too much. Best you be getting ready.'

'I appreciate your words, Tirsik. I'm a stranger, and they help.'

'Are we still going?' asked Daffyd, loudly.

'Why not?' Anna smiled brightly as she turned.

'I heard ... last night.' The player glanced toward the central hall structure.

'That doesn't change anything. I talked with Menares this morning.'

Daffyd shook his head. 'The armsmen won't be happy.'

'Spirda is a lancer. He reports to Hanfor,' Anna pointed out.

Daffyd shrugged, an expression that did not signify full agreement.

Anna walked to the stall, where Farinelli neighed. 'Good morning to you, beast. You seem to be the only one besides Tirsik who's pleased to see me this morning.'

The gelding neighed again.

'Except you just want to be groomed.' She laughed as she slipped into the stall, setting her feet carefully. The area still held the faintest residual odor of charred meat and straw. Anna tried not to think about it as she brushed the palomino, then saddled him, and strapped her gear in place.

Farinelli almost pranced as she led him from the stables out into the courtyard where Daffyd waited, a sober expression fixed in place. He shook his head minutely as Anna rechecked the saddle.

'Why are we riding to Pamr?' Spirda asked, as he led his mount into the courtyard and stopped beside Anna.

'So I can figure out some way to stop the Ebrans before they kill you,' answered Anna. She wanted to apologize for being short with the clueless young subofficer, but she didn't. She was tired of explaining and apologizing.

'But the Prophet ...'

'The counselor and the Prophet have already agreed.' Anna turned to Farinelli and checked saddlebags, water bottles, and the lutar case a last time before mounting.

Daffyd scrambled into his saddle, as did Spirda.

Anna slowly eased Farinelli across the stones of the courtyard toward the portcullis gate.

Except for the half squad of duty guards, there were no armsmen moving in the tents beyond the liedburg walls. The horses in the temporary corral stood almost motionless. Even in the meanest stretch north of liedburg, the early-morning light fell on streets that were all but deserted.

A wisp or two of smoke drifted from a handful of scattered chimneys, and Anna had to guide Farinelli to the east side of the street to avoid an enthusiastic maid dumping chamberpots. But far too many shutters were fastened tight, or ripped open and hanging askew on iron brackets.

Spirda rode stiffly behind Anna and Daffyd, but Anna was in no mood to cheer anyone up. How could she figure out how to use a river and land to stop the dark ones? And did her inability to see Mario mean something terrible? Or that she was losing her talent for sorcery? Or that, as Brill had intimated, too much trying to see the mist worlds – her earth – would cost too much? Or start a raging blaze?

She straightened in the saddle and pushed the thoughts away. She had to do what she could do.

74

The endless sun beat down on Anna, on the dusty road as she led the riders up the long incline from Sorprat and the ford across the Chean River. Sweat oozed into her hair and down onto her brow no matter how often she used the soggy square of cloth that once had resembled a handkerchief.

At the top of the incline, where the road flattened into a

dusty strip heading eastward toward Mencha, Anna turned
Farinelli back west for a few paces, along a narrow path
wide enough for perhaps two horses. There she reined up
and studied the road. The main road from Mencha and the
east swung down through the cut in the hillside to the ford
– essentially a stone causeway over which a handspan of
brown water flowed. On the low hill on the north side of the
river stood the handful of houses that represented Sorprat.
On the south side, where Anna, Daffyd, and the armsmen
had reined up, the dry river bluffs were empty, except for an
abandoned stone watchtower less than fifty yards across the
road from Anna. The watchtower offered a clear view of both
ford and town, and the flat highway that stretched through
scattered brown grass, creosote bushes, and bare reddish
ground toward the eastern horizon. Anna edged Farinelli
slightly closer to the bluff edge and leaned forward in the
saddle, trying to study the curve of the river.

'*Still waters run deep . . .*' The song's words echoed in her
thoughts and were gone. The Chean might run smoothly, but
it certainly wasn't deep, and that was part of her problem.

'Why are we headed out this way?' asked Daffyd. 'No
one is stupid enough to fight a battle with their backs
to a cliff.'

Anna wanted to glare at the player. Too often, he was
still the condescending undergraduate who hadn't figured
out how much he didn't know. 'You're right, but I don't
know the road. I need to check it out.'

Daffyd looked puzzled. 'Check out?'

'Look at it.' Anna paused, then continued, absently patting
Farinelli on the neck. 'If the Prophet's forces are in Pamr,
how will Eladdrin bring his troops?'

'He'll take the high road along the bluff here,' answered
Spirda from Anna's right. 'He wouldn't want to put them
on the exposed low ground down there, especially since
he knows you're a sorceress. They'd be sitting geese for
archers, too.'

Anna would not have called the narrow dusty trail that

wound westward – almost paralleling the curves of the river itself – a road, although perhaps it had been a highway once, before the rains had ceased. The trail was flat, level, and ran through low brush and brown grass, leaving any who traveled it visible for deks or leagues . . . . or whatever. Her eyes flicked back downhill to the Chean River, a thin line of brown water almost lost in wider banks that announced it had once been far greater.

As Spirda had said, the Ebrans certainly would not wish to lead their troops downhill into the ford – even if they knew the area contained no troops.

What if Behlem drew up his forces as though to defend Pamr – a good part of a day's march farther west? With their water-scrying, the Ebrans would certainly know where the Prophet's forces were.

Anna frowned. The Ebrans could take the narrow trail that once might have been a road and follow the river to hold the high ground – and they wouldn't have to worry about mud or rain. Even so, how near would they stay to the river? She rubbed her forehead.

'Spirda? If Hanfor were leading his troops, how close would he stay to the river?'

'It's hard to say.' The subofficer pursed his lips, then scratched the back of his head. 'He'd want to see the river and the plain there. I don't know, but I'd bet he'd pretty much follow this road we're on. You can see riders from a long ways, and there's higher ground on this side as you get toward Pamr.'

Anna looked at the bluffs – they seemed to be normal clay and soil, not sandstone or the redstone of the Ostfels. Could she turn the bluffs into something more dangerous? She remembered listening to Sandy and his endless lectures on aquifers and groundwater and sinkholes. But could she create something that the Ebrans couldn't see? Couldn't sense? Something that seemed natural even to magic sensors?

'We'll be here awhile.' Anna took out the second water bottle, uncapped it, and swallowed a good third of it before she replaced it. Even with the bedraggled floppy-brimmed hat and the long-sleeved shirt, she felt the sun beating through her.

Spirda looked surprised.

'I need to do some prep work. Just make sure we're not disturbed.' She slowly dismounted, handed Farinelli's reins to the subofficer, and began to unstrap the lutar. 'Daffyd?'

'Yes, Lady Anna?' The player eased the mare over beside Spirda.

'I'm going to need some help.' She pulled out several scraps of paper and the battered greasemarker that she'd lugged all across Defalk. 'After I figure out the right kind of spell.'

Daffyd nodded and began to dismount.

Spirda gestured, and one of the other armsmen, older, black-bearded, rode closer. 'Take these, Fhurgen.' The subofficer handed Farinelli's reins to the bearded man. In turn, Daffyd handed the mare's reins to the older armsman.

Anna set the lutar case beside the road, and began to hum, trying to match what she had in mind to the melody. She sat on a patch of ground between two bedraggled creosote bushes that seemed clear of ants and insects, pushing the hat back slightly, her back to the mid-afternoon sun.

She was probably crazy to be out in the heat, but she felt there wasn't that much time. So she just kept drinking lots of water.

The first line didn't work, and she scratched it out.

'What's she doing?' whispered Fhurgen to Daffyd.

The other armsmen just watched, and Anna could feel all the eyes on her. She wanted to shake her head.

'Creating a spell . . . I think,' the player muttered back.

Anna glared at them. It was hard enough without intrusions. Both men closed their mouths, but she caught the exchange of glances. More unspoken shit about moody or bitchy women. Men were creative or eccentric, but women were difficult or bitchy. She snorted, ignoring the second set of glances, forcing her thoughts back to the spell rhyme.

Her neck burned by the time she had the four verses she needed scrawled out on the paper. Her knees creaked as she stood.

'All right,' she said, turning her head toward Daffyd, who was blotting his sweating face. 'You can tune the viola. I'm just about ready to try this.'

'That's good. I'm hot.'

'So am I.' Her back was soaked where the shirt and tunic had rested against her skin.

As Anna brushed off her trousers, and began to tune the lutar, and Daffyd the viola, Spirda rode back toward the ford, not more than fifty yards, before announcing loudly. 'There's no one coming.'

Although the sorceress felt like telling Spirda that such announcements were unnecessary, that she could see that herself, she just nodded and finished tuning the lutar. Then she cleared her throat and ran through a set of vocalises. Her throat was dry, and she stopped for more water before resuming.

Finally, she turned to Daffyd again, catching him wiping his forehead. 'Here's the song.' She hummed the round, once, then again. 'Can you do that?'

'Of course. It's a simple tune.'

'I won't be playing the same thing,' she pointed out. 'The chords are harmony.'

Daffyd nodded again, and fiddled with his bow.

The sorceress looked toward the river, cleared her throat, nodded to Daffyd, and began.

> 'Cut, cut, cut your bed
> deeply through the ground
> easily, easily, easily,
> with water yet unfound.

> 'Leave, leave, leave the road
> covered by the ground . . .

'Carve, carve, carve
deep beneath the ground ...'

Despite the support of Daffyd's playing, by the time she strummed the last chord, Anna had to sit down – abruptly – on the dusty day of the road, her head swimming, and her skull throbbing. The lutar on beside her, and stars flashed across her eyes.

A low rumbling, or groaning, filtered up through the ground, and little puffs of dust burst upward along the road.

'Are you all right?' asked Daffyd, kneeling beside her.

'I need something to eat,' she admitted. 'And drink.'

Fhurgen eased his mount back as Daffyd rummaged through the saddlebags of his mare before returning to Anna with a chunk of bread and her water bottle.

'Here.'

First, she drank, and then began to chew the stale bread.

Spirda rode slowly back to the two. Even through the sparkles of her intermittent vision, Anna could see the subofficer was pale.

'The river's gone. It's just gone. What did you do?'

'It's working for us,' she answered, her mouth partly full. She had another long swallow of warm water. It still tasted good. She broke of another piece of bread and put it in her mouth.

The ground trembled once more. Anna smiled faintly.

'Now what, Lady Anna?' asked Spirda.

'We wait awhile.' The images in front of her eyes still sparkled, and she turned to Daffyd. 'I need more bread and some cheese.'

He nodded and went back to the saddlebags.

Anna kept eating, as more small puffs of dust rose along the line of the road.

Daffyd's mare whinnied, and Farinelli sidestepped, drawing the reins held by Fhurgen tight. The other armsmen rode in tight circles on edgy mounts. Daffyd glanced from Anna to the armsmen and back to Anna. She had to force herself to finish all the bread and cheese. She felt like a hog. Was that the way anorexics felt – as though normal nourishment were stuffing them? Yet her dietary needs were far from normal, and she could tell she was too thin – but how on Erde could she keep eating all the time?

'You keep it up or you'll die, either from starvation or because you can't do sorcery,' she mumbled to herself.

Spirda rode back and forth, to look at the river, then back to survey the sorceress and the player, then back to the river. While he rode, and Daffyd fidgeted, Anna made her way through almost another half loaf much before the sparkling motes before her eyes died away. She had to have been hungrier than she'd thought – either that or her spellcasting involved a great deal more than she had considered. She felt ready to retch before she felt strong enough to stand.

The faint groaning and the dust puffs continued.

In time, when she felt matters had proceeded long enough – and she had no way of knowing, but had to trust her feelings – Anna finished the water bottle and stood, lifting the lutar. Her fingers touched the gut strings once more. She nodded and looked at the younger player. 'We need to do it again.'

Duffyd raised both eyebrows, but extracted his viola and bow from their case.

Anna waited until he nodded, and then she cleared her throat and organized the second version of the song that had started as a nursery-rhyme round.

> 'Leave, leave, leave the road
> covered by the ground ...
>
> 'Hold, hold, hold the road
> firm above the ground ...'

Spirda eased his mount back toward the road cut to the ford, watching until after Anna and Daffyd had finished.

Then he rode back to the waiting squad – and to Daffyd and Anna.

'The river's back, but it's even muddier,' announced the subofficer.

'It may be for a while,' Anna conceded. 'It may be.' She felt exhausted, and hoped she was up for the long ride back toward Pamr. Slowly, she walked toward Farinelli, and even more laboriously, fashioned the lutar and case in place, then mounted.

'What did you do?'

'Enough, enough.' She hoped it had been enough, and that it would held, and that Eladdrin would indeed follow the course of apparent common sense. So much was based on hope, and so often hope was disappointed.

Anna took a deep breath and turned Farinelli back toward the ford and the still-shallower and muddier Chean River. She'd have to eat again, before long, and she hoped the churning of her overstressed stomach would subside by then.

75

Looking ahead to the bridge across the river, Anna reflected that the Chean River wasn't even a river, but more like the Platte in August – a thin stream lost in wide banks cloaked in browning vegetation. Because of all the irrigation in the river valley, the Chean carried less water than it had at Sorprat.

The sorceress had not slept well the night before, perhaps because they had stopped short of Pamr and bedded down in an abandoned barn, perhaps because her digestive system was having trouble coping with all the food her sorcery demanded, or perhaps because she continued to worry about her sorcery itself. She was relying on what she *felt*, and after her failure to scry Mario in the mirror, she'd begun to wonder. Was sorcery as reliable as it had seemed? Had she accomplished what she had tried with the river bluffs – or was she deceiving herself? Had her earlier successes been based on her ability? Or had she been lucky? Or was sorcery just unreliable in trying to view an earth based on technology? That didn't even deal with what she *knew* about people. Too many in authority – like Avery or Behlem – demanded proof for others to justify their actions, while conveniently ignoring it for their own. Proof that Virkan was abusing people, proof that Delor would have kept trying to kill her – and the only proof of that would have been her death.

There remained so much she did not know. She took a long, slow breath, and let it out equally slowly, trying to settle her churning stomach. Her eyes drifted northward, drawn by ... something. She squinted as the morning sun caught the corner of her eye, but despite the glare she could see a line of armed horsemen waiting silently on the low hill above the green fields of some sort of beans.

'Lady ...' said Spirda softly. 'To our right ...'

'I see them. Let's keep riding.' The bridge wasn't that far ahead.

Anna glanced to the bridge, then back to the hill. A single rider rode slowly downhill at an angle, so that he would cross the meadow ahead to Anna's right and meet them on the road.

'One rider,' said Daffyd.

'They want something,' affirmed Spirda.

Again, Anna wanted to strangle them both for stating the obvious as though she had no brains at all. Instead, she contented herself with a single word. 'Obviously.'

A low guffaw came from one of the armsmen riding behind. Fhurgen? Or one of the others – Hirreno, perhaps? She couldn't tell without looking, and she didn't need to, since whoever it was happened to be laughing at the self-officiousness of Daffyd and Spirda.

She checked the larger body of riders motionless on the hill beyond the irrigated bean field. They had not moved. By now, Anna, Daffyd, and the squad of armsmen were closer to the stone bridge across the Chean than to the armed riders. As they neared the mown meadow, the single rider, wearing a blue sash and bearing a white banner, trotted toward the squad.

'What is your pleasure, lady?' asked Spirda.

Anna studied the weathered but thin face of the man who rode ever closer. Except for reins and banner staff, his hands were empty.

'Let him close enough to speak.'

The rider, clearly unsure of his reception, reined up a good twenty yards from Anna and her group.

'I bear a message for the lady Anna.'

Anna eased Farinelli away from the others only slightly. 'I'm Anna.'

'The lord Jecks begs your indulgence and would like a word with you.' The rider bowed.

'Should you?' asked Spirda. 'He hasn't declared his allegiance to the Prophet.'

'That might be a good reason to meet him. I talked with him before, briefly, and he seemed honest.'

'Seemings are not always truths.'

'I'll risk it.' Anna turned to the messenger. 'I'll meet him on the open meadow there. Alone. Everyone else must stay well away from us.'

'No arms,' hissed Spirda, behind Anna.

'I will bear no arms, except my knife, and I trust that Lord Jecks will also bear no arms.'

'He will be alone.' The messenger nodded. 'Without his blade or bow.'

'He is keeping his armsmen well beyond bow range,' said Spirda. 'He must want to speak with you badly.'

'Very badly,' added Daffyd.

Anna watched as the messenger urged his mount up the low hill and as a single rider eased away from the mounted armsmen there. As Jecks rode downhill, Anna eased Farinelli into the middle of the meadow and reined up.

The stocky white-haired rider drew up a few yards from Anna, keeping his bare hands in plain view.

Farinelli whuffled, then sidestepped.

'Easy . . . easy . . .' Anna patted his shoulder.

'Lady Anna.' The white-haired man inclined his head. 'I took this risk in the hopes that you would not employ your sorcery to destroy me. It is a risk, from what I hear, but at my age, you discover that everything is a risk.'

'What you do want?' Anna asked. 'I'm sorry if I'm too blunt, but I know little about you, except that we spoke briefly before the battle of the Sand Pass, and that you seemed honest. The few common people who knew you thought you kept your word.'

Jecks smiled briefly, an open smile that Anna liked, although she kept her distance, her eyes occasionally checking the horsemen on the ridge. Spirda had said they were well out of bow-shot, and she hoped he was correct.

'I have heard the same about you, and also that you are a sorceress who has great power, and dislikes using that power.'

He wouldn't have said that if he'd been around Falcor lately, thought Anna. 'The situation here seems designed to force me to employ everything that I know,' she admitted aloud. *And much that I don't*, she added to herself. *It isn't Kansas, Dorothy, or even Ames, Iowa.*

After a puzzled look, Jecks added, 'You, and Lord Brill, served Lord Barjim in trying to stop the dark ones. You may recall that my daughter was his consort.'

'I recall.' Anna had liked Alasia, certainly a point in Jecks' favor.

Jecks nodded. 'I managed to recover half my forces from the battle. The dark ones were reluctant to pursue after your efforts. Instead of returning directly to Elhi, I rode to Falcor and escorted my grandson from the liedstadt to his ancestral home – where he now remains.'

Anna could feel her forehead knitting in puzzlement. 'What do you want from me?'

'Might I ask why you have chosen to serve the Prophet Behlem? If you would not mind telling me?' Jecks offered another wry smile, looking much younger than the silver-white hair initially had indicated.

The sorceress pursed her lips for a moment, scanning the horizon again, but neither her squad nor Jeck's horsemen had moved. 'I didn't see anyone else trying to stop the dark ones. After that battle, I felt someone had to. Those people are . . . They're evil,' she concluded, much as she hated to pin that label on anyone.

'Why do you feel you must fight them?' Jecks asked. 'Humor me, please, with these questions. I am an old man, trying to protect his only grandson.'

Jecks, for all the white hair, didn't look that old, prob-ably not any older than Anna was, and he was stocky, muscular, and doubtless quite a fighter. In fact, Anna con-cluded to herself, he was a lot more attractive than any of the men she'd seen so far – clean-shaven, honorable, and willing to stand up for what he believed in. Plus . . . he seemed to have a wry sense of humor, or some-thing like it.

'I saw terrible things in my world, and they only got worse because no one would stand up to stop them. There, because magic was different, I could do nothing. Here I can.' She laughed, not quite harshly. 'You might say that life has called my bluff.'

'Thank you, Lady Anna.' Jecks bowed his head. 'I would beg your leave to talk with you again. The Prophet sent a messenger, but I would reply first through you. You may tell the lord Behlem that while I will not join his forces, I will not fight him, and I will do all that I can to hold back the dark ones.' The older lord offered a more wintry, but still open smile. 'Florenda, the player Liende, and Albero wish to be remembered to you. It was their idea that I speak with you, and I am glad I heeded it. A good trip back to Falcor to you, Lady Anna.'

'I will tell the Prophet, and I will do my best to persuade him of your goodwill.'

'I would not deceive you, lady. I bear neither goodwill nor evil will for Lord Behlem. I wish to save Defalk.' Jecks inclined his head, then turned his mount toward the east.

What was that last bit all about? wondered Anna. She shook her head as she eased Farinelli back toward her squad.

'Will you destroy them?' asked Spirda as Anna reined up Farinelli.

'No. He had a message for the Prophet, and the Prophet should hear that message and make his own decision.' Anna reached for her water bottle. Suddenly, her throat was dry, and she was thirsty. Since Jecks had agreed to fight the dark ones, she didn't believe that Behlem had so many armsmen that he could afford to spurn the offer. Still, she wasn't sure, and she wasn't about to blurt it out.

'The Prophet may not be pleased.'

Anna finished drinking and eased the water bottle into the straps, then nudged Farinelli enough to start the gelding on their interrupted course toward the bridge. 'The Prophet has requested allegiance, and Lord Jecks has asked me to deliver his reply. The Prophet should make his own judgment on Lord Jecks.' *And he'd be a fool to take on a fight he doesn't need to right now.*

Spirda rode silently beside Anna, frowning. The sorceress ignored his displeasure, wishing the subofficer would grow up. Then, she reminded herself, Spirda had not seen or felt that dark massed power of the Ebrans, and some people learned only from what they experienced personally. Was she like that? She hoped not, but self-delusion was the easiest of all deceptions.

76

ESARIA, NESEREA

The raven-haired woman leans forward, stopping short of where the top of the low-cut pale green gown would reveal too much to the officer in the maroon uniform of a lancer of Mansuur. 'You have followed the dispatches from Falcor?'

'Yes, my lady Cyndyth.' The officer remains erect, his voice polite, formal.

'Is it true that this sorceress who has joined the Prophet killed many of the darksingers at the battle for the Sand Pass?' Cyndyth leans back in the dark polished wooden arm-chair that is not quite a throne, her green eyes the same shade as the brocade trim of the chair's head-high upholstery.

'So it is said, my lady.'

'And she has joined the Prophet's forces in Falcor?'

'Yes, my lady.'

Cyndyth lifts the crystal goblet, sips the pale red wine, then replaces it on the silver tray that sits upon the table to her right. Long slender fingers lift a candied almond from the silver dish on the tray. 'Is she beautiful?'

'She is said to be young and blonde.' The lancer's forehead crinkles ever so slightly as he adds, 'Yet it is also said that she has children as old as you are, my lady.'

'Does she have scars, great gashes on her skin?' asks Cyndyth. 'I heard the dark ones nearly killed her.'

'The dark ones seek her, or so says the counselor Menares, and she was thrown from the walls by their attack. Yet she lives.'

'You do serve the Liedfuhr, do you not?'

'As I must, Lady Cyndyth. As my family has ever.' A faint sheen of perspiration coats the officer's forehead.

'And you know that my father is ever vigilant?'

'The vigilance of the Liedfuhr is legendary.'

Cyndyth laughs, softly, throatily, and lifts the goblet for another sip of the wine. 'It is legendary. You are so comic, Nubara. So formal. So careful.'

'I understand my duties, lady, and do my best to fulfill them.'

'So you do.' Cyndyth's voice turns lazy, slow, as she continues. 'A sorceress who is young and blonde . . . a battle against the dark ones that must be won . . . and after that?' She shrugs and a smooth-skinned shoulder is momentarily uncovered. 'Once the mighty Eladdrin is vanquished, will the Prophet need a sorceress? Will the Liedfuhr?' She straightens in the chair and reaches for another almond. 'Oh, you might wish to inform my sire that we will be departing for Falcor.'

'"We," my lady?' asks Nubara.

'You are the envoy of the Liedfuhr to the Prophet, and the Prophet – and the sorceress – are in Falcor. How could you possibly deal with the sorceress from here? Or serve the Liedfuhr?' Even, white teeth delicately crush the almond, and Cyndyth takes another sip of wine. 'You will serve the Liedfuhr, will you not, by ensuring that the next battle of this sorceress is her last battle?'

'I serve the will of the Liedfuhr.' Nubara's forehead is even brighter with sweat.

'I am so sure you do, Nubara.' Cyndyth smiles slowly, showing white teeth framed by reddened lips. 'So very sure that you will not misunderstand his will in this. We leave tomorrow.'

77

Anna dried her just-washed face, then straightened her last clean set of riding clothes. Again, the night before, they had

418 • • • L. E. MODESITT, JR.

ridden late to reach Falcor, and she had probably overslept, but at least a covered tray of bread and cheese had been waiting when she rose, a heaping tray, thankfully. From Skent, she suspected.

She looked at the pile of the floor and the two buckets of water beside them. With a sigh, she took out the lutar. Sorcery to do laundry? Was it worth the headache it would cause? What else could she do? The last time she'd asked for it to be done, the clothes had been returned brushed clean of dust and dirt, but still stained and smelly.

After too long a time, and the headache she had antici-pated, Anna hung the two sets of trousers, tunics, and shirts around her room, as well as twice that many undergarments. The idea of her room looking like a Chinese laundry bothered her, but not so much as dirty clothing.

She put the lutar away and sat down to a goblet of water and the one chunk of bread left over from breakfast. Almost before she finished the bread, she jerked the bellpull, and waited.

Birke arrived almost immediately.

'Birke? I'd like to talk to Garreth.'

The page swallowed.

'Don't worry. I just want her to draw something for me.' Anna held in a grin. 'Do you like her?'

'She draws well,' answered the page.

Meaning yes, Anna inferred.

'I also need you to take a message to Counselor Menares. I have a message from Lord Jecks to the Prophet.'

'You have a message from Lord Jecks?'

'To the Prophet,' Anna added. 'I'll be either here with Garreth or upstairs with Lady Essan.'

'You do not intend to come directly?' Birke's brows lifted.

'That would waste my time and his.' Anna smiled. 'Garreth first.'

'Yes, Lady Anna.'

Anna said nothing, though she could sense the youth's disapproval. Would he disapprove of every contact she made? She shook her head as she closed the door to the landing.

Even before the sorceress had finished her second goblet of purified water, the door knocker thunked, announcing Garreth.

'Birke said you had requested my presence,' said the thin-faced brunette, her eyes on the stones of the landing before the door.

'Please come in.' Anna motioned to a chair, but the young woman barely sat on it, almost perching on the edge. Garreth's eyes wandered around the room, glancing at the garments draped around.

'Laundry,' explained Anna.

The brunette frowned. Anna didn't explain, feeling that she'd come across as arrogant and condescending if she attempted to discuss cleanliness, especially since the room had gotten dusty in her absence.

'Your room is cold. How be it so?'

'Sorcery,' Anna admitted. 'Erde gets too hot to be comfortable for me.'

Garreth shivered, but said nothing.

'I had a request of you,' the sorceress finally said. 'Could you draw a picture of me, say on the tower, with some of Falcor behind me? It doesn't have to be fancy, but something that's recognizable as me.'

Garreth frowned, ever so slightly, her green eyes slightly hooded.

'I'd pay you for it,' Anna added. 'I don't have that much coin, but . . . would a silver or two help?'

'It is not that, Lady Anna. I not be that good.'

'You're better than most of the pretenders who call themselves artists.'

A faint smile flitted across Garreth's lips and vanished.

'I would also consider it a great favor.'

'If you would explain that to Lady Essan . . .'

'I would be happy to – very happy.'

'How big?' ventured the brunette.

'It must be small, to fit in an . . . a packet.' Anna framed a space with her hands. 'And soon, if that's possible.'

'I could come back this afternoon, when Lady Essan rests.'

'Good.' Anna smiled, and stood. She still needed to see Essan, preferably before Menares and Behlem. 'Is Lady Essan in now?'

'She usually be in, Lady Anna.' As she stood, Garreth's voice was polite, but Anna felt stupid. Where would the widow of the former Lord of Defalk go?

'I'll talk to her now.'

'Then I will return to my corner.'

Anna waited until Garreth's steps died away down the tower steps before she headed up toward Essan's room. The stairwell was hot and close, even before mid-morning, and smelled faintly of urine and worse from the jakes on the level below Anna's quarters. She wrinkled her nose, but kept climbing.

She paused outside the lady Essan's room, then rapped on the door.

'Yes? What is it?'

'It's Anna, Lady Essan.'

The older woman opened the door. 'You have returned safely. Do come in.' Essan turned to the stocky woman with white-streaked black hair. 'You may go, Synondra.'

Synondra bowed her head, first to Lady Essan, and then to Anna, as she stepped out of the room.

Anna followed Essan toward the pair of purple uphol-stered and embroidered chairs. The polished table held the small silver platter, empty except for a few of the almonds, and the same pewter pitcher and paired goblets.

'What happened on your journey, sorceress woman-girl?' Essan settled herself into the chair with the pillow. 'Have you found a way to defeat the dark ones and thus ensure Defalk as a province of Neserea?'

Anna wanted to wince at the bitter undertone.

'Don't mind me, Anna.' Essan lifted her goblet. 'I am old

enough to say what I please – in my own small quarters, anyway.'

Anna still didn't know how to answer. After a moment, she spoke. 'I *might* have created something that will help defeat the Ebrans, but until I try it, how will I know?' She forced a shrug, feeling slightly dishonest as she did. 'Even if it does work, will that ensure that Lord Behlem can hold Defalk?'

'I would wager, naive-wise woman, that whether the Prophet holds Defalk rests solely upon you.' Essan popped one of the two remaining almonds into her mouth and pointed to the remnant. 'The last is for you.'

'Go ahead,' Anna said. 'I'm not hungry now.' *Not too hungry, and I need to let my stomach settle, if it will.*

'I hope you enjoyed the ride,' Essan went on. 'The liedburg staff, those left from earlier days and not rooted out, have made you into a warrior hero. Your knife has grown to a yard in length, and you destroyed half the stable in your fury. You also cursed all the Prophet's captains – those that you did not burn to ashes – and even the Prophet has doubled his Guard against you.'

'Oh ...'

'These things happen. Harmony knows they need a champion, and now even a sorceress from the mist worlds will do. Until you win and they discover you are a woman,' Essan added dryly.

Two quick raps sounded on the door, and a frown crossed Essan's wrinkled forehead. 'Not even up here is there peace, not with that clown of music in the hall.'

Anna started to stand, but Essan waved her back to her seat. 'I would get it. You are a guest, and small as my kingdom is, guests answer no summonses.'

Anna held in a grin as Essan marched to the door.

'It's Birke, Lady Essan. Is Lady Anna there? The Prophet wishes to see her now.'

'She is here, young Birke, and I will tell her.'

'Thank you, Lady Essan.'

Anna could hear Birke's steps on the stones of the tower stairs before Essan closed the door.

'Oh, the Prophet wishes to see you.' The white-haired woman's eyes twinkled. 'Even Donjim at his drunkest was not that peremptory. But then, you did not present yourself at his chamber and wait and wait upon his pleasure.'

'I don't do that anymore.'

'You have experienced more than that youthful face shows. What it does not indicate . . . your voice does. Best you be careful with that tongue.' Essan smiled as she warned Anna. 'Still . . . you should not keep our present lord and master waiting too long.'

Anna wasn't certain she held back the grin as she stood. 'I appreciate your thoughts, Lady Essan.'

'Another thought, sorceress. For all your age you are far too honest to play with power.' The older woman shook her head. 'Yet Defalk could ill afford to lose such honesty – it is so rare. Best you be on your way. Lord Behlem is not long on patience, especially with women.'

Anna nodding, thinking as she walked toward the door that few men in Liedwahr seemed to be patient with women – or anyone else.

'We must hurry,' Birke insisted as Anna stepped out onto the landing. 'The counselor was very insistent.'

'That may be,' Anna said, 'but it won't do anyone any good if we fall down the stairs and kill ourselves.' She steadied herself on the rough stones of the stairwell wall.

Once they reached the main corridor beyond the tower, Birke began to walk faster and faster. 'Counselor Menares said to hurry, Lady Anna.'

After taking the wide steps and heading halfway back along the unlit hallway where the glass mantles on the wall sconces for the candles were smudged and dusty, Birke stopped short outside a doorway. An armsman stood on each side, and a page by the door handle.

Birke bowed to the older, black-haired page. 'Seckar,

announce to the Prophet that the lady Anna has arrived in response to his summons.'

Seckar eased the door open. 'The lady Anna.'

'About time!' came from beyond the door.

The sorceress thought the Prophet's voice sounded more petulant than commanding, but she stepped past Seckar.

Behlem sat in a high-backed wooden chair placed on a dais. Menares sat on an armless chair on the floor level, but rose as Anna entered. The Prophet did not. His hand touched his beard briefly, then dropped to the padded arm of his chair.

The receiving room was hot and smelled of sweat. The row of high windows on the left-hand side all remained closed. Anna wanted to wipe her forehead. Instead she bowed slightly. 'I came as soon as I received word.'

'Where were you earlier this morning?' asked Behlem.

'We returned last night. I sent word to Menares right after I rose.' Anna bowed toward the white-haired counselor.

'Time is important, Lady Anna. The last of the Ebran reinforcements are in the Sand Pass,' Menares said. 'In two days they will be in Mencha, and in four Eladdrin will be on his way to Falcor – unless he heads north to Elhi first.' The counselor looked to the Prophet.

Behlem fingered his reddish blond beard, but shook his head.

'What have you to offer the Prophet?' asked Menares, reseating himself. Neither man suggested Anna sit, and there was no chair obvious.

'I believe I have a way in which I may be able to cripple the armies of the dark ones.'

'What does it require? Masses of gold?' Behlem's voice remained high and sarcastic.

'No. All you have to do is mass your forces somewhere in the neighborhood of Pamr, enough so that Eladdrin will take the trail south of the river rather than cross into the river valley.'

'He would not cross the ford in any case,' snapped the Prophet.

Anna shrugged. 'You know the military terms. If he travels the bluff trail, then I have a chance of hurting his forces.'

'A chance? You wish me to commit my forces on a chance?'

'My lord,' offered Menares smoothly, 'the ford is two days from Pamr, more for large bodies of armsmen.' The counselor turned to Anna. 'You intend to be near the ford, with a small guard?'

'Yes.'

'The sorceress is willing to put herself in danger, while your armsmen are not.' The counselor shrugged. 'That does not seem so bad a bargain.'

Behlem fingered his beard. 'Perhaps not. We must discuss this and consider it.' His eyes hardened. 'Subofficer Spirda reported that you met with a Defalkan lord. You did not mention this.'

'That was one of the reasons I wished to speak with you.'

'Oh . . . now you tell me.' Behlem's lips curled.

Anna forced herself to remain calm, even as she could sense the withdrawal into her shell, the professional calm, the Plexiglas shields of the soul, drop around her. 'You haven't given me much chance to explain anything,' she said reasonably. 'It wasn't a meeting. He had a large body of troops, and we spoke for a few moments in an open meadow.'

'That is what Spirda said,' ventured Menares.

'Menares . . .' said Behlem warningly.

'Lord Jecks asked me to convey a message to you in response to your message.'

Behlem raised his eyebrows. 'What was his message?'

'He said that he would not fight you and that he would fight the Ebrans.'

'But he would not support our claim to Defalk.'

'No.'

'And you let him live?' asked the Prophet silkily. 'You let him offer such insolence and live?'

'Whether to kill him or not isn't my decision, Lord Behlem. I didn't see much point in trying to kill someone who is a potential ally against the Ebrans.'

'You forget yourself, Lady Anna,' snapped Behlem.

Menares put a hand on the Prophet's sleeve, but Behlem shook it off. 'I am the Prophet. You are a stranger. You know nothing of Defalk or Liedwahr. How can you tell me what is wise?'

'I have seen the dark ones,' Anna said, forcing herself to remain calm, even though Behlem reminded her of all too many arrogant graduate students. 'I have fought them. You have not.'

'You did not defeat them.'

Anna remained silent, seething.

'No . . .' added Menares slowly. 'Yet she destroyed more darksingers than anyone ever has, as you yourself have said, my lord. And she killed several thousand Ebran armsmen – more than our armies have.'

Behlem twisted toward the older man, then smoothed his face. 'And?' he asked Anna. 'Why did you let him live?'

The sorceress couldn't quite believe that the Prophet had heard nothing of what she had said – like so many junior DMAs who thought their doctorates counted for more than a lifetime of experience. She rephrased her answer. 'Lord Jecks has agreed not to fight you, and he has agreed to fight them. You lose nothing.'

Behlem fingered his beard. Finally, he looked directly at her. 'Have you told *anyone?*'

'No. The message was for you. All I told Spirda was that you had requested Lord Jecks' alliance and that I was asked to deliver his reply.'

'Are you sure of that, Lady Anna.'

'I'm sure,' Anna said coldly, 'and when I say something is true, it's true.'

Behlem's eyes smoldered, but his fingers brushed the beard again.

Menares swallowed, easing back from the Prophet.

Abruptly, Behlem laughed. 'So! Well, nothing's changed. He isn't a friend, and he isn't an enemy, and he won't attack, and you told Spirda the decisions were mine. There are worse things.'

Anna waited.

After a moment, Behlem nodded. 'You may go. We will discuss your idea.' His eyes went to Menares.

The sorceress got the message and bowed. 'By your leave.' Then she turned and left, opening the door for herself on the way out, barely managing not to slam it.

In his childish way, Behlem was dangerous, paranoid. He'd baited her just to see if he could find a reason to distrust her, and then he'd almost tossed her out.

He'd learn. Anna knew what battles to fight, and when, and Behlem's turn would come.

In the meantime, she wanted Garreth to start drawing. With the way Avery was behaving and the agony on Elizabetta's face, Anna had to do something – or try. Her instincts – Brill's cautions – told her that her communications with earth were likely to be very limited.

78

MENCHA, DEFALK

The songmaster rises from the table in the salon as the lancer officer enters through the unused main dining area. The officer glances around and shakes his head.

'Opulent for a mere wizard,' notes Eladdrin. His eyes focus on the spare figure, in the dusty gray black uniform. 'What did you find, Ghurey?'

'Begging your pardon, Songmaster . . .'

'You found nothing?'

'We found traces of horses. We got the tale from the local farmers, but . . .' The dark lancer with the line of blacker braid across his shoulder shrugs. 'The blonde bitch rode out to Sorprat and crossed the ford. She rode up to the top of the bluffs, and she stayed there for maybe a glass. Then she rode back.' Ghurey smiles. 'We did find out something else interesting, though.'

'Oh?'

'She met with a local lord – Jecks – outside of Pamr. They met in a meadow, just the two of them. Then she rode back to Falcor.'

Eladdrin rubs his temples, then shakes his head.

'You think, ser, she was expecting to meet him at Sorprat? He's from Elhi, and Sorprat's two days' ride closer than Pamr.'

'It's hard to believe she rode four days for a short meeting in a meadow.' Eladdrin drawls out the words. 'You are certain there was no sorcery at the ford?'

'None so as I could detect. The highway was sound, and the stones of the ford were firm. We tested 'em with spells and iron rods. Not that I liked to running forces along any road with a sorcerer or sorceress around.' Ghurey shifts his weight from one dusty boot to the other.

Eladdrin nods. 'What about the river?'

'How could you tell? It's running water. Your darksingers didn't feel a thing.' Ghurey pauses, then asks, 'Can you say when we be heading out?'

'Not long. Not long.' The Songmaster smiles, briefly. 'Thank you.'

'Sorry we found nothing.'

'You did what you could.'

'Thank you, ser.' The lancer bows, turns, and makes his way through the dim structure toward the heat beyond.

After the other leaves, Eladdrin turns to the small mirror basin he has set up in the corner, and after doing the necessary, studies the image in the waters again, but the shimmering waters only show the road up from the ford at

Sorprat and the river bluffs that have not changed in years, only brown grasses and empty spaces to the east, only a farming valley to the west.

The Songmaster shakes his head again.

79

Anna shifted on the stool as Garreth worked on the sketch.

'Most sorcerers or sorceresses would not wish their likeness to be taken,' said the young woman, pausing to study Anna intently before dipping the fine-pointed stylus in the ink again.

'I can see why.'

'It's so pleasant here,' Garreth said, glancing from Anna to the paper before her again.

Anna nodded.

'Virkan is even nice now.' Garreth paused. 'Birke says that you bespelled him. Is that true?'

'I put a spell on him that told him to be kind to people.'

'It be unfortunate you could not do that to more souls.'

'That would not be a good idea. I only did it because Virkan was hurting people. Doing it still bothers me. I don't like meddling with people.'

Garreth shook her head minutely, but dipped the stylus again.

Anna wondered if the young woman disapproved of Anna's qualms or Virkan. The sorceress suspected that Garreth would like more than a few people bespelled, as if that kind of sorcery would solve anything. It was only another kind of force, and force always led to force.

'How soon can you be finished?' Anna asked after a time.

'It is almost done – a poor likeness, but you had stressed speed, lady.'

Anna walked over and looked down at the board. She couldn't help smiling as she saw the face Garreth had drawn – almost a young face, yet one with character, with features carrying the refined sharpness of experience, the character that never showed in the faces of those truly young – but a face that was too thin.

She shook her head ruefully.

'You do not like it? I should have taken—'

'No. You did a good job. Especially for just two sessions. You can take more time on another one, but I need this one sooner rather than perfect.'

'"Sooner rather than perfect"?' Garreth laughed. 'When you speak suchly, it is easy to tell that you are a stranger.'

Thunk.

With the rap on the door, Anna crossed the room and opened it.

Cens stood outside. He bowed. 'Lady Anna, the Prophet has requested your presence at a more formal dinner honoring Lord Dencer this evening. He has requested that you attire yourself appropriately.' As the page finished repeating the words, his face reddened.

'Thank you, Cens. The words aren't yours, and I know that. You may tell the Prophet or Menares that I will be there.' Anna smiled.

Cens looked at the stones of the landing, then looked up. 'Thank you, Lady Anna.'

She waited until he had turned and started down before closing the heavy door. She felt like slamming the iron bolt closed or screaming. Instead, she walked to the window and looked out at the heat of midday. Beyond the walls of the liedburg, Falcor looked dusty, even more deserted. A pair of crows flapped across the sun-bleached sky away from the river.

Dress appropriately indeed! That was nothing more than a request that she look more feminine, and a not-so-subtle power play.

'You look displeased,' offered Garreth.

'I'm not exactly overjoyed to be ordered into what I wear,' Anna said wryly as she turned.

Garreth's face went blank.

'I know, Garreth. It seems small enough to you, when you worry about being cast aside, or worse. But it's not as small as it seems. What would you feel if the lady Essan told you she did not like what you wore?'

'Oh . . .'

'Lord Behlem likes to control all those around him. That can't be a secret, can it?' Anna forced a grin.

Garreth gave a quick smile, then dipped the stylus in the ink again as Anna sat back on the stool.

In time, the young artist set aside the stylus and corked her ink bottle. 'That be what I can do this way.'

Anna uncramped herself from her perch on the stool and stood, stretching. 'Thank you.'

Garreth eased the small drawing off her board and laid it gently on one of the few clear spaces on the bed. 'This should dry for a time.'

Anna studied the images again, amazed at how closely the woman resembled her, and yet how different the sorceress was from the singer she had been. Then she turned and fumbled in the belt wallet until she came up with a pair of silvers that she pressed into Garreth's hand. 'These aren't enough, but I hope they help.'

'Lady . . . I could not.'

'Garreth, your work is worth that. Don't let anyone tell you otherwise. Save the silvers until you need them. I hope you don't, but I doubt that either Lady Essan or I stand highly in the Prophet's liking.'

'He respects you, lady. All know that,' protested the artist.

'Respect and liking are not the same.' Anna's eyes flicked to the picture. 'I like it.'

'I be glad.'

'Me, too. Now, I have to worry about appropriate attire.'

'You could use a maid, lady.'

'I probably could,' Anna answered, ignoring the implication, 'but that's something that will have to wait.'

Garreth bowed.

'I'll put you first, if you still want it, when the time comes,' Anna added as the younger woman's hand touched the door. 'I'm not making too many long-range plans at the moment.'

'Thank you, Lady Anna.' Garreth's voice was warmer.

After the girl left, Anna went back to the bed and studied the picture. The ink needed to dry a bit, but it would do. As she had requested, Garreth had drawn her sitting on a stone bench on the tower roof, with a sketchy view of Falcor behind. Now . . . if Anna's planned sorcery worked . . .

She glanced to the door, then to the two gowns hanging from the pegs in the corner. 'Attire yourself appropriately!' Chauvinist pig!

After a deep breath, she slipped out into the heat of the landing, and began to climb the stairs. When she reached the upper level, Anna knocked on the door. Synondra opened it fractionally, started to speak, then stopped as she recognized Anna. 'She . . . was resting, Lady Anna, but I will see if she will take company.' The door shut, then reopened immediately.

'Anna . . . come in, if you don't mind a rumpled old lady. Synondra, go play for a bit.'

Synondra looked at Anna and mouthed, 'Not too long.'

'I saw that, Synondra. I won't keep Anna that long, but she be a stranger here. She will listen because I have not yet bored her to death.' Essan waved toward the door again.

Synondra bowed. 'I will be back before long, ladies.'

'A stubborn woman she be,' groused Essan. 'Stubborn.'

Anna smiled. To deal with Lady Essan required stubbornness and then some, she suspected.

As the door closed, the older woman looked at Anna. 'What need ye?'

'I've been summoned to a more formal dinner as sorceress and who knows what else because a Lord Dencer is here.'

'Behlem cannot awe him with his own power.' Essan nodded. 'Dencer lords Stromwer, and those are the southernmost holdings in Defalk. If need be, he could pledge to Ranuak, and that would give the Ranuans a foothold west of the Ostfels.'

'I have been requested to attire myself appropriately.' Anna slipped into the unoccupied chair.

'What did you do to Behlem?' asked the older woman. 'Pretty as you are, he only has you in his company when your power is vital, and Behlem has bedded every pretty skirt in the hall.'

'He could not bed me,' said Anna ruefully, 'except by great force.' *And maybe not even then, I hope.*

'So . . . he does place his power above his bed,' cackled Essan. 'At least, sometimes. He should listen to his counselor more often.' She shrugged. 'If he did, he would be stronger still.'

Anna wondered. Menares was playing a deeper game, but for whom she did not know, not yet. 'I wore trousers to his last dinner.'

'Ha! Sorceress girl . . . I would wager that he did not like. Like as to telling him you were equal to any man. No, he would not be pleased.' Essan laughed again. 'Anna, I like you. A woman such as you could rule Defalk, and far better than those dunces, save perhaps Jecks, and he is wise enough to know he cannot hold Defalk by mere skill at arms.'

Anna just looked at the wrinkled countenance.

'Some device you might need, but,' Essan shrugged, 'you could do it. And if ever you have the chance, woman, you take it, or the harmonies and I will haunt you eternally.'

'I doubt I'll ever have a chance like that.'

'You being here says the times are changing and the tunes are new.' Essan refilled her goblet with the strong-smelling brandy. 'You use your skills to see your children?'

'It was hard. I may not be able to do it many times.' Anna nodded. 'Yet . . . I worry.'

'A mother you be not, if there is no worry. They will endure, though, without you, and if they could not, you could not save them, like as we would that it were other.'

Anna still worried.

'An' ye still worry. That be always the lot of us who bear. Not that worry helps.' Essan took a deep swallow from the goblet. 'Not that it helps, sorceress woman, not that I need tell you.'

The sorceress agreed there.

'Ye be here now, and here be where ye must stand. Poor Barjim. Always was he wishing it were otherwise. Otherwise it is never, and we must live the melody played. Even you, sorceress. Even you.' Essan fell silent.

'The melody played . . .' mused Anna, in the silence that followed.

The door creaked, and Synondra peered in. 'Lady Essan . . . you needs must rest.'

'Rest? Rest be all I have left.' She winked at the sorceress, then added. 'Visit an old woman again.'

'I will,' Anna promised as she stood. 'I will.'

As the sorceress walked back down to her own room, she felt the tower shudder, as if the ground beneath were a string vibrating in sympathy with a massive chord plucked from the depths of Erde. Sweat beaded instantly on her forehead, and her hand went out to the stones of the wall. The wall was warm and firm.

She paused on the stone steps for a moment, but all was hot and still, without a trace of motion. Had she imagined the tremor?

She shook her head. She had felt *something*, even if she couldn't identify it.

80

Anna set down the pen and capped the ink bottle, laying the sheet aside to dry. As the note lay on the table, she read the note once more, her eyes skipping across the words.

Elizabetta—

This will not seem believable, and I do not know how else to reach you – magic here works through song, but it is strange . . .

I can send this, but I cannot send myself. Sometimes, I can watch you, in a sort of magic mirror – like the time you sat on the deck of the New Hampshire house and told your father – I think – that I wouldn't willingly leave you. I wouldn't, and I didn't. I was summoned by a sorceress . . . and now I am stuck here. So far, I have found no way to return . . .

I love you and Mario, and I miss you both terribly, and I do not know if this is the right thing to do. I do not know if I can ever figure a way back from here, and it is a terribly savage place in many ways. Yet I can't just let you think that I left you willingly. I don't know if this will reach you, but I must try.

For whatever reason, I cannot seem to see Mario. My 'magic window' does not show everything I wish, and I may not be able to do this much longer. Please tell him that I am well, and that I love him, as I love you.

I leave it to you whether you tell your father. I worry that if you do tell him he will accuse you of being irrational and making it all up because you could not face my disappearance, but you must do what you think is best for you . . .

> If this letter does reach you, and if I can see it ...
> I will try again, but if I do not, it will be because I
> cannot, not because I have not tried.

Once she was certain the ink was dry, Anna folded the
letter and slipped it back into the envelope, along with the
gold and silver coins, her watch, and the small drawing of
her on the tower.

Then she took out the lutar, and began to sing the
mirror song.

All that appeared in the mirror was a towel on the lake
beach, and the mirror frame began to smolder. Anna closed
off the spell hastily, and sank onto her bed.

She sighed. She hoped Elizabetta was swimming, or
water-skiing, or whatever, although she had the sense that
it should be fall in New England, or close to it. For whatever
reason, the spells did not show matters well around water,
which Anna found abstractly amusing since she could use
spells to purify and cool water.

She slipped the envelope under her pillow. While there
was really no place in her room safe from search, she didn't
want to leave it out in plain sight, either.

She paused to look out the window. To the west rose a
high plume of dust, whipped higher by the late summer –
or was it early fall? – winds. No, Falcor certainly wasn't in
Iowa – or Kansas.

Her cool-air shield/spell protected her room, but she could
hear the whistling of the rising winds, and see dust and small
pieces of wood swirling through the courtyard below.

She watched for a few moments as the dust turned the
late-afternoon sun red, nearly blood-red. Then her eyes went
back to the gowns in the corner. Two, and once she had had
dozens. Yet the dozens had not brought her control of her
own life.

She shrugged. Neither had the two, and she needed to eat.
She hated having to eat all the time, even more than she'd
hated never being able to eat without gaining pounds.

Why was life like that – always on the extremes?

81

WEI, NORDWEI

The dark-haired woman stands at the window to the north, its shutters drawn back despite the chill of early fall, and looks down from her hillside vantage point at the swirling brown, debris-filled water that surges into Vereisen Bay and has flooded the dock district and the warehouses.

At a discreet cough, she turns.

'Honored Ashtaar? You requested my presence?' asks the heavyset Kendr.

'I did. Please come here.'

'As you wish, your mightiness.' The seer with the plaited muddy-brown hair waddles forward on thick legs.

Ashtaar opens her mouth, then closes it, and waits for Kendr to reach the window.

'This wasn't normal.' Ashtaar gestures through the open window to the expanse of water that covers the lower sections of Wei. 'I sent you a message.'

'Yes, honored Ashtaar. I received it.'

The spymistress gestures to the armless chair that sits on the far side of the high table she uses as a desk. 'Sit down.' She closes the shutters before seating herself.

Kendr waits.

'Did you find out how it happened?'

'It was the Evult, I think,' offers the seer. 'The ice is gone from the peaks above the headwaters of the River Ost.'

Ashtaar's fingers slip around the polished finish of the dark agate oval. 'How did this happen without a warning?'

'The sorceress from the mist worlds.'

The spymistress shakes her head. 'What does that have to do with the Evult?'

'The sorceress is powerful, and many of her spells shake the harmonies, even the earth deep beneath. She has done something to the Chean River, I think, but I cannot see what that might be.'

'The Evult?' prompts Ashtaar.

'We cannot trace every great sorcery ... not and obey the duties the Council has laid upon us.'

'Why not?'

Kendr pales and her mouth moves silently. Finally, she stutters, 'I ... none ... of us ... is that strong.'

'Do we need more seers?'

'We have needed more seers for seasons, your mightiness.'

'I know. I know.' Ashtaar waves away the comment. 'You say you are not strong enough. How does this excuse your failure to discover that the Evult was planning mischief?'

'The blonde sorceress had sung many spells – she was trying to see the mist worlds, we think – and when another blow to the harmonies rang through the waters, I had no strength ...'

'And you thought, foolish seer, that it was the blonde sorceress again?'

'Yes, Ashtaar.' Kendr looks to the floor.

'Then, you feared to tell me?'

Kendr does not answer.

Ashtaar's fingers tighten around the black agate oval, and her lips clamp together. She stares at the seer, but the heavyset woman does not lift her eyes to the spymistress.

'Kendr?'

'Yes, your mightiness?'

'We all get tired. We all can make mistakes when overtired. If you ever let your fear of one failure lead you to make another or fail to tell me in a timely fashion, you will indeed learn that I am "your mightiness." Do you understand me?'

'Yes, honored Ashtaar.'

The spymistress looks toward the door, her fingers still tight around the black agate oval.

Kendr backs out of the room.

82

After struggling through yet another medieval-style sponge bath, where she wondered once more about using sorcery to create a bathroom, Anna studied herself in the mirror. In addition to the youthfully idealized mature face, still too thin, she also had little body hair, except in the more obvious places, and what she had was fine and so blonde it was almost transparent. She'd originally thought that might have been a temporary result of the youth spell, but only the hair on her head grew.

Then, there was another troubling thing. While Anna clearly had the body and physical attributes of a young woman in her mid-twenties, she hadn't had a single period since she'd been in Liedwahr. First, she'd thought it was stress, but everything else was normal, except her cycle. She didn't have one, and she didn't have an explanation ... unless ... unless ...

Brill's sorcery had frozen her physically so that she'd never have a cycle ... and, young body or not, no chance at children. She wasn't sure she wanted to bring children into Liedwahr, and she certainly hadn't met anyone she would have wanted to love or father them – but she would have liked the choice! And it didn't look like she was going to get that, either.

She took a long slow breath and looked from the mirror to the two gowns once more.

In the end, she donned the green one, the more modest of the two, though neither was as daring as the recital gown that still lay in Loiseau, probably moldering, or plundered by the Ebrans.

Skent answered the bellpull, his eyes wide, and they headed down the stairs toward the middle dining hall.

Did she really look that good? Anna wanted to shake her head – his reaction had to be a youthful crush.

'How is Cataryzna?' she asked.

The page blushed.

'All right, young man. I won't embarrass you too much. Will I ever get to meet her?'

'She lives with her aunt in the south tower. That's the guarded one.'

'I take it that her father is important?'

'Geansor is the Lord of Sudwei, and Sudwei is the gate to the South Pass.'

Anna frowned. So Geansor was the key to the main trade route to Ranuak? Why was Cataryzna so valuable as a hostage, apparently for both Barjim and Behlem, when women didn't count for that much? 'I find it hard to see why a daughter—'

Skent stopped and turned, lowering his voice. 'Lady Anna . . .' He looked up and down the tower staircase.

'She's a hostage. I understand that. But why her? Doesn't Lord Geansor have any sons?'

'Lord Geansor was . . . wounded in the peasant uprising when she was small. She was his firstborn, the only one that lived. He can have no more children. The lord's only brother was killed by raiders two years ago.'

Anna understood. Cataryzna was literally the only blood relative or possible heir, and that meant she would be married off – probably as soon as the mess with the Ebrans was resolved. She shuddered at the thought of a world where a young girl was effectively imprisoned, if in a golden cage, until she could be imprisoned by marriage once more. Then, much of earth had been like that – and some still was. She put a hand out to Skent and squeezed his shoulder. 'I'm sorry, Skent. Does she like you?'

The page forced a nonchalant shrug. 'Who could say? I only deliver meals and such when Hestyr is ill or on other errands.'

The sorceress could tell. Love had found a way, and that love seemed hopeless to both.

'Don't worry yet,' she cautioned, as she continued down the steps toward the main level. 'Nothing will happen for a time.'

'Lord Behlem was talking of consorting her with Over-captain Delor.' Skent grinned. 'You didn't know, did you?'

'No.' Now that strange exchange between Skent and Birke the day she had left made sense. Of course, so did Behlem's plan to marry Cataryzna to Delor, because an officer would owe loyalty to Behlem more than would any lord from Neserea. Anna snorted. Barjim probably had worked out something similar with one of his own trusted officers. Men! 'But I understand more.' Anna forced a smile, hating what she was about to do, even if it was true. 'You know, I'm the only one who would oppose what Behlem has in mind.'

'You would?' Skent's tone was skeptical.

'I don't believe women should be barter chips in power games.' Anna laughed harshly. 'At least, we ought to have the right to barter ourselves.' After all, wasn't that what she was doing? The thought left the taste of bile in her mouth.

Skent pursed his lips, but said nothing, and Anna let it ride. There was nothing she could do at the moment.

Only half the lamps in the long corridor to the dining hall were lit, and the air remained hot and dusty as Skent and Anna approached the double doors where Giellum stood, flanked by two armsmen with drawn blades. Both wore Neserean cream and blue, and Anna wished she had worn her dagger, and brought the lutar. Instead she smiled at Giellum.

The younger armsman swallowed and eased open the left-hand door. 'Lady Anna.'

Anna nodded to Skent and stepped into the dining hall, again lit only dimly by three candelabra upon the single long table.

'My lady!' called Menares from beside the head of the table. Beside him stood a tall and gangly man whose thinning hair was far too long, with a lock dangling forward over his left eye.

As Anna stepped forward, the handful of officers eased away, almost as if she were a leper, and the man beside Menares pushed his hair off his forehead. Ignoring the officers, she walked the length of the table and stopped a few yards short of the counselor.

'Lord Dencer, this is the lady Anna, the sorceress from the mist worlds,' Menares said. 'Lady Anna, Dencer is the Lord of Stromwer.'

Dencer inclined his head ever so slightly, enough to convey his impression that Anna was far beneath him.

'I'm pleased to meet the lord who holds the key to the south,' Anna lied, wishing she could simply incinerate the condescending bastard.

'Lady Anna is the sorceress who destroyed much of the Ebran forces at the Sand Pass.'

'A pity she could not destroy them all.'

'I don't recall seeing you there, Lord Dencer,' Anna said smoothly. 'Were you engaged in important business elsewhere? Perhaps in Ranuak?'

Menares swallowed a gulp almost soundlessly, then turned at the sound of a chime to see Behlem, resplendent in a new or refurbished tunic of blue and gold.

'Lady Anna, would you be so kind as to light the chandeliers?' asked the Prophet, his voice smooth.

'It would be my pleasure.' Anna put even more butter in her words than Behlem had in his. She wanted to toast both the supercilious Dencer and the Prophet, the first for his arrogance and Behlem for his cavalier use of her as a tool. Instead, she cleared her throat and sang the candle spell, projecting as much force as possible and visualizing the blaze of light.

The sudden illumination was almost as good as a bank of flashbulbs, Anna felt, and the paleness of Lord Dencer reflected the effectiveness of Behlem's ploy.

'Thank you, Lady Anna,' said the Prophet. 'We should be seated while the food remains warm.'

'Rather impressive,' admitted the Lord of Stromwer. 'Yes . . . rather impressive.'

'And without players,' added Menares as he sat down beside Lord Dencer and across from Hanfor, who had slipped into the seat to Anna's right.

'Congratulations,' whispered Hanfor, his lips not moving, the words barely reaching Anna as he poured her wine.

'Thank you, overcaptain.'

'It is surprising to find a . . . sorceress of such power . . . in the hall of . . . one such as the Prophet of Music,' said Dencer. 'How did you come to be here?'

'It was not exactly my idea,' began Anna, as she quickly summarized her arrival in Mencha and her encounters with the Ebrans, concluding with, '. . . and Lord Behlem seems to be the only leader with both the resources and the desire to stop the dark ones.'

'The lady Anna is too kind,' said Behlem ironically. 'Far too kind, but her talents allow her the luxury of kindness.'

'I give you only your due,' Anna answered graciously, adding, 'You are the sole lord who has stepped forward against the dark ones.'

Behlem's fingers touched his beard, and a smile flitted across his mouth and vanished as he said. 'We must also defeat them.'

'Indeed you must,' added Dencer, brushing a longish lock of mostly brown hair off a sweaty forehead. 'If Defalk is to remain intact.'

'Defalk will remain intact,' promised Behlem, 'especially with your assistance and that of Lady Anna.'

Dencer smiled blandly and lifted his goblet.

'Your player said that in an earlier skirmish with the Ebrans you took a war arrow full through the shoulder and yet within weeks you fought at the Sand Pass.' Hanfor smiled with his last words.

'Is that true?' asked Dencer.

'Mostly. It wasn't a skirmish. It was an ambush.' Anna paused as the surcoated servers slipped the platters and the baskets of bread onto the long table.

'He also said you deflected the arrow barehanded or you would have been killed,' added Hanfor.

'Yes. I was unfortunate enough to try that. Those arrows hurt.' Anna lifted her goblet and took the smallest of sips.

From his position on the table below Hanfor, Zealor grinned and whispered, 'Especially if you live through them.'

'You do not look as so many women warriors do,' offered Dencer, his tone neutral.

'Ha! Tell that to Delor's kin, or the armsman she gutted with a dagger.'

Anna couldn't tell who had offered the sotto voce comment, but she could see that Behlem was caught between amusement and anger.

'Ah . . . you seem to have garnered quite a bit of respect,' Dencer finally replied.

Anna speared two thick slabs of meat, then held the platter for Hanfor. As usual, she was hungry, as she had been the entire time in Liedwahr. She hoped her stomach wouldn't churn all night, either from the nourishment she needed or the politics she loathed.

'The lady Anna is highly respected,' interjected Menares. 'She has even scouted and served as an envoy for the Prophet since her arrival in Falcor.'

'Enough of this talk of arms,' ordered Behlem with a laugh. 'Everyone will want to tell a tale, and we will never eat.'

Dencer smiled again, faintly and falsely, and served himself two slabs of meat.

'Since I am a stranger here,' Anna began, 'I know little of Defalk. Tell me about Stromwer.' She didn't bat her eyelashes, but she might as well have. Still, what she didn't know would fill a book, and it wouldn't hurt to thaw Dencer out of his shock. She might also learn a lot, and everything helped.

Hanfor nodded minutely, and Anna took a small sip of

wine, knowing she needed to keep the sips small indeed over the long evening. Then she forced herself to take another slab of the meat.

83

ENCORA, RANUAK

'The Evult unleashed the headwaters of the Ost. Much of Wei was flooded,' reports Veria. 'The entire trading area will have to be rebuilt.' She seats herself on a low cushion to the left of the Matriarch's chair.

'He is a little man. Every time his plans are thwarted, he wants to destroy something,' observes the Matriarch. 'He will have to unleash something even worse on Defalk before long.'

'Why? People still flee Falcor, and the border lords must buy our grain. Each week the land suffers more from the heat, and the harvest would hardly repay a third of what you loaned Barjim and lost.'

'She never loses,' points out Ulgar. 'You only lose when you stop playing.'

Veria's eyes flicker to the silver-haired consort who is bent over a board filled with pieces. 'Father . . . this is not a game.'

'It is not . . . not exactly, but he is right, dear,' says the Matriarch, her round face still cheerful. 'Lord Behlem plays the Lord of Defalk now, and he still holds the soprano sorceress.'

'I'd say she holds him, though neither knows it,' opines Ulgar.

'None of this makes sense,' protests Veria.

'Oh, it doesn't make sense; but the parts of the harmonies are there, and there will be a harmonic resolution. That's why the Evult is only making matters worse with all his fussing and fuming.'

'Mother—'

'Matriarch, dear. We are speaking officially.' The Matriarch offers a serious face for a moment, but the smile returns to the cherubic cheeks as she speaks. 'Eladdrin will fail against the sorceress because he expects her to fight, and she will not, not on his terms. That will upset the Evult even more, and he will fly into a rage, and do something even more dissonant, and that will strengthen the rebounding harmonies. Really, it is quite clear.'

'What about the golds?' pursues Veria.

'I do not know, but a debt is a debt, and it will be paid one way or another.'

Veria looks to her father, but he only smiles.

84

Even before she washed or dressed, Anna was at the mirror, lutar out and envelope in hand, the envelope heavy with her letter, the gold and silver coins, her watch, and the small drawing.

'Mirror, mirror . . .'

This time the image was clear. Elizabetta was alone, standing in front of the dresser in the guest room at Avery's vacation house, rubbing her eyes. Anna didn't wait, but strummed the lutar and began the spell, hoping, somehow, that it would work.

'Bring this to my daughter, in her land,
Deliver it safely to her hand,
let her know that I love her ...'

The envelope vanished, and the tower room around Anna
shivered, as though a distant chord had been plucked on
a gigantic harp and reverberated through the entire tower,
through all of Falcor. Yet Anna sensed she alone felt that chord.

Her head ached, and sharp needles stabbed through her
eyes. Still, Anna, though her head was pounding, started to
repeat the first spell, but the words caught in her throat as
cracks rippled across the mirror and flames flickered along
the wooden mirror frame.

She barely managed to empty the water basin across the
burning wood before her knees shivered into jelly, and she
half staggered, half fell toward the bed.

85

When Anna woke again, her head ached, and her whole
body ached, and her room was hot and dusty from the hot
wind coming through the window. She could barely open
gummy eyes and struggle upright.

Drinking nearly an entire pitcher of water – slowly, so
slowly – helped reduce the headache. After easing the
cloth-covered breakfast tray from the landing, she began
to eat. The stale bread and hard cheese helped, and, by
the time she had finished, she only felt like Farinelli had
ridden over her, as opposed to an entire army.

Ignoring a too-damp forehead, she looked to the window,
no longer blocked by the unseen cooling filter she had earlier
ensorcelled into place, then to the blackened and sagging
rectangle that had been a mirror. She'd have to get another.
Apparently, sending even the smallest package to earth had

taken tremendous effort. Anna shivered, despite the heat. Everyone said she was the strongest sorceress around, and if she had that much trouble . . . She shivered again, then forced herself to her feet.

She needed clean water, and she needed a mirror. Slowly, she reached for the bellpull, and then shuffled to the door.

When she opened the door for the page, Skent's mouth opened as he saw the wall past her shoulder.

'These things happen to sorceresses,' she said. 'I need a new mirror – an old one – any kind of mirror – immediately, and I need more water.'

'Yes . . . Lady Anna.'

'I'm sorry, Skent. It's hard, sometimes.' She stepped aside. 'Could you take what's left of the mirror?'

Skent just gawked for a moment.

'Not all spells work the way they should. People forget that.' She rubbed her forehead. 'And, if you wouldn't mind, could you bring me something more to eat?'

The page almost shook his head, but looked dumbly at the spidered lines and the blackened frame of the mirror before he stepped toward it.

After Skent left, Anna sat down and drank some more water while she waited for the wash water, the food, and another mirror. From the way she felt, she didn't even want to consider how she looked.

Before long Birke brought the wash water, and a small tray of dried apples and bread.

'Thank you.'

The page nodded and backed away.

When she had eaten some of the apples, she spelled the water. Laboriously, she washed and began to pull on her clothes.

She stood dressed but barefooted in the middle of the room, forcing more of the rubbery apples past her lips, when the knocker thunked.

'Yes?' She half walked, half staggered toward the door.

'It is Menares, Lady Anna.'

She suppressed a groan and opened the door.

With a smile, the white-haired counselor marched into the chaos of the room and looked around. 'What mighty sorcery have you tried this morning?' asked Menares pleasantly.

'What?'

'Lady Anna, I am not powerful, but I am not without wit. You appear as though you have wrestled with dissonance. Your room is hot, and your composure is less than perfect.' The counselor smiled. 'And your page has removed a burned mass of glass and wood.'

'Trying to bridge worlds,' Anna admitted. 'It takes more effort than I thought.'

'Were . . . you successful?' Menares's eyes narrowed.

'Not so much as I would have liked.' Anna didn't want to say more. So she walked to the table and took another swallow of water. 'What did you have in mind?'

'Since you will lead the vanguard, the Prophet wanted to inform you that you will leave at dawn tomorrow.'

'What is the vanguard?'

'You will have some two companies of lancers, in addition to Subofficer Spirda and your personal guard.'

'A company?' asked Anna.

'Five squads.'

Anna tried to calculate mentally, then just approximated – something like one hundred and fifty mounted armsmen.

'You will be ready?'

'I'll be ready.' She paused. 'Wait. I'll need messengers, some sort of way to communicate, and once we get there—'

Menares held up a hand. 'You should talk to Overcaptain Hanfor. He will be coordinating the Prophet's forces.' The counselor stood. 'You have much to do, as do I.' He bowed once more before departing.

Anna closed the door slowly, rubbed her forehead, then the back of her neck, far too tight and stiff. She didn't pretend to be a military expert, but what Menares had told her didn't seem to show any great organization. Either that or, once again, the good old boys were trying to keep her in the dark. She rubbed her forehead and looked around the room for her boots. She definitely needed to see Hanfor.

But where had she left the boots?

One was under the bed, the other in the corner half-covered by laundry she had meant to do. The thought of doing anything else with sorcery sent another stab of fire through her eyes. Who would have thought . . . ? She started to shake her head, then stopped. Why was it so damned hard just to send one lousy envelope to Elizabetta? She could churn up the subsurface, murder people, and destroy armies, but sending one message to her daughter put her out of commission and ruined her ability to do sorcery.

Her eyes burned. *Stop it!* she swore at herself. *You can't change the way this stupid world works.*

After blotting her eyes, she yanked the bellpull, almost angrily, and waited for a page to appear. This time, the unlucky youth was Birke.

'Birke, do you know where I can find Overcaptain Hanfor?'

'He stays somewhere in the east quarters.'

'Fine. Let's go.'

Birke looked at the floor stones with resignation. 'Yes, lady.'

Anna followed the redhead down the tower steps and into a courtyard filled with the chaos of supply wagons, armsmen seemingly riding back and forth endlessly, dust, and the odor of fresh horse dung. They hugged the hall walls to avoid the riders that seemed to fill most of the space. Over the clicking of hoofs, and the growl of armsmen's voices, Anna could hear the muffled *brawwk*ing of the liedburg's chickens, although she saw none.

'Might I help you, Lady Anna?'

She looked up to see a familiar, black-bearded face mounted on a dark chestnut.

'We're headed to see Overcaptain Hanfor.' Anna paused.

'Over there.' Fhurgen pointed to the open-shuttered building to the east of the hall. 'Just walk beside me.' The armsman raised his voice. 'Give way. Give way.'

Anna almost blushed, but Fhurgen knew what he was doing, and she walked straight across the courtyard, faintly amused as the mounted armsmen halted for her.

Outside the designated door, she turned. 'Thank you, Fhurgen.'

'My pleasure, Lady Anna.' The armsman gave a head bow and turned his mount away.

Anna walked through the door and into a narrow hall-way. Less than five yards back was a closed door with a sentry.

As she neared, the young armsman looked from the page to Anna, then swallowed, and said, even before Anna could speak. 'The overcaptain is expecting you, lady. Might I tell him you are here?'

Anna nodded. Somehow it didn't surprise her that Hanfor expected her; it would have surprised her if he had not.

The guard opened the battered and stained wooden door. 'The lady . . . sorceress is here, ser.'

'Have her come in.'

Anna inclined her head to Birke, then to the guard, and stepped into the dark and low-ceilinged room that contained little more than a pallet in the corner, a three-legged table, four stools, and Hanfor's arms and gear, neatly stacked against the wall on the inside corner.

The two younger officers with Hanfor stood abruptly, yet stiffly, as Anna entered the small room, stuffy despite the open window.

'Lady Anna.' Hanfor bowed. 'Might I present you two of my officers? Captain Alvar.' He nodded to the short, wiry man with the black hair and beard. 'This is Lady Anna.' He turned to the taller and stockier man with curling sandy hair, clean-shaven except for a curling and drooping mustache. 'Captain Himar, Lady Anna.'

'My pleasure, Lady Anna,' responded Alvar. His black eyes showed a trace of a twinkle, and he had a warm voice.

'My honor,' said Himar, more formally.

Hanfor nodded, and the two bowed again to Anna and

eased out of the room. Alvar bowed once more and shut the door.

'These are the best I can offer.' Hanfor gestured to the stools.

Anna sat, gratefully. 'We need to talk.'

'I would agree.' Hanfor's voice was droll, but not condescending.

'Menares just told me that I would be leading some lancers out of here tomorrow morning. I'm a sorceress and a few other things, but I'm not a military leader.' Anna paused. 'Menares said you were in charge.'

'Subject to the orders of the Prophet,' the weathered officer answered. 'But I am the one who will get the blame should anything go wrong. I try to avoid that.'

'What are the plans, and how do you suggest I handle my part?'

'I was told you were very effective at the Sand Pass.'

'So I'm told. But I went where I was told, and I did my best to destroy the enemy.' Anna shrugged. 'It worked.'

'Menares told me that you had wanted the Prophet's troops marshaled in Pamr? Is that so?'

'Not exactly . . .' Anna explained, without giving details of the spells or their precise hoped-for effect, how she would try to use the river to decimate the Ebran forces, but how that required that Eladdrin stay on the south side of the Chean, and close to the bluffs.

Hanfor spread out a small map. 'Show me.'

'Here – see, there's the ford, and the trail runs along here. This map doesn't show it, but it's there.'

The overcaptain pursed his lips, then asked as he straightened from the map on the small table, 'So you do not have any real tactical plans?'

'Heavens, no. I thought that was up to whoever commanded the troops. And I probably messed things up because I'm not a military person.' Anna spread her hands. 'I should have come to you sooner, I suppose, but I was trying not to do anything to offend Lord Behlem. A few things have happened, and I'm not used to everything in Liedwahr.'

'Lady Anna, I had hoped it would be a pleasure to work with you, and it appears as though it will be.' Hanfor smiled, warmly.

'Why?' Anna tried not to sound skeptical at Hanfor's pleasure.

'You know what you need to be effective. You tell me, but you do not insist on how I must create the situation. You do not pretend to know what you do not. That makes my life much easier. It is also much easier on the armsmen.' Hanfor stood and paced to the small window, not looking at Anna. 'I can see certain problems, however.'

'Such as?'

'You need an escort strong enough to fend off their heavy scouts, yet you will need to be close enough to where you do your sorcery, and you do not wish to be detected. Can you throw a concealment spell?'

'I don't know. I've never tried.' Anna frowned. 'I could test one later today. I have time. What else?'

'I see that as the single largest problem.' The overcaptain turned. 'You can ride, quickly, I hope.'

'I have learned that.'

'Can you use spells while riding?'

'I have used them from the saddle, not while riding.'

'Hmmm ... that should work with that beast of yours. You are taking just the one player?'

'Daffyd? Yes. I need his support.' *And more, but if I had to rely on players like Fiena ... forget it.*

'What if the Ebrans do not come near your river, but detect your actions and circle around you?'

'Then I move back and use what I have. It won't be as effective, but it should work as well as at the Sand Pass. I have some other spells as well, in case they have some way of stopping what I used there.'

'I wish some armsmen thought in those terms.' Hanfor shook his head. 'I must think about the best way to work this out. I will talk to you in the morning before you go. Now . . . you should know the order line—'

'Order line?'

'Captain Alvar will be the senior captain, and all orders actually must go through him to the lancers.'

'So I don't order anything stupid?'

'He is a brave man, Lady Anna. And experienced.'

Anna thought for a moment. Anyone who agreed to serve under a sorceress in this culture was probably brave – to say the least. 'Did you choose him?'

'I told him that you were reasonable, and that you were loyal to those who support you. Was I wrong?'

'No,' Anna admitted. 'I don't think so.'

'In his absence, or if something occurs to him, the orders would go through Captain Himar – except for your personal guard under Subofficer Spirda. Spirda answers to you, directly, and I will emphasize that to him again, and to the captains. You will not have trouble there.'

Looking at the weathered face, Anna was certain she wouldn't.

'Is there anything else?' she asked.

'I do not think so, but we can talk in the morning. I will be there to see you off.'

'You don't—'

'I see off all detachments, Lady Anna.'

'I'm sorry. I told you I was no military person.' She rose from the too-hard stool.

'Unlike some, lady, you acknowledge that,' answered Hanfor, his lips twisting into a sardonic smile, as he inclined his head and walked to the door opening it for her.

'Thank you, overcaptain,' said Anna as she left the small space.

The sentry remained frozen in place as she left, heading for the courtyard – still bustling with activity. She could still hear the chickens, and she wondered if all the horse hoofs on the stones stirred them up. Was it because travelers meant slaughtered chickens? Anna shook her head and dashed across to the north tower.

Back in her room, she rubbed her temples and then her neck. A concealing spell? How could she do that? And what if other magic would see through it? Somehow, she had to set it up so that both sorcerers and nonsorcerers could not see where she was – even if she appeared in a scrying glass or pond.

How?

Camouflage? She filled her goblet, deciding against cooling her room until she was certain her headache had passed. Besides, she had to work out the concealment spell.

First, she took a long swallow of the lukewarm water. Then she dragged out the greasemarker and some of the paper Skent had dredged up for her. It could be a long day.

86

Anna patted Farinelli and turned in the saddle, looking away from the sun that still almost touched the eastern horizon. Spirda rode at her left, Alvar at her right, and Daffyd to the right of the captain, almost on the shoulder of the road.

Behind them, the dry road dust rose like a plume, cloaking the few roadside trees in brown, and most of the lancers in the rear of the column. Moving troops by horse in Defalk certainly was easy enough to detect. The dust could be seen from deks or leagues away. They were less than three deks east of the Falche River, and already the heat haze and the dust had cloaked both the stone bridge across the Falche and Falcor, as if they had vanished, as had most of its people over the previous weeks.

Anna turned her gaze back to the dusty road ahead that

stretched into the rising sun. Her eyes squinted against the glare. Her stomach growled; her system had not enjoyed bread and cheese before dawn, especially in the quantities required. Then, she seldom enjoyed anything that early, something Sandy had never understood, with his chirp-bird early-morning chatter.

She readjusted the battered, floppy-brimmed hat, but the sun was too low for the brim to block all the glare. Her fingers brushed the hilt of the dagger at her belt, then dropped away.

'The rest of the Prophet's forces will begin to march tomorrow morning,' Alvar said, drawing his dapple fractionally closer to Farinelli and Anna.

The sorceress nodded politely, although Hanfor had told her as much as she had saddled Farinelli in the predawn grayness. Absently, she patted the gelding again.

'They will be two days behind us by the time we reach Sorprat,' Alvar continued.

'The armsmen on foot?' Anna asked, to give him the chance to explain.

'Aye, and the supply wagons. The land is too poor to forage, and besides, if we foraged, the locals would shoot arrows at our backs as much as at the Ebrans. Perhaps more, for they fear us less.'

Anna hadn't thought about supply wagons. Then, she hadn't thought about the logistics of waging war in a medieval culture. There was too much she still had not considered, far too much.

'*Kkchheww!*'

At Daffyd's sneeze, Anna glanced to her right. 'Are you all right?'

'Fine, lady, fine, except for the dust.' The player rubbed his nose and sniffed as if trying to stifle a second outburst.

'Dust – we will breathe plenty of that before we reach Sorprat,' Alvar said with a laugh. 'I have been in the rear, and being in the van is better, far better.'

'Until the arrows fly,' answered Spirda.

'If they fly,' said Daffyd.

With that indirect reminder, Anna felt her shoulders sag. Her choices were abysmal. If she were totally successful, thousands of Ebrans would die. If she were unsuccessful, she and thousands of Nesereans and Defalkan levies would die. If she were partly successful, thousands on each side would die. Why did it have to be that way?

Her mouth twisted. She could bemoan her situation, but the days ahead were no time to be self-sacrificing. She'd done that, and with little enough to show, in her years in academia.

She leaned forward and thumped Farinelli's shoulder again.

87

WEI, NORDWEI

'Yes, Gretslen?' Ashtaar motions the blonde woman into the room.

Through the open window at her back come the sounds of hammers, saws, and the scattered curses of carpenters and masons beginning the rebuilding of the dock quarter.

Gretslen stops opposite the table and waits.

'You may sit.' The dark-haired woman's fingers fold around the polished oval of black agate. 'What have you to report?'

'Both the Ebrans and the Nesereans are moving toward Pamr. The Prophet has nearly eight thousand of his best armsmen, plus a number of Defalkan levies. Eladdrin has about ten thousand under arms, as well as his darksingers.' Gretslen shifts her weight in the hard chair.

'What of the blonde sorceress?'

'She rides ahead of the Prophet's forces, perhaps two days.'

'Alone?'

'With a personal guard and several companies of crack lancers.'

'Behlem must put great stock in her.' Ashtaar laughs softly. 'Or he needs her and mistrusts her.'

Gretslen does not answer the observation.

'Can you detect any spellcasting?' pursues the spymistress.

'Before the sorceress left, she nearly rent the chords of harmony. She opened a small gate to the mist worlds, briefly. We could not see what was involved or why.'

'And she is well enough to ride?' Ashtaar asked.

'She was walking later that day.'

Ashtaar's fingers tighten on the polished rock. 'You are certain? No burns? No fire?'

'Very certain, honored Ashtaar. She is mighty and knows it not.'

'I would like a written report on this matter. By tonight.'

'Yes, Ashtaar.'

'Is there anything else I should know?'

'Eladdrin is trying to seek out the sorceress, also.'

'The man is no fool. He knows his greatest danger. What else?'

'The lady Cyndyth is traveling to Falcor with the envoy from Mansuur.'

'And?'

'That is all . . . but we will continue to scry.'

Silence seeps across the room, blotting out the noise from the city repairs.

Her fingers still caressing the black agate oval, the spymistress's eyes focus on the door behind the blonde woman, and she says quietly, 'That is all. The report. By tonight.'

'Yes, honored Ashtaar.' Gretslen eases out of the room, not quite backing, but not turning away from the spymistress either.

88

Anna rode closer to the dozen armsmen who sweated and toiled in the heat with the small spades. She felt almost guilty as they worked, but she wouldn't have lasted an hour – a glass, she corrected her thinking – digging in the heat of Defalk.

Her eyes turned eastward, down the gentle rise that was barely perceptible to the highway from Mencha. To her left was the road cut down to the Sorprat ford. She studied the waist-high sun-browned grass in front of the trench – she'd insisted that no one walk or ride on the down-rise side – and then the trench itself.

'That's deep enough,' Anna said to Alvar, after inspecting the trench. Even Farinelli and several mounts would fit into the sloped endramps angled into the center part of the excavation, and with the spell, she hoped Eladdrin would not see them – at least until it was too late.

'Clean it up, square it out,' ordered Alvar. 'Then mount up.' The captain turned in his saddle toward Anna, as if to speak, then paused.

In the slightest of breezes, a few stalks of brown grass whispered, not enough to cover the mutterings from the trench.

'. . . glad she is pleased . . . not the one digging . . .'

'. . . sshh . . . you want to be up here with her . . . when the dark ones . . .'

'. . . better dig than die, Fifard . . .'

Anna pursed her lips, then waited for Alvar.

'I still do not fully understand the need for a trench.'

The sorceress didn't, either, but her feelings told her it was necessary, and she'd learned years ago that every time she disregarded her feelings she ended up in trouble. Here trouble meant death.

'What is the difference between this grassland and that?' Anna gestured from where the trench gaped to the grasslands more to the south of the bluffs. 'Or those?'

'None, save their closeness to the river.'

'And if I am not on the ground, but beneath it, and the dark sorcerer can tell only that I am surrounded by grass and dirt, how will he know where I am?'

'He will not.' Alvar nodded. 'But if you sat in the grass, would he know, either?'

'Captain Alvar, sometimes you have to follow your feelings. This time I have to follow mine.' She gave a slight shrug, watching as the last of the armsmen scrambled from the trench, then turning in the saddle to ease the lutar out of its case.

'Now?' he asked.

'A concealment spell.' Anna took a deep breath and began to strum, then to sing.

When any trace of the displaced grass and the trench vanished, gasps whispered from the squad of armsmen waiting on the west side of the rise.

'Your orders?' asked Alvar.

'We head back to the others,' said Anna. 'We will camp at least four deks west – over those rises there. Even if the sorcerer sees us in his glass now, he will not know exactly where I will be later. Then, when they near, Daffyd and I and a few riders will come back here.'

The captain frowned.

'How can we protect you?'

'By not being too close.' Anna turned Farinelli westward, toward where Captain Himar held the main body of Anna's company.

She hoped she wasn't being too brave, or too foolhardly, but what seer could miss two companies of lancers? And what would Eladdrin think if they were perched on top of the ford?

89

WEST OF MENCHA, DEFALK

Eladdrin studies the mirror on the ground, though the image wavers. Finally, he packs the mirror into its leather case and straightens.

'Ser?' asks the mounted subofficer.

'Behlem seems to have split his forces. Half are on the north side of the river, to the east of Pamr. The others are on the south side, on the high ground at the southernmost bend in the river.' Eladdrin eases the leather case into the oversized saddlebag and swings up onto the black. 'The sorceress is somewhere in the grasslands, but she could be anywhere within fifty deks of either army. She's probably in front of them somewhere, but close enough to retreat after she's done her worst.'

The subofficer looks at the Songmaster inquiringly.

'No, Gealas, I cannot discern where she is. She has used a concealing spell. While it reveals its use, she is in the middle of brown grasses that could be anywhere in Defalk.'

Gealas nods. 'Which way should we go?'

The Songmaster blinks, then looks to the west, away from the mid-morning sun. 'We do not have to decide yet. They are more than a half day from the ford, no matter which way they go.' Eladdrin flicks the reins and heads toward the front of the long black column. 'We will attain the ford, and pause, and scout.'

When the subofficer catches up and settles his mare into a trot beside the Songmaster, he finally asks, 'Why would the Prophet split his forces?'

'They are split now, but they will not be when we meet. The Prophet is drawn up defensively. If we go north and cross the river, then he can pull back the southern forces and cross the river at Pamr to support the northern body. The same of the northern forces if we go south.'

'What is the point in that?'

'The point,' explained Eladdrin, his voice slightly hoarse, 'is that half his forces are well rested and dug-in no matter what we do, and that we will have to come to him.'

'That does not sound like the Prophet.'

'Oh, it does. Remember, this is not his land, Gealas. He can sacrifice territory to save soldiers, as he could not do in Neserea. He also has some local levies. He fights us where his own people are not harmed and makes us work. The bulk of the harvests are beyond the river valley, or in it. He is guessing that we will not take the ford, and he is probably right. Going down in that kind of lowland against a sorceress is dangerous. That's why she's out from their forces, to try and trap us if we do. But we won't.'

'What do you mean?'

'Suppose we take two days to cover a long half-day march, then stop several deks away. We are in no hurry, and perhaps I can find the sorceress. She is not a warrior, no matter how powerful she may be.' Eladdrin snorts and flicks the reins. 'In any case, no sorceress alone can stop our forces.'

Gealas nods again.

Eladdrin's eyes focus on the clear western horizon.

90

Despite the heat that had seeped into the chest-deep trench where she and Daffyd – along with Spirda, Fhurgen, and another armsman named Mysar – had waited since early morning, Anna could smell a shift in the weather, a hint of something like fall.

Whhnnnnn! From the north end of the trench came the

sound of Farinelli's displeasure, echoed by a similar sound from one of the mares.

'Quiet!' hissed Anna.

Whhhnnnn!

She sang the word, lingering over the syllables, and surprisingly, the horses quieted.

Beyond Daffyd, to her left, she could see Fhurgen jab Mysar in the ribs. The younger armsman handed a copper to the black-bearded man. Anna felt amused and irritated simultaneously.

'How much longer?' whispered Spirda, leaning toward her from her right, his breath smelling of something like garlic.

Anna shrugged. 'I don't know, and I'm not about to use another spell. If Eladdrin is close, he might be able to tell where we are.'

The sun inched higher, and over the faint and intermittent whispers of the grass came the calls of something like a meadowlark. The sorceress smiled, recalling the time she and the children had spent a week in the Garrisons' cabin in Estes. So long ago . . . so far away.

She swallowed and looked up at the grass that hung on its brown stalks, still in the mid-morning heat – so still, as if the world were hanging on a thread, waiting for her to act.

Anna snorted. Delusions of grandeur! She was a singer, lucky enough to have talent, and hardworking enough to have mastered technique and repertoire, and those talents enabled her to cast spells, not manipulate worlds.

Daffyd sniffed, stifled a sneeze, and rubbed his nose. Was he allergic to grass, wondered Anna, or getting sick?

Perhaps another glass passed before Anna readjusted her hat once more, blotting away the sweat that gathered under the band and oozed onto her forehead. Her hair was damp as well, and she wanted a bath or a shower. Washing her hair in a basin left it feeling still unclean, but cleanliness wasn't high on the priority lists in Defalk.

She cocked her ears. Was that a dull thudding, a rumbling in the soil?

'Something out there,' hissed Fhurgen.

Spirda eased past the mares and partway up along the earthen ramp, peering through the grass. After a time, he slipped back. 'There are a good four companies of lancers, but they've halted back a dek or so.'

Anna eased past the blond officer, careful not to make contact with him in the narrow confines of the trench. While he wasn't her type, she still didn't want to convey any ideas. Except for a few like Alvar and Hanfor, most of the armsmen seemed so young. Then, they were. People on Erde lived fast and died young, except for lords and ladies. Lord Jecks was probably the only one near her age. He was almost like a white-haired Robert Mitchum. She'd liked the actor, thought he was sexy, and so was Jecks. She pushed away the thoughts and concentrated on the present.

She studied the distant horsemen, and the two drooping black banners. They were on the fringe of the area she had prepared, but only on the fringe, and they clearly waited for someone or something.

The sun climbed higher, and the horsemen waited, and Anna read-justed her hat and blotted her forehead and neck, and Daffyd sniffed. The two armsmen looked at each other, and Spirda rocked from one foot to the other, and the grass hung limply in the hot air.

Then a single horn sounded, and the horsemen turned toward the ford, letting their mounts walk slowly toward the bluff. They were within a dek of the concealed trench before the first dark figures of the main body appeared on the eastern rise of the highway.

'What's she waiting for?' whispered Mysar.

'For all of them to get close enough to destroy them!' hissed Anna at him. She shouldn't be whispering, she realized. So she eased the lutar from the case, and began to check its tuning, as quietly as she could. Following her example, Daffyd took out the viola and did the same.

A whisper of wind ruffled the grasses and was gone, and Anna shivered, sensing the unnaturalness of that seeking wind and feeling vindicated that she had insisted on the trench. A grim smile appeared and vanished.

To the east of her vantage point, the horse troops reined up again, this time at the top of the bluffs, a good half-dek east of Anna, at the beginning of the road cut down to the ford. Several dismounted and stretched, walking around and pointing to the river and the valley, talking, although she could not hear their voices.

The next set of horsemen, leading the main body, became more than outlines, became real men in black, bearing sabres. Some had lances. From the concealment of the trench, Anna looked through the browned grasses at the oncoming mass of armsmen. The dark ones had even more troops than she had seen at the Sand Pass. In the van were the dark horse, hundreds of them, followed by a long column of foot, then wagons, dozens of wagons, followed by more foot.

Anna wanted to shake her head. The Ebrans were too strung out. She hadn't realized how far a marching army would stretch along the road, especially a large one.

'Dissonance! How many are there?' murmured Daffyd.

'There might be five hundred-score.' Spirda wiped his forehead.

Ten thousand troops? Could she? Anna swallowed, thinking about what ten thousand troops would do to Pamr, and Gatrune and Firis – or Falcor. Could she not?

'Lady?' ventured Spirda.

Anna shook her head.

Another sweep of the dark, seeking wind ruffled the grasses and passed, and yet more horn signals echoed across the grass toward the bluffs. With the signals the scouts who remained afoot remounted, and formed their mounts into two rough lines.

A square of black banners borne by black-coated armsmen appeared. The column split to allow the bannered group to advance.

Eladdrin? Anna swallowed, then turned to Daffyd and motioned. She eased up toward the south end of the trench, hoping the concealment spell would hold, stopping where the excavation was only knee-deep.

The wind swirled around her, and several of the banner-bearers turned toward them.

'Now! The sinking song.'

Daffyd stroked the bow, twice, then began the song, and Anna chorded the lutar, trying for the maximum volume, not belting, but fullvoiced opera technique, launching into the first spell, the one that she hoped would neutralize the Ebrans. *Neutralize?* her mind asked. She pushed away the nagging thought, and concentrated on spellcasting, matching lutar and voice with Daffyd's viola.

> 'Sink, sink, sink the land
> deeply through the ground
> easily, easily, easily,
> mud is all around.
>
> 'Churn, churn, churn the rocks ...'

Even before she hit the second stanza – and her perverse mind insisted on pointing out that spells were strophic – the ground trembled – once, twice, and then even harder.
BBbrrrrrrrrrr ...

She shifted her feet and kept singing.

At least two squads of horsemen galloped toward her, but they seemed to move in slow motion, and several horses stumbled, throwing riders, as the ground swayed under them.

Still, five or six riders thundered toward Anna and Daffyd.

Spirda ran past Anna, his blade out, followed by Fhurgen, who carried a sabre in each hand. Both staggered as the ground rumbled and lurched, and another Ebran rider went down.

Anna could sense some sort of activity around the Ebran

black banners, a gathering of power, but she kept her
voice and mind on the spellsong, concluding with a perfect
on-key finale.

'. . . swirled underground!'

A massive chord seemed to vibrate both through the
ground and across the clear blue-green heavens, even casting
a flickering shadow over the sun momentarily. Anna's ears
rang with that timeless, yet instantaneous, vibration.

Then the grasslands seemed to whirl around her, and a
ground wave rippled the grass and the soil as it spread
outward from somewhere to the east of Anna, just as
though it had been caused from the impact of a stone on
a quiet pond.

RRRRUuuuuuurrrrrr . . .

That rending, grinding roar paralyzed Anna's hearing,
as the second set of ground waves rumbled across the
grasslands and brought her to her knees. Somehow, she
kept from going all the way down and crushing the lutar.

Hammers slammed at her skull, and the ground kept
trembling.

Somewhere before her, Spirda slashed at an oncoming
Ebran armsman who had struggled off a fallen mount,
while Fhurgen flailed through the grass toward the blond
subofficer.

Anna tried to rise from her knees, but had to put a hand
out as another tremor raced through the ground. She blinked
as she realized that the grasslands ended not more than thirty
yards in front of her. They just . . . ended.

A vast chasm, more than a dek long and slightly narrower
in width, centered on where the highway to Mencha had been
and ran down where the road cut to the ford had been, so that
water from the Chean was already oozing into the depressed
area, across the mass of mud and grass-covered patches of
earth that filled the sinkhole.

Slowly, her head pounding, and her ears ringing in the

aftermath of the subsidence of her massive sinkhole, Anna struggled to her feet.

In front and to her right, Fhurgen slashed at the Ebran lancer, who had not even seen the second armsman. The Ebran's blade dropped, and he stood for a moment, then wavered, before crumpling into the waist-high grass.

The sorceress forced herself to walk toward the edge of the bluffs and to study the mess. She swayed as she looked down and out across the churning, bubbling mass of mud and chunks of grassland that bobbed in the mud. On the intact sections of land below, especially near the eastern side of the depression, armsmen on foot scrambled away from the gooey mass, only to find themselves facing sheer, if crumbling, dirt walls. Perhaps a thousand troops, or more, seemed to have survived the drop of her undermined sinkhole.

On the far side of the depression, a fewscore armsmen, mostly on foot, scrambled eastward through the grasslands and along the highway, back toward Mencha.

Slowly, she glanced down at the lutar she had not even been aware that she carried, then, despite her headache, lifted it and touched the strings. 'The river song, Daffyd.'

There was no answer, and Anna turned. The player stood a dozen steps behind her, his mouth open, his eyes wide.

'We need the river song,' she repeated.

'But . . .'

'The river song!' Again, her feelings drove her. While the men below were pawns, Eladdrin might be among them, and she could not chance his escape.

After a moment, Daffyd, his eyes not meeting hers, lifted the viola and began to play, raggedly.

'We have to do better than that. Start again!' Anna hated herself for the hardness in her voice, but she didn't have that many reserves left, and she didn't want to fight yet another battle with the Ebrans.

As Daffyd started the melody over again, Anna's fingers touched the lutar strings, and she began to sing, letting her voice fill the troubled air.

'Ol' man riber . . .'

She tried to visualize the mighty power of the Mississippi,
a brown torrent filling the banks of the Chean, sweeping into
the vast circular sinkhole that lay before her, swirling and
covering all that lay there.

The ground trembled yet again, and shivered, and shivered. With that second shiver, her feet slipped, but she kept
chording, kept singing, her thoughts firmly on that image
of a brown torrent.

Almost . . . almost, she could sense the waters rising and
plunging toward the circular sinkhole that adjoined the river
where the ford had been.

Screams rose from the sinkhole, but Anna shut them out,
singing . . .

'. . . he just keeps roiling along . . .'

Her voice and chording were along. Daffyd had stopped
playing midway through, but she had to finish, had to get
to the end of the section. She gave the lutar a last strum, and
tried to swallow. She couldn't, so dry were her mouth and
throat. She licked her lips, but even her tongue was woolly
and dry.

Swwwussssss!

A thin sheet of spray, almost like fine rain, cascaded
across her, and the screaming ended, as if choked off. A
second, heavier, sheet of water slammed across her, half
spinning her around, and she staggered backwards three
or four steps before she could catch her balance, standing,
gasping, thrusting the lutar out like a balance pole for a
moment to steady herself.

A last, finer spray flared from the crumbling cliff edge
less than twenty yards in front of Anna, then subsided.

The sorceress forced herself back toward the muddy
caldron, where she gazed into her own hell – or discord,

or dissonance. Already, the waters were draining from the oval sinkhole, pouring back into the Chean, carrying timbers, dead horses, and unmoving uniformed figures. Anna could feel the odor of death building, though she knew it had to be her own imagination. Her eyes narrowed against the burning and the knives that jabbed into her skull, and she turned, putting one foot before the other as she trudged, slow step after slow step, toward Farinelli.

She automatically stepped around the dead Ebran lancer, who lay sprawled face-up, and past Spirda.

The blond officer staggered up and away from the spot in the grass where he had been bent double, wiped his mouth with the back of his hand, and tottered back toward the trench and the mounts, slightly behind Anna. His complexion was pale underneath his tan.

Mysar stood, unmoving, where he had since the first spell, his face blank, his mouth unmoving.

Anna stopped and let Spirda catch up.

'We need to mount up, I think,' Anna suggested to the blond sub-officer. Her stomach was twisted inside out, and half the time she kept her eyes closed because, everywhere she looked, they hurt. Several large hammers pounded at her skull, and her cords felt trashed, though she had not, in terms of concerts and recitals, sung that much – not at all.

'Mount up ... Oh, yes, lady.' Spirda turned toward the immobile Mysar. 'Mount up, Mysar.'

The lancer shuddered, then slowly closed his mouth, turned, and walked toward the trench and his mount.

The hot sun, oblivious to the deaths and destruction, had already begun to dry the muddy splotches that dotted Anna's clothes, and the dampness created by the sprays from surges of water into and out of the sinkhole.

Daffyd was mechanically easing his viola into the case, but his fingers trembled as he did. Anna led Farinelli into the grass west of the trench and looked across the grasslands to the south and west. They seemed unchanged – hot and dry and dusty. She turned back to Farinelli and rested against the big gelding's shoulder for several moments. Farinelli *whuff*ed, but did not move.

Then Anna straightened and lifted the lutar to pack it into its case.

'Anything I can do, Lady Anna?' Fhurgen practically groveled toward her as Anna fastened the lutar case on Farinelli's back.

'No. Not now. Not now. We need to tell Alvar – and the Prophet – of their great victory.' *And mine – all the destruction was mine.*

'Great victory, lady, a great victory.' Fhurgen marched back toward his horse.

It took Anna two attempts to mount, her legs were so wobbly and her balance so uncertain. Why? Because of the magnitude of her sorcery?

Her mass murders was more like it, yet, once again, what could she do? Like Hitler, like so many others, the Ebrans were determined to force others to their will. She had the means to stop them. How could she refuse?

As Farinelli carried her westward, her eyes drifted northward from the trail, to her right where the Chean, swollen to twice its former size by the muddy outflow from Anna's devastation, carried dark splotches that could have been everything from houses shattered in Sorprat to dead armsmen and their mounts.

Anna swallowed. She hadn't meant to hurt the people of Sorprat, and the sinkhole hadn't reached them, but the backlash of her raised torrent had, smashing houses like a giant sledge and spreading mud out into the river valley. Her mouth filled with bile, but she swallowed again.

Then she steadied herself in the saddle and urged Farinelli westward, closing her eyes to shut out the pain of seeing, ignoring the pounding in her skull, trying to shut out the memory of the screams and the vision of mud-flattened Sorprat.

The five rode westward in silence.

91

Alvar and a squad of lancers met Anna halfway back to the camp. Anna reined up Farinelli. The gelding dropped his head and began to graze. Anna let him.

'What happened?' The captain's eyes traversed the group. 'Are you all right, Lady Anna?'

No. My head is splitting. I'm hot and sick inside, and I don't want to be here, and I'm tired of the killing, and see no way out. 'I'm tired. The Prophet has his victory.' She could feel herself slump in the saddle, and she was afraid almost to move, for fear she would topple out of the saddle.

'I saw the river rise and fill with bodies.' Alvar fixed on Spirda.

'The Ebrans are dead, all but a score. Those are running toward the east. They will never fight again.' Spirda's voice was flat, dead.

Anna could feel the perspiration dripping down her face, oozing into her hair, but she didn't care.

'Never,' echoed Fhurgen.

Mysar said nothing, and Daffyd kept his eyes on his mare's mane.

'There are none left?' Alvar asked.

Of the six armsmen behind him, a young redhead smirked.

'Do not laugh,' said Fhurgen, his voice on the edge of cracking. 'Ride east. Ride until you see a huge hole filled with mud. There lie the Ebrans. Ride back, and then laugh. Then laugh.'

'Terrible ... terrible ...' muttered Mysar. 'She is terrible.'

'Is it as they say, Subofficer Spirda?' asked Alvar.

'No. It is worse.' Spirda shook his head slowly. 'Best you see for yourself.'

'You are sure there are no Ebrans?'

'Not alive. Not west of the ford.'

'You come with me, Spirda,' Alvar insisted. 'Lady Anna, please ride to the camp with the player and your two armsmen. The rest of us will rejoin you before long.'

Anna nodded. She did not have to go east to the ford. She knew what was there. Yes, she knew.

She watched blankly as the captain, his escort, and Spirda headed eastward again, back along the grass-bordered river trail, back along the trail above the death-swollen Chean.

'Lady?' offered Daffyd. 'You must ride to the camp.'

Ride to the camp? Of course, she must ride to the camp. Anna barely lifted the reins, and Farinelli raised his head and began to walk westward again, along the narrow trail toward the vanguard's camp. Her ears still rang with the chords she had struck from within Erde, and all that she heard was muffled and distorted by that ringing.

Daffyd rode silently beside her. Occasionally, he massaged his temples or his neck with his free hand. Anna could not have lifted either hand. Farinelli walked steadily, and she just rode.

As they neared the hills that should be familiar, Daffyd looked up and said something that Anna missed – or couldn't hear, but since he kept riding, so did she. She had to ride to camp.

Daffyd glanced at Anna, beyond her to her left. She turned her head, and it was an effort.

There, Alvar drew his horse abreast of Farinelli. His swarthy face was immobile, and the two rode for nearly half a dek, to the lower slopes of the gentle hills, before the captain spoke. 'I apologize, Lady Anna. I did not know.'

'You don't have to apologize, Alvar,' Anna said slowly, trying to force each word out against the overpowering fatigue that tugged at her. 'You did what you thought best. So did I.'

'I cannot believe ... I cannot believe ... but it is there, where there were only grasslands this morning at dawn.'

Alvar kept looking over his shoulder and then ahead to the grassy hilltop. 'Now ... now there is but mud and death, a new lake filled with death ... cannot believe ...'

Anna could believe. She was getting good with death. Then she saw the tents. They looked familiar.

At some point as they neared the vanguard's camp, she could no longer hold off the darkness.

92

'Lady Anna, Lady Anna ...'

Anna swam up through the darkness, trying to recognize the voice. Mario? But she wasn't a lady. No, she hadn't been lucky like Kiri.

'Lady Anna ... please wake up. You need to drink.'

A drink was the last thing she needed, the very last thing. Her head throbbed, and her mouth was dry. What had she done?

White needles stabbed through her eyes as she opened them, and her stomach wanted to turn over, or inside out, or something – and probably would have, had there been anything in it. She was lying on a narrow cot of some sort in a small tent, but she closed her eyes before she saw more. Seeing hurt too much.

'Please drink.' The voice of a young man wavered in and out of her hearing.

Water slopped across her mouth and she licked it, realizing that despite the tightness in her stomach, she was thirsty.

'Here.' Something was placed in her hands.

Her fingers recognized the water bottle, and she struggled into a half-sitting position, her eyes still closed. Someone helped her. Then Anna took a long sip from the water bottle, then another. She said nothing, but slowly sipped her way through the water.

Memories flicked into place: Irenia's death, the fund-raiser she'd never made, Daffyd and Jenny, Brill, the Sand Pass fort, Farinelli, Behlem, and all the sorcery. All of it.

'Be you better?' asked the voice she recognized as Daffyd's.

'A little,' she croaked.

'You've slept almost a day and a night,' Daffyd explained. 'But you must wake up. The Prophet is no more than a glass away.'

'A glass?' Anna said, her voice still rasping. 'Shit . . . I feel like shit.'

'You destroyed all the Ebrans – almost all, anyway, and the Prophet is moving his forces to Mencha. That is what Alvar says.'

When she finally set aside the bottle, Anna squinted through slitted eyes. Seeing still hurt, but she could see, sort of.

'We did manage to get a bucket and some water for you to wash in.' Daffyd pointed.

Anna nodded, then said, 'I need to pull myself together.'

'I told you that.'

If she hadn't been still so exhausted, she would have . . . done something, preferably naggingly annoying, if she could have thought of it. Instead, she waited for him to leave.

Alone in the tent, she used the water to remove the worst of the grime, especially from her face and hair. Heaven, what she wouldn't have given for a hot bath, even in the heat of the tent.

She pulled on the second set of riding clothes, thankful she had used sorcery to clean them before she had gone to the ford, and then her boots. She couldn't have sung 'Come to Jesus' in whole notes, or any other way.

She stuffed her dirty clothes into the empty saddlebag and fastened it. Her stained and battered hat lay on her gear. She bent and picked it up, then folded it into her belt. She felt like gritting her teeth every time she bent over, because the headache intensified and her stomach cramped. Her trousers were even looser. Shit! She was going to die of anorexia even while she was stuffing herself.

The lutar seemed fine, but she left it in its case by her saddlebags.

'Lady Anna?' called Daffyd from outside the tent.

'Yes?'

'I brought you some cheese and bread.'

'Come in.'

Anna sat on the cot and ate slowly, deliberately, drinking more water. The food helped, reducing the pounding inside her skull to something less, but more than a dull ache. She still had to close her eyes periodically to relieve the pain associated with seeing, and she had to force herself to eat every scrap of enough food for two people, telling herself that she didn't want to die of starvation, and wanting to laugh at the terrible irony of it all.

A horn call echoed across the camp. Anna struggled to her feet.

By the time the blue-and-cream banners reached the center of the camp, Anna was waiting.

'Lady Anna,' offered Behlem from the gilded saddle on the palomino stallion, a mount nearly as big as Farinelli. 'We understand that you have delivered the Ebrans to us.'

'Most are dead, Lord Behlem. A handful may have escaped.'

'How large a 'handful' might that be?'

'Less than twoscore.' Anna waited.

'We are grateful.' The Prophet nodded. 'Would you join us? We ride east to Mencha to remove the yoke of Ebra from all of Dcfalk.'

Anna wouldn't have phrased it quite that way, but she nodded. 'It will take a moment to get my mount.'

Behlem frowned.

'She collapsed after vanquishing the Ebrans,' volunteered Alvar.

Beside and slightly behind Behlem was Hanfor – weathered face and graying hair. The tall overcaptain nodded for Alvar to continue.

'It was a great sorcery, Lord Prophet. You will see,' asserted the wiry and dark-bearded captain.

'I will see, and I do hope it was great.'

Anna looked around. She had no idea where Farinelli was. Daffyd, standing by the tent where she had lain, pointed to the right.

Anna walked over to where he was tethered. Someone had gotten the gelding's saddle off, but that was all. While Daffyd gathered her gear and lutar, Anna gave Farinelli a quick grooming.

'I'm sorry, but I'm not at full voice, fellow.' Even talking to her mount created a throbbing in her skull.

The gelding whuffled.

While it seemed like it took forever, Anna was saddled and mounted beside Behlem before long.

'It would have been better had you been ready,' the Prophet said mildly.

'I was not made aware of your desires, Lord Behlem,' Anna countered. 'But I am here.'

Behlem snorted. Beyond and behind him, several horses back, Anna caught sight of Daffyd's quickly suppressed smile. She hoped the player was laughing at Behlem and not at her.

Behlem nodded, and the entourage resumed, while behind them Alvar supervised the packing of the camp. Anna wondered if she should have pleaded illness. No – without visible signs, that would have been regarded as a womanly weakness, and she couldn't afford that.

After they had covered several deks in relative silence, Behlem looked toward Anna. 'So we will see this evidence of destruction?'

'It's right ahead.' Anna pointed toward the depression.

The Prophet stood in his stirrups as they rode closer to the ragged edge of the sinkhole.

'That? That hole? Or is it a muddy lake?'

Anna repressed a sigh.

From his mount on the other side of the Prophet, Hanfor said smoothly, 'You can see where the road was sheared off up there. And the river has filled the pit, but you can see all the bodies.' He paused. 'And smell them.'

Anna tried to ignore the sour stench, faint as yet, but certainly the result of mud, water, death, and the unending heat of Defalk.

'There are quite a few bodies,' Behlem finally admitted. 'It is a pity that the road and the ford were destroyed.'

Despite her headache, Anna wanted to throw sorcery at the spoiled brat. What did he expect? Then she pursed her lips and looked at him, catching the half-smile. She understood. He was beginning the political effort to discredit her. She'd seen it before, at the university, where other professors who felt threatened always found little faults with what she had done, generally right after she'd accomplished the impossible.

'Once the ground settles,' she said, forcing a smile, 'we can rebuild the road and the ford.'

'"We"?' asked Behlem pointedly.

'Daffyd and I.'

'Why not now?'

'Because I would have to do it again later,' Anna said. 'There are limits, you know?'

Behlem smiled. 'I would have to take your word for that.'

'Please do.'

'All our forces are on the south side of the river,' interjected Hanfor blandly. 'So we will not need the ford anytime soon.'

'I would hope not, overcaptain. I would hope not.' The Prophet smiled. 'Well ... we have seen the sight of a most glorious victory, and we must push on to secure the border.' He nodded sharply at Hanfor, then flicked the reins. Anna followed his example, since she was clearly expected to ride close to Behlem, and be subjected to periodic indirect abuse.

If only she felt better.

They continued eastward, and the sinkhole vanished behind into the seemingly endless grasslands and scattered trees, the abandoned steads, and the clumps of dying trees that had once been woodlots.

In time, the knives and chisels driven by massive unseen sledges returned to pound through Anna's skull, but she forced her knees against the saddle, holding herself erect as she rode beside Behlem toward Mencha.

How long can I trust him? Not long at all.

Her cords were tight, and if she had to sing, she'd have nothing, no protection at all. She needed rest, and she couldn't afford to let down her guard at all.

She'd destroyed the Ebran forces, and she had no way to protect herself, except that Behlem didn't know that, and she couldn't let him know.

III

VERLUSTTRAUM

93

VULT, EBRA

The silvered waters shimmer and show a blonde woman on a palomino, the waters imparting the only light to the darkened room, casting a faint glow on the face hidden in the black cowl.

'Never . . .' murmurs the man in the dark cloak.

He gestures, and a chime rings – once, twice, three times.

In a few moments a second cloaked figure enters. 'Yes, Evult?'

'Yurelt, you are Songmaster now. Summon the master-singers, and the horns.'

'As you wish, Evult.' Slightly lifted shoulders accompany the acquiescence.

'We will bring down the storms and the ice upon Defalk! Upon those who accepted that wench of the mists.'

'Now, Evult? Now . . . when we have lost . . . so much?' stutters Yurelt.

'Now! Once we have shattered her city, then your charge is to rebuild our forces. You must destroy the blonde sorceress.' The deep-set eyes burn toward the younger man – burn so much that his face is bathed in light.

'Yes, Evult.' Yurelt swallows.

'Bah . . . it is simple, so simple that brilliant Eladdrin could never have thought of it. First, she cannot be in more than one place, and we will ensure she must be in Falcor. Second, she must sleep. Third, without her, no armsmen of Liedwahr can stand against us. Fourth, we are not bound by honor. Do you understand?'

Yurelt nods. 'Whatever it takes, I must send men from

so many places and locations that she cannot sense them all—'

'Not yet. First, we must raise the fires of the earth, and the mighty storms. Then, after the devastation, you must move the eastern army to Synek, to make her worry about our forces. Then . . .'

'Then,' Yurelt agrees. 'Then.'

94

When Behlem's vanguard had reached Loiseau, Anna had stabled Farinelli quickly and headed toward the hall. She laughed to herself as she climbed the dusty stone steps in the late-afternoon gloom. That was one advantage with the big gelding. Few would bother him or try to move him.

The captains and overcaptains were gathered around Behlem in the back courtyard. She hadn't been invited and had decided against crashing.

Anna opened the door and glanced around the bedchamber. Surprisingly, almost everything was as she had left it, except for the heat and dust. The one exception was her green recital gown, and it lay upon the bed.

She crossed the chamber and peered into the robing room, noting the spare sets of riding gear. She could use them.

As she crossed back into the main chamber, she heard steps through the open door.

'Lady Anna?' Hanfor peered inside. 'Oh . . .'

'This is my room. Does the Prophet intend to dispossess me here?' As she spoke, Anna wished she hadn't been quite so sharp. Hanfor had been more than fair. 'I'm sorry.'

'Ah . . . I think you are entitled to your own room.' Hanfor stepped inside and shut the door. 'More than entitled. A sorceress of your stature certainly ranks with senior officers.' The weathered face offered a tight smile. 'I will note that this is yours. There are more than enough rooms for the Prophet and the overcaptains.' He grinned. 'One of the chores of the senior overcaptain is quarters – because senior officers listen to no one lower.'

'Brill's suite is at the end of the corridor,' she offered. 'It would be appropriate for the Prophet.'

'Most appropriate,' Hanfor agreed. 'Thank you.'

Anna inclined her head. 'Thank you.'

Hanfor paused, then added, 'Do not get too comfortable.'

'You don't think I should stay here?' Anna asked. 'I suppose I'm as much Brill's heir as anyone these days.'

'The Prophet has already claimed the hall,' Hanfor noted dryly. 'He wishes it were in Falcor, instead of the liedburg. We will be leaving for Falcor tomorrow or the next day.'

Anna frowned.

'The lady Cyndyth is there already. She has requested the Prophet's presence, and yours. Since her sire is the Liedfuhr of Mansuur, Lord Behlem is most cautious.'

'I take it Mansuur is powerful.'

'Perhaps mightier than Nordwei.' Hanfor nodded. 'I must finish my survey and chamber assignments. My duty – to avoid further difficulties.' He bowed again.

After Hanfor left, Anna walked around the room, too hot really, but she decided against trying her cooling spell yet. She still had the vestiges of a headache, and she needed to save her ability to spellcast, especially with Behlem – and possibly his consort – out to get her.

She slumped into the chair and looked at the blue-tinted windows.

There came another rap on the door.

'Yes?'

'It's Daffyd.'

'Come in.'

The player slumped into the room, pausing to close the heavy door.

Anna blotted her forehead, glancing at the empty pitcher

on the table before her. She needed more water. She always needed water.

'They killed her,' Daffyd said slowly, as he walked toward Anna.

'Killed who?' *Will it never stop?* 'Sit down and tell me.' Anna gestured to the other chair. Her legs hurt.

'Jenny.' Daffyd dropped into the heavy blue iron-framed chair.

The sorceress frowned, then lowered her voice. 'Why would Behlem—'

'It happened weeks ago. No one knows who. It could have been the dark ones. There were two strange riders – that was what Lisbey told me. Some say they rode horses with brass on the harnesses.'

'That doesn't sound like the dark ones.' Anna rubbed her forehead.

'The Norweians use brass that way.' The young player shook his head. 'But why? Why Jenny?'

In the pit of her stomach, Anna knew. Jenny had proved she could summon a sorceress from the mist worlds, and someone wanted no more sorceresses that powerful.

Anna wanted to laugh, an urge almost hysterical. Were they after her? Who in this godforsaken world wasn't?

Lord! It never ended. Never.

'I'm sorry,' she offered. 'You liked her.'

'I liked her well enough. But she didn't do anything. She didn't do anything.'

'Except fetch me,' Anna said.

Daffyd's mouth opened. 'They would kill her for that?'

'No. Someone killed her because they did not want another sorceress in Liedwahr or Defalk.'

'But you're already here.'

'I can be killed, Daffyd. People have already tried. If Jenny could bring more . . .'

'I never thought . . .' The dark-haired young man looked down. 'I wanted Brill dead, 'cause of what he did to Da. Brill's dead, and things are worse than ever.'

Anna nodded. Both she and Daffyd had gotten ill-chosen wishes, and she had effectively lost her family, while he had lost his father, perhaps his sister because of Anna's spell on Madell, and now a close friend.

95

The morning sun beat down on her back, and the shadows of the banners borne behind her flickered across her and Daffyd. Three rows of horse ahead, Behlem rode with Hanfor to his right and Zealor to his left.

Anna couldn't believe that she was riding back across Defalk once again. Still, she'd appreciated two nights' sleep on a bed, and the chance to think about spells. From what Hanfor said, she'd need them.

The whole time at Loiseau, Behlem had dined alone, and basically avoided her, and the rest of the senior captains. He had merely left word that he had 'matters to consider.' Matters to consider? Anna almost snorted out loud as she rode. He couldn't eat with his senior captains and exclude Anna without seeming ungrateful. So he was conveying, indirectly, the message that the power that had delivered him was not to be trusted.

She patted Farinelli on the neck and reached for the water bottle, having to reach under the thin cloth bag that held her green recital dress. Why she had brought it, she wasn't sure, only that her feelings said she should. Was that her unwillingness to abandon good clothes? She didn't think so.

'All you do is drink,' said Daffyd.

'Mayhap that is what is necessary for her spells.' Spirda, on her left, pushed back a lock of blonde hair. 'I would drink the entire Saris River if it gave me even half her powers.' He wiped his forehead with the back of his hand. 'This Defalk is hot for harvest time.'

'Most of the harvest is in now,' Daffyd noted. 'Except for that . . .' His eyes strayed to the north, across the Chean River, whose waters were both thinner and more reddish brown than ever.

Anna understood. Her efforts against the Ebrans had created the unintended side effect of washing out many of the lower-lying fields – although worst of the damage had been confined to the area within a day's ride of the ford and where poor Sorprat had once stood.

Now the river ran with even less water, although Anna wasn't quite sure why. Had she messed up the groundwater, or was her sinkhole lake draining off some of the flow?

'Then it is hotter than it should be,' said Spirda. 'Why have the rains not returned if you defeated the Ebrans, Lady Anna?'

'Their forces are gone, not their sorcery,' Anna pointed out.

'Then what is to prevent them from rebuilding?' Spirda scratched the back of his neck, then wiped his sweating forehead again. 'Must we destroy their entire land?'

'I don't know,' Anna admitted. 'I'm a stranger here, remember, and I don't know exactly why the Ebrans do what they do.' Inside, she was all too afraid she did, that they were like all the other tyrants in her own earth's history who continued until they were destroyed. Was there really something to the obsolete idea of a national character? Some countries just changed tyrants, without changing anything else. Was Ebra like that? Or were all people like that deep inside, wanting whatever people would let them take? Here she was, using enormous powers she'd never dreamed possible. Some would have said she was already abusing those powers. Would she do even worse? She shivered, even as she perspired, and sweat and road dust mixed on her forehead.

'They will try again,' Daffyd predicted dourly.

Anna looked forward toward where the Prophet was riding. Hanfor had pulled away from the Prophet and was turning his horse, probably for one of his periodic inspections up and down the column. In his absence, Zealor had drawn his mount closer to that of the Prophet, and bent closer to Behlem.

The sorceress didn't like Zealor's whole body position, particularly his drawing closer to Behlem so soon after Hanfor had ridden away. Zealor, she felt, was Delor with more brains, and with Behlem wary of her already . . .

Was she getting paranoid? Had she always been paranoid, but not recognized it?

She shook her head.

'Is something wrong, Lady Anna?' asked Daffyd.

'No, nothing,' she lied, knowing there was nothing the young player could do. 'Nothing.'

96

Anna shifted her weight in the saddle and readjusted her soggy hat. Then she glanced over her shoulder. The dust raised by the horses and the supply wagons not only reached back to Zechis, but was probably choking the armsmen on foot, enough that some might have wished to be among those few who had been left to garrison Loiseau and to rebuild and garrison the Sand Pass fortifications.

'Lady Anna?'

The sorceress turned in the saddle as the wiry Alvar eased his mount into the moving column. Spirda held back his horse, and let the darkbearded senior captain ride in beside Anna.

'Captain Alvar. How are you?'

After a glance ten yards farther up the road, where Behlem rode with the overcaptains, followed by his personal guards and armsmen bearing cream-and-blue Neserean banners, Alvar offered a guarded grin. 'Right well, lady. Unlike some, I am uninterested in fighting when it can be avoided. And unlike others, I do not mind if someone else garners the credit.' He paused, then added, 'In your case, it may not entirely be a credit.'

Anna smiled, but bristled inside momentarily before realizing that Alvar's words were not meant exactly as spoken. 'So you think destroying the Ebrans did me little credit.' She tried to warm her smile.

'For me, I would give you great credit.' He shrugged, a hand brushing the black beard. 'There are those who find a victory without arms and offered by a . . . sorceress . . . less than desirable.'

'In short, they find a woman's solution degrading to their honor. Were you assigned to support my efforts because of your "practicality"?' asked Anna, lowering her voice slightly.

'Overcaptain Hanfor understands,' answered Alvar.

'But the Prophet and some of the others do not?'

'Like as I said, Lady Anna, the overcaptain and I, we see things much alike.'

'I like your viewpoint,' the sorceress answered. 'But it doesn't seem that common here.'

Alvar glanced down at his mount's mane.

Anna wondered, then spoke, 'For what it's worth, I appreciate your support. And I'd like you to know that . . . what I did . . . it wasn't easy for me, and I did it because there didn't seem to be a better way. But,' she was the one to look down, 'most of the Ebrans were people like us, I think.'

'That is what makes war hard,' Alvar said, black eyes somber.

'Who's that?' asked Daffyd, gesturing toward a rider on the road ahead.

Anna turned.

'Someone is riding hard,' observed Alvar, standing in his stirrups. 'It's one of our messengers. From Falcor, I would wager.' He snorted. 'The lady Cyndyth has stubbed her toe. Or wants to execute the cook for mispreparing fish.'

'Lord Behlem! Lord Behlem!' The rider, apparently smeared with what seemed to be dried mud, reined up short of the Prophet, barred from nearing more by Zealor and Behlem's guards. The messenger's mount was lathered and clearly almost run into the ground.

Anna peered over the crowded mass, trying to hear the messenger.

'A wall of water – a torrent – never so much – the entire Fal River – half of Falcor is no more. The liedburg is whole, but water covered the courtyard knee-deep. The lady Cyndyth bid me find you.'

'Our men?' asked Hanfor.

'All are safe, save one squad on patrol.'

Behlem turned in the saddle and motioned to Anna. She rode forward slowly, reining up short of the Prophet, aware that the entire column was slowing behind her.

'I am told that a great river flood has destroyed much of Falcor. What do you know of this?' Behlem fingered his beard.

'Nothing.'

'Why not?' Behlem gestured vaguely over his shoulder. 'Your ... work ... devastated the crops east of Pamr. Yet you know nothing about the river torrents that have struck Falcor?' The calculated irony of his tone was loud enough to carry to the captains around him.

'Lord Behlem,' Anna said carefully, 'I spent all my power defeating the Ebran forces. I couldn't have detected anything afterwards.' She paused, then added, 'You can see that my use of the rivers only went a day's ride.'

'That is true,' offered Hanfor.

Zealor's eyes slitted.

Behlem's eyes went to Anna. 'Yet you did not warn me?'

'I did not know. I cannot be everywhere.'

'You are a sorceress.'

'You are a Prophet, Lord Behlem, yet you did not know.' Behlem stiffened in the saddle, and his eyes blazed. After a moment of silence, he said, harshly. 'Go, sorceress ... I must think.'

Anna eased Farinelli out to the shoulder of the road, letting the Prophet's imperial party resume their ride, before she edged back to Alvar, Daffyd, and Spirda.

Before they had covered another dek, a tall officer in Neserean blue rode along the shoulder studying faces. Then he motioned. 'Lady Anna.'

'Hanfor.'

The overcaptain turned his horse so that it matched steps with Farinelli, and Spirda and Alvar nodded and dropped back.

'I could not help but overhear. It took me a bit to persuade Lord Behlem that I needed to check with my officers.' He shook his head slowly. 'Never has a ruler been delivered a triumph so absolute.'

'He does not seem pleased,' Anna pointed out.

'Those in power, they fear power,' Hanfor said. 'You are powerful.'

'And a woman,' Anna said dryly.

'He was most wroth when you pointed out his limitations.'

'I shouldn't have, but he's trying to devalue me every chance he gets.'

'Half his guards snickered. While your words were true ...' Hanfor shrugged, concern mirrored on the weathered countenance.

'I know.' Again ... more politics. Those in power wanted to fault her for not saving them from one disaster when she'd been busy doing what they wanted somewhere else – like department chairs who wanted her to perform and teach full loads and then complained that she hadn't published enough or warned them that some instrumental professor was dissatisfied and had left with no notice – as if she had anything to do with it.

Hanfor gave a quick smile and eased his mount out of the column, heading rearward.

At least, Anna reflected, a few people respected her. There were always a few, but they never seemed well-placed enough, or powerful enough, to save her from her own straightforwardness.

Farinelli *whuff*ed, and she patted his shoulder. 'Easy there, big fellow. Too bad more men don't have your soul.'

She could sense Daffyd raising his eyebrows, but she didn't care, not at the moment.

97

WEI, NORDWEI

'Did you personally scry what she did to the dark ones?' Ashtaar glances toward the dark agate shape on the wood surface before her, but her hands remain on table, fingers steepled.

'She buried most of Eladdrin's forces in liquid mud, and then she cast a flood over the rest. Perhaps two-score survived.' Gretslen shudders. 'The woman is a monster.'

'Do you think she must be killed, then?' The spymistress winces ever so slightly at the barrage of hammers and metal-working that the wind carries up from the harbor, where the rebuilding continues.

'Is there any question, honored Ashtaar? Can we allow that sort of twisting of Erde's chords?'

A frown momentarily flickers across the dark-haired woman's face, followed by a bland smile.

'You think we can?' asks the blonde.

'You question whether we should allow her that power and, yet, by suggesting that we curtail her use of it – does that not suggest equal arrogance on our part?' The spymistress's fingers reach out for the black agate oval.

'We seek but harmony . . .'

'For our tune,' answers Ashtaar. 'Let me ask you a question, Gretslen. What happens if we try – and fail?' She smiles brittlely. 'And a second question. How comfortable will the Prophet be with such power at his elbow?'

'Neither he nor his consort will be happy ... if they survive.'

'Do we care?'

'But she is a monster, and you do not care. I see now the wisdom of the strictures. How could anyone bury armsmen in liquid mud?'

'You are young, and still innocent in some ways. Most died more quickly than from blade wounds. Is it more glorious to kill a man with a blade? Why? Is he any less dead?'

Gretslen's eyes harden, but she does not speak.

'No,' Ashtaar continues. 'Let others draw her wrath, and they will. The Evult has already visited his devastation upon Elhi and Falcor, and he is taking steps to rebuild.'

'The floods? The Evult? Kendr said nothing.'

'I bid her keep silent. When he saw the destruction of his armies, he released all the heat under the Ostfels west of Vult, and caused the storms to gather.'

'Monsters to the south of us, wherever we look,' mutters the blonde.

'Each of them would say something similar about those to the north of them,' notes Ashtaar. 'Your job is to scry, and to report. To communicate and to follow orders.'

'Yes, Ashtaar.'

'You do not have to face the Council. Be thankful you don't.' Ashtaar smiles self-deprecatingly. 'And try to remember this conversation before you have to.'

Gretslen glances at the polished floor.

'Now ... send word to your 'influence' in Falcor that the dark ones killed the travel sorceress.'

'But ...'

'Who else knows the killers were ours? Let the Evult take the blame. Oh, and make sure that your friend knows about the massacre of Synek – and that the tale is told to the sorceress.'

'That was five years ago,' observes the blonde.

'Do as I say. She feels as well as thinks. We must use that.'

98

'Not more than a dek to the river,' Spirda observed.

'Don't see the old toll booth,' Daffyd added from where he rode near the right shoulder. 'Some of the trees are down.'

From where she rode, almost directly behind the Prophet's guard, Anna couldn't see all that much directly ahead, although she recalled that the east bank was slightly lower than the west, at least where the bridge was.

Before long, the vanguard slowed, and Anna peered through the heads and banners before her, using the advantage of Farinelli's height. She tried not to gape. The stone bridge across the Falche was no more. Only the foundation piers remained, and those massive blocks had been twisted in their bases. The river bed was nearly empty, an expanse of mud where, with the endless sun and heat, the stench of dead animals, vegetation – and people – was already beginning to rise.

Anna swallowed, hard, looking across the devastation, as the lead lancers picked their way down through a trail already packed through the mud. Farinelli carried her after the Prophet and his guards, the gelding setting his feet almost delicately, if firmly.

Why? What had caused such a flood? It couldn't have been her sorcery, not unless there were links she didn't understand. The effects of her muddling with groundwater and whatever had died out long before Zechis. From her studies of the Defalk maps, the Fal River rose in the north-east, in the Ostfels between Ebran and Defalk, far from the Chean's headwaters.

Had the legendary Evult raised the flood somehow in retaliation for her destruction of the Ebran army? Did that mean even more destruction and bloodshed? How much, and how soon? She tried not to shiver, despite the late afternoon heat.

In the square beyond where the bridge had been, the pedestal stood without its statue. Around the buildings on each side of the two streets closest to the river – of the five branching off the square – were piled branches and timbers and barrel staves and other debris, but a narrow way had been forced through the river road barricade.

As she passed into the shadows where the dampness of mud and worse lingered, Anna looked to the left side of the street, where a barefoot woman in soiled trousers rolled up to the knees and a mud-smeared tunic dumped a basket of muddy water into the street where the open sewer had once been.

Her dark eyes flicked toward the slow-moving column.
'. . . western bastards . . . your fault . . .'

Only a comparative handful of people toiled in the mud. As she rode past the cross-street beyond the trading quarter, Anna looked westward. The slight grade was enough that the buildings more than a few hundred yards west appeared untouched.

'Just in the river plain,' she murmured to herself.

The liedburg, its eastern side buttressed by its rocky promontory, sat above a sea of cracked and drying mud that filled the depression between it and the city. The walls showed watermarks less than a yard high beside the portcullis gate. Armsmen struggled to brush off the mud from the collapsed tents and re-erect them on the flat. That indicated to Anna that the liedburg had only been touched by backwaters or something like them.

Menares stood just inside the gate, in soiled trousers,

supervising the squads of armsmen who continued to carry out baskets of mud from the courtyard.

The column lurched to a halt as Behlem stopped and spoke to the counselor. Anna strained to hear the interchange.

'Lady Cyndyth suggested I was in charge, and that I had best be out here.' The heavy-set older man shrugged. 'It was easier.'

'And quieter,' muttered Alvar from his mount beside Anna.

She turned. Alvar smiled blandly, as if he had said nothing.

'What does Cyndyth look like?' Anna asked.

'I have not seen her at close quarters, lady, but she has raven hair, and her lips are very red, and she is slender.' Alvar's words were low, and he glanced nervously toward Behlem and the courtyard beyond.

The sorceress was beginning to dislike Cyndyth, and she had never met the woman.

After reining up when the Prophet's party entered the stables and blocked the doorways, she eased Farinelli toward the western wall enough to get into the shadow. Then she glanced sideways toward Daffyd. The player shrugged expansively and rolled his eyes.

Not too much later, when Behlem had dismounted and paraded into the hall, followed by Menares, neither man looking in her direction, Farinelli carried Anna to the stables. She was glad the Prophet hadn't lingered, and from Alvar's sigh as the sandy-haired ruler had departed, she gathered she wasn't the only one.

Anna dismounted by the doors, led the gelding into the stable, and half-smiled. The stable floors had already been cleaned and fresh straw laid. Tirsik fussed with two stable boys in a corner.

'If it be taking a warren to muck out the corner stalls, then be taking a warren—' The wiry stable-master glanced toward Anna as she stopped with Farinelli, trying to stretch out the stiffness in her legs and thighs. 'How is your beast, Lady Anna?' Tirsik's eyes remained on the sorceress.

'He's in better shape than I am.' Anna laughed, genuinely pleased to see Tirsik.

'His stall is clean. I made sure it was one of the first. After those for the Prophet, of course,' the stablemaster added as Spirda and Daffyd appeared behind Anna with their mounts.

'Of course,' said Spirda flatly.

Anna looked sideways at Tirsik as Spirda led his mount toward the rear of the stable.

'Poor lad,' said Tirsik. 'Tis hard to see your idols tarnished. I will wager he will recover.'

A strange look passed across Daffyd's face, and Anna wanted to nod.

'You, too, Daffyd?' she asked softly. 'Have I tarnished your images of what sorcery and sorceresses are all about?'

'No . . . no.'

'I think that probably means "yes." I'm sorry.'

'I had best get her stalled,' Daffyd temporized. 'Others are waiting.' He led the mare away.

'I was not hinting of you with Spirda,' pointed out Tirsik.

'I know,' Anna said as she led Farinelli toward his stall and as the stablemaster walked with her. 'But the same is true of Daffyd. He created this image of the perfect beautiful sorceress – and I'm not. I don't fit his woman image or his mother image, and he's upset and doesn't know why.' As she spoke, Anna wondered why she did, except that she had to tell someone, and Tirsik would tell no one. That she could feel.

'Aye. You understand. Unlike some.'

'Stablemaster!' came a shout from the doors.

'Take care of yourself and that beast.' Tirsik nodded and walked quickly back toward the front of the stable.

Anna unsaddled Farinelli, and carefully set the awkward bag containing the green recital dress over the stall wall, along with the saddle-bags. The lutar case went above the manger. Then she forced herself to take the time to groom Farinelli thoroughly.

Once the gelding was as clean as she could get him, she lifted her gear, throwing the saddlebags over one shoulder, the wrapped gown over the other, and carrying the lutar case in her right hand. She struggled through the heavy horse traffic in the courtyard.

'. . . stop pushing, Girsto!'

'. . . easy with that beast . . .'

'. . . way for the sorceress! Give way for the sorceress . . .'

That might have been Fhurgen, but Anna couldn't see. Whoever it was, she was grateful as she slipped through the double column and made her way along the wall to the north tower of the hall.

'Lady Anna . . . you . . . returned.' Skent hopped off the stool and looked at the stones of the tower floor as Anna stepped inside the lower entry. 'Oh . . . might I help you?'

'Yes. The saddlebags.' She kept the lutar and the gown bag.

Her room was hot – like everything else in Defalk, but not so hot as when she had left. Perhaps fall was coming. And unlike the courtyard, the room didn't smell muddy – just dusty. Anna set the lutar on the narrow bed and glanced around, frowning after a moment. Although she couldn't say why, the room *felt* different, as if things were not quite where she had left them, as though everything had been examined and then replaced, not quite perfectly.

She sighed. That somehow figured, and she couldn't do much about it immediately. The sorceress turned to the page. 'Set them on the floor there. Can you get me some water – lots of it?'

'Ah . . . the flood, the wells are bad,' Skent said.

'I don't care if it's dirty. Just not too muddy – and plenty. All right?'

'Yes, Lady Anna.'

'How have things been?' she asked.

'Quiet, mostly, except in the main hall.'

'The Lady Cyndyth?' guessed Anna.

'She brought her own pages. They sent Resor here to the north tower. The others are cleaning a lot, like sculls. It be better here, I think.' Skent looked down.

'Cataryzna?'

'She be fine, I think.'

'I take it you haven't had much chance to see her?'

'Not since you left.' Skent shifted his weight from one foot to the other. 'Best I get your water, Lady Anna.'

'All right.' Something was bothering the youth – that was clear – but he wasn't ready to say.

After Skent departed, Anna first hung out the recital gown, then looked through things. The writing paper, and some spells were arranged under the stone paperweight more neatly than she had left them, but all seemed to be there. Her gowns were hung off-center. The pallet on the bed had been shifted, not that she'd hidden anything there, but someone had checked.

Was she getting paranoid?

Thunk!

'Lady Anna, I got two buckets.' As he stepped into her room, his eyes went to the green gown hanging from the wall pegs. 'Oh, that be beautiful!' Skent struggled in with two large buckets of water, which he set on the stone floor beside the wash table. 'These be as clean as I could get. And I have to go because Virkan says all the pages have to get the big dining hall ready.'

'Thank you.' Anna paused. 'Ready for what?'

'There's a big dinner planned for the night after tomorrow night. Virkan said it was a victory dinner.' Skent brushed his longish dark hair back off his forehead. 'Cens told me that you destroyed the Ebrans all alone.' The page lowered his voice. 'Is that so?'

'I had some help from Daffyd – and Spirda, and captain Alvar, and overcaptain Hanfor,' Anna said.

'But you did most of it?'

The sorceress nodded reluctantly.

'I don't understand—' Skent stopped, almost embarrassed.
'Understand what?'

'Oh, nothing, lady. I guess I do.' Skent glanced at the
floor. 'I needs must be going.'

'You mean why Lord Behlem gets the victory dinner?'
Anna laughed. 'Isn't that always the way it goes?'

'Lord Barjim was fairer.' Skent's eyes do not meet Anna's.

'He probably was. He seemed straightforward. I liked
Lady Alasia, too.'

'She kept Jimbob trued to the stone.' Skent's eyes drifted
towards the door, and he added, 'I will be late.'

'Go ahead. I won't tell anyone you told me about the
dinner. It was supposed to be a secret, wasn't it?'

'You ... thank you.' Skent flashed a grin of relief and
edged toward the door.

'Go.'

So she wasn't supposed to know about the dinner. What
else wasn't she supposed to know?

After unpacking the saddlebags and stacking them in the
corner – the tower room lacked closets, the closest thing
being the wall pegs and hungers that were sufficient only
for her two gowns – Anna looked at her smudged visage
in the wall mirror. Lord, she was a mess.

Thunk!

Now what? Anna resignedly walked to the door and
opened it. 'Lady Essan ...'

'Might an old woman trouble a young sorceress for a
moment?'

Anna had trouble not grinning, and stood aside as Essan
swept into the room wearing her purple trousers and a light
purple shirt. Anna shut the door and turned.

'You have obviously been undertaking items of a less
than lady-like nature.' There was a twinkle in Essan's eyes.
'Otherwise, the liedburg – the staff, I mean – for proper
people would not stoop to such gossip – would not be
buzzing so about the blonde sorceress. To think that your
burying all those awful Ebrans in mud deprived the Prophet

of a glorious victory, and that you did not fall to your knees and beg forgiveness. Well,' mock-huffed Essan, 'I am but an old woman, but you mark my words, there will be trouble, not that anyone listens to an old has-been who rattles around the distant north tower and only listens to what the pages and maids say.' Essan settled herself into one of the chairs.

'People will talk,' Anna agreed, sitting down across from the older woman.

'And Nelmor, Gatrune must have told you about him, he was kind enough to send his boy Tiersen as a messenger. You know, Nelmor's daughter Ytrude, she is the water's own image of Gatrune. Tiersen, I was talking of him, he said that his father – that's Nelmor, and he has holdings at Dubaria – why Nelmor said that he was a dutiful lord and pledged to the Prophet, seeing as how Lord Behlem held the liedstadt. Tiersen told me his sire hoped someday that Defalk could be proud again, and, imagine this, that he would even rather see a woman or a stranger who had laid his life on the sword's sharp edge for Defalk than one who claimed his power by lineage or by consortship.' Essan shook her head. 'Imagine that, the widow of Lord Donjim being told such. And a widow who had pledged to Lord Barjim.'

'Imagine that,' echoed Anna, her mouth dry.

'There be others that feel that way, too. Strange times, Lady Anna, these be most strange times.' The older woman's eyes grinned behind the somber facade. 'Then, too, they have been inspecting the towers. Some folks, servitors of the Lady Cyndyth, I would imagine, peered through every room, like as not so she can reorganize it all. Changes everywhere. They even took my poor Garreth, not even telling me for what, just that the Lady Cyndyth needed her, and I have not seen her since.' Essan's eyes were cold, but she continued. 'I would be hoping that they would not turn out an old lady, or worse, but who have I to turn to? I came down the stairs soon as I heard you are returned, and I prattle on, and you have not even had a chance to prepare yourself for all that will come with the victory.'

Anna wanted to wince at the slight hardening in Essan's last words, but she only nodded. Clearly, these walls had ears, or the lady thought they did, as did Skent. 'I've enjoyed your company, and your insights from the beginning, Lady Essan, even if I am a stranger and a woman. I do feel for the land, and it was hard for me when I saw the destruction from the river.' She bowed her head momentarily. 'I had not thought . . . about all that has befallen you, the widow of a great lord, and I feel blessed that you have shared your thoughts with me.' How could she get across what she was trying to say without giving it totally away?

'I must leave you to . . . whatever . . . whatever sorceresses do.' Lady Essan rose, her face blank, and Anna knew she had to say more, somehow, even as she stood.

'My children, you know, are far, far away,' Anna began, 'but I understand, and perhaps I can act as your daughter, as you would have her act now.' Anna smiled. 'But you'll have to keep acting like a mother. There's too much I don't know, and even adopted daughters need guidance, especially now. I hope I can live up to Nelmor's expectations. I'll certainly try.'

The light in Essan's eyes told Anna that she had been understood, even before Essan stopped by the door. 'You be sure that I be no old woman, badgering and bothering you?'

'If you did not talk to me, how would I learn about Defalk? Or the liedburg?'

'Much you have to do, sorceress-girl. Much, but don't you worry. I'll be back, and it is good to see you in health. See that you stay that way. I will tell you that though you were mine.' Essan nodded affirmatively and opened the door. 'Now get that pretty face clean.' Her eyes went to the recital gown. 'And wear that gown when you want all eyes on you.'

'I hope so,' Anna answered ambiguously.

After she watched the older woman climb up the stairs, firmly but slowly, Anna closed the door.

She needed to clean up – quickly – and then to develop

and cast some sort of protection spell – or something. And that was just the beginning. The Lady Essan had made it clear – very clear.

One thing was very clear. She was running out of time. She had to do something – either leave or fight, and she really wasn't a fighter.

Anna laughed. She hadn't been a fighter, but something about Erde had changed her from being a survivor to a fighter. Was it that the worst had already been done to her children? That her actions couldn't be used against them?

So be it. She would fight Behlem. But in her own way and on her own terms.

99

FALCOR, DEFALK

'You could not keep that uniformed fop Nubara . . .' Behlem breaks off and paces across the corner of the room, brushing away a spider web that has tangled in his reddish-blond beard. He pauses by the window, pushing the shutters wide. 'Double moons, to boot.'

'How would you have me do that?' asks Menares, ignoring the Prophet's comments about the ominous moons. 'You wish to offend the Liedfuhr?'

'You don't consider the doubled moons a problem?'

'The moons are not in our control, Lord Behlem.' Menares pauses, then adds deliberately, 'I was . . . surprised to see the sorceress.'

'What would you have me do? My own officers, except Zealor, worship the bitch. She put herself out in front of the army, almost got killed by some lancers, and destroyed dissonance-near the entire Ebran force. And you want me to have her executed, if I could? For what? I should have let her have that sorcerer's hall and pensioned her off, but no, I had to listen to your advice about all Defalk rising with her.' The Prophet turns from the window and steps toward the table. 'What on Erde was I thinking about?'

'Replacing one danger with a greater one,' murmurs the white-haired counselor.

'I am supposed to believe that?' Behlem ignores the nearly-empty goblet and lifts the bottle to his lips.

'You are the Prophet. You can do as you wish.' Menares shrugs. 'You will anyway, once you have heard me.'

'Go ahead.'

'You have noted how respected she is, and how few she knows. Some already love her, except that they do not love her, but her image. Who respects and loves the Evult? Yet none know him, just his image. Eladdrin was the only Ebran respected, and the sorceress has vanquished him. If you left her in Mencha, even if she helped you again, even if she defeated all of Ebra and laid it at your feet, a season, a year, from now who would be respected? You – or her?'

'Why are matters so complex?'

'Because you are a ruler,' replies Menares. 'You know that. Things are simple for a farmer or a peasant.'

'Fine. What do I do now?'

'Let events take their course.'

Behlem's eyes flicker to the door at the side of the room. 'Already?'

'Cyndyth saw Lady Anna this afternoon, but I believe her mind was made up already.'

The Prophet's tongue licks his lips. 'And if her schemes fail?'

'How can you lose? You had no part in it, and there never is anything to link them to her.'

'She will inform Konsstin that it is once again my fault, and his assistance will halt,' Behlem points out.

'Only for a time. He cannot afford to stop aiding you, not when he wishes you to take the brunt of the effort in destroying the Evult and weakening Nordwei.'

'You don't have to live with her. I had thought by undertaking this campaign . . . perhaps get some peace, some affection without politics and more politics.'

'She knows that. Why else would she be here?' Menares toys with his goblet but does not lift it.

'Enough. She is waiting, and she will need her say.' Behlem shakes his head. 'Enough.'

Behlem walks to the side door without looking back.

Menares smiles sadly and looks at his own untouched goblet. Then he stands.

100

Anna looked out her window, craning her neck. She smiled. Clearsong and Darksong – the twin moons – were close together, one silvered gold, one dark silvered red. Two moons – the idea still fascinated her, even while it reminded her that Erde was far different from earth.

Voices rumbled from the walls, carried in the night stillness.

'. . . dissonant moon near the other . . . an omen of bad things . . .'

'Bah . . . happens every year or so . . .'

'. . . tell you, that was when they killed Mikell . . .'

'. . . died in his sleep . . .'

'. . . tell you . . .'

The sorceress yawned. She felt paranoid, as though she were using sorcery for every little thing. She'd even sung a spell over the rather dry and boring beef pie Skent had brought her for dinner. She could have sought out the players and eaten with them, she supposed, but that sent the wrong signal, somehow.

Omens, deaths, what else? She stiffened, turning from the window toward the sole flickering candle in its mantle on the table.

Garreth! What had Essan meant about Garreth? She'd been so absorbed in trying to read through the words and frame the right kind of response, and then to hurry and come up with spells for what lay ahead that her concerns about the girl had been submerged.

For a moment, she thought, then mentally figured the words, before she faced the mirror and lifted the lutar.

She cleared her throat and sang.

> 'Mirror, mirror, on the wall
> show me Garreth from this hall,
> where she is or last did lie
> if she live or if she die.'

The mists swirled across the mirror, then revealed a patch of bare earth covered with weeds flattened by the river. Anna thought the space might be the land sloping to the river to the southeast of the hall, but the location really didn't matter.

Her eyes burned, and her jaw clenched for a moment. Why hadn't she paid attention sooner? Except . . . it wouldn't have mattered.

She turned from the newer mirror, with its painted green frame, laid the lutar on the bed, and walked to the window. The light wind, cooler now than when she had left Falcor, ruffled her hair, hair that had more natural curl than it had ever had before. Another image of Brill's?

She shook her head, thinking again that she had the gift of youth because she had gone to Brill's side when he died – she and not Liende, and from that much else had flowed. And she was here in Falcor because two innocents – Daffyd and Jenny – had tried the impossible. If ever there had been a case of fools rushing in where angels feared to tread . . . but they had, and Jenny was dead, and Daffyd in the middle of intrigue that made Brill an angel by comparison.

Anna pulled the handkerchief from her belt and blew her nose. She sniffled too much when she was upset. Why had they killed Garreth? Because the poor girl was associated with both Anna and Lady Essan? Because of what she might know?

Garreth had been seated there, and drawn Anna on a stool, even doing the background so that Elizabetta would know something about where Anna was. And now Garreth, who had wanted little except to be safe, was dead.

Anna glanced to the door where the bolt was drawn. It seemed to fade in and out in the flickering light from the candle.

What else did Anna need to worry about? Her eyes went to the door, and she carried the candle as she crossed the floor.

Anna studied the sliding bolt on the door, closely, first inside, then outside. She nodded. Maybe she was paranoid, but there were two small holes in the wood on the outside, and a thin slit between them, just enough that something slender could open the bolted door from outside silently.

That needed to be remedied, but she needed to redesign the bolt first. Brill had said that inanimate materials were easier.

Before long, she had a drawing of a double drop bolt – strong enough that it would take several men and a battering ram some time to break down the door. She hoped that would be all she needed.

Next came the first spell.

She grinned as she completed the last words,

'. . . iron hard and fixed in place!'

As she set the lutar on the bed, her eyes straying to the window and the almost locked moons, she had to wonder. Should she just leave? Why was she tempting fate to stay in a hall where the walls had ears and where who knew how many souls plotted against her?

Because she would be on the run . . . and because . . . because she was tired of running. What was the point of youth and a new world if she just repeated the old?

Anna took a deep breath and reached for another piece of paper. Not running was getting complicated, and her head was beginning to ache again.

Before too long, she wrote out another set of simple words, based on the fire spell, then worked on memorizing them, not that they were much different, but she might well need them in a hurry.

Then she laid the striker by the candle, the words there as well, with the lutar on top of its case and waiting.

She hoped she needed none of them, and feared she would.

She did not sleep, not at first, not with her thoughts of poor Garreth, possibly tortured, and her own imagination about shadowy figures creeping up the steps and pounding down the door. In time, she dropped into the darkness.

Clang! Clang!

The reverberations of the hammers, or whatever they were, woke her out of a nightmare where she kept riding, and riding, and found nowhere to rest. Her whole body was drenched in sweat, and now . . . now someone was trying to break into her room.

Her fingers trembled as she fumbled with the striker.

Clang!

'. . . get on with it . . .'

'. . . boys'll keep it clear long enough . . . bitch . . . center it, frig it!'

As the candle flamed, she lifted the lutar, and let her fingers caress the strings, clearing her throat, and hoping, just hoping she could make trembling hands, and trembling voice work.

Clang!

The first note told her she wasn't lucky. Her throat was clogged with mucus, and she coughed it clear.

Clang! The door shivered.

Anna ran through a quick vocalise, stopping halfway through to cough up more junk. Shit! Shit! Shit! What a time for an allergy attack!

'What was that?' muttered the voice beyond the door.

After another set of coughs, she sang, chording the simple structure to match her spell.

> 'Attackers there, attackers strong,
> turn to ashes with this song.
> Be you right or be you wrong,
> death take you all along.'

'AEiii! . . .'

The tools dropped on the stones of the landing. The screams did not last long, but Anna only half-dozed the rest of the night, the candle burning, the lutar at hand.

The tower remained silent, eerily silent, as though abandoned, and Anna dozed, and woke, and dozed.

101

FALCOR, DEFALK

The raven-haired woman shakes Behlem's shoulder.

'Wha . . .' He blinks and tries to open his eyes, although the sun has barely cleared the horizon, and the room is dim, its shutters closed tightly.

'We need to talk, dear consort and Prophet.' She wears a silk robe of dark blood-red, tucked in to show a narrow waist and more than ample breasts.

'At this glass?' he groans, dropping his head back on the sheets.

'What I do not understand, Behlem,' says the raven-haired woman, almost languidly, as she perches on the foot of the bed that had once belonged to the lords of Defalk, 'is why you always think you can deceive me when you go off and leave me.'

'Deceive you?' He struggles up into a sitting position. 'What on Erde are you babbling about. I told you everything.'

'In the middle of the night, some . . . intruders . . . entered the north tower. They were apparently bent on some mischief with your dear sorceress.'

Behlem rubs his eyes. 'What are you talking about?'

'There were screams, I am told, but they were not from the sorceress. I was led to believe that she was unprotected.' Cyndyth smiles. 'After last night, I almost believed you, until this morning.'

'You used your father's . . . resources, and they failed?' Behlem laughs. 'The resources of the great Konsstin failed?'

'You would be wise to remember, consort dear, that he is paying for the arms and supplies for this expedition.' Cyndyth shifts position, and her eyes smolder. 'In the interests of everyone's safely, I inspected many of the lockbolts throughout the liedburg, rustic place that it is. The sorceress's was singularly inadequate. 'Yet . . .' Cyndyth shrugs. 'So I would like to know why you warned her.'

Behlem shakes his head, almost sadly. 'I did not. I would wish I had, just to see you frustrated, dear plotting consort, but had I, your tame seers would know already.'

'You slept with her.'

'I would rather sleep with a grass-snake.' The Prophet grins momentarily.

'As pretty as she is? Have you lost all manhood?'

'Cyndyth, I have no idea what happened to your assassins, but I saw what she did to Delor, as I am certain Menares informed you. I had no desire to end up as he did.' Behlem shrugs and sits up farther in the bed. 'Since you would be displeased at the results and since I would also, I did not think that you would mind.'

'Good. Then you will not mind our devising a way to remove her?'

Behlem holds up a hand. 'Only one stipulation. That her removal be quietly handled – after the victory dinner. Her

demise before it would not set well with many of the captains
and their troops. She must appear . . . low on the table, below
all the overcaptains and senior captains. And I will delicately
suggest that her victory, while welcome, created significant
additional problems that are entirely her fault.'

'You worry about peasants?'

'They have more weapons than we do, Cyndyth, and even
the densest of them will suspect us – especially after this
botch of yours.'

'Mine? I had nothing to do with it.'

'Yours. Now go get something else to chew on and let me
get dressed and talk to Menares. We will work out something
quiet – perhaps in Mencha. I will give her the sorcerer's hall,
as compensation, despite her failings.'

'You what?'

'Then she will have to travel there. The dark ones will
be waiting, to avenge their losses. Something like that.
Now . . . go find someone else to annoy.' Behlem staggers
to his feet.

Cyndyth smiles as she sways toward the door.

102

Lady Anna?'

'Yes?' the sorceress answered without unbolting the door.
Despite washing up, eating, and dressing, she still felt
tired.

'It's Menares. Might I come in?'

'You and who else?'

'There is no one else here.' A pause followed. 'Do you
think anyone else would dare?'

After using the mirror spell to verify that Menares was
indeed alone, and feeling untrustworthy about it, Anna
opened the door.

Menares stepped in slowly, glancing around. He licked his lips.

'I won't incinerate you, Menares,' Anna promised, closing and bolting the door behind the counselor.

'I would . . . appreciate that.'

'I've never wanted to kill anyone here,' she added. 'That's why it's so hard to understand why so many people want to kill me.'

'Lady Anna . . . the Prophet is distressed.' After another sweep of the room, his eyes halting on the uncovered lutar on the bed, the counselor settled into one of the chairs.

'Menares, I'm distressed. Do you think I enjoy having people trying to break into my room in the middle of the night?' Anna paused, then sat on the bed beside her instrument. 'Do you know who they were?'

'No, Lady Anna. No one is missing from the Prophet's retinue.' Menares' eyes flickered, and Anna knew a lie would follow. 'It could have been the dark ones. At Synek, when they came, the streets were filled with bodies and they hacked to death those who would not follow.'

'These didn't feel like dark ones,' Anna said.

'There is no way to tell. They had blades and daggers and coins in their purses. Everything else . . .' The counselor shrugged.

'And some sort of hammer and chisel?' prodded Anna.

'Ah . . . how did you know?'

'When someone takes a hammer to an iron hinge, it is loud.' Anna smiled. 'I also found it interesting that no one came to investigate until Skent brought my breakfast tray and found the . . . remains. Was he supposed to find mine?'

'Lady Anna, I swear I had nothing to do with this.' The white-haired counselor licked his lips. 'And the Prophet is most unhappy about this . . . occurrence.'

Anna almost nodded. She believed most of his statements. There had been a massacre in Synek, and Menares had known, or suspected, someone was out to assassinate her, but had had nothing to do with it, and the Prophet wanted her out of the way, but more subtly, and probably after his victory dinner.

Lord, how many people wanted her dead?

'Can't you find out who they were?' she asked.

'Lady Anna,' the white-haired counselor said with a shrug, 'you did not leave much except their leathers and their weapons. And their tools.'

'I'm sure they would have left little of me, Menares.' Anna smiled coldly. 'What do you want?'

'To reassure you, and to offer a solution mutually agreeable to you . . . and everyone, I hope.'

Anna didn't like the term 'solution,' because it meant she was a problem, and she'd already had enough experience with being a problem. Dieshr had been a wonderful Music Chair, forever offering 'solutions' – each one of which either had or would have isolated Anna more, like suggesting that Anna give up her non-credit performance classes because she was 'working too hard.' That would have left her students unprepared for their performances in recitals, and in turn, that would have allowed Dieshr to fault officially their preparation by Anna.

'Lady Anna?' asked Menares.

'Sorry. I was thinking. Your solution?'

'It is the Prophet's solution. He has been thinking and reconsidering the situation as well. He is granting you the estates and hall of the late Lord Brill, in recognition and recompense for your services.'

Anna managed to keep her jaw in place. Just like that? After earlier insisting that they would be his? 'That's most gracious,' she said slowly. 'I had understood that he would retain them.'

Menares looked toward the door and lowered his voice. 'The Prophet and his consort both agree that you should be rewarded and that you should take possession soon after the victory celebration. In fact, he and the Lady Cyndyth would like to meet with you in the hall slightly before the dinner to convey his appreciation and respect.'

Anna was beginning to see *all* the elements of the 'solution.' She allowed herself a deep breath, trying to consider how to respond. Clearly, the Lady Cyndyth had it in for Anna, and the assassins of the night before had probably been her doing, and that had upset Behlem, who couldn't afford to have anything happen to Anna just yet. Behlem liked things smoothly and quietly done, at least in public, and he just avoided Anna when he feared matters would not be smooth.

'Lady Anna?' asked Menares nervously.

'I'm sorry,' Anna lied. 'Loiseau is such ... such a ... gesture. It's hard to believe.' And things too good to believe usually were.

'Lady Anna, might I be frank?' The counselor's eyes flicked around the room. 'You have done much for the Prophet. And you are beautiful. And powerful. Mencha is near the border, and you would doubtless use your abilities to protect that border. The lady Cyndyth is most devoted to her consort, and would also wish that he not be any more ... committed to spending time away from Falcor – or preferably Esaria – than absolutely necessary.' The white-haired man offered a smile. 'So you see ...'

'I think so. I can't put it quite so delicately. Cyndyth would prefer my absence and Lord Behlem's presence, and he would like a strong first-line defense against any future Ebran attacks on the borders of his new expanded lands. He can reward me and please her and strengthen his position, all at once.'

'Most precisely. Now ... I would appreciate your discretion until the dinner, for there are those among the overcaptains ...' Menares shrugged, and his eyes flickered. 'You are a woman, if a sorceress.' He heaved himself out of the chair.

'I understand.' And she did, hopefully far more than Menares understood that she did. She walked with him to the door, opening it. While treachery was still theoretically possible, she doubted that anything would happen to her, not until Behlem could get her out of Falcor, or until more time passed.

'Thank you, Lady Anna.' Menares bobbed his head up and down. 'Thank you.'

'Thank you, Menares. I appreciate all the efforts you have made to resolve what could have been a difficult situation.' Anna lied with yet another smile, hoping it didn't seem too false.

After she dropped the bolt in place, she walked to her chair and sat down, trying to figure out the situation. If she'd been offered Loiseau while she was in Mencha, she probably would have taken it and never thought otherwise. But this latest turn of events . . . while she couldn't say why, she knew it was all a ploy to put her on ice, or worse. Was she being unreasonable? Menares' explanation made sense; it made a lot of sense, and she might have done the same thing had she been in Behlem's position. But Behlem was the type not to give up much of anything, and though she had never met Cyndyth, Garreth's death told her all she needed to know.

'Aren't you being unfair?' she asked herself.

Besides, even if Behlem's offer were honest, that meant she'd end up killing more and more Ebrans – or someone – while he got the credit and Cyndyth pulled her cruelties on more and more innocents. She'd be the butcher of Mencha, and people like Virkan would become more and more common.

She had a chance – a slim one – to make a difference.

'You also have a chance to get thoroughly killed,' she whispered under her breath. The sorceress shook her head. One way or another, she would die if she accepted Behlem's 'offer.' She felt that coldness down to the pit of her stomach, a coldness that was more solid than any form of 'proof.'

She laughed nervously. Anna Mayme Thompson, born off the holler in Cumberland, Kentucky, and here she was, at the center of a mess that involved half a continent in a world she'd never dreamed existed. Even Avery wouldn't have believed it. He would have wanted proof. Damn proof!

She looked at the bellpull, then yanked it and waited.

Birke was the page who responded.

Anna met him on the landing. 'Birke? Have you seen Garreth?'

'No, Lady Anna.' Birke's eyes slipped to the floor.

Cold inside, Anna said, 'If you do, would you tell her I'd like to see her.'

'They said she's with the Lady Cyndyth, and I'm not allowed up there, Lady Anna.'

'If you do . . .' Anna nodded in a perfunctory fashion.

'Yes, Lady Anna.'

'That's all. Thank you.'

Birke went downstairs slowly, his eyes drifting back to the landing.

That might confuse someone . . . maybe.

Next came Hanfor.

She took a deep slow breath, then straightened, and opened the tower door. After crossing a courtyard crowded with armsmen cleaning away mud, she found the tall senior overcaptain in the same small room where she had gone before.

'Lady Anna. I must say I did not expect you.' The overcaptain rose from the stool. A map was spread on the small table, and Anna could hear horses and men through the open window.

'Did you hear about last night?' Anna dropped onto one of the stools.

'Last night?' Hanfor's face showed total confusion.

'Good, I'm glad you didn't. Last night some assassins attempted to enter my chamber. I had noted that the door bolt had been weakened, and I repaired it before I went to sleep. They attempted to use a sledge and chisels to snap off the hinges.'

'The hinges were outside?'

'At one time, long ago, I suspect that the room was used for other purposes. It is not large.'

'I forgot. The north tower has those marks, but they have removed the bars from the windows.' Hanfor nodded. 'I take it that you were successful in routing them?'

'I turned them into a pile of ashes. Now, the Prophet is somewhat distressed, so distressed that he has offered me lands. Through his counselor.'

'A good distance from here, I would wager?'

It was Anna's turn to nod. How far could she go? She frowned. 'As a matter of fact, you know the lands.'

Hanfor's eyebrows rose. 'You worry about such a gift horse?'

'The idea had occurred to me,' Anna admitted.

'I do not know what to say, Lady Anna.' The overcaptain's hand touched his graying beard, then scratched the back of his head. The weathered brows knit together for a moment. 'You saved many of my men, even me. But I must tell you frankly that I do not *know* the cause of this mischief, nor do I believe that the Prophet would have anything to do with such an event at this time.'

'Rumor has it that his consort is jealous of any woman who is the slightest bit attractive.'

'I could not deny such a rumor,' mused Hanfor, offering a quick grin that vanished.

Anna forced herself to relax. 'What do you like about what you do, Hanfor? Or do you like it at all?'

Again, the overcaptain looked startled. 'I am sorry?'

'What you do – why do you like it?'

'At times, I do not. I am the third son, with no lands and no ear for music, though my sire was sure to see that I knew my letters. That helps.' He shrugged. 'Except with weapons, my hands are clumsy, and I am not terribly clever. I understand that many men have these problems, or ones like them, and I found I can lead them.' Hanfor's eyes narrowed. 'Why ask you?'

'I'm a stranger. I'm faced with the problem of trying to

sort out what's right. You must know that it was hard to kill the Ebrans.'

'Alvar said you were prostrate for more than a day.'

'It was hard to decide to do it, too,' Anna mused. 'If I didn't kill them, then I'd die, and so would you and a lot of men. If I hadn't slaughtered the last thousand, who were helpless, then Eladdrin would have escaped. Was that right?'

'Hmmmm.' Hanfor scratched his head again. 'All armsmen must answer questions like that.' He laughed. 'The easy answer is that it is better to live than to die. That is as far as most go.'

'I'm not most people,' Anna pointed out.

'You are not. You are a sorceress and a warrior and a beautiful woman. That makes it hard.'

'I appreciate the compliments. I don't know that I'm either beautiful or a warrior.'

'But you are, and now you seek justice.' Hanfor shook his head. 'I fear you may not find it, not in this world.'

'I might have a chance, a small one.' Anna looked at the honest, weathered face. 'Should I try?'

Hanfor laughed wryly again. 'Do you have any choice? You are who you are.'

'I suppose not.' His reaction would have to do. She hoped she was reading the overcaptain right. 'But it's scary.'

Hanfor was fidgeting. Was everyone afraid to be caught alone with her? If only it were for different reasons. Anna rose and bowed slightly. 'I did not mean to take so much of your time, Hanfor, but I appreciate your thoughts.'

'I will do what I can, Lady Anna.' The tall, graying officer bowed.

'Thank you.'

Anna walked back toward the north tower, noting that the west side of the courtyard was filled with wagons, supply wagons, possibly for the great feast.

'. . .' Ware the roan! Easy there!'

'. . . keep that team back . . .'

In between the teamsters' calls, she could hear the chickens, *brawk*ing from the mud-crusted corners of the walls and by the heap of straw outside the stables. At the sight of the stables, she paused, then turned toward the players' quarters.

Although the day was marginally cooler than those of the long summer, she still had to fan her forehead as she stepped through the doorway. Daffyd was alone in the small common room practicing a songspell she had not heard, with a melody that seemed vaguely familiar.

'That's lovely,' Anna noted.

'It be no spell, just a tune. Most are longer, and you can make a mistake without a sorcerer yelling. No offense, lady.' The dark-haired player grinned sheepishly as he glanced up, then around. 'They say that some folk tried to enter your room last night and you left them a pile of ashes.'

Anna nodded. 'They tried to break down the door.'

'No one heard?'

'No one came,' she pointed out.

'That be strange. Most strange, especially for a sorceress who delivered the Prophet's victory.'

'Strange things seem to happen in Erde,' she observed.

'Yes.'

'Where are the other players?' she asked.

'The counselor sent for them.'

Anna didn't like that, either, but she wasn't liking much of what went on in the liedburg. 'Do you know why?'

'Whenever he uses the mirror, he needs them all. So does the Prophet.'

'For a mirror spell?'

Daffyd shrugged, then asked, 'Are you going to the big dinner?'

'I've been asked. How about you? Do you want me to get you a seat?'

'That would be nice, but the players made a place for me, and that might be best.'

'You're sure.'

Daffyd nodded. 'I don't like Zealor or some of his ilk. You would have to worry about me then, and you may have to worry about you.'

'You think so?'

'I have never trusted the Prophet, and now is no time to begin.'

Anna laughed at his sour tone. 'If you hear anything that I should know, would you let me know?'

'Most certainly.'

'And would you play that tune again? I like music that's not a spell.' She stood and listened, and the young player went through three other songs before he stopped and wiped his forehead.

'You're tired?'

'I practiced all morn.'

'Oh ... I'm sorry.'

Daffyd grinned. 'Would you join me for something to eat?'

'Of course.'

'It be but bread and cheese, and dry beef.'

'That sounds wonderful.'

They walked to the small low-ceilinged room where they had eaten before, and Anna heaped her plate with mostly cheese and bread, but, knowing she needed the concentrated protein, she added two slabs of dry meat. Daffyd had several slabs of the dried beef and a warm sour ale that Anna forwent in favor of a vinegary red wine.

'Lady,' ventured Daffyd, sitting on one side of the wobbly trestle table, 'be it safe for you to remain here?'

Anna finished a mouthful of the stale and almost musty bread before answering. 'Everywhere in Defalk is as safe as anywhere else, I think.'

'That be an odd way of putting it,' mused the violist, his mouth partly full. 'Odd and true. But no great comfort.'

'Life isn't meant for comfort, sometimes. Especially if you want to do something.' Anna took a tiny sip of the acid-bitter wine. 'You just wanted to avenge your father, didn't you? And you got me, and look where we are.'

'Never thought I'd be a player for a sorceress in Falcor.'

'I never thought I'd be one.'

Daffyd looked at her for a moment. 'There be many here who would rather you be more, than less.'

Anna swallowed. Even Daffyd? 'I am a woman, Daffyd, and your sister's consort had troubles with that.'

'He was no true man.'

At the creaking of the door, Anna glanced up to see a handful of players filing into the room. Fiena was the second one, and, as Anna's eyes fell on the strawberry-blonde, the Prophet's player looked down.

'Aye, an' we know where that mirror looked,' muttered Daffyd. 'Strange times, indeed.'

The five other players gathered at the far end of the second table, eating silently, while Anna and Daffyd quickly finished their food.

Outside, Daffyd nodded and said, his voice muffled by the continuing traffic in the courtyard, 'Best ye do what needs to be done. No sense in being . . . well . . . the great mountain cats must die in their own skins. Sorceresses, too.'

'Thank you.' Anna thought she knew what he meant. She had lots of cheerleaders, but then, she'd always wanted to be onstage, rather than in the audience. Now, she had little choice.

As she walked toward the tower, more supply wagons, and more yelling teamsters, seemed to appear, but Anna saw no familiar faces among the Neserean guards posted around the courtyard.

Skent nodded as she entered the tower and gestured to the sandy-haired page beside him. 'Lady Anna, this is Resor.'

'You're from the main part of the hall? Skent had said you were working here now.'

'Yes, Lady Anna.' Resor measured Anna with his eyes, appraisingly, yet warily.

'You wonder how one small woman can create consternation?' She tried to keep the laugh light.

'Not many as would call you small, Lady Anna, either in stature or deeds.' Resor nodded his head. 'Some say you have claimed Defalk as your home, having no way to return to your own.'

'They do?' Anna smiled. 'What do you think, Resor?'

'I would beg your indulgence, Lady Anna.'

The sorceress pondered for a moment, then responded. 'There are sayings where I come from. "Home is where the heart is." And "Actions speak louder than words." I hope I have acted correctly.' Anna turned and started up the stairs.

'. . . no answer . . .' muttered Resor

'Has she ever raised a hand against any of Defalk?' asked Skent. 'Ever?'

'Oh . . .'

Skent was too bright and too vocal, Anna reflected. Still, he had spunk, and he'd managed to survive. Both said something. She walked past her landing and up to the top level, where she rapped on the door.

'Who be it?'

'Anna.'

Essan opened the door herself.

Anna raised her eyebrows.

'Now they have gone and taken Synondra. They say that the lady Cyndyth needs her – as if I do not?' Essan snorted, but her eyes were damp. 'Come in, if the mess will not bother you. I am old, too old for cleaning and other such foolishness.' She trudged back to her chair and sank into it.

Anna had not been able to halt her stiffening at the mention of Cyndyth and Synondra, but she slipped into the room, closed the door and made her way to the other chair. What could she say? Especially with all the players and Menares around a mirror, scanning the whole liedburg? 'I just wanted to thank you for your courtesy the other day.' She paused, then added, 'I will have to repay your

warmth and courtesy in another way, but as would your
daughter I will.'

'Now . . . do not go upsetting an old woman.' Tears seeped
from the corners of Essan's eyes. 'You are a gracious lady,
taking care to talk to me when few will, and you being
from afar.'

Gracious? It was more a cross between being stubborn,
a damned fool, and terrified. 'You are too kind, lady.'

Essan's eyes crossed to the wall mirror, then back to Anna,
before the older woman took a handkerchief and blew her
nose, loudly. Then she said, 'I am sickly, and tired, and you
are kind to look in on me. Best you go before you catch my
malady.'

'As you wish, lady.' Anna rose. 'Perhaps I can come again
before long and call upon you or your friend Nelmor.'

'He would be glad, I am sure. Now . . . off with you.'

Anna bowed and left, gently closing the door and walking
down to her own quarters. This time the room appeared
untouched, but she dropped the new bolt in place, then
walked to the window. She looked out, down at the portcullis
gate and the rows of tents beyond the walls. Thousands of
men, and she thought spells would work?

The sorceress smiled. Was that to cover the fears within,
the fear of what she must do, and what she might become?

103

FALCOR, DEFALK

'You are sure she plans nothing?' Behlem paces across
the sitting room, resplendent in his formal blue-and-cream
uniform.

'We have exhausted all your players using the mirror to
watch her every move. Yesterday, she went to see Hanfor.

He was scrupulously polite and excused himself after but a few moments. She ate with her player, and they talked of nothing. She passed a few words with the pages, and then stopped to see Lady Essan, who rather bluntly suggested that the sorceress leave, even after Lady Anna made overtures to her.'

'And today?'

'Much the same. She practiced upon her instrument, but said no spells. She made another overture to Lady Essan, which was rejected. She ate with her player, and they talked of music that was not linked to spells – apparently that is possible in the mist worlds, even with words. She groomed her mount, walked around the upper battlements of the north tower, then washed up—'

'How does she look out of those riding clothes?' Behlem grinned.

'She is beautiful, perhaps even as beautiful as the lady Cyndyth, in a different way.' Menares flushes, then clears his throat. 'Then she washed up and cast a small spell to clean and press that green gown she brought back from Mencha—'

'So she plans to wear a gown tonight,' muses Behlem. 'Good.'

'You ordered her to,' points out the counselor.

'She is obeying. That is good.' Behlem paces toward the window again. 'So I will inform everyone that she is leaving on the following morn to rebuild the old sorcerer's place – Loiselle or whatever it's called. Will that be enough?'

Menares spreads his hands. 'Even if the assassins fail, they cannot be traced to you – or Cyndyth – and she is out of here. If she survives, you call on her to repulse the next attacks of the Evult. She will.' Menares shrugs. 'You cannot lose, sire. She either dies or replaces thousands of armsmen.'

'What if she throws in with Ebra?' The Prophet pauses by the shuttered window.

Menares laughs. 'She cannot. The Evult hates her, and he

hates women. Those lands are surrounded by your holdings
in Defalk, and only Ebra is close.'

'I still worry about the old man, and the lord-pretender.'
Behlem turns toward the center of the room and fingers his
beard again.

'Lord Barjim's brat is twelve years old, and Lord Jecks
has all of tenscore in armsmen and levies. Remember, Jecks
sent a messenger and met with her in a open field without
weapons. That does not sound like they are exactly close.
Also, the lady Anna is clearly from a place where intrigue is
seldom practiced. She is most straightforward, even blunt.'

'That seems apparent.' Behlem straightens his uniform. 'It
nears the glass when we formally bestow the lands upon the
lady Anna.'

'And your officers will understand that the private pres-
entation, announced later at the dinner, effectively terminates
her service as the equivalent of an armsman.'

'Exactly.' Behlem smiles. 'So does Cyndyth.'

The counselor nods. 'That is good.'

'You do not know how good. No ... do not respond,
Menares. Not a word.' Behlem's hand touches the gold hilt
of the ceremonial blade.

104

After running through a full set of vocalises, Anna took down
the green recital gown from the corner wall pegs. She didn't
have to struggle into it. She didn't even need the longline bra.
In fact, she had wondered if the gown would be too large,
but it wasn't – even though she knew she was slimmer. Was
she more muscular? Or had she subconsciously tailored it
with her cleaning-and-pressing spell? After dressing, she
tried more vocalises, but the gown let her breathe easily,
unlike when she had worn it in Ames.

She looked in the mirror, but couldn't see any real difference. The gown fit, almost perfectly, and she knew it would have the desired effect. Her eyes dropped to the open note on the table.

She was to meet with the Prophet in the small receiving hall – the note from Menares was quite specific – and then proceed to the main hall for the dinner. She was not to approach the Prophet during the dinner itself. One way or another, that would not be a problem.

Beside the open note was a sealed one, with the name *Hanfor* on the outside. What it said was simple enough, just requesting that the overcaptain meet the sorceress outside the small receiving hall following her meeting with the Prophet in order that she might express her gratitude in an open and proper fashion.

Thunk!

'Coming.'

Anna turned and picked up the lutar case, careful to hold it away from the gown's skirts. The sealed sheet was in her other hand. When she opened the door, the dark-haired page stood on the landing. His eyes widened as Anna stepped out.

'Ah ... Lady Anna. You ...' Skent blushed.

Anna touched his shoulder. 'You're good for a lady's ego. Thank you.' She paused. 'Would you please carry this for me?'

The page looked at the lutar case, then took it, even as he said, 'Of course.'

'Is Birke below? Or Resor?'

'They both are.'

'Good. I have a message for Birke to deliver.' Anna went down the stairs carefully, although she wore the green dress slippers she had created, rather than the heels. She wasn't used to heels anymore, and the gown didn't drag with the slippers – another change? Or was she somewhat taller?

Both Birke and Resor gaped as had Skent when she turned the corner and came down the last steps to the main level.

Anna handed the folded and sealed sheet of paper to the redhead. 'This is to be delivered directly and immediately to Overcaptain Hanfor. You are to hand it to him directly. Dire consequences will befall you or anyone else if it does not go to his hand. Remember,' Anna smiled, 'it is from a sorceress.'

Birke looked at the envelope and gulped.

'Thank you, Birke.' Her voice softened, and she offered a smile, though her heart was pounding, as it always had prior to a performance, and this was going to be quite a performance if she could pull it off.

'. . . is beautiful . . .' murmured Resor.

'. . . got to get going . . .'

The sorceress hoped Birke would have no trouble finding the overcaptain, but if he did not, she would go solo.

For once, all the lamp mantles in the hall's corridors were clean and shimmered with the flames of trimmed and lit lamp-wicks. Armsmen in clean uniforms were positioned at every corner, standing stiffly – or relatively stiffly, Anna reflected.

A pair of guards and the ubiquitous Giellum were drawn up outside the small receiving hall.

Anna smiled at Giellum. 'Is the Prophet ready?'

'He said to show you in, lady.'

'A moment.' Anna turned to Skent. 'This case is important, young man. You wait right here with this until I summon you. It probably won't be long.' She forced a smile. 'Certainly no longer than until the dinner itself will begin. It is part of the ceremony after I meet with the Prophet. Don't go anywhere.' Anna looked over at Giellum. 'Make sure he doesn't, Giellum. The Prophet would be displeased, and so would I.'

Both nodded.

'As soon as the doors open, you be ready with this. Do you understand?'

'Yes, Lady Anna.' Skent nodded seriously, tightening his grip on the brown leather handles.

'Good.' Anna glanced at Giellum.

The young armsman and de facto herald opened the door. 'The lady Anna, as summoned by the Prophet, Lord of Defalk, Sovereign of Neserea, and Protector and Prophet of Music.'

Anna blanked her face and entered the long and narrow room.

Behlem stood before a high-backed and gilded wooden chair. A raven-haired woman sat in gown of brilliant blue in a lower-backed but also-gilded chair to the left of Behlem's. Cyndyth's eyes fixed on Anna as the sorceress stepped forward and as the door closed behind her. On right side of the dais stood Menares, in dark Neserean blue. On the left, beside Cyndyth, stood Hanfor, in a formal blue uniform.

Behlem smiled broadly as Anna approached. She stopped and curtsied – à la Metropolitan Opera, Anna reflected to herself, all style and no heart. She stood and waited.

'Menares has informed you, Lady Anna, that you are gifted, for your life, the estates and lands of the late Lord Brill?'

'Your grace is most kind,' Anna murmured, her heart pounding, almost hoping that Behlem would provoke her, wondering if she could do what was necessary if he did not.

'This strikes me as a most reasonable compromise,' Behlem continued. 'You have rendered me service in your efforts against the Ebran forces, but those services have been costly in other ways.' The Prophet provided a condescending smile, the kind she hated.

'First, the road to Mencha and the only good ford across the Chean have been greatly damaged. Second, the flow of the river has diminished and that has reduced the harvest. Third, there is the devastation to Sorprat and to Falcor itself.'

Anna waited. Hanfor's face was weathered stone. Menares looked grave, as if trying to emulate some great jurist. Cyndyth smiled, faintly, triumphantly.

'I would talk about the devastation wrought by the great flood. Could you not have stopped this?' asked Behlem.

'They say you are the greatest sorceress in the history of Liedwahr.'

'Your trust in my abilities is most touching, your majesty,' Anna said with a smile, but not taking her eyes off either the Prophet or Cyndyth. 'I am one person. I cannot be in two places at one time.'

'Then it is for the best.' Behlem nodded. 'I would request that, tomorrow morn, you make your way to Mencha to take possession of your holdings. You may take all that you require, and your player, and any of your personal guard that may choose to accompany you. Like all lords, you will pay liedgeld, but because your lands have been neglected, not until after the next harvest.'

'Is that all?' Anna asked.

'All? You have been rewarded, rewarded beyond the dreams of most singers or sorceresses.' Behlem looked incredulous. 'Do not press me, sorceress.'

'Nor me . . .' murmured Cyndyth.

Menares shook his head minutely.

Anna sighed, hummed one note, and sang, full-voice:

> 'Prophet strong, prophet wrong,
> turn to flame with this song.
> Singing turn, music burn,
> die the death you've earned!'

'No! You bitch!' Behlem stumbled forward, his right hand groping for the ceremonial blade for a moment before he began to tear at his uniform. Then slowly, like a falling tree in a forest fire, he toppled slowly.

Even as she stepped to her left, Anna felt like retching, both at the shrieks of agony, and the stench of burned meat. Instead she gathered herself together, as cold inside as Behlem was hot, hummed again and sang.

'Scheming lady, scheming wrong
turn to fire with this song.
Your schemes have you burned,
die the death you've earned!'

Cyndyth stared for a moment, then opened her mouth, rising and lurching toward the sorceress, but she, too, flared into flame, and then toppled into a burning charcoaled heap.

Anna swayed, but managed to stay on her feet, swallowing the bile in her throat.

The old advisor – Menares – opened his mouth.

'Don't,' Anna croaked.

Menares shut his mouth.

Anna turned to the overcaptain. 'Will you serve me, Hanfor?'

Hanfor stood for a long moment. 'Do you threaten me, lady?'

'No. I am asking, because you have ability, and because I'd rather there not be any more killing and deaths. Defalk has had enough, and there's no one left capable of commanding armsmen here.'

'I will serve you,' Hanfor bowed, 'so long as I do not have to lead troops into Neserea.'

'Thank you.' Anna appreciated his wording. 'I suppose you had best gather the officers immediately in the main dining hall. Do not mention the Prophet yet. I will announce that.'

'What . . . of me?' Menares croaked.

'Come along, and say not a word,' snapped Hanfor, touching his blade.

Anna opened the door, and motioned Menares out, glancing at Hanfor. She let him close the heavy door.

'Let no one enter,' Hanfor ordered Giellum.

The young armsman's eyes flickered, and his nose twitched, and he swallowed. 'Yes, ser.'

Across the hall, Birke stood looking around, note in his hand. Then he rushed for Hanfor and pressed the paper into the overcaptain's hand. Hanfor glanced at Anna. She smiled briefly, then took the lutar case from Skent, as

Hanfor opened and read the note, which he then tucked into his belt.

'The Prophet has commanded that all enter the dining hall,' Anna said quietly. She took the lutar case and extracted the instrument, then handed the case back to Skent.

As she walked toward the open double doors thirty yards down the corridor, she could hear low voices, and voices not so low. Her mouth was dry, and her heart pounded. Was it murder? Of course it was. Was it necessary? Lord, how many people justified themselves that way? She kept walking.

The great hall was already half filled with the Prophet's officers when Anna walked to the dais. Holding the lutar, she glanced around, waiting.

'. . . beautiful . . .'

'. . . beautiful like a sharp blade with no hilt . . . no matter how you handle her . . . get sliced six ways to market . . .'

'. . . never seen her in a gown . . . looks different . . .'

'. . . like her better in the field . . .'

More officers entered, then Hanfor, and the doors closed. Hanfor moved across the room, and the officers parted as he neared Anna. He offered a quick bow. 'They are all here, I think.'

'Thank you. Stand behind me. Please.'

The weathered officer frowned, but obeyed.

Anna's fingers flicked three loud chords, and the murmurs died. Would she have enough time before someone charged, or would her reputation hold them at bay? She slipped into Rosina's words quickly, almost effortlessly.

> *'Ma se mi tocano dov'e il mio debole,*
> *sarouna vipera, sa ro,*
> *e cento trapole*
> *prima di cedere*
> *faro giocar, faro giocar . . .'*

Then she followed up with the revised version of the spell used on both Virkan and Madell.

'Captains here, captains strong,
keep me safe with this song.
Captains warm, captains cold,
faithful be till dead and old.'

Even before she stopped singing, Zealor stepped forward, trembling, and opened his mouth. Then a violent shaking took him, and he collapsed on the floor writhing. Soon . . . he was still.

Anna nodded. So much hate that his system could not stand the conflict.

She turned to the others. 'As I am sure some of you know, Delor attempted to have me killed. Don't believe that I didn't understand that Behlem kept others around to try again once I had defeated the dark ones.'

She paused. She was sounding stupid, getting ahead of herself, and her mouth was still like cotton. 'The lord Behlem had requested I leave Falcor and planned to have me killed once I left tomorrow. He and his consort killed and tortured innocent women. She set at least two assassins after me. Yet I never opposed him. Not until today. All rulers do some terrible things, but Lord Behlem would have become little different from the Evult of Ebra.' She swallowed. 'Those of you who know me, you know I do not like killing. Those who know me know I do not speak in fancy phrases. I have done what I thought best. I killed many to save you, and I have destroyed the Prophet and his Consort to save Defalk and perhaps Liedwahr. I don't know, but I have done what I felt was right.'

Silence filled the hall, the silence of men stunned beyond immediate belief. Men who could not believe a woman was cold-blooded and direct enough to kill their ruler and face them.

The sorceress looked out across the faces of the officers, seeing Alvar's swarthy face, and Spirda's strained pale face. 'I do not intend you harm, as most of you must know by now. There are some who have meant me harm, and the spells were to keep them from harming me. Any of you may leave, with your armsmen, but I command those who do depart to leave Defalk and never to return, save with my written permission.

'Now,' Anna gestured to the tables, 'there was a victory. You have paid for it. Best you enjoy it.' She turned to Hanfor. 'It is time I leave the hall.'

'Lady Anna!'

A swarthy figure made his way through the stunned officers – Alvar.

'I be no lord. I be no overcaptain. I captained the lead lancers. I watched the lady Anna stand in a dirty trench with a player and three guards and face ten thousand Ebrans alone. I watched her almost die from that effort, and I watched Lord Behlem insult her.

'I talked to others. They watched her stand on a broken wall and try to hold back the Ebrans when all others fled. She near died then, too, and was carried away 'cause she spent herself to save others.' Alvar coughed. 'I be from Firscor, and for generations, my folk be there. I never saw a lord put himself in front of his men one time. The lady did twice. That be all I have to say.' He knelt.

Anna's eyes burned, but she took Alvar's hand and insisted he rise.

'Lady Anna ... Lady Anna ...'

The murmured words were not a booming acclamation. Neither were they bitter, but an acknowledgment that she was Lady Anna, worthy to be called such.

'Eat and enjoy it,' Hanfor said. He turned to Alvar. 'It's your job to get them not to waste good food. I will return shortly.'

'Yes, ser.' Alvar smiled. 'You heard the overcaptain! To the tables.'

As Anna and Hanfor stepped into the corridor outside the hall, followed by a dazed-looking Menares, Giellum knelt, as did the two pages. The two guards looked to Hanfor.

'The lady Anna holds Falcor,' Hanfor said, 'and all the Prophet's officers support her. You guard her, with your lives, or I'll have them.'

The two young guards blinked.

'You heard them acclaim Lady Anna.'

The guards' faces relaxed. 'Lady Anna.'

Anna turned to Skent and Birke, still kneeling. 'Up. You need to spread the word. Just what the overcaptain said. I hold Falcor. No more, no less.'

As the two pages scurried off, and as overcaptain, the sorceress, and the white-haired counselor walked toward the receiving room, followed by the two guards, Hanfor said, 'Neatly done, my lady. Are you going to claim any special title? The Sorceress of Defalk?'

'No.'

Hanfor's face blanked.

'It's not time for a woman to be lord, not officially. Young Jimbob will have to be lord.'

'He is but a child.' Hanfor stroked his beard. 'Yet your words about women have a bitter wisdom.'

'This poor land doesn't need another lineage.' Anna looked at Hanfor. 'My children are worlds away, and I can have no more. For now, I am acting as regent – in the absence of anyone in the lineage of Defalk.' Anna smiled. 'Do you mind serving an acting regent, Hanfor? I will release you . . .'

'I will stay. My life would be worthless in Neserea.' The weathered face cracked into a smile. 'Matters here will be interesting, anyway.'

'You will have much to do. We need to summon Lord Jecks . . . and take care of all sorts of details, such as the transport and burial of Lord Behlem and Lady Cyndyth.' She nodded toward Menares. 'It might be best if most of the armsmen, particularly the Prophet's Guard, were returned to Esaria as soon as possible to ensure the safety of Rabyn. Isn't he the Prophet now?'

'Ah . . . that would have to rest on the lords of Neserea, Lady Anna,' mumbled Menares.

'You would know better than I, but shouldn't young Rabyn be offered some protection?'

'I would be happy . . .' stuttered Menares.

Anna shook her head. 'Your assistance will be needed here, Menares. And I suspect you will be far safer here. Far safer.' She paused, shaking her head. 'There's so much, and I don't know where to start. I feel you're playing a deeper game. I don't know who else is involved, but I'd suggest you tell me. Before I use sorcery to find out.' Her eyes bored into his.

'The Council of Wei . . . they . . . my sister . . . the story is long . . .'

Hanfor's mouth opened, then closed with a smile.

'You work for me,' Anna said. 'Hanfor and me. Or you leave tonight for Wei.'

Menares gulped and looked down the corridor. 'I work for you . . . Lady Anna.'

'Do not forget it. Ever.'

'No, Lady Anna.'

'Do you intend to take the lord's quarters?' asked Hanfor.

'Not tonight. Maybe not ever.'

The overcaptain raised his eyebrows.

'I'm too tired to worry. My own quarters are comfortable enough, and,' Anna smiled, 'I can defend them.' Her fingers tightened around the lutar. 'Later, I might get a room with a bath. Later. I haven't slept much lately.'

'That will not get any better,' offered the overcaptain.

'No. It won't. But I hope other people will sleep.' She turned toward the north tower, and Hanfor turned with her.

'You left some confused officers,' he pressed.

'I know. I'm not demanding loyalty. They gave it to the Prophet. Most of them should go back to Neserea and defend his son. He's their duty now.'

'Can I tell them that?'

Anna rubbed her forehead. 'Yes. I should have thought of that. I should have. There's so much I should have thought about.'

'You have made a start, and that is more than most.' Hanfor

inclined his head, with a look at Menares who tagged along like a lost old dog. 'You can't think of everything, lady.'

I'm going to have to, especially now. Especially from now on.

After Hanfor left, with the two guards remaining outside her door, Anna shook her head. Why? She still didn't know exactly why. Was she power-hungry, just like every other woman who protested loudly that only men were? Or was she just tired of reacting when she had the chance to do more?

She didn't know, really, and she might not ever. *We all deceive ourselves, with the best of motives.*

In time, she slept, most uneasily, waking and wondering how many things she had forgotten and left undone, then dozing.

105

Anna stood at the tower window in the stillness of dawn. Could she have somehow just exiled the two? Then the officers would have remained loyal. Loyalties were more personal than national on Erde, and only death dissolved them. Sandy had argued that modern war was insane, that thousands died because no one would kill a madman who happened to be a ruler. But Behlem hadn't been a madman. He and his consort had just wanted to kill Anna, or use her until she died for their purposes.

She shook her head and looked out beyond the walls at the lines of tents in the gray light. Now what?

Messengers to Lord Jecks, and to all the lords announcing her temporary regency. Should she invite them to Falcor? Was she prepared? Would they come?

First . . . Jecks.

And what about all the armed Nesereans? How could she

disarm that situation? Should she rely on the officers she had ensorcelled? That didn't feel right.

Anna turned back to the basin. She heard occasional clankings and that meant she had guards. With a sigh, she yanked the bellpull.

Rather than stand in a thin gown on the landing with two strange guards, she waited until the door knocker thunked.

Resor and Birke and Skent all stood on the landing, crowded indeed with three pages and two guards.

'How about some buckets of water and some breakfast?'

'Yes, Lady Anna!' The three chorused before departing on their errands.

The guards, if they looked at her disheveled state, did so so surreptitiously that she did not notice.

After eating and washing, and dressing in clean riding clothes, she sent Skent to request Hanfor's presence. While she waited she began to draft her letter to Lord Jecks. That had to be handled quickly so that the message was traveling while she attended to other matters.

Hanfor was punctual, and she had barely finished her proposed note to Lord Jecks before he arrived, with another thunk of the knocker.

'How did it go last night?' Anna asked, after she had closed the door, and gestured toward one of the chairs.

'Well enough,' Hanfor shrugged, sitting on the front edge of his seat. 'You were right about not being there. Most appreciated the freedom to talk. Except they whispered at first, as if Alvar or Spirda or I might overhear something.'

'And?'

'They are still confused.'

Anna shook her head. 'From what I've read, and heard, this sort of thing happens here. Why are they confused? Behlem tried to conquer a neighbor, and he didn't succeed. The sorcery might be new . . .'

'It be not that. They are not used to that kind of directness from a woman. Ladies are either not heard, or they are like Cyndyth or the bitches of the south.'

Anna raised her eyebrows.

'Ranuak,' he explained. 'They spent much time talking to Himar. He confused them more, the honest wright, for he confirmed what Alvar said.'

'Will they go home peacefully?'

Hanfor snorted. 'All will go home peacefully. Only poor officers would want a fight against a sorceress. But Konsstin will hate you. Nubara will see to that.'

'Nubara?' Again, Anna felt in over her head, with names she had never heard.

'He was Konsstin's envoy to Neserea. He came to Falcor with Lady Cyndyth, but he and his retinue left at dawn this morning. In great haste, I might add.'

Anna nodded. 'The assassins?'

'I would expect so.'

'How is Menares?'

'He appears wrung and plucked with dissonance. He will obey you, though, for no others would have him.'

'If his deviousness serves me, fine, but I'll need other counselors, too.' Anna brushed back the blonde curls that were getting far too long. 'And what about Behlem? Shouldn't the bodies go back to Neserea?'

Hanfor nodded. 'I put Himar in charge of that. That detail of lancers will leave this afternoon, but he will stay. He asked to. The sooner the coffins are out of Defalk, the better.'

'All of their personal servants go also,' Anna added. She handed the two sheets of paper to Hanfor. 'I thought I would send this to Lord Jecks. What do you think?'

'It is not—'

'Hanfor. How can we work together if you're not free to be honest with me?'

The overcaptain read slowly, and Anna thought, wondering about what else she had forgotten. She needed to act quickly, before people got ideas, while they were still stunned.

Perhaps some sorcery in parts of Falcor – to rebuild some of the damage from the floods?

'Will he believe you?' asked Hanfor.

'We have met twice. I could have destroyed him the second time, and the Prophet would have preferred that I did. He knows that.'

'Then . . . he may come. But if he does not?'

'I must go to him.'

'You feel strongly.'

'About some things.' *About a lot of things, these days. Or is it that I'm letting myself feel strongly?*

Hanfor waited.

'That leaves one problem – how to deal with the armsmen. I think I should talk to them.'

'That could be dangerous. What do you gain?'

'Respect.'

'Is respect from those who will soon be gone worth the risk?' asked Hanfor gently.

'That's not it. If I stand up to all those armsmen, then . . .' Anna shrugged. She couldn't explain, but somehow it was important, and not just to her. It had to do with the people of Defalk and the armsmen who would guard the liedburg and . . . everything else.

'What will you do if one expresses open disrespect? Best you think of that. And the Prophet's Guard . . .' Hanfor paused, then said. 'Many are like Zealor.'

'A compromise,' Anna said. 'All except the Prophet's Guard? I ride Farinelli, and I carry the lutar.'

Hanfor frowned again.

'It's a feeling, and it's important.'

'I would not go against strong feelings,' answered Hanfor in his dry voice. 'Not those of a sorceress.'

Anna smiled, briefly.

'There is a question of the banner,' Hanfor offered.

'Banner?'

'Whose ensign shall the liedburg fly? Do you wish to design one?'

'No.' Anna frowned. 'Is there one of Lord Barjim's?'

'That would not be proper ... He no longer lives.'

'Was one ever designed for Jimbob?'

'I would not think so.'

'All right. Put a black border on Lord Barjim's and fly it. Would that work?'

'For a time.'

'And have someone design one for Jimbob, and then have them add whatever device is necessary to indicate a regent for him.'

Hanfor nodded slowly. 'You remain tied to that view?'

'I feel that it's right, and that it will work.'

'Will Lord Jecks and the other lords accept that?'

'I don't know,' admitted Anna, 'but it seems they would prefer that to losing everything.'

'Lords are not always reasonable,' said Hanfor.

'That's true. We'll wait and see. Now ... what about seeing the armsmen?'

'You still believe—'

'Yes.'

Hanfor shrugged. 'Then I would do it quickly, without notice.'

'Fine. I'll meet you in the stable shortly. Or is that too soon?'

'Lady Anna, the sooner this idea is past, the happier I will be.' Hanfor rose, and Anna escorted him to the door.

Open disrespect? What could she do?

For a time, she pondered, then finally jotted down something on a scrap of paper. She tried the chords, and said the words, separately, several times before she was satisfied.

Then she gathered the lutar into its case and stepped out onto the landing. Anna carried the lutar, feeling almost self-conscious with the pair of guards tramping down the stone steps behind her.

It got worse as she crossed the courtyard. Although there were but a handful of armsmen, and Behlem's players, standing about, all conversation ceased. She could hear the echo of her boots and those of the guards, and it seemed like every eye was on her.

She'd thought that the attention a ruler received might be like being onstage, but she didn't like the idea of being onstage all the time. *You'd better get used to it*, she told herself as she entered the stable.

'Lady Anna.' Tirsik almost went to his knees.

'Enough,' she said softly. 'I'm the same Lady Anna I always was. How's Farinelli?'

'He is as usual – feisty to the rest of us.'

'Good. I think.' Anna paused and drew the stablemaster aside. 'Hanfor is looking for good Defalkan armsmen. We need them. Do you know of any?'

'Me?'

'Tirsik, I've tried to tell everyone. I am an acting regent only, regent for young Jimbob. Defalk belongs to Defalk. Now . . . I'm going to groom Farinelli.'

Why was it that no one ever believed what she said?

Farinelli *whuff*ed and pranced sideways, as she set the lutar aside and opened the stall door.

'It's only been two days,' Anna remonstrated, as she ran the brush across her mount's shoulder.

The gelding *whuff*ed again.

'All right.'

The time seemed caught in molasses, and grooming Farinelli took forever, but Hanfor had barely arrived with Spirda and a full squad of guards when she led Farinelli out of the stables.

'. . . more of a lord than any of them . . .' murmured Tirsik.

She doubted that, even as she appreciated the sentiment.

'The officers are drawing up the ranks now,' Hanfor announced. 'They were not told why. I thought that was better.'

If he were right, Anna reflected it certainly was. If not, it made no difference.

Somewhere, in the corner of the courtyard, as various

armsmen and Behlem's players still watched silently, a
chicken *brawk*ed. Anna wanted to laugh. Only the chicken
had the right outlook. Life went on, and chickens *brawwk*ed,
and the sun turned things hotter, and sometimes the wind
blew, no matter who held what city or liedstadt.

She mounted and rode toward the gate, Spirda pale-faced
and to her left, Hanfor to her right, the squad behind.

The portcullis was up, and Anna turned Farinelli across
the cracked and dried ground that had been mud.

'The first group there.'

Anna's eyes followed Hanfor's gesture.

She reined up Farinelli in front of the next line of tents,
her eyes going to the walls of the liedburg, and then to the
loose formation of men.

'Armsmen! Ranks!'

Several armsmen slouched. One, at the end, spit on the
ground.

Anna picked up the lutar, concentrating on the two.

> 'Armsmen lax, armsmen strong,
> turn to order with this song.
> Armsmen lax, armsmen bold,
> respect and fear my hold!'

Both men stiffened, and Anna could sense the fear, fear
from more than the two.

'I could have turned you two into ashes. I didn't, but
I could have. Ask around. Ask what happened to Lord
Behlem, or Captain Zealor, or Captain Delor. I don't sneak
around. I also don't kill people for no reason, but I will be
obeyed.

'Some of you may have seen me before. Some may not.
You have heard, or been told that I hold the liedburg, and
that your officers respect my claim. I am not asking you
change your loyalties or theirs. I am telling you face-to-face
that times have changed. I risked my life to stop the Ebrans,
and that saved many of your lives. I could treat you as I did

them. I will not. You invaded our land. That choice was not yours, but the Prophet's. He has paid for that. Too often the everyday armsman pays for others' mistakes. Instead, you will have to march home, without dying in a battle you did not choose. I'm telling you that because you deserve to hear it from me.' Anna nodded, and waited a moment, trying to gauge the reaction. 'That's all.'

'. . . guts . . . where they find her . . .'

'. . . keep her and the dissonant Prophet . . .'

'. . . nervy bitch . . .'

'. . . shit . . . four weeks marching for shit . . .'

Anna couldn't expect to like all that she heard, but she wished, knowing that it was a futile hope, that the armsmen would see that she was as straightforward as anyone. She pursed her lips and turned Farinelli toward the next line of tents.

'One down,' murmured Spirda, his eyes raking across the tents.

Fhurgen and Mysar followed, the rest of the squad behind.

Anna looked over the next row of blank faces and wanted to scream.

Maybe Hanfor was right. Maybe, but she had to try. Her mouth was dry as cotton, and she swallowed as she drew up Farinelli for another performance, another duty.

106

WEI, NORDWEI

'What is it now?' asks Ashtaar.

'Gretslen, my lady. She insists that she must see you now.'

The words tremble from the guard's mouth.

'Show her in.' Ashtaar set the bed tray aside and props

herself up with the pillows, then straightens the coverlet.

Gretslen steps into the bedchamber, eyes downcast.

Ashtaar waits.

'I fear great troubles, honored Ashtaar.' Gretslen's voice is hard, hard with the effort of suppressing uneasiness.

'Don't tell me your fears, not so early in the morning. Tell me the facts.'

Gretslen swallows. 'Last eve, from what I scried, the blonde sorceress killed Lord Behlem and Lady Cyndyth and now holds Falcor.'

'Are you certain?'

'Yes, Ashtaar.'

'How did a stranger who knows no lords, bears no blade, and beds no man, manage this feat? With what sorcery did she manage this extraordinary occurrence?' Ashtaar's voice is dry.

'I do not know. I have tried to discover how, but there were no great spells, and no large chord tremors.' Gretslen licks her lips. 'There are always tremors around her, all the time, and we cannot . . .'

'I understand that. No large disruptions of the harmonies?'

'None.'

'And she holds Falcor?'

'The ensign of Lord Barjim flies, bordered in black, and already Neserean armsmen and wagons march westward.'

Ashtaar shakes her head.

'It is most puzzling, and we cannot determine how this occurred. Her chamber remains a small tower room, and yet the overcaptain of the Nesereans serves her, as does Lord Behlem's counselor.'

'Your influence remains, then?'

'I do not know. That mirror is shattered.'

The spymistress raises her eyebrows.

'She has discovered our influence, I fear.'

The spymistress smiles. 'It is extraordinary, and unforeseen, but to our advantage. Rather than Behlem uniting two countries into one stronger land, we have a stranger ruling Defalk, and that is bound to create more dissension. She must still face the Evult, who is gathering yet another army, and she has an occupying army she must see out of Defalk – leaving with no defense but her sorcery, and she cannot be in more than one place at a time.' She laughs. 'Unforeseen, but not unfortunate. Not unfortunate. Now go.'

Gretslen bows and turns.

107

Anna looked out the window into the gray of dawn. She'd never awakened so early so often. Did it come with trying to run a country? She wasn't so much running it, she felt, as it was running her. Somehow, she had to get a better handle on things. She took a deep breath.

The view from the room that had formerly been a guest suite beside Alasia's private study was uninspiring, just the merchant quarters beyond the south wall, but it met Anna's needs – the bath, a large wardrobe in the bath, and access through a single heavy door with a large iron bolt. The double bed was wider, and there was a writing table, and both a small mirror in the main chamber, and a full-length one in the bath, plus a small conference table with chairs, and two large dressers. The tub still had to be filled by hand, but it did have a drain. The night before, Anna had enjoyed her first bath in weeks, even if it had taken sorcery to heat the water.

In the courtyard below, another section of officers readied their mounts for the long march back to Neserea. Already, the number of tents in the flat north of the liedburg had been more than halved, and Anna would be happier once the Nesereans were gone.

The last two days had gone by all too quickly, but she

kept feeling as though she were forgetting too many details – far too many.

She turned to the writing table and the letter upon it – one of the reasons she was up early. If her effects succceded, she would need to rest.

The second letter to Elizabetta was brief – from what she felt and what she had learned from the old volumes in the near-abandoned liedburg library, the stronger the sorceress, the greater the heat and power involved with opening what the older volumes called a 'weltsperre.' She walked to the table and reread her words.

Elizabetta—

From what I am learning and being told, sending these will get harder and harder.

I have enclosed more gold coins. They are for you and Mario – no one else. I don't know law very well, but there is insurance for you both. Since there is no body – obviously you will have to wait to collect that. You may have to claim that I have died now. I don't know. I'm sure you can discuss that with your father – or any attorney if you prefer. The gold is to help in the meantime. I cannot send much, and I may not be able to send more, but I hope this arrives.

I love you both, and I did not choose to leave you
. . . All of you were special . . .

The sorceress sealed the envelope and set it on the table before the mirror. She picked up the lutar and began the chording, then the song to call up her daughter's image. The mists swirled, and Anna could feel heat radiating from the glass as the mirror showed Elizabetta lying in the guest bed, her eyes wide open.

Anna began to sing the sending spell. She was shaking by the time the envelope vanished, despite the full chording of the spell with the lutar, and the mirror was a flaming mass.

She set down the lutar, her head ringing, her legs tingling. She took a half step, and felt her legs crumple as the darkness swept across her. *Shit* . . .

It was full light when she woke again, her head pounding, her mouth dry as though it were stuffed with cotton. Her eyes burned when she opened them, and kept burning, needles jabbing into her skull.

After a time, she staggered toward the mirror, then stopped. There was no mirror, just charcoal and glassy slag on the stone floor.

How much longer could she even view her daughter, let alone send messages? Each time it seemed worse, and she'd waited weeks between messages.

She used the clean water in the washroom basin to wash her face, and she dressed slowly, pulling on the purple-shaded cotton riding trousers and shirt, topped with a darker purple vest she had discovered. She had gathered together some additional sets of shirts and trousers, and those, she had decided, would be her 'uniform' as regent – dressier than normal riding clothes. Except for special occasions when she might wear gowns, she wanted a comfortable but half stylish, no-nonsense look, for practical reasons, and since she had gained what support she had from being straightforward.

Skent was waiting with her breakfast tray when she pulled the bell cord.

'Just put it on the table there, Skent.'

'Yes, Lady Anna.' He kept his eyes away from the darkened mass on the floor.

'I'll need another mirror,' she said ruefully. 'Could you have someone find me one?'

Skent nodded.

Anna laid her list beside the tray, ready to read it as she ate and before she met with Menares and Hanfor. While she had managed to cross off some items from the top, she was adding to the bottom faster than she was managing the top – and that was with Hanfor, Alvar, Himar, and Menares all

helping. She forced herself to begin eating before she keeled
over again.

Skent remained standing by the table after setting the
tray in place. He licked his lips. 'Ah ... Lady Anna?'

'Yes?' she mumbled through a full mouth.

'You remember Lady Cataryzna?'

'Oh ...' Anna hadn't, not until Skent reminded her. 'Yes.'
'Is there ...?' The page looked at the polished stone
floor.

'I've been busy, Skent. I'll look into it, but I can't promise anything until I do.' Anna held up her hand. 'You'll
be able to see her, maybe more. I can't do everything
at once.'

'Thank you.' Skent looked both relieved and skeptical.

Anna wanted to sigh. Everyone wanted something, and
they wanted it *now*! Sorceress or not, she remained but one
person, and one with too much to learn. Still, after the door
closed and she sat at the table and had a long drink of water,
she added *Cataryzna/hostages?* to the list. After she finished
nearly half a loaf of bread, some sliced early apples, and
hard cheese, the throbbing in her head had dropped to a
dull pounding, and her eyes were only irritated, rather than
agonizing.

She added another item to the list – *ford at Sorprat*
– although she had no idea when she could get to that.
After a last swallow of water from her purified stock,
she stood, straightened her vest, and, list in hand, headed
out.

Now she had permanent guards by her bedroom, and
Fhurgen followed her whenever she left, which was probably a good idea – Hanfor's – since her mind was flitting
everywhere.

Hanfor and Menares waited for her in the small main-
floor receiving hall, now more of a formal conference room
with the addition of a large circular table and relatively
comfortable chairs. The dais remained, as did a single
high-backed gilt chair. Anna didn't feel all that comfortable

in the chair that was effectively a throne, but Hanfor and Daffyd had both suggested that she needed some trappings of power.

'Lady Anna . . .'

'My lady . . .'

Anna motioned for them to sit, took her own seat, and laid out the list. 'First, what problems have occurred since yesterday?'

'Tirsik found me this morning. We have but a week's supply of grain for the horses,' Hanfor said. 'He can buy more from local farmers, but . . . he needs gold.'

'I should have asked earlier. Gold – is there any? Didn't Behlem and Barjim have a treasury?'

'The paychests are in the strongroom,' Menares volunteered. 'And there was a small chest for expenses.'

'Who was in charge?'

Menares's face remained grave, blank.

'You were?'

'Yes, lady.'

'Are the chests still there?'

'The paychests are. I . . . ah . . .'

'—took the small one into personal custody for safekeeping? Do you still have it? Safe, I mean?' Anna asked pleasantly.

Menares nodded.

'Hanfor, we'll need trustworthy guards, and a lock that only you have the key to.'

'Me?'

'I can use sorcery, and no one else needs it.' Anna added *grain* to the bottom of the list.

'Were there any coins left from Lord Barjim?'

'Perhaps a score of golds in a small chest.' Menares added quickly, 'The chest and golds are still there.'

'How much is in those paychests?' Anna asked.

'Several months, perhaps,' offered the older counselor.

'Hanfor, tell the soldiers they will be paid for the next month—'

'When they reach Denguic,' interjected Hanfor. 'We need no disruptions here.'

'All right,' Anna agreed. 'Can we get it there for those who have already left?'

'Those are mostly all foot, and the lancers have to stay with them. The wagons should catch up. That highway's good, but it's still six days, maybe seven, by foot.'

'It's fair to keep the rest of the gold, isn't it? According to the way things go here?'

'You would have the right to keep it all,' said Menares.

'I think it's better to pay the armsmen what they are owed, but only that,' Anna said. 'That should leave us some to pay our own.' She turned to Hanfor. 'How is that coming?'

'Slowly. It will take time. There are nearly twentyscore who would claim service to you.'

'How many should we take?'

'Most of them, except those from the Prophet's Guard.'

Anna nodded. 'The grain. How many golds does Tirsik need?'

'He said that Jisplir had been giving him two golds a week.'

'Menares, when we're done, you get the expense chest and meet Hanfor in the pay strongroom.' She turned to Hanfor. 'Is this all right for now? You can't do it all forever, but ... for a few more days?'

'A paymaster?' Hanfor sighed. 'Responsible for the treasury of a whole land?'

'It'll make a good story someday.'

'You are a slavemaster, Lady Anna, but I will do it.' Hanfor grinned.

'Next ...' Anna looked at the list.

They met until nearly midday, when Anna stopped. 'That's more than enough. First, take care of the gold and the armsmen's pay, then the grain, and the payments to the cooks for supplies ...'

When Hanfor started to stand, Anna smiled. 'There's something else.'

'My lady, we cannot rebuild a land in a day.'

'This is simple. There are a number of women – hostages of sorts – housed in the south tower. They should have the freedom of the hall.' Anna rubbed her forehead. 'Bring them – no, have someone else bring them here first, though.'

'That we can do.' Hanfor nodded slowly. 'I feared you would ask for the market square to be rebuilt.'

'Perhaps we should,' the sorceress offered, deadpan.

Hanfor looked slowly at her. Finally, the weathered face split into a grin. 'You can be wicked, Lady Anna.'

'Not me.'

The de facto chief of staff and armsmen shook his head. 'I'll have Himar take care of the women.'

'Right after I grab something to eat.'

The sorceress wolfed down some cold beef tucked between black bread, some cheese, an apple, and more water, before returning to the receiving room.

Four women stood up from around the table as she entered.

'Lady Anna . . .'

'Sorceress . . .'

'Lady of Defalk . . .'

'Please sit down.' The sorceress walked to the dais and took the gilt chair, still not comfortable in what amounted to a throne, but trusting in Daffyd's and Hanfor's sense of the proper for Defalk. Then she studied the four women.

One was young and had straight blonde hair, square-cut just above her shoulders. Close beside her sat a narrow-faced and square-chinned woman in dark brown. Cataryzna and her aunt? Another woman, almost as young, but red-haired and freckled, sat on the far side of the table. The fourth was brown-haired and very pregnant.

'Which of you is Cataryzna?'

'I am,' answered the blonde.

'You are her aunt?' Anna asked.

'Yes. I am Drenchescha,' said the narrow-faced woman.

The sorceress turned her glance to the redhead.

'Lysara.'

'I am Wendella,' volunteered the pregnant woman. 'My consort is Dencer.'

Anna nodded. How Behlem or Barjim had gotten the woman was one question, but it certainly explained Dencer's nervousness when the sorceress had met the lord. 'You have all been hostages. I do not know all the reasons, but I do know some. You will have to remain in Falcor for at least a time, but I see no reason that you should be confined to the south tower. Your quarters will remain unchanged, but you now have the freedom of the hall, if you wish. I would ask that you remain within the walls.'

'Do you intend to keep us hostage?' asked Drenchescha.

'Until this morning, I only knew that you and Cataryzna were being held, and, honestly, I have been trying to undo the mess I found here.'

'Why are you flying Barjim's banner?' questioned Lady Wendella. 'He kept me here by trickery.'

Even if she were pregnant, Wendella and her attitude bothered Anna. 'I'm inclined to believe that was in response to Lord Dencer's trickery, but I will look into it. As for the banner, I am acting as regent for young Lord Jimbob, and the banner is the best we can do at the moment.' Anna didn't miss the knowing glance that passed between Lysara and Cataryzna, but she turned to the redhead. 'Why are you here?'

'I am the daughter of Lord Birfels of Abenfel.'

'You're Birke's sister?'

'Half sister,' Lysara corrected.

Anna wondered why Birke never mentioned his sister, or had the glances between the two pages been a warning to Skent not to mention Lysara? Things just kept getting more complicated. The sorceress stood. 'I was reminded of your situation only this morning, and I cannot do everything at once, but I did wish to give you a greater degree of freedom.'

'What if we leave the hall?' asked Wendella. 'What then?'

Anna frowned, then turned and sang softly, hoping she was not breaking the form too terribly:

> 'Wendella all too snide,
> never go the walls outside,
> unless I give you all my leave,
> and my pardon you receive.'

The sorceress smiled. 'You do not have my pardon or my leave.'

Wendella flushed. 'You're no better than either of those . . . men. You're a singer. A darksinger.'

Again, Cataryzna and Lysara exchanged glances.

'Defalk cannot afford treachery on its southern borders,' answered Anna. 'I tried to act in good faith, and you've attacked and accused me.' She shrugged. 'And the spell will hold as long as you live. So it wouldn't do much good to try to kill me, would it?'

Hatred poured from Wendella's eyes, before she looked away from Anna.

After the group had left, Anna sat for a time in the chair, collecting herself, glad she had a few moments before Lady Essan arrived. She thought she could work with Lysara and Cataryzna, but she'd need to talk with them alone, and she had neither the time nor the knowledge she needed.

'Lady Essan.' Giellum made the announcement, while Skent brought in the tray with the goblets and the amber brandy.

'Thank you,' Anna murmured to the page. She wondered if Skent had thought up the brandy or Lady Essan. Lady Essan, probably.

Anna rose and walked toward the older woman, leading her toward the nearest two chairs by the ancient, if slightly battered, inlaid wooden table.

Anna poured some of the amber brandy into the other's crystal goblet.

'My, and being served by a regent.' Essan took the goblet and sipped.

The sorceress refrained from wincing. 'Acting regent,' she said mildly.

'Careful you are being, and that be good.'

'It wasn't careful to take on Behlem.'

'What would you have of me?' asked Essan. 'Not that you be needing much.'

'I said you would be as my mother, and, while I may not always be able to take your counsel, I value it.' Anna waited, then added, 'I would also like to ask if you would wish to return to your former quarters.'

'The tower steps, though I walk them seldom, are hard on my bones.'

Anna nodded.

'What else have ye on your mind?' Essan laughed, almost a cackle. 'Even devoted daughters have ideas.'

Anna grinned briefly. 'Some questions.'

'Ask, sorceress-regent. For what I know I will answer.'

'Lady Wendella?'

'A true wench, even more devious than her consort. A tongue like a viper. Rumor has it she poisoned her own sister, who was betrothed first to Dencer. Her sire was Lord Mietch. He held the lands north of Abenfel. His eldest, Mietchel, now holds them.' Essan took another long swallow of the brandy.

'Abenfel – why both Birke and Lysara?'

'Lord Birfels had two consorts. Lysara was by his first, and most beloved. After Lady Trien died, he consorted again for sons. Birke is his eldest, but a younger son – his name I forget – lives at Abenfel.'

'So Barjim needed both as insurance?'

'Insurance?'

'Surety.'

'Exactly.'

Anna paused for a swallow of water. 'Did Lady Alasia manage the finances of Defalk – the coins – for Lord Barjim?'

'None other. Who else could he trust, besides Jecks? And Lord Jecks wanted no part of Falcor. What else?'

Anna plugged through her list of questions. At least there was someone who knew where some of the skeletons lay.

When Essan left, Anna sent Skent for Daffyd. Her head was beginning to pound again. More water and nearly half a loaf of dark bread helped, but Skent rapped on the door even before she finished.

'The player Daffyd.'

She rose from the conference table and swallowed the last mouthful of bread.

'Lady Anna.'

'Sit down.' She motioned him to the table. 'I haven't forgotten you. You're in charge of the regent's players. We'll work out some suitable payment for you, and you can have your own quarters in the hall proper – something not too grand, but nothing dingy, either.'

'Even your old quarters, Lady Anna—'

'Fine. Take them. Later, we'll see.' She paused. 'I'm sorry if I hurry. Every day seems like this, and I get edgy by the end of the day. I have a special job I want you to start on.'

'Me?' The young player's eyebrows rose.

'I want you to develop and train a group of players, not less than eight, and no more than fifteen. But I want horns – lots of brass, and the kind that carry. No more than two other string players besides you. The players have to be young – and strong. I don't care if they're men or women, but they have to have a clear, strong tone in their instruments, and they have to be in good physical condition. They'll have to travel, as soon as you have them trained, but I'd prefer you not tell them when, only that travel is expected.'

Anna waited.

'For that . . . you must pay . . .'

'I'll pay. Just start work on it tomorrow. As soon as you have enough to practice, let me know, and I'll come up with the arrangements you need to learn – the spell tunes.' Anna paused. 'This isn't something I invented for

you to do, Daffyd. It's important. Very important. It's so
important that I can't tell you more yet. It's so important
you can't tell people it's important. You can tell them I'm
busy, that we don't talk much, or whatever, but not that
you're doing something important.

'And it must be done quickly. I want a group that can
begin rehearsing in a week. No more than two weeks at the
outside. Do you understand?'

The dark-haired player swallowed. 'Ah ... yes ... Lady
Anna.'

Anna smiled. 'Good.'

The smile dropped away after Daffyd left, as she thought
of the next meeting with Hanfor, Alvar, and Himar as they
tried to figure out the best way to structure the permanent
force of armsmen for the regency.

108

Anna scuffed her boot across the mold-covered floor and
looked at the square-faced man in brown. Her nose wrinkled
at the smell from the storeroom, a combination of rot, damp
mold, and manure.

'Jussa, this has to be cleaned before we put any more
grain in here.'

'Never been cleaned before, Lady Anna. My da, he never
cleaned it.'

'And most of the grain at the bottom spoiled, I'd bet.
Except that you never went to the bottom except in hard
times, and no one complained.'

That got a blank stare at the ground.

Anna walked out of the granary area and back into the
courtyard, shaking her head. 'Why do I have to be the expert
on everything? Why don't people see that clean rooms and
clean grain bins make a difference?'

Behind her, she could sense the wiry Alvar and the stockier Himar exchanging glances, the kind that said, 'Here she goes again.'

She turned. 'I want the granary clean before our grain goes in.' She paused, thinking of moisture. 'I don't know if it will work, but talk to Tirsik. See if he thinks that a layer of clean straw at the bottom would help. If he does, tell Jussa to do it.'

'Yes, Lady Anna.'

Anna turned, headed for the main smithy, when the horns sounded, announcing someone's arrival, presumably someone important, a lord probably. She sighed and began to walk toward the portcullis area.

Behind her, Alvar and Himar shrugged and followed.

She reached the north side of the courtyard as the first horsemen rode in, an armsman bearing a blue banner with a gold bear, and a white-haired man bearing a huge sword in a shoulder harness.

'You do me honor, Lady Anna!' shouted Jecks.

The rest of the guard behind him reined up.

'I'm glad you came,' the sorceress said quietly. 'I have been inspecting granaries. I'd like to wash up while you stable your mounts. Then you could join us for something to eat.'

'As you wish, Lady Anna,' offered the white-haired and tanned lord.

The sorceress nodded and left.

Washing not only got the grime off her hands, but the grit from her eyes, grit carried on the hot wind that had swirled through the courtyard. She swept out of the room she seldom saw except early in the morning and late in the evening, and headed back down to the middle hall.

Jecks, Hanfor, and Menares were seated at the sides of the table in the hall when Anna entered. All stood.

'Please sit.' She took the end chair, the one Behlem had used, hoping that it wasn't a dangerous tradition.

'Since when do lords or . . . regents . . . inspect granaries?'

Despite his travel-worn blues, Jecks still reminded Anna of a white-haired Robert Mitchum, and she'd always had a crush on Mitchum. *Careful*, she warned herself.

'When they're trying to get a handle on what needs to be done, and there's little experienced staff left.' Anna broke off a chunk of the heavy dark bread she liked. These days her bread was fresh, at least. 'You might help there.'

'Me, inspect granaries?'

Anna laughed. 'No, know or lend people who could.'

Jecks looked at Anna. 'Your message said you had defeated Lord Behlem and were acting as regent. Regent for whom? Has that changed? What will you do?'

Anna met the deep eyes. 'I had thought to turn Defalk over to you as regent for Jimbob. You're the only one worthy of holding it.'

Hanfor swallowed hard.

'You cannot do that, Lady Anna. Nor could I accept,' answered Jecks slowly. 'As I suspect you already know. But I appreciate the kindness of the offer and the thought behind it.'

'Why not?'

'Then Ysel, acting as regent for young Rabyn, will persuade Konsstin to send his armies here. Or the Norweians will propose a partition . . .' Jecks shrugged. 'Or many other things I cannot foresee.'

'What should I do, Lord Jecks?' Anna asked, still holding a chunk of bread in her hand.

'Defalk must have a leader who is respected and powerful.' The white-haired warrior laughed. 'I flatter myself that I might be respected, but I lack the power to impress any of those on our borders. Only you can claim that. So you must proclaim yourself regent. Or lord.'

Anna frowned. 'I have a better idea.' She smiled.

'Oh?'

'You and the other lords request me to act as regent until Jimbob reaches the appropriate age.'

'Some of us in the north had already discussed that,' admitted Jecks.

'And you remain as my advisor. At least, for a time.'

'You drive a hard bargain, Lady Anna.'

Anna hoped so.

'She does,' admitted Hanfor, his eyes momentarily as gray as his hair.

'Very hard,' added Menares.

Anna surveyed the three, each in turn. 'I have power, of sorts, and knowledge of a different sort. I am a woman, and whether I like it or not, I would have to fight too many people to rule outright. As I have already told Hanfor, I can have no heirs. So there's no point in claiming the title of lord. It's better that I prepare the way for someone who has a blood claim. Even that won't be easy. It can be done, if you will help.'

'How could I not help, when you propose restoring my grandson?' Jecks paused. 'Do you wish his immediate return to Falcor?'

'Not immediately. I would like to stabilize things a bit more. In no more than a few seasons, I hope we'll have everything in place.' Anna lifted her goblet.

'There is another matter,' Menares coughed, then handed a rolled scroll to Anna.

The sorceress set down her goblet.

'It arrived by messenger this morning. I do not know how the witches of the south knew.' The heavyset counselor shook his head.

Jecks raised his eyebrows.

The sorceress unrolled the parchment and began to read. After the flowery opening, she read aloud.

'"While we applaud the restoration of the lineage of Defalk under the new regency, we would note that the time for harvest is past and that Defalk now owes the Bank of Ranuak two thousand golds . . ."' She paused. 'There's more, but it's all rhetoric, calling for acting in good faith and suggesting adverse and unnamed consequences if we don't.'

'They could be great,' suggested Jecks.

Anna still wasn't as clear on relative coinage values as she should have been. She was a singer, not an economist. 'How much do we have in the chests?' she asked Hanfor.

'About four thousand golds – it took almsot three thousand to pay the Neserean armsmen.'

'Do you know how this debt was incurred?' Anna glanced first at Menares.

'It is said that Lord Barjim had to borrow funds in order to move his small force to the Sand Pass.'

'He did. I did not know it was that much,' admitted Jecks.

'Do we have to pay?' Anna asked bluntly.

'If you do not,' opined Jecks, 'then you, or your lords will not be able to buy Ranuan grain.'

Anna thought about the lords Hryding, Dencer, and Geansor, and about the deserted condition of Falcor, and about the ravished harvests along the Fal and Chean rivers. 'Does anyone know what the debts supposedly owed by Defalk are?' She dragged out something from her conversation from Behlem and added, 'And how much is due and owed in liedgeld or other fees?'

'The liedgeld is due at the start of winter, roughly five weeks from now,' said Jecks. 'It differs from lord to lord.'

Anna managed a wedge of cheese, some of the meat, and a sip of water before pursuing the liedgeld. 'How many lords are liable?'

'Why . . . all of them.'

Anna repressed a sigh. 'I'm a stranger, remember, Lord Jecks. I do not know how many lords there are in Defalk. I have met perhaps ten or fifteen, but are there twenty-five or a hundred?'

'Thirty-three. There have always been thirty-three.'

'Do you have any idea how much the average—'

'Herstat handles my coins. I do not know.'

'Is Herstat dependable and honest?'

'Extremely.'

'Does he have an assistant?'

'Of course.' Jecks looked warily at Anna.

'Is he honest?'

'It is his eldest daughter, and she is most honest.'

'Good. I would like the use of her services, since Alasia handled the liedstadt accounts, and there seems to be no one left. Would that trouble you too much, Lord Jecks?'

'No.' Jecks offered a wary and wry smile. 'Will I have any of my lands and people left when you are done?'

'I only need those you can spare.' Anna offered what she hoped was a demure smile.

Hanfor put a hand to his mouth to cover a smile.

Menares kept his face blank.

Anna picked up her goblet and drank before returning her gaze to Lord Jecks. 'If you do not mind, Lord Jecks, my first task for you as my advisor is for you – and Herstat's daughter – to develop a budget—'

'Budget?'

'Sorry. I want to know what Defalk owes and what people owe us. I want an estimate of what the next year will cost, you know, running the liedburg, paying armsmen, repaying loans, debts, and what other revenues we might receive.'

'I am not a sorcerer, lady.'

'No. But you know what it costs you, and with your knowledge, I am sure you and the young woman can put it all on paper.' Anna looked at them. 'Surely, you don't expect me to make decisions when I don't know what they cost?'

'Costs – you . . . That sounds like a merchant's approach,' offered Hanfor.

'Menares?' Anna asked. 'Isn't Nordwei the most powerful land in this part of Liedwahr?'

'Why . . . certainly now, although Ebra . . .'

'Don't you think the Norweians know to the last copper what their ships and armsmen cost?'

'Absolutely,' said Jecks. 'All laugh at them.' Was his smile more like Sean Connery's? Anna wondered absently. She forced her thoughts back to coins.

'Of course,' pointed out Menares.

'Gentlemen,' offered Anna. 'Doesn't that say something?' She smiled. 'I certainly wouldn't want to have Hanfor recruit armsmen and have them leave about the time Ebra or someone attacks because we could not pay them. Or have lords decide to pledge allegiance to Ranuak because I was forced to raise the liedgeld or lean on them for heavy use of levies. All of you know more about the details, I am sure, but how can I support you if I have no idea where the money comes from and when?'

The three exchanged glances.

'Next ... does anyone know how much grain we can expect from Lord Barjim's holdings – I mean, young Lord Jimbob's?'

The afternoon was going to be long, Anna reflected, as she studied their faces. Every afternoon would be, for a time. She had too much to learn, far too much.

109

ENCORA, RANUAK

Ulgar's fingers fly across the fretboard of the mandolin, yet each note resounds individually, without slurring. He finishes with three gentle chords that draw all the notes he has played together in both a resolution and a promise.

'You play well, dearest,' offers the Matriarch. 'Then, I have known that for years. You would make a great player, or even a sorcerer.'

'I would rather not pay those prices.' Ulgar slips the

mandolin into its case, and places the case in the cabinet
on his side of the large bed. 'Most do not live that long, and
those that do seldom sleep – not well, anyway.'

The Matriarch sets aside the scroll she has been reading
and rubs her forehead. While her face is as round as ever, the
somberness of her eyes removes any cherubic impression.
'The prices of such power are high. I feel for the soprano
sorceress.'

'Why did you send her that demand for payment, then?'
Ulgar sits on the left side of the bed, pulls off a silken
slipper and massages his right foot.

'The debt must be paid, one way or another. She must know
all her debts. Otherwise, how can she address them? Debts
off-key the harmonies more if they are hidden or ignored,
and if she chooses to ignore them, then her harmonies will
turn dissonant.'

'You are sometimes cruel, dear,' Ulgar reflects.

'No ... I would be cruel if I did not let her know the
debt existed. If she does not pay, the exchange will stop
selling grain in Sudwei, and then more will suffer.' She
rubs her forehead again. 'She can postpone paying, if she
will acknowledge it, without too great a consequence, but
if she tries to repudiate it, she and her people will suffer –
the debt is that of Defalk, not of Barjim.'

'That seems harsh. She seems to be acting in good faith.
She did not have to uphold young Jimbob's claim.' Ulgar lays
his vest on the chair and begins to unbutton his wide-sleeved
silk shirt.

'The harmonies do not care about faith or belief. You know
that. That is something that neither the Evult nor Behlem
have understood. Any use of sorcery creates dissonance, and,
in time requires greater dissonance for harmonic resolution.'
The Matriarch takes the scroll from the coverlet and lays it
on the table.

'I am for harmonic resolution,' Ulgar offers with a smile.

'Then snuff the lamp ...'

110

In the gray predawn light, the only time Anna was likely to have time to herself, she strummed the lutar, cast the looking spell, and studied the mirror – the third mirror since she'd come to Falcor. She was seeing why sorcerers used water pools, but she'd never had time to set one up.

Elizabetta lay reading on the bed. A large white square sat on the foot of the bed, propped up by the stuffed white tiger that had come off the love seat in Anna's bedroom in Ames.

Even through the faint heat waves that rippled across the mirror, Anna could make out the word *Mom!* on the envelope. She swallowed and blanked the image immediately, noting that the wood frame of the mirror was literally steaming.

The sorceress sat down at the table. What could she adapt? The spell she had used to send her messages? She began to write, slowly, striking out words and substituting.

The sun had cleared the horizon by the time she took out the lutar and began to play. She ran through the chords twice, then spoke the words. She stopped and changed a phrase, and tried again.

'Better.'

Finally, she was ready to try. She cleared her throat and sang.

> 'Bring my daughter's letter from her land;
> deliver it safely to my hand,
> as she knows that I love her . . .'

As she struck the last chord, the entire room seemed to rock with a second unseen, unheard chord that shivered the sky outside.

Clinnnk!

Anna threw up her arms as the wall mirror shattered and sprayed glass across the room, staggering back, feeling – *knowing* that she was the only one affected, as if that chord were almost a magic harmonic directed at her.

She did not make the bed before she went down.

Thump! Thump! Thump!

What was the noise? Between the pounding in her head and the thumping somewhere in the room, Anna had trouble figuring out the sound, and when she opened her eyes they burned.

Thump!

'Lady Anna! Lady Anna!'

Slowly she rolled over onto her knees, then levered her way up the footboard of the bed until she stood tottering.

'Lady Anna!'

'Just . . . a moment . . .' she croaked.

'Lady Anna! Lady Anna!'

She finally recognized Daffyd's voice. Ignoring the throbbing in her skull, she forced her voice louder. 'I'm all right. Just a moment.'

A look down showed cuts and dried blood across her forearms below the three-quarter-length sleeves of her riding shirt. Glass shards from the wall mirror lay across the polished floor, and the outline of the mirror was literally burned into the stones of the wall. Only ashes – on the floor – remained of the frame and glass.

When she opened the door, Daffyd gaped. So did the guards behind him. Did she look that awful?

'I could feel something . . . something . . . terrible,' he stuttered.

'A little sorcery backlash . . .' she said. 'It was more than I planned. I need to get cleaned up – again.'

'Are you sure you're all right?'

'I'll be fine. Send up some breakfast, and tell Menares and Lord Jecks that I will be delayed.'

She closed the door and walked slowly – very slowly –

toward the bath room, but she stopped as she saw the white oblong on the bed.

Elizabetta's letter? Had it gotten through? She picked it up. The edges of the envelope were almost brown, as though they had been scorched, but the letter was there. The letter was there. Her fingers trembled as she opened it and began to read, forcing her eyes, burning as they did, to pick out the words.

Mom—

Everyone would say I'm crazy to try this, but they didn't see your envelopes arrive. They don't know, and they don't know you.

I had already showed the first coins to Mr Asteni, and he said the gold one was solid gold, but he'd never heard of Neserea, and he wanted to know if that was some new African country. I didn't tell him . . .

Mario's nice about it, and he's fine. I don't know why you can see me but not him because he's doing great. He worries that I'm crazy. I'm not, am I? I mean, writing letters to answer letters that appear by magic is strange, but it isn't crazy. And I knew you wouldn't just go off, no matter what Dad said about your going off the deep end . . .

I guess it must be hard, magic or not, to send these. I couldn't read part of the second letter, because it was sort of charred. Are you sure you didn't get burned when that wizard pulled you where you are?

Anna had to stop reading because she couldn't see . . . but at least Elizabetta knew. At least, she knew.

After closing her eyes and taking a deep breath, she picked up the letter again.

I got permission to take off the fall semester without losing my scholarship – I told them I'd come back if it made a difference, but the dean was understanding,

for once, and I'm working at the Homestead until
Christmas. Dad and Paulina are back in New York,
and it's nice to have the space, but I MISS YOU!!!!

Anna swallowed, and sniffled, and blotted her eyes with
her sleeve, and noted the dried blood flakes that rubbed onto
her sleeve. She'd take care of them in a minute.

I don't know if this letter will reach you, and if it does,
if I can send another. So I wanted you to know that
I love you, and that, even if we did argue sometimes,
that wasn't because I didn't love you. It was because
I was trying to be me, and you're a hard act to follow.
Irenia and I talked about it, a lot, and you're the kind
of person who draws up tight inside when you're
hurt. You don't bleed or gush. You get formal and
professional. Dad never understood that, and I think
Sandy did, but he couldn't understand why. Irenia and
I understood, but sometimes it was still hard, and I'm
sorry that I sometimes didn't make more of an effort.
It's hard to say everything in a letter, and especially
when you're not a letter-writer, but this is the only
way I'll get to say it. You were there when it counted,
and you cared, and I even remember when I got the
chicken pox, and you left the audition in San Francisco
that you might have won to come home because Dad
said he had to open at the Met.
    There are a lot of other memories, good ones, and
I'll always hold on to them.

Anna didn't realize she was sobbing until one of her
tears dropped on the *I love you – always* scrawled above
her daughter's signature.
    In the end, she sat on the bed clutching the letter, and
letting herself cry, knowing, as only her guts could tell her,
that the black-etched rectangle in the wall stones signified
the closure of all her portals to the mist worlds.

111

Even by midday, when she forced herself to march into the receiving room where Daffyd, and lunch, waited, Anna felt like she'd been run over by Farinelli. She looked worse than she felt, with several scratches across her left temple, and more than a few across her hands and arms. None of the cuts were deep, but several hurt, if not as much as her aching head, and heart.

'You look better, Lady Anna,' offered Daffyd as he stood.

'I look like shit. And I feel worse.'

Daffyd's mouth opened, then closed.

'That's all right.' The sorceress pointed to the table. 'Sit down. We need to eat. I do, anyway. My blood sugar's so low it wouldn't register.'

Daffyd looked blank at the reference, but she didn't bother to explain. She sat at the back side of the conference table, where she could see both doors, and immediately broke off a chunk of the dark bread. As she did, a head peered inside. Anna motioned. 'Resor, bring in whatever we have besides the bread. I hope we have something else. Lots of it.'

'Beef and onions and peppers,' said the page, setting the platter midway between Anna and the player.

The sorceress nodded and finished her bread before serving herself. Were regents supposed to be served? Not this one.

After several mouthfuls, she swallowed and cleared her throat. 'How are you coming with the players?'

'I have seven, lady, and soon . . . You did say you would pay . . .'

'Fine. You need silvers?'

'A silver a week for each.' The young player nodded.

'And two for you?' Anna grinned.

Daffyd tried to shrug nonchalantly.

'I'll get them to you later today or in the morning.' Anna stuffed more of the meat into her mouth. She was hungry, and then some, but that was clearly the result of sorcery. After eating for a time, and letting Daffyd eat, she resumed. 'I hope to have the songs ready for you in the next day or so. Then we can practice, and I hope you'll be able to rehearse them a lot when I can't.'

'Me?'

'Why not? What am I paying you for?' She asked deadpan.

'Lady ... oh ... you jest.'

'Not entirely. Once you know a song, you ought to be able to get it put together. I won't have that sort of time, not the way Lord Brill did.' Anna snorted. 'I don't have enough time to get organized, let alone do anything.' She took a deep breath. 'You'd better go. I need to work on spells before I get interrupted again.'

Daffyd nodded and rose.

'Daffyd, I'm not displeased or upset. I am busy and frazzled.'

'Yes, lady.'

She wasn't sure he understood, but then, men always expected women to understand. It was different when they had to, even as young men.

As Daffyd left, the sorceress called, 'Resor! Someone?'

Skent peered in. 'Yes, lady?'

'Can you cart off the platters and plates?'

Skent started to gather them up.

'How is Cataryzna?' Anna asked playfully.

The dark-haired page blushed. 'Fine, lady. She is appreciative, but she would like the freedom to return home.'

'I know. Matters aren't that simple, though, as I keep discovering.'

'Wendella – she hates you, and she tells everyone how awful you are.'

'Am I?'

'No, lady. Even Drenchescha thinks you are fair. She told Wendella she was lucky to keep her head. She wouldn't have been near so charitable. That shut her up for a time.'

That would change, Anna knew, and probably before she had a solution.

'Thank you, Skent. I'll think about it.' That she could promise.

As the door closed, Anna pulled the paper and ink stand before her and began to jot down song ideas – she had to come up with something quickly so that Daffyd could get his players practicing.

She had managed only a few ideas when there was a gentle thump on the door and Birke peered in. 'Lady Anna, Lord Jecks is here with Dythya.'

'Have them come in.' She set aside the spells and stood. Who was Dythya?

'Dythya, this is the lady Anna,' offered Jecks. Anna could not help but note that his blue tunic was stained. 'She is Herstat's daughter . . .'

Dythya was older than Anna had anticipated, in her mid-thirties, dark-haired, with a touch of gray, and solid but not overweight. Her gray eyes were appraising as she bowed. 'Lady Anna, I am at your service.'

'I hope so. Did Jecks tell you about my needs?'

'He said you had no one to do the accounts for the liedburg.'

'Or the liedstadt. I also want to set up a budgeting system, where we can estimate what future revenues and expenditures may be.'

'How—'

'A simple system to begin with, but I have no idea right now what we owe, what we may owe, or even what many things I would like to do might cost. How can I plan when I don't know what anything might cost?'

Dythya looked to Jecks, who nodded.

'My lady,' said Dythya, 'I can tell you how much you have

spent and where. Or I can find out. Beyond that, one must foresee the future.'

'If you can figure out the past, I can show you how to plan for the future.' Anna paused. 'What kind of numbers do you use?'

'Numbers?'

Anna pointed to the chair across the table. 'Sit down. If you would also, Lord Jecks?' As the two took chairs, she pushed the ink stand and a sheet of paper across the table. 'Write the numbers, digits, from one to twenty there.'

Dythya wrote.

It was as bad as she feared. They weren't exactly Roman numerals, but they weren't Arabic either, and it didn't look like there was either a decimal system or place value. Would she have to reinvent double-entry bookkeeping? She only had the faintest idea of how it worked. Why was everything so hard?

'We have a lot of work to do, Dythya, including a better system of numbers that will make it a lot easier.' *I hope.*

The sorceress lifted the bell on the table and rang it. It bothered her to be summoning people hither and yon, but the bell made more sense than yelling.

Birke opened the door. 'Yes, lady?'

'I would like to see Menares for a few moments.'

Birke bowed and closed the door.

Anna turned to the white-haired lord. 'Lord Jecks, how have you had young Jimbob tutored?'

'As best I could, lady. He learns his numbers from Herstat, his horsemanship from Hylar, his letters from Restak . . .' Jecks frowned. 'Why ask you?'

'I am going to offer more regular instruction to some of the children of the lords.'

'Here in Falcor?'

'Where else?'

'Why . . . lessons are the prerogative of the lords. They always have been. Who else would know what their offspring would need to learn?'

'Oh, I don't intend to force this down anyone's throat. Not directly. And I intend to see that instruction is offered to young women as well.' Anna looked up as the door opened.

'Menares for the lady Anna.'

'Take the other seat, Menares.'

'Yes, Lady Anna.' The white-haired counselor looked around the table warily, then eased his bulk into the remaining chair.

'Have you found out who taught young Lord Jimbob when he was here?' asked Anna.

'Tirsik taught him about horses, and his mother taught him his letters and numbers. Someone named Isosar taught him heraldry and emblems and the basics of tactics. I believe he was the sire of young Skent. One of Lady Alasia's maids taught him about manners.'

Anna winced at what was considered education.

'We will be doing more here, in the future.'

'That may not go well,' cautioned Jecks.

'Did Barjim save his son's land – or did I? I am a woman, you know.'

'Very much so.' Jecks offered a smile, but his eyes did not quite appraise Anna.

For a moment, Anna was most aware of the near sexual tension between them, but she knew where that could lead, and now was not the time.

'Defalk is too poor to waste half its talent and brains. Lord Barjim would have failed before he started without your daughter.'

'I have been so told,' Jecks said.

Menares and Dythya looked from Anna to Jecks and back again, following each speaker, but offering nothing.

'Knowledge is power, or so it's been said . . . in the mist worlds. Since we don't have much of any other kind of power, we'd better use what we can. I intend to add all the knowledge I can.'

'You have other reasons for such instruction, I would wager,' suggested Jecks.

'Of course.' Anna smiled. 'They will be closer than if raised on their own lands or fostered in a single other hall.' The smile vanished. 'They'll also have a better idea of whom to respect and whom not to.'

'You are a dangerous woman.' Jecks shook his head.

So did Menares. Dythya smiled faintly.

'Menares? Dythya?'

'Yes, lady?'

'Two things. Menares, first, find Hanfor and dig up twenty silvers from him. Get them to Daffyd so that he can pay the players. Then, you two find a quiet corner and some paper. I want you to come up with two lists – one that gives all the possible expenses we have faced or could face. The second list should show all the sources of revenue that the liedburg has, or might have. Then come back here.'

The two looked at each other.

'Just do it. I'll explain when you return.'

Both nodded.

'You are even more dangerous than I thought,' Jecks said with a laugh. 'When neither of those two can think ahead of you . . .' He shook his head.

Anna waited until the door was closed.

'I intend to destroy the Evult.'

'How could you do that? And why? You have destroyed his armies.'

'The Evult is putting together more darksingers and another army. I intend to put a stop to him now.'

'I have heard of and seen your powers, Lady Anna, but you risk everything you have gained by such an effort.' Jecks frowned. 'You do not have the coins to send an expedition into Ebra, and the Evult will not return to Defalk for another year.'

'In time to ruin next year's harvest, if we have one. We need rain, and we won't get it without destroying the Evult. Besides, I have another idea.' Anna forced a smile she did not feel. While her body felt less sore after eating, her head still throbbed. Why was it that even trying the littlest spells across the worlds cost her more than far larger efforts on Liedwahr? Another one of those physical laws she had never learned, she supposed. It made sense, but she didn't have to like it.

Jecks raised his eyebrows.

'It will take only a small expedition.'

'If it is small, you will have to lead it,' the white-haired man pointed out, 'and that is dangerous.'

'Not as dangerous as suffering another year of drought followed by another invasion. And I can get halfway there without anyone knowing. No one will expect it. I can visit your lands without suspicion. Wouldn't everyone expect me to make such visits? I'll let it be known that I intend to visit many lords.' Anna shrugged. 'You're right, though. It's not reasonable. It's not prudent – but, as the saying goes, it's better than the alternatives. And there's another thing. Everyone is watching. Sooner or later, someone else will try. We cannot fight more than one enemy at once.'

'No ... we have few arms and fewer armsmen and only one sorceress,' admitted Jecks.

'I intend to move quickly, within the next few weeks.'

'That be awfully soon, and close before winter.'

'We are surrounded on all sides,' Anna pointed out. 'But if Ebra is rendered permanently helpless, that will stop one threat, and from what everyone says, that will buy a lot of time. Neserea, even under Konsstin, cannot do anything until next year. I don't know about Nordwei.'

'The Norweians like to plot carefully. They will wait, I think.' Jecks fingered his chin. 'You have not said how you will accomplish this.'

'I want maps showing the shortest feasible routes from Elhi to Vult and to Lake Aulta.'

'Surely you do not think armsmen could travel the Ostfels? In late autumn, when the snows begin to fall?'

'I have a plan. Let's leave it at that.' Anna smiled tightly. 'Can you come up with the maps?'

The older lord shook his head. 'No one has ever tried such a . . .'

'Lord Jecks,' the sorceress said tiredly, 'unless the Dark Monks are totally destroyed these senseless battles will go on and on.'

'You destroyed their entire army at the river.'

'They lost their best . . . general . . . and they're already rebuilding. Even if the Evult were killed, the system would create another. That's what systems do. Isn't that what's happened all over Liedwahr? You kill a despot and get another. I bought a year, perhaps two, and then I'll have to do it again. I won't live forever. Do you want your grandson to suffer his father's fate?'

'You talk as though he will live to be lord.'

'He will be,' insisted Anna. 'I intend to see him married, to Secca or one of the other suitable fosterlings.' Anna finished the last of the water in her goblet.

Jecks rubbed his forehead. 'You walk to tunes unplayed and spells uncast, as if they were already ringing in the air.'

'Can you get me maps? Good maps? Can your scouts find me what I need?' Anna asked again.

Jecks bowed his head. 'We will make your maps.'

As the white-haired lord left, Anna wanted to scream. What was it with these people? Couldn't anyone look ahead? Didn't anyone believe that anyone else kept their word?

In the meantime, she had to give arithmetic lessons, develop a rough budget outline, meet with Hanfor, and come up with tunes for Daffyd's players, not to mention setting up a school, figuring out what sort of answer to give the Matriarch of Ranuak, and a dozen other items she hadn't even gotten to yet.

The meeting with Hanfor would be long, because she had to ensure that the armsmen – or some of them – could be used for some work around the liedburg, maintenance, and the like. She didn't have the coins to pay any good-sized force that was limited just to occasional battles. Yet she didn't want maintenance workers who carried arms.

Later, she should talk to Lady Essan, if for no other reason than to see where else she might have made a mistake or overlooked something. She hoped there weren't too many mistakes or oversights ... but she wouldn't have bet a clipped coin – or an off-tune key-harp – on it.

112

Anna walked to the single high rear window in the receiving room, where the base of the sill was nearly chest-high. She needed to rearrange the place, put the receiving/conference area somewhere with more ventilation and light. She sighed – another item for the list.

Outside, in the oblong between hall walls and the outer walls, the sky remained clear and blue. While the daytime temperatures were more moderate than before the harvest, in most places in the U.S., the day would have had people headed to the beaches or the pools.

After a last look at the blazingly clear fall sky, she walked back to the table where the scrolls were laid out for her signature – at least Menares had a decent hand and didn't mind acting as a scribe-secretary. The row of scrolls sat there – for Secca, for Kyrun, for Cataryzna, for Nelmor's daughter Ytrude, for Birke and his sister, and the rest generally worded to various lords, inviting them to consider sending a child to Falcor for the opportunity to study under her and various other experts.

Then she shook her head – all for what ... so she could try to bring some stability to a place that had never had any? And how many lords would accept? She had to try, even if it meant fostering a child from every major and minor lord in Defalk, or if it meant only a handful.

576 · · · L. E. MODESITT, JR.

She smiled grimly. That handful would get every advantage she could give them.

She also had to decide about Cataryzna. Should Anna send the girl home? While she had made an offer to Lord Geansor, would he see it as a veiled threat, or seize the opportunity to bring her home? Skent had told her that the crippled lord seldom traveled.

If Cataryzna loved Skent, perhaps Anna could set up a match between the two. Skent would more likely be loyal to Anna, and thus Jimbob, either through fear or gratitude, and that might keep some other ambitious lord from consolidating holdings. The last thing she or Jimbob needed was a growing barony or the equivalent on Defalk's southern border.

Anna wanted to shake her head. She was thinking like Machiavelli. Then she smiled bitterly. Why not? She had the problems that the old Florentine had addressed.

A squeaking sound caught her ear, and she walked back to the window. A wagon laden with grain and pulled by two bony horses creaked through the courtyard.

With a sudden gesture she turned and walked to the door, opening it. Skent, Birke and the guards stiffened.

'I'm headed to the granary. Skent, you come.' She didn't have to tell the guards. Both followed.

The glass mantles along the main corridor had been polished, and the floor mopped and wiped dry. She sniffed. Did the place smell cleaner? She hoped so.

As she stepped into the courtyard, the armsmen practicing blades in the exercise square stiffened.

'Lady Anna!'

'Keep practicing,' she called.

'You heard the sorceress!' snapped Himar, offering a half salute to her before he turned back to his charges.

The sorceress nodded in return and walked along the walls. One of the ubiquitous chickens hopped onto the shafts of a cart drawn up beside the wagon shop and *brawwked* twice.

Anna passed the open door where the wagonmaster struggled with a harness.

'Good day, Mies.'

'Good day, Lady Anna.' The brawny man shook his head. 'Armsmen, they never take the time . . .' His eyes dropped to the leather in his hands.

Anna looked at the wagon that stood by the granary.

Both the teamster and the granary man looked at Anna, then looked down.

When Anna stepped into the granary, the floor was still dirty, and damp in spots where the clay had been scooped out over time, and the storage area smelled more like manure than grain.

Stepping back out into the sunlight, the sorceress turned to the hauler. 'You'll have to wait to unload.' Then her eyes went to the square-faced man in brown. 'I told you to have this clean. That was a week ago. Parts of it are damp, even wet. And it still stinks.'

The square-faced man looked at the floor. 'Da never . . .' he muttered.

'I don't care about your da . . . and what he did or didn't do.' Anna looked at the sullen figure. 'Is there any reason why you haven't cleaned this?'

The man looked at the dark moldy floor.

'Have you been sick? Did you have to do repairs on something else?'

'No . . .' mumbled the man.

Anna shook her head, trying to hold back the anger.

'Never did before . . .'

That did it. The words almost leapt into her mind, and she squared her shoulders and sang.

> 'Grainman wrong, grainman strong,
> Forever leave this place with my song!'

'No . . . You can't.'

'Some would have had you killed. I'm just sending you

away.' Anna glanced at Skent. 'Find me Alvar or Himar or
Spirda. No, Himar's conducting arms practice. Try Spirda
first. Tell him that I need a dozen men to clean up at least part
of this so that they can start to unload the winter's grain.'

'Yes, Lady Anna.'

The teamster fidgeted on his seat, and his eyes were
downcast.

Anna fumbled in her purse and turned to the granary
man. 'I don't want it said that I'm totally heartless. You've
worked for a long time here, and that merits something, but
you won't change, and we have to change.'

The man looked bewildered as she stepped up and pressed
two golds into his hand. 'There are places to live in Falcor or
elsewhere. Use these until you can get settled. But you must
be out of the liedburg by the day after tomorrow. Do you
understand?'

'Yes, lady.' The brokenness of his voice tore at her, but
she steeled herself. If she let people disobey or refuse to
change their ways, then all the lives that had been spent
already would have been lost for nothing. She had to keep
that in mind. She had to.

Anna turned and headed back toward the receiving room
and the scrolls she still had not signed and dispatched, hoping
that she had time before she wrestled with the accounts and
Menares again.

113

Anna squelched a yawn. How long since she'd had a decent
night's sleep? She'd tried again the night before to use the
mirror to see Elizabetta – but all she had gotten was the
damned white mists and another splitting headache. Had
the letter been her last contact? It couldn't be . . . could it?

She forced her thoughts back to the conference table.

Menares scratched his head. 'I am too old for this. Where the number goes is as important as what it is?'

Anna wished she knew more about explaining place value. A year of teaching fourth grade twenty-five years earlier wasn't enough.

'Oh, Menares,' snapped Dythya, ''Tis not that difficult. Where you put words when you speak changes their import. Each position you put the number to the left increases its value tenfold. You can have two eggs or twoscore eggs – it is the same thing.'

Anna was glad that Dythya understood. She even had grasped the idea of double-entry bookkeeping, although Anna had a feeling that Dythya's bookkeeping would require as much learning on Anna's part as the would-be accountant's.

'I'd like to categorize what we spend coins on.'

They both looked blank.

Anna scrawled on a piece of paper. 'Look. We buy food. That could be eggs, meat—'

'You slaughter from the herds of the liedburg,' interjected Menares. 'And we have chickens.'

Anna kept forgetting that examples not rooted in the clear and factual reality didn't work. 'Weapons,' she said. 'We buy weapons. Hanfor says we do. I know we have bought pikes, blades, and some spears.'

'You wouldn't, if you had a weaponsmith.'

'We do, and, Menares,' Anna said sweetly, 'that is a good point. Why don't you send out word that we need one?'

'I should talk . . .' mumbled the white-haired counselor.

'So,' Anna pushed on, 'I want numbers, how much we spent, for pikes, for blades, and for spears. Then I want a number that sums the three. I want all the expenditures set up like that, with subtotals gathered for each general grouping.'

'Like families of costs, almost,' mused Dythya.

Anna sighed. All she had wanted was a way to track what was spent so that they could project future costs. Did local lords just spend what they had and then tax or take from their landholders? She wanted to shake her head.

'If you did that for several years,' Dythya went on, 'you might learn enough to guess about the years ahead.'

Most accountants would have winced about the term 'guessing,' but it was close enough for Anna. 'That's one of the reasons. Another reason is that we'll have a record of what we were charged, and . . .'

'You can see if they are trying to cheat you. You would not have to rely on your memory.' Dythya nodded. 'Can I show my father these ideas?'

'Absolutely – after we get them working.'

'Lady Anna,' said Menares, 'are you sure you do not come from Ranuak? You sound like their traders.'

'Most people who are successful in managing coins are similar to others who are successful.' Anna just hoped she would be successful in handling finances. Avery had always said she had no head for figures, even more so after he became the great Antonio, but that was the king of the comprimarios. No one had any head for figures and analytical thought but Avery.

'Do you know what I want, now?' she asked.

'Yes, Lady Anna.' Dythya bowed her head.

'Yes, Lady Anna.'

'Fine. Take all the papers and get to work. By tomorrow I want to look at all the accounts of the liedburg, laid out the way I told you.'

'Tomorrow?' blurted Menares.

Even Dythya looked grave.

'The day after tomorrow, then.'

The two nodded.

After they left, Anna picked up the scroll that had arrived by messenger earlier in the day and glanced through it. The bottom lines were the important parts.

   . . . we recognize that your regency has restored the
   Defalk we had hoped would always be, and therefore,

so long as you stand as regent behind Lord Jimbob, we stand fully behind you, and offer our honor, our arms, and our levies in support of your regency.

The signature was that of Nelmor. Pretty clear, Anna reflected, and her guesses had been on target. The chauvinistic lords of Defalk would support a female as regent for an underage lord, only if she were powerful, a sorceress, and a regent, and some, unlike Nelmor, were balking at that. If her expedition succeeded – when, she corrected herself – she needed to visit some of them, like Lord Fustur, whose holdings bordered the Nordbergs – and Nordwei, in the north.

She rerolled Nelmor's scroll, with its flowery words, and veiled references to Gatrune. She snorted. Nelmor didn't even want to admit in writing that he might have listened to his sister.

Then she stood and left the conference room, taking the stairs up to the second floor of the main hall, heading north until she reached Lady Essan's door.

'You can wait out here, Blaz,' she told the guard.

'Yes, Lady Anna.'

She rapped on the door to the corner suite, almost a duplicate of her two rooms, except Essan's were on the north end of the hall.

'Yes?' asked Synondra.

'Lady Anna to see Lady Essan.'

The door flew open. 'Oh, she was resting, but she will certainly see you.'

'No . . . I can come back.'

'Stop your protesting, sorceress-lady, and come in and see an old woman,' snapped Essan.

Anna grinned and stepped into the room. The white-haired woman had her feet up on a stool, and despite the warm temperatures – Falcor still remained as hot as late spring in Ames – a lap robe over her legs.

Anna eased into the chair across the low table.

'I do be liking my old haunts,' offered Lady Essan.

'I'm glad.' The sorceress paused. 'What do you think of Lord Nelmor?'

'He be good-hearted enough, not so as you would know at first meeting.'

'He listens to his sister, but won't admit it in public?'

Lady Essan laughed. 'He listens to his lady, as well, and she is quick-witted, but in public she is silent, and all credit is his.'

Anna chuckled, but her heart wasn't quite in it. For a moment, silence filled the chamber.

'You be going off to do something desperate, before long?' asked Essan.

'Why do you say that?'

'I been around long enough to see the signs. Your temper is sharp, and you rush from one matter to another. Everything must be done now. You insist on hiring tutors, and you have that poor Menares copying and recopying the liedburg accounts. You have your arms commander straining his wits to guess what battles he must fight in the year ahead, and you are trying to order iron stocks and find a weaponsmith, but you find time to insist on a clean granary.' Essan smiled. 'They say women are sentimental, but neither Donjim nor Barjim could release the granary keep.'

'I didn't want to,' Anna admitted, 'but I could tell Jussa wouldn't change. He'd just hang his head and do it the same old way, and the grain would spoil. I talked to Tirsik and asked him.' She gave a sharp laugh. 'He told Jussa to do something like that nearly ten years ago.'

'That be what I mean, sorceress-lord-lady. You feel, but you do what needs to be done. Do you want to tell this old heart what great venture you plan?'

'I'd rather not give any details. Let's say I'm planning a surprise for the Ebrans.'

'I will ask no more.' Lady Essan nodded. 'You are decisive, willing to risk everything for the proper outcome. Harmonies! I wish I were young again, and could ride with you.'

'You rode with Donjim?'

'Often. I remember the first peasant uprising, save that it was none of that. They had fresh-forged blades from Ranwa, and some even had breastplates, and they said they were peasants. I carried the shorter twin blades. Saw no sense in a shield that was as heavy as I was, and I was a mite in those days, even after childbearing . . .'

Anna leaned back to listen. She deserved some time just to listen to someone who didn't need something, want something, or wasn't scheming.

114

Anna looked up from the revisions to her spellsongs at the knock on the door.

'Lord Birfels of Abenfel to see you,' announced Giellum, stepping inside the room. 'He is the sire of the page Birke,' added the young armsman in a lower voice, 'and Lysara.'

'Show him in.'

Anna stood and moved toward the center of the room, her eyes shifting toward the high-backed gilt chair on the dais, the chair she avoided whenever possible. She still hated the idea of guards never more than a few feet from her, and she tried to make them appear as ceremonial as possible, but there still were some people she was sure didn't take kindly to a woman regent who came from beyond Erde. Her mouth creased momentarily. And there were crazies everywhere.

The man who stepped through the door looked hard at Anna, then bowed. His red hair was liberally streaked with white, and his ruddy complexion was blotched from too many years in the sun. 'Regent Anna.'

'Lord Birfels.'

'My son did not lie when he said you were beautiful.'

'Birke is generous,' Anna said.

'Generous? I think not. Even Lysara said you were beautiful.' The older man smiled wryly. 'I am here to visit them, and to escort Lysara home for a brief visit.' He paused. 'She will return for your schooling. She told me that she has already learned more about numbers in the past few weeks from that woman who does your accounts than she has in all her life.' Birfels shrugged. 'How can I offer her more? Besides, she is safer here, as is Birke.'

'Here? With an upstart regent?' Anna motioned to the table. 'Please be seated.'

Birfels took the chair closest the door, then replied. 'An upstart would declare herself Lady of Defalk and start with executions. I have spent the morning talking to the people of the liedburg . . . You are a sorceress. They say you are concerned about everything, and when you released a man for a terrible failure, you did not execute him, but sent him off with enough coins so that his family would not starve.' The red-haired lord smiled coldly. 'Yet Lysara and Birke also said you were fair, considerate, and—' Birfels paused. '—vindictively just against those who are evil.'

Anna wasn't sure she liked being considered vindictively just.

'I am here, simply, to offer my allegiance to you as regent for young Jimbob.'

'I appreciate your support.'

'What would you say if I asked you to release my son?'

'I will not retain him here if you need him,' Anna said slowly. 'I would prefer that he, or one of your offspring, son *or* daughter, remain here in Falcor. As Birke may have told you, I have resumed tutoring for those fosterlings—'

'Birke said that.' Birfels shook his head. 'He said that you insisted that they all learn to write, and to read, and learn other things. I cannot say I understand it all.'

'I have a few things in mind, Lord Birfels. First, the world is changing. The more knowledge those who will be lords and ladies hold, the better they will serve themselves and their lands. Second, they will come to know each other, and that will help knit Defalk together more tightly. Third, the more they see beyond their lands – before they are responsible for their lands – the more objective they will be later.' Anna shrugged. 'I hope, at least.'

'I could leave Lysara, rather than Birke?'

'Yes. Or both, or neither. That is your choice. In time, I believe that people will come to realize that the rule of a wise lady is preferable to that of a fool who rules merely because he is a man.'

'Some believe that already.' Birfels's tone was cool.

'I did not say that would happen now,' Anna said, forcing her voice to remain warm, 'but half of Defalk is women, and Defalk stands against much of the world. Our enemies use the skills of their women. Can we afford to do less?'

Birfels bowed his head briefly. 'Some would say that such a course would leave us little different from them.'

'I believe,' Anna answered, 'that those who lead should be the best because they are the best, not because they are either men *or* women.'

'You have daughters?'

'I have a daughter and a son – but they're on earth – the mist world, and neither will benefit from what I do here.'

'I must think for a bit, Lady Anna, before I decide about Birke. It is clear that Lysara will benefit. I do not know about my son.'

'Think as long as you want,' the sorceress responded. 'I like Birke, but I will neither reward him nor punish him because of that liking. Nor will I reward nor punish you because of it.' She rose from the table.

'I respect you, Lady Anna. I am not prepared to like you, or what you represent.'

'I appreciate your honesty, Lord Birfels, and that you said what you felt. I hope, in time, you will find it easier to like what I stand for.'

Birfels bowed.

Anna inclined her head in return.

After the red-haired lord left, Anna sank back into her

chair at the table. How many more interviews and meetings would it take? How many more years before *some* of them recognized that women were people, competent people? Or would her success, if she were successful on the coming expedition, make the lords even more wary?

She had no choice, not as she saw it. She rose. Time for more work with Daffyd and the players.

115

'This arrived by messenger, Lady Anna.' Skent bowed as he offered the scroll.

'Thank you.' She paused. 'Has Birke left?'

'He rode out this morning.' The dark-haired page paused, as if to speak, then closed his mouth.

'Was he all right?'

'His sire was pleased.'

That meant Birke wasn't totally happy about something. Anna hoped the stiff-necked redhead would be back, but she had her doubts, especially after meeting Lord Birfels. 'Thank you, Skent,' she repeated. After the page left her alone in her receiving room, she broke the red wax seal, unrolled the scroll, and began to read.

Lady Anna—

I apologize if the title is not correct, but word is slow to reach the south. I have received your invitation and messages from both Cataryzna and Drenchescha. They both confirm that you immediately gave them the freedom of the hall.

From my own sources, I have learned that you have kept your word in all matters. This is a rare trait in these days, and especially for one so powerful. While I would like to have Cataryzna come home to visit as soon as possible, I also feel that her future would be better assured in Falcor under your guidance. I do not say this to spirit her away, for I know that my defenses would avail me little against you. I assure you that she will return after her visit. I do wish to see her, but my ability to travel is most limited.

I recognize your power and appreciate your efforts to return Defalk to order and to the eventual hand of young Lord Jimbob ...

The precise signature read *Geansor*. The sorceress nodded, then lifted the bell. 'Skent? Would you ask if Lady Cataryzna and her aunt are free to see me?'

'Now?'

'If they can.'

Skent stood rooted there, and Anna took pity on him.

'It's nothing to worry about, but it's only fair you learn it from Cataryzna. She should hear first.' *If she doesn't already know.* 'Now ... go, you imp.'

Skent gave the sorceress a quick grin. 'Yes, Lady Anna.' He was still grinning as he left the room.

While she waited for the two, the sorceress pulled out the first listing of Dythya's 'families of costs' and began to read where she had left off. Some made sense. The accountant – that was how Anna thought of Dythya, for want of a better local term – had managed to get all the crop revenues in one category. But on the expense side, there were too many categories – cooperage, baskets, pots were listed separately and in totally separate parts of the list, as were cutlery and glassware. She jotted a note to create subcategories for domestic operations of the liedburg, as opposed to similar costs for Hanfor's forces. She wanted to know what it cost to maintain the liedburg proper, in comparison to the armsmen.

She lifted the quill pen and began to write – laboriously, since the ink took forever to dry, and the slightest brush of her hand turned whatever she touched to illegibility.

She hadn't gotten even through reorganizing the major cost categories the way she wanted them before Giellum knocked and then pushed the door ajar.

'The ladies Cataryzna and Drenchescha, responding to your summons, Lady Anna.'

'Send them in.' Anna sighed and stood, moving toward the chair on the dais. Everything ran into everything else, but she had to remember to deal with people first. She could reorganize lists while others slept.

Cataryzna, blonde as ever, and the narrow-faced Drenchescha eased into the receiving room. Anna did not invite them to sit, instead standing on the dais beside the gilt chair and looking down at the two.

'When we last talked, you asked me what I would do about your situation. I have decided. As you know, I have mentioned your continuing lessons here in Falcor, and I sent a message to that effect to your father, Cataryzna.' Anna lifted the scroll. 'I have received a message in return.' Her eyes surveyed the two, and she smiled faintly. They were not surprised, which meant that they also knew, one way or another. That didn't surprise her, either. Despite the lack of modern communications, everyone seemed to know everything. 'Your father has requested that you visit him immediately for some period of time. He also feels that after that visit you should return here for lessons.'

Anna cleared her throat. She was talking as much now she was a regent as she had when she'd been teaching, or so it seemed. 'You should make arrangements for your trip home, if your sire has not already. If you need an escort, I can find some worthy armsmen to accompany you.'

'You mean it?' burst out the blonde.

'Yes.' Anna held up her hand. 'If you return, and that must be your choice, you will have not only the freedom of the liedburg, but of Falcor – with one stipulation. Since you are a young woman, whenever you leave the liedburg, you must have adequate companionship and a guard for your own protection. If your father wishes, you may bring a guard back of his and your choosing. I only ask that such a guard be devoted to you and physically able to defend you.'

'You cannot defend her in Falcor?' asked Drenchescha.

The sorceress looked coldly at the pinched face of the aunt. 'I can guarantee her safety within these walls. In any liedstadt, there are thieves and brigands. While I will do my best to ensure everyone's safety, a few precautions don't hurt. I cannot be everywhere.'

Cataryzna laid a hand on her aunt's arm. 'The regent is far more forbearing than either Lord Barjim or Lord Behlem.'

Drenchescha glanced at her niece, but the blonde's eyes were steady.

Anna suspected that Lord Geansor was also a determined man. He had to be in this society, to hold his lands together while crippled.

'Cataryzna . . . if you need any assistance, please let me know. I would appreciate knowing exactly when you intend to leave and if you need any escorts.'

The blonde bowed. 'I will, Lady Anna. And thank you. My sire will be most pleased.'

After the two had departed, Anna tucked her accounting list away and headed for the middle hall – trailed by the ubiquitous Blaz. She hoped that Daffyd's players were still there and she would be able to determine their progress. The acoustics weren't all that bad in the middle hall, unlike the great hall where the hard plaster threw echoes every which way.

After the rehearsal, she had to meet with Hanfor to go over the plans for the trip to Elhi – and beyond. She glanced at the wall lamps – the glass mantles were dirty again, and the floors were dusty. She needed to talk to Virkan. Actually, she needed a lord chamberlain or a liedburg butler or something like that. Maybe Lady Essan would have a suggestion.

Anna opened the middle hall door and tried not to wince at the inadvertent squawk from one of the horns. The young redheaded player looked guiltily at Daffyd, then at Anna as he lowered the horn – something shaped like a cross between a Wagner tuba and a French horn, but with less elaborate tubing, and a slightly bigger mouthpiece than a French horn.

'Sorry ... Lady Anna,' said Daffyd.

'I am most sorry,' said the offender.

Anna held back a smile. 'That's all right, Ristyr. So long as you don't make that sort of mistake when we go to Elhi.'

Glances went around the group.

'Elhi?'

'It's cold up there already.'

'... told us we'd travel.'

Anna let the comments roll around the hall for a moment, then spoke. 'We have some work to do for Lord Jecks – that's where Lord Jimbob is staying. I'll be visiting a lot of the lords in the next year. So will you.' She nodded at Daffyd. 'Let's hear the battle hymn.'

'Battle hymn,' repeated Daffyd.

Feet shuffled, and the players repositioned themselves – Anna had insisted that they play all pieces standing, since that was likely to be the case in the wilds of the Ostfels.

As they dropped into the melody, Anna hummed along, testing her ears against the players.

'Too slow!' Anna interrupted. 'After the first measures, you're dragging. The tempo is upbeat! And the spell won't work if I have to slow down or try to drag you with me.' She nodded to Daffyd, whose forehead had begun to shimmer with perspiration. 'Again, from the top. Keep it moving!'

Getting the tempo right all the way through took nearly half a glass – and for a three-verse spellsong that lasted less than four earth minutes for all three verses. Except, this time it had to be perfect for what Anna had in mind. She was hoarse, as if she were teaching music appreciation to meet general-ed requirements once again.

'All right. You'll need to work more on that. Now ... the fire spell.'

That was even shorter – and worse, although how a

twenty-second tune could be that bad, Anna didn't understand. She was beginning to have more sympathy for orches-
tra conductors – they had to get hours' worth of performances right.

The sorceress was soaking wet by the time she dismissed
the players.

Daffyd waited until the others had left before he spoke.
'You were hard on them.'

'Daffyd, I'm not asking a lot. I want five spellsongs. I
want them perfect. All together, they don't last longer than
a third of a glass – if that. I've had to learn hours' – glasses'
– worth of songs, and sing them perfectly almost without
breaks.'

'The horns – they say it is hard on their lips.'

'Their chops . . .' muttered Anna. The French horn professor at Ames had always been talking about his chops
and who had the chops. With a glint in her eye, she looked
straight at the young violist. 'What's the difference between
a horn and an onion?'

'What?'

'At least you cry when you chop up an onion.'

Daffyd just looked puzzled.

'Never mind. Just get them to play. There's not much time
left.' She paused. 'Do you need more silver?'

'It might help.'

'Fine. Tell them they each get a silver bonus if I'm pleased
the next time. I'll tell Dythya to have the silvers ready.'

'It is that important?'

'It's that important,' Anna affirmed. She touched his
shoulder. 'I know I'm being difficult, but you'll understand
why when the time comes.'

'If you say so, Lady Anna.'

'Believe me. Believe me.'

She left the bewildered player and headed back down to
the receiving hall and the accounting lists she still had not
had time to revise. Outside, the pre-sunset shadows from
the west wall had cloaked the courtyard in gloom.

Before she had even dipped the quill in the ink, Giellum was knocking.

'Lady Anna, there's someone to see you. A lord, and he has his daughter with him.'

'Send them in.' The sorceress sighed and stood, not caring that she was still perspiring or that the room remained too warm for her.

The two stepped into the receiving room. Both wore still-dusty riding clothes, but the big-boned blond lord held a floppy cap in his hand. The daughter, also taller than Anna, still wore a green scarf that set off the fine blonde hair. Both had straight, strong noses, more fitting on the father than the daughter.

The blond man bowed. 'Lady Anna, my sister Gatrune bid me see you.'

Anna tried not to frown. Who would he be? She didn't nod, either, as she guessed. 'I don't know all the names I should, but would you be Lord Nelmor? And Ytrude?'

Nelmor bowed. 'At your service.'

Anna gestured to the table. 'Please sit down.' She rang the bell and waited for a response.

'Yes, Lady Anna?' asked Resor.

'Some pastries, if we have any, and something to drink – perhaps some of the apple brandy that Lady Essan favors and some cold water for me.'

Resor nodded.

'You do not favor the brandy?' asked Nelmor, easing himself into a chair.

'Not if I want to function.' Anna studied the girl while Ytrude sat. As Essan had said, Ytrude was almost a younger version of Gatrune, except Anna thought her features were finer, even with the strong nose. 'You look like your aunt.'

'Many have said so, Lady Anna.' The brown eyes darted away from meeting those of the sorceress.

'What might I do for you, Lord Nelmor?'

'You had sent a scroll to me, and so had Gatrune.' Nelmor shrugged. 'Also, I have spoken with Lady Essan, and she

favors you and your regency greatly. I fear that Dubaria is
... somewhat distant, especially for Ytrude.' The big blond
man stopped with a smile.

The sorceress wanted to kick him. The oaf wasn't about
to ask for anything, and he was setting up Anna to ask or
state something, and she was too tired to play courtly word
games. 'In short, you can't offer a good education for your
daughter; there's no one suitable nearby for a match; and
your sister is pressuring you to let Ytrude come to Falcor
and study with me?'

Nelmor's brown eyes turned flat. 'Mayhap I misunderstood.'

Anna smiled, professionally, bright and hard. 'Lord Nelmor, I
ask your pardon if my words offend. I am a stranger. I do not
always know the polite way to say things, and I have all too
often found that attempting to be blandly polite creates more
confusion than understanding. I am attempting to provide a
better education for the children of Defalk's lords. I am also
attempting to rebuild the ability of the regency to protect
its people. I am more interested in actions than words. So,
if I offend, pardon me, but understand that I act from the
best reasons.' After a pause, she added, 'I am also tired,
because my predecessors left a mess – or as you would say
it, a mighty dissonance.'

The faintest of smiles creased Ytrude's face, and Anna
wanted to hug the girl for it. Instead, she waited.

Nelmor turned to Ytrude. 'The choice be yours, daughter.'

Anna really wanted to kick Nelmor, because he was
washing his hands of the situation.

Resor slipped through the door with a large tray, bearing
two pitchers and three goblets. Behind him, Skent bore a
platter of pastries.

'Please, help yourself.' Anna smiled more warmly.

Nelmor's eyes went from Anna back to Ytrude, and then
to the pitcher. He filled a goblet all the way to the top. Anna
took the pitcher and asked, 'Wine or water, Ytrude?'

'The wine ... if you please, Lady Anna.'

Anna half filled the girl's glass with the wine, better than vinegar, but not much, and refilled hers with water. 'Would you like to stay here for a time, and see if you like it?'

'Ah,' reflected Nelmor with a smile. 'A trial. That might be best.'

'I would . . . like that,' Ytrude said slowly, her eyes darting to her father and then back to Anna.

Poor girl's never had a real choice, thought Anna. 'You can stay now, or you can return at your leisure.'

'Your ways are strange, Lady Anna,' Nelmor said after draining half his goblet. 'You suggest, in a veiled way, I have no choice, yet you offer my daughter a choice.'

'I do not deal in veiled words, Nelmor,' Anna said. 'They cause trouble. I offered you an honest choice, both for Ytrude and Tiersen – that is your son's name?'

'Tiersen – yes.' Nelmor refilled his goblet and eased a pastry into a hamlike hand.

Anna nodded to Ytrude. 'Please have one. You must be hungry after such a long ride.'

The blonde girl took the smallest, eating it in quick small bites, as if she could not believe she were allowed to do so.

'Gatrune said you were not like other women,' offered the big man. 'She said that even her armsmen respected you.' He swallowed the pastry in one huge bite, jaws moving ponderously.

'I can see you have had a long journey,' Anna said. 'I would be most pleased to have you join us for the evening meal. There we could continue our discussion.'

'Thank you. We would be honored.' Nelmor smiled.

'While you refresh yourself, I, unfortunately, must attend to a few other needs before dinner.' Anna forced a smile as she stood. 'I look to see you later.'

Nelmor took the hint and rose. After a moment, so did Ytrude.

The sorceress waited until they had left before she hurried

through the hall, across the courtyard, and up the open steps in the east-wall quarters, with Blaz hurrying along behind his regent. While her guard set himself outside the door, Anna stepped into the largest room in the east barracks. Hanfor had insisted on a space there, rather than a space in the hall proper, as a measure of his independence. Anna had agreed, but insisted that he take the largest space for his de facto command center and conference room.

She also made a point to meet with him there at times, to reinforce his position.

The tall Defalkan arms commander looked up from his small and battered conference table – the same one he had used in his smaller room below – then started to stand.

'Sit down. I've got another visiting lord, and we'll have to be charming and entertaining at dinner tonight. You, especially.'

Hanfor groaned. 'I'm still trying to figure out how to cover everything, and Himar's having trouble with the local smiths. Dissonance, they're not even smiths, just excuses for smiths.'

'We'll have to buy our own, sooner or later, then?'

'If we can even find one. To find a good weaponsmith is uncertain, not like wagonwrights or the like.'

Anna dropped into the ancient wooden chair across from the weathered commander. 'I've been thinking . . .'

Hanfor waited. His gray hair was mussed.

'What about Himar taking a trip, and some force out to Mencha?' Anna asked. 'While I'm visiting Lord Jecks.'

'You want the Evult to have to concentrate on more than one place?' asked Hanfor.

'That was my thought. Would it work? Do we have enough armsmen to do it and not leave your forces stripped?'

'Our walls are not exactly overflowing with armsmen, Lady Anna, as I was about to tell you. There are still many who are uneasy about a regency controlled by a sorceress.'

Anna knew. The liedburg had less than two hundred professional – semiprofessional, really – armsmen, and since her regency was viewed as a continuation of Barjim's, she had no right even to call up levies until after the liedgeld payments were made.

'Hmmm . . .' Anna poured the vinegary wine into the spare goblet, lifted it, then lowered it without drinking. 'If I could pry some out of somewhere else?'

'I have no problem with your idea, but I would have no armsmen left here. You must take fivescore with you.'

'Threescore should be enough.'

'Four,' insisted Hanfor. 'That leaves only sixscore, and you would have to move that many to Mencha even to get the Evult to spend a few extra moments viewing them in his glass.'

'Let me see what I can do.' Anna stood. 'I'll see you at dinner.'

As she walked back across the courtyard, followed by Blaz, their booted steps echoing from the stones, she wondered how anything got done in a society where almost everything had to be handled and supervised face-to-face.

She laughed. And she'd been the one who thought her earth had been too impersonal – now she was trying to run things in an all-too-personal manner.

116

The conference room was hot, even with the single window wide open, and the hot air enveloped Anna like an oven. Would winter ever come? *Not yet! You need good weather*, she corrected her wishes.

'What should we do about the Matriarch's demand for repayment?' Anna asked, her eyes going from Hanfor to Menares to Dythya.

'That was two thousand golds, was it not?' asked the white-haired counselor.

Was it her imagination, or was Menares thinner? She looked to Hanfor.

'If the Norweians and Konsstin mount an attack at the same time next year, we will need additional golds. We also need a weaponsmith and iron stocks for him.' Hanfor coughed softly. His weathered face had circles under the deep-set eyes, deeper circles, and his hair was grayer.

'And?'

'I do not know what else, lady, save that armsmen, their mounts, and their weapons always take more coin . . . and more than that.' Hanfor offered a twisted smile.

Anna scanned the hand-drafted list of liedburg expenses and projected outlays – well over 10,000 golds for the year ahead, with only about 3,500 on hand, but none of the liedgeld had been received, and Dythya's 'guesses' showed that with the harvests of Jimbob's lands and the liedgeld, Anna should receive around 8,000 golds, although some of it might be seasons in actually arriving.

She'd arbitrarily decided on a financial year that started with the liedgeld payments, since that date was as fixed as any for receiving revenues, and it was easier not to project from negative numbers.

Her eyes looked over the numbers again. No reserves for extra materials, and repaying 2,000 golds . . . that didn't look good at all, especially since her little expedition would doubtless cost several hundred golds.

'All right. Menares, draft me a letter to the Matriarch. Tell her that while the debt incurred by Lord Barjim was not of our doing, we will respect that debt, but that it will have to be paid over time. We will send five hundred golds with the scroll as the first payment and as a token of good faith.'

'Five hundred golds in return for their reminder.' Hanfor nodded. 'That will keep them from getting ideas of invading.'

Anna hoped so.

She glanced toward the open window. Before long she would have to go to the middle hall and check on the players' progress. Another few days, and they would have to leave, and that would be pushing it – a lot. But they could practice on the road, and they had to reach the Ostfels before the winter snows began. And she still hadn't heard from Lady Gatrune. The loan or rental of Kysar's – Gatrune's now – levies would help stretch the liedburg's armsmen without incurring permanent overhead, if Gatrune and Firis would only agree.

The sorceress took a deep breath and tried to bring her thoughts back to the accounts and all the details she had to handle before she could head out into the disaster she was about to create.

117

The sorceress lifted the scroll from Lady Gatrune off her table and read through it again. She nodded to herself, glad that she had stopped to see Gatrune, and glad that one Captain Firis remained grateful.

Then she set it aside for later, when she would meet with Hanfor, and looked at the first map that had arrived from Lord Jecks, showing the route along the upper Fal River into the Ostfels.

For a time, she studied it, trying to get a feel for the geography, until there was a rap on the door.

'Yes?'

'Lady Anna, it is past the fourth glass of the morning . . .' offered Blaz.

'Oh . . . I'll be right there.'

The sorceress rolled the map back up and slipped it into the case, then straightened her tunic and the purple sash that Lady Essan had recommended as a suitable mark of a regent. Anna only wore it in the hall. Outside, it just made her a target, and after her introduction to the assassins of

THE SOPRANO SORCERESS • • • 599

the dark ones, she didn't need to give them any easier ways of picking her out.

Then she stepped into the corridor and headed toward the large hall, noting that Virkan had gotten the lamp mantles clean again. Blaz followed, stationing himself at the door to the hall as Anna entered.

The youngsters gathered there and slumped around the uncovered banquet tables leaped to their feet.

In the light cast by the two lit wall-lamps, Anna looked out across the pages and girls she knew – Skent, Lysara, Resor, Cens, Barat, Hoede, the pale blonde Ytrude, and Secca, the youngest redhead, sitting on a stool in the corner, her eyes darting to Anna, and then away.

Too bad Nelmor hadn't let Tiersen stay, but it seemed that the blond lord wasn't about to have all of his heirs and himself in the same place – or something like that. He'd warmed up a little after a long dinner, but he was far too traditional for Anna. She almost shook her head.

Cataryzna hadn't returned from Sudwei, if she ever would. Anna still hadn't heard about Birke. And she worried whether Secca was too young, but Hryding would not have understood if she had excluded the little redhead, and Lord Hryding's bitchy consort would have made another issue Anna couldn't afford.

'Sit down,' she said after a moment, taking a chair and setting it in front of them, then seating herself. 'I'm sure you all wonder what terrible reason there is for you all to be gathered here.' Her eyes swept the group.

She saw a faint nod from Skent, ever the pessimist, but then, he was the only one not a scion of a lordly house.

'There's no terrible reason. Starting tomorrow, part of your day will be taken up with lessons. Dythya will teach you something about numbers and accounts, and if you can learn what she has to offer, you will be better prepared, when the time comes, to manage or oversee your own accounts or those of your lands.' Anna paused. How could she put what she had to say in an acceptable way?

'Since I have been here, I have seen talent in all sorts of people. There are bright lords and not-so-bright lords; there are bright peasants and dumb peasants. There are bright armsmen and stupid armsmen.' The sorceress paused and looked at Skent. 'What does that tell you?'

'Ah . . . anyone can be smart or . . .' Skent faltered.

'And anyone can be dumb. Right. Some of those who will teach you are not lords or from lordly blood, but they are talented. I hope you will judge them, and all those you meet, by who they are and what they do – not by how or where they were born.'

'But . . .' protested Hoede, 'you mean I have to learn from a peasant?'

'No,' Anna said. 'That's your choice. You don't have to learn anything. Where I come from, the teachers give tests. I'm not inclined to do that. If you don't seem interested in learning, I'll just send you home and let someone else take your place. And they'll learn all the new things, and you won't.'

'You talked about accounts . . .' ventured Lysara. 'My sire has a clerk.'

'And I do, and you will. So does Lord Jecks,' answered Anna. 'And how will you know if he is managing your accounts well or poorly? If he does it well, you should know enough to reward him so that he will remain loyal and grateful. If he does it poorly, shouldn't you know?'

Skent nodded. So did Resor and Cens. Ytrude smiled faintly and briefly.

'You, young ladies, why do I want you to learn things that have normally been reserved for men?'

Lysara looked blank, and Anna turned to Ytrude and waited.

'You want me to answer?'

'I wouldn't have asked if I didn't.' The sorceress's eyes flicked across the pages. Skent looked interested, watching Ytrude, waiting for an answer. So were Resor and Cens, again. Hoede and Barat appeared puzzled. Secca just watched, bright-eyed.

'I am not certain,' Ytrude finally said.

Anna wanted to sigh, and then scream. Instead, she asked, 'Who holds the lands of Pamr?'

'They were Lord Kysar's.'

The sorceress did not grit her teeth, much as she wanted to, but asked, 'And who affirmed allegiance to the regency and administers those lands?'

'Lady Gatrune,' admitted Ytrude.

'And who is the regent of Defalk?'

'You are.'

'Who controls Ranuak?'

'The matriarchs.'

'Lady Anna . . .' Hoede looked down, as if he could not finish the question.

That was going to be a problem, Anna had realized. Because she was regent, few were going to question her. So she would have to read faces and guess.

'No, Hoede, I am not suggesting that women will take over Defalk or that there will be many ladies holding lands – but there will be some. I would rather have a strong lady than a weak man, and the people of Defalk need and deserve good leaders. Also, look what happened in many holdings. When a lord dies in battle and his children are young, shouldn't his consort know enough to administer those lands? Would you want your lands to go to a stranger because your consort wasn't able to handle them? Or to some distant relative?'

Barat looked shocked, as if the idea had never crossed his mind, *If he has one*, Anna thought. The process would be slow, if she got anywhere at all.

'You will also spend some time in the stables with Tirsik. Most of you know how to saddle and care for horses, and you will do some of that, even you ladies, but I've also asked him to talk to you about how the whole stable should be run. I'm sure that some of you know some of what he will say, but I doubt any of you know all that he knows.'

'I'll have to saddle my own mount?' asked Lysara.

'Yes,' Anna answered, 'and Cens will probably have to learn about chickens and a few other unmanly things. A good lord or lady should know something about everything, and we're going to try to have you learn more than you would at home.'

'Will we learn . . . magic?' asked Ytrude.

'I will teach you the principles of magic, and its uses and limits.' That was all she would promise in that area, and even that bothered her. In this culture, too much knowledge too young could create disasters, as Daffyd had already discovered. At least, she hoped he'd learned that magic had special pitfalls, although she wasn't certain.

She shifted her weight in the hard-seated chair. Now what? After a moment, she stood. 'That's all for the moment.'

Behind her, she could feel the mix of puzzlement and interest. Before long, she needed to spend time, a little, at least with Secca . . . but not too much, or everyone else would be offended.

From the great hall she headed for Hanfor's office. Hanfor, Alvar, and Himar were seated around the table when she entered.

'Just keep your seats,' Anna said as she crossed the room and took the free seat. It was the chair that wobbled, but she wouldn't be there that long, anyway.

'You require us?' asked the stocky Himar.

'Actually, yes.' She turned to Hanfor. 'Did you talk to Himar about the possibility of taking armsmen to Mencha?'

'I did not wish—'

'Fine. Himar, in another few days, you'll be headed to Mencha. Alvar, you'll head up the lancers that go with me to Elhi.' She could feel the light breeze through the window, cooler and refreshing.

'Hanfor had said that you would be going to Elhi at some time,' affirmed the swarthy, wiry captain. 'I assume Spirda will be coming.'

'And nine players.'

'Ah . . . Lady Anna . . . I recall concluding that we had no armsmen to accompany Himar to Mencha.' Hanfor touched his beard.

'I still agree with you, but I received a message from Lady Gatrune earlier this morning. She will support us. We would still need several squads. Could you spare two?' the sorceress asked.

'Would she be willing to offer us enough armsmen to make . . . an impression?' Hanfor glanced at Anna and raised his eyebrows.

'According to Lady Gatrune, Captain Firis will lend Himar some considerable fraction of the Pamr levies for three weeks, provided we pay for their food and travel expenses.'

'That is not cheap,' said Hanfor.

'But it won't cost that much, and we don't have to worry about hiring mercenaries that we might not be able to pay in the future.'

Hanfor fingered a beard that was getting more white than gray, seemingly by the week. 'That might work. It would certainly give the . . . the Ebrans something else to worry about.'

'That's all we can hope for, right now.' Anna looked at Himar. 'You don't mind taking levies to Mencha, perhaps doing a little maintenance on the hall there, as if you were getting ready for a larger force to follow?'

'That would be no problem, and the squads I took from here would be happy to be on the move, I think.'

'Good. Plan to leave in a week.' Anna stood. 'That's all I had, for now.'

The three exchanged glances as she left, and she could sense the combination of puzzlement from Himar and Alvar and amusement from Hanfor.

As she marched back to the receiving room, she felt her mind splitting in different directions – maps, routes, the accounts system that still wasn't the way she wanted it, the chaotic state of her proposed private schooling for the sons and daughters of the lords – and her continued inability even to see her daughter for even a moment – not if Anna didn't

want to destroy every glass in the liedburg and risk fatal
cuts from flying glass even before she finished the spell.

'Shit . . .' muttered the sorceress. 'Shit . . .'

118

Anna took another sip of water and a mouthful of bread
as she studied the scroll again, hoping that it didn't say
what it did.

> . . . will always remain loyal to Lord Barjim and to his son
> Jimbob, and have great sympathy for the task which you
> have undertaken. While Lord Jecks and other respected
> lords of Defalk have reluctantly endorsed the expediency
> of a prolonged regency, as have I, some concerns remain
> about the continuity of such an arrangement . . . Defalk
> has a long and glorious tradition . . . up-held even recently
> by the bravery of Lord Barjim and Lord Jecks, not to
> mention the sacrifice of Lord Kysar and others . . .

The words rambled on for pages, saying nothing overtly
damaging, but clearly implying that the writer was not exactly
pleased about the way Defalk was being governed, since all the
great warriors and leaders of the past had been great *men*.

The signature was not a signature, but a sealmark, a
name written beside it – that of Arkad, Lord of Cheor.

Anna snorted. The last thing she wanted to do was visit
Lord Arkad of Cheor, but in some way she had to put an
end to such garbage, preferably without putting an end to
the writer. The clearly illiterate writer? She paused. Did Lord
Arkad even know what his scribe had written?

She sighed. That was another problem in a semiliterate
society. How much power was really held by talented and
scheming subordinates, like Virkan had been? She didn't like

the idea of such a weaseling message coming from someone who couldn't – or wouldn't – sign his name personally.

The sorceress cut a wedge of cheese – a late breakfast for another day that was likely to be all too long. But she had so much trivia to attend to before she left on the day after tomorrow, and she wanted to spend some time with Lady Essan, getting the equivalent of a briefing on Lord Jecks, Jimbob, and the situation in Elhi. Even eating enough to keep from wasting away took more time than she wanted to spend.

Hanfor wanted to discuss last-moment details about what supplies she would need, and she still needed to talk to Tirsik about how to handle his training in stables, horses, and the like for her pampered darlings, some of whom couldn't bear the thought that their underlings knew more than they did.

She snorted. That – in a society where some lords could barely write and others questioned the wisdom of learning how.

She also wanted to hear what Hanfor and Menares had been able to find out about events in Neserea. Perhaps their information would enable her to make sense out of her own scrying efforts.

'Lady Anna . . . the overcaptain and the counselor.' Skent bowed as he delivered the message.

'Have them come in.' She swallowed the last of the water in the goblet and refilled it before standing. With the weather returning to the hotter days that had ushered in the harvest weeks earlier, a warm breeze blew in through the high rear window.

'Lady Anna . . .' murmured Menares, barely loud enough for her to hear.

'Lady Anna—' Hanfor clipped off the salutation briskly.

'Sit down.' She reseated herself and waited for them to settle around the conference table before she asked, 'What do you know about what's happening in Neserea?'

'Nubara seems to be acting as regent for Rabyn,' offered Menares.

'Nubara – he's the one who set the assassins on me?'

'Ah . . .' coughed Menares. 'He was close to Cyndyth, but . . .'

'That's good enough for me,' said Anna. 'Why is it unexpected that he is regent?'

'We had thought that Ysel would be regent, but it appears that the Liedfuhr has insisted on Nubara . . .' The heavy white-haired counselor shrugged. 'Ysel would have been more . . . temperate.'

'Ysel has disappeared,' said Hanfor dryly. 'As many do when Konsstin becomes involved.' The weathered overcaptain glanced at Menares. 'Better you took service with Lady Anna.'

'That I can see,' replied Menares. 'Still . . . one never thinks it might happen.'

'I can't detect any armsmen headed in our direction from there,' Anna said. 'Not with a glass. Would Nubara send them now?'

'Not now,' said Hanfor. 'Even he would have to consult with Konsstin, and I would wager that Konsstin would not wish to start a war with a sorceress with winter coming on.'

'You are hard on glasses, Lady Anna,' offered Menares. 'You might consider a pool.'

'After I return from my visit to Lord Jecks, I'll consider it.' Anna regretted not letting Menares in on the full details of her 'visit,' but she still didn't fully trust Menares. He wouldn't act against her, but he might pass on information, and the more information that was out, the less the chance of her efforts providing a surprise to the Evult. Her expedition couldn't be a surprise once she neared the Ebran border, but no army could catch her if she could reach Ebra before the Evult knew, especially not where she was headed. Hanfor's suppositions about Nubara and Konsstin reinforced her determination to try to defeat the Evult immediately. She could not fight on two borders at once.

'Is this visit wise?' asked Menares. 'You have not had a chance to complete ...'

'I know. Things aren't really nailed down here, but I am the regent, and if I don't visit young Lord Jimbob pretty quickly, the other lords are going to start saying that I'm really trying to be lord or master of Defalk in my own right. We just got a scroll from Lord Arkad of Cheor pretty much suggesting that.'

'Some say he is a windy soul,' offered Menares.

'Perhaps,' agreed Anna, 'but what he says, others are thinking.'

Hanfor nodded.

'You have met with many lords – even Lord Nelmor recently,' said Menares.

'There's a difference between their coming here and my visiting them. I visited Lady Gatrune, and now we have the use of her levies – some of them. We also have a pledge of support from Lord Hryding, and he even sent his daughter to join us.'

'When did that come?'

'Last week, with her, I think,' Anna answered. Absently, she remembered that she hadn't groomed Farinelli, either, and that seemed to be one of the things that she couldn't delegate. Tirsik could partly clean the stall, but none of his stable boys, and no one else could so much as touch the palomino, only hold the reins once he was bridled and saddled.

She smiled faintly, trying to pay full attention and to shuttle everything else she needed to do to the back of her mind – again.

119

Anna led Farinelli out into the courtyard, her eyes once more checking the saddlebags and the extra water bottles, her left hand touching her belt and overlarge belt wallet, and then her knife.

Hanfor waited in the long shadows and gloom of dawn, his fingers going to his trimmed salt and pepper beard. Behind him, Alvar stood on the stones of the courtyard, reins in hand.

Anna could sense the mounted lancers of Alvar's company beyond the portcullis, waiting for her and the players.

'You didn't have to see us off,' Anna began as she stopped short of Hanfor. Then she smiled. 'You're the armsmaster of Falcor and arms commander of Defalk. You have to, don't you?'

'It would be remarked upon – not favorably – if I failed to be properly respectful to the regent of Defalk.' The older-looking man smiled wryly. 'Never let it be said that I am not respectful.' The smile dropped. 'I cannot say I am pleased to remain here while others bear the brunt of what must be done.'

'I know.' Anna looked at her commander. 'But if you accompany me, especially with armsmen . . .'

'I understand, and I agree. I do not like it. You are wagering on surprise and your own powers. I can only hope to the harmonies that they will be enough.'

'They have been before, but this will probably be the last chance. If this works, then every movement I make will be followed through all the scrying ponds and glasses of Liedwahr, and the fishbowl will be even worse.'

'Fishbowl?'

'Everyone will watch – forever. Also, I can't fight the Evult and Nubara both next year. We know that. So I have to go.' Anna shook her head. 'And how could I leave anyone else in charge? Everyone knows you are honest and that you represent me. The armsmen will obey you, and even Lady Essan wishes that her consort had had a commander such as you.' She shrugged. 'That means you're the one.'

'Such an honor I had not expected.' The commander

accented 'honor' slightly, and followed his statement with a gentle laugh.

'You earned it.'

'I must be more careful in the future.' Hanfor lowered his voice. 'Do take care, lady. Much rests on you, much more than you wish to believe.'

The sorceress didn't need that reminder. It was easier to believe she was just a stranger who had a few useful talents. 'I also don't need such honor.'

Hanfor smiled briefly.

A light breeze, almost cool, wafted down from over the walls, and she hoped that the Ostfels would not be too cold. Was she totally insane to try her campaign?

Not totally, but what else could she do? The Evult continued to rebuild the Ebran armies, and enlist more and more souls into the massed darksingers. As time passed, more and more would be pressed on Anna and her regency.

Anna mounted Farinelli, then bent forward in the saddle and patted his shoulder, getting a *whuff* in response. 'I know. You're ready for more exercise than I've been giving you. We both may be getting more than we want before it's over.' She looked around the courtyard as the gray sky lightened.

The players were already mounted, as was Daffyd. As she surveyed the group inside the walls, Alvar and Spirda vaulted into their saddles.

'The regent's players are ready, Lady Anna,' said the young violist.

'Are you ready, lady?' asked Alvar.

'Let's go,' she said, and flicked the reins, urging Farinelli toward the raised portcullis, with Daffyd, Alvar, and Spirda closing up behind her.

Once they were outside the liedburg walls, the rest of the lancers eased their mounts in behind Anna, and the sound of hoofs echoed from the stones of the road.

A few faces peered from a handful of windows in Falcor as the regent's party rode northward through the still mostly

deserted city. The sorceress wanted to shake her head. She
had so much to do.

Could she use sorcery to rebuild the bridge across the
Falche? And the ford at Sorprat?

Those would have to wait – but not long, because the
Falche would regain its normal flow by the spring runoff,
if she were successful. Nothing was likely to wait, not long
enough, anyway. She tightened her lips, then forced herself
to relax.

She patted Farinelli, which somehow helped, and continued to study Falcor, from the red dust in the corners
where walls and ground met, overlying dried mud, to the
cracking and unrepaired mortar, to the broken and dangling
shutters on too many windows.

120

Anna readjusted the floppy-brimmed hat. Disreputable as it
looked, even after some sorcerous cleaning, it was comfortable and did the job. Besides, any hat worn on the dusty
roads of Defalk would end as a worn and dirty mess.

The cool breeze still blew out of the north, and the sun
still shone through clear blue-green skies, and the dust still
rose from the hoofs of the horses. The one better thing
about being regent was that she didn't have to eat anyone
else's dust.

She studied the road ahead – a long arcing curve to the
east, following the course of the almost-empty Fal River.

'I take it the river was once much larger?' Anna asked
Daffyd, who rode directly to her right.

'Much larger. Even two years ago, well after the rains
stopped, the water covered the center there, the sandy part.'
The player pointed to the sand flats where only a thin trickle
of brown water had etched a narrow curving channel in the

middle of the river bed. Dried grasses, broken and bleached tree limbs lay scattered across the depression that had once held a far larger and mightier river.

'It is not much of a river now,' observed Alvar.

'No,' Anna agreed. From what she could tell, most of the flow of the Falche River at Falcor now came from the Chean River – and she hadn't exactly helped that.

Somehow, as her explorations of the upper Fal with her glass had shown – she had no problems scrying so long as she confined her attempts to Erde – the Evult had created the flood that had rampaged down the Fal by melting off most of the snowpack of the Ostfels around the headwaters. Since the headwaters weren't that far from Vult, the Evult's action might make Anna's efforts easier – there certainly wasn't any snow to block them – not yet.

'It is sad,' Alvar said.

Beside him, Spirda nodded.

The sorceress repressed a smile. From all his initial complaining about providing a protection detail, the blond subofficer had certainly changed, and Anna doubted that he would ever willingly give up his position. She found it interesting how she had less trouble with the professionals than with the amateurs, but that had been true back on earth. She had developed great relationships with conductors and performers – it was only the academics who were mediocre performers, and often worse teachers, who created the problems.

She chuckled to herself as she reached for her water bottle. Some things didn't change.

The chuckle stopped as she looked along the seemingly endless red clay road that stretched to the northeast horizon, bordered on the left by empty lands filled with browned grass, bleached weeds, and dust, by empty peasant cots, and by low hills crowned with dead and dying trees.

After two full days, they still had not reached Ohal, the small hamlet supposedly two thirds of the way to Elhi.

She opened her water bottle and drank, slowly, then

stoppered it, and replaced it, before patting the palomino.
'A long ways to go, fellow. A long ways.'

That was true in more ways than one. She straightened
in the saddle and blotted her forehead.

121

'That'd be Elhi, I wager,' offered Alvar.

Anna glanced from the red clay of the road and to her left
at the Fal River, still but a muddy trickle winding through
sun-bleached devastation, and then beyond the river to a
collection of structures rising above the river farther to
the east.

Closer to the regent and her lancers and players, on the
north side of the river, were what appeared to be wharves,
long stone piers that had survived the Evult's flood – except
even the base of the stone pillars stood at least two yards
above the thin line of water that ran through the river bed.
A closer look revealed to Anna that some of the piers had
been planked, and that the planks had been ripped away.
The irregular piles of debris – branches, boards, and mud
– above and behind the piers represented the remains of
warehouses, Anna surmised.

The river docks were yet another measure of how much
Defalk had suffered from the magic of the Ebrans.

'Dissonant mess,' said Spirda, his voice rising above the
dull clop of hoofs.

Anna brushed away a fly – once, twice. Now that the
breezes had subsided, and the temperature was higher, the
flies were back, and they were horseflies with a nasty bite.

'This poor land.' Alvar shook his head and glanced sideways at Anna.

What had she gotten herself into? Had she had much
choice? She nodded. Everyone had choices, but she couldn't

stand back, in the way she felt Brill had, and let things go to hell – or dissonance.

She glanced eastward along the road as Farinelli continued to carry her at an even pace.

Upstream, to the right of where the river docks stood, were a set of redstone piers – all that remained of the bridge that had led into Elhi. A rough path or trail, as at Falcor, wound down through the river bed and then up to the town. On a low rise, north of the town itself and barely visible above the roofs of Elhi, rose another set of low walls, presumably those of Elheld, Lord Jecks's hold.

As the sorceress reined up at the top of the path through the river, she turned to Alvar. 'It's probably time to bring out the regency banner. We don't need to have someone thinking we're another invasion force.'

'Some may think that with the banner,' said Daffyd.

'The regency banner!' called the swarthy captain.

'Ready arms,' called Spirda.

'Ready it is,' answered Fhurgen.

A young armsman trotted up beside Spirda, riding on the shoulder of the road, and unfurled the purple oblong that bore the golden crossed spears of Defalk – the basic design of Barjim's ensign – with a golden crown beneath. The only indication of the regency for Jimbob was an R under the crown. If he wished, Jimbob would only have to remove the R to have a banner derived from his sire's, yet his own.

Farinelli picked his way down the trail and back up onto the dried mud that covered the stone pavement that led to the washed out bridge.

Anna looked at the bridge, wishing she could repair it with sorcery. She shook her head. Not now. Not yet. Using that much power would only further alert the Evult and call attention to where she was. Better that she keep any demonstrations of her abilities minimal until she had dealt with Ebra.

The line of riders followed the main street past structures

that seemed mostly abandoned structures – until Anna could see the central square ahead. By then, the shutters of the structures hung squarely, and even a few had been painted recently.

The central square of Elhi, like that of Synope, squatted around a dusty, oblong redstone platform with a balustrade that ringed the two short sides and one long side. *Another roofless town bandstand*, Anna thought, easing Farinelli along the street on the north side of the square.

The handful of people in the square just stopped. A thin, white-haired woman pointed toward the banner.

'. . . the sorceress . . . the regent . . .'

'. . . what's another one? Won't stop the dark ones . . . no sense in getting hopes up . . .'

Anna understood, but wanted to wince. Instead, she forced herself to study the square as Farinelli carried her onward.

Chandler proclaimed a dull black sign bearing two crossed candles. Under the sign was a shop with recently washed and white-trimmed windows. To the south of the chandlery was a smaller building, with an open door, but no signs. Across the square from the chandlery was an inn, with a sign bearing a golden bear, clearly an attempt to curry favor with Lord Jecks. Some things didn't change, Anna reflected.

A tall and lanky woman in calf-length gray trousers and a gray work shirt hurried across the square toward the regent. Her feet were bare.

'Welein . . . she be mad!'

'. . . little enough to lose . . .'

The woman began to run, ignoring the comments from the other townspeople, then stumbled to a halt several yards before Farinelli.

The sorceress reined up, even as she could sense Spirda's and Fhurgen's blades being raised. 'Let her talk.' Behind her, the clop of hoofs died away as the lancers halted their mounts.

The lanky and barefoot brunette offered a rough bow,

but her gray eyes immediately met Anna's. 'Lady? You are the new regent?'

'I am.'

'You are said to be a sorceress. Can you not bring back the rains and the river? My sons have died, and my consort has fled. You say you are the lady of Defalk. You must do something, or we cannot be your people.' The gray eyes were firm, fixed on Anna, who scarcely felt regal or like a regent.

'You're right.' That was easy enough, but what else could she say? Especially without promising more than she could deliver or without tipping off the Evult?

The woman waited in the dusty stillness of the square, and Anna felt like the whole world was filled with people holding their breath, looking to her.

Finally, she spoke. 'The dark sorcery took years to bring down Defalk. I am working to undo that evil, but I cannot undo those evils all at once.' Anna fumbled in her wallet, then came up with a silver. She eased Farinelli toward the woman who watched, eyes still cold and gray. 'I hope this will help until times are better.' She extended the coin. 'You may take it or not, as you wish, but you have my word that I have not forgotten what must be done.' The sorceress continued to look at the supplicant.

After a moment, the woman reached out and took the silver, her eyes still on Anna. 'For good or evil, regent or lady, you have given your word. If you keep it, none will ever gainsay your rule. If not, no sorcery will save you.'

The sorceress nodded. 'I agree.'

After a moment, the woman stepped back. 'Harmony be with you, lady.'

'And with you,' Anna answered, feeling as though everyone in the square had begun to breathe again. She flicked the reins, and Farinelli *whuff*ed as he stepped forward.

Two workmen in soiled trousers and ragged shirts stacked barrels in front of the cooper's, less than a dozen yards away.

Neither even looked up as the column resumed its walk through the streets of Elhi toward Jecks' hold.

'The people despair, but they hope,' said Alvar quietly. 'You cannot afford to disappoint them.'

'The people are fickle,' Daffyd said. 'Once they cheered Lord Barjim, and some even cheered Lord Behlem.'

'Some are. Some aren't,' Anna said, thinking about the bleak gray eyes of the barefoot woman, a woman younger than Anna, yet who had suffered more, far more, and who had to put her faith in a stranger and a sorceress.

The houses beyond the square seemed newer, and were, as in the south, generally finished on the outside with a plaster or stucco. Some were gray, others painted.

Beyond the north end of Elhi, where the houses began to spread, and where more abandoned cots appeared, the fields swept upward from flat bottomland filled with stubble or recently-turned dark earth to higher, hillier fields, most of which were covered in browned grass or weeds.

Thinking once more about what lay ahead, Anna turned in the saddle toward Daffyd. 'How are your players doing?'

'Well enough. Well enough, though they question, and I have no answers.'

'We'll have answers before too long.' *Unfortunately ... unfortunately*.

'I await them, but I fear those answers,' answered the young player.

So do I. 'We can't avoid them.'

'I would rather not rush to find them.' The corners of Daffyd's mouth curled into a sardonic smile.

The sorceress glanced over her shoulder, seeing both the dust and the line of horsemen that stretched all the way back into the town. Had she ever dreamed she would be leading such a group?

Her head went from the lancers to the banner at her right and to the well-kept road ahead that curved to the right and then back to the left as it wound up to the hall.

Although dusty, the road to the hall was well kept, and

Anna could see where potholes had been filled and tamped smooth. The fields had been turned or harvested, and the wooden fences, if darkened by weather, remained sound, with occasional cross-beams of newer and lighter-colored wood.

The well-maintained red stone walls, which ran about half a dek on a side, were short for a Defalkan hall, Anna judged, no more than four yards high – enough to present a defense against casual attacks and to create an impression of strength – and well away from the central hall – at least a hundred yards.

The iron-bound wooden gates were open, and two guards stood in the shade of the arch as Anna reined up.

Both guards bowed.

'Welcome to Elheld, regent and lady,' offered the shorter, gray-haired armsman. 'Lord Jecks awaits you in the hall.'

'Thank you. We appreciate the welcome.' Anna offered a smile, hopefully warmer than merely professional, despite her weariness. 'Lord Jecks is known for his fairness and hospitality.'

'He is a good lord,' acknowledged the greeter.

With another smile, Anna eased Farinelli through the gate.

The outbuildings, also of red stone, were set about twenty yards inside the walls and paralleled them all the way around the red stone barrier, except directly behind the gates.

By the time Anna reached the front of the hall, the white-haired Jecks stood on the long columned portico that extended the length of the hall front. The hall's combination of squared-off stone pillars, heavy stone walls, and red stone conveyed to Anna an impression of a cross between Egyptian and Southern antebellum architecture.

Beside Jecks were a heavyset and clean-shaven man with jowls and iron-gray hair, and a boy with mahogany-colored hair, already broad shoulders, and a strong-boned face.

'Greetings, Lady Anna. We are honored that the first visit of the regent is to Elheld.' Jecks offered a bow, respectful, but not mocking.

'You're the one who honors me, Lord Jecks.' Anna dismounted and, reins in hand, stepped forward toward the boy.

'Lord Jimbob?'

'Lady Anna.' The boy bowed. 'My grandsire tells me that I have much to thank you for.'

'You may not thank me so profusely,' Anna said wryly, 'once you take your patrimony in hand. Enjoy being young while you can.'

Jecks laughed. 'I have told him that, but he is serious beyond his years.'

Anna wondered what child wouldn't be, given his parents' death, and given the possibility that he could have been killed by Lord Behlem.

'This is Gelen, Jimbob's tutor and counselor.' The white-haired Jecks inclined his head toward the heavy man. 'Gelen, this is Lady Anna, the regent who has reclaimed Jimbob's patrimony.'

Anna turned. 'Alvar commands the lancers who accompanied me.' She gestured toward the swarthy officer, who had dismounted and bowed. 'And Daffyd is the leader of the regent's players. He was with us at the Sand Pass.'

Daffyd bowed. 'I'm honored, Lord Jecks.'

'I am pleased your head player has experienced the full might of the dark ones – and survived,' replied the Lord of Elheld.

'Surely you do not intend magic . . .' began Gelen.

'The Lady Anna has assured me,' Jecks said smoothly. 'But if Defalk needs her magic, what good are her players if they are in Falcor and she is here?' He motioned to a stocky figure in a blue-and-gold tunic. 'Tunbar?'

'Ser.'

'Captain Alvar commands the regent's lancers. If you would ensure that their mounts are taken care of and that they are quartered in the barracks . . .'

'Captain.' Tunbar bowed to Alvar.

'The players will guest in the hall. Captain Alvar . . . you

are most welcome in the hall . . . or the barracks . . .' Jecks'
voice was neutral, yet concerned. 'I must insist, however,
that you dine with us, as will the subofficer who is the
regent's personal guard chief. And of course, the chief of
players.'

The sorceress wanted to smile. She could still learn a lot
from Jecks.

'Thank you, ser,' responded Alvar. 'Best I quarter with
the lancers, if there is a suitable space.'

'There is, better than some rooms in the hall, captain,'
offered Tunbar. 'Leastwise, Captain Sepko always said so.
And there's one for the guard subofficer, too.'

A faint smile crossed Spirda's face

'Might we spend a few moments. in conference, Lady
Anna, before you refresh yourself for dinner?' asked Jecks.

'That might be best,' Anna said. If the older lord requested
such a meeting, he had his reasons. 'But I will have to groom
Farinelli first.'

A frown crossed young Jimbob's face, then vanished.

Jecks laughed, and he turned to the boy. 'The palomino
may be a gelding, Jimbob, but he is a raider warhorse,
and none can touch him save the lady Anna. She may
look like a delicate lady, but more than a few have died
at her hand.'

Anna wanted to wince at that, but she understood, and
only nodded slightly.

'How many, Lady Anna?' asked Jimbob.

'Best you ask how many thousands,' answered Jecks.

'No. I don't mean with sorcery in battle.'

'She killed one man with that dagger at her belt,' said
Daffyd. 'Three attacked her. They all died. She also rode two
deks with a war arrow all the way through her shoulder.'

'I saw the scars,' Jecks confirmed. His eyes blazed at
the boy.

'I apologize . . . if I have offended, Lady Anna.' Jimbob
bowed again.

'Jimbob,' Anna said slowly. 'Some women are weak, and

so are some men. Other women are strong, and so are some men. Never assume that a woman is weak because she is a woman.'

'Some have, and they are all dead,' added Alvar. 'She has stood on a broken wall and faced the Ebrans when all around her were fleeing. She walked into a hall, after killing the Prophet of Music barehanded, and faced down all the officers of Neserea.'

'If you can do that, without an army at your back, as she did,' added Jecks, 'then perhaps you will deserve to inherit what she has saved for you. You may excuse yourself until dinner.'

'By your leave, Lady Anna? My lord?' Jimbob bowed, and Anna could sense the anger and humiliation.

'Jimbob . . .' Anna's voice was gentle. 'You will be a ruler, and we all want you to be a good ruler. Your sire's greatest strength was his willingness to see things as they were. When he met me, he greeted me as an equal, and I wanted to help him for that kindness. To my knowledge, he was always that way, and that is why he almost accomplished the impossible. He might have, if I had known then what I know now, but I was too new to Liedwahr.' Anna paused. 'He was a good man, and he would want you to be a good man also.' After a moment, she added, 'You have my leave, and I look forward to seeing you later.'

The boy bowed, and Anna could still sense tears close to the surface. So she bowed slightly in return and waited until he turned and left. After a moment, Gelen eased away.

'Lady Anna?' asked Alvar.

'Please do what you have to, Alvar. You, too, Daffyd.'

She waited until Tunbar and Alvar began moving the lancers away, and Daffyd and the players followed.

'I can see why you are effective, lady.' Jecks chuckled. 'Jimbob will remember what you said, and after a bit, realize that you mean well.'

'I hope so.'

'Let us get your mount stabled.' Jecks turned and began to walk around the east side of the hall.

Anna walked after him, leading Farinelli to the stable – another stone building as dry and clean as Tirsik's, if longer and narrower.

Farinelli's stall was in the front, and larger than all but a handful.

There were two pages waiting as well.

'Did you have a baggage beast?' asked Jecks, as Anna began to unstrap the lutar, the saddlebags, and the light but bulkier bag that contained a single green gown – not the recital gown, but one of those she had created.

'No. There's one gown, slippers, and riding clothes.'

'You travel like a warrior, too, like my own daughter. I'll have to tell Jimbob that.' He turned to the pages. 'Take these to the great guest quarters.'

'Not the lutar,' Anna corrected.

Jecks nodded to the pages.

Anna set the lutar case aside, then unfastened the saddle and laid the saddle on the rack. Jecks straightened it, and Farinelli neighed.

'I know,' Anna said. 'You're hungry, but you need grooming.' Then she answered Jecks. 'I liked Alasia. I wish I'd had a chance to know her better.'

'She said you might save Defalk.'

Not soon enough for her, if I do, Anna thought. 'I tried.'

'You still seem to be trying.'

Anna gave a short laugh as she began to curry Farinelli.

Later, once the gelding was settled, they crossed the stone-paved expanse back toward the hall, and in the twilight, Anna could hear chickens. All halls seemed to have chickens – chickens and dust.

She stifled a sneeze, half shaking her head. 'It's so dusty here.' The lutar case seemed heavy, but that was because she was tired.

'We had dust before in the summer, but not like this.'

Like Brill's hall, Elheld was clean, with only a light coating of dust on the stone floor, and the lamp mantles shone, as if they had been polished for her arrival. They probably had been.

Jecks opened the heavy wooden door and beckoned. 'This is my workroom.'

Anna stepped inside. The room was comparatively small, especially for a lord, no more than five or six yards square. A desk table sat before the open double windows at the right end of the study. The area directly before the door contained a small circular table and four carved wooden chairs.

'It's not meant exactly for comfort.'

'That's fine.' Anna sat in one of the four chairs, setting the lutar by her feet.

'I'm told you prefer water after riding.' The lord poured some from a pitcher into the goblet before Anna. 'This has been orderspelled. Hyutt can do some small spells, but that is about it.' Then he filled his own goblet and sat.

'Thank you.' Anna drank most of the goblet in two swallows. 'I get thirsty here.'

'How was your journey?'

'I had not realized how hard the Evult's revenge fell on you and your lands,' Anna admitted.

'It was close enough to harvest that we did not lose too much. Three weeks earlier and we would have lost most of the crops.' Jecks offered a wintry smile. 'You can see why I have mixed feelings about your ... expedition. If you fail, all will be lost for Jimbob. But if you do not try, within another two years, perhaps sooner, all will be lost for Defalk. You are a stranger, and you have never seen Defalk as I have known it most of my life – with fertile fields, wide-leafed trees and orchards on the hills, rivers filled with green water, towns and hamlets filled with laughing and happy souls.

'Even young Jimbob finds it hard to remember, for half

his life has been spent in this parched land, and that is the half that he remembers.'

'I take it that tonight is purely social?'

'It would be expected.' Jecks nodded. 'And, unlike many lords across Liedwahr, I have no complaints with my liege. Complaints are usually the business of such visits,' he added. 'I have taken the liberty of inviting a neighbor, Lord Clethner. Will that displease you?'

Anna refilled the goblet and shook her head.

'I also have a favor to ask, a small one.' His eyes twinkled slightly.

'Oh?'

'I would like you to light the candles.'

Anna nodded. 'You think a small demonstration would be in order?'

'Clethner – and even Jimbob – have trouble believing what they cannot see.'

'I can manage that. Even the Evult wouldn't be surprised, if he's watching.'

Jecks rose and walked to the table. There he lifted a cylindrical leather case and carried it back to Anna. 'Here are the maps you requested. They are the best we have.'

'Thank you.'

'How long will you stay?' Jecks reseated himself.

'How long should I stay?' Anna countered.

'Some great lords inflict themselves on their loyal retainers for weeks.'

Anna winced. 'I can't wait much longer. How about two days?'

'With a promise to return shortly . . . that would suffice. Clethner will praise my luck. He has already been here two days, waiting to meet you.'

'Just my luck.'

'And his.' Jecks glanced toward the window.

'It must be getting late. I need to get ready. I would like some water . . .'

'The tub is filled.' Jecks smiled. 'I have heard.'

'Thank you.' Anna rose. 'Until dinner.'
Jecks rose also. 'Until dinner, Regent Anna.'

122

Anna stretched, after having enjoyed the first hot bath in four days, and wrapped the dressing gown around her, brushing her hair back away from her face. In the dry air of Defalk, the hair she had cut short of necessity would dry quickly – she hoped.

Then she walked from the bathing chamber into the main room and studied the single gown she had brought. The simple green dress lay across the purple coverlet of the triple-width bed.

The sorceress turned and, for a moment, stood at the window, looking out across the lands shrouded in shadow, toward a reddish purple sunset that faded into dark gray and purple as she watched. Both moons were visible, but separated by half the width of the sky, with Darksong nearly at the zenith, its reddish glow like an ember in the sky.

Clearsong was almost an evening star, a point of light above the horizon.

She turned back toward the dress on the bed, then dropped into the big easy chair, wondering if Alasia or Barjim had preferred the chair, trying not to think about so many things, from Mario and Elizabetta to the expedition ahead, from the disapproving presence of Gelen to the questions posed by Jimbob. Had the tutor set up the boy? Sooner or later, she'd have to do something about that – assuming she were around to do it. And then there was the question of why Jecks had stated her accomplishments so clearly, even to the point of nearly humiliating his grandson. Was there more there than ensuring that Jimbob didn't get an inflated opinion of himself?

Anna wanted to shake her head. Right now, she didn't need those kinds of complications – and there was no reason to look farther, at least not until she dealt with the Evult, assuming she could, and she returned.

Finally, she rose and began to get ready.

She had dressed, and brushed her hair, and added what little makeup she had when the rap on the door was followed by a feminine voice. 'Lady Anna?'

'Yes?'

'Lord Jecks would like to know if you are ready to join us, or if he should hold the dinner for a time?'

'I'll be there shortly.'

She put on the faintest hint of lipstick – too much wouldn't be good in this culture and it didn't hurt to stretch her meager two tubes – checked her image in the glass, and headed for the door.

Fhurgen smiled as Anna stepped out of the room.

'You have guard duty?'

'I volunteered, lady.' The dark-haired guard paused. 'That was a kind thing you did out front. With the boy.'

'I don't know, Fhurgen. I don't want him automatically thinking women are weak, but I also didn't want him humiliated before me, and he still might resent me.'

'He has time to learn.'

I hope so. 'It's hard to learn some things when you're young and powerful, and Lord Jecks doesn't want him to get too big for his britches.' Anna turned toward the grand staircase and Fhurgen followed.

Jecks was waiting at the foot of the staircase, with a broad smile. Definitely like Sean Connery, she decided. His eyes took in Anna, all of her, and she almost found herself blushing as the tanned and white-haired warrior extended a hand.

'It is hard to believe you are the same regent who rode in on a mighty mount.'

'I feel better,' she admitted.

'Are you hungry?'

'Very.'

Jecks escorted her along the short hall to the first door on the right, where Alvar waited. Fhurgen stationed himself by the door, his hand close to the hilt of his blade.

'This is a mighty hall,' Alvar noted, his wiry frame bowing to Anna as she entered the dining room.

'Not so mighty in these days,' answered Jecks dryly.

Anna looked to the chandeliers, unlit as Jecks had indicated.

'Would you honor us, Lady Anna?' Jecks stood back and raised his voice in asking, as if to make an announcement with his question, with only the slightest twinkle in his eye.

'I would be honored, Lord Jecks.' The sorceress smiled, hummed, hoping she had the pitch right, and sang the candle spell, with concert vigor.

Obediently, the chandelier blazed.

Jimbob's mouth opened, but the redhead shut it quickly, his eyes flicking to his grandfather as if to ask whether Jecks had seen his astonishment, then to Gelen, standing beside the young lord. Gelen's eyes widened, but only momentarily.

The whipcord-thin man who had moved from beside the dining table until he stood behind and to the right of Jecks nodded, as if to affirm to himself that the Regent of Defalk was indeed a sorceress.

'Thank you, Lady Anna. May you bring light – and rain – back to our lands.'

Anna inclined her head slightly. 'I'll do the best I can.'

'Knowing you, that will be good indeed.'

The sorceress wanted to squirm at what she viewed as a setup, but only smiled politely.

Jecks stepped back and gestured to the thin man with the lank brown hair. 'Lady Anna, might I present Clethner, Lord of Nordland?'

'I'm pleased to meet you, Lord Clethner.'

'Clethner, Lady Anna. I am a plain man.' Clethner bowed.

'You are most impressive in person.' His eyes glittered, and Anna stiffened inside.

'People expect a regent to be impressive, I've gathered.' She nodded politely.

'This is a small dinner, Lady Anna, in keeping with the times.' Jecks gestured. 'Besides those you know, and Lord Clethner, I have also asked Herstat to join us, since I thought you might like to meet him.'

'His daughter has been very helpful.'

'She has written her sire that you have been most effective in reorganizing the accounts, and that you have suggested major improvements in holding accounts.' Jecks shook his head slightly, reminding Anna once again of the combination of Robert Mitchum and Connery.

Careful . . . you can't think like that, not now.

'A sorceress who can improve accounts and who is deadly with both spells and daggers, and who rides a raider beast no one else can touch?' Clethner laughed, a gentle laugh. 'You are the stuff of legends, Lady Anna.'

'I doubt that.' *I couldn't be, not a country girl from Cumberland, Kentucky.*

'If you would do the honor?' Jecks inclined his head toward the table.

Anna smiled and eased herself toward the table, finding she was seated at the head, with Jecks at her left, and Jimbob at her right. Clethner sat beside Jecks, and Alvar beside Jimbob, with Daffyd flanking Clethner and Spirda flanking Alvar. Gelen was seated beside Daffyd and Herstat beside Spirda.

'Before we begin . . . although it is not customary, I would like to propose a toast for the honor we have in our regent visiting us.' Jecks lifted his goblet. 'To the regent! To her success in restoring Defalk to health and honor.'

'To the regent,' echoed the others.

Anna worried more about the honor part than the health part. Honor among men was a nebulous concept, often continually redefined. She held back a snort. She should complain, when all too often she'd found women – like Dieshr – had no concept of honor at all. Either way, restoring honor was a chancy business.

The whole business of being a regent was chancy, and getting chancier.

She smiled.

123

VULT, EBRA

As the echoes of the mirror-pond spell die away, the white mists give way to the image of a blond woman in a green gown, seated at the head of the table.

'That is not Falcor,' observes Yurelt, unaware of the sidelong glance the Evult bestows upon him.

'She guests at Lord Jecks.' The Evult nods. 'What does that tell you, Songmaster?'

'She is trying to gain his support? Or strain his purse and hospitality. Perhaps she has need of coin, and is letting Jecks support her and some of her forces? Why, she is no different from Lord Behlem.'

'All possible,' admits the cloaked leader of the Dark Monks. 'But she is more devious than that, I fear. She will strike at us, as soon as the roads clear in spring.'

'She will not be ready. Defalk is in ruins. Falcor is a shambles. She destroyed the roads and the ford across the Cheor.' Yurelt shakes his head.

'She will be ready, and we must be ready before her.' The Evult smiles, but only white teeth show from under the dark hood. 'I will melt the winter snowfall and cast down more floods – down both the Cheor and the Fal, and you will march even as those floods ravage Defalk.'

'She is beautiful,' says Yurelt.

'She is evil, and older than you. She may be older than I am. Do not be misled by appearances. She is resourceful.' The hood turns as if he shakes his head. 'It is too bad this has gone on so far, and we have few choices. I would almost like to see her take on the Liedfuhr. Would that not give the mighty Konsstin fits?' A harsh laugh follows. 'Or those plotting fools in Wei.'

'Why can you not wait?' asks the Songmaster.

'Because she has declared herself our enemy, and she will not believe any envoy we send. Besides . . .' The Evult does not finish the sentence.

'She is a woman?'

The Evult touches the harp strings, and ripples cross the pond, fragmenting the image of the blonde soprano. 'I want your supply lists and your march plan for the spring two weeks from today. No later.'

'Yes, Evult.' Yurelt bows.

124.

On the third morning after leaving Elheld, as Anna and her expedition orde first eastward, and then more toward the north, the dark smudges on the horizon slowly grew taller, and more distinct, until the outline of the Ostfels rose clearly above the brown and dusty hills of eastern Defalk. The riverbed dwindled to the point where it no longer dwarfed the thin line of water that wound down from the mountains, and scattered junipers began to dot the sloping banks of the Fal.

In time, Anna could see patches of brown where evergreens, or some trees, had died, almost like she imagined might be the impacts of acid rain. From each side of the river stretched deks and deks of browned and bent grass. Close up, Anna could see the grass consisted of clumps separated by reddish dirt, but the more distant grass appeared unbroken.

She shook her head. Even the grasslands were slowly dying. Her eyes lifted to the Ostfels. Were there clouds to the east of the tallest peaks? Anna squinted, but she could not see any. What she did see was that the peaks to the northeast were rocky and barren, while the taller peaks to the south bore some snow cover.

A faint smile crossed her lips. Had the Evult used warm rain or something to melt the snow cover to fuel the flood that had devastated Elhi and Falcor? Perhaps she wasn't so insane to try to strike now. By spring there would be more snow.

'We are going over those?' Daffyd asked again.

'Yes. According to Jecks, there is a trail, an old road, but it's narrow.' Anna upstoppered the water bottle and drank, then replaced the bottle and patted Farinelli on the neck.

'Had I not seen what you did to the Ebrans before, I would say this is foolhardy.' Daffyd volunteered.

'It is foolhardy,' Anna admitted. 'Totally foolhardy. It's just that not doing anything is even worse. You've seen Defalk. The whole land is dying. I'm hoping to surprise the Evult in his lair . . . his den . . . whatever.'

'Do you know he is there?'

'So far.' When Anna had used the glass the night before, only briefly, very briefly, the shadowed figure had been in Vult, eating at a dark table, alone.

She also had the feeling that he would still be in his den, and she had to trust the feeling, not that she had any intention of getting too close to that den. The idea behind the battle hymn – rivers of fire, not water – that should let her spells create their havoc from farther away. She winced. If the spells worked, there would be havoc. If not . . . another kind of havoc. War, whether through technology or magic, created havoc, but she had to wonder why arms were regarded as more acceptable. *Or are you self-justifying again?*

She patted Farinelli absently. Why was it always so hard to figure out what was truly right – and still survive?

'I'm sore,' said Iseen, one of the horn players, as she tried to stand in her stirrups. Then she called to Alvar, who rode to Anna's left. 'Captain, isn't it about time to water the horses?'

Alvar grinned at Anna, who smiled back, then shrugged. 'In a while, lady player. We will need a more gentle slope down to the river.'

'In a while, he says . . .' muttered Iseen, just loud enough for Anna to hear.

'All those silvers . . . too good to be true . . . now we know.'

'Stop mouthing, Iseen. You were told you would travel. Did you expect a carriage?'

'They sound like lancers,' observed Alvar. 'Nothing is ever quite the way they would like it.'

'Nothing ever turns out quite the way any of us would like it,' Anna said dryly. 'It's just that the young ones feel that they deserve it that way.'

Daffyd frowned, but Anna ignored the expression. The chief player had found that out already, but he still didn't like it. Neither did she.

125

WEI, NORDWEI

The spymistress steps into the tower room where Gretslen sits before a mirror pool, chanting. The blonde does not falter, but finishes the spell, and watches the clear waters gather white mist, before silvering and displaying an image.

Both women watch the image.

A long line of horsemen ride up a road flanked by woods filled with dry and dying evergreens. To the left of the column is a gorge, through which trickles the thinnest of streams.

'Where?' asks Ashtaar.

'The upper Fal, on the ancient road to Vult.' Perspiration beads on the blonde woman's forehead. 'They are nearing the outer pass, and the weather barrier set by the Evult.'

'She is brave.'

'Foolhardy!' Gretslen continues to study the image in the glass, her eyes on the palomino and his rider – who leads the winding column. 'She risks everything.'

'Perhaps . . . and perhaps not. Now, what has she to lose? A land that dies as she watches? Neighbors who speculate which bones to pick clean? Lords looking for allegiances elsewhere?'

Gretslen starts on her stool, and the image wavers and then dissolves in ripples. 'You sound fond of this . . . sorceress . . . this abomination.'

'I only try to see things as they are, Gretslen, not as I wish to see them. This sorceress . . . this regent . . . whatever you wish to call her . . . she does not think as we do.'

'Her thoughts will not stop the Evult from crushing her,' points out Gretslen.

'She has lost everything dear to her, from what your influence reported. And even your source, you may recall, severed his ties with us – mostly politely, most reluctantly, but most firmly. He fears her power. Yet what restrains that power? All she has is her beliefs. She must do what she feels is proper . . . and with no children to protect . . . Defalk is her child . . . and she will gamble to ensure it survives long after her death.' Ashtaar looks up from the pool that is now only clear water. 'If her foolhardiness pays off, then Ebra may be the land suffering the long dry years indeed.'

'She has overreached.'

'That could be. We should hope so, but now that she is almost within Ebra, there is little enough we can do – or should. Keep watching, as you can.' Ashtaar nods and turns.

'Yes, most honored Ashtaar.'

Ashtaar's lips tighten, but she does not turn her head

as she steps through the door and onto the landing above the stairs.

126

Anna readjusted the floppy hat and the unfastened oiled leather jacket and shifted her weight in the saddle. A cold mist – not quite rain – fell from featureless gray clouds that dwindled into nothing over the high pass that lay more than two days and a dozen leagues behind them.

The sorceress glanced back along the road that wound along the mountainside down from the pass, then at the gorge to her left. In the base of the gorge was a brook, already almost as wide as the diminished Fal had been at the point where Anna and her expedition had entered the Ostfels. Above the brook were scattered firs and pines – healthy firs and pines, growing out of rocks and crevasses.

Her lips tightened, and she forced herself to take a deep breath, looking forward. Just ahead, the road curved right around a jutting spire of rock. Beyond the rock spire rose a sheer cliff, stretching at least several hundred yards straight up.

Beside the sorceress rode Alvar, bareheaded, but smiling. The road was little more than a rock-and-clay track scratched out of the mountainside and capable of holding but two horses abreast, even though Jecks' maps had indicated that it had once been part of the northern land route to Ebra in centuries past.

'The mist feels good,' said the lancer captain.

'It feels cold,' answered Daffyd from his mare.

Anna agreed with Alvar. 'You've gotten too used to that dissonant heat in Defalk.'

Farinelli slowed as he neared the tight curve around the red stone spire, and Anna peered forward, abruptly reining in the gelding.

'Halt!' ordered Alvar his hand in the air, and his voice echoing back along the rocky gorge. 'Halt!'

'Now what?'

'No one said anything about rain . . .'

Anna stared at the sheer drop-off where the road ended. Near the end of the cliffs to the right, she could see where the road resumed, but there was no road, not even a pile of rubble, connecting the two points. The entire mountainside had peeled away, leaving just a vertical extent of rock connecting the two points.

'Now what?' asked Daffyd. 'We'd have to go back leagues to find another road.'

And that road won't lead where I need to go, thought the sorceress.

'The rock below is more than fifty yards down,' added Alvar. 'We might be able to lower horses and people, but there is no way to cross the jumble of rocks . . . no way to climb up on the other end.'

'More sorcery,' Anna sighed, hating the idea. Any sorcery she could use would be like setting an alarm and alerting the Evult. Then, he might already know, and retracing their steps and trying another route would certainly alert the Dark Monks' leader, if he weren't already waiting.

For a time, she sat on Farinelli, thinking. What song could she adapt? Not 'The Long and Winding Road.' A long and winding road was the last thing she needed. 'On the Road Again'?

She smiled and began to formulate possible spells.

'What is she doing?'

'. . . just sitting there in the mist . . .'

'. . . nowhere to go, and she is looking into the sky?'

Anna ignored the players' comments. After a few more mumbled verses, or semiverses, she dismounted and took out the lutar, then handed Farinelli's reins to Alvar. 'Would you?'

'If you can repair the road, I can hold reins.' The swarthy captain's face showed no sign of humor, except for the glint in his eyes.

'Let's hope I can.' She walked toward the point where the road ended abruptly, then stopped a yard short of the drop-off and looked down at the tumbled red rock. In places, weather-stripped fir trunks protruded, indicating that the avalanche had occurred some years earlier.

After tuning the lutar and running through several vocalises, she spoke the words slowly, trying to fix them in her mind. Then ... she lifted the lutar and began to strum, adding the words of the spell, trying not to hear Roger Miller in her mind.

'Fix the road again ...'

As the words and chords tumbled out, rock dust spewed from the cliff ahead, and the mountain beneath the road trembled. Anna finished the spell, and stepped back from the swirling dust.

The sense of a chord on a giant harp vibrated across the slopes, and a groaning rumble endured long after Anna's words had died away. A dull throbbing pounded at Anna's skull, and she closed her eyes. That didn't help. When she opened them, the misting rain had begun to strip away the curtain of rock dust.

Instead of ending at a sheer drop-off, the road now continued, easing to the right and following a newly-cut shelf that extended almost half a dek along the sheer cliff that had once seemed impassible, continuing the descent from the pass behind them.

'Dissonance!'

'... begin to see why she's regent ...'

'You still want to complain, Iseen?'

Anna walked back toward Alvar and Farinelli.

'Most impressive – again – Regent Anna,' offered the lancer captain.

'Thank you.' She rubbed her temples with her left hand, still holding the lutar in her right, trying to massage away the worst of the headache, and understanding once more the strain involved in handling both words and instrumental support.

She took a deep breath. If the Evult hadn't known that Anna was headed into Ebra, then he certainly would by now. That was the bad news. The good news was that they were only a day or two from where she wanted to be.

I hope it's the good news, she thought as she wiped the mist off the lutar and slipped it back into its case. Her eyes stabbed, and her stomach churned.

'I'll need something to eat.' As if she weren't always eating, always stuffing herself, and always on the brink of starvation and/or collapse.

127

VULT, EBRA

The image in the pool reveals an empty mountain road, almost like a stone shelf cut from the rock of a sheer cliff, that connects two sections of older, time-worn highway.

The hooded figure studies the image for a time, then shakes his head, barely moving the dark hood.

The faintest glissando shimmers across the strings of the harp on the pedestal in the mirror pool, then fades as the Evult lifts the bell.

Shortly, another figure in dark robes, unhooded, appears.

'We seem to have underestimated the foolhardiness of the sorceress,' rasps the Evult.

'I feel the harmonies ring. What has she done?' asks Yurelt.

'Repaired the rift in the old highway to Elhi. I am about to summon her image again, and I wished you to be here so that you may ready your forces, Songmaster.' The older man laughs, then cuts off the laugh and begins to chant.

In the pool at his feet the white mists swirl and then disclose a woman in oiled leathers and a worn, floppy-brimmed hat, riding through a light rain that leaves the clay-and-rock roadway glistening, slick looking.

Another chant, and the mirror pool reveals a view, as if seen by a bird.

'There – she has already reached the upper ponds. Three more days, and she could enter Vult.' The Evult pauses. 'But she will not have three days.'

Yurelt waits.

'She must descend the ramp road to at least the third river falls for her voice, powerful as it is, to reach even the outskirts of Vult. Her voice may surprise us yet. You will take no chances. Set your traps just above the first valley falls. Not even the harmonies could touch Vult from there. I will move to the third falls. Think upon how you may best trap them, and we will meet again after evening meal.'

'Yes, Evult.' Yurelt bows.

'In her haste, she has opened Defalk to us.' The Evult laughs again. 'Even by next spring, no one will have risen to challenge us. The traders of Nordwei and the cowards of Ranuak will grasp a few bones from the corpse of Defalk, but by next harvest we will hold both Defalk and Neserea. You see, our tradition and our ways are beyond the loss of great commanders. Patience and the way will triumph, unto the centuries.'

Yurelt's eyebrows rise fractionally.

'Yes. She had no patience, and her haste was her undoing,' concludes the Evult. 'Her undoing.'

128

Vult shouldn't be that far ahead.' Anna's eyes went to the curve ahead, where there was a break in the scattered firs and pines that flanked the road on both sides.

Despite the sunlight, a cool dampness filled the late morning. In the light breeze, she enjoyed the fragrance of the pines, the first time she had smelled them in ages. There hadn't been any evergreens to speak of in Ames, and Defalk was so mummified that the trees had no scent at all. Even the withered berries on the few Defalkan junipers remaining had no scent.

'We have been riding downhill for leagues,' Daffyd added from behind Anna and Alvar. 'And the road is not that good.'

'What do you expect from an abandoned highway? Also, the Ostfels are not exactly a small mountain range, friend player. Even Vult is in the middle, with leagues of rocky peaks to the east. You can see the taller peaks there.' Alvar gestured.

'Too many mountains,' Daffyd said with a slight grin.

'How are your players doing?' Anna asked. 'It may not be too long before I'll need them.'

'They are ready, once we stop,' the violist answered.

'Lady Anna,' said Alvar in a low voice, bending in his saddle toward the sorceress, 'you have been saying that all morning.'

'The maps aren't as good as I'd like.' The sorceress flushed. She still hated not being certain of things – like where she was – especially now that everyone looked to her. Yet, once again, she was partly at the mercy of someone else – Jecks' scouts and maps – and she hated that, too.

'No maps are that good,' said Alvar.

'They need to be better.'

'Honored regent, if you live another ten centuries, you will still be attempting to improve the world.'

The sorceress eyed the wiry captain, then grinned. 'I suppose so.'

As they neared the curve in the mountain road, the trees thinned. After slowing Farinelli, Anna eased the gelding to the left side of the road and over some low bushes out onto a rocky outcrop, perhaps five yards square, that jutted out from the road and the pines that clung to the steep slopes below the road.

'Halt! Rein up!' ordered Alvar. Then he eased his mount almost up beside Farinelli, reining up slightly back to allow the sorceress an unobstructed view.

For a time, Anna studied the valley below. While the river still followed the road, the water – easily five yards wide – was nearly fifty yards below the roadbed, and tumbled through the valley that was not quite a gorge. Less than two deks to the southeast and several hundred yards lower, the rushing water smoothed into an almost lakelike surface. Even farther east, hidden in the hills and trees into which the river wound, a waterfall of some sort existed, sending a mist of spray into the morning, a misty fog barely visible above the endless evergreens.

Overhead, the scattered clouds were white and gray, scudding south-ward in a brisk cool breeze that ruffled Anna's hair as she sat on Farinelli on the outcrop – a breeze much stiffer than the barely moving air that favored the tree-lined and uneven ancient road behind her.

The sorceress attempted to match the terrain below with the small map she held, turning it and then comparing inked images to the reality of gree, and brown and gray, that stretched out to the northeast.

Two gray stone towers – barely pinpricks above the trees – stood near the fork where the river the road had followed joined another.

'I think that's Vult,' Anna said as Alvar reined up beside her.

'Almost a day's ride.'

Anna shook her head. 'We're almost near enough now.' She folded the map and replaced it in her belt wallet.

The lancer captain frowned, then leaned forward in his saddle. After a moment, he gestured to the south. 'There are the armsmen of the dark ones,' added Alvar, pointing to the line of brown that rose from the valley floor, an exposed section of road no more than a league away.

Anna had to strain to see the dark dots that represented a long column of horse winding upward along the lower sections of the old road that would eventually reach the Defalkan group. She glanced around. The outcrop where she had reined up was just about the only clear vantage point on the road – at least that she could see.

Farther down the road, the trees thickened enough that she would be unable to see the Ebran forces until they were practically on top of the small Defalkan force.

'How long before they get here?' she asked.

'A glass,' opined Alvar. 'Less, if they push their mounts. Should we make ready?'

'Just a moment,' the sorceress temporized. What should she do? Was she close enough?

An even colder wind gusted out of the north, accompanied by the faintest of brass chords. Anna glanced up, and, even as she watched, the scattered clouds began to darken, to expand, massing in the north above the sharp-toothed Ostfels. On the slope below the outcrop where she sat on Farinelli, the suddenly stronger wind whistled through the dark firs, bending the tops of their crowns.

'It is not dry, like Defalk.' Daffyd eased his mare up beside Alvar. 'Defalk was green like this once.'

Anna hoped it would be again. Her eyes went to the Ebran horse, but they seemed no nearer, and then to the sky, her ears still on the rising wind.

'Oh . . .'

Alvar glanced up, following Anna's inadvertent comment.

The clouds, now all gray and darkening toward black moment by moment, covered more than half the sky. The late-morning sunlight dimmed as the spreading blackness cut off Anna's view of the ice-covered peaks beyond Vult to the east.

For better or worse, Anna decided, she had lost any real options. Besides, if the Evult's magic could reach her, hers should be able to reach Vult. She hoped.

'Players!' Anna snapped, turning Farinelli and riding back onto the road so that she faced her expedition, an expedition that seemed pitifully small compared to the endless lines of Ebran horse. 'There!' She pointed back to the rocky outcrop that jutted out from the curve in the road, the spot where she had reined up shortly before and from where she had surveyed the valley. She hoped that the outcrop had a solid rock base, solid enough for what she had planned. But she had no more time, not the way the Ebrans were moving, and the black clouds massing.

'Players!' reiterated Daffyd. 'On the point, ready to play!'

Anna motioned to the players, then turned to Alvar. 'Get half the lancers down the road. I hope they won't be needed, but—'

'Purple company! Purple company! To the standard.'

Anna hadn't seen the regency banner unfurled, but it flapped in the gusting wind that blew colder with each moment, and the young armsman who bore it joined up with Alvar, then trotted down the road, followed by Defalkan lancers.

At the edge of the road, the players struggled off their mounts, some moving stiffly, others more fluidly, all grasping for instruments.

'Green company! Green company! Hold the uphill road! Hold the uphill road!' Alvar's voice was strong and carried, despite the whistling of the wind.

The mounts of the purple company clattered past the dismounting players.

'Fhurgen!' ordered Spirda. 'Get the players' mounts up there! Out of the way. You too, Mysar!' The blond subofficer rode toward Anna.

As she dismounted, Anna handed Farinelli's reins to Spirda, then hurried out toward the end of the outcrop, trying to clear her throat. Once again, she felt like she was being hurried, caught not totally prepared, and it wasn't anyone's fault but her own stupidity.

You idiot! Of course, the Evult would just let you ride up and try your magic! Idiot!

Behind her, Spirda started to ease the palomino after him back up the road, following Fhurgen and Mysar. Farinelli whuffled, then neighed, sidestepping but trailing the subofficer, who slowed, then stood in the stirrups and half turned toward the sorceress, shouting, 'Do you want the lutar?'

'No. Leave it on Farinelli.'

Spirda nodded and gestured toward Fhurgen. 'Tie the mounts there.'

As her guards tethered the players' mounts to a pine branch that extended along the downhill side of the road up from the outcrop, Anna stopped just short of the end of the point, running through a vocalise as she took another look at the valley and tried to clear her mind, easing the written spells from her wallet. She hadn't wanted to trust her memory totally, but she hoped she wouldn't have to look at the words, that she could focus her mind on the images she wanted to call forth.

Even in the space clear of the evergreens that flanked the road, the day had turned more like twilight as the black clouds continued to spread and churn. The wind on the point was nearly a gale that lashed around her.

Idiot! Talk about spellcasting with disruptions!

The players scurried into position, their eyes straying toward the darkening clouds, their hair blown by the increasingly bitter wind. Iseen blotted an eye, as though dust or grit had lodged there.

'Warm-up song! Warm-up song!' called Daffyd, struggling with tuning pegs even as he spoke.

Anna turned from the group and tried not to wince, either at their sounds or at the sight of the Ebran forces trotting up the road. The Ebran van had vanished into the trees, but that meant the dark riders were just that much closer. She hoped – always hoping – that Alvar could hold them off until she did what she had to – and that it worked.

The sorceress forced herself to take a deep breath, forced herself to wait as the discord behind her began to resemble music.

'Warm-up song – one more time!'

Cracccckk! A single yellow lightning bolt struck the road a dek farther downhill from Anna's force, sending a faint vibration through the rocks and soil. With the lightning bolt came another of the underlying bass chords, so deep that the air groaned.

The sorceress and regent hoped the Evult had struck his own lancers, but doubted she'd be that lucky.

No casualties from friendly fire here. The fire isn't at all friendly, not here.

The sorceress turned to Daffyd. 'The hymn! Have them do it once – that's all the more warm-up we'll have time for.'

'The hymn ... now!' Daffyd snapped, his voice rising slightly. 'One and two ... and ...'

The sound was ragged, but not too bad. Anna hoped – prayed – it would suffice as she turned her back to the wind, and, after clearing her throat, tried another vocalise.

Crracck! The second lightning bolt was less than a half dek away, and the groans and rumbles were even more pronounced – and a deep, counterpointed chord, somehow harmonically dissonant, rumbled beneath everything.

You can't have harmonic dissonance, insisted part of Anna's mind. *Except in modern music, and that doesn't count here.* She pushed away the thoughts.

A blackish yellow pallor, darker than twilight, cloaked the valley, almost as though a dome had capped the area. In the deepening gloom, the long lines of mounted Ebrans continued to ride up toward the pitifully small Defalkan contingent.

The wind cut through Anna's leathers like a knife, and ripped her hat off her head as she turned back to the players. Her eyes followed the battered felt as it fluttered out beyond the outcrop.

Craaacckkk!!! The blinding yellow bolt struck less than two hundred yards below the outcrop, and the hiss of stream from the river momentarily drowned out the whistling of the wind and the creaking of the firs as they bent in the wind, a wind that smelled metallic, foreign, sorcerous.

Anna blinked away the glare and the momentarily blindness and cleared her throat. 'The hymn. Now!'

'One . . .' shouted Daffyd, easing his viola under his chin and gesturing with the bow.

The raggedness cleared after two bars, and Anna sang, sang as though it were the Met or Carnegie Hall or Covent Garden, with all the years of training that had never been fully utilized.

'I have sung the terror of the power of all sounds,
I am bringing forth the magma from the deeps where it resounds,
I have loosed the fateful tremors of the plates beneath the grounds.
My songs will smash the earth.
Glory, glory, halleluia; glory, glory, halleluia;
Glory, glory, halleluia; my songs will smash the earth!

'In the terror of the tremors, death is freed from all its locks,
with a slashing through the hillsides that flattens trees and rocks.

As I spelled to keep men free, let us see Vult fall in
   shocks.
My songs will smash the earth.
Glory, glory, halleluia; glory, glory, halleluia;
Glory, glory, halleluia; my songs will smash the earth!

'With the rising of the waters, streams are loosed from
   all their banks,
and their torrents through the hillsides will drown the
   darkest ranks . . .'

Even before she had finished the last chorus – strophic-
spell, some part of her mind insisted – that great harp
behind and within the world had vibrated with a frequency
so deep it felt like her bones had been jellied – harmonic,
yet disharmonic.

Crracck! The bale-yellow lightning slammed the mountainside less than a hundred yards away, and Anna started
to put her hands to her ears to shut out the pain.

Yet, powerful as the lightning was, painful as the blast
of sound and energy was, she could sense a finality, a
desperation. She blinked and turned back to the players.

Daffyd held his viola and bow, staring past her toward
the still-swirling and dying clouds, as if he expected the
world to end.

Iseen's mouth hung open, her horn almost dangling from
her hands, and, beside her, Ristyr's eyes bulged.

In the background, Anna could hear blades ringing, and
shouts, as if through a muffled curtain. Were the Ebrans
upon them?

'The fire song! The fire song!'

Daffyd looked blank.

'The fire song, damn it!' Anna shrilled.

'The fire song!' Daffyd repeated.

The notes were more ragged, but they would have to do.
There was no more time, not with all the mounted Ebrans
hacking at Alvar and his lancers.

Anna sang – sang as if it were the last song.

> 'Armsmen brown, armsmen black,
> not flame nor ashes shall you lack . . .

> from the strings, from the sky,
> fire flay you till you die!'

Crackling bolts – golden red – flared like snapping harp strings from the still-dark clouds, whipping across the evergreens, a line of endless down-pointed fireworks raking the long road down to the valley. A second line of fire followed the first, and then a third, and fourth . . . until the sky seemed hatched with lines of fire.

And yet the ground beneath heaved and groaned, and the rocks shrieked.

Anna's arms fell to her sides, as she stood there dazed. Too battered even to wince at the screams that seemed to go on and on, too stunned to cover her ears, too flash-blinded to see what she had unleashed.

Before her, Daffyd staggered, and two others staggered and went to their knees, as the ground rumbled and shuddered, with a shrieking grinding from deep beneath the rocks that went on and on and on.

The rumbles and the shudders made those that had occurred around the Sorprat sinkhole seem like nothing. Small cracks ran down the middle of the narrow road, and dust puffed into the air above the cracks.

Anna could vaguely hear horses neighing, some screaming, but those sounds were lost in the deeper shrieks and rumbles of the earth itself. The entire world seemed to vibrate, the clash of harmony and disharmony shaking the very bones of the earth.

The sorceress shifted her weight, trying to keep from being toppled. She looked eastward toward the valley. Had the clouds stopped rising?

Anna swayed on her feet as the earth rolled under her, and as a fissure split the bottom of the valley in a jagged line that crept uphill, back toward the river below the outcrop where she stood. Both the red glare and the heat from that chasm seared her face, and she staggered back and threw up her hand.

A wall of flame, blue and red, wavered out of the chasm's depths, growing and fountaining with each instant, and the fallen trees vaporized into ashes as the almost living fire marched down toward the toppled gray-stone towers of Vult and up toward Anna.

As she braced herself against the tremors that continued to shake even the solid rock of the mountain beneath her, Anna's mouth dropped open as she saw curtains of steam rise, ghostly white against the swirling black sky, from both rivers as their waters poured into the rising wall of golden red magma that welled out of the earth in dozens of spots.

The wind dropped from a northern gale to intermittent gusts from the southeast carrying waves of chill and waves of heat, sulfur, and ozone, all swirled together, and carrying the odor of steamed vegetation and steamed meat.

Oh Lord, no, thought the sorceress as her stomach churned at the sickening odors that she had created, as she choked back the bitter bile, and straightened, despite the needle-knives that stabbed at her eyes and the hammering through her skull.

Down the valley, the dark pines began to fall, row by row, impossibly uphill, as though scythed by an invisible blade that left none standing.

The screaming of a horse overrode the other cries and shrieks.

Farinelli? Anna turned and staggered toward where she thought the palomino might be.

WWHHHUMMMP!!!!!

The shock wave threw Anna flat across the trail, skidding her on her back toward the boulders on the mountain side of the trail.

She struggled to her knees at the edge of the road, and lurched upward. No one else could calm Farinelli. No one.

Another rending shriek of tortured rock bombarded her ears as the sorceress took another step through the unearthly haze of powdered rock, of steamed vegetation and fire-flayed armsmen, of dust, and sulfur, and . . .

WWHHHUMMMP!!!!! WWHHHUMMMP!!!!!

The two massive ground shudders lifted her into the air, and she half turned, throwing her hands out before her as the boulders seemed to fly toward her, ever so deliberately, ever so slowly.

Yet she could not even find time to open her mouth before she could feel the impact, the white-fired pain cascading up her outstretched arm like the most dissonant of chords slamming through her whole body.

Then there was silence . . . and darkness.

129

ENCORA, RANUAK

'You see,' offers the Matriarch. 'The harmonies are reknitting.'

'The entire world shuddered. The winds screamed, and the sea smashed the front line of shops in the harbor.' Black-haired Veria frowns. 'Vult is a pile of molten rock and steam. The north of Ebra is devastated, and most of Synek has been washed away by the rains and melted snow and ice. The Evult has been destroyed, as have all the darksingers, and almost all the dark armsmen in Liedwahr. That is harmony?'

'I would call that dissonance,' says Alya coolly. 'Dissonance the like of which Erde has never seen.'

'If your mother and matriarch says the harmonies are rechording,' says Ulgar, 'then they are.'

'Father . . . saying it is so does not make it so,' protests Veria.

Alya looks toward the round-faced, gray-haired woman and offers the slightest of shrugs, as if to indicate that there is little point in arguing the issue.

'Might I point out, daughters, ever so humbly as a worthless old male whose views are doubtless beneath notice, that the soprano sorceress called upon Harmony, has attempted to rebuild Defalk, and renounced immediately any thoughts of building a dynasty. Might I also point out that the rains have begun to return to Defalk and that the sorceress has survived, while the Evult did not.'

'How long will she linger?' asks Veria.

'She will live, and prosper. The harmonies will see to that,' offers the Matriarch.

'Mother ... you keep making these grandiose statements, and you never explain.'

The Matriarch ignores the slip in salutation, instead offering a warmer smile before speaking. 'The sorceress has acknowledged Defalk's debt justly, not as hers, but as one for which she assumes the responsibility.' The round-faced matriarch smiles even more broadly. 'Since when did either Lord Behlem or the Evult acknowledge anything? The sorceress acknowledged her debt to Lord Barjim, and she was willing to put herself in the way of dissonance. We will rebuild a few shops, and the harmonies will not fail her – or us.'

Ulgar coughs, hiding a grin with the hand that covers his mouth.

130

'She's so good with young voices ...'

Young voices, young voices ... what about older voices? What about opera? What about ...

'Could you not have stopped this? You are the greatest

sorceress . . .' Greatest sorceress . . . greatest sorceress . . . greatest sorceress . . .

'I MISS YOU!!!'

Miss you, too, littlest redhead, miss you, miss you . . .

Something jolted Anna, and she moaned. She didn't mean to moan, but she did. She tried to open her eyes, but even attempting to lift her eyelids sent lances of pain through her skull, and the darkness came up and swallowed her.

What's a furl . . . furl . . . furl?

'There is the question of the banner.' *Whose banner . . . whose?*

'Will we learn magic?'

No such thing as magic, except there is.

'Can you not bring back the rains and the river?' *Can you not . . . not . . . not?*

'Most impressive – again – Regent Anna.' *Most impressive . . . impressive . . .*

What was impressive? Going out and getting yourself killed?

She could feel her body being moved, somehow, and again, the pain was enough to drive her under – for a time.

'Drink . . . lady . . . drink.' Each word out of the darkness echoed in her ears, each syllable burning, boring like a dull dentist's drill into her skull and brain.

She drank, she thought, though she could not feel anything but a hot liquid spilling across her face. Hot liquid and soft sounds that burned through her ears and into her brain.

131

In time, Anna recognized where she was – in the great guest quarters in Lord Jeck's hall, and for the time that flowed around her, she drank and ate mushy stuff and dozed – it hurt too much to sleep, really sleep.

Her right arm was encased in the medieval equivalent of a splint, a leather-and-wood contraption that weighed on her stomach if she rested it there, and hurt, besides making her feel lopsided, in any other position.

Finally, she could stay awake – sort of.

The door opened.

'You are awake,' offered the white-haired lord, standing at the foot of the triple-wide bed. Beside him stood Alvar, with what looked to be burns across half his face.

'Partly.' She winced. Even her own words hurt her ears. So did the sight of the injured captain.

'The women – they were reluctant to let us in. Even the healer. She rode from Ohal when she heard you suffered.' Jecks shook his head, then gestured to the grayness outside the half-open window. 'Do you see the rain? We have had no rain in more than four years.' He laughed. 'I feel for you, lady.'

'It's not that bad,' lied Anna. Her mouth felt like it had been lined with mildewed blankets. She didn't even want to think about the havoc she had unleashed, not yet.

'Between the spells from Lord Brill and the healer, you will heal. That is not why I pity you.' Jecks looked at her thoughtfully. 'You have done the impossible, and your people – they have claimed you, now – will expect that and more. You are the destroyer of dissonance, the savior of the land, lady and sorceress, great Regent of Defalk.'

Destroyer, that was about right. The greatest destroyer in history . . . because there were no other options, but who would remember that? You will . . . She closed her eyes.

'They will expect miracles and more,' Jecks reiterated.

Anna groaned. 'Forever, I suppose.'

'No . . . thank the harmonies. I do not know exactly what sort of spell rendered you forever young, Lady Anna,' said Jecks, 'but even an old warhorse like me knows that no spell creates immortality. Did you think you could not be killed . . . to attempt such a massive destructive spell in the midst of the Ostfels?' He shook his head, still looking like Robert Mitchum, Anna thought. 'Such youth spells only mean that you will remain young until you die. Because you have more vitality you may live a decade or two longer, but you will still have a human lifespan. That, you will find, may be all too long.' He shrugged. 'Then perhaps your youthful energy will support you. I am only glad that it is you, and not me.'

Alvar nodded.

Anna coughed, wincing at the shock through her chest and arm. 'What happened . . . afterward? Spirda? The players?'

Alvar swallowed, moistening his lips. 'Vult is . . . no more. All . . . The whole valley steams with the fires of dissonance. The rivers . . . they became torrents with the melted snow and ice and the mighty rains.' He shook his head. 'Synek is mostly gone. Even half of Elawha was destroyed. The mountains still shake, and a new peak rises, a volcano. They call it Zauberinfeuer.'

Anna struggled with the word. *Zauberflotte* was a magic flute – Mozart; so 'Zauberinfeuer' had to be a magic fire, didn't it? 'The players? Your lancers?'

'About half the purple company survived, and most of the green company.' The wiry captain swallowed again. 'The outcrop where the players . . . It split off the mountain.'

Anna's eyes burned even more. 'All . . . of them?'

Alvar nodded.

'Even Daffyd.'

The slightest of affirmations followed. 'Spirda and Mysar, too. Fhurgen dragged you clear.'

'Is he all right?'

'He will be.'

The sorceress closed her eyes for a moment, then opened them. Both men waited. 'Thank you,' she whispered.

'You are tired, regent, and I talk too much, but I too wanted you to know that I am in your debt, and all you need do is ask.' The Lord of Elheld bowed. 'We are all in your debt.'

'All of us.' Alvar bowed.

Anna blinked, or thought she did, and the two were gone. On the breeze that drifted in from outside, she could smell the dampness, even hear the rain. Was there ever such a price for rain?

And Daffyd? Had a man ever paid so much to revenge his father? Without even really getting it?

As she lay on the pillows, the pain still pounding through her skull, and her broken arm still throbbing, questions flooded her mind.

Too tired to even lift her good left hand, she hurt too much and was too awake to sleep. She closed her eyes. That way, they didn't hurt, but her thoughts continued to spin through her mind.

Magic was far from easy, but even with all the constraints, there should have been more than three sorcerers in Defalk. Why weren't there more sorcerers, or sorceresses? Once she'd gotten the hang of it, sorcery hadn't been *that* difficult.

After a while, the answer floated out of the depths inside her, and she could have kicked herself – except that would have hurt even more, and she was tired of pain. It was so obvious. It wasn't the lack of a good voice, or of intelligence, or even knowledge. The limit was the lack of human kindness.

If any song could potentially invoke magic, training a voice could be potentially fatal, given the ungrateful nature of most students – literally murder. Also, given the consequences of a bad spell, and the arrogance of many gifted youngsters, trying to learn sorcery alone could be equally fatal. That limited sorcery to those with strong natural voices, the ability to craft words, and match them to music – and there just weren't many who could do that – even on earth. Add in the need to visualize the results of a spell . . . you couldn't even create an iron chair without knowing what it looked like.

That left few enough with the talent. But from whom could they learn? Without teaching, few would go beyond the rote of sorceresses like poor Jenny, and no one with any brains would touch a potentially ungrateful student. Here, sorcerers had to have brains and power ... so they didn't have to teach the ungrateful.

Kindness, consideration ... the ultimate limits, because they were so very rare in their deepest forms.

She wanted to laugh, but it would have hurt too much. *You talk of kindness, of consideration ... after the thousands you've killed?*

She sank deeper into the pillows. Sorceress, savior, and regent – she was trapped in what she had created, and then some – and every part of her body still hurt. Her soul ... she didn't even want to consider that, not anymore, not given the deaths that rested on her.

132

WEI, NORDWEI

The two women watch the mists clear, and the vision appears.

A blonde woman sits carefully upon a palomino and rides slowly down a wide street. Her right arm is heavily bound, but she smiles. Flowers and grains of rice rain upon her, as do cheers.

Behind her, a white-haired lord rides, his eyes shifting from her to the redheaded youth who rides beside him, but the lord's eyes linger more upon the regent than upon his grandson.

'How?' whispers Gretslen, her eyes on the shimmering water. 'How? She was helpless, and they carried her back. She could not have lifted a hand in her own defense, and Lord Jecks, and Nelmor, and even stern Birfels stood by her, and they all carried out her wishes when she could sing nothing, spell nothing. She is a stranger, and made no secret of it. She is a sorceress, and she did not hide it in a land that has killed sorceresses. She shivered the world, almost rent it in twain with her sorcery, and they hail her as a deliverer.'

'Because . . .' Ashtaar offers slowly, 'because we have not seen enough good in the world and did not recognize it.'

'Good? She is nearly an absolute ruler, and you call her good?' questions the blonde. 'She brought fire upon the Ostfels and drowned two cities in fire and floods, and that is good?'

'She raised harmony against disharmony, and the conflict rent the world. There is a difference.' The spymistress shrugs. 'We thought she wanted power like Behlem, or that because she sought to help people she would be weak like Barjim. She has already begun to bind together the lords by raising their younger children and providing them with more learning than Defalk has seen ever before. She has returned the rains to the fields, and she does not raise taxes or levies. She treats everyone fairly and does her best to destroy greed and evil. She raises the honest lords to power, and keeps her word. She is the Liedfuhr of the North, and she would not have the title. Do you have a better definition of a good ruler, Gretslen?'

The image in the shimmering waters vanishes.

'I can explain it to you well enough,' says Ashtaar wryly. 'Explaining it to the Council may be more difficult.'

'They will not see her as good, but as a threat.'

'Goodness in another ruler, especially when successful, and backed with great power, is about as threatening a danger as they could imagine. Nor would I wish to be her.' Ashtaar forces a smile to hide the shiver that takes her.

The golden-haired Gretslen frowns.

Ashtaar smiles sadly. 'You will learn, as has she.'

133

Anna stood in the twilight on the east tower, looking out toward Mencha, toward Loiseau, away from the invisible webs that spun in and around Falcor, understanding once more Brill's attachment, and wondering if she would ever be able to return there for more than a brief visit – at least in the ten years or so before Jimbob could rule in his own right.

She had Brill's papers, and she could even decipher the crude codes and some of the spells and doubtless would learn more in the seasons and years ahead.

A yard or so away, a redheaded figure leaned against the parapet and gazed through the cold mist toward the Fal River, already more than the trickle it had been just weeks earlier, but still dwarfed by the banks it had yet to refill.

The boy turned. 'Lady Anna?'

'Yes, Jimbob?'

'Can I go down to the fire? With grandsire?' He grinned. 'I am not from the mist worlds.'

'Go join your grandsire. I'll be down in a while.'

'Will you be all right?'

'I just need time alone.'

'By your leave?'

'You have my leave.'

The redhead bowed. 'I will have your cider ready. With all that funny spice in it. And more nuts and cheese. Grandsire says you must eat more.'

'Go.'

'I hear and obey, honored Regent.' With a last grin, the youth turned, his steps hard on the damp stones.

Anna looked out through the gray and damp, through the

rain that was slowly revitalizing Defalk. For the first time in her life, she had power, real power. For the first time in her life, she could direct at least some of her own destiny. And yet she could not, not without considering the destinies of others, not being who she still was.

She thought of Jecks and smiled, briefly. She even could have the local equivalent of Robert Mitchum or Sean Connery – and perhaps she would, in time. In time ... if he would, and that was far from certain in a world, like any, where little indeed was certain, even for a woman of power.

For now ... she shook her head slowly, thinking, letting the cool mist shroud her.

What had it all cost her? Her life on earth. Her son and daughter, for she was dead to them, and their lives went on. Every time she glanced at the black-etched rectangle on her chamber wall, she was reminded of that. And there was young Daffyd, who had given her the lutar, helped and trusted her. Brill, who had given her youth in body again. Innocent Jenny, killed by the dark ones to prevent her from summoning another sorceress. Spirda, the young players, all the innocents swept away by the fires and floods she had unleashed. Even the guilty, like Delor and Behlem, had marked her, in anger for giving her no choice, and in regret that she had found no other way than the force she deplored – and continued to use.

The list was long ... and she had the feeling it would get longer ... no matter what she did, and how hard she tried. No matter what amends she tried to make, no matter how many years Brill's spell sustained her.

Dropping her head in her hands, in the cool damp misting rain of early winter, Anna, destroyer of dissonance, savior of the land, Lady and Sorceress, Regent of Defalk, wept, silently, and in great shuddering sobs.

And the cold, soft rain fell. Cold and soft, like sorrow, the mists of Defalk shrouded the sobbing sorceress.

In time, she would go to the hearth below, her face clear, her voice clear.

Now ... with the silvered rain that had cost so dearly, she wept.

THE MAGIC OF RECLUCE

L. E. Modesitt, Jr.

The first volume in a stunning epic fantasy adventure.

'Fascinating! A big, exciting novel of the battle between good and evil, and the path between'
Gordon R. Dickson

'Entwining issues of magic with maturation, Modesitt's thoughtful coming-of-age tale is adorned with a finely drawn, down-to-earth yet dangerous world, and an intriguingly ambiguous view of how good and evil interact'
Carole Nelson Douglas

'A complex world based on a plausible system of magic and peopled with engaging and realistic characters'
Publishers Weekly

'Extremely interesting . . . unique . . . a refreshing use of the traditional fantasy elements'
Andre Norton

All available from Orbit

THE BAKER'S BOY

The Book of Words: Volume I

J. V. Jones

At vast Castle Harvell, where King Lesketh lies dying, two fates collide. In her regal suite, young Melliandra, the daughter of an influential lord, rebels against her forced betrothal to the sinister Prince Kylock. In the kitchens, an apprentice named Jack is terrified by his sudden, uncontrolled power to work miracles. Together they flee the castle, stalked by a sorcerer who has connived for decades to control the crown, committing supernatural murder to advance his schemes.

Meanwhile, a young knight begins a quest, leaving behind his home and family to seek out the treacherous Isle of Larn, where lies a clue to his desperate search for the truth.

And a wondrous epic of darkness and beauty begins . . .

Praise for J. V. Jones:

'J. V. Jones is a striking writer . . . wonderful'
Robert Jordan

THE WHEEL OF TIME

Robert Jordan

The Wheel of Time turns and Ages come and go, leaving memories that become legend. Legend fades to myth, and even myth is long forgotten when the Age that gave it birth returns again. In the Third Age, an Age of Prophecy, the World and Time themselves hang in the balance. What was, what will be, and what is, may yet fall under the Shadow.

THE WHEEL OF TIME SERIES

All available from Orbit

'Solid as a steel blade, and glowing with true magic'
Fred Saberhagen

Orbit titles available by post:

☐	The Magic of Recluce	L. E. Modesitt, Jr.	£6.99
☐	The Towers of the Sunset	L. E. Modesitt, Jr.	£6.99
☐	The Magic Engineer	L. E. Modesitt, Jr.	£6.99
☐	The Baker's Boy	J. V. Jones	£6.99
☐	Master and Fool	J. V. Jones	£6.99
☐	The Barbed Coil	J. V. Jones	£16.99
☐	The Eye of the World	Robert Jordan	£6.99
☐	The Great Hunt	Robert Jordan	£6.99
☐	The Dragon Reborn	Robert Jordan	£6.99

The prices shown above are correct at time of going to press, however the publishers reserve the right to increase prices on covers from those previously advertised, without further notice.

ORBIT BOOKS
Cash Sales Department, P.O. Box 11, Falmouth, Cornwall, TR10 9EN
Tel: +44 (0) 1326 372400, Fax: +44 (0) 1326 374888
Email: books@barni.avel.co.uk.

POST AND PACKING:
Payments can be made as follows: cheque, postal order (payable to Orbit Books) or by credit cards. Do not send cash or currency.

U.K. Orders under £10	£1.50
U.K. Orders over £10	**FREE OF CHARGE**
E.E.C. & Overseas	25% of order value

Name (Block Letters) _____

Address _____

_____

Post/zip code: _____

☐ Please keep me in touch with future Orbit publications

☐ I enclose my remittance £_____

☐ I wish to pay by Visa/Access/Mastercard/Eurocard

Card Expiry Date